ABSOLUTELY NAT

MARIA SCRIVAN

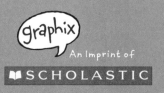

graphix
An Imprint of
SCHOLASTIC

For Courage

Library of Congress Control Number: 2020946616

ISBN 978-1-338-71540-8 (hardcover)
ISBN 978-1-338-71539-2 (paperback)

10 9 8 7 6 5 4   21 22 23 24 25

Printed in the U.S.A.   40
First edition, August 2021
Edited by Megan Peace
Creative Director: Phil Falco
Publisher: David Saylor

CONTENTS

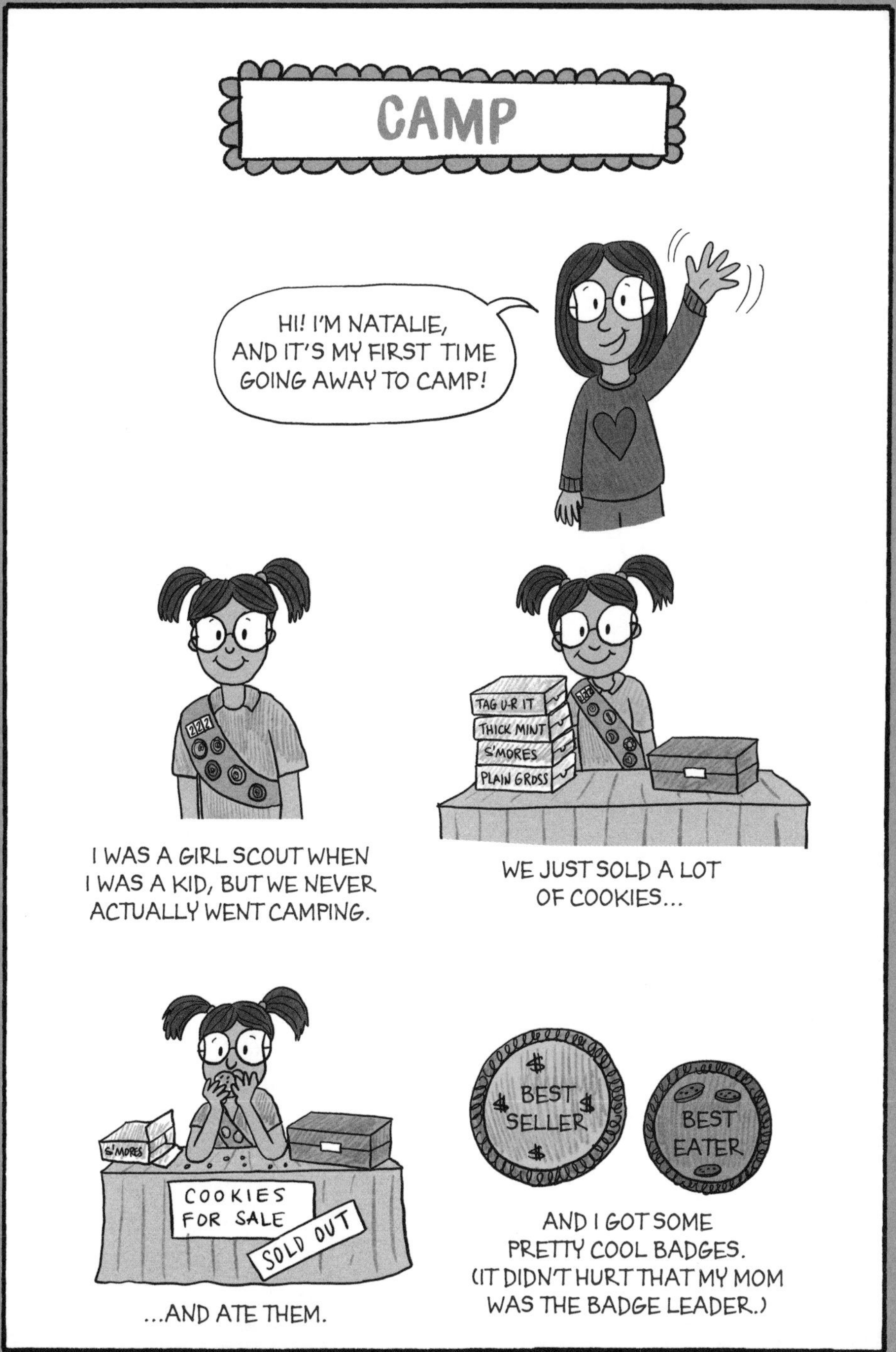
CAMP
HI! I'M NATALIE, AND IT'S MY FIRST TIME GOING AWAY TO CAMP!
I WAS A GIRL SCOUT WHEN I WAS A KID, BUT WE NEVER ACTUALLY WENT CAMPING.
222
TAG U-R IT
THICK MINT
S'MORES
PLAIN GROSS
WE JUST SOLD A LOT OF COOKIES...
S'MORES
COOKIES FOR SALE
SOLD OUT
...AND ATE THEM.
BEST SELLER
BEST EATER
AND I GOT SOME PRETTY COOL BADGES. (IT DIDN'T HURT THAT MY MOM WAS THE BADGE LEADER.)

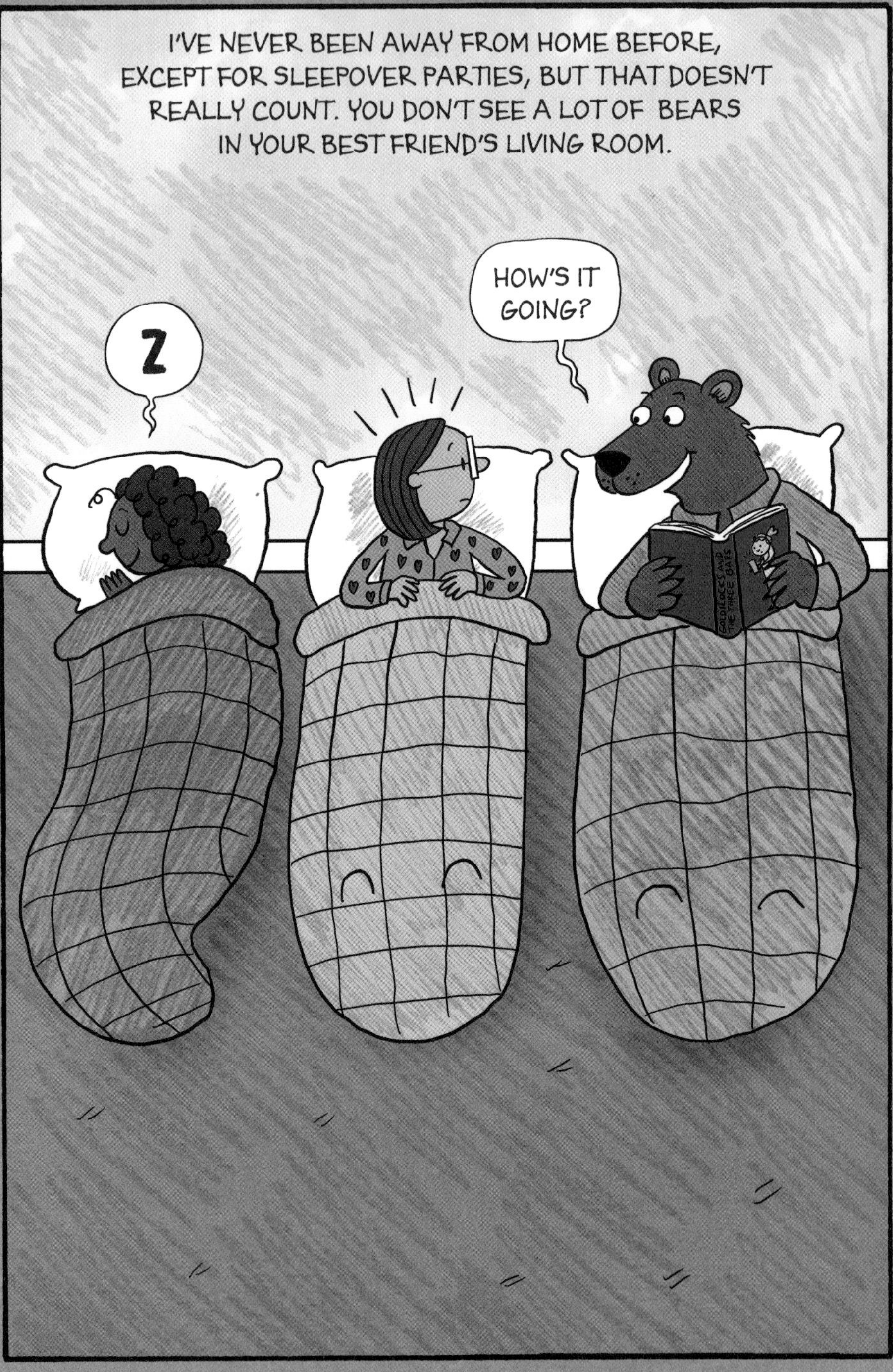
I'VE NEVER BEEN AWAY FROM HOME BEFORE, EXCEPT FOR SLEEPOVER PARTIES, BUT THAT DOESN'T REALLY COUNT. YOU DON'T SEE A LOT OF BEARS IN YOUR BEST FRIEND'S LIVING ROOM.
Z
HOW'S IT GOING?
GOLDILOCKS AND THE THREE BEARS

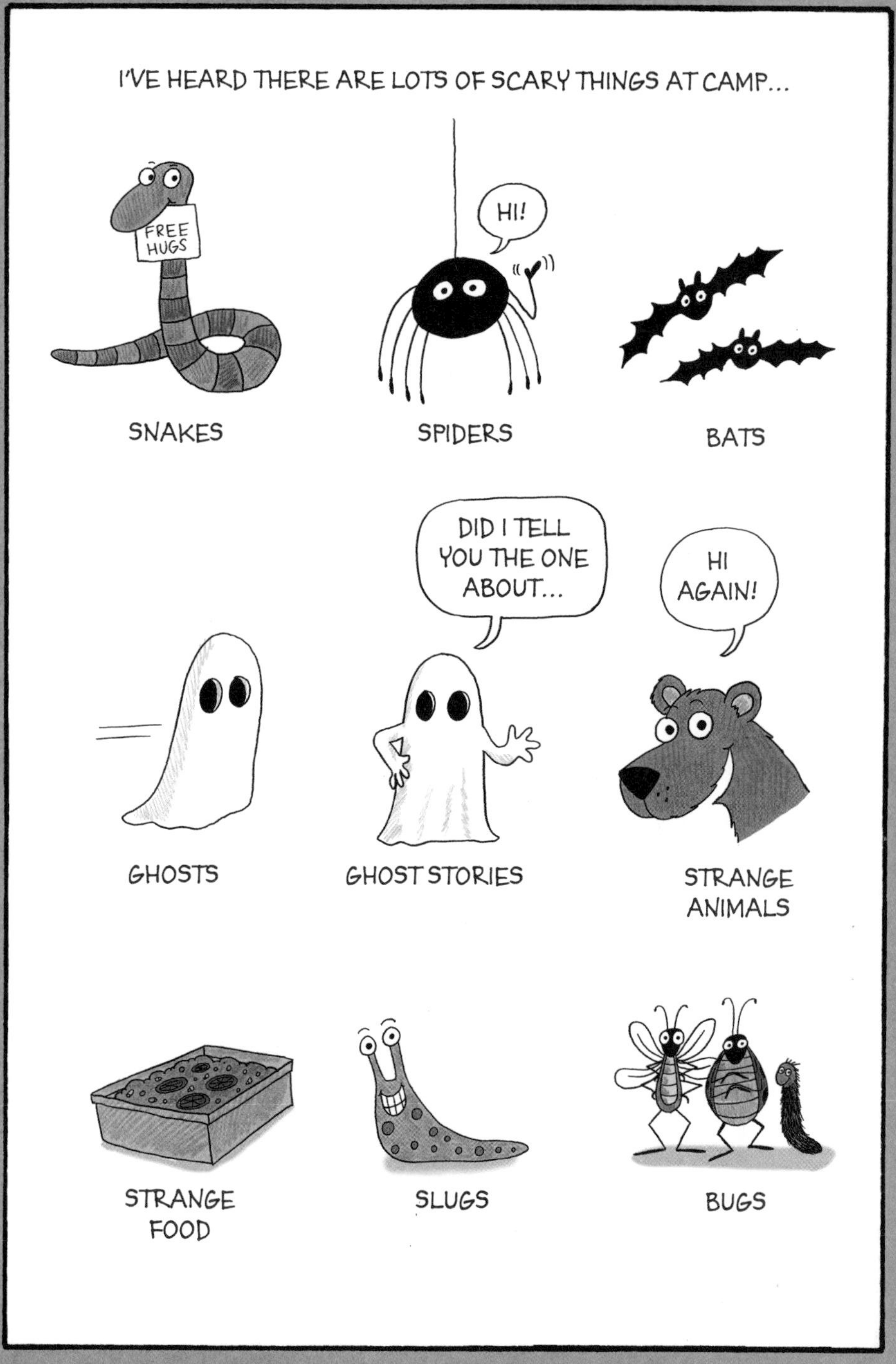
I'VE HEARD THERE ARE LOTS OF SCARY THINGS AT CAMP...
FREE HUGS
SNAKES
HI!
SPIDERS
BATS
DID I TELL YOU THE ONE ABOUT...
HI AGAIN!
GHOSTS
GHOST STORIES
STRANGE ANIMALS
STRANGE FOOD
SLUGS
BUGS

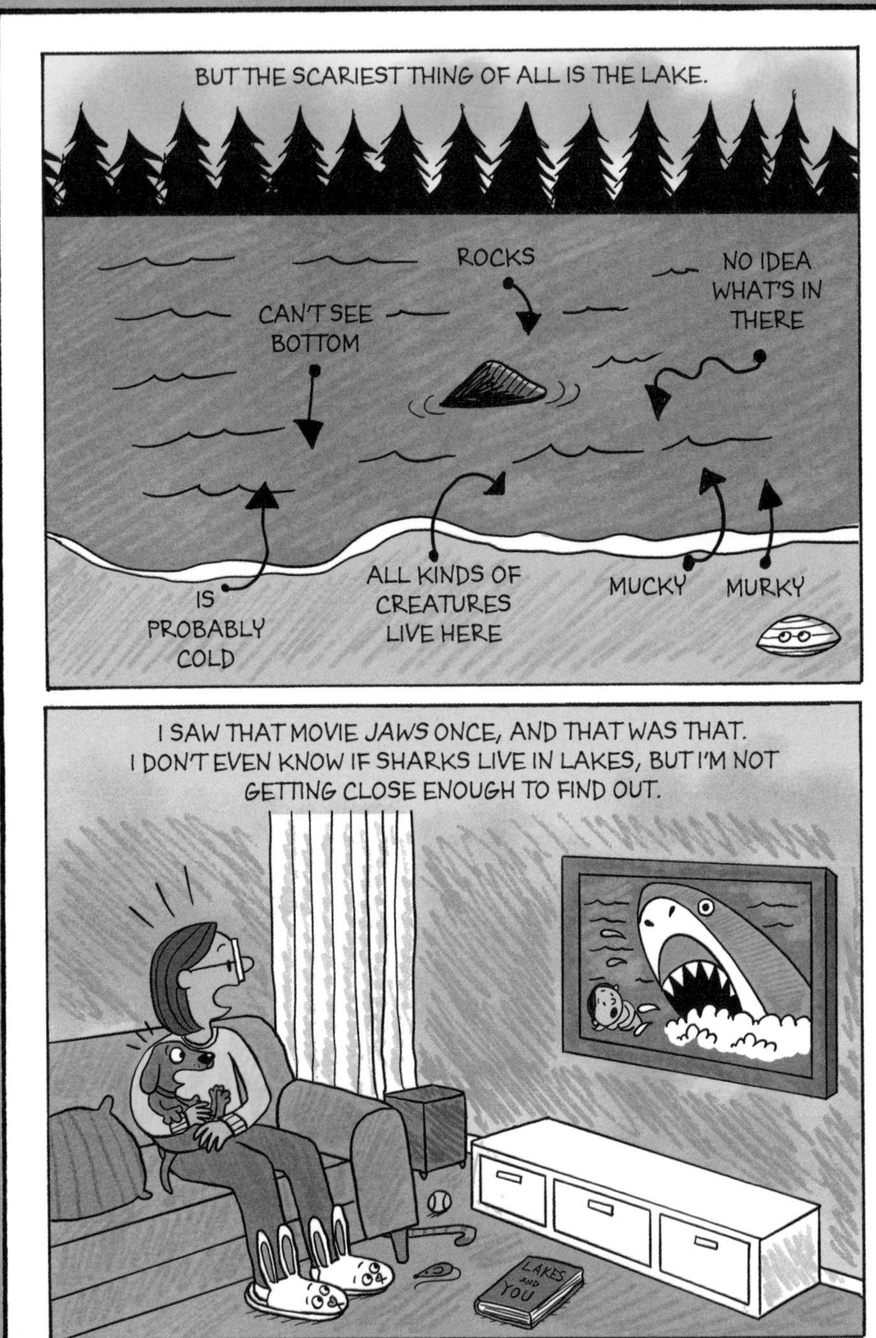
BUT THE SCARIEST THING OF ALL IS THE LAKE.
ROCKS
NO IDEA WHAT'S IN THERE
CAN'T SEE BOTTOM
IS PROBABLY COLD
ALL KINDS OF CREATURES LIVE HERE
MUCKY
MURKY
I SAW THAT MOVIE *JAWS* ONCE, AND THAT WAS THAT. I DON'T EVEN KNOW IF SHARKS LIVE IN LAKES, BUT I'M NOT GETTING CLOSE ENOUGH TO FIND OUT.
LAKES AND YOU

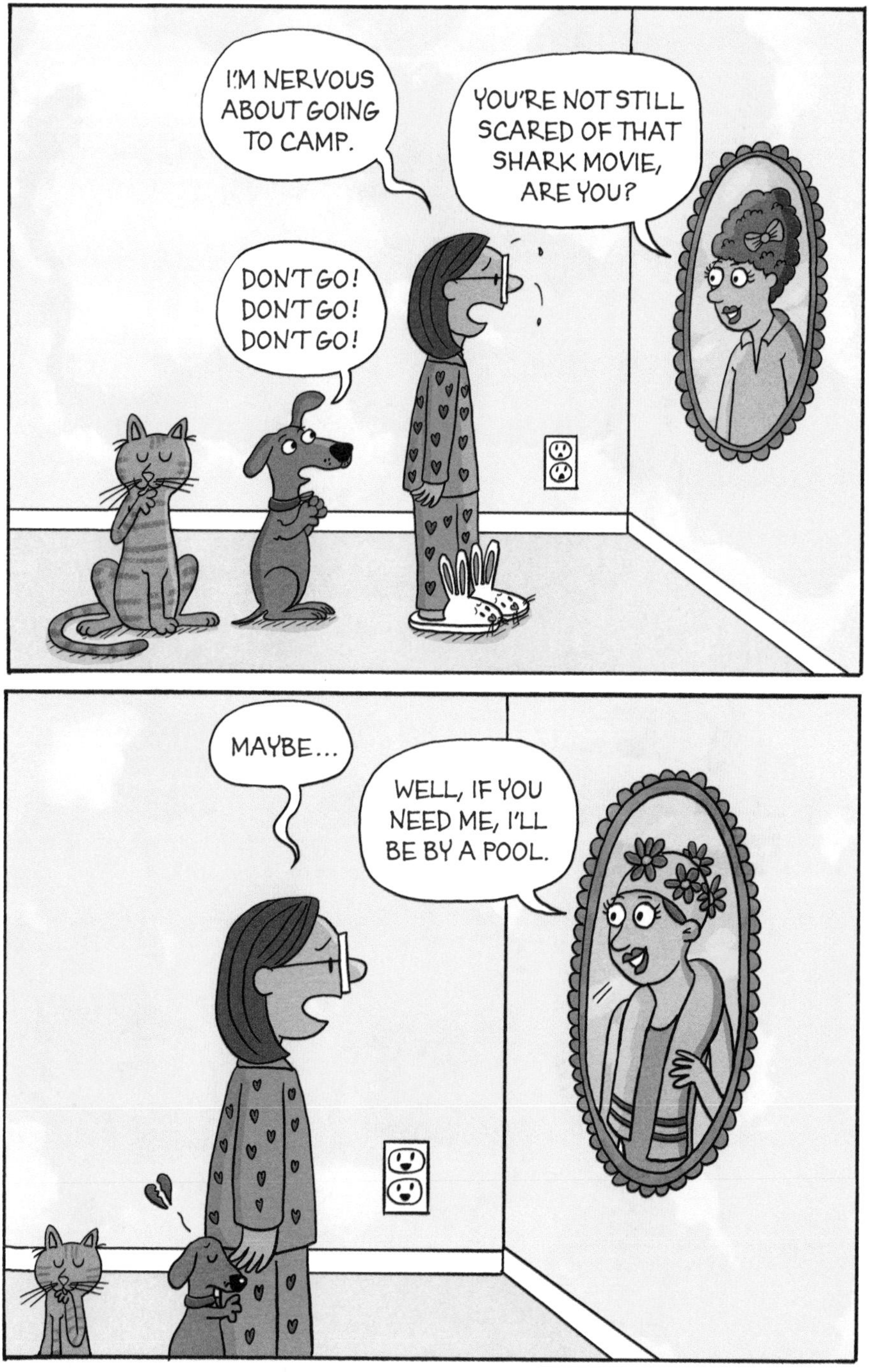
I'M NERVOUS ABOUT GOING TO CAMP.
YOU'RE NOT STILL SCARED OF THAT SHARK MOVIE, ARE YOU?
DON'T GO! DON'T GO! DON'T GO!
MAYBE...
WELL, IF YOU NEED ME, I'LL BE BY A POOL.

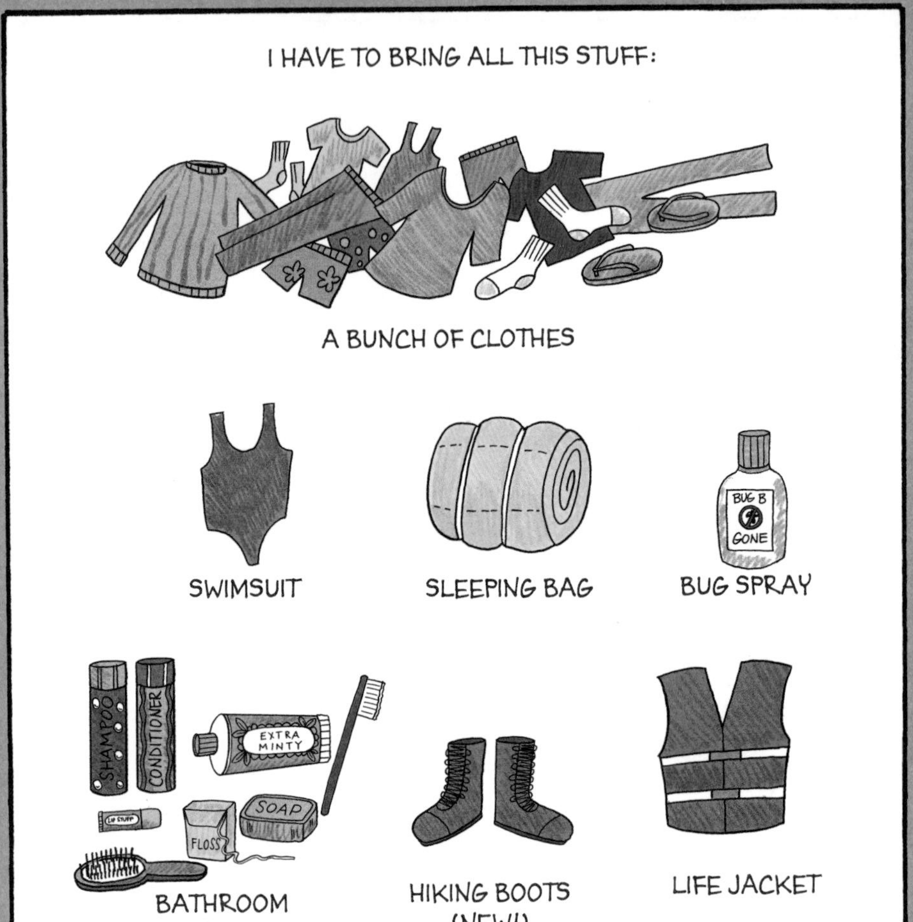
I HAVE TO BRING ALL THIS STUFF:
A BUNCH OF CLOTHES
SWIMSUIT
SLEEPING BAG
BUG B GONE
BUG SPRAY
SHAMPOO
CONDITIONER
EXTRA MINTY
LIP STUFF
SOAP
FLOSS
BATHROOM STUFF
HIKING BOOTS (NEW!)
LIFE JACKET
SKETCHBOOK (AND PENS)
EXTRA SKETCHBOOK (JUST IN CASE)
TOO MANY MOSQUITOES
A POISON-IVY PRIMER
BOOKS (LOTS)

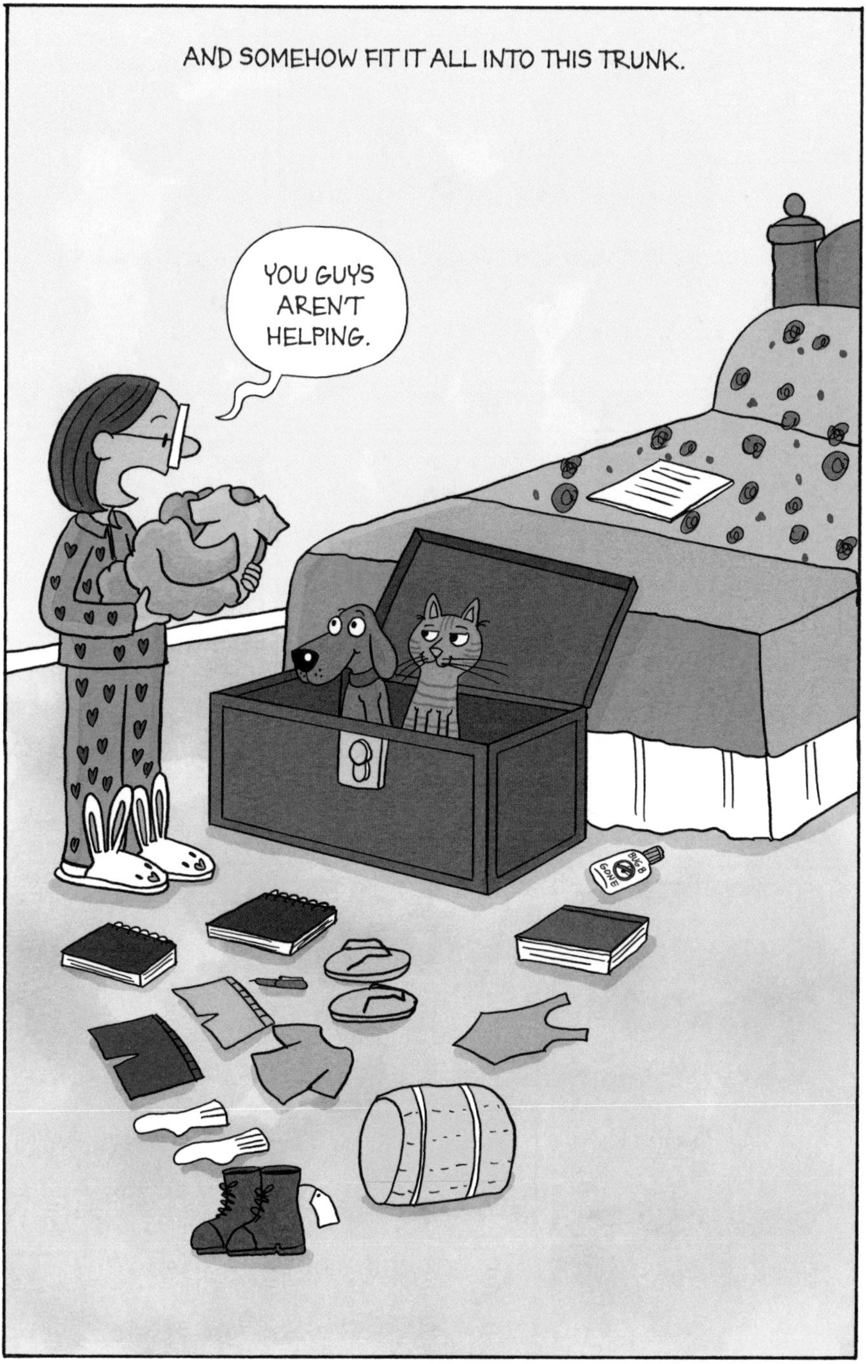
AND SOMEHOW FIT IT ALL INTO THIS TRUNK.
YOU GUYS AREN'T HELPING.
BUG B GONE

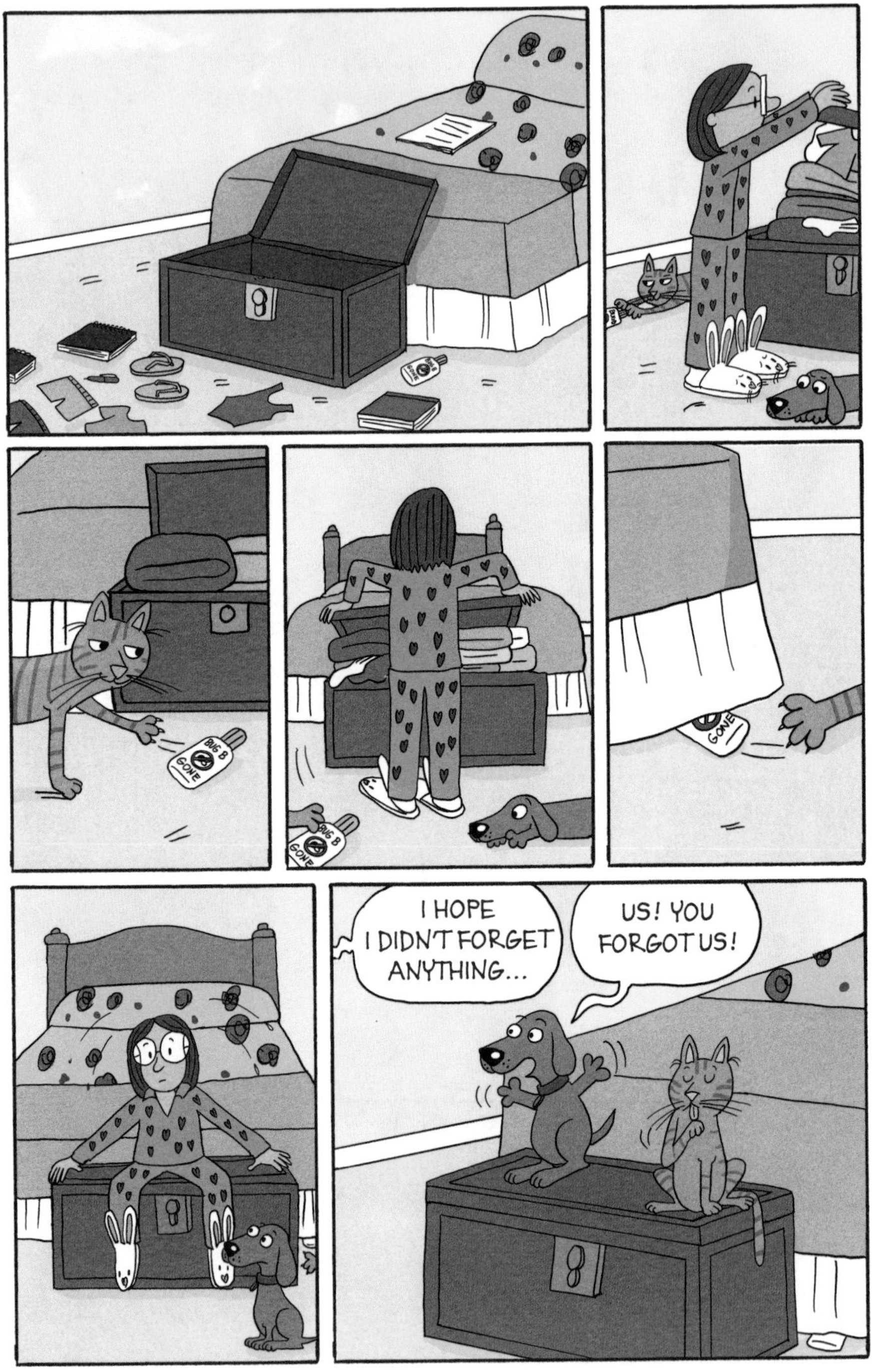
BUG B GONE
I HOPE I DIDN'T FORGET ANYTHING...
US! YOU FORGOT US!

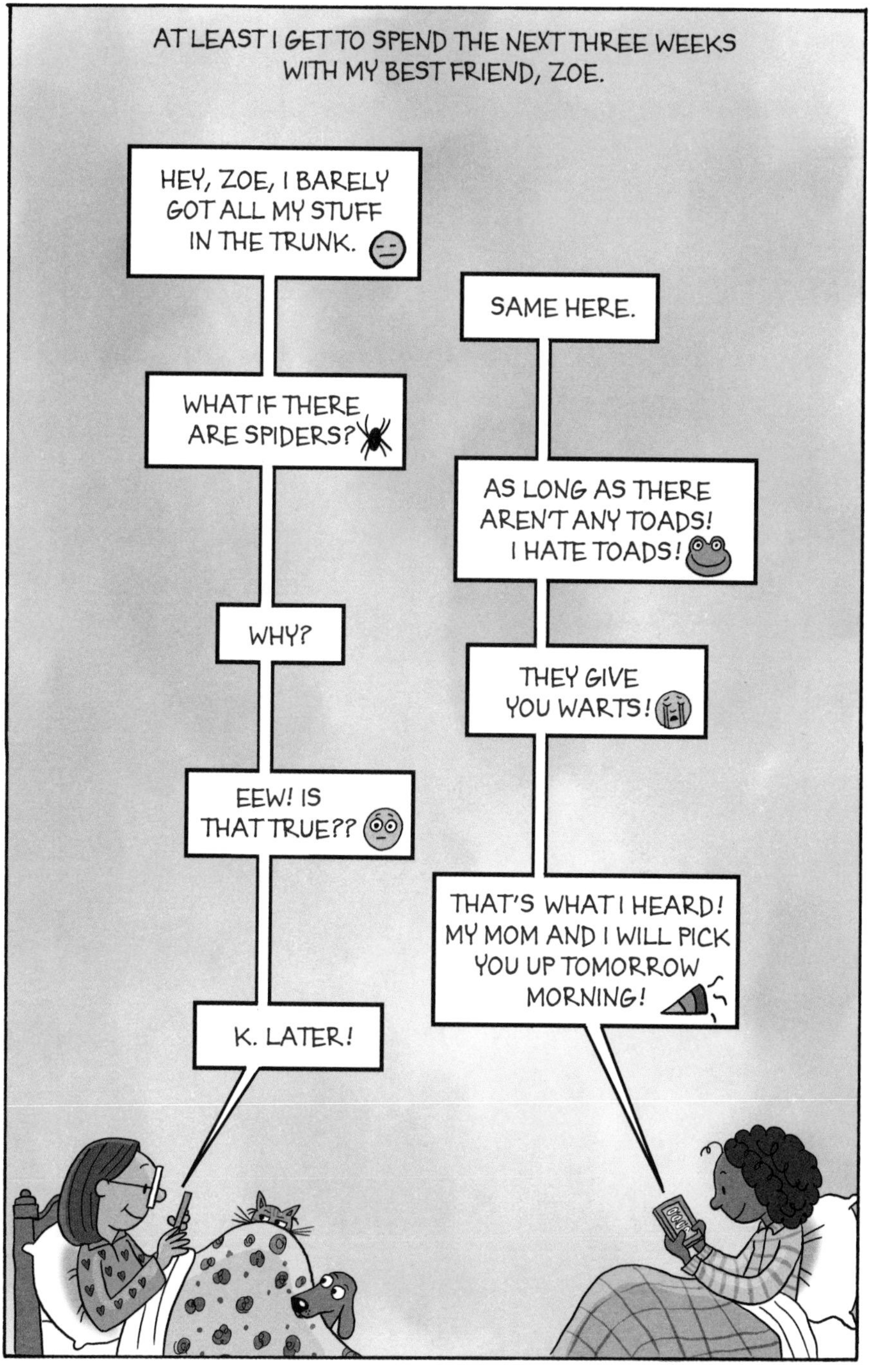
AT LEAST I GET TO SPEND THE NEXT THREE WEEKS WITH MY BEST FRIEND, ZOE.
HEY, ZOE, I BARELY GOT ALL MY STUFF IN THE TRUNK.
SAME HERE.
WHAT IF THERE ARE SPIDERS?
AS LONG AS THERE AREN'T ANY TOADS! I HATE TOADS!
WHY?
THEY GIVE YOU WARTS!
EEW! IS THAT TRUE??
THAT'S WHAT I HEARD! MY MOM AND I WILL PICK YOU UP TOMORROW MORNING!
K. LATER!

I JUST HOPE IT'S AS GOOD AS IT LOOKS IN THE BROCHURE.

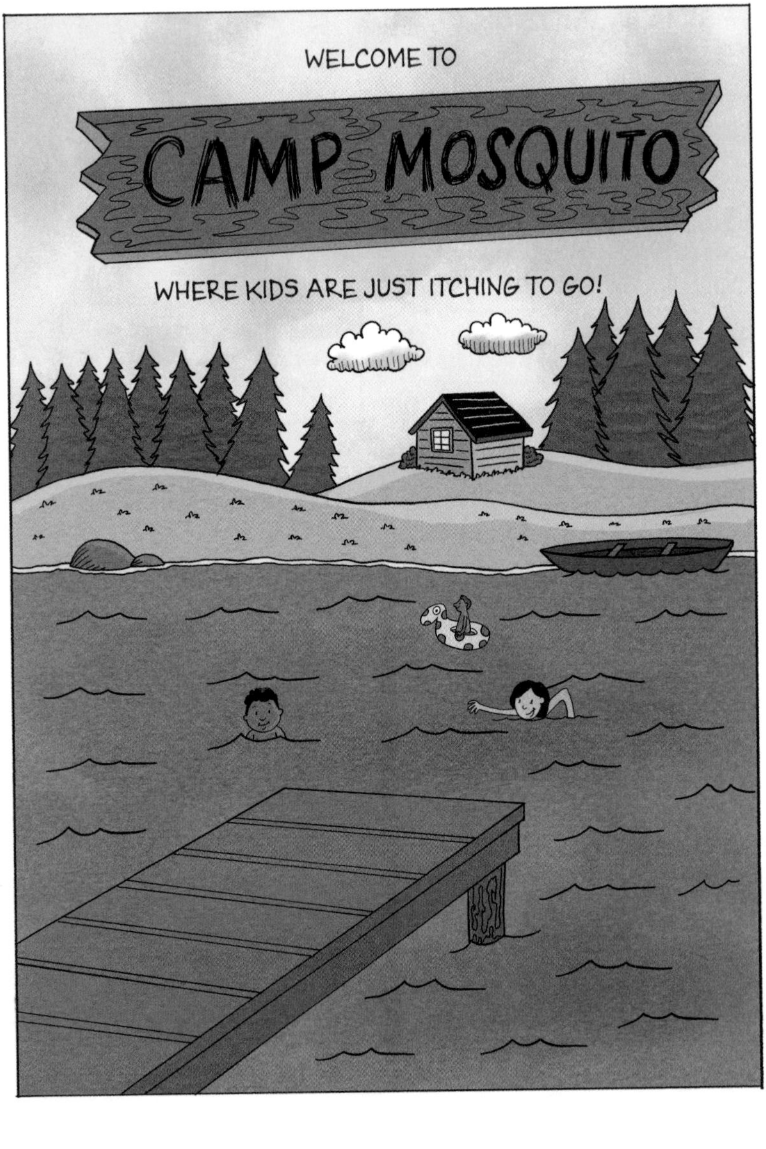

WELCOME TO
CAMP MOSQUITO
WHERE KIDS ARE JUST ITCHING TO GO!

CHAPTER 1
CHECK IN

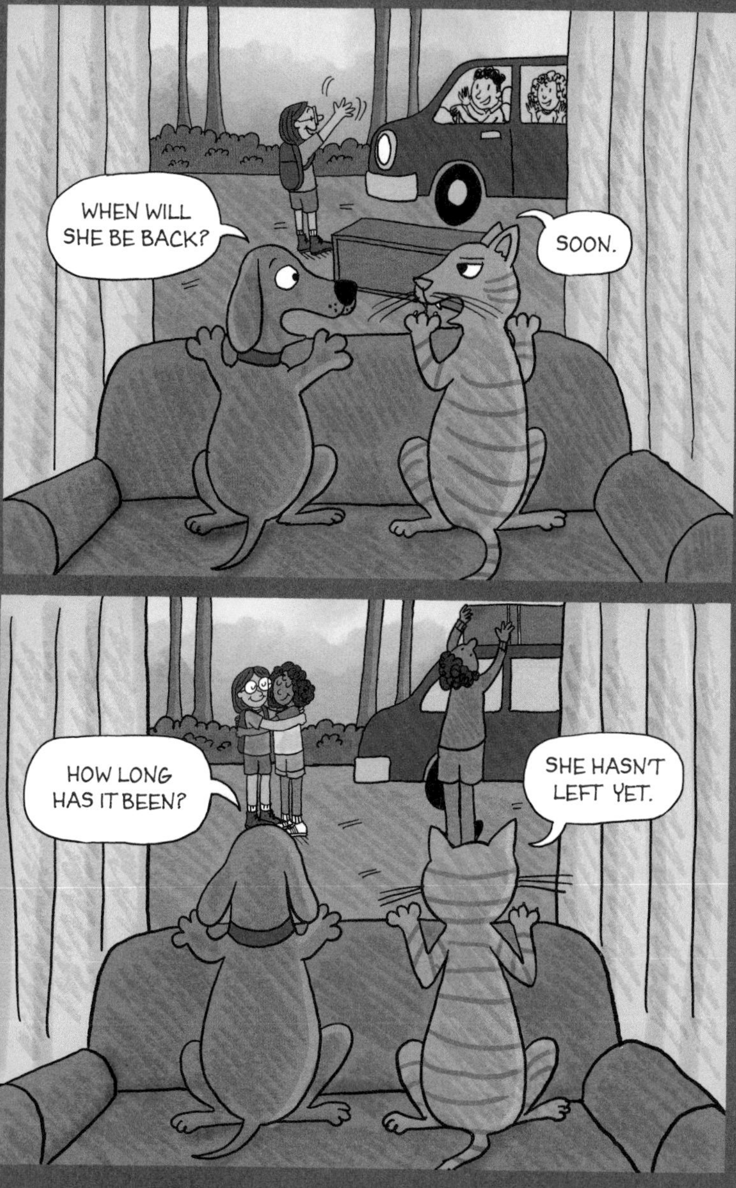
WHEN WILL SHE BE BACK?
SOON.
HOW LONG HAS IT BEEN?
SHE HASN'T LEFT YET.

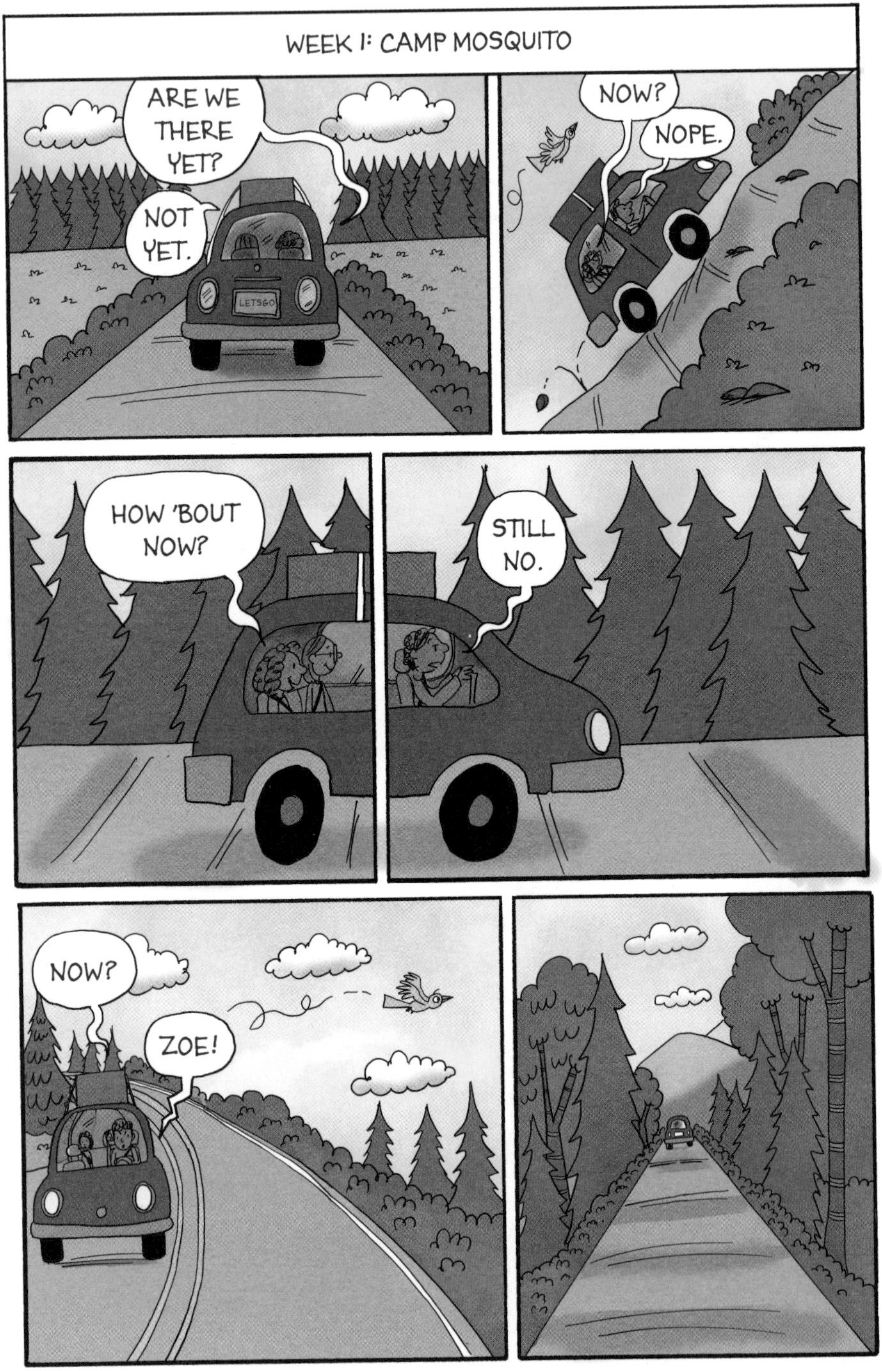
WEEK 1: CAMP MOSQUITO
ARE WE THERE YET?
NOT YET.
LETSGO
NOW?
NOPE.
HOW 'BOUT NOW?
STILL NO.
NOW?
ZOE!

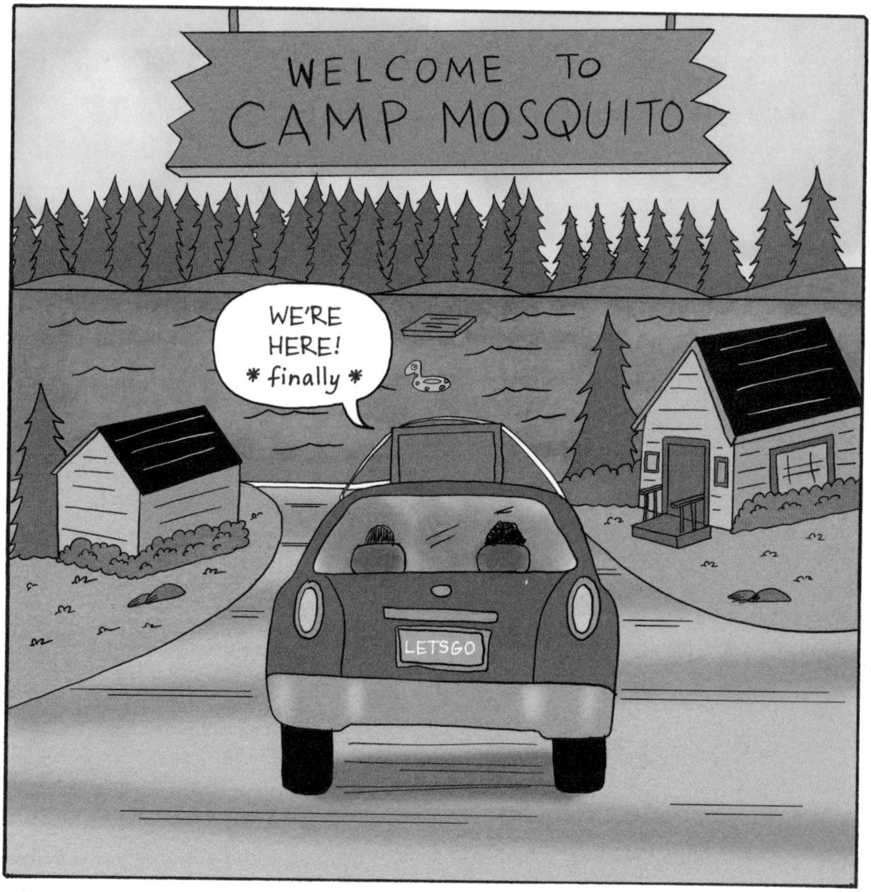
WELCOME TO
CAMP MOSQUITO
WE'RE HERE! * finally *
LETSGO

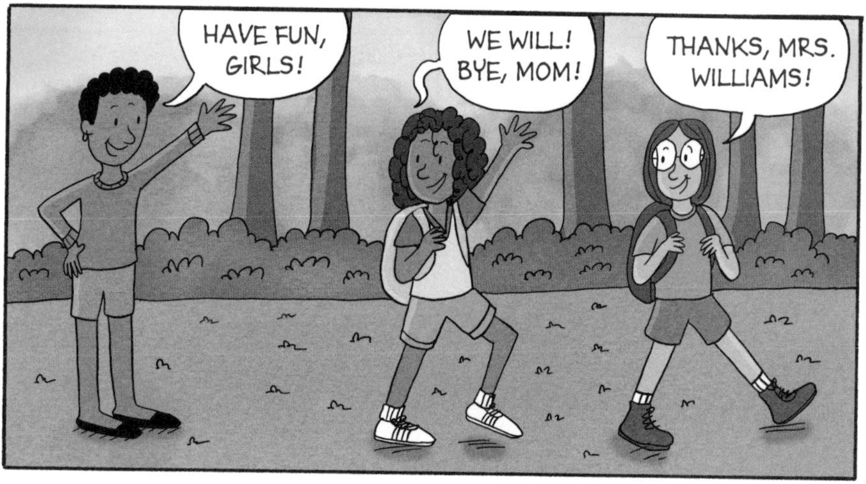
HAVE FUN, GIRLS!
WE WILL! BYE, MOM!
THANKS, MRS. WILLIAMS!

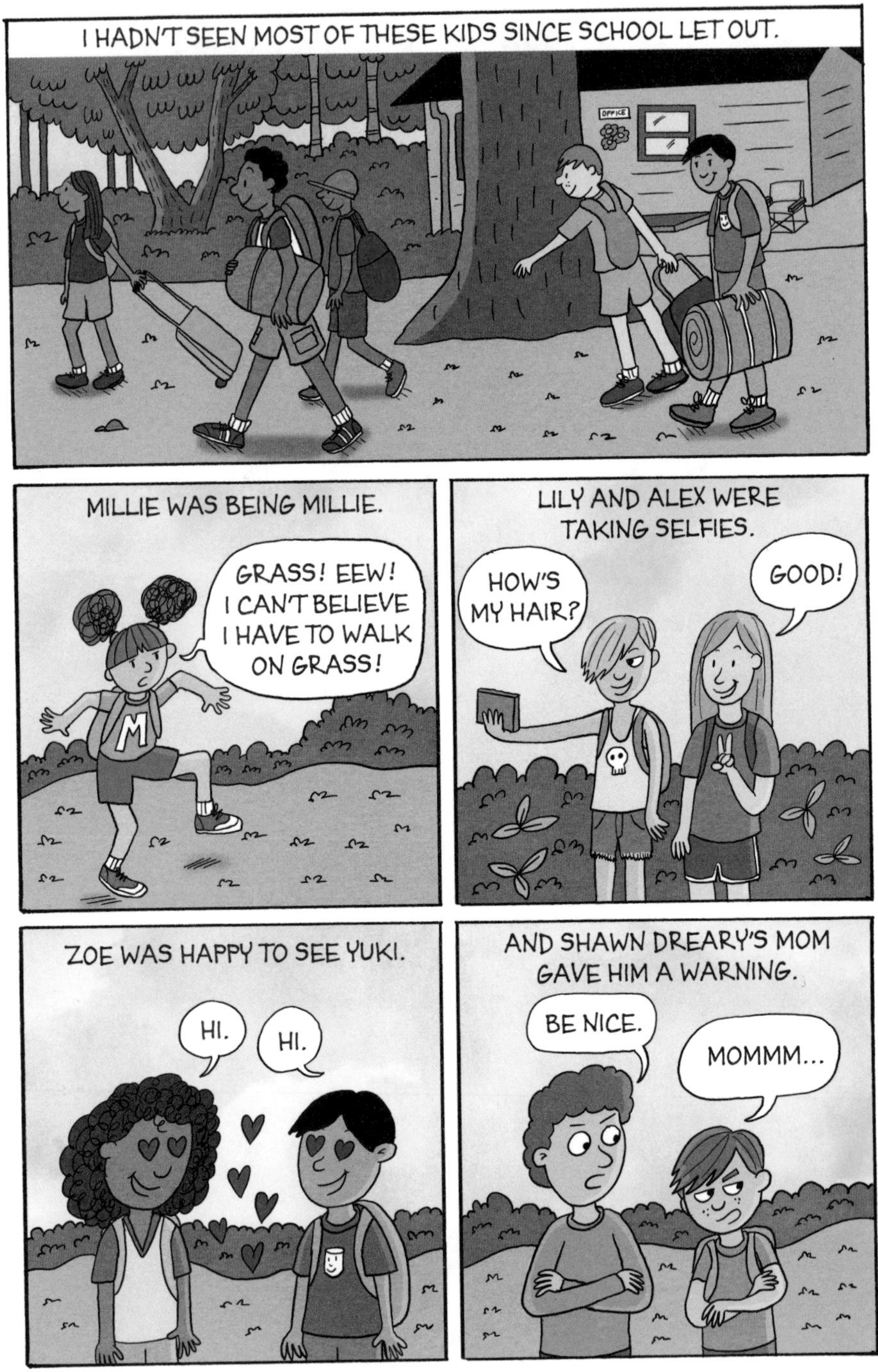
I HADN'T SEEN MOST OF THESE KIDS SINCE SCHOOL LET OUT.
OFFICE
MILLIE WAS BEING MILLIE.
GRASS! EEW! I CAN'T BELIEVE I HAVE TO WALK ON GRASS!
LILY AND ALEX WERE TAKING SELFIES.
HOW'S MY HAIR?
GOOD!
ZOE WAS HAPPY TO SEE YUKI.
HI.
HI.
AND SHAWN DREARY'S MOM GAVE HIM A WARNING.
BE NICE.
MOMMM...

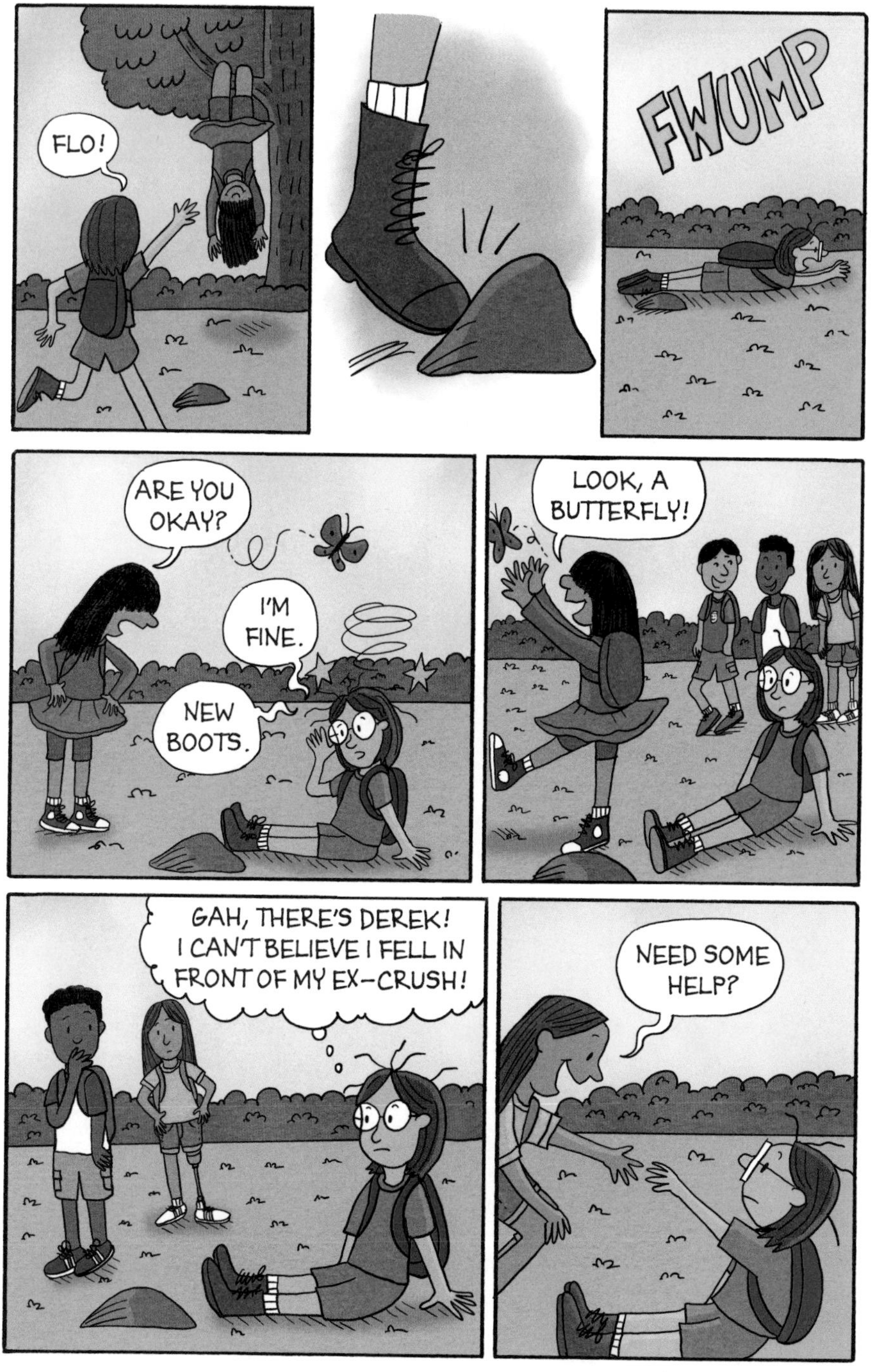
FLO!
FWUMP
ARE YOU OKAY?
I'M FINE.
NEW BOOTS.
LOOK, A BUTTERFLY!
GAH, THERE'S DEREK! I CAN'T BELIEVE I FELL IN FRONT OF MY EX-CRUSH!
NEED SOME HELP?

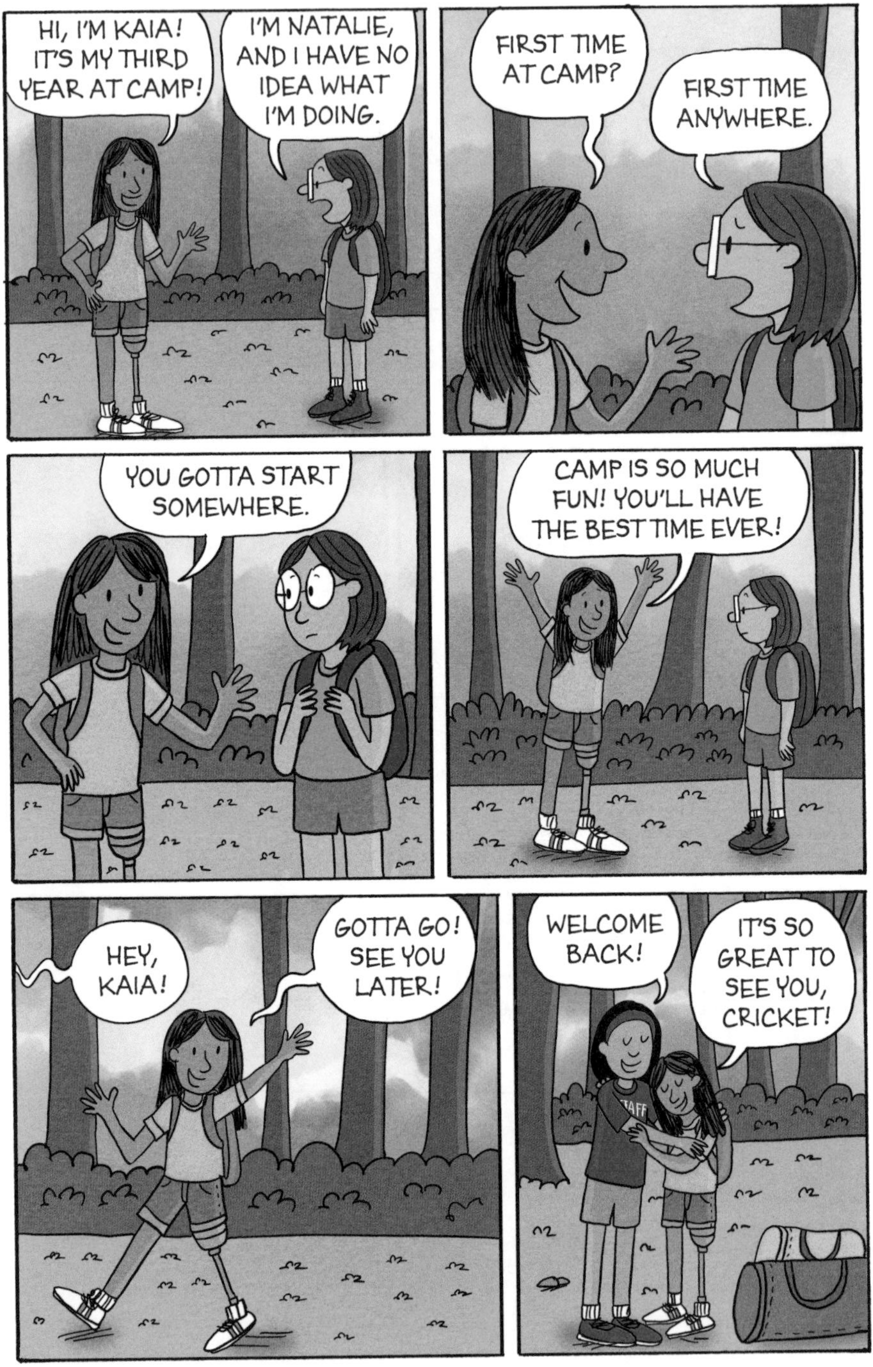
HI, I'M KAIA! IT'S MY THIRD YEAR AT CAMP!
I'M NATALIE, AND I HAVE NO IDEA WHAT I'M DOING.
FIRST TIME AT CAMP?
FIRST TIME ANYWHERE.
YOU GOTTA START SOMEWHERE.
CAMP IS SO MUCH FUN! YOU'LL HAVE THE BEST TIME EVER!
HEY, KAIA!
GOTTA GO! SEE YOU LATER!
WELCOME BACK!
IT'S SO GREAT TO SEE YOU, CRICKET!

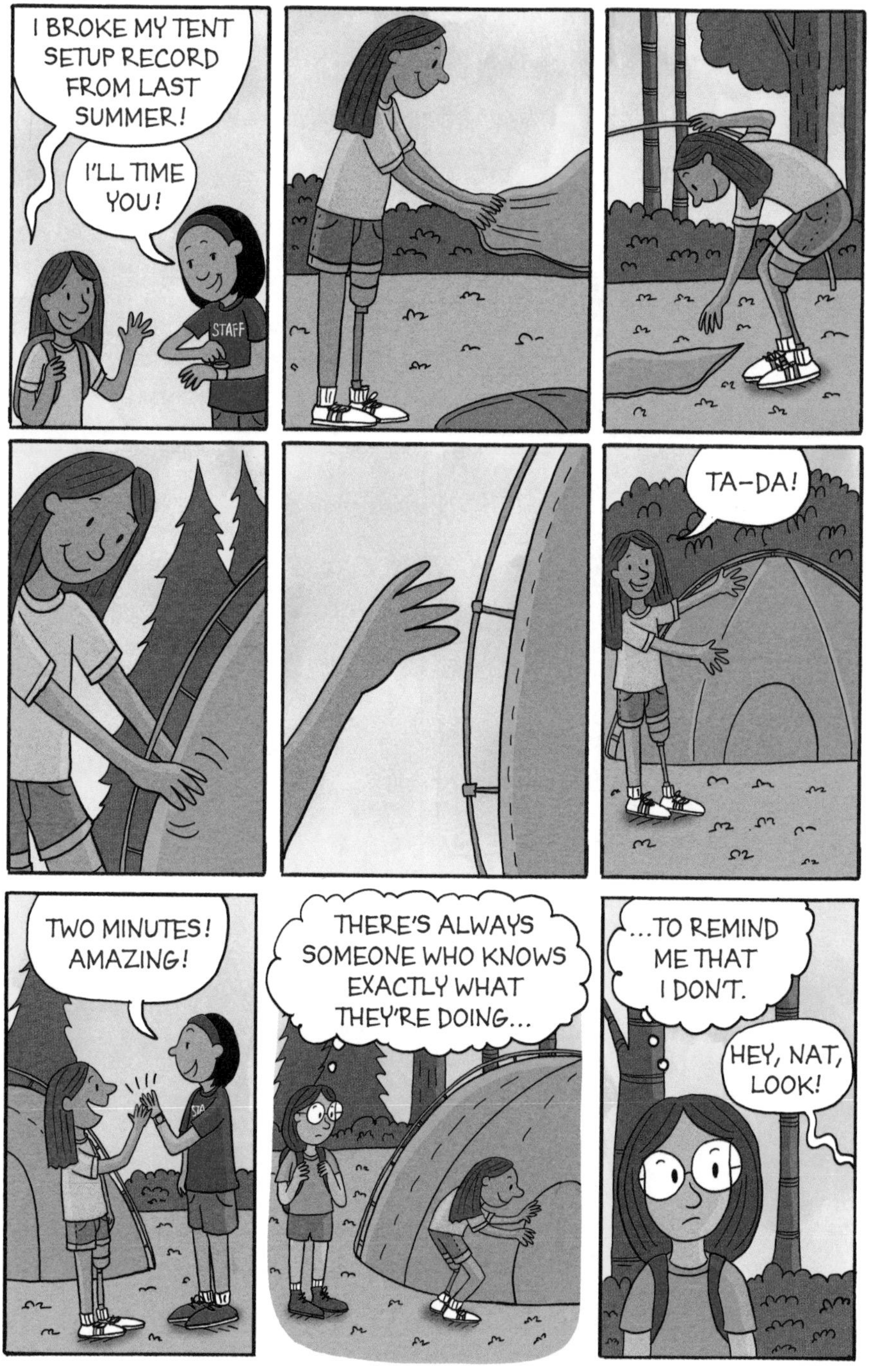
I BROKE MY TENT SETUP RECORD FROM LAST SUMMER!
I'LL TIME YOU!
STAFF
TA-DA!
TWO MINUTES! AMAZING!
THERE'S ALWAYS SOMEONE WHO KNOWS EXACTLY WHAT THEY'RE DOING...
...TO REMIND ME THAT I DON'T.
HEY, NAT, LOOK!

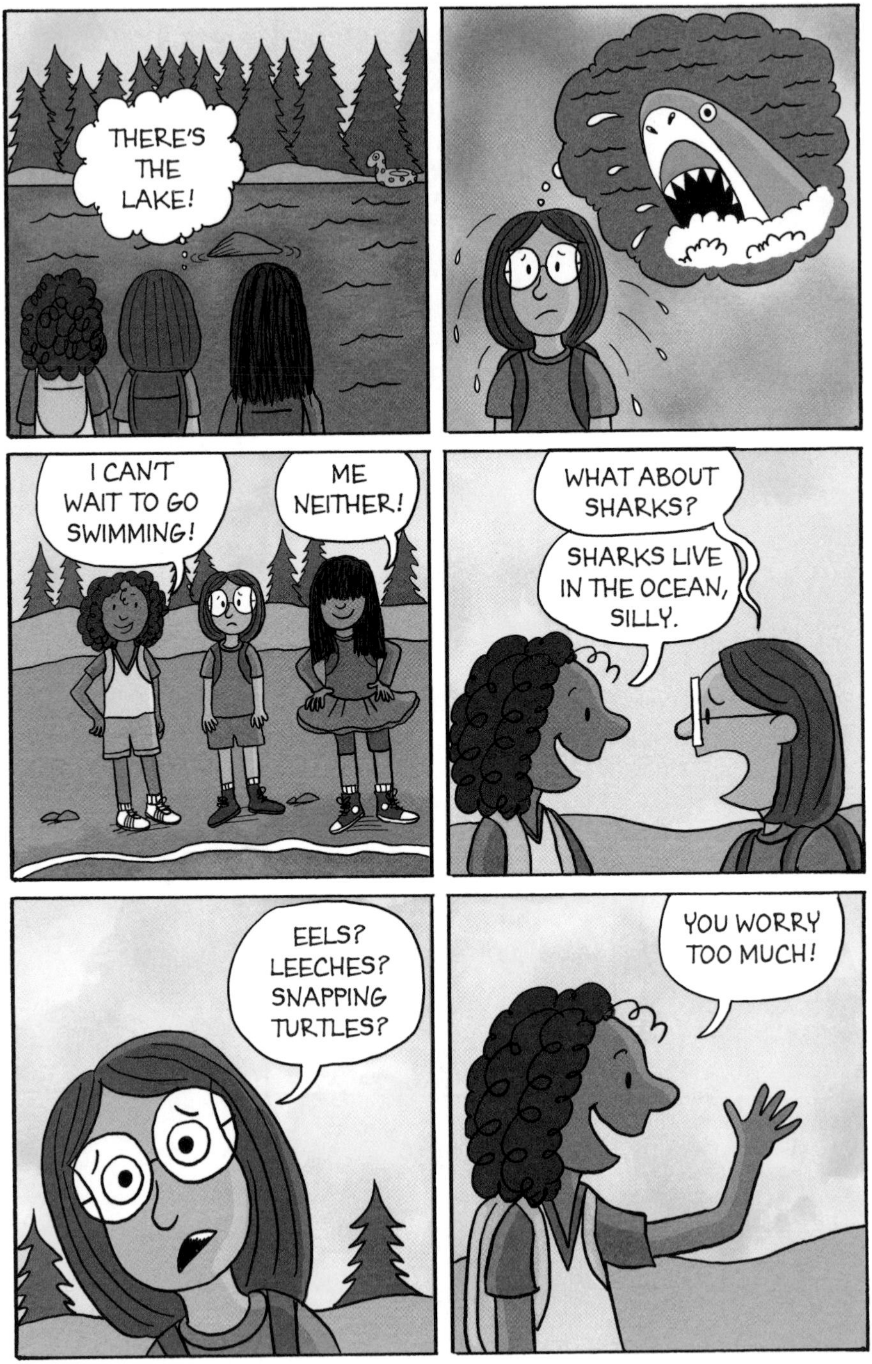
THERE'S THE LAKE!
I CAN'T WAIT TO GO SWIMMING!
ME NEITHER!
WHAT ABOUT SHARKS?
SHARKS LIVE IN THE OCEAN, SILLY.
EELS? LEECHES? SNAPPING TURTLES?
YOU WORRY TOO MUCH!

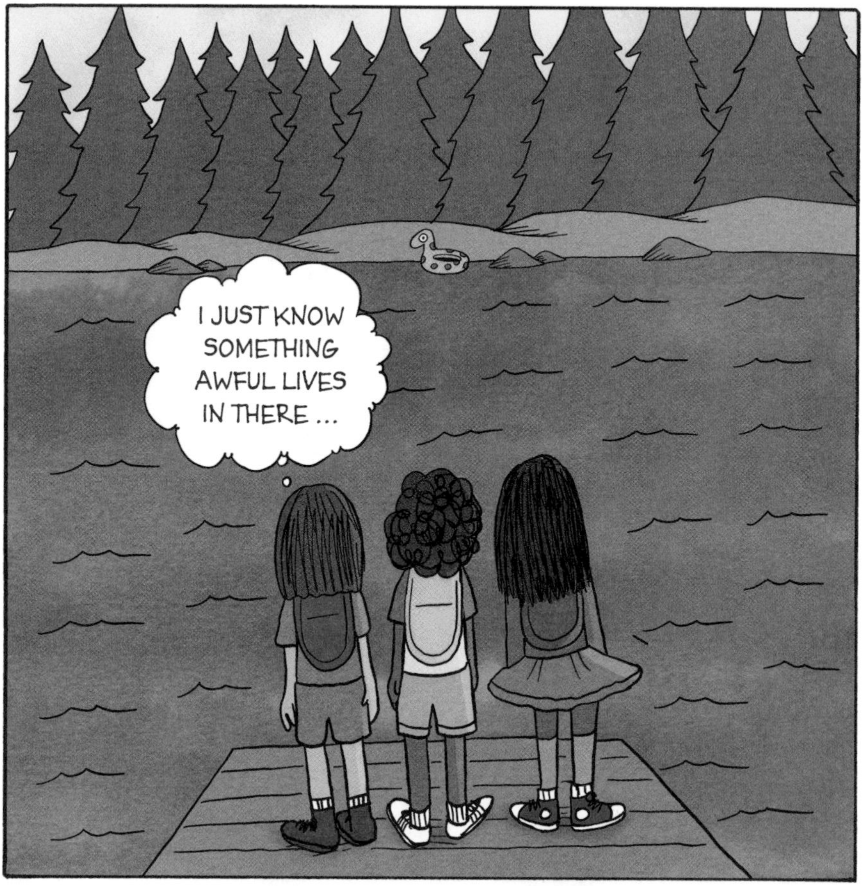
I JUST KNOW SOMETHING AWFUL LIVES IN THERE ...

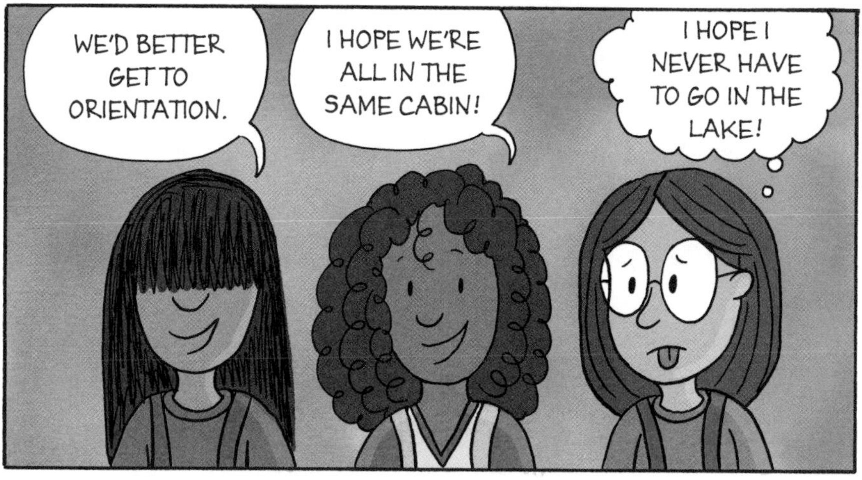
WE'D BETTER GET TO ORIENTATION.
I HOPE WE'RE ALL IN THE SAME CABIN!
I HOPE I NEVER HAVE TO GO IN THE LAKE!

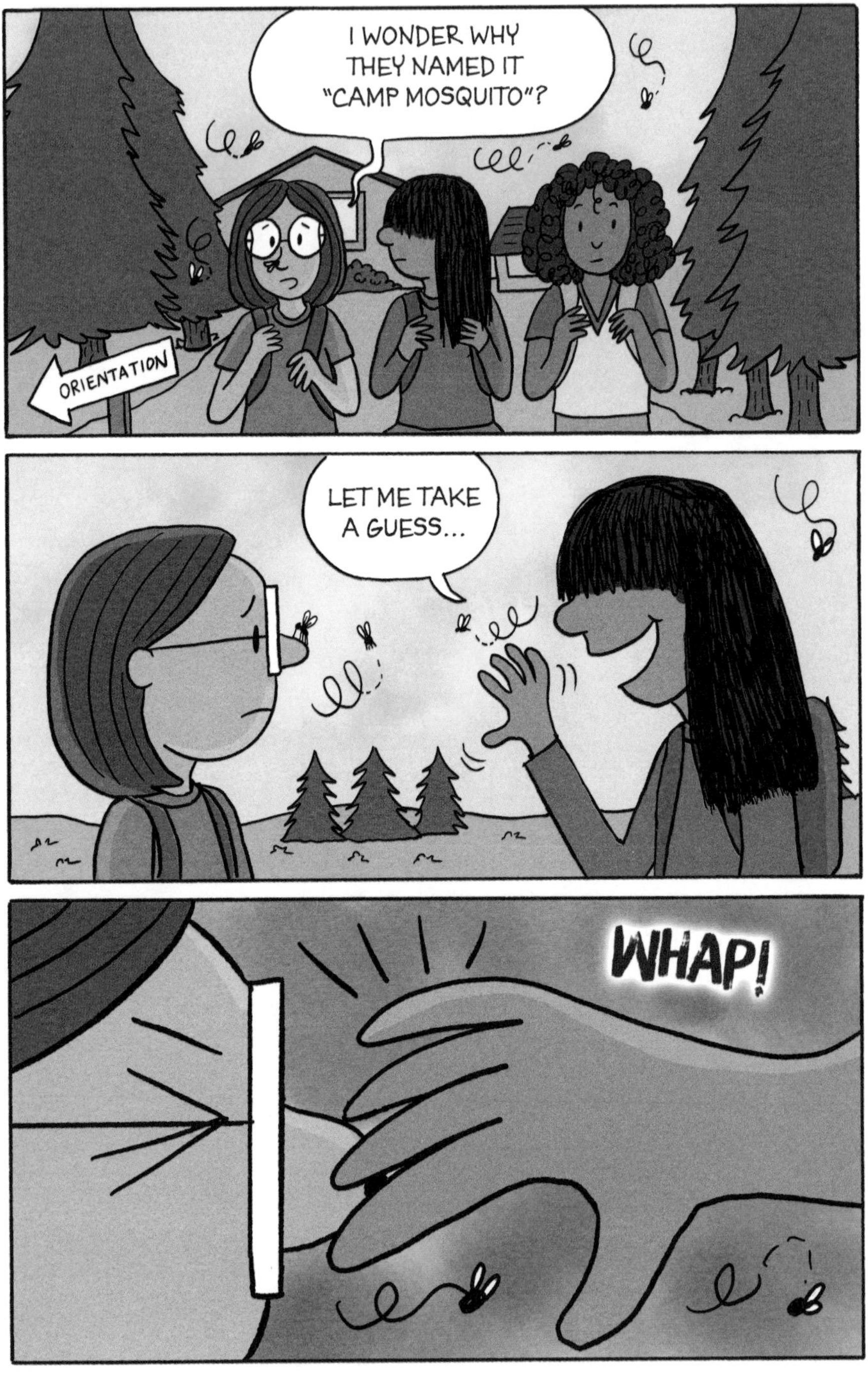
I WONDER WHY THEY NAMED IT "CAMP MOSQUITO"?
ORIENTATION
LET ME TAKE A GUESS...
WHAP!

CHAPTER 2
ORIENTATION

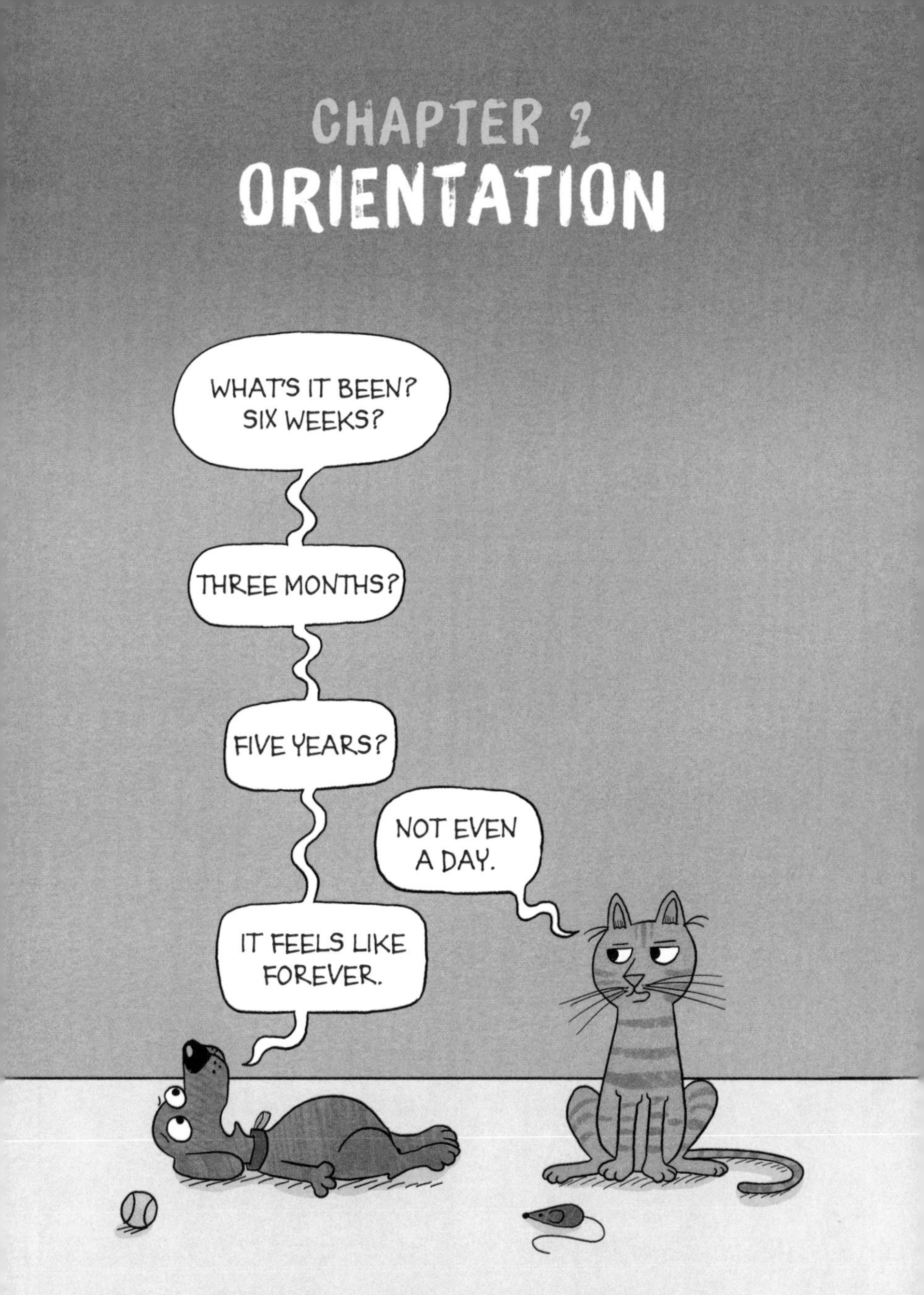
WHAT'S IT BEEN? SIX WEEKS?
THREE MONTHS?
FIVE YEARS?
IT FEELS LIKE FOREVER.
NOT EVEN A DAY.

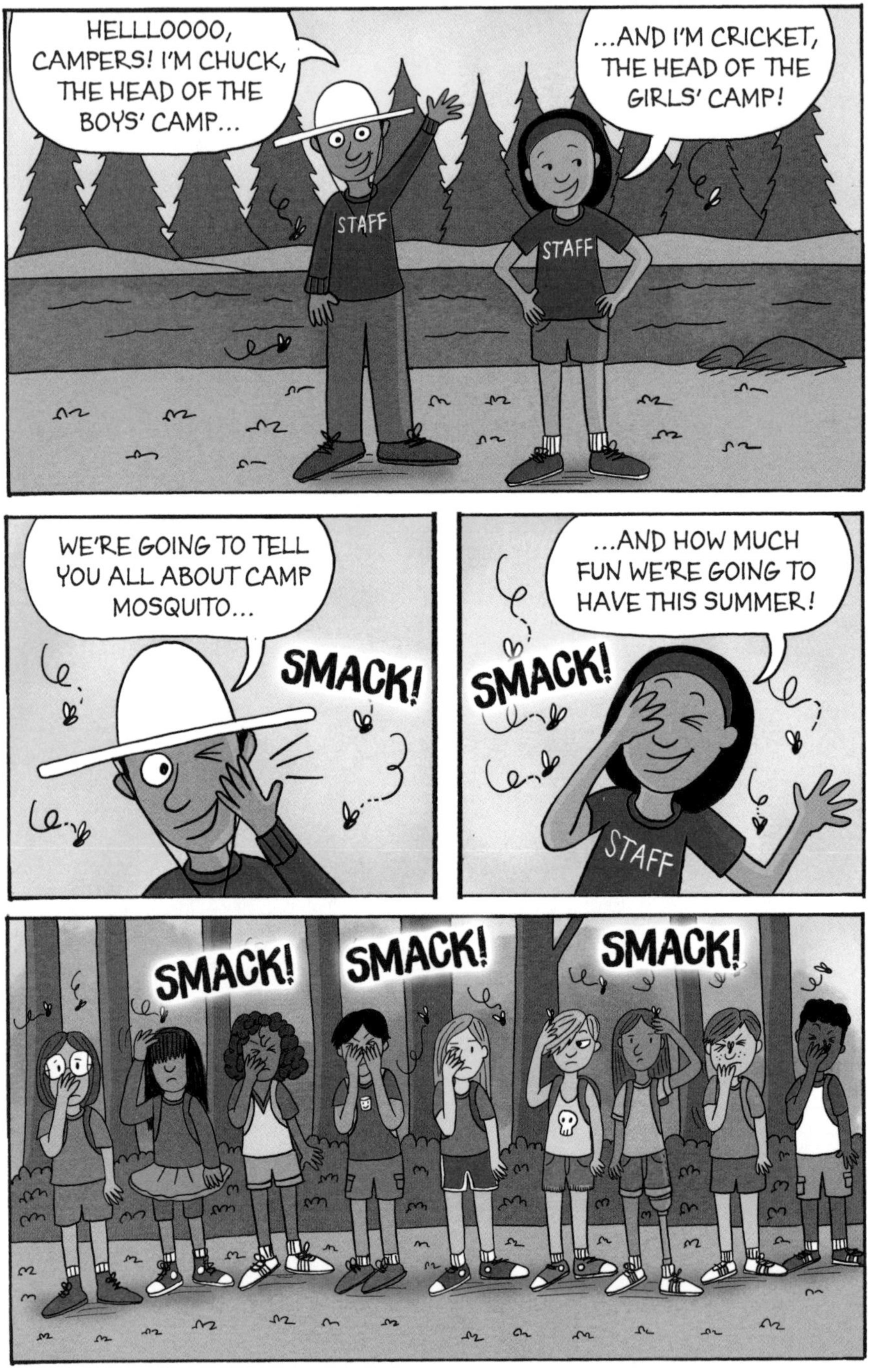
HELLLOOOO, CAMPERS! I'M CHUCK, THE HEAD OF THE BOYS' CAMP...
...AND I'M CRICKET, THE HEAD OF THE GIRLS' CAMP!
STAFF
STAFF
WE'RE GOING TO TELL YOU ALL ABOUT CAMP MOSQUITO...
SMACK!
...AND HOW MUCH FUN WE'RE GOING TO HAVE THIS SUMMER!
SMACK!
STAFF
SMACK!
SMACK!
SMACK!

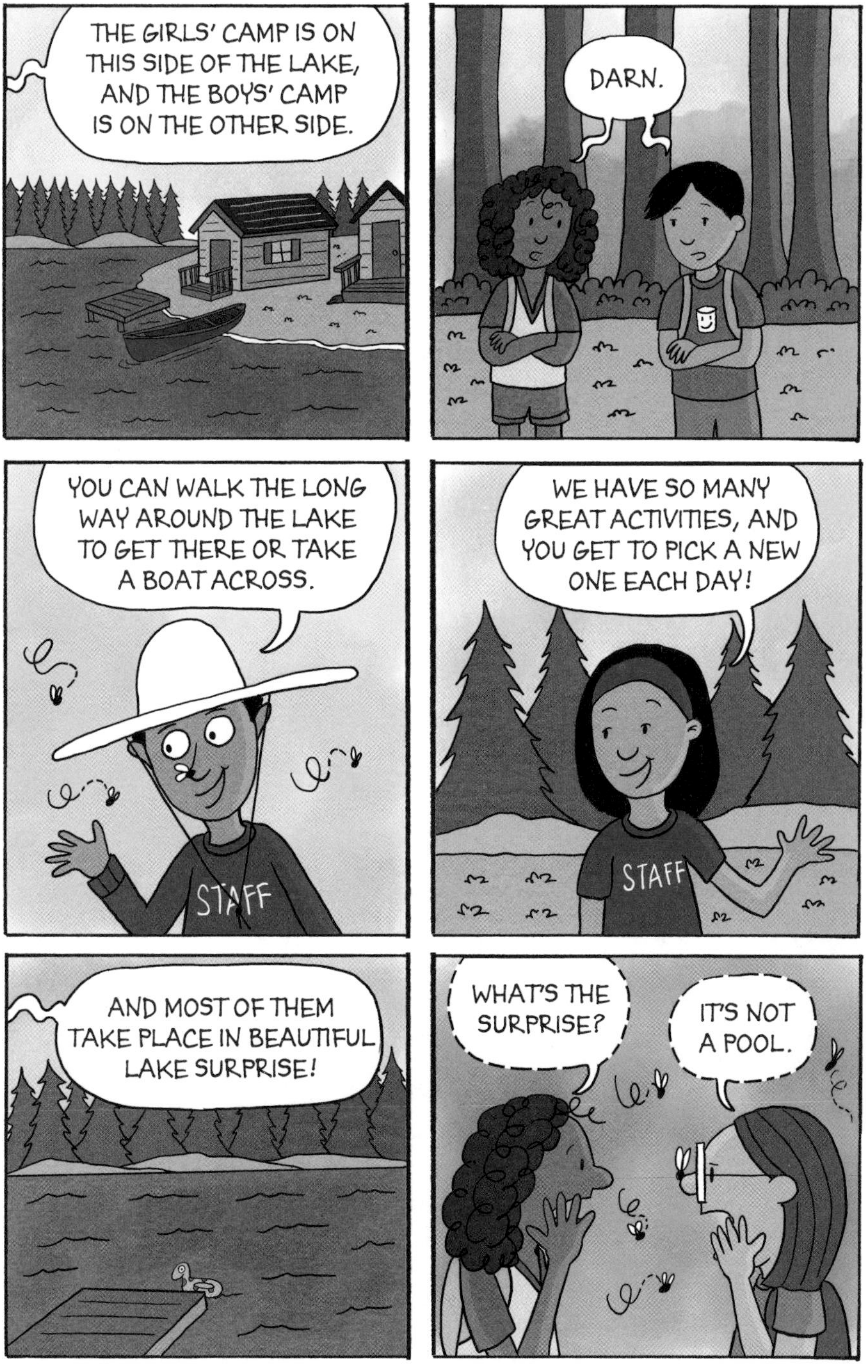
THE GIRLS' CAMP IS ON THIS SIDE OF THE LAKE, AND THE BOYS' CAMP IS ON THE OTHER SIDE.
DARN.
YOU CAN WALK THE LONG WAY AROUND THE LAKE TO GET THERE OR TAKE A BOAT ACROSS.
STAFF
WE HAVE SO MANY GREAT ACTIVITIES, AND YOU GET TO PICK A NEW ONE EACH DAY!
STAFF
AND MOST OF THEM TAKE PLACE IN BEAUTIFUL LAKE SURPRISE!
WHAT'S THE SURPRISE?
IT'S NOT A POOL.

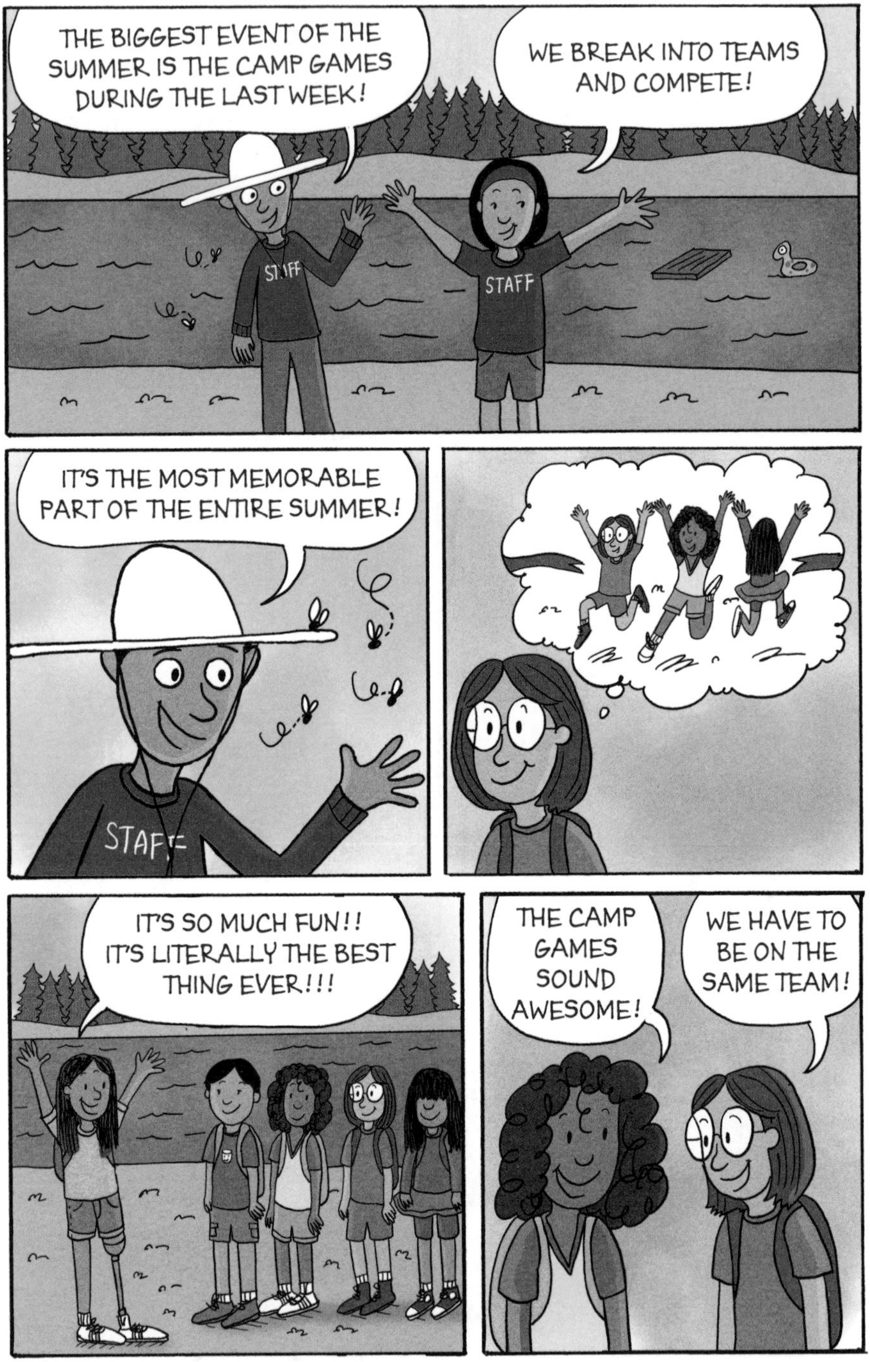
THE BIGGEST EVENT OF THE SUMMER IS THE CAMP GAMES DURING THE LAST WEEK!
WE BREAK INTO TEAMS AND COMPETE!
STAFF
STAFF
IT'S THE MOST MEMORABLE PART OF THE ENTIRE SUMMER!
IT'S SO MUCH FUN!! IT'S LITERALLY THE BEST THING EVER!!!
THE CAMP GAMES SOUND AWESOME!
WE HAVE TO BE ON THE SAME TEAM!

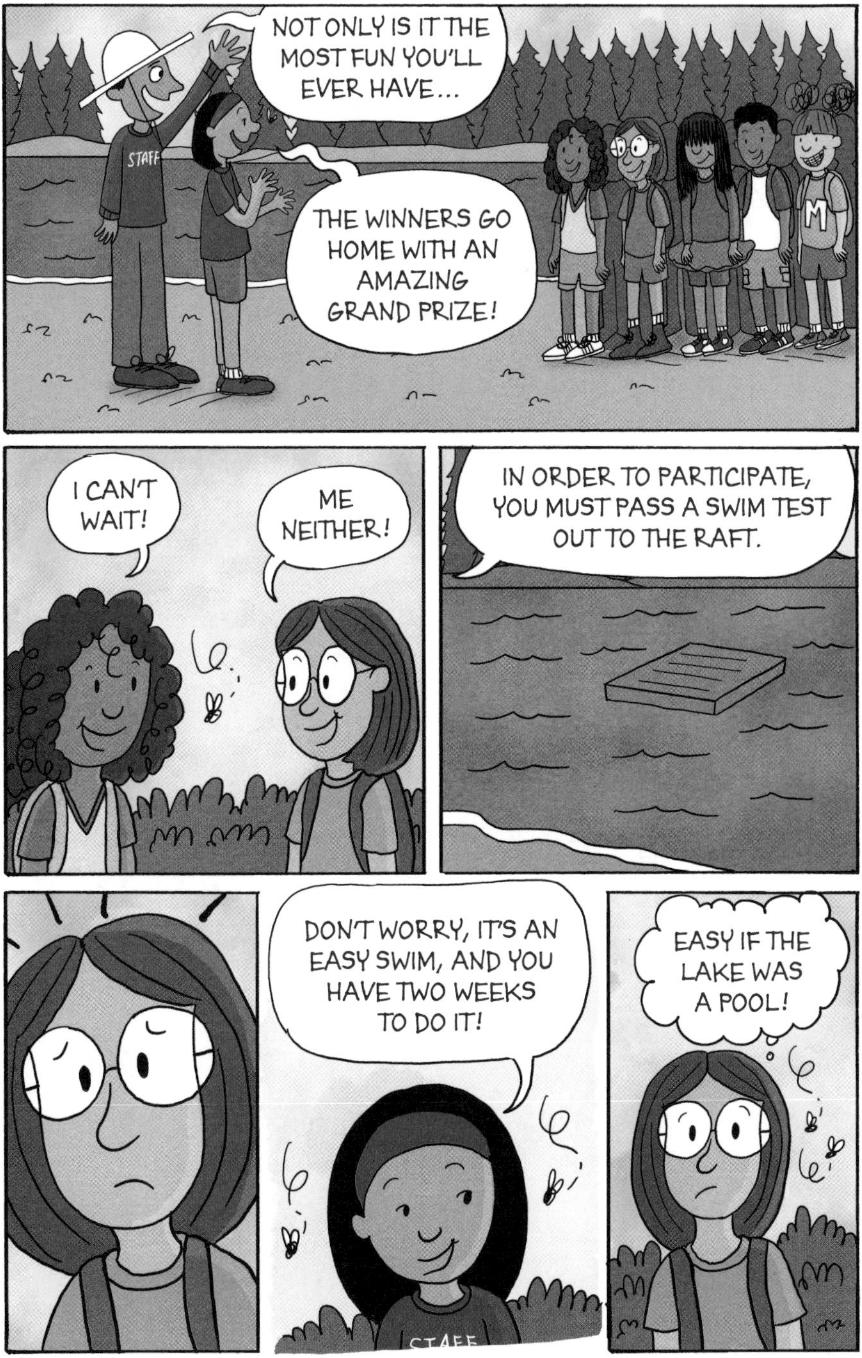
NOT ONLY IS IT THE MOST FUN YOU'LL EVER HAVE...
STAFF
THE WINNERS GO HOME WITH AN AMAZING GRAND PRIZE!
M
I CAN'T WAIT!
ME NEITHER!
IN ORDER TO PARTICIPATE, YOU MUST PASS A SWIM TEST OUT TO THE RAFT.
DON'T WORRY, IT'S AN EASY SWIM, AND YOU HAVE TWO WEEKS TO DO IT!
EASY IF THE LAKE WAS A POOL!

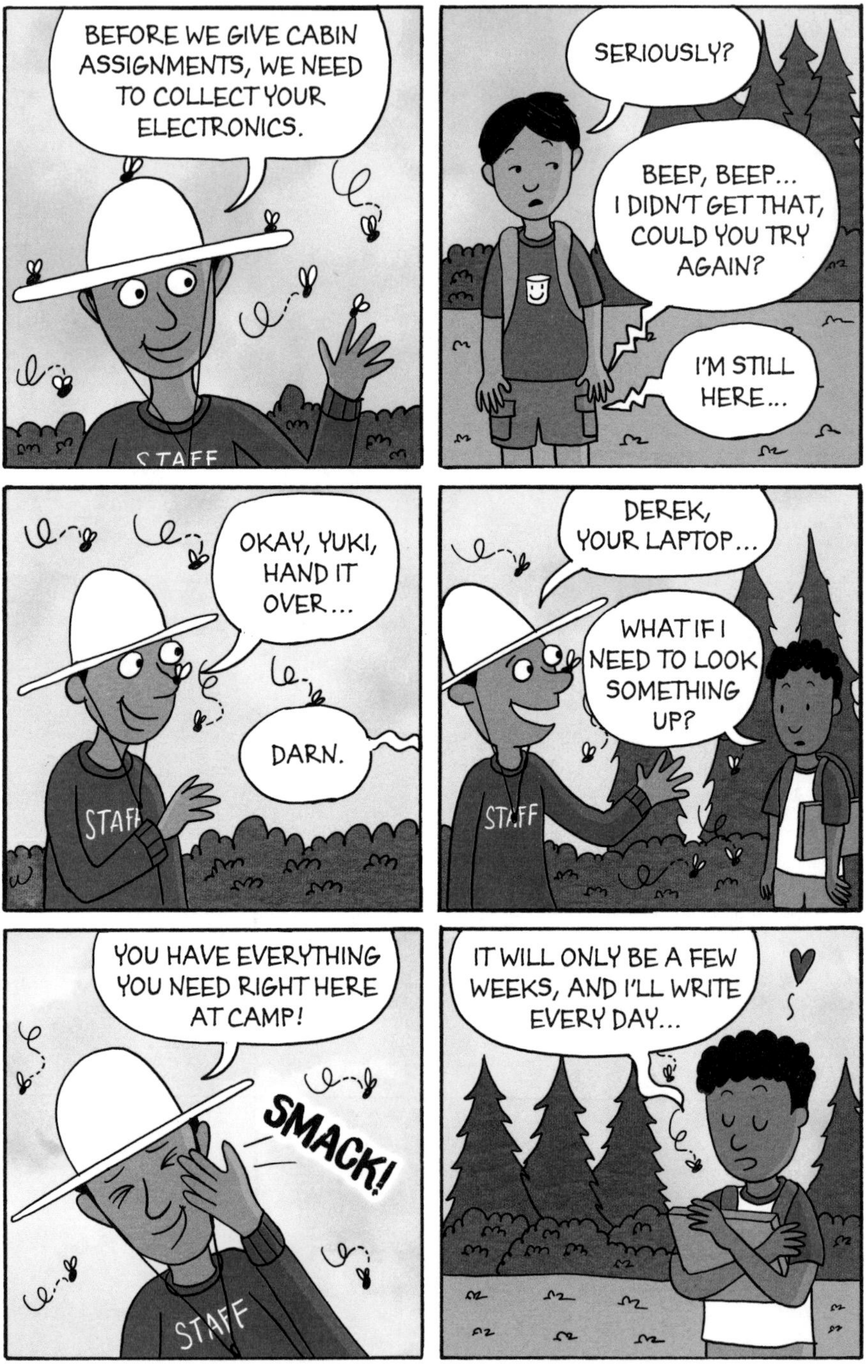
BEFORE WE GIVE CABIN ASSIGNMENTS, WE NEED TO COLLECT YOUR ELECTRONICS.
STAFF
SERIOUSLY?
BEEP, BEEP... I DIDN'T GET THAT, COULD YOU TRY AGAIN?
I'M STILL HERE...
OKAY, YUKI, HAND IT OVER...
DARN.
STAFF
DEREK, YOUR LAPTOP...
WHAT IF I NEED TO LOOK SOMETHING UP?
STAFF
YOU HAVE EVERYTHING YOU NEED RIGHT HERE AT CAMP!
SMACK!
STAFF
IT WILL ONLY BE A FEW WEEKS, AND I'LL WRITE EVERY DAY...

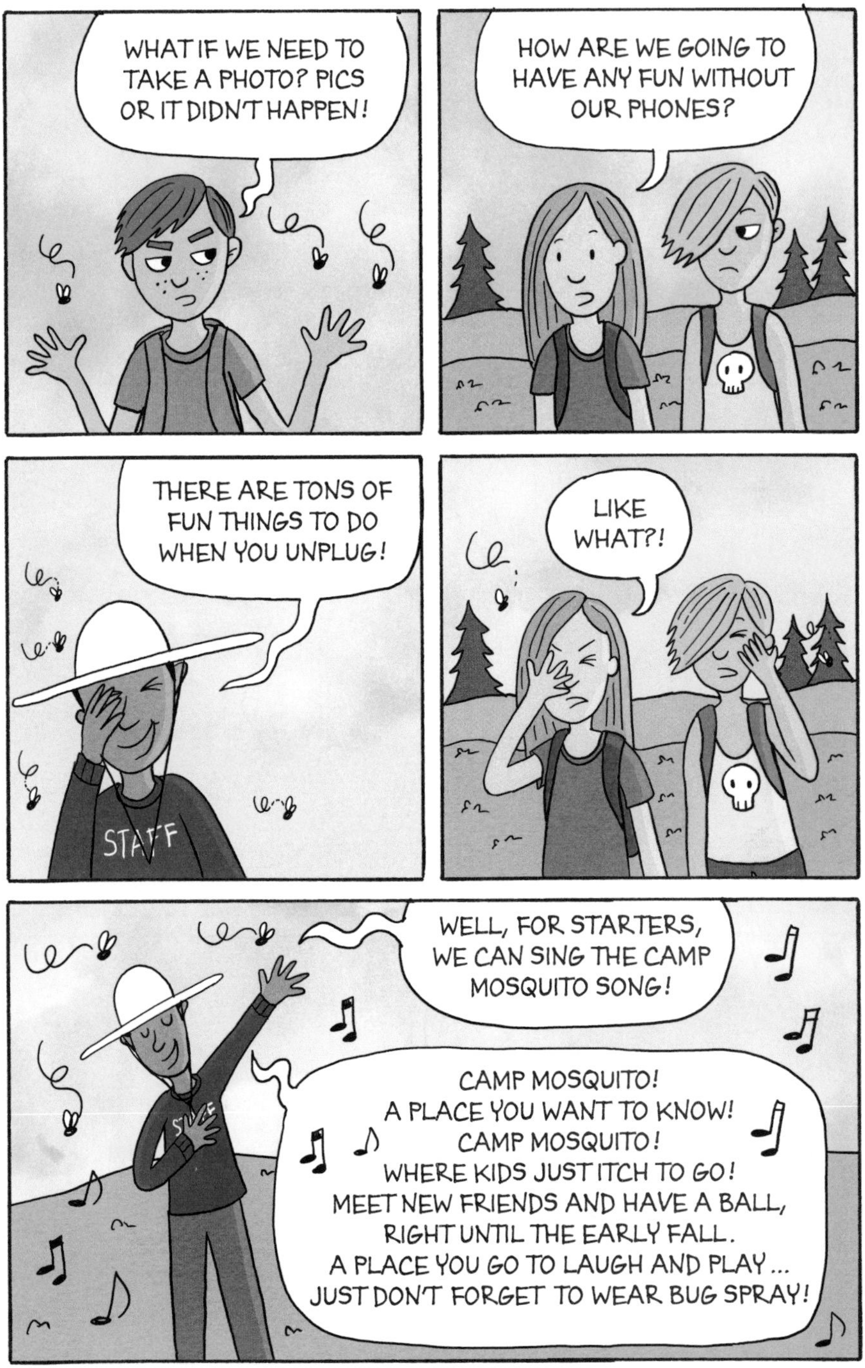
WHAT IF WE NEED TO TAKE A PHOTO? PICS OR IT DIDN'T HAPPEN!
HOW ARE WE GOING TO HAVE ANY FUN WITHOUT OUR PHONES?
THERE ARE TONS OF FUN THINGS TO DO WHEN YOU UNPLUG!
STAFF
LIKE WHAT?!
WELL, FOR STARTERS, WE CAN SING THE CAMP MOSQUITO SONG!
CAMP MOSQUITO!
A PLACE YOU WANT TO KNOW!
CAMP MOSQUITO!
WHERE KIDS JUST ITCH TO GO!
MEET NEW FRIENDS AND HAVE A BALL,
RIGHT UNTIL THE EARLY FALL.
A PLACE YOU GO TO LAUGH AND PLAY...
JUST DON'T FORGET TO WEAR BUG SPRAY!

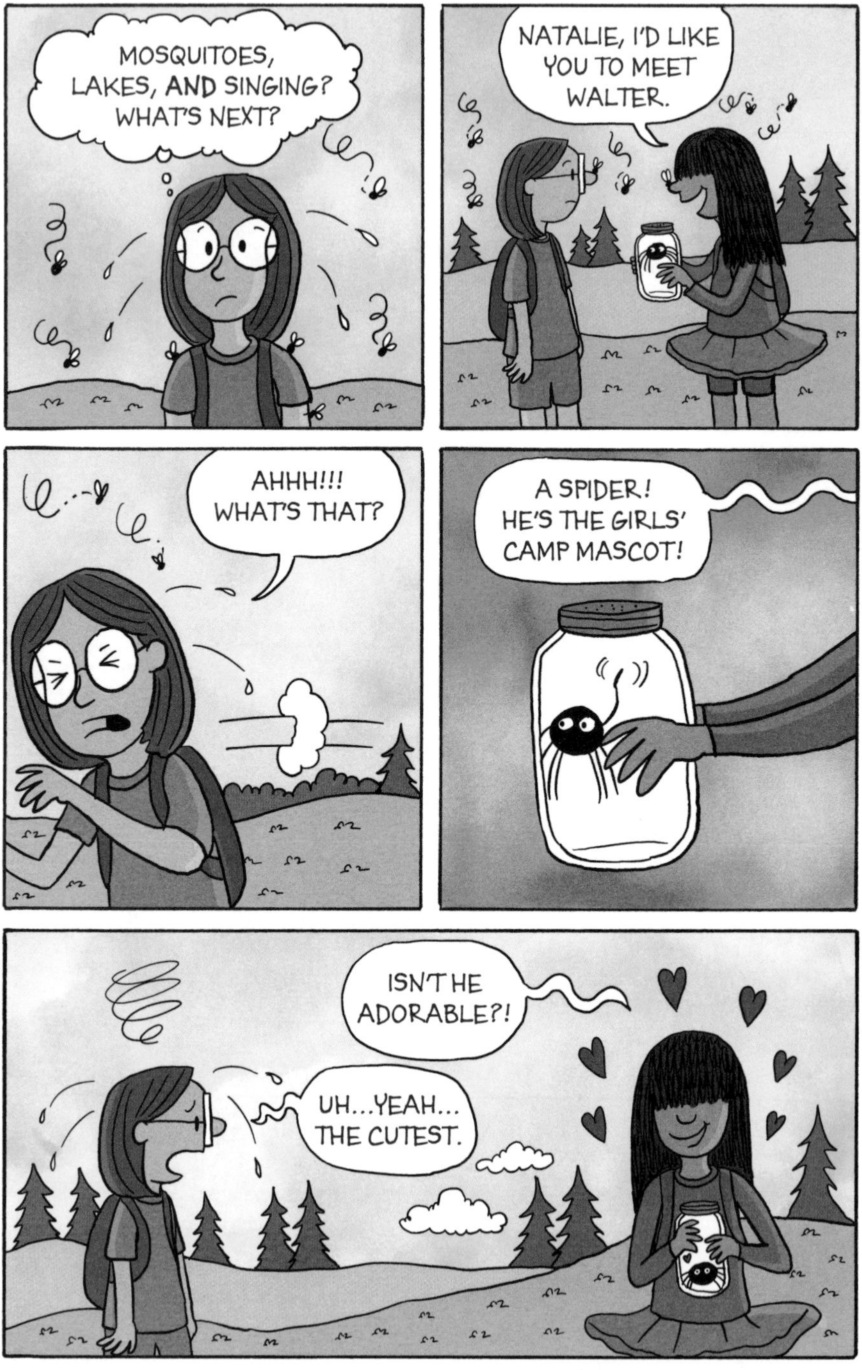
MOSQUITOES, LAKES, AND SINGING? WHAT'S NEXT?
NATALIE, I'D LIKE YOU TO MEET WALTER.
AHHH!!! WHAT'S THAT?
A SPIDER! HE'S THE GIRLS' CAMP MASCOT!
ISN'T HE ADORABLE?!
UH...YEAH... THE CUTEST.

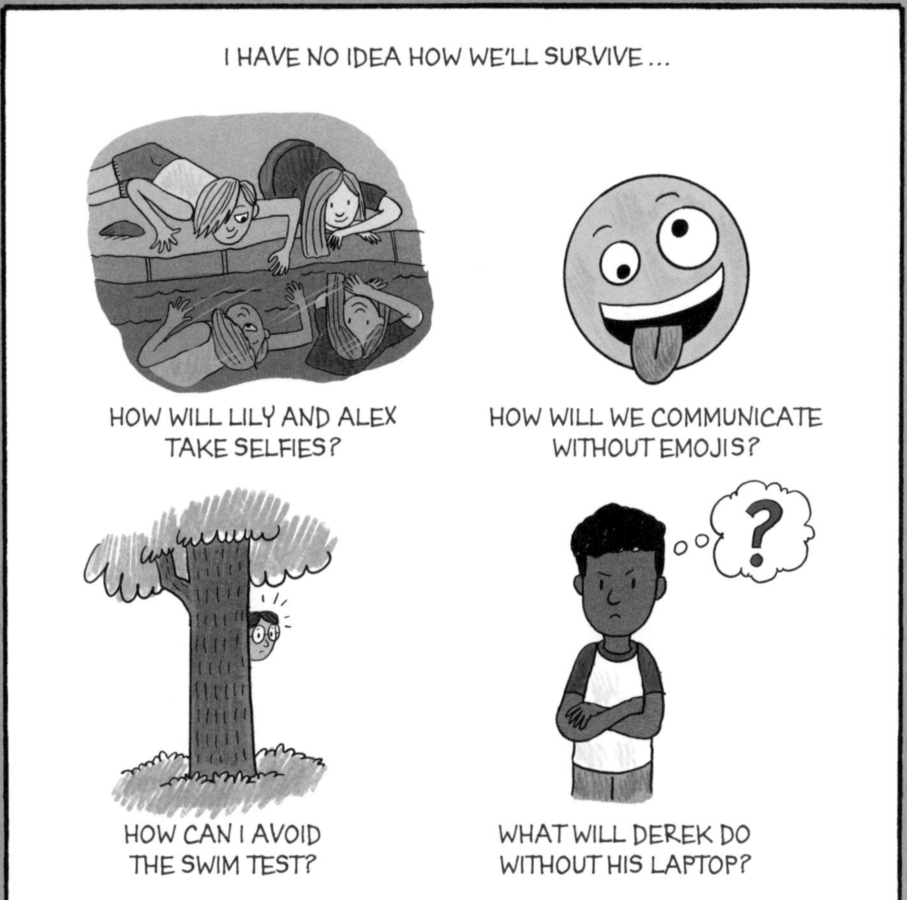
I HAVE NO IDEA HOW WE'LL SURVIVE...
HOW WILL LILY AND ALEX TAKE SELFIES?
HOW WILL WE COMMUNICATE WITHOUT EMOJIS?
HOW CAN I AVOID THE SWIM TEST?
WHAT WILL DEREK DO WITHOUT HIS LAPTOP?
HOW WILL I DEAL WITH A SPIDER BEING THE GIRLS' CAMP MASCOT?
CAN I BE IN THE CAMP GAMES WITHOUT EVER GETTING IN THE LAKE?

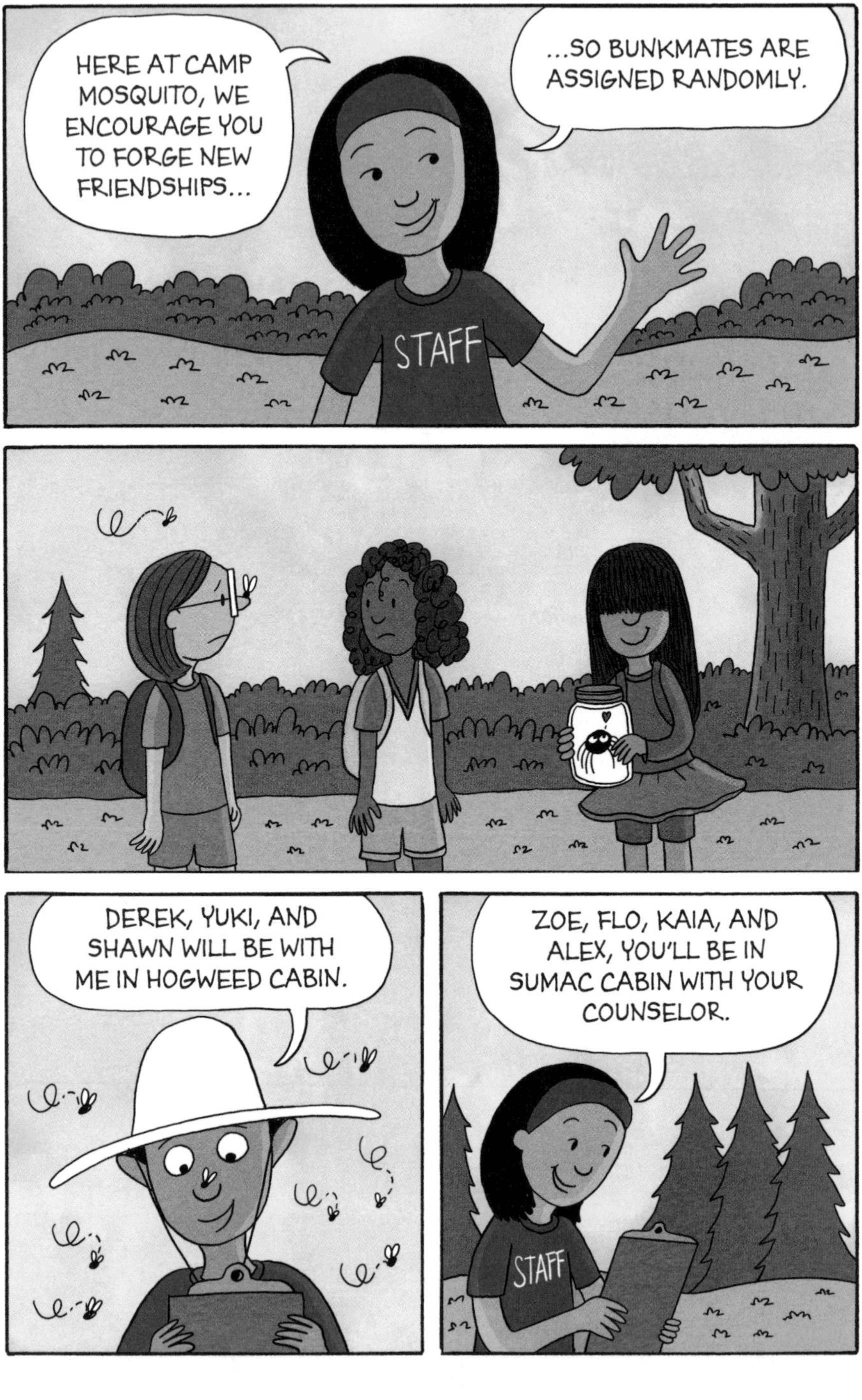
HERE AT CAMP MOSQUITO, WE ENCOURAGE YOU TO FORGE NEW FRIENDSHIPS...
...SO BUNKMATES ARE ASSIGNED RANDOMLY.
STAFF
DEREK, YUKI, AND SHAWN WILL BE WITH ME IN HOGWEED CABIN.
ZOE, FLO, KAIA, AND ALEX, YOU'LL BE IN SUMAC CABIN WITH YOUR COUNSELOR.
STAFF

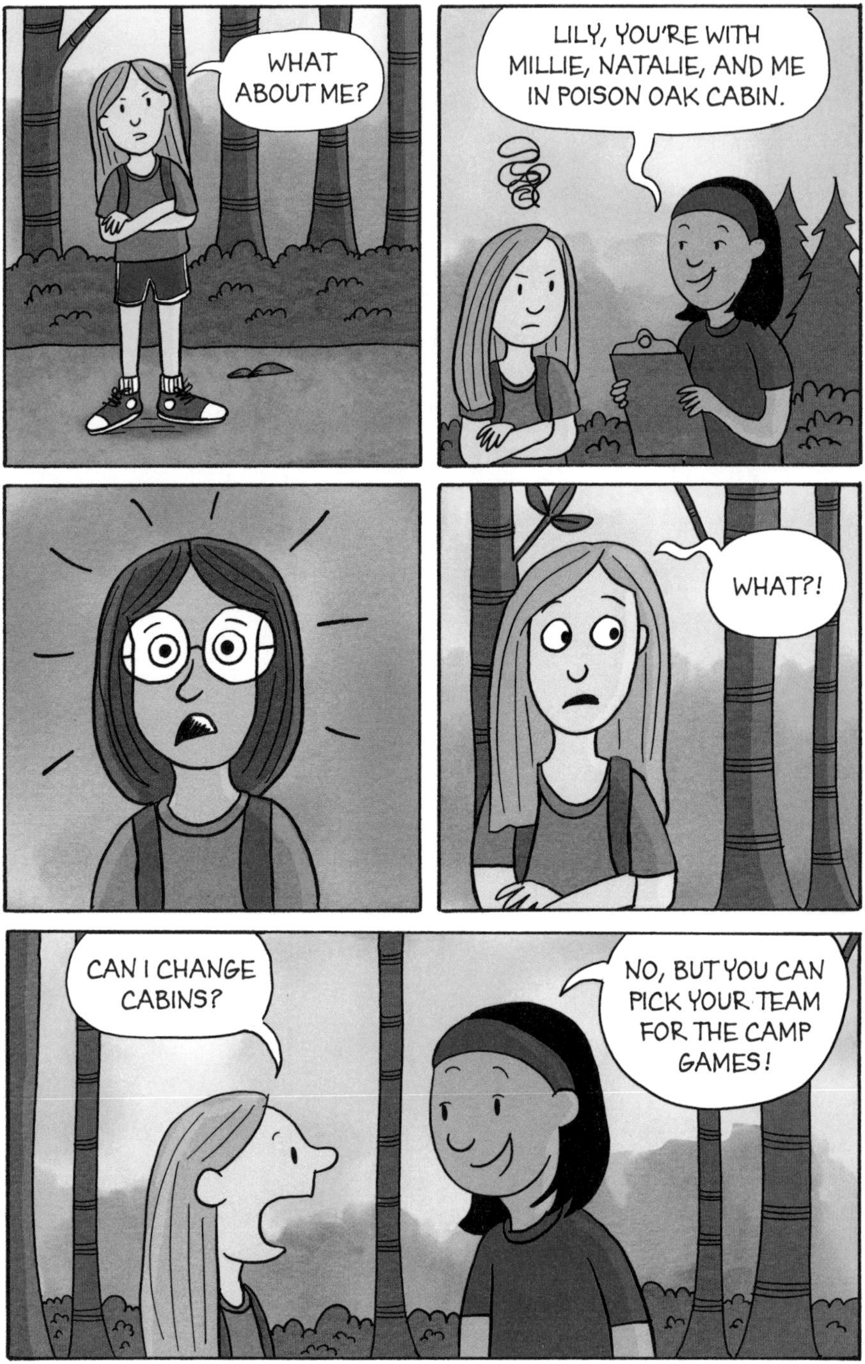
WHAT ABOUT ME?
LILY, YOU'RE WITH MILLIE, NATALIE, AND ME IN POISON OAK CABIN.
WHAT?!
CAN I CHANGE CABINS?
NO, BUT YOU CAN PICK YOUR TEAM FOR THE CAMP GAMES!

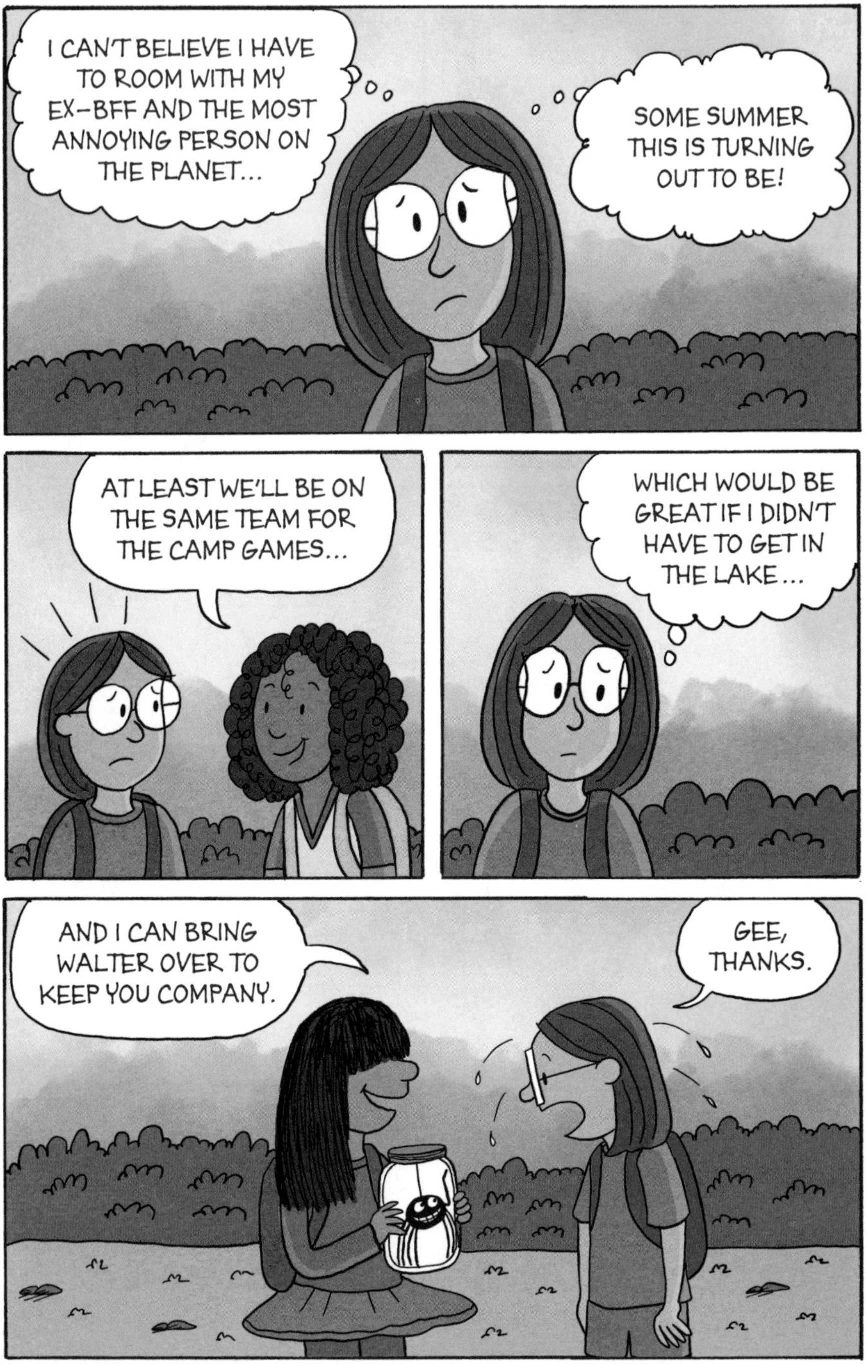
I CAN'T BELIEVE I HAVE TO ROOM WITH MY EX-BFF AND THE MOST ANNOYING PERSON ON THE PLANET...
SOME SUMMER THIS IS TURNING OUT TO BE!
AT LEAST WE'LL BE ON THE SAME TEAM FOR THE CAMP GAMES...
WHICH WOULD BE GREAT IF I DIDN'T HAVE TO GET IN THE LAKE...
AND I CAN BRING WALTER OVER TO KEEP YOU COMPANY.
GEE, THANKS.

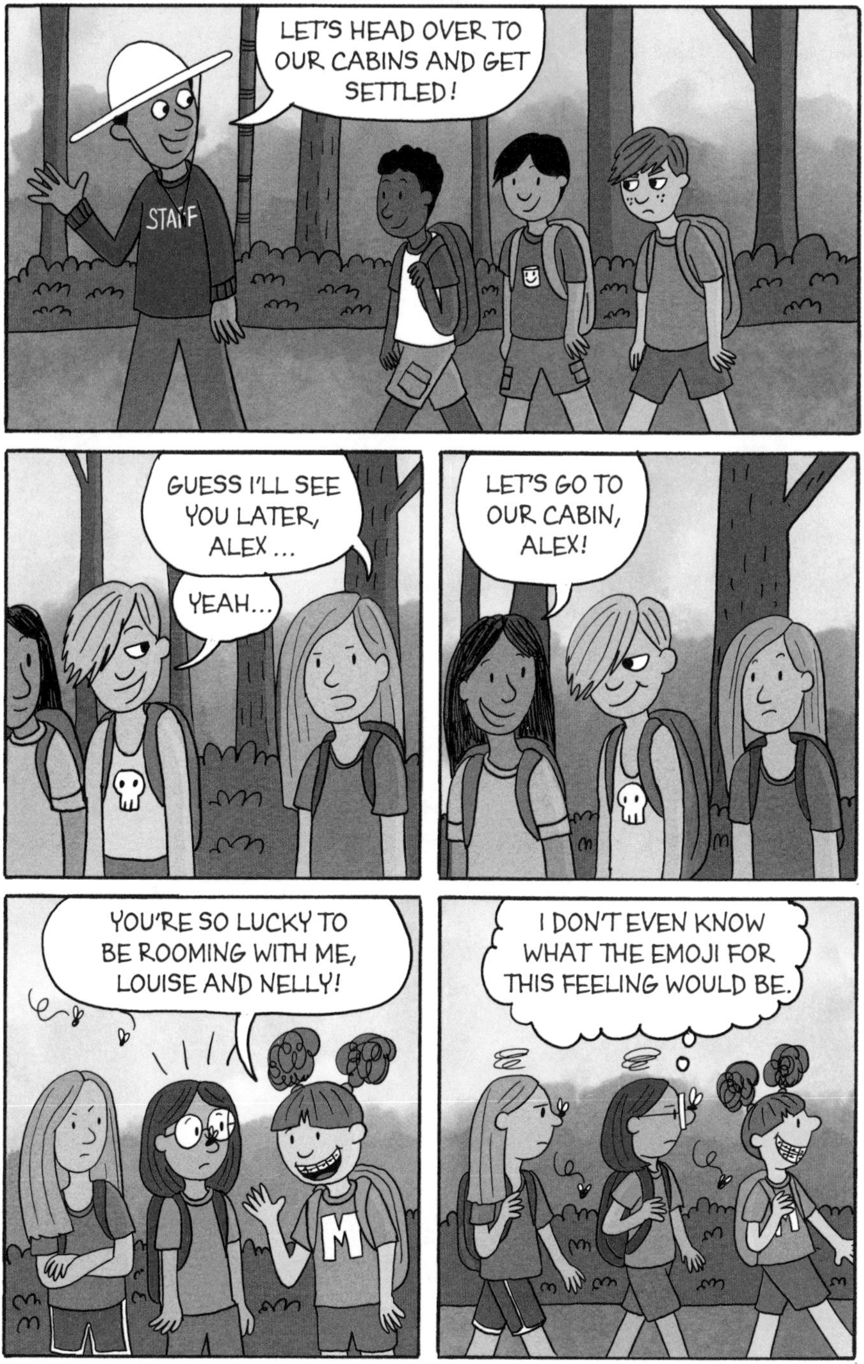
LET'S HEAD OVER TO OUR CABINS AND GET SETTLED!
STAFF
GUESS I'LL SEE YOU LATER, ALEX...
YEAH...
LET'S GO TO OUR CABIN, ALEX!
YOU'RE SO LUCKY TO BE ROOMING WITH ME, LOUISE AND NELLY!
M
I DON'T EVEN KNOW WHAT THE EMOJI FOR THIS FEELING WOULD BE.

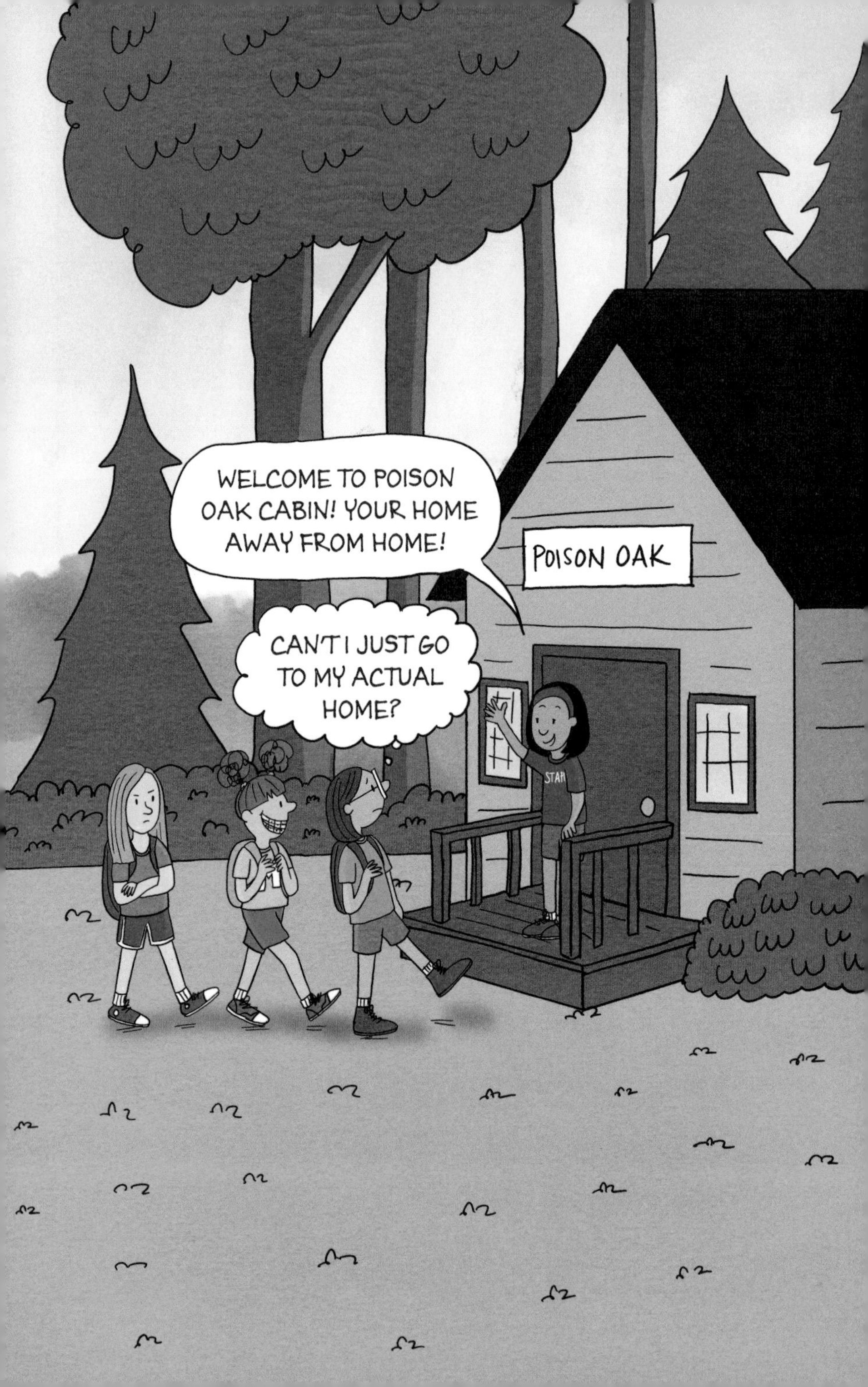
WELCOME TO POISON OAK CABIN! YOUR HOME AWAY FROM HOME!
POISON OAK
CAN'T I JUST GO TO MY ACTUAL HOME?
STAFF

CHAPTER 3
GHOST STORIES

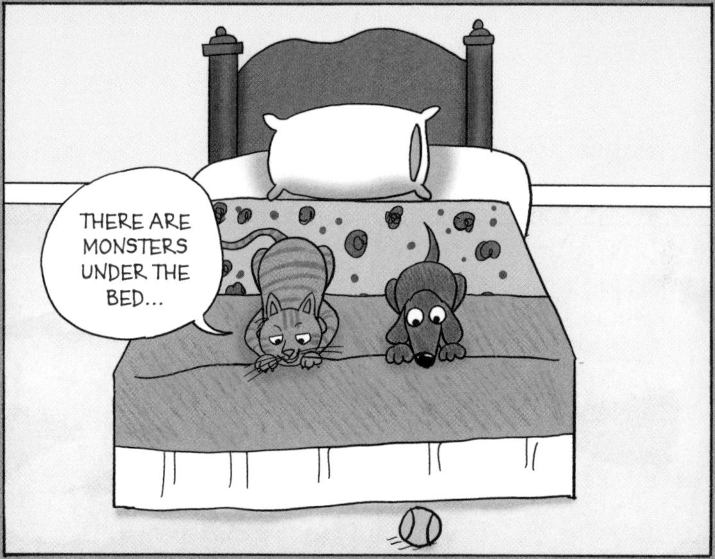
THERE ARE MONSTERS UNDER THE BED...

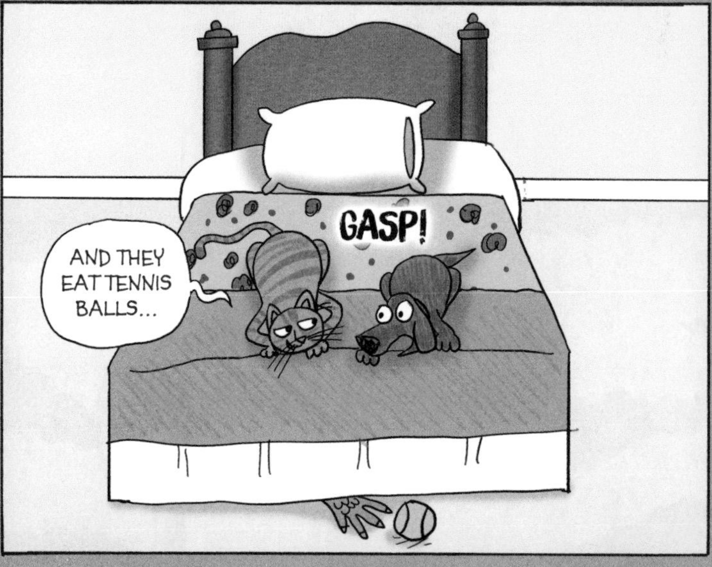
AND THEY EAT TENNIS BALLS...
GASP!

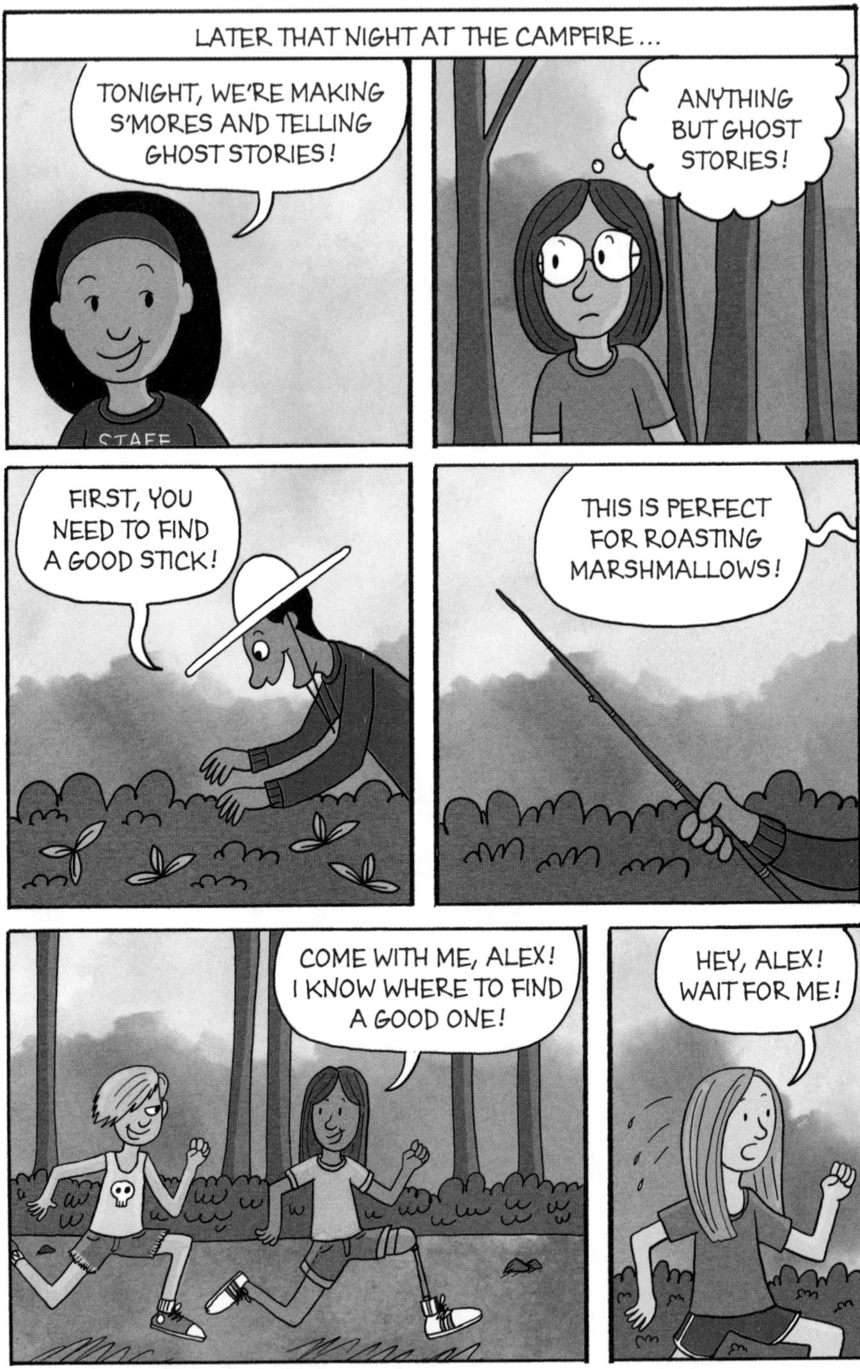
LATER THAT NIGHT AT THE CAMPFIRE...
TONIGHT, WE'RE MAKING S'MORES AND TELLING GHOST STORIES!
STAFF
ANYTHING BUT GHOST STORIES!
FIRST, YOU NEED TO FIND A GOOD STICK!
THIS IS PERFECT FOR ROASTING MARSHMALLOWS!
COME WITH ME, ALEX! I KNOW WHERE TO FIND A GOOD ONE!
HEY, ALEX! WAIT FOR ME!

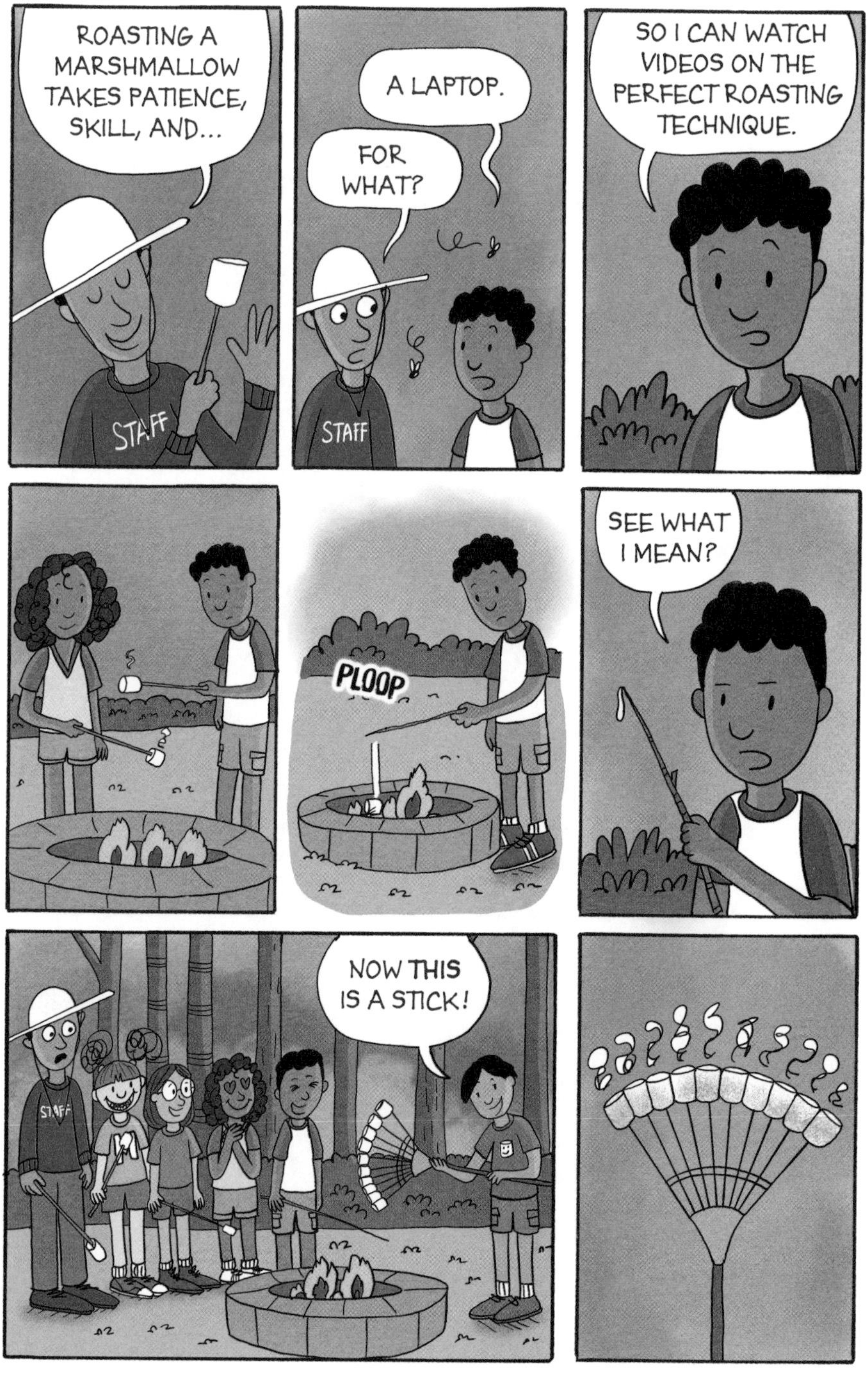
ROASTING A MARSHMALLOW TAKES PATIENCE, SKILL, AND...
STAFF
A LAPTOP.
FOR WHAT?
STAFF
SO I CAN WATCH VIDEOS ON THE PERFECT ROASTING TECHNIQUE.
PLOOP
SEE WHAT I MEAN?
NOW THIS IS A STICK!
STAFF

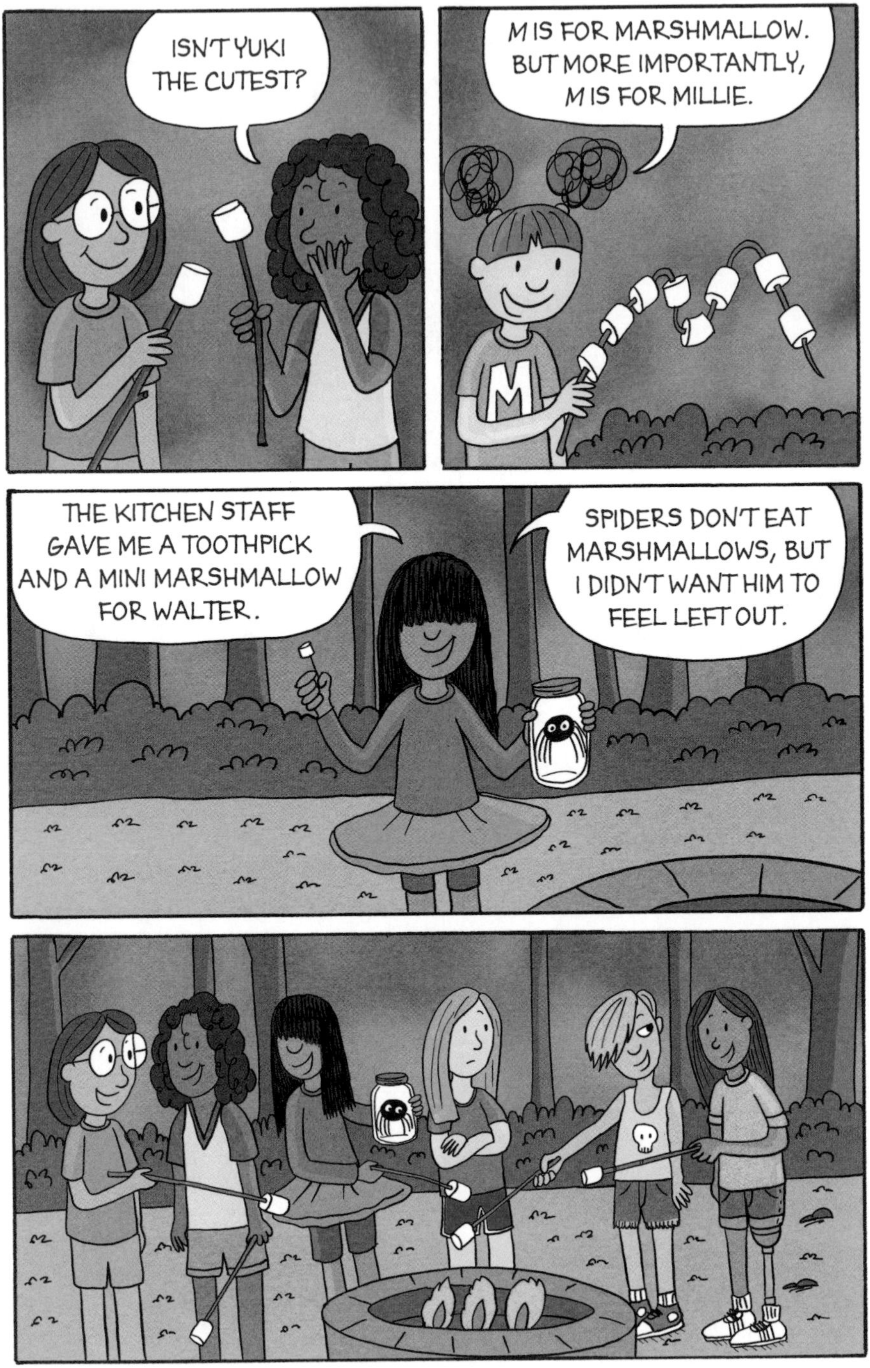
ISN'T YUKI THE CUTEST?
M IS FOR MARSHMALLOW. BUT MORE IMPORTANTLY, M IS FOR MILLIE.
M
THE KITCHEN STAFF GAVE ME A TOOTHPICK AND A MINI MARSHMALLOW FOR WALTER.
SPIDERS DON'T EAT MARSHMALLOWS, BUT I DIDN'T WANT HIM TO FEEL LEFT OUT.

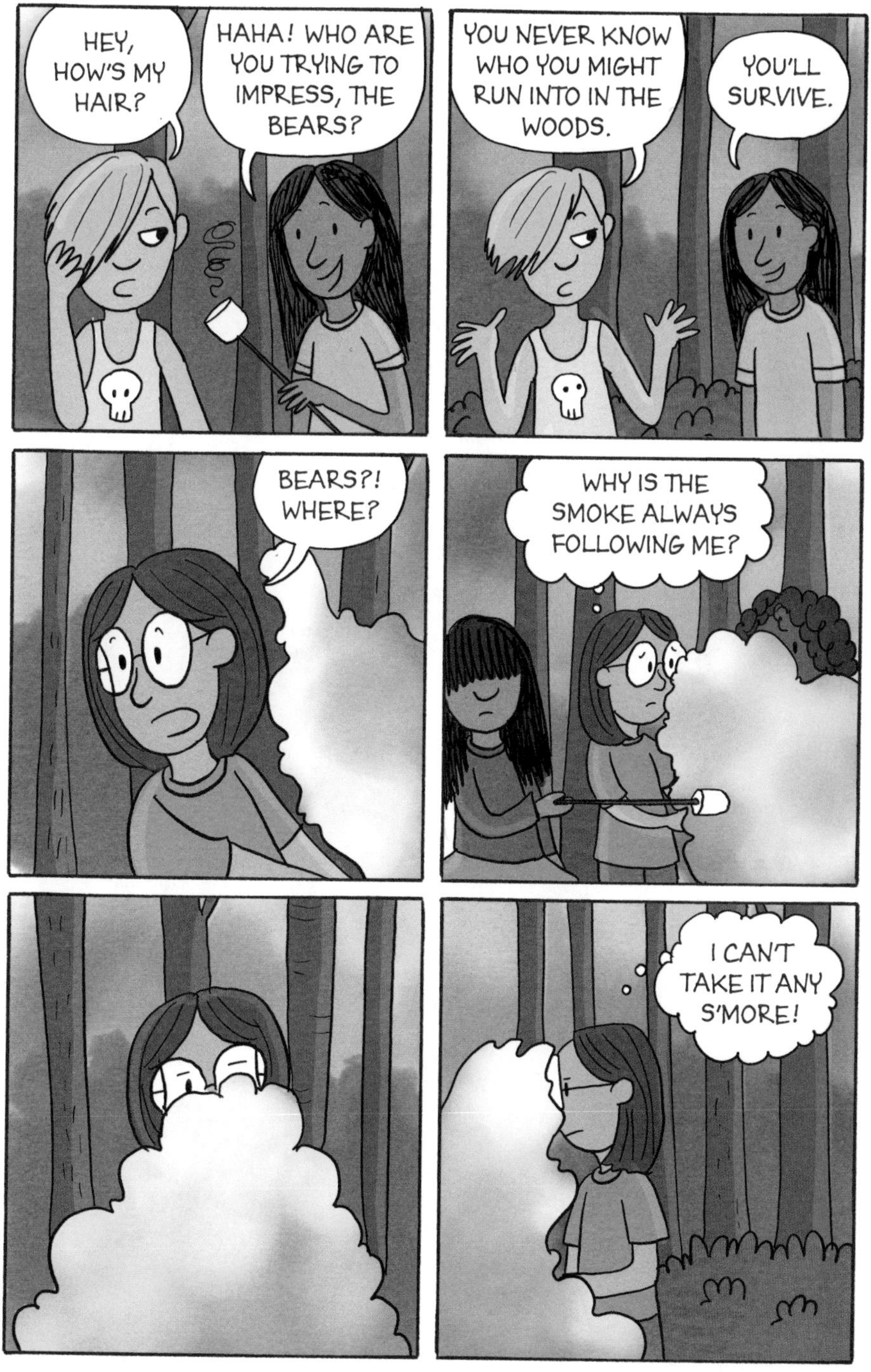
HEY, HOW'S MY HAIR?
HAHA! WHO ARE YOU TRYING TO IMPRESS, THE BEARS?
YOU NEVER KNOW WHO YOU MIGHT RUN INTO IN THE WOODS.
YOU'LL SURVIVE.
BEARS?! WHERE?
WHY IS THE SMOKE ALWAYS FOLLOWING ME?
I CAN'T TAKE IT ANY S'MORE!

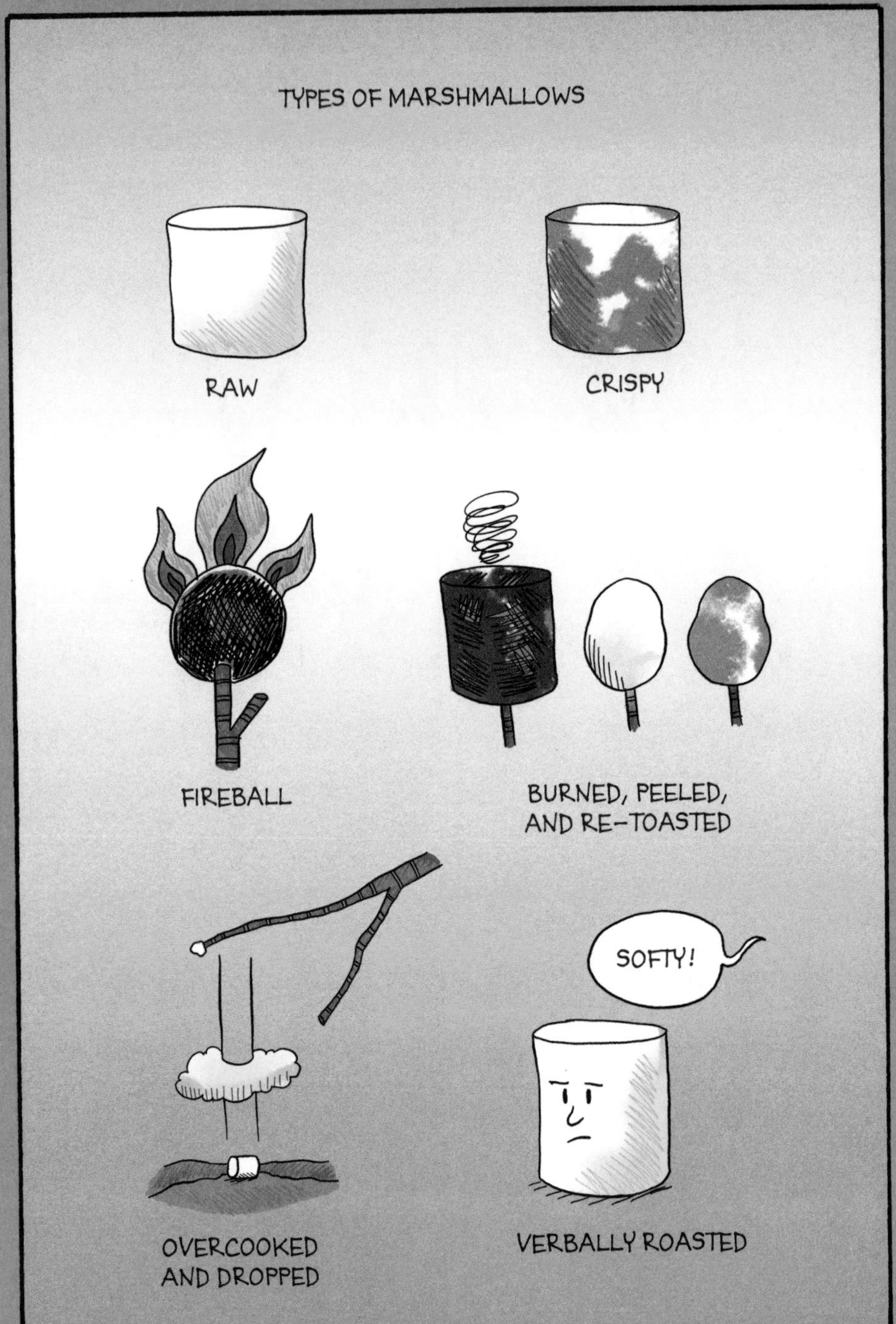
TYPES OF MARSHMALLOWS
RAW
CRISPY
FIREBALL
BURNED, PEELED, AND RE-TOASTED
SOFTY!
OVERCOOKED AND DROPPED
VERBALLY ROASTED

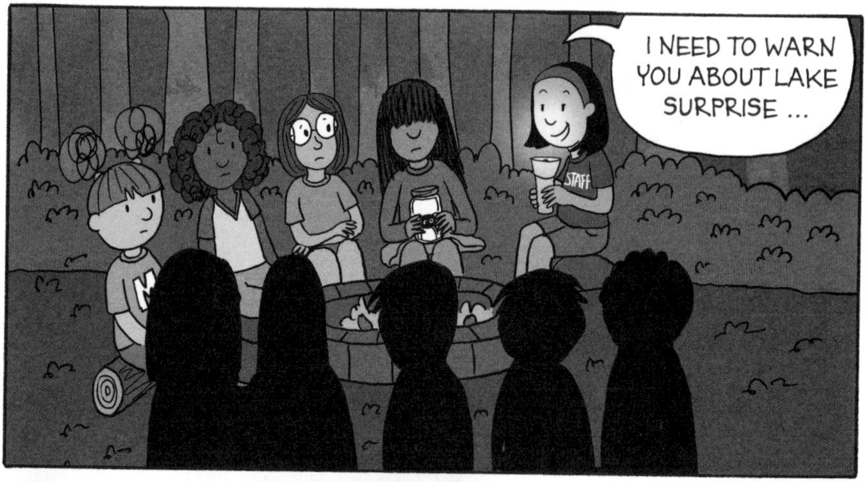
I NEED TO WARN YOU ABOUT LAKE SURPRISE ...
STAFF

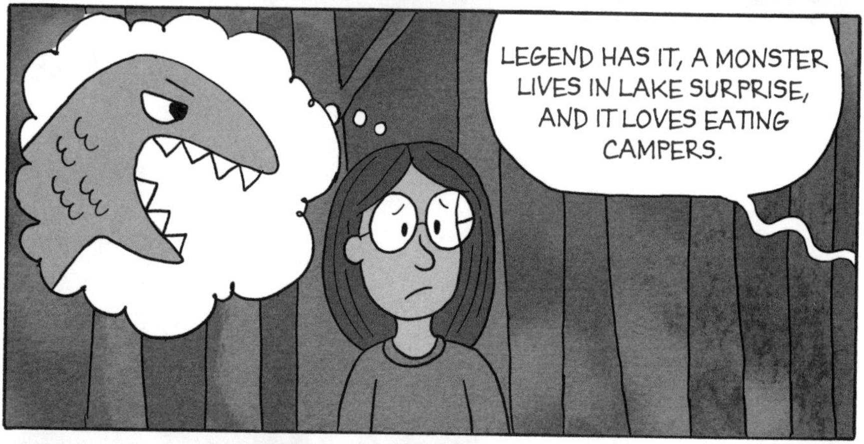
LEGEND HAS IT, A MONSTER LIVES IN LAKE SURPRISE, AND IT LOVES EATING CAMPERS.

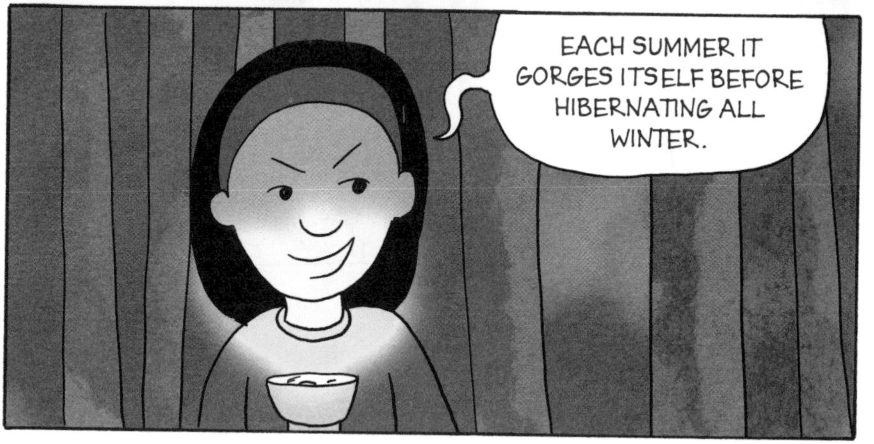
EACH SUMMER IT GORGES ITSELF BEFORE HIBERNATING ALL WINTER.

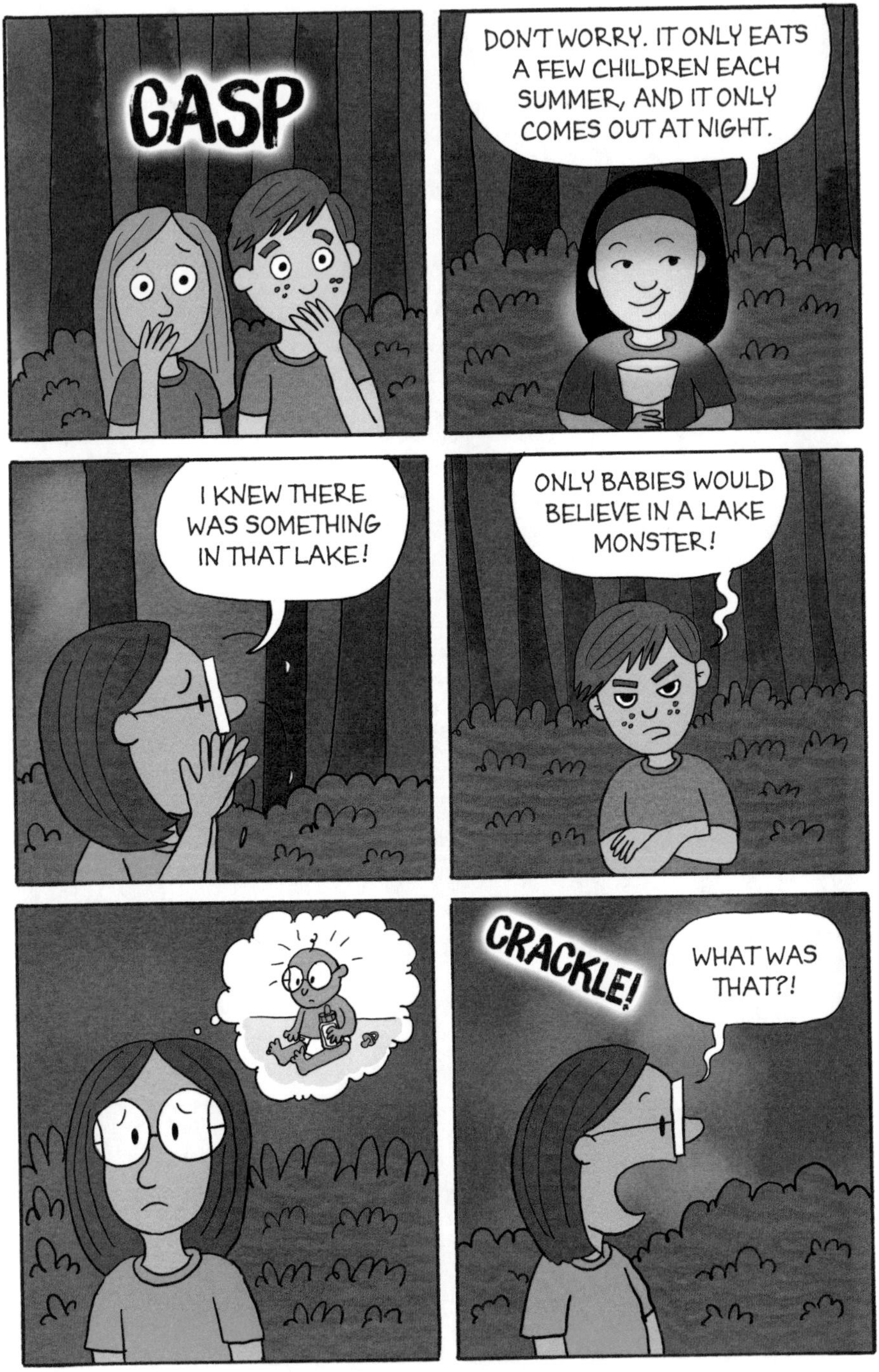
GASP
DON'T WORRY. IT ONLY EATS A FEW CHILDREN EACH SUMMER, AND IT ONLY COMES OUT AT NIGHT.
I KNEW THERE WAS SOMETHING IN THAT LAKE!
ONLY BABIES WOULD BELIEVE IN A LAKE MONSTER!
CRACKLE!
WHAT WAS THAT?!

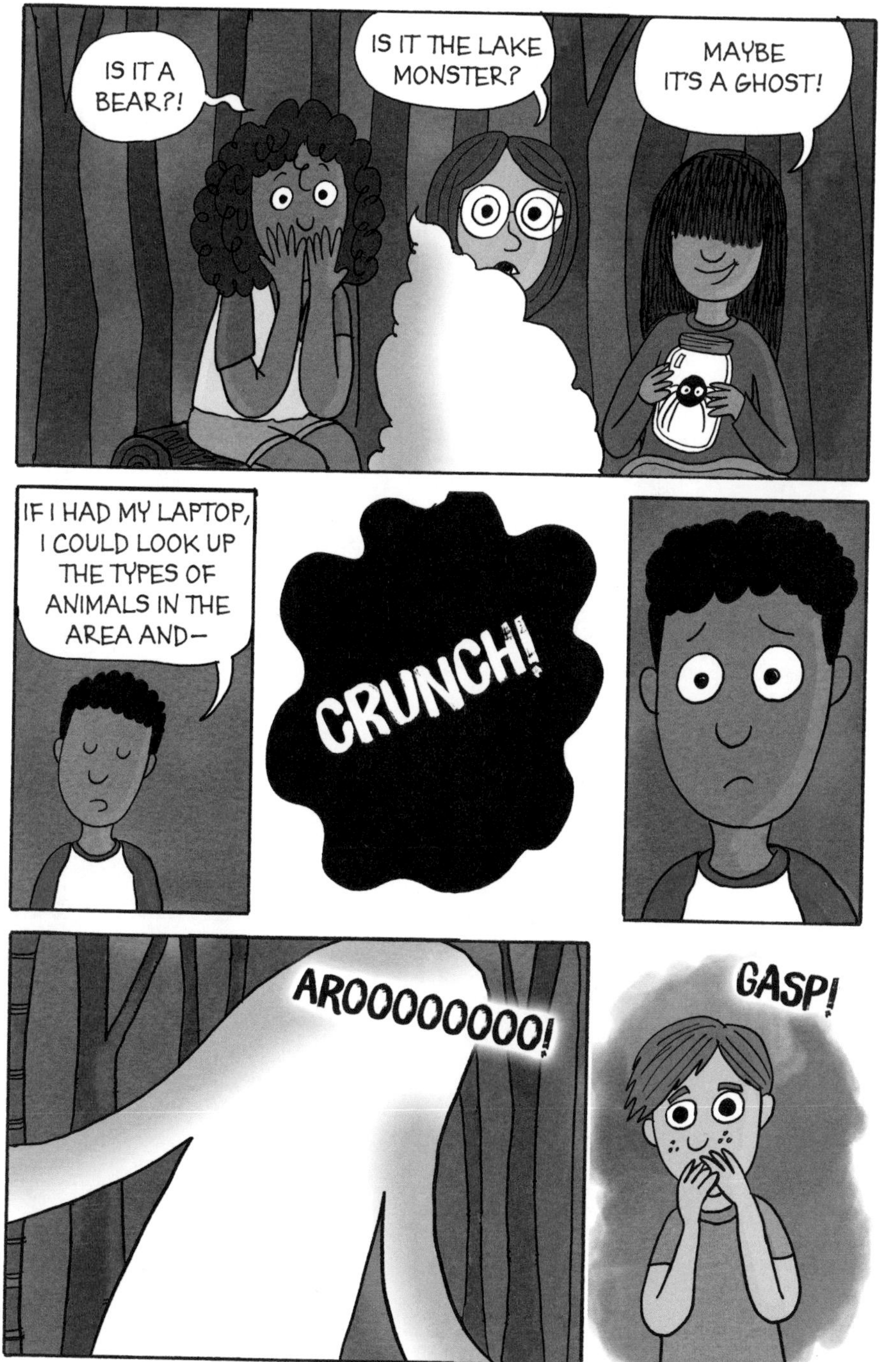
IS IT A BEAR?!
IS IT THE LAKE MONSTER?
MAYBE IT'S A GHOST!
IF I HAD MY LAPTOP, I COULD LOOK UP THE TYPES OF ANIMALS IN THE AREA AND—
CRUNCH!
AROOOOOOOOO!
GASP!

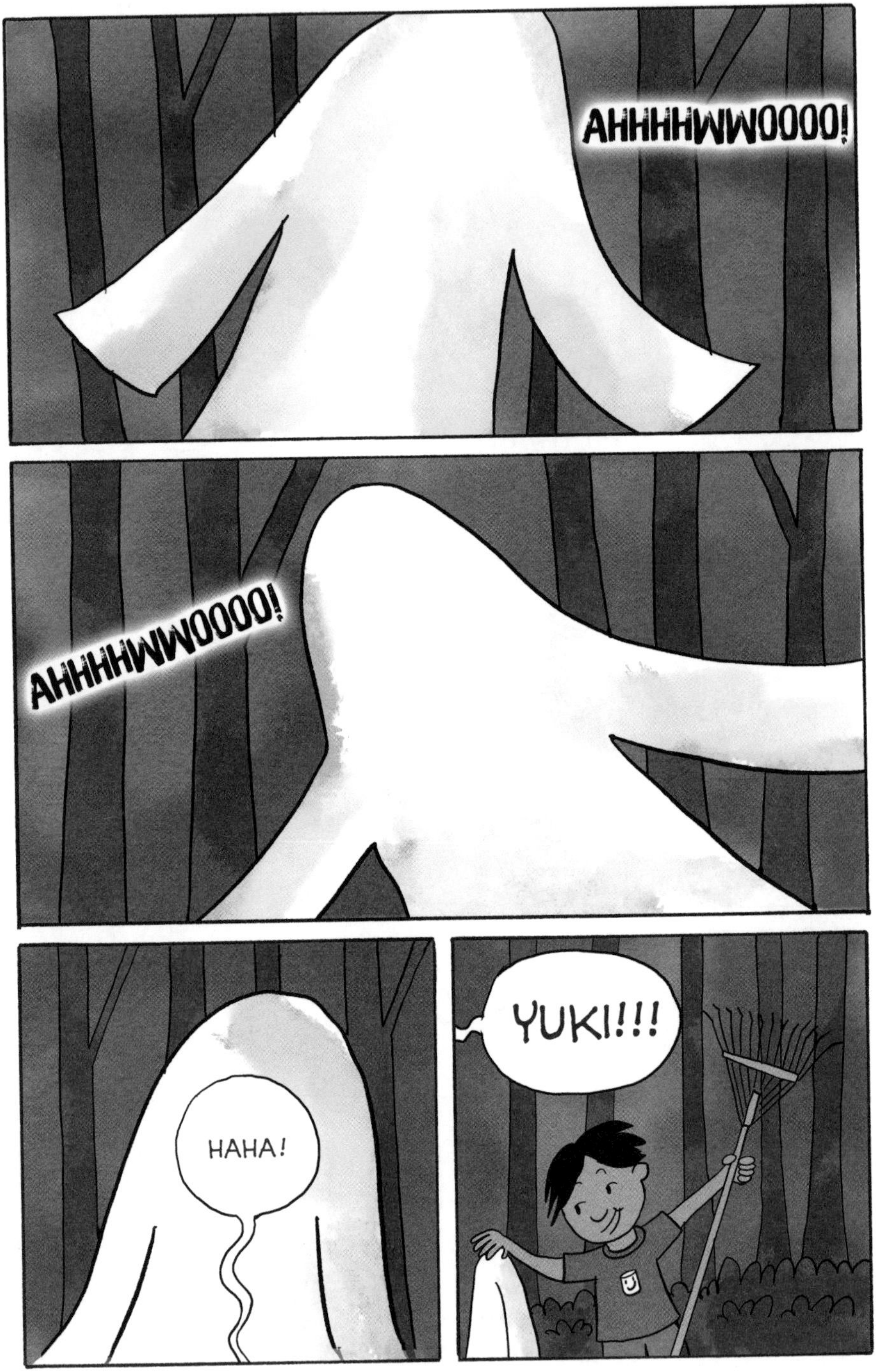
AHHHHWWOOOO!
AHHHHWWOOOO!
HAHA!
YUKI!!!

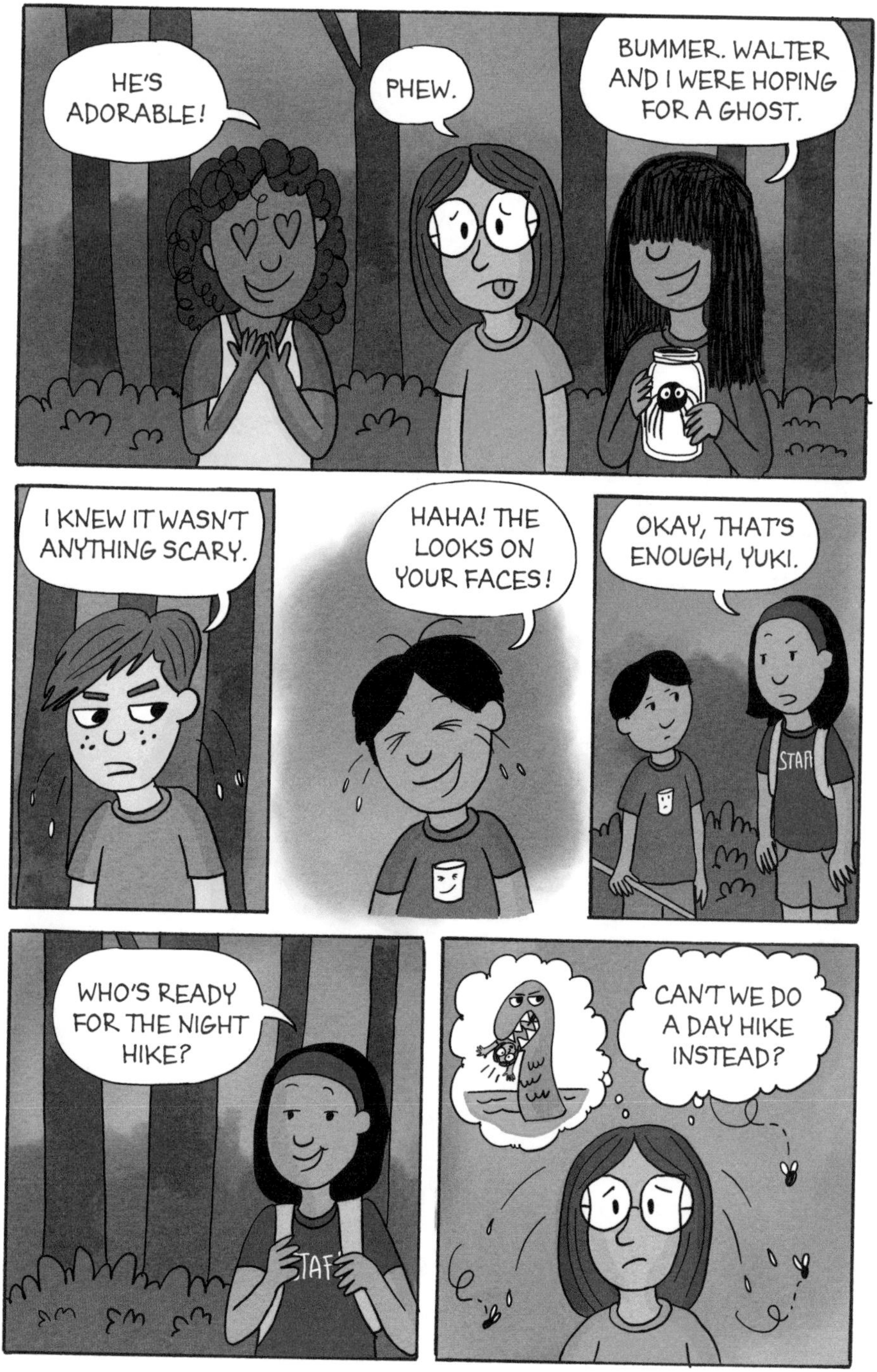
HE'S ADORABLE!
PHEW.
BUMMER. WALTER AND I WERE HOPING FOR A GHOST.
I KNEW IT WASN'T ANYTHING SCARY.
HAHA! THE LOOKS ON YOUR FACES!
OKAY, THAT'S ENOUGH, YUKI.
STAFF
WHO'S READY FOR THE NIGHT HIKE?
CAN'T WE DO A DAY HIKE INSTEAD?

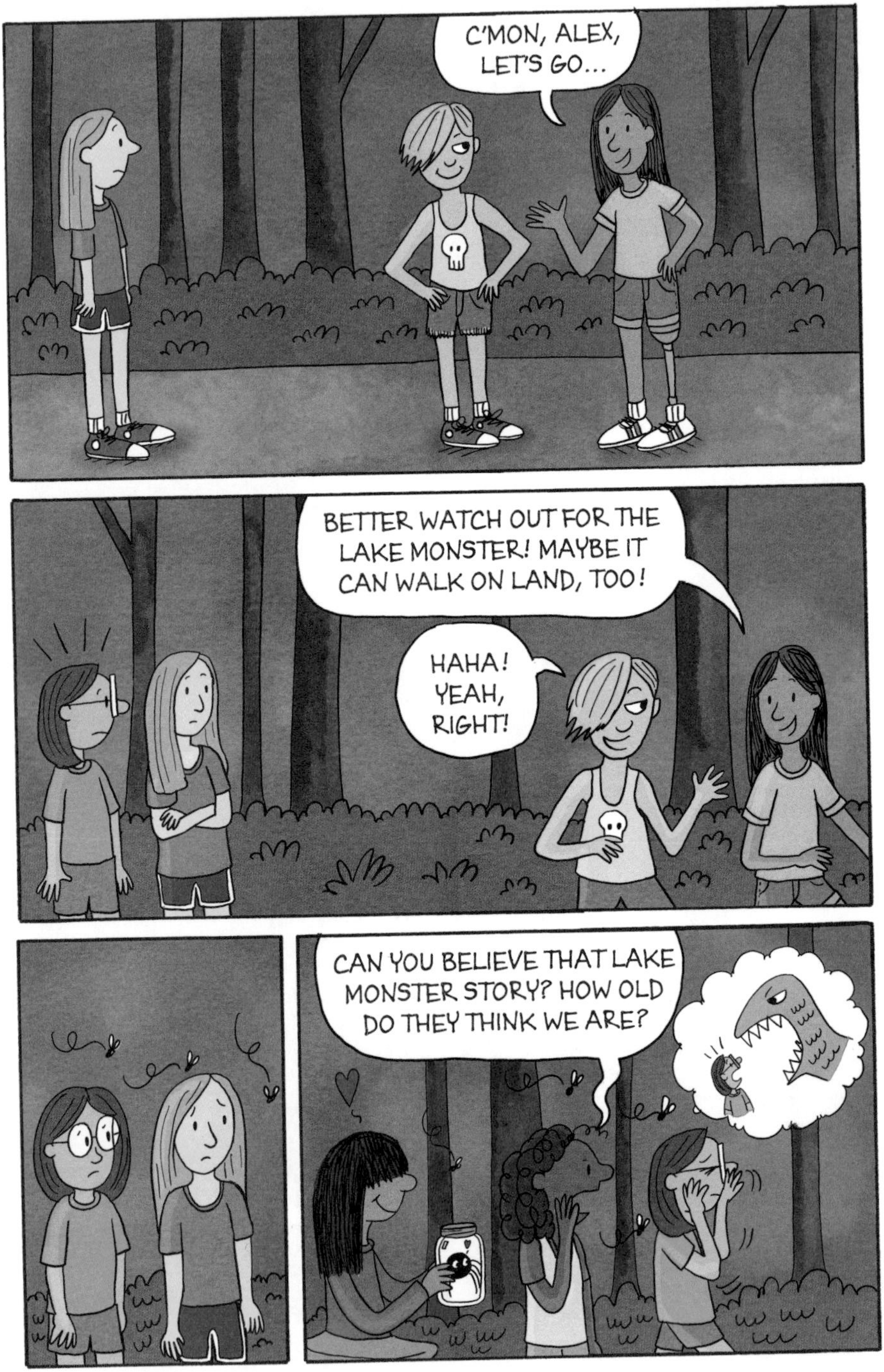
C'MON, ALEX, LET'S GO...
BETTER WATCH OUT FOR THE LAKE MONSTER! MAYBE IT CAN WALK ON LAND, TOO!
HAHA! YEAH, RIGHT!
CAN YOU BELIEVE THAT LAKE MONSTER STORY? HOW OLD DO THEY THINK WE ARE?

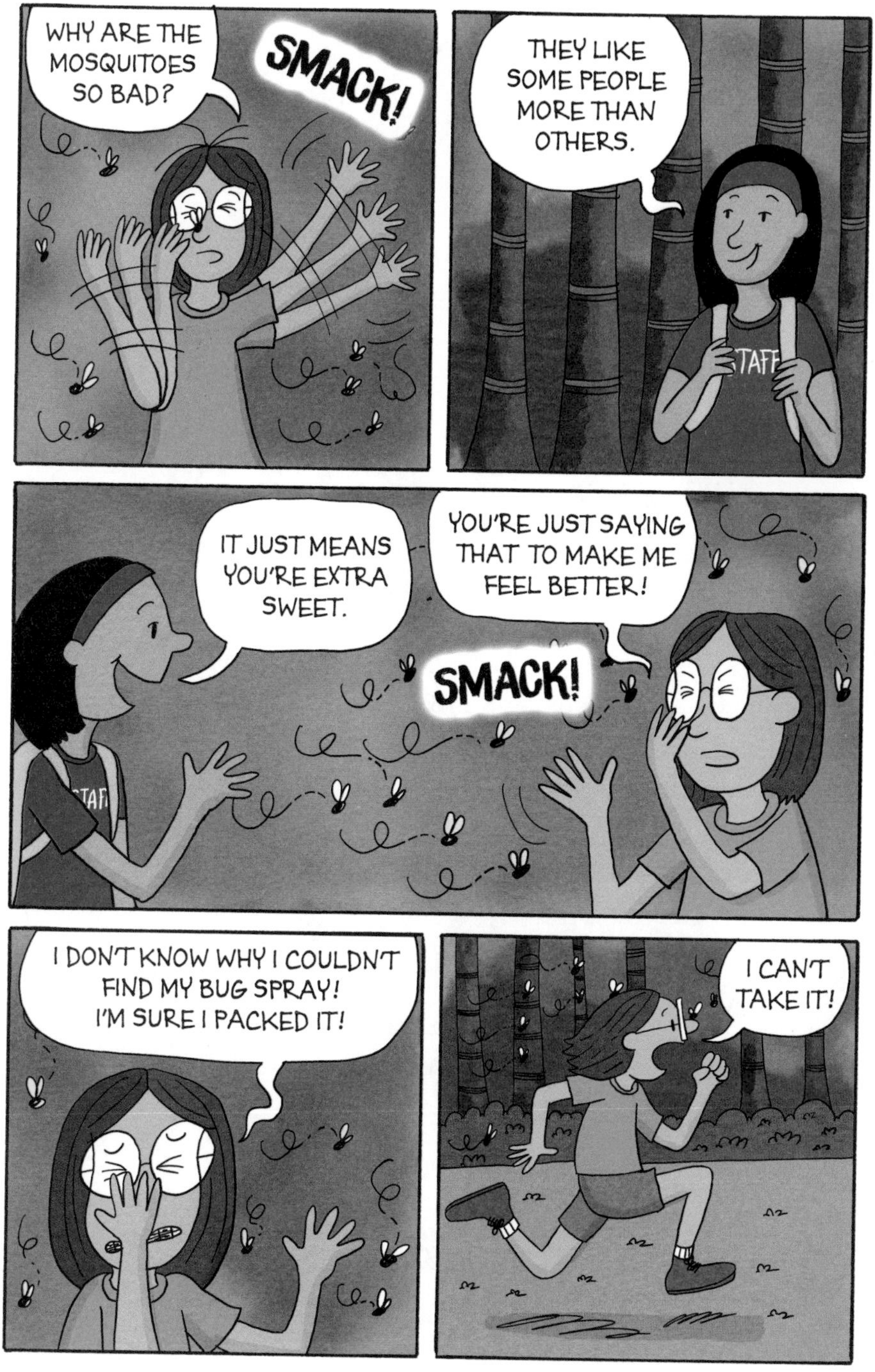
WHY ARE THE MOSQUITOES SO BAD?
SMACK!
THEY LIKE SOME PEOPLE MORE THAN OTHERS.
STAFF
IT JUST MEANS YOU'RE EXTRA SWEET.
YOU'RE JUST SAYING THAT TO MAKE ME FEEL BETTER!
SMACK!
I DON'T KNOW WHY I COULDN'T FIND MY BUG SPRAY! I'M SURE I PACKED IT!
I CAN'T TAKE IT!

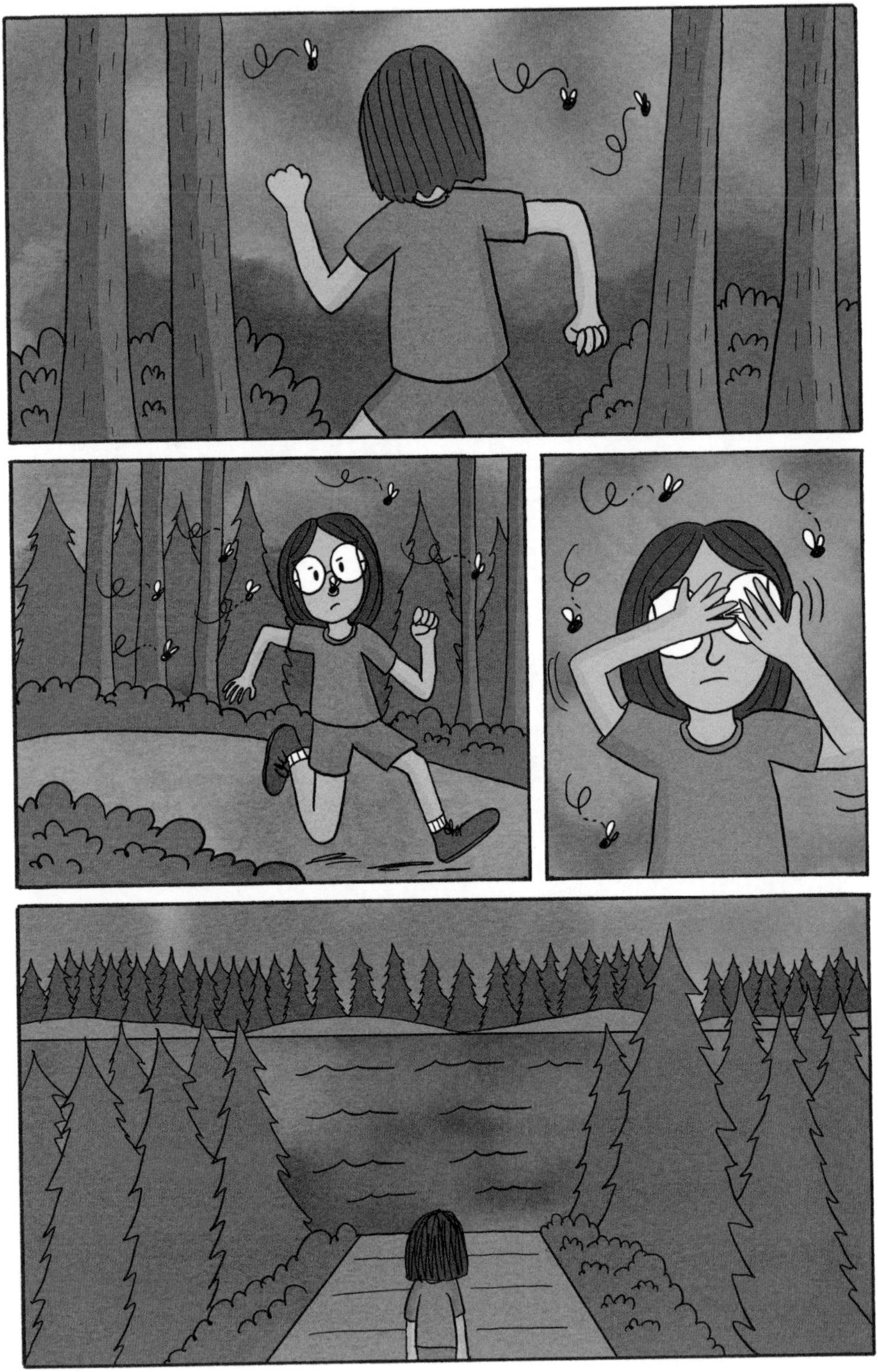

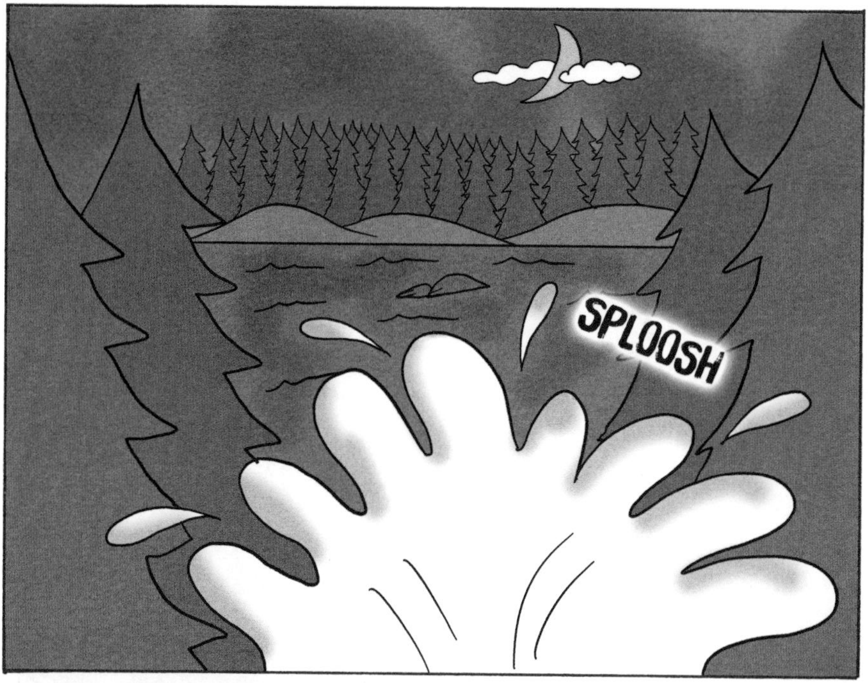
SPLOOSH

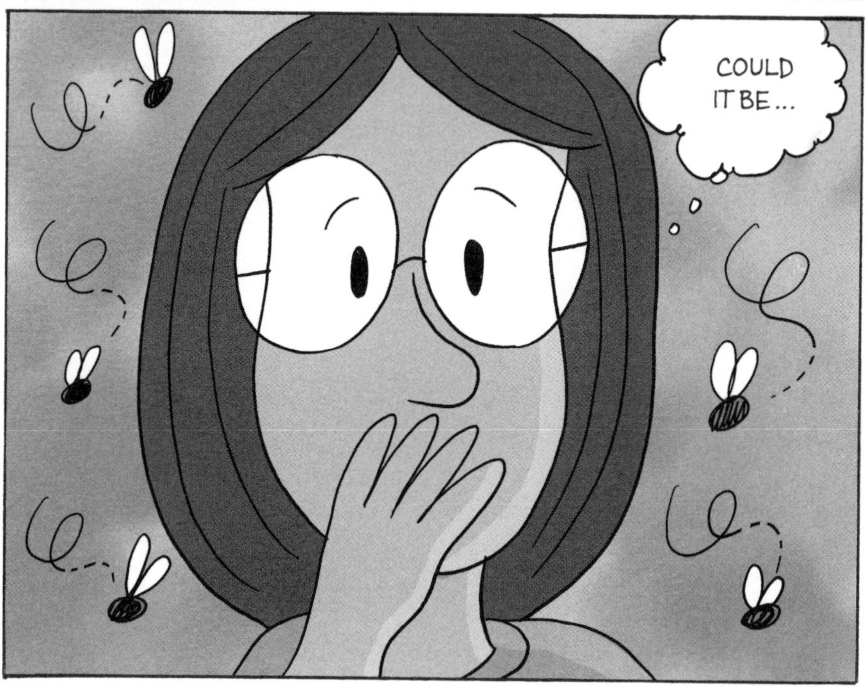
COULD IT BE...

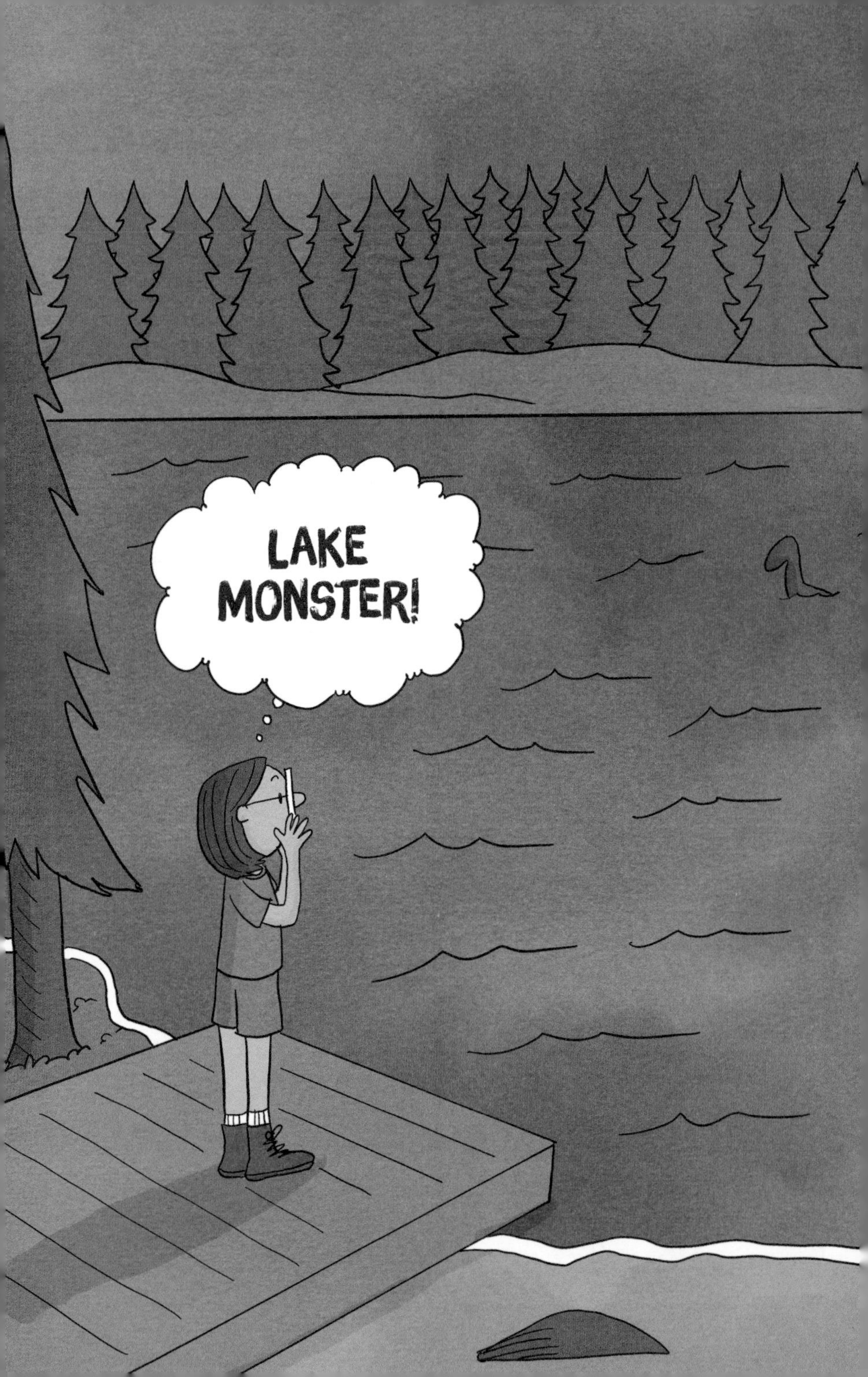
LAKE MONSTER!

CHAPTER 4
SNOOZE BUTTON

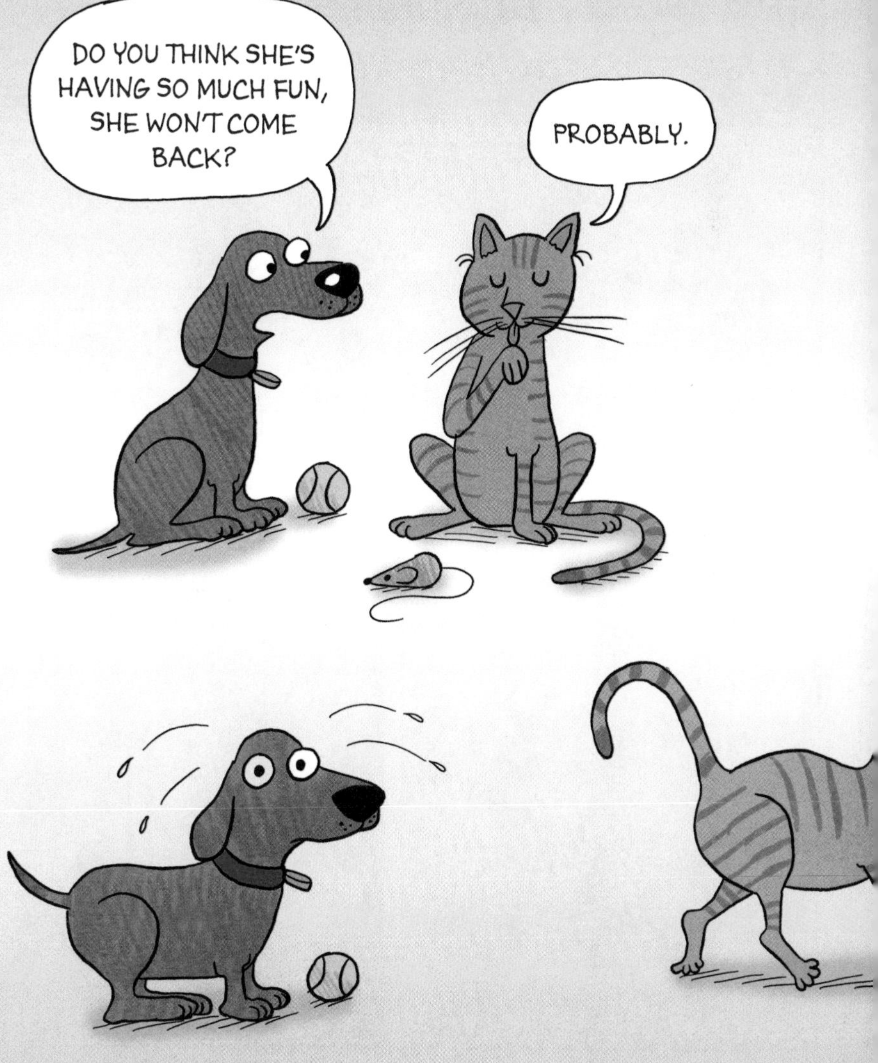
DO YOU THINK SHE'S HAVING SO MUCH FUN, SHE WON'T COME BACK?
PROBABLY.

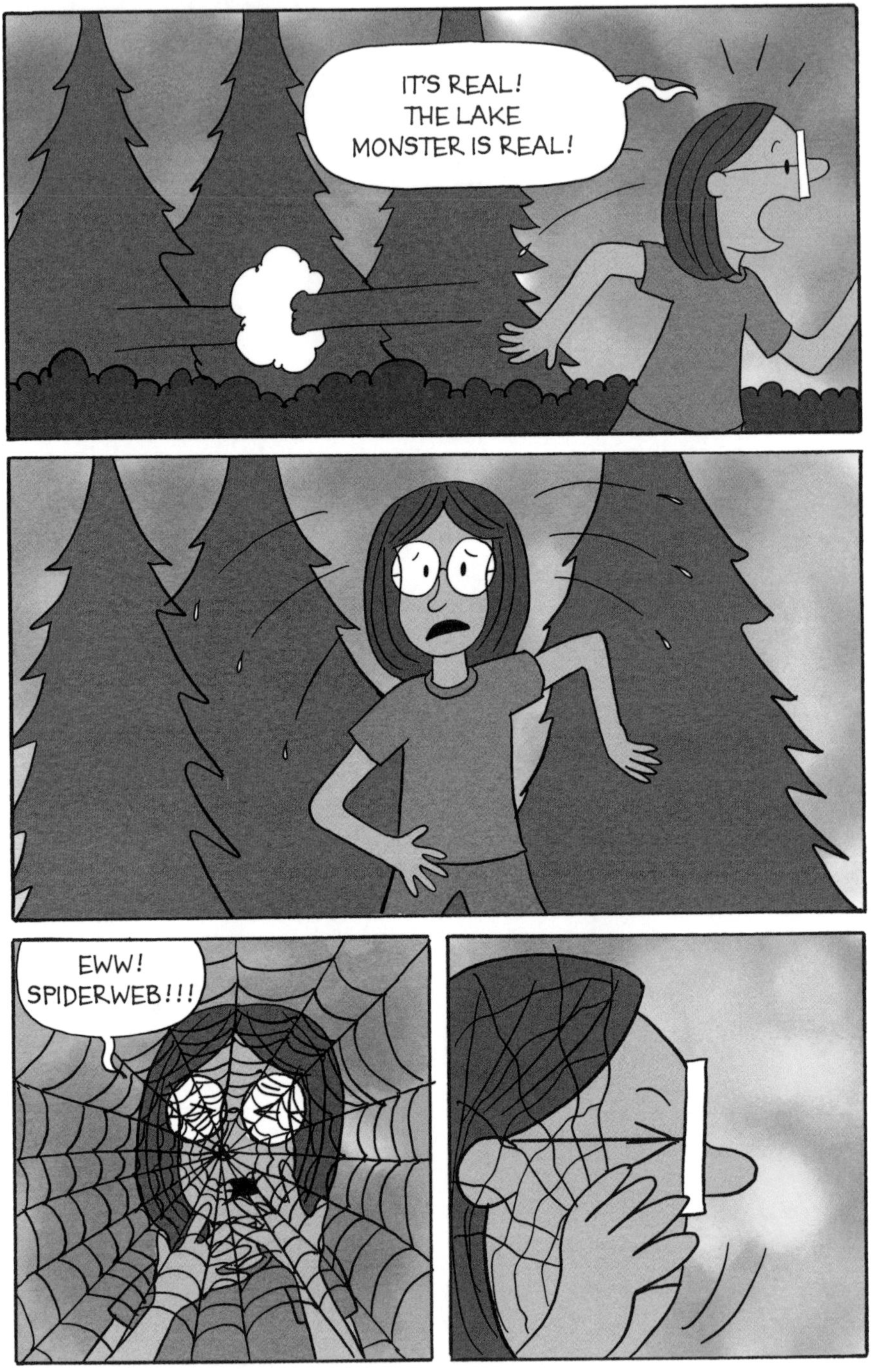
IT'S REAL! THE LAKE MONSTER IS REAL!
EWW! SPIDERWEB!!!

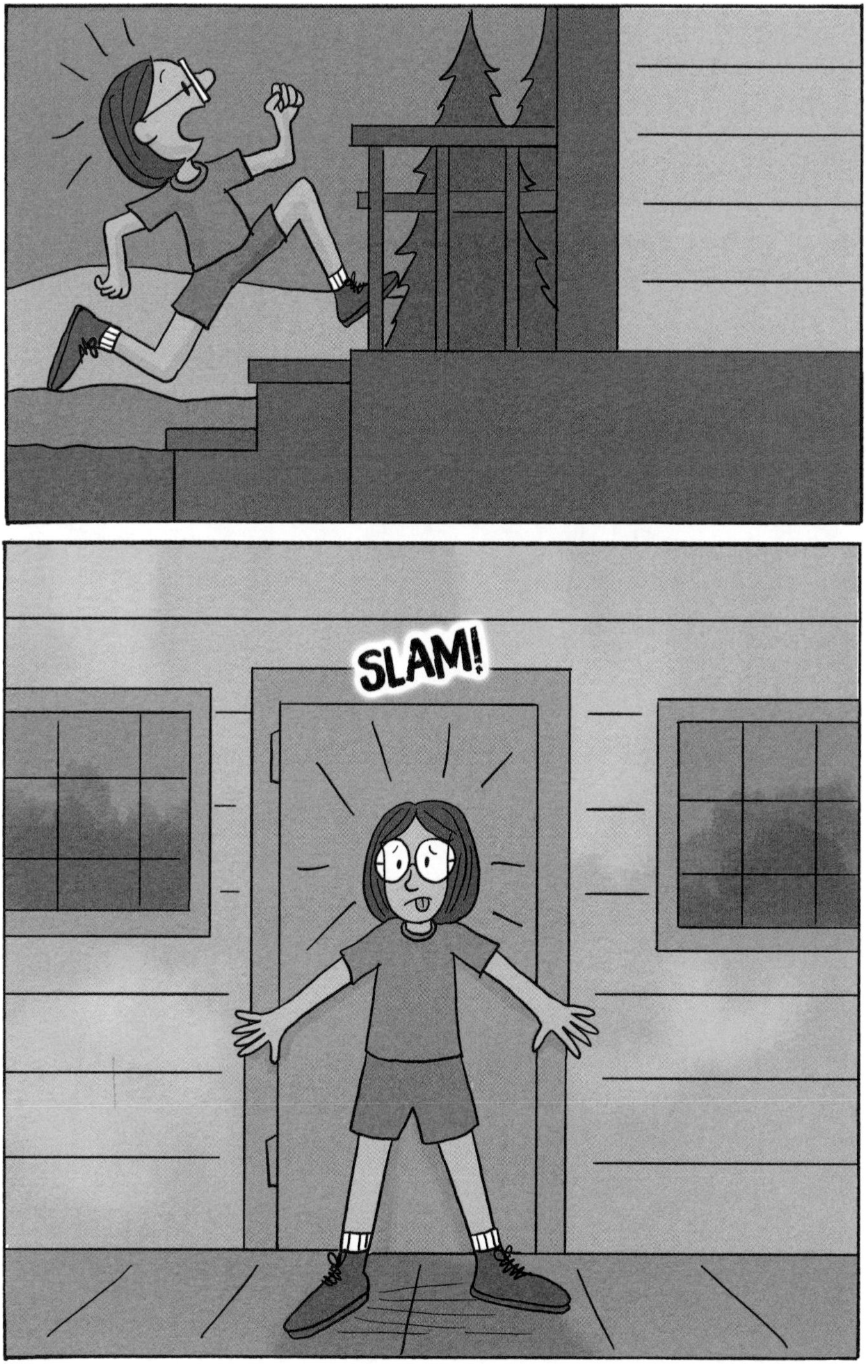
SLAM!

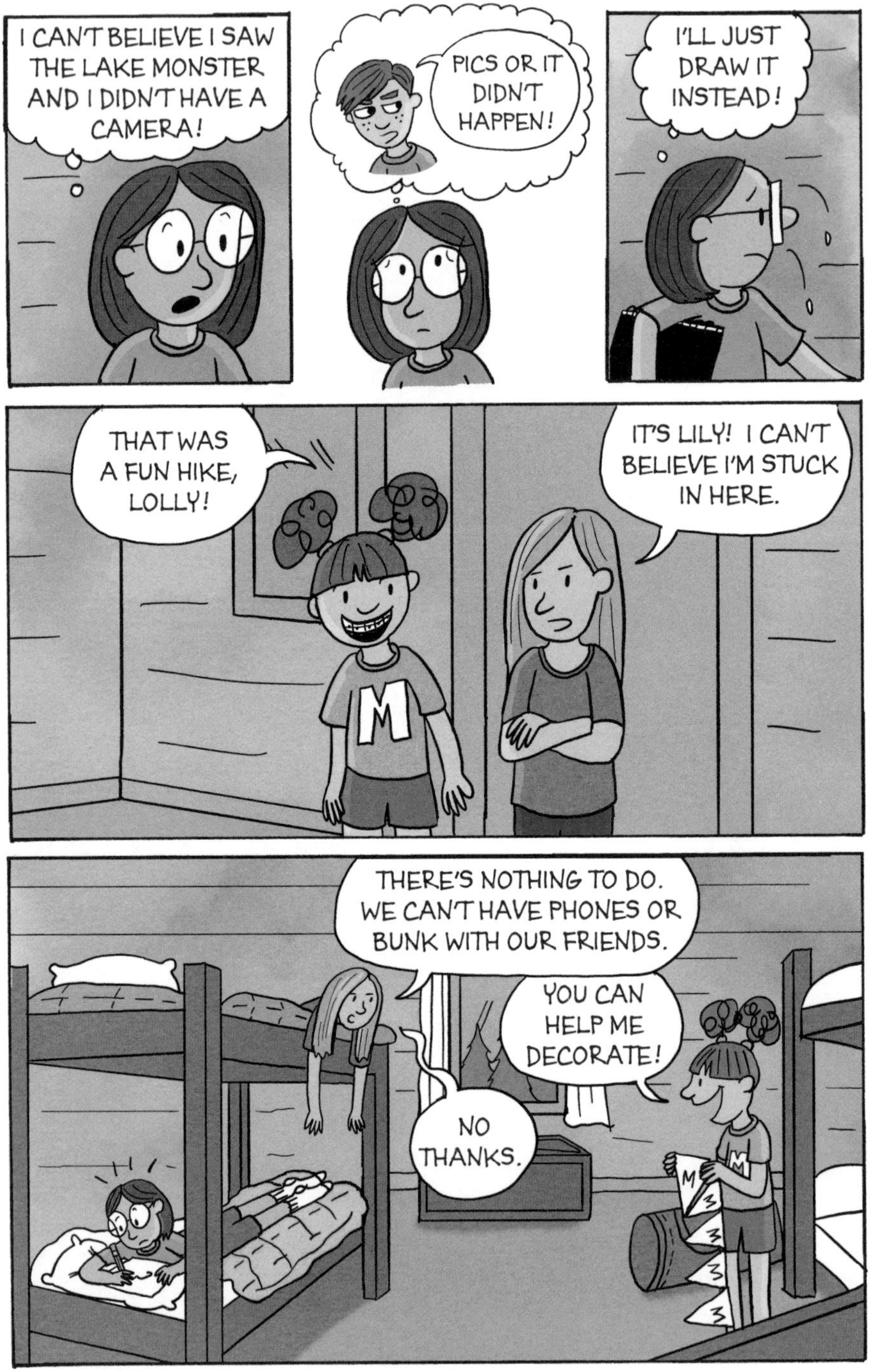
I CAN'T BELIEVE I SAW THE LAKE MONSTER AND I DIDN'T HAVE A CAMERA!
PICS OR IT DIDN'T HAPPEN!
I'LL JUST DRAW IT INSTEAD!
THAT WAS A FUN HIKE, LOLLY!
IT'S LILY! I CAN'T BELIEVE I'M STUCK IN HERE.
THERE'S NOTHING TO DO. WE CAN'T HAVE PHONES OR BUNK WITH OUR FRIENDS.
YOU CAN HELP ME DECORATE!
NO THANKS.
M

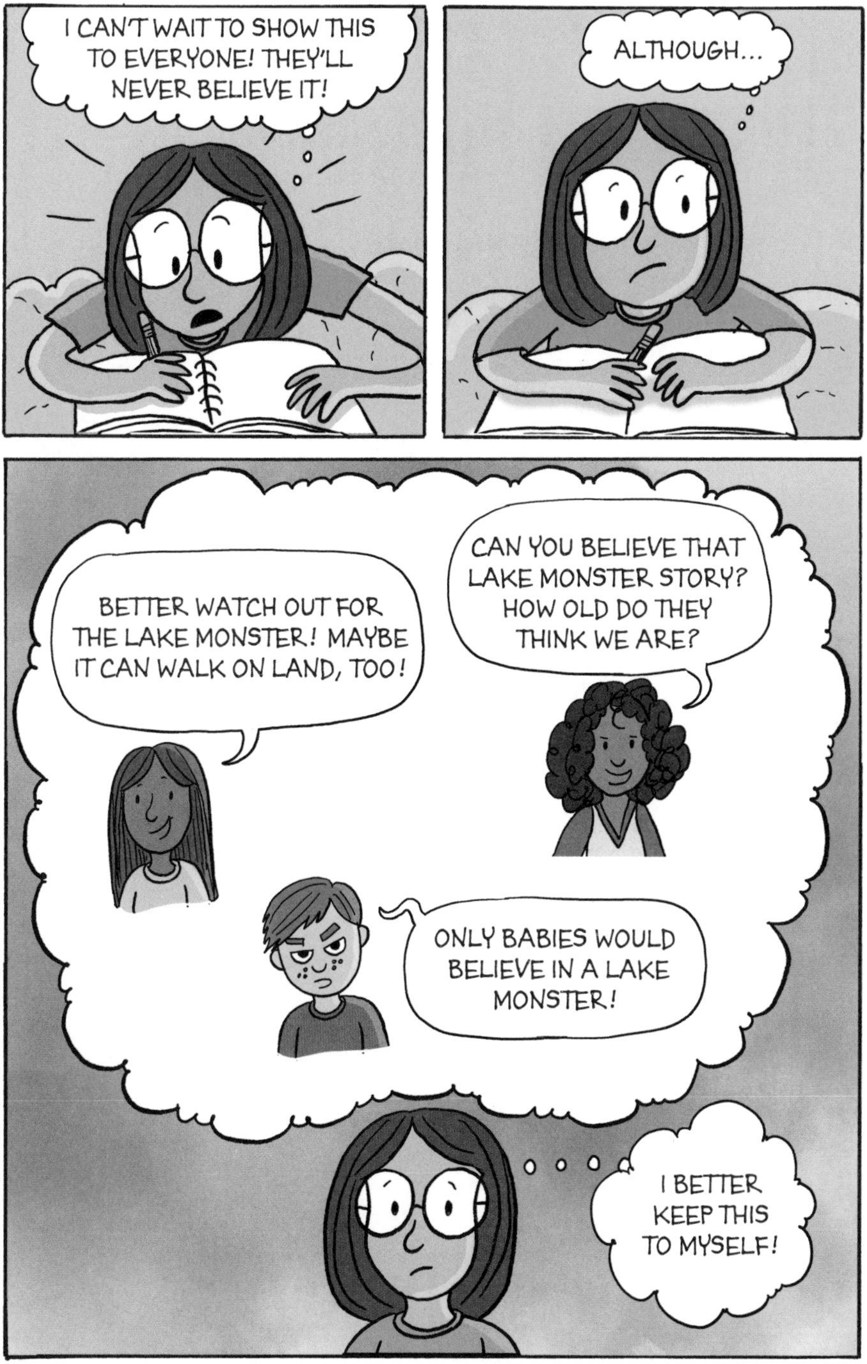
I CAN'T WAIT TO SHOW THIS TO EVERYONE! THEY'LL NEVER BELIEVE IT!
ALTHOUGH...
BETTER WATCH OUT FOR THE LAKE MONSTER! MAYBE IT CAN WALK ON LAND, TOO!
CAN YOU BELIEVE THAT LAKE MONSTER STORY? HOW OLD DO THEY THINK WE ARE?
ONLY BABIES WOULD BELIEVE IN A LAKE MONSTER!
I BETTER KEEP THIS TO MYSELF!

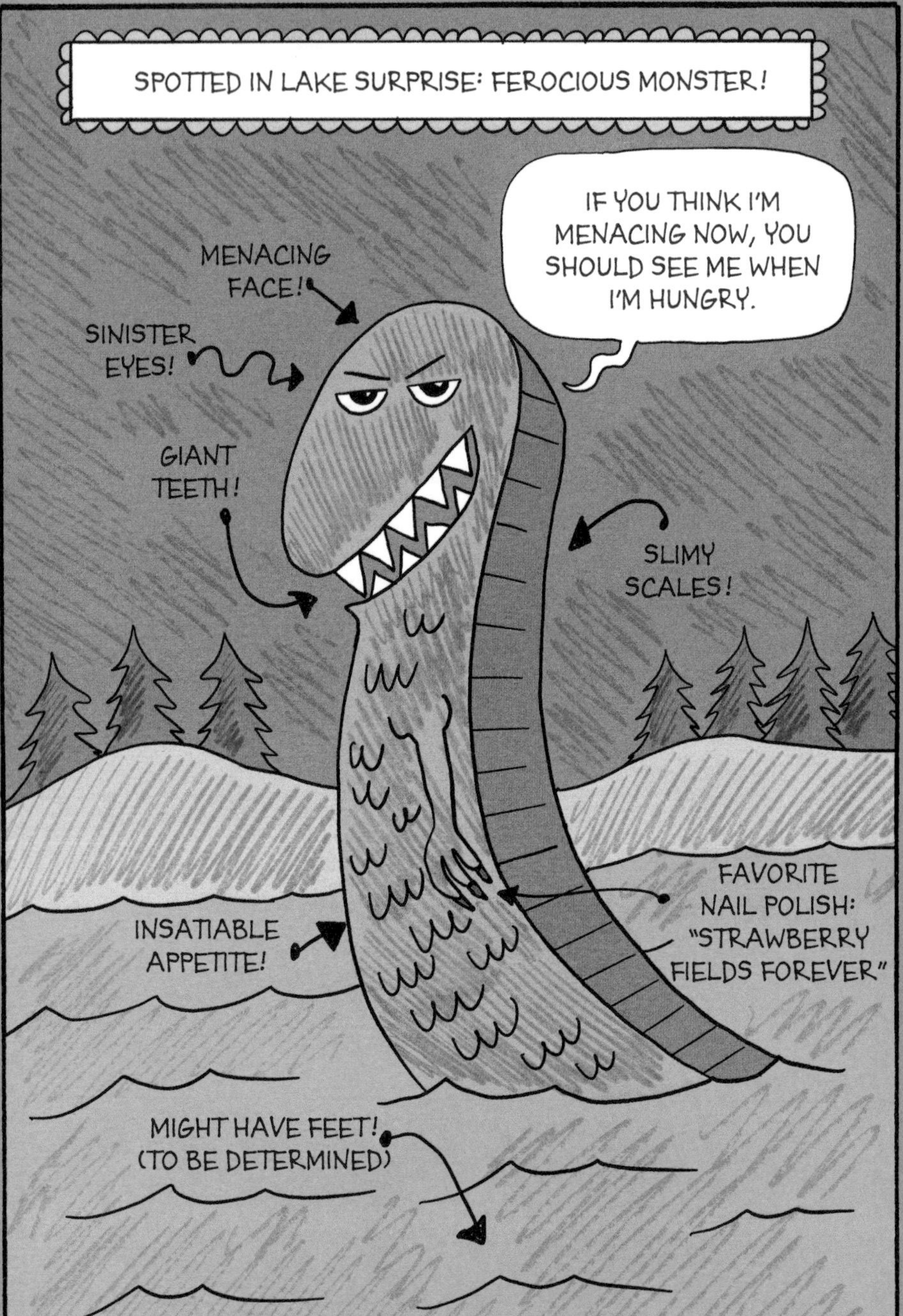
SPOTTED IN LAKE SURPRISE: FEROCIOUS MONSTER!
IF YOU THINK I'M MENACING NOW, YOU SHOULD SEE ME WHEN I'M HUNGRY.
MENACING FACE!
SINISTER EYES!
GIANT TEETH!
SLIMY SCALES!
FAVORITE NAIL POLISH: "STRAWBERRY FIELDS FOREVER"
INSATIABLE APPETITE!
MIGHT HAVE FEET! (TO BE DETERMINED)

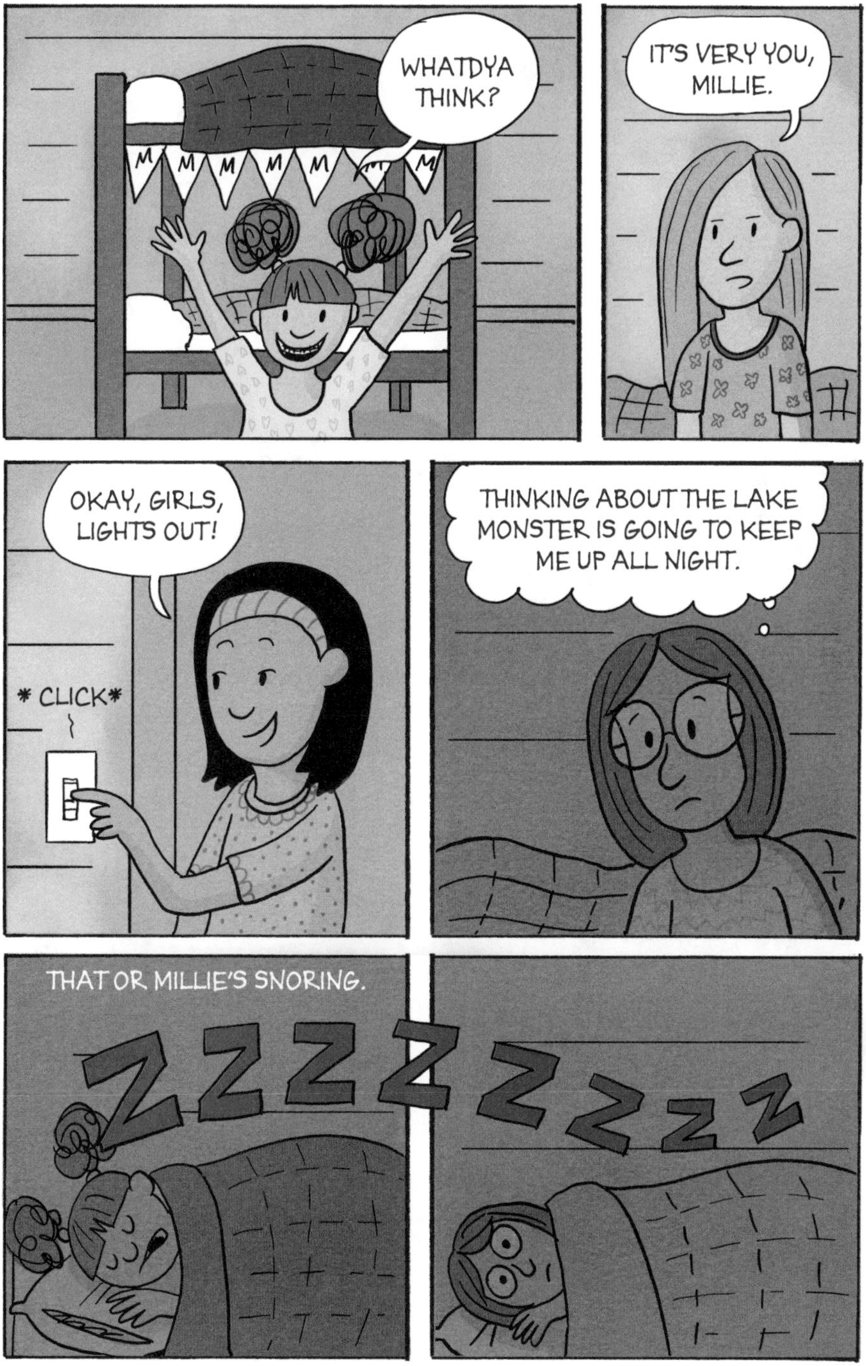
WHATDYA THINK?
IT'S VERY YOU, MILLIE.
OKAY, GIRLS, LIGHTS OUT!
* CLICK *
THINKING ABOUT THE LAKE MONSTER IS GOING TO KEEP ME UP ALL NIGHT.
THAT OR MILLIE'S SNORING.
ZZZZZzzz

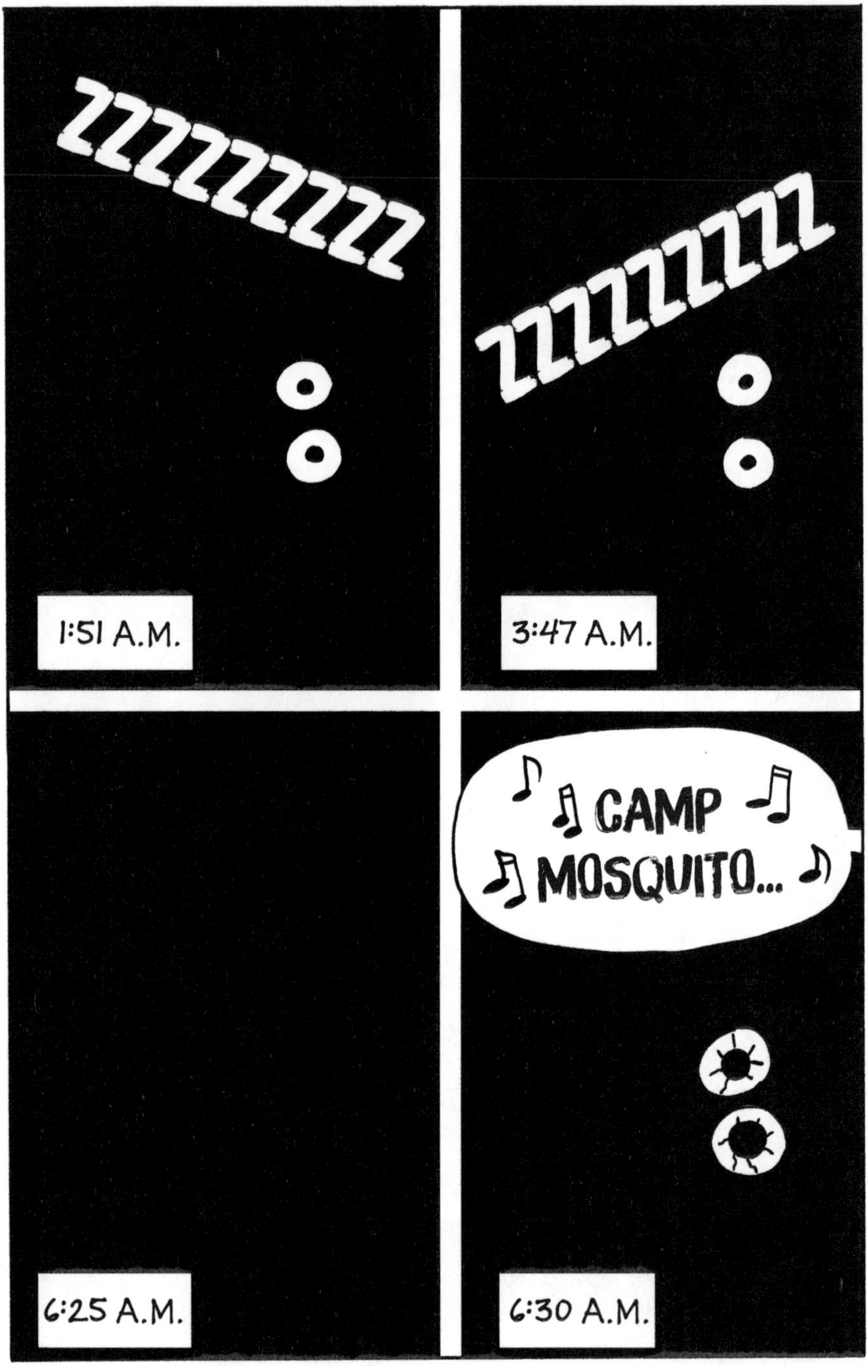
ZZZZZZZZZ
1:51 A.M.
ZZZZZZZZZ
3:47 A.M.
6:25 A.M.
♪ ♫ CAMP ♫
♫ MOSQUITO... ♪
6:30 A.M.

CHAPTER 5
GET LOST

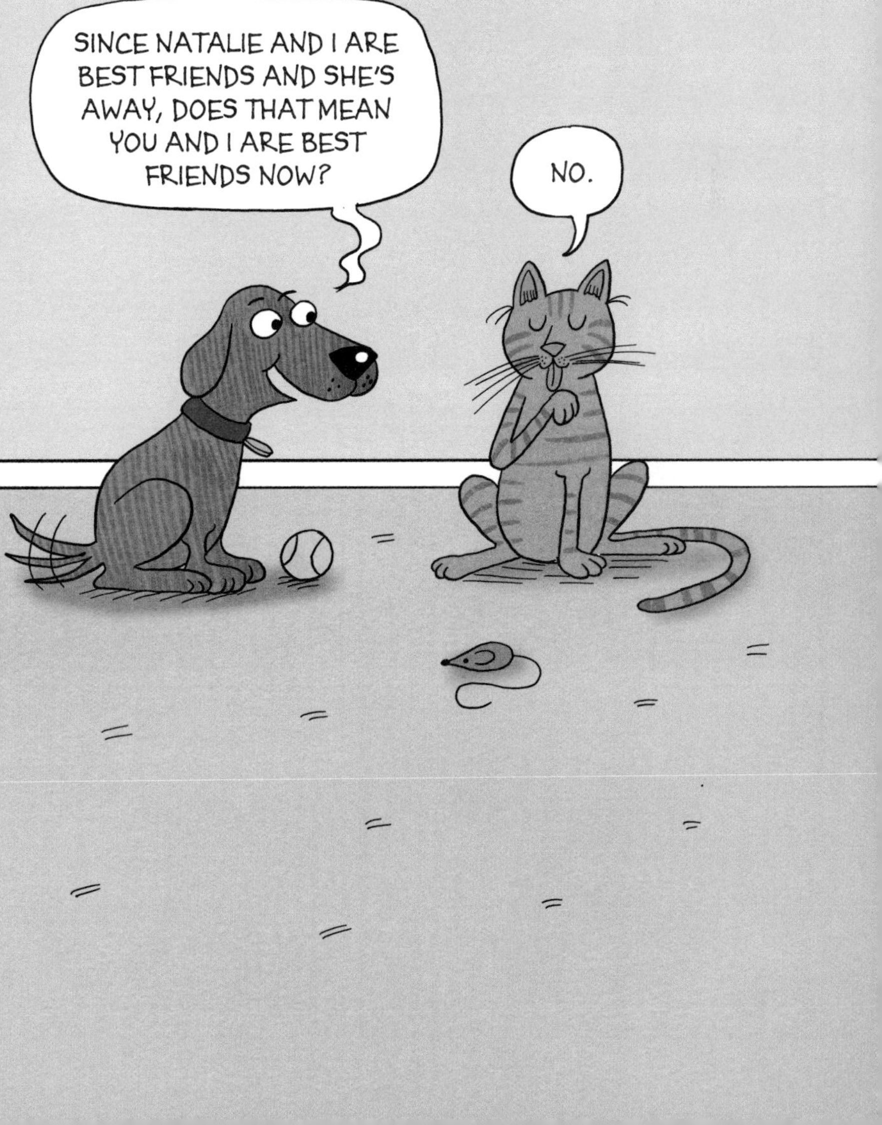
SINCE NATALIE AND I ARE BEST FRIENDS AND SHE'S AWAY, DOES THAT MEAN YOU AND I ARE BEST FRIENDS NOW?
NO.

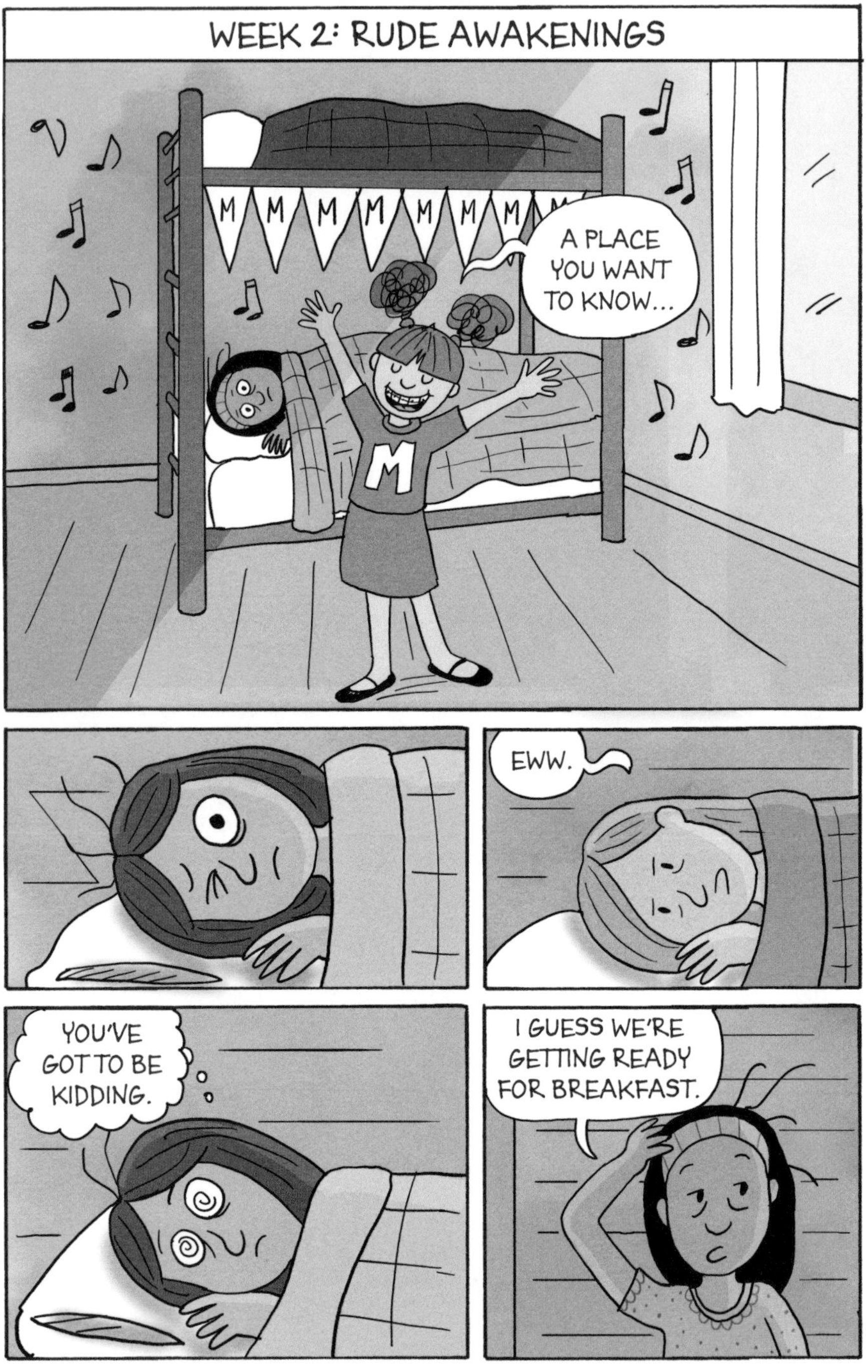
WEEK 2: RUDE AWAKENINGS
M M M M M M M M
A PLACE YOU WANT TO KNOW...
EWW.
YOU'VE GOT TO BE KIDDING.
I GUESS WE'RE GETTING READY FOR BREAKFAST.

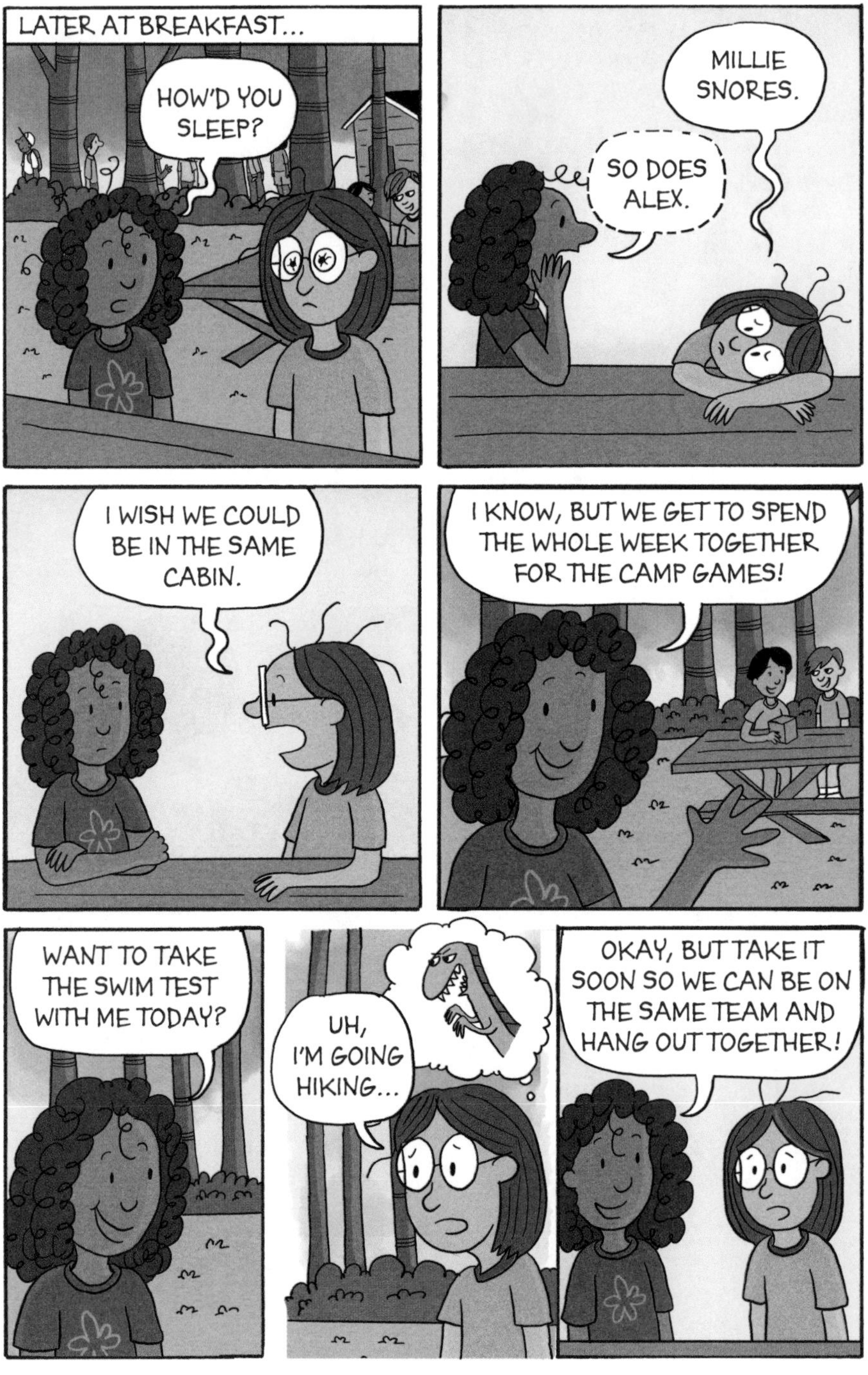
LATER AT BREAKFAST...
HOW'D YOU SLEEP?
MILLIE SNORES.
SO DOES ALEX.
I WISH WE COULD BE IN THE SAME CABIN.
I KNOW, BUT WE GET TO SPEND THE WHOLE WEEK TOGETHER FOR THE CAMP GAMES!
WANT TO TAKE THE SWIM TEST WITH ME TODAY?
UH, I'M GOING HIKING...
OKAY, BUT TAKE IT SOON SO WE CAN BE ON THE SAME TEAM AND HANG OUT TOGETHER!

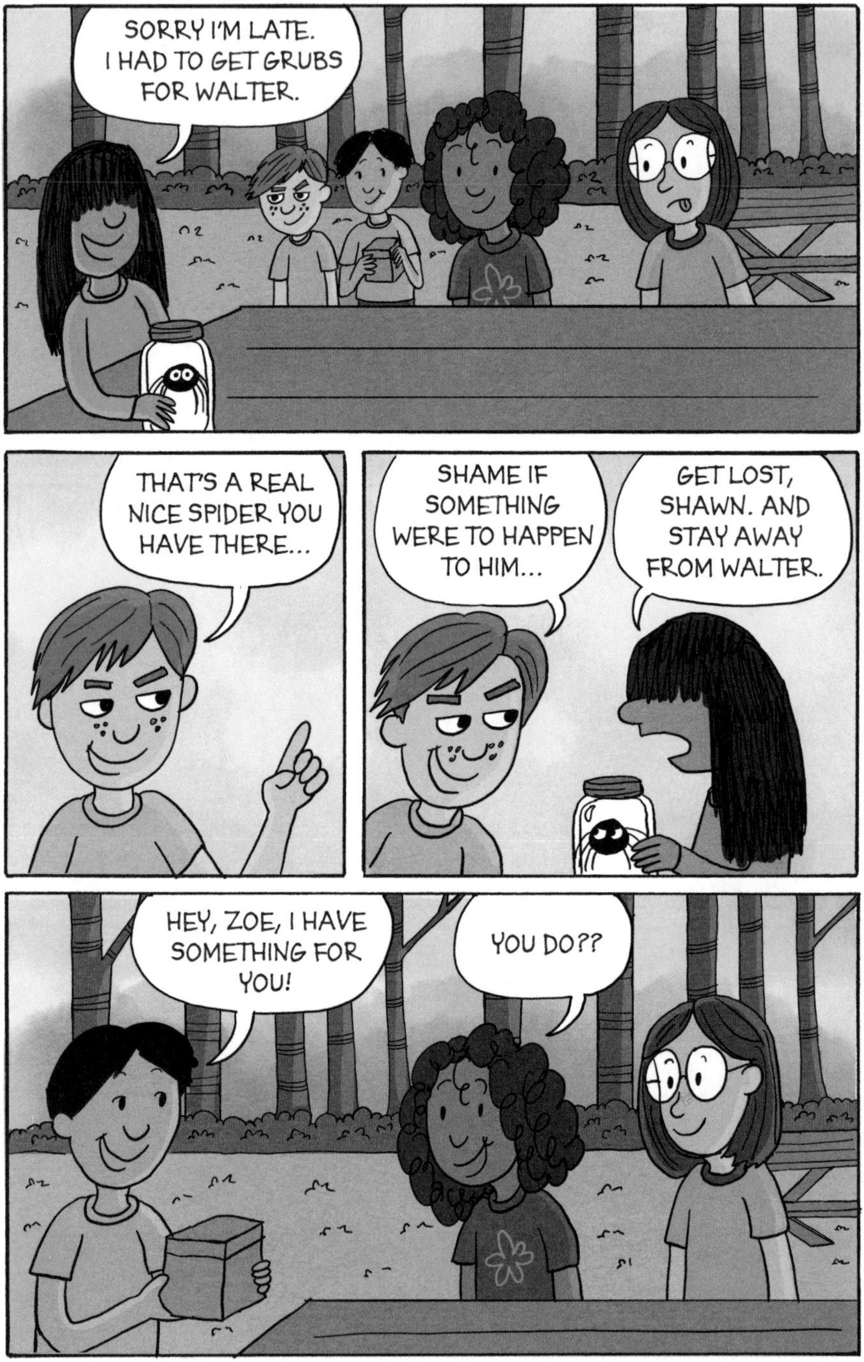
SORRY I'M LATE. I HAD TO GET GRUBS FOR WALTER.
THAT'S A REAL NICE SPIDER YOU HAVE THERE...
SHAME IF SOMETHING WERE TO HAPPEN TO HIM...
GET LOST, SHAWN. AND STAY AWAY FROM WALTER.
HEY, ZOE, I HAVE SOMETHING FOR YOU!
YOU DO??

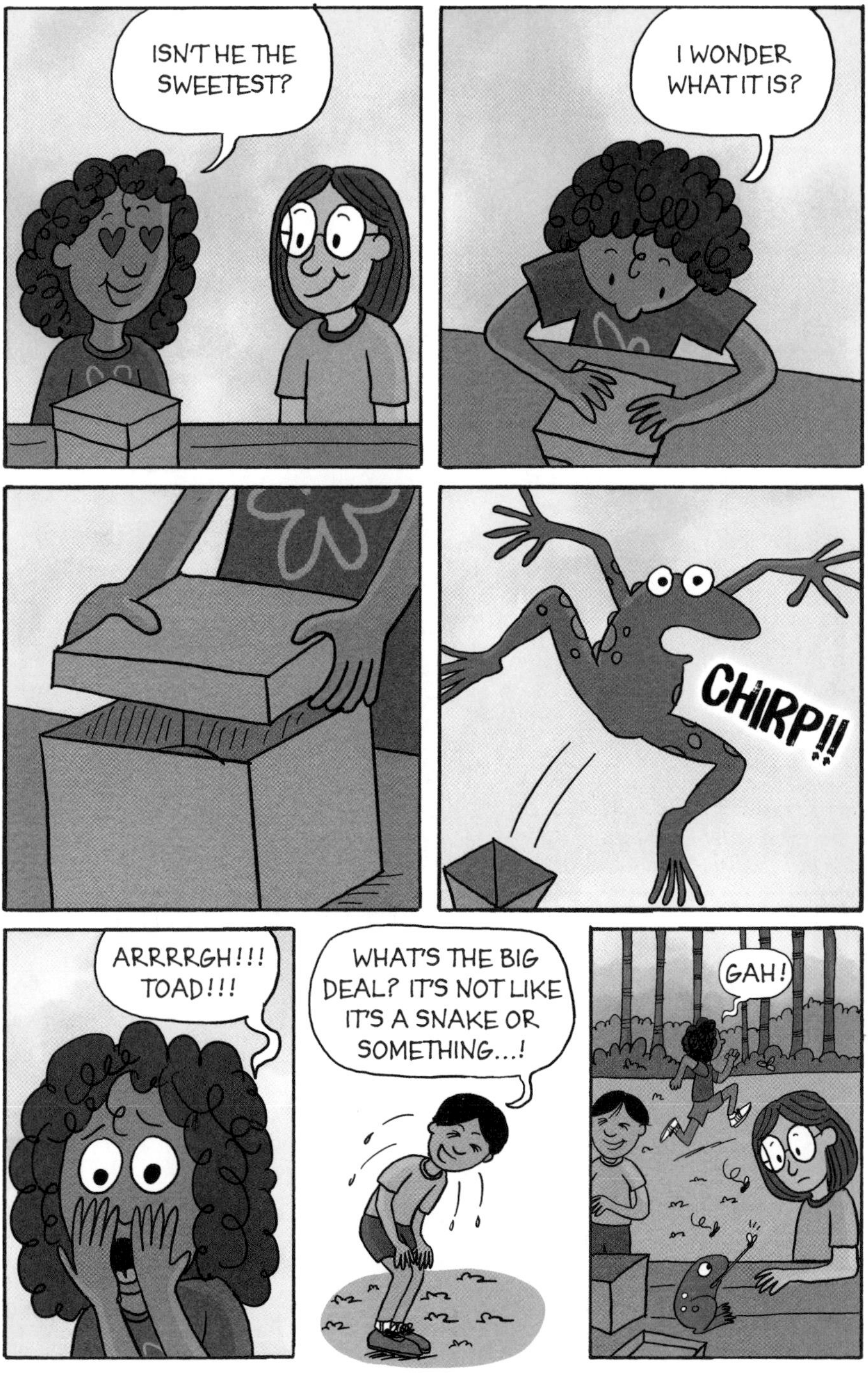
ISN'T HE THE SWEETEST?
I WONDER WHAT IT IS?
CHIRP!!
ARRRRGH!!! TOAD!!!
WHAT'S THE BIG DEAL? IT'S NOT LIKE IT'S A SNAKE OR SOMETHING...!
GAH!

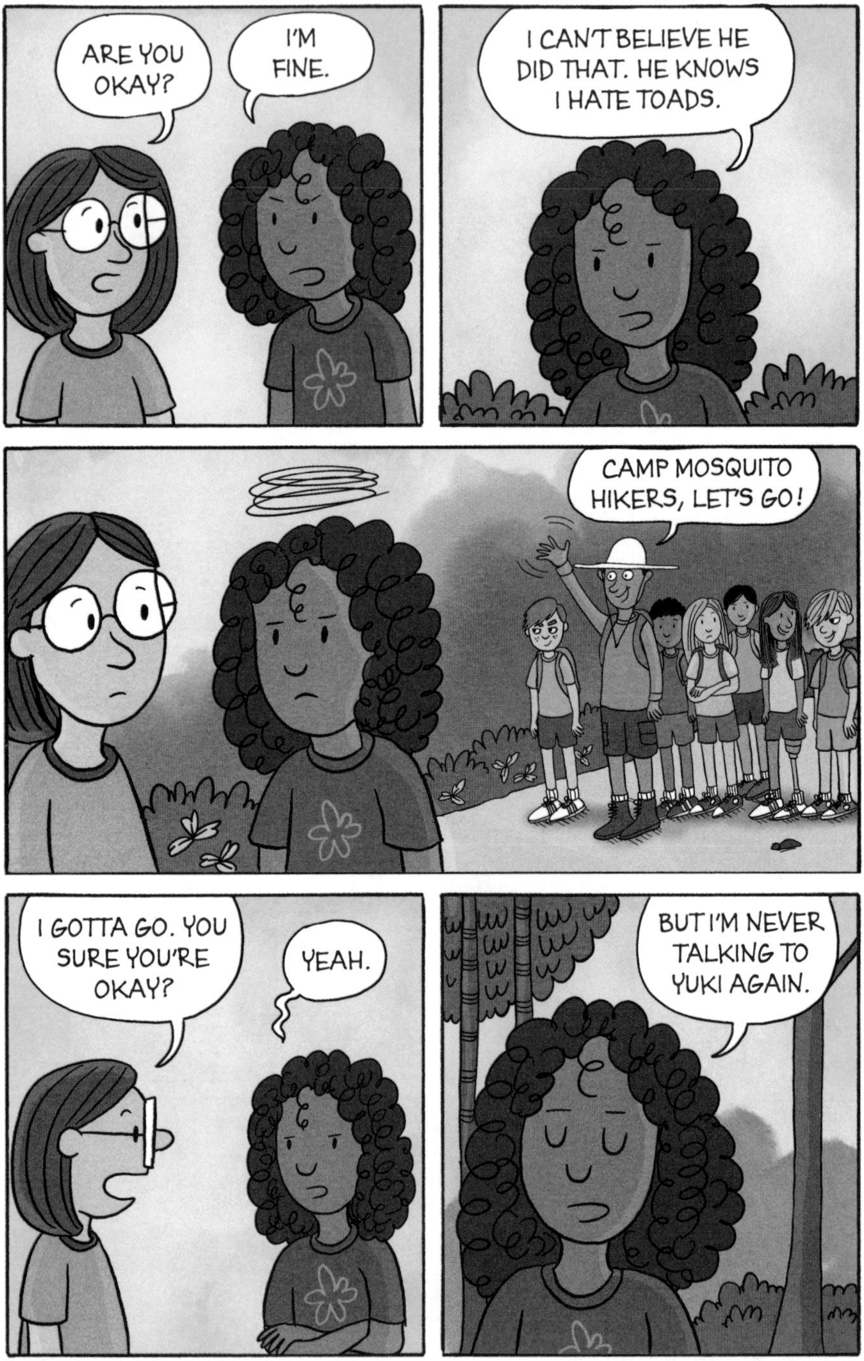
ARE YOU OKAY?
I'M FINE.
I CAN'T BELIEVE HE DID THAT. HE KNOWS I HATE TOADS.
CAMP MOSQUITO HIKERS, LET'S GO!
I GOTTA GO. YOU SURE YOU'RE OKAY?
YEAH.
BUT I'M NEVER TALKING TO YUKI AGAIN.

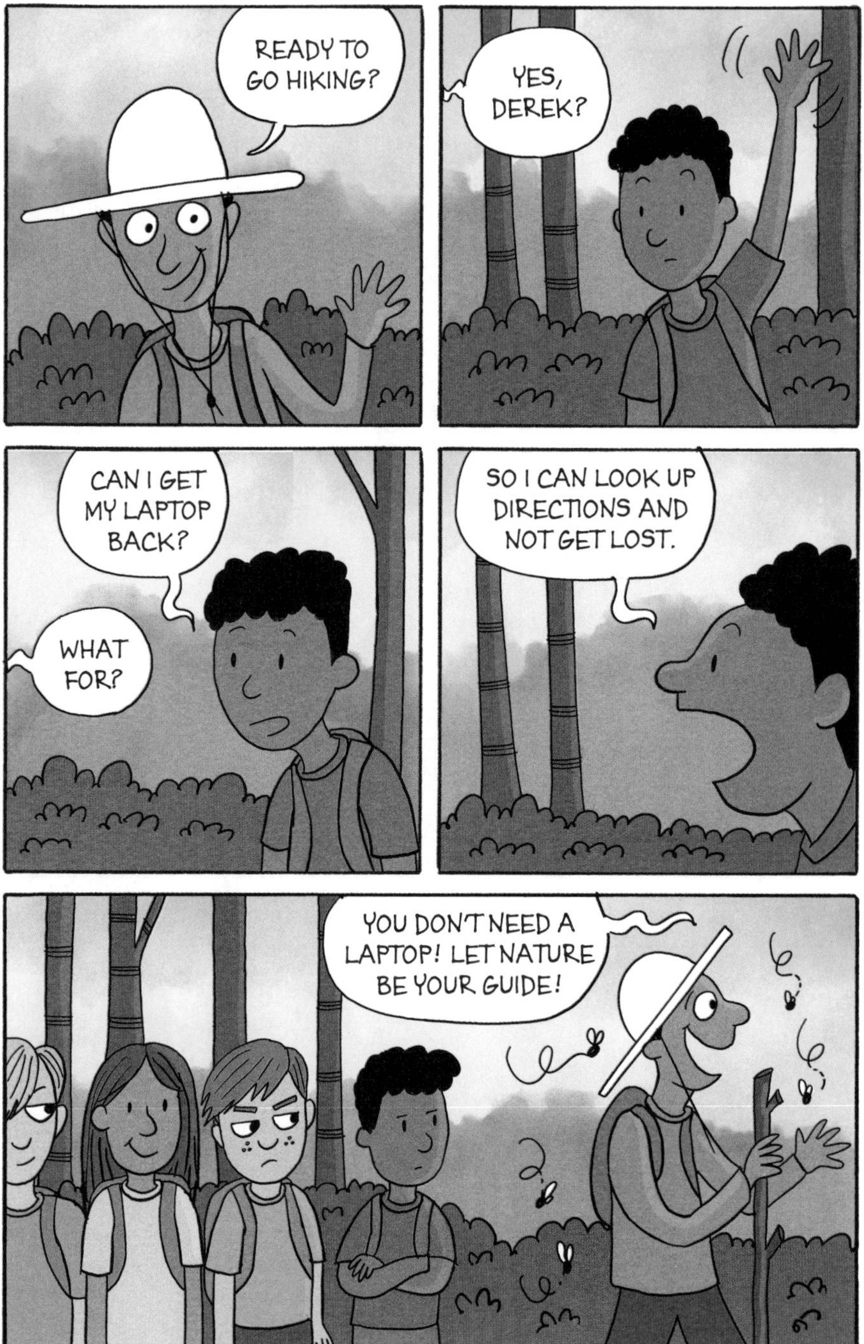
READY TO GO HIKING?
YES, DEREK?
CAN I GET MY LAPTOP BACK?
WHAT FOR?
SO I CAN LOOK UP DIRECTIONS AND NOT GET LOST.
YOU DON'T NEED A LAPTOP! LET NATURE BE YOUR GUIDE!

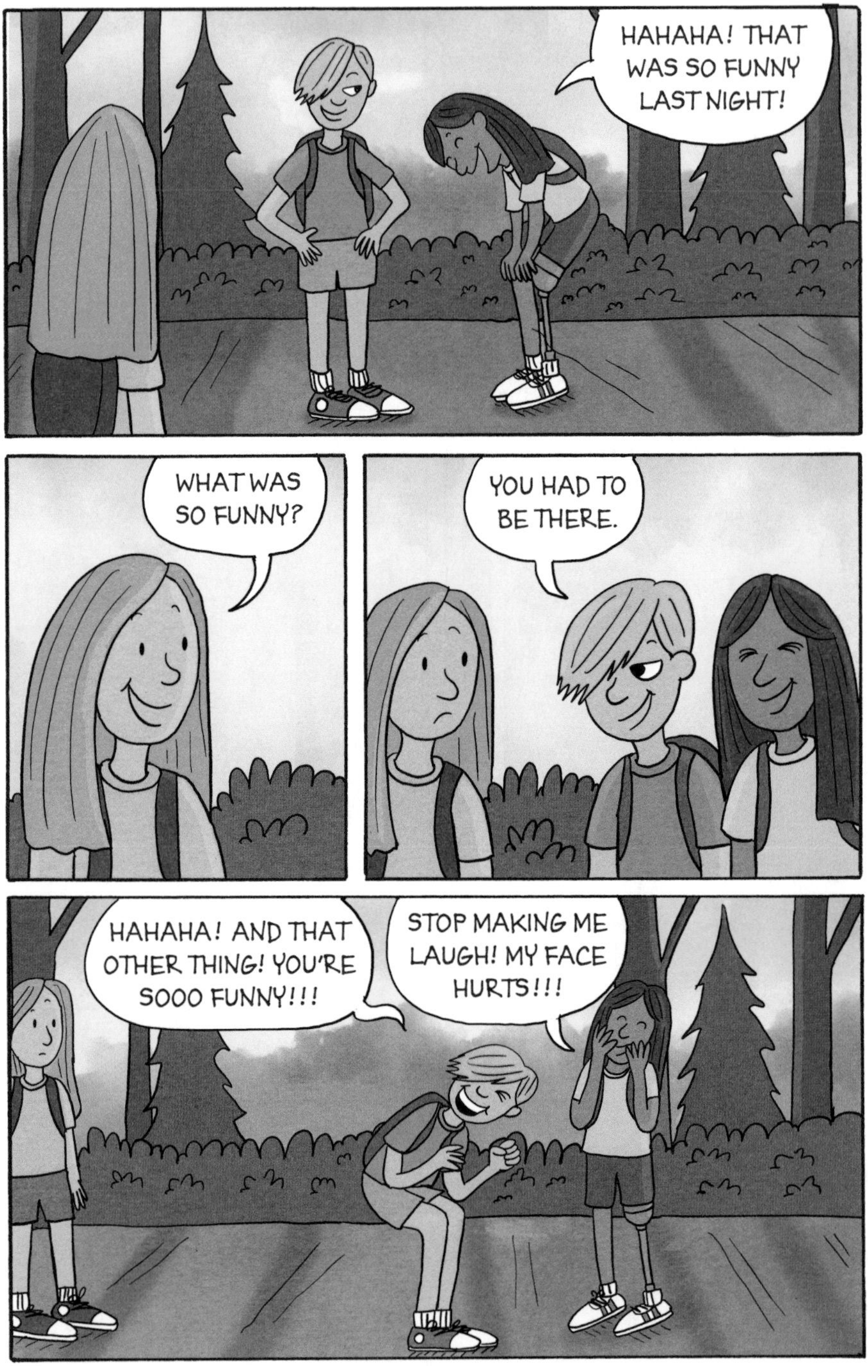
HAHAHA! THAT WAS SO FUNNY LAST NIGHT!
WHAT WAS SO FUNNY?
YOU HAD TO BE THERE.
HAHAHA! AND THAT OTHER THING! YOU'RE SOOO FUNNY!!!
STOP MAKING ME LAUGH! MY FACE HURTS!!!

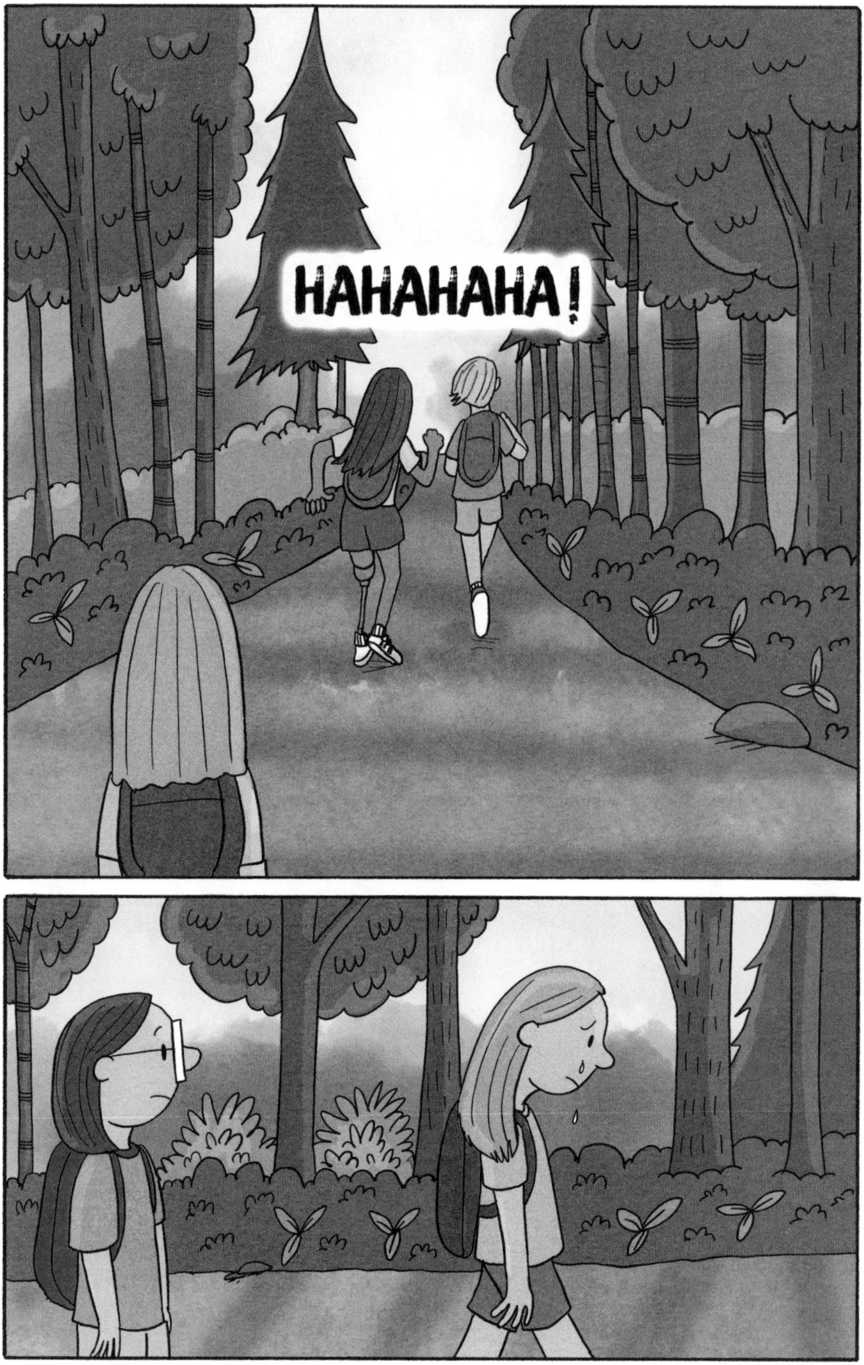
HAHAHAHA!

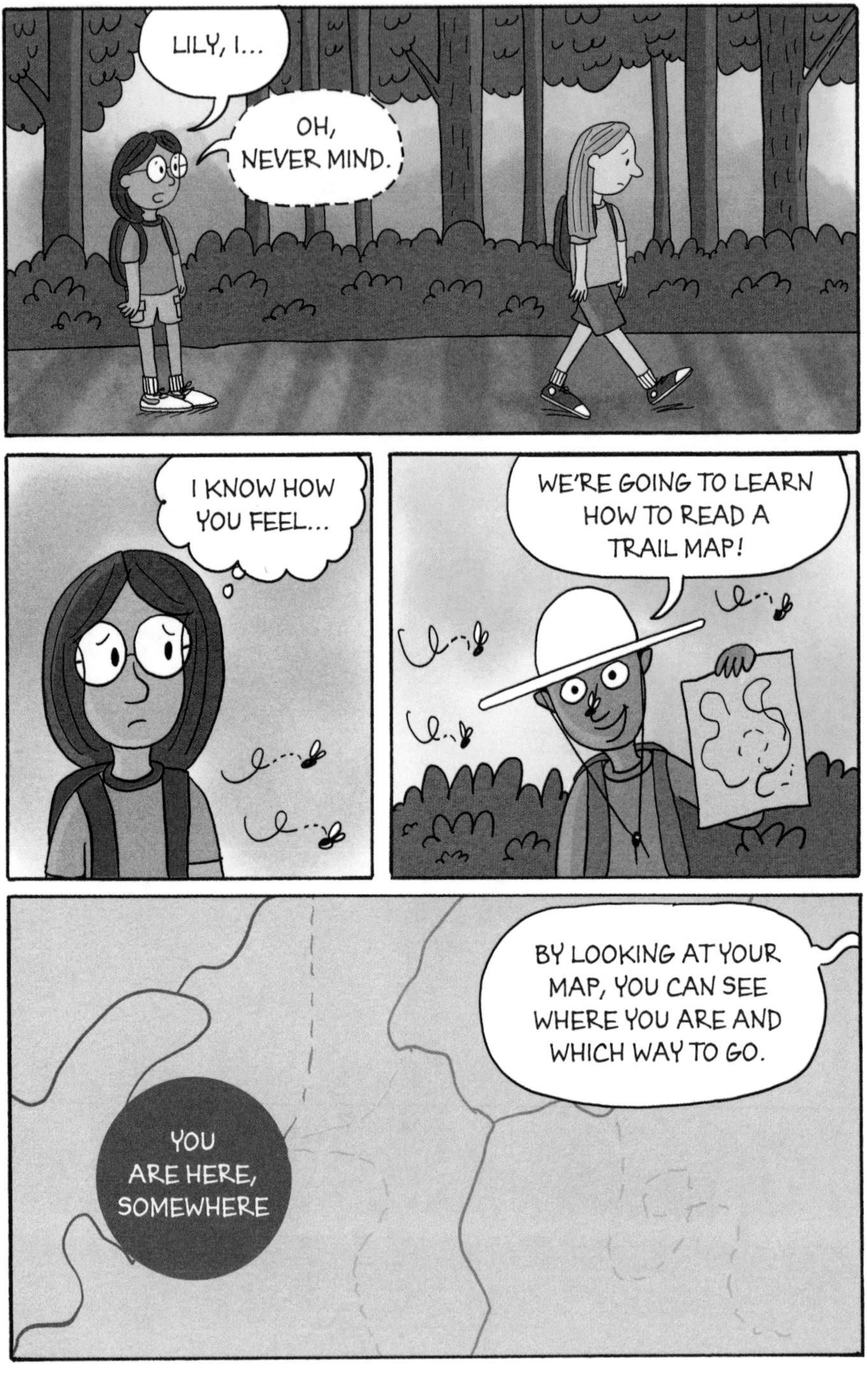
LILY, I...
OH, NEVER MIND.
I KNOW HOW YOU FEEL...
WE'RE GOING TO LEARN HOW TO READ A TRAIL MAP!
BY LOOKING AT YOUR MAP, YOU CAN SEE WHERE YOU ARE AND WHICH WAY TO GO.
YOU ARE HERE, SOMEWHERE

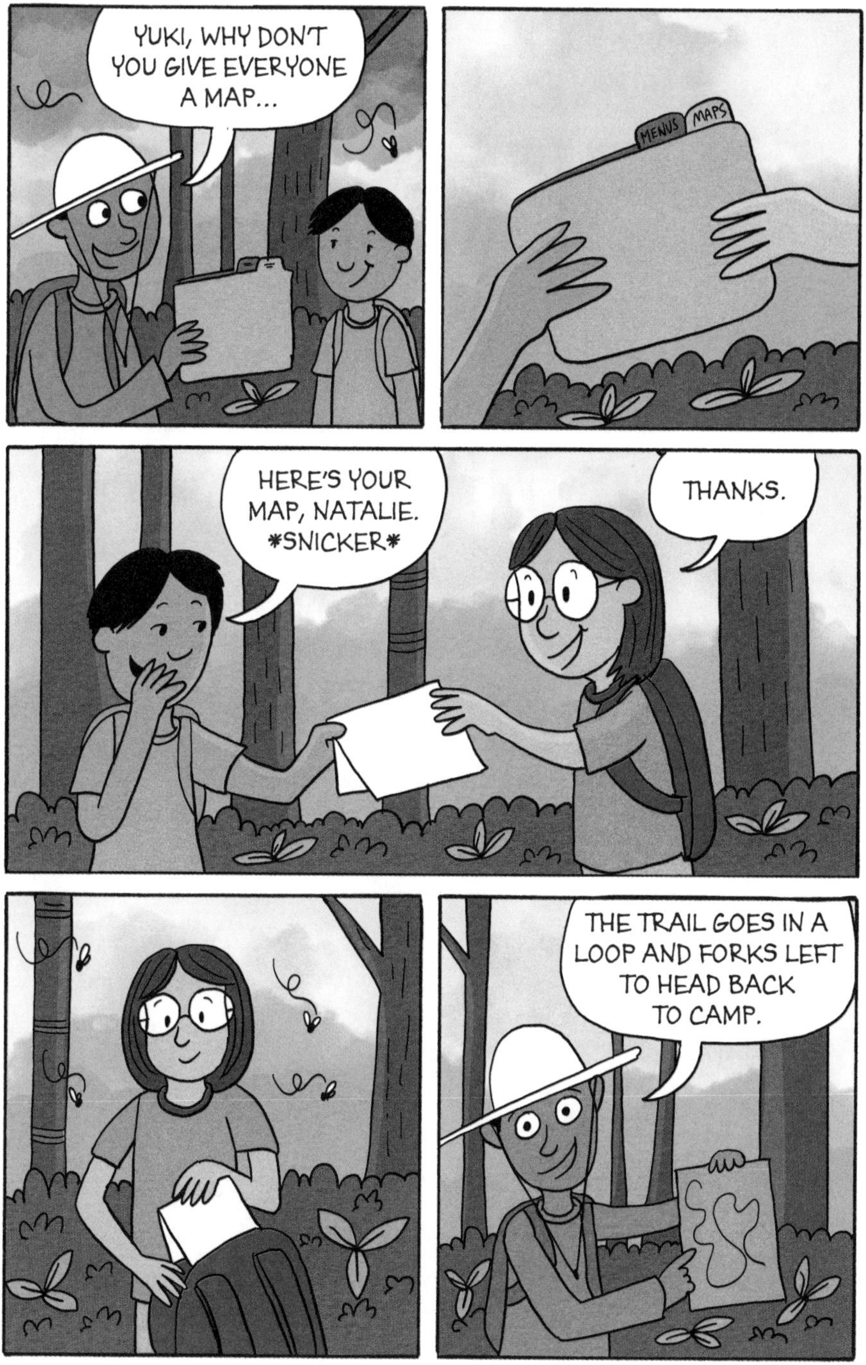
YUKI, WHY DON'T YOU GIVE EVERYONE A MAP...
MENUS
MAPS
HERE'S YOUR MAP, NATALIE. *SNICKER*
THANKS.
THE TRAIL GOES IN A LOOP AND FORKS LEFT TO HEAD BACK TO CAMP.

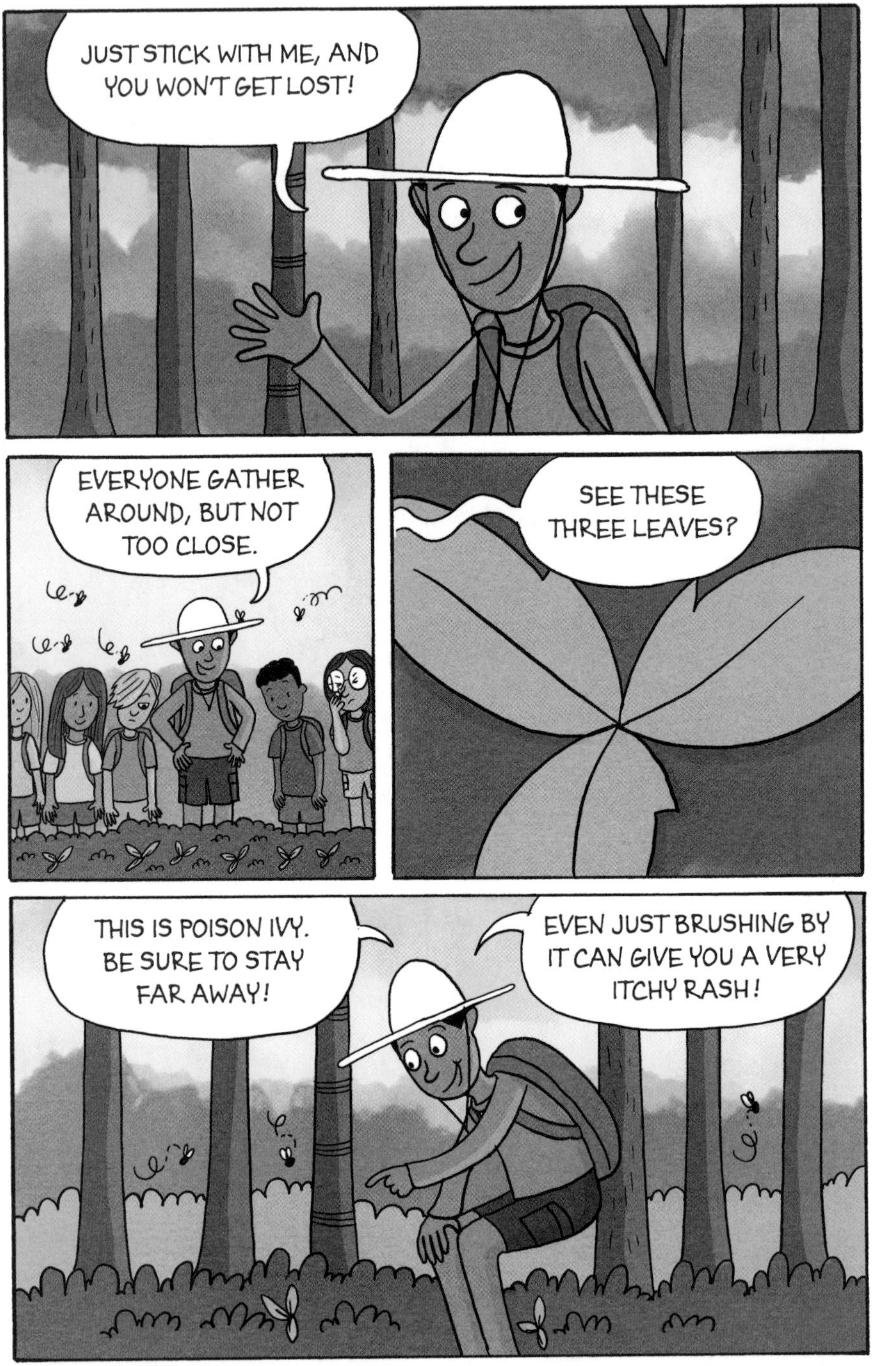
JUST STICK WITH ME, AND YOU WON'T GET LOST!
EVERYONE GATHER AROUND, BUT NOT TOO CLOSE.
SEE THESE THREE LEAVES?
THIS IS POISON IVY. BE SURE TO STAY FAR AWAY!
EVEN JUST BRUSHING BY IT CAN GIVE YOU A VERY ITCHY RASH!

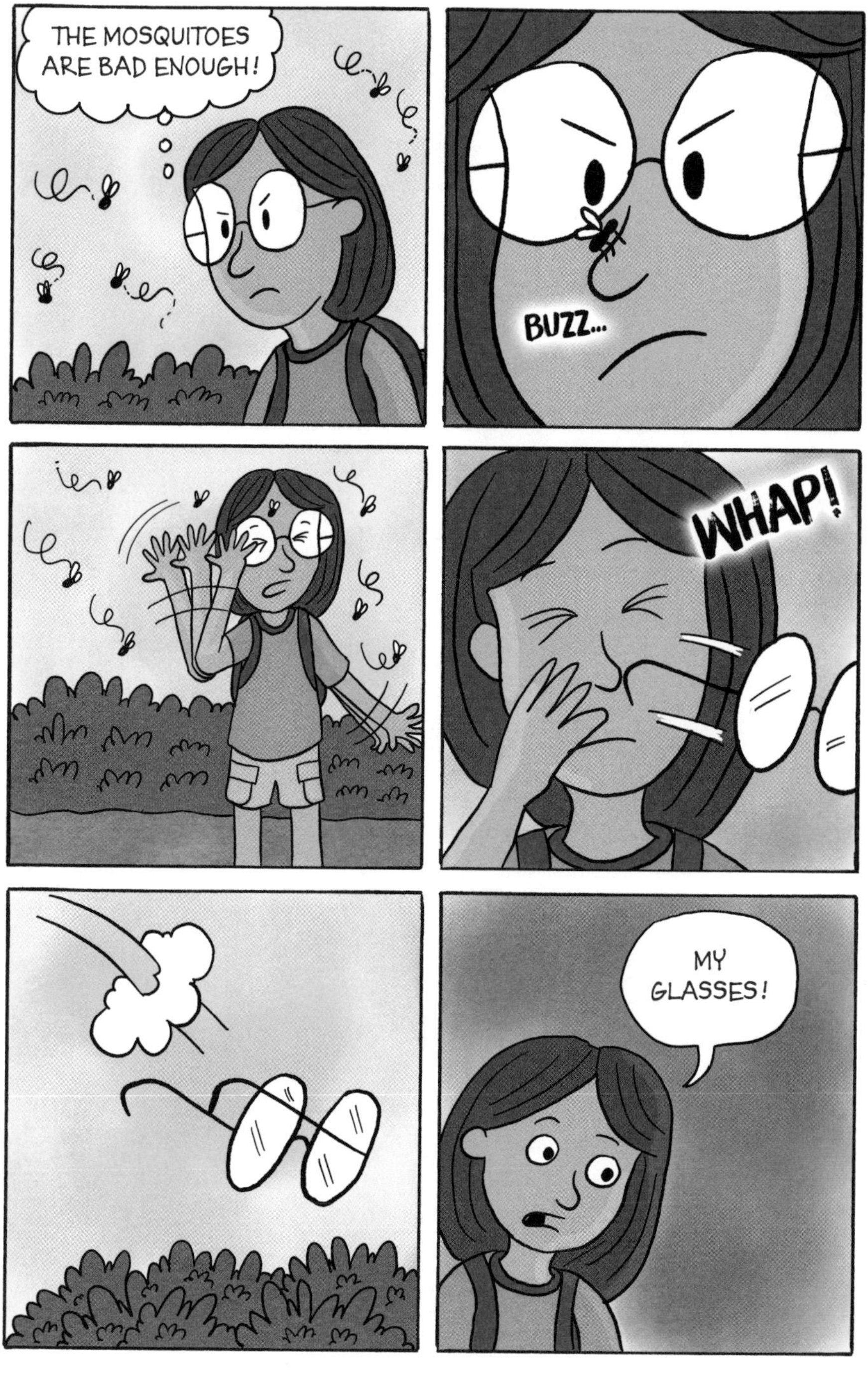
THE MOSQUITOES ARE BAD ENOUGH!
BUZZ...
WHAP!
MY GLASSES!

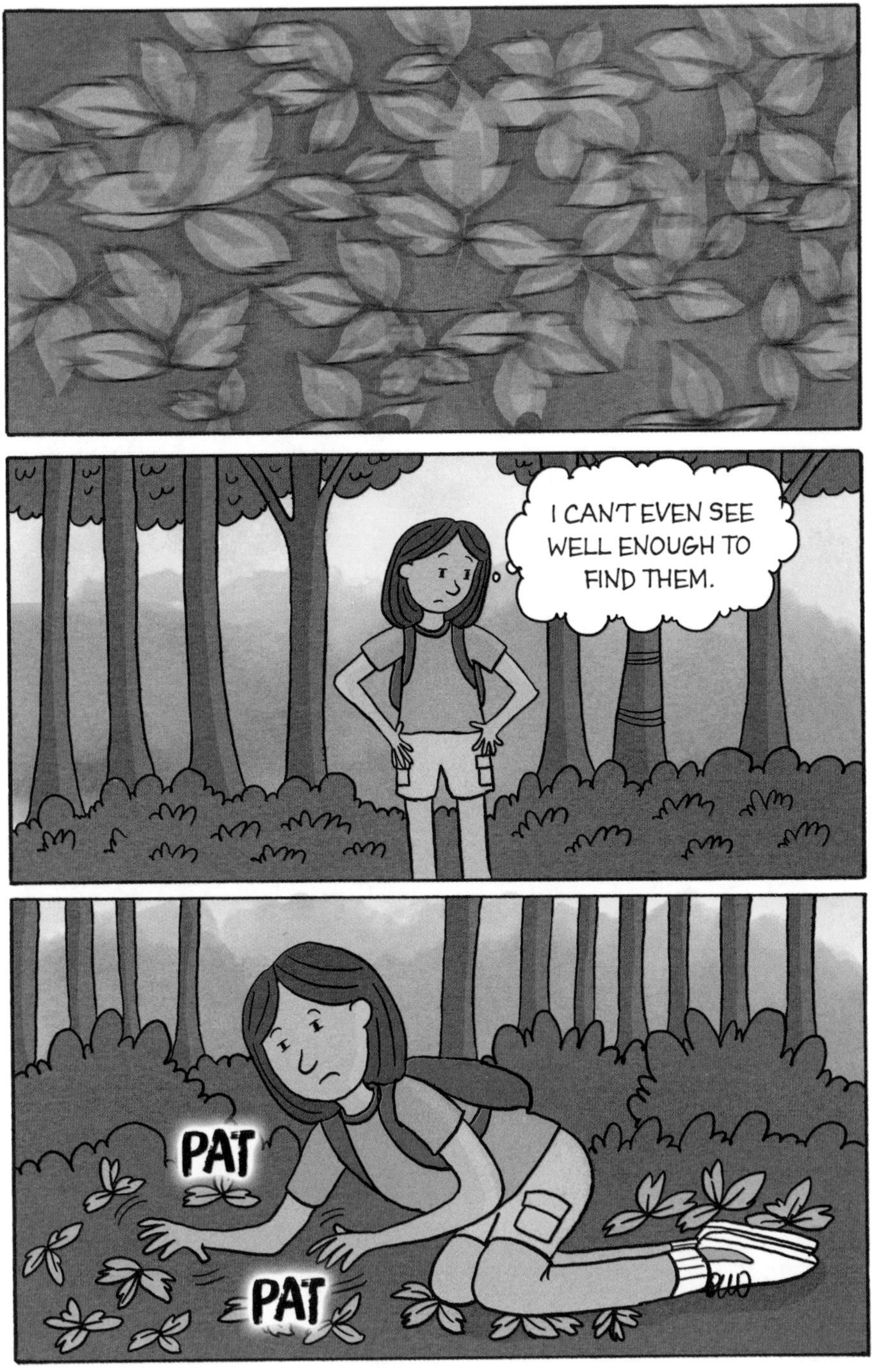
I CAN'T EVEN SEE WELL ENOUGH TO FIND THEM.
PAT
PAT

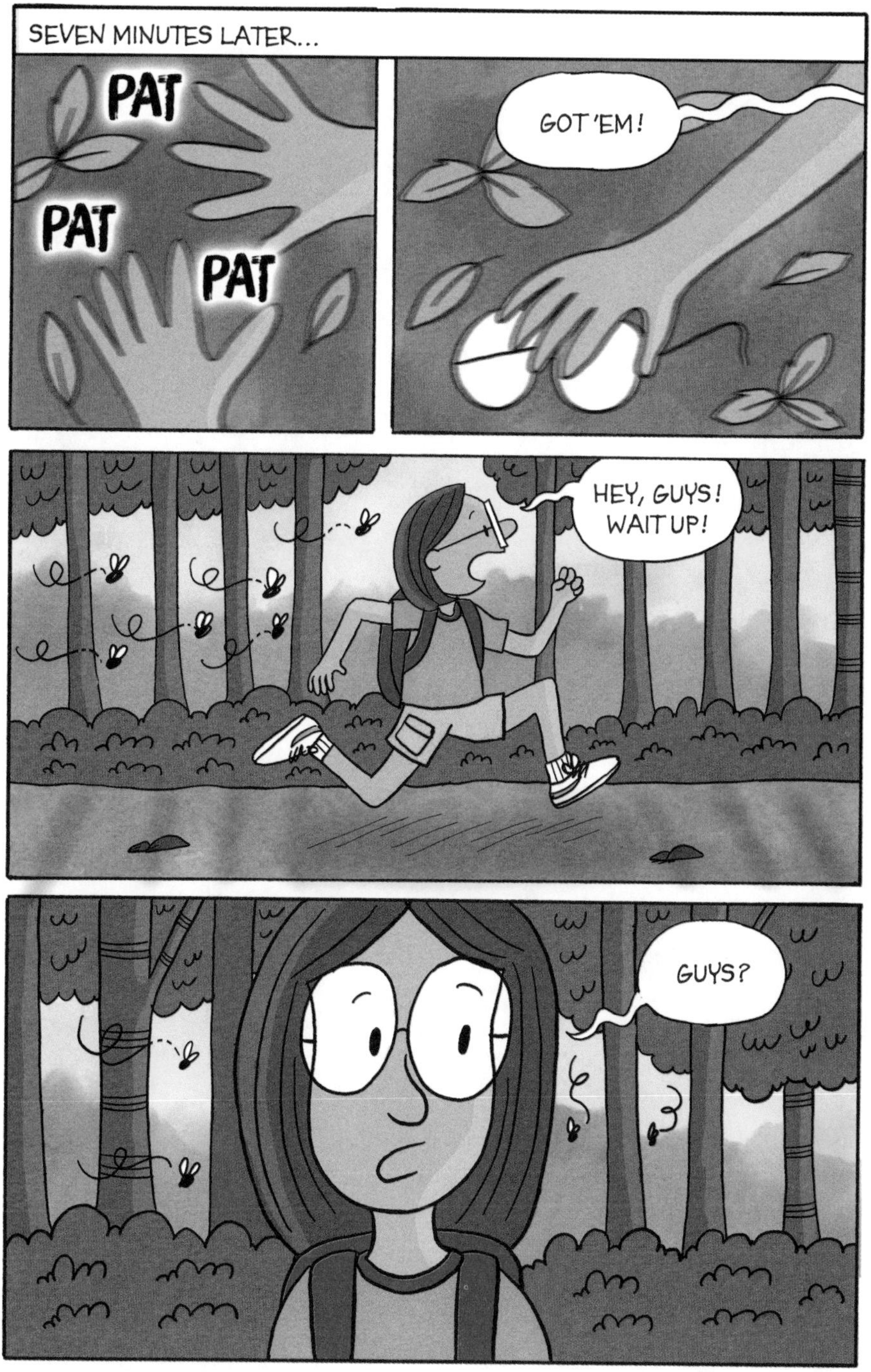
SEVEN MINUTES LATER...
PAT
PAT
PAT
GOT 'EM!
HEY, GUYS! WAIT UP!
GUYS?

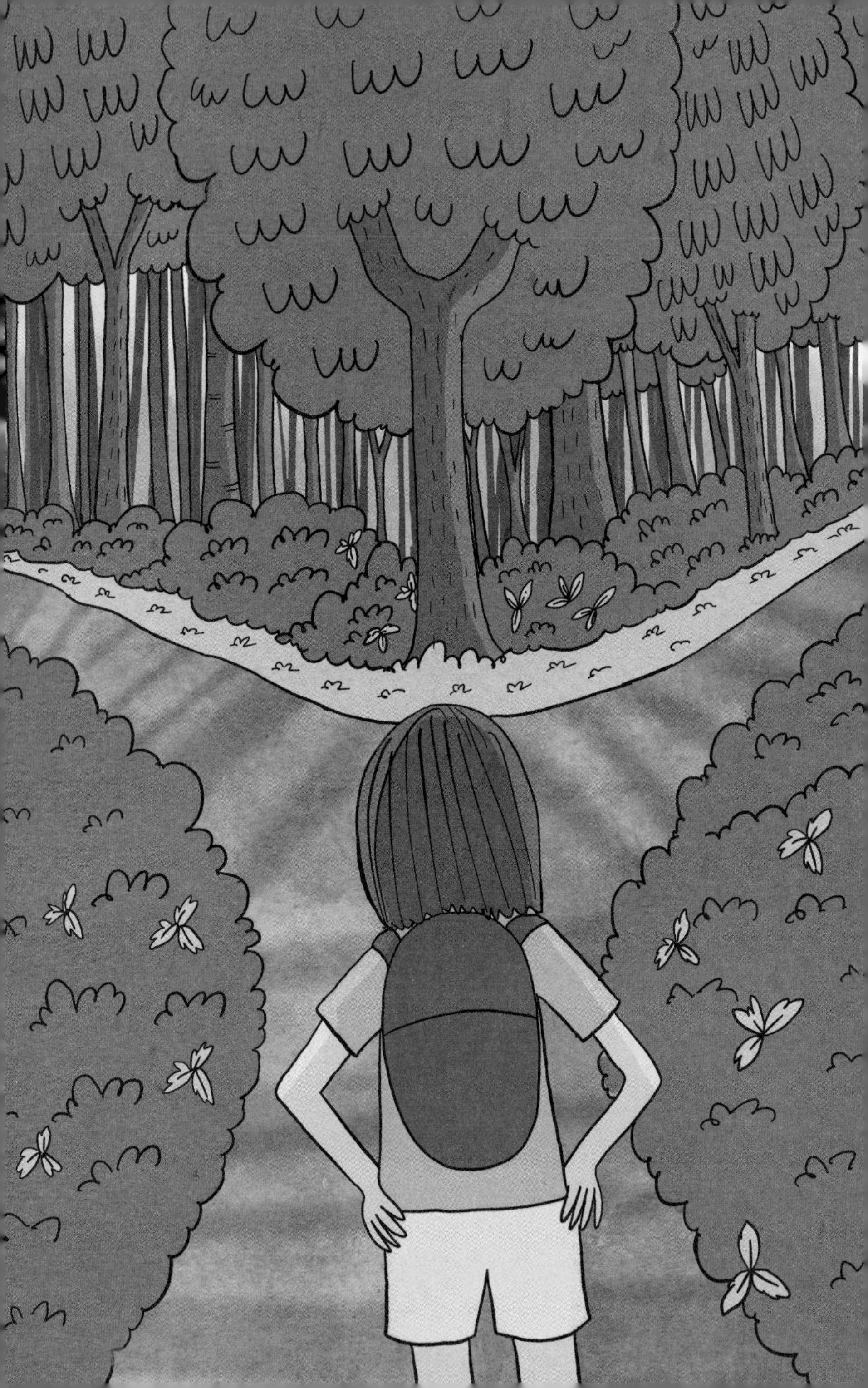

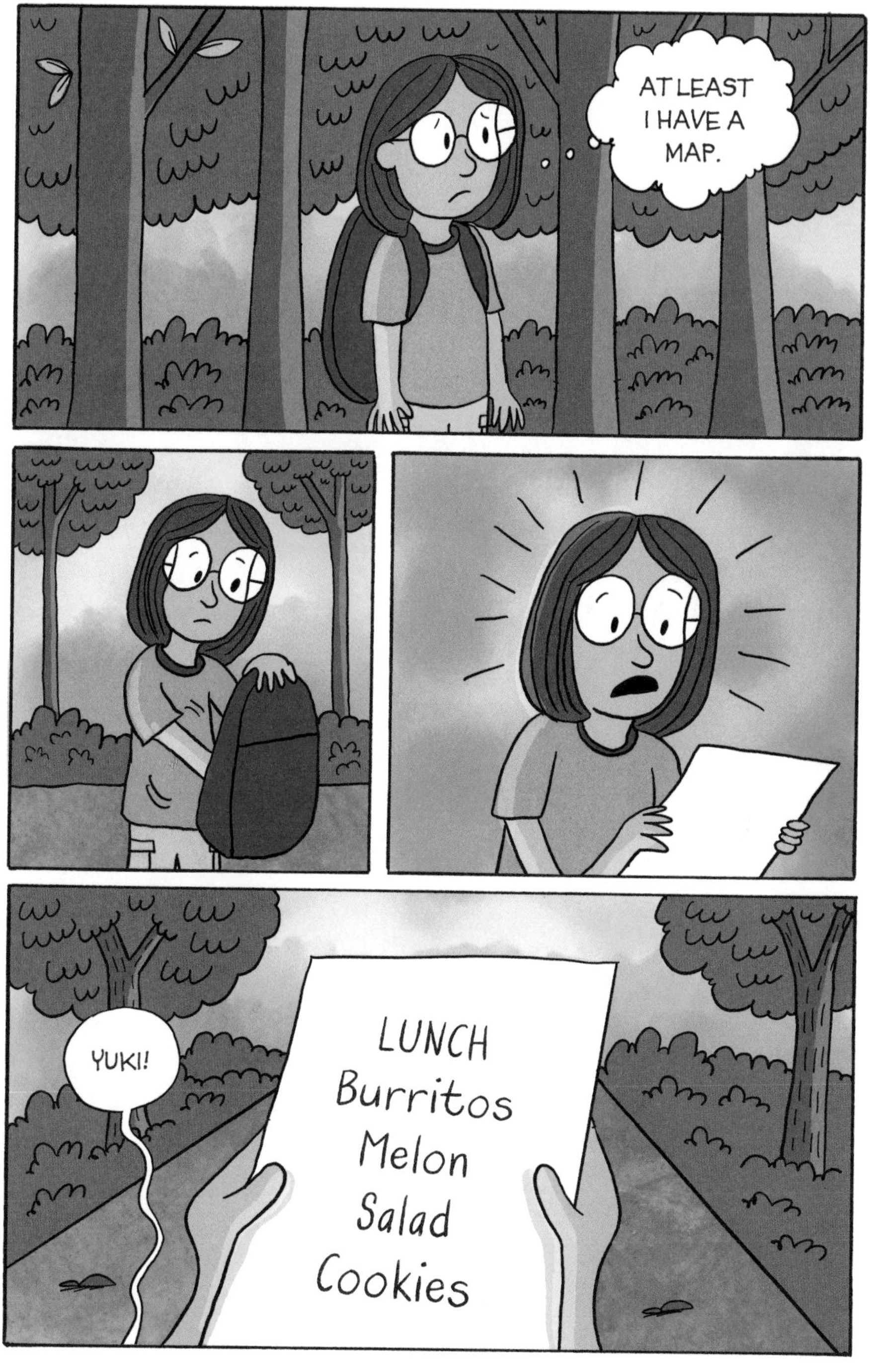
AT LEAST I HAVE A MAP.
YUKI!
LUNCH
Burritos
Melon
Salad
Cookies

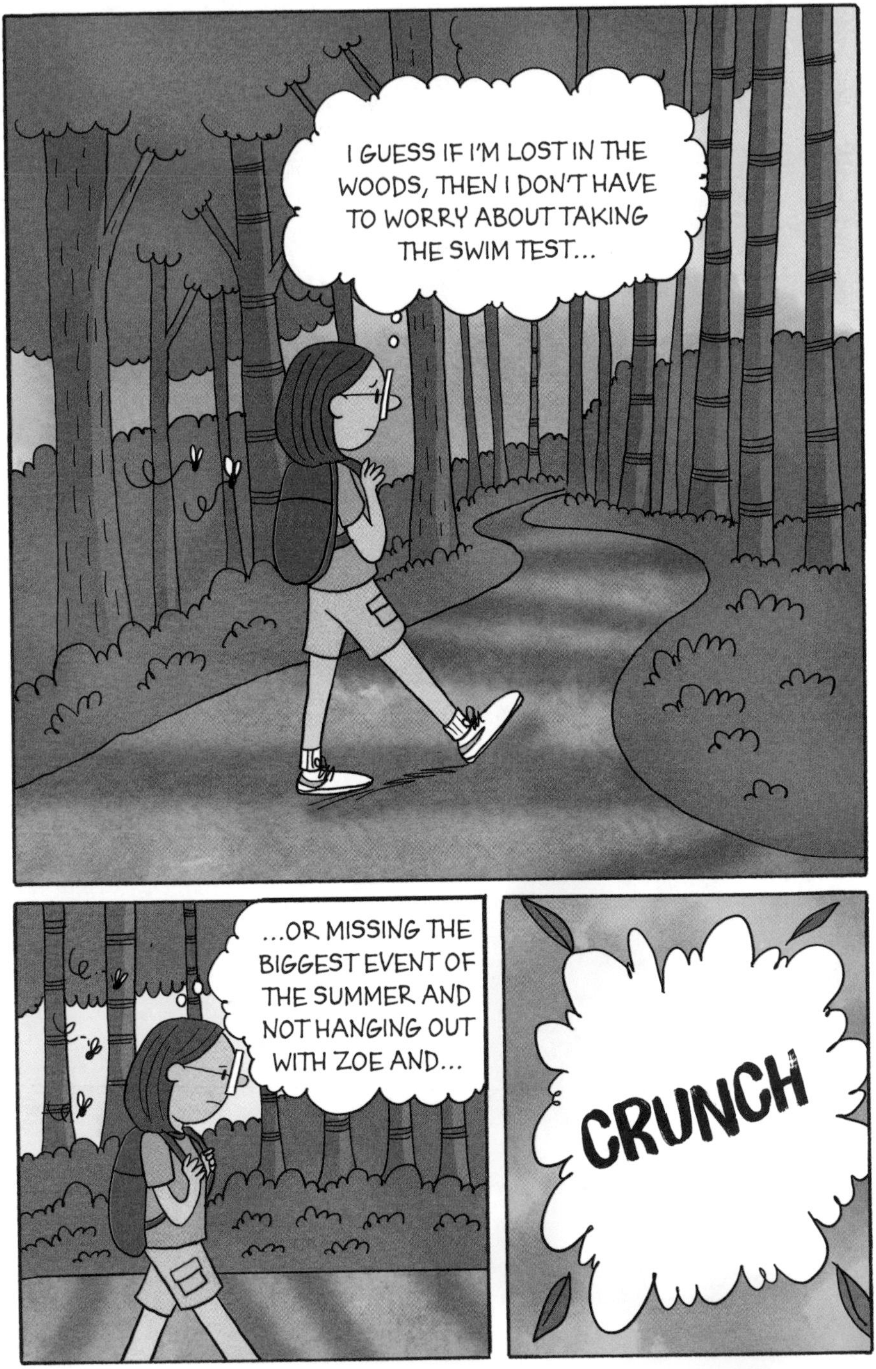
I GUESS IF I'M LOST IN THE WOODS, THEN I DON'T HAVE TO WORRY ABOUT TAKING THE SWIM TEST...
...OR MISSING THE BIGGEST EVENT OF THE SUMMER AND NOT HANGING OUT WITH ZOE AND...
CRUNCH

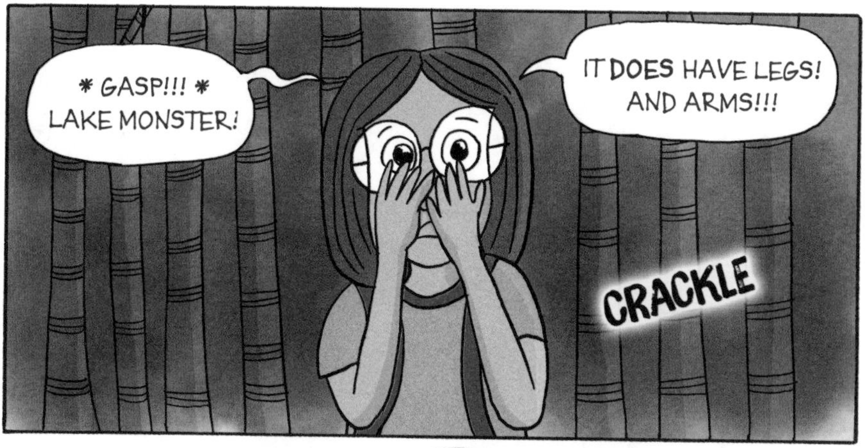
* GASP!!! *
LAKE MONSTER!
IT DOES HAVE LEGS!
AND ARMS!!!
CRACKLE

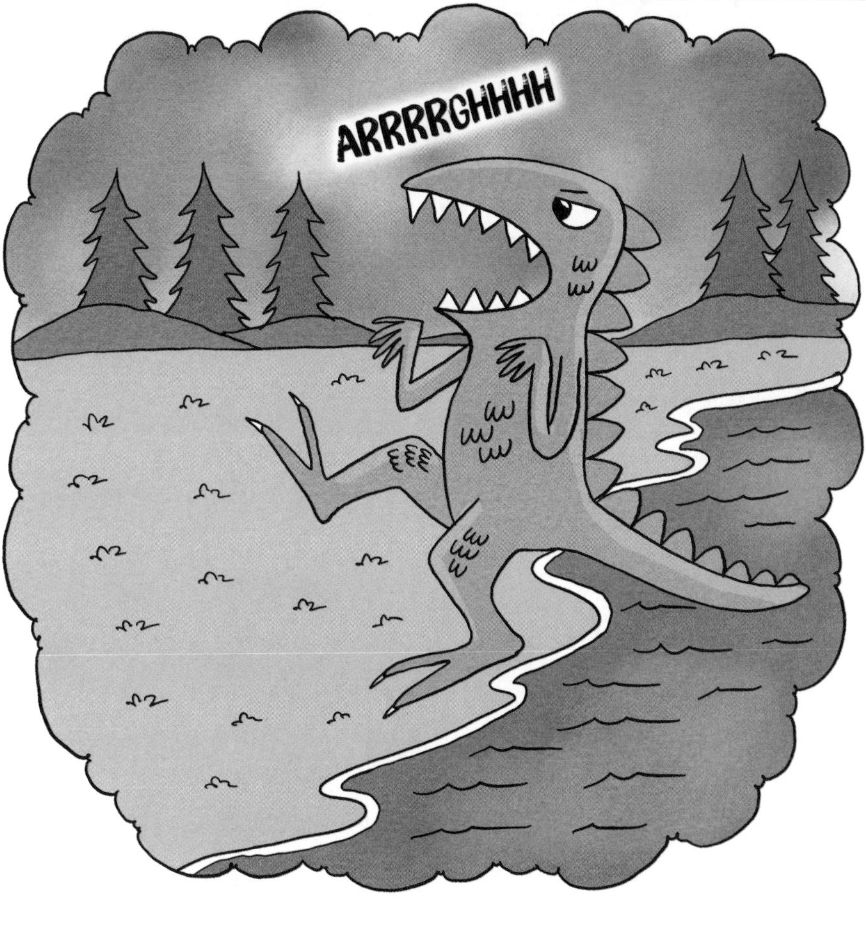
ARRRRGHHHH

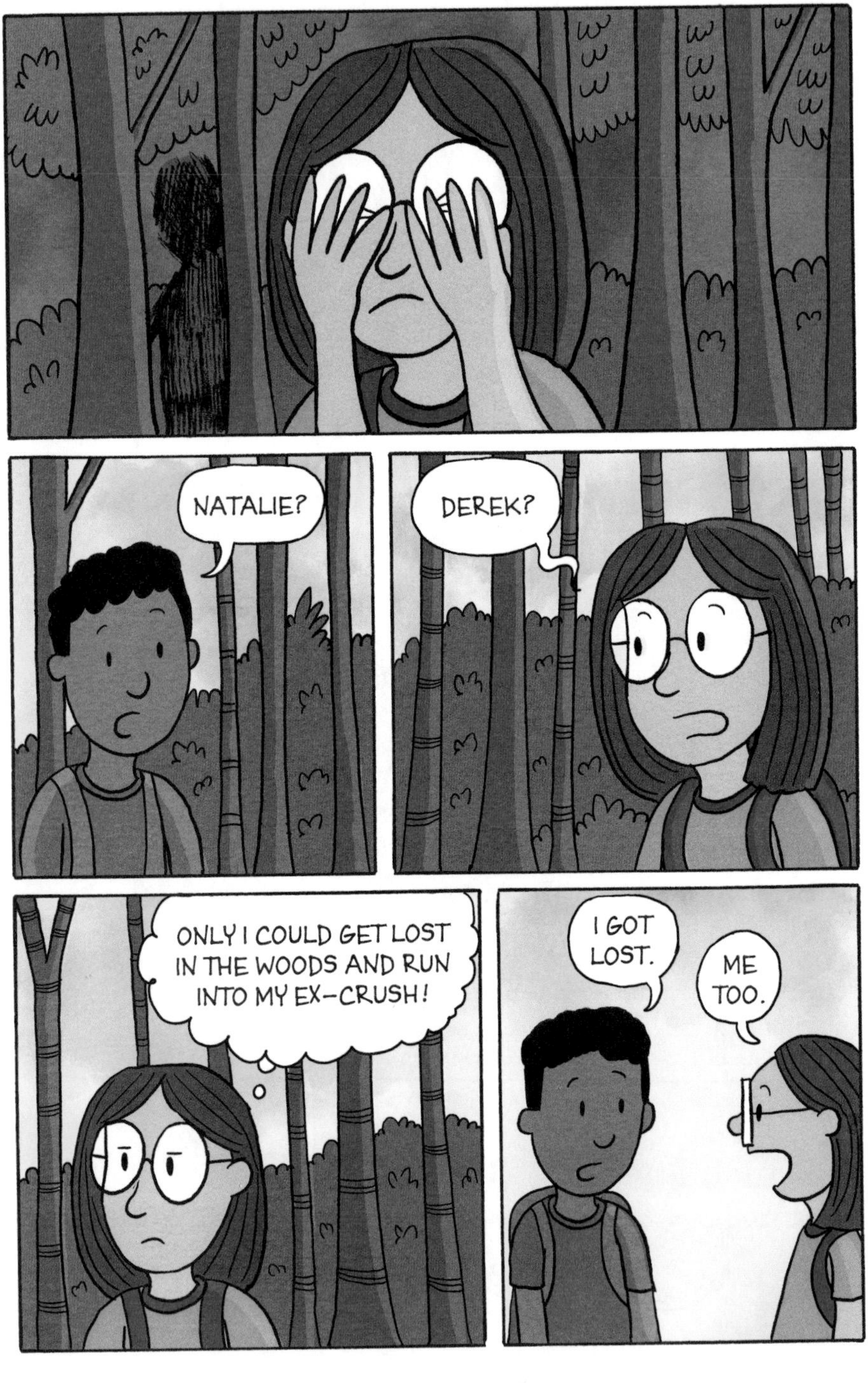
NATALIE?
DEREK?
ONLY I COULD GET LOST IN THE WOODS AND RUN INTO MY EX-CRUSH!
I GOT LOST.
ME TOO.

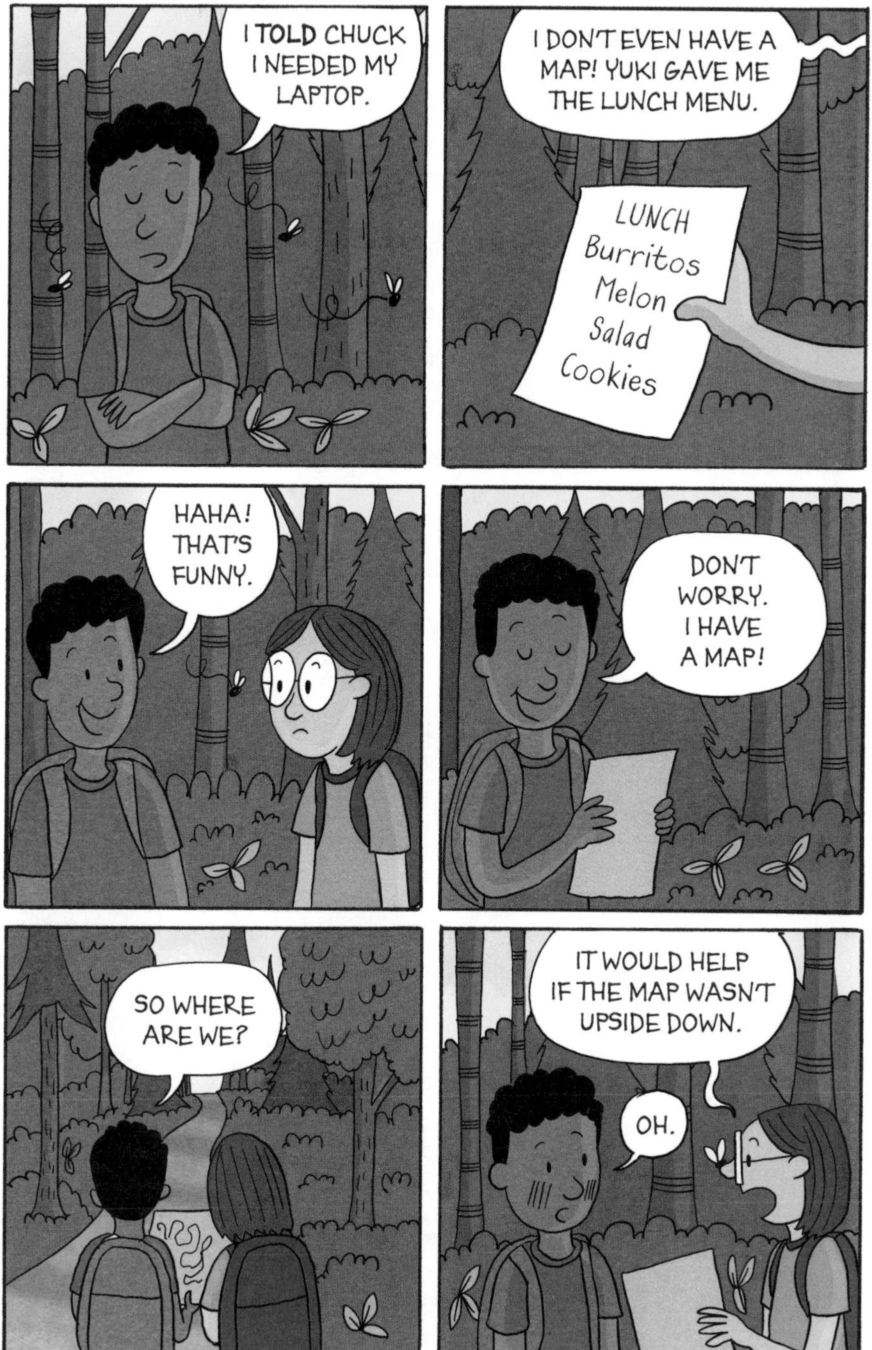
I TOLD CHUCK I NEEDED MY LAPTOP.
I DON'T EVEN HAVE A MAP! YUKI GAVE ME THE LUNCH MENU.
LUNCH
Burritos
Melon
Salad
Cookies
HAHA! THAT'S FUNNY.
DON'T WORRY. I HAVE A MAP!
SO WHERE ARE WE?
IT WOULD HELP IF THE MAP WASN'T UPSIDE DOWN.
OH.

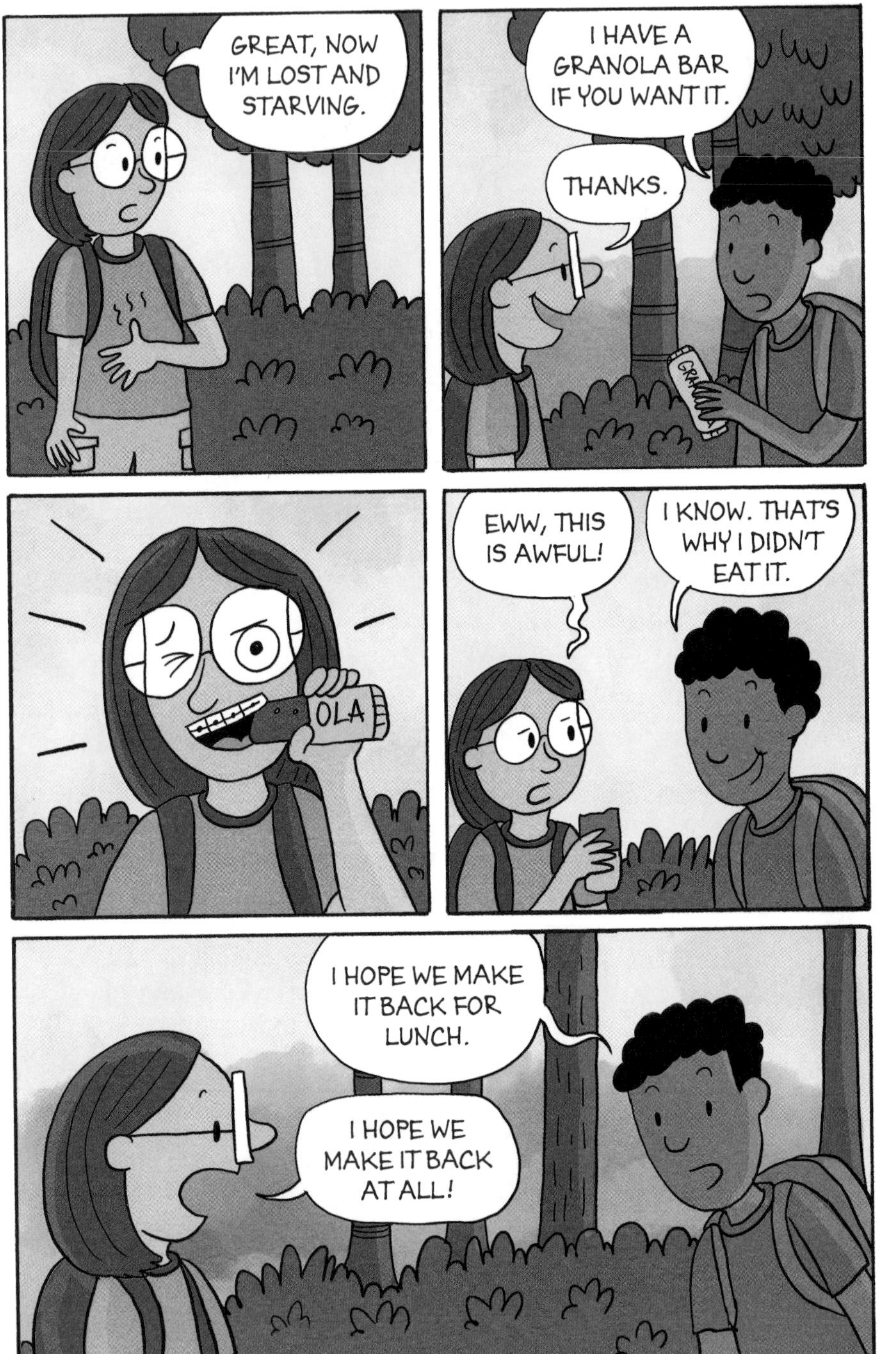
GREAT, NOW I'M LOST AND STARVING.
I HAVE A GRANOLA BAR IF YOU WANT IT.
THANKS.
GRA
OLA
EWW, THIS IS AWFUL!
I KNOW. THAT'S WHY I DIDN'T EAT IT.
I HOPE WE MAKE IT BACK FOR LUNCH.
I HOPE WE MAKE IT BACK AT ALL!

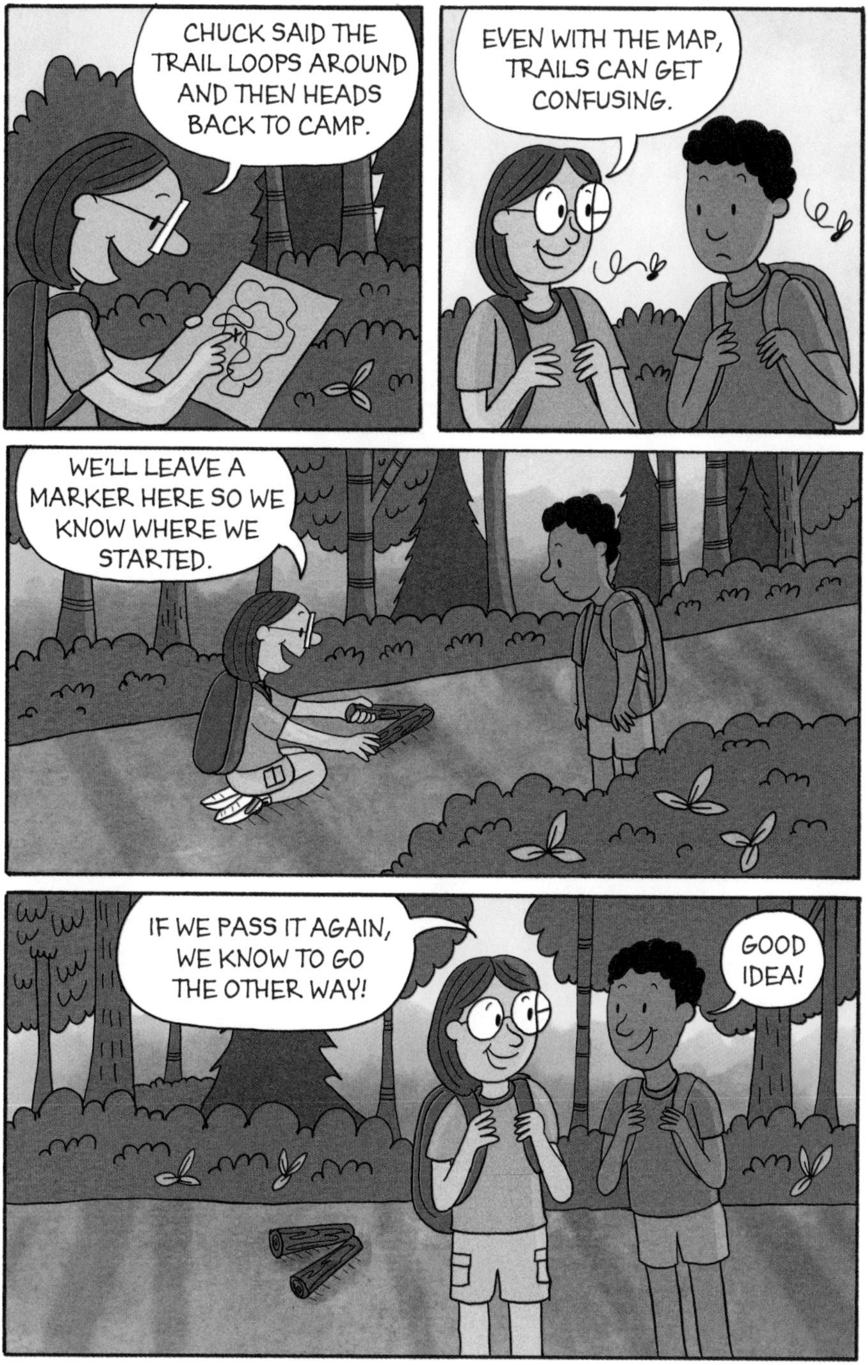
CHUCK SAID THE TRAIL LOOPS AROUND AND THEN HEADS BACK TO CAMP.
EVEN WITH THE MAP, TRAILS CAN GET CONFUSING.
WE'LL LEAVE A MARKER HERE SO WE KNOW WHERE WE STARTED.
IF WE PASS IT AGAIN, WE KNOW TO GO THE OTHER WAY!
GOOD IDEA!

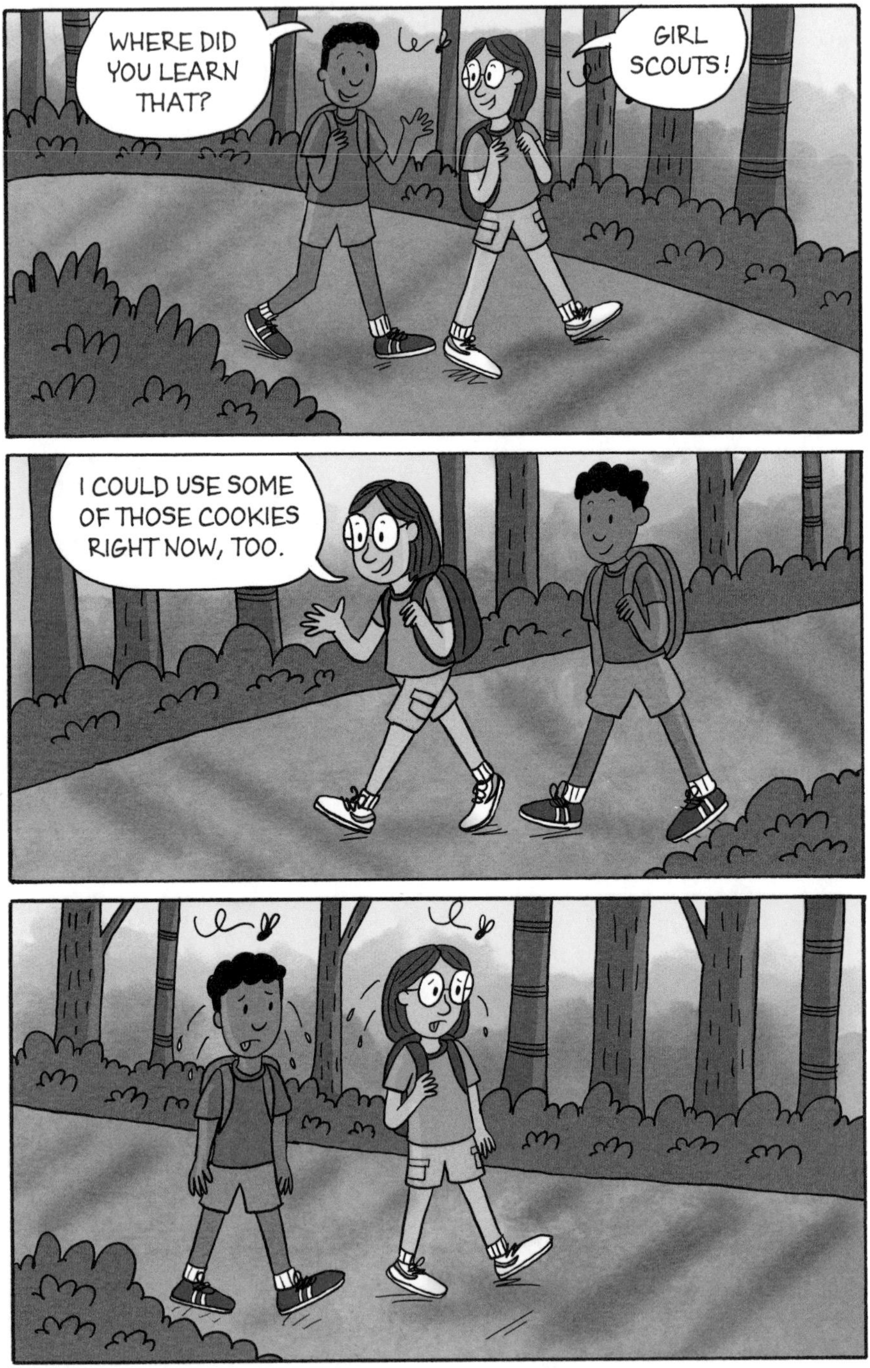
WHERE DID YOU LEARN THAT?
GIRL SCOUTS!
I COULD USE SOME OF THOSE COOKIES RIGHT NOW, TOO.

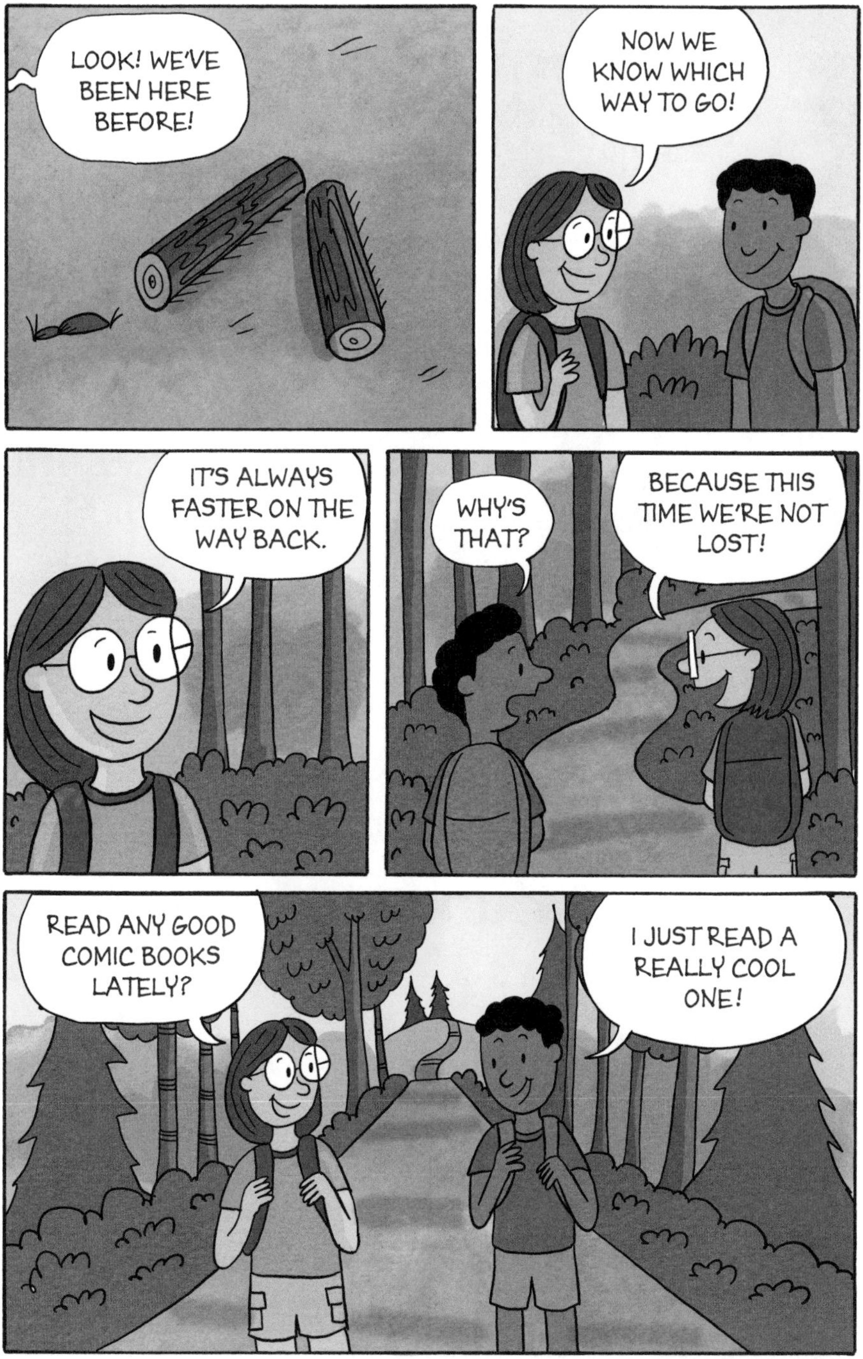
LOOK! WE'VE BEEN HERE BEFORE!
NOW WE KNOW WHICH WAY TO GO!
IT'S ALWAYS FASTER ON THE WAY BACK.
WHY'S THAT?
BECAUSE THIS TIME WE'RE NOT LOST!
READ ANY GOOD COMIC BOOKS LATELY?
I JUST READ A REALLY COOL ONE!

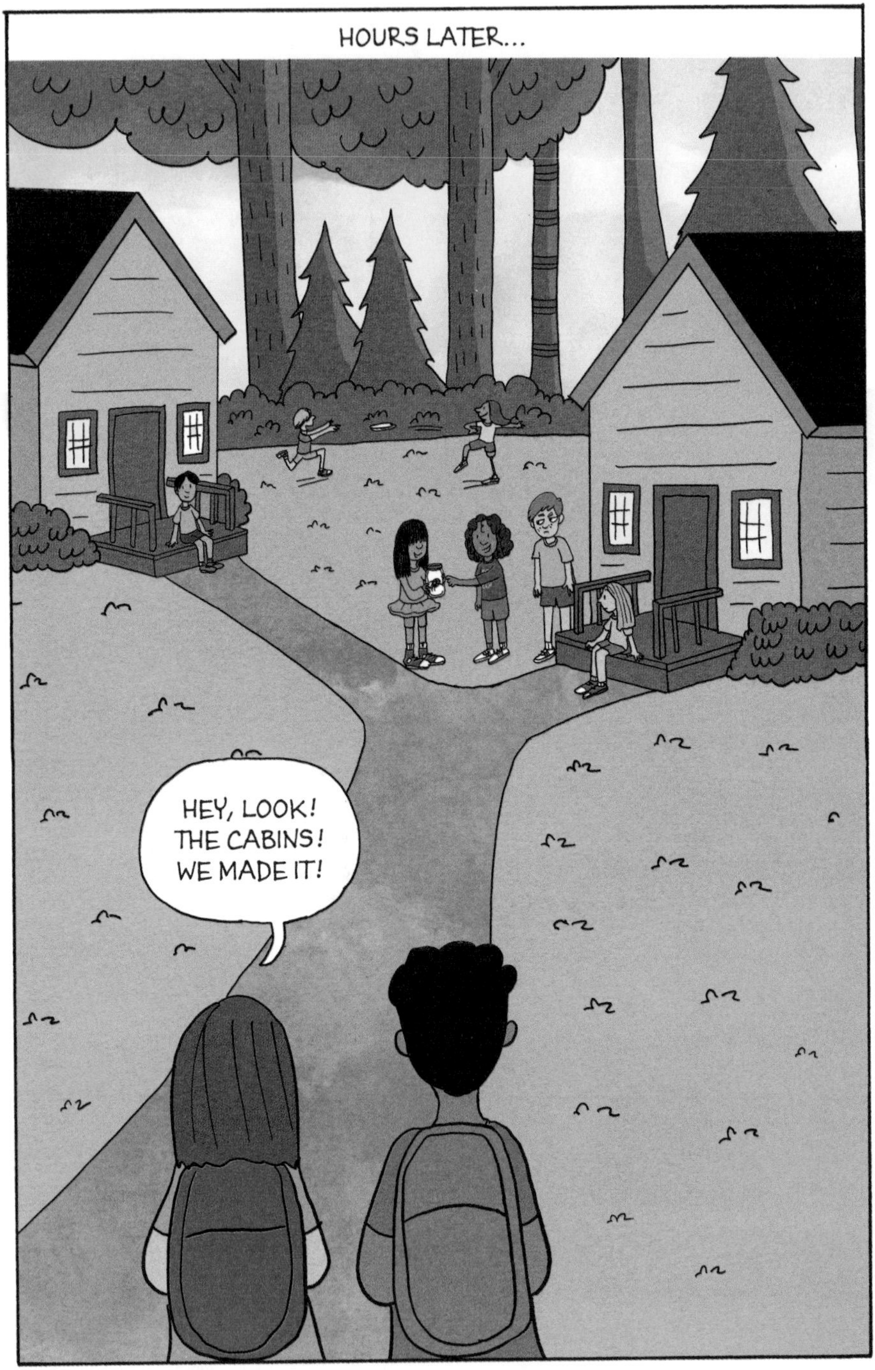
HOURS LATER...
HEY, LOOK! THE CABINS! WE MADE IT!

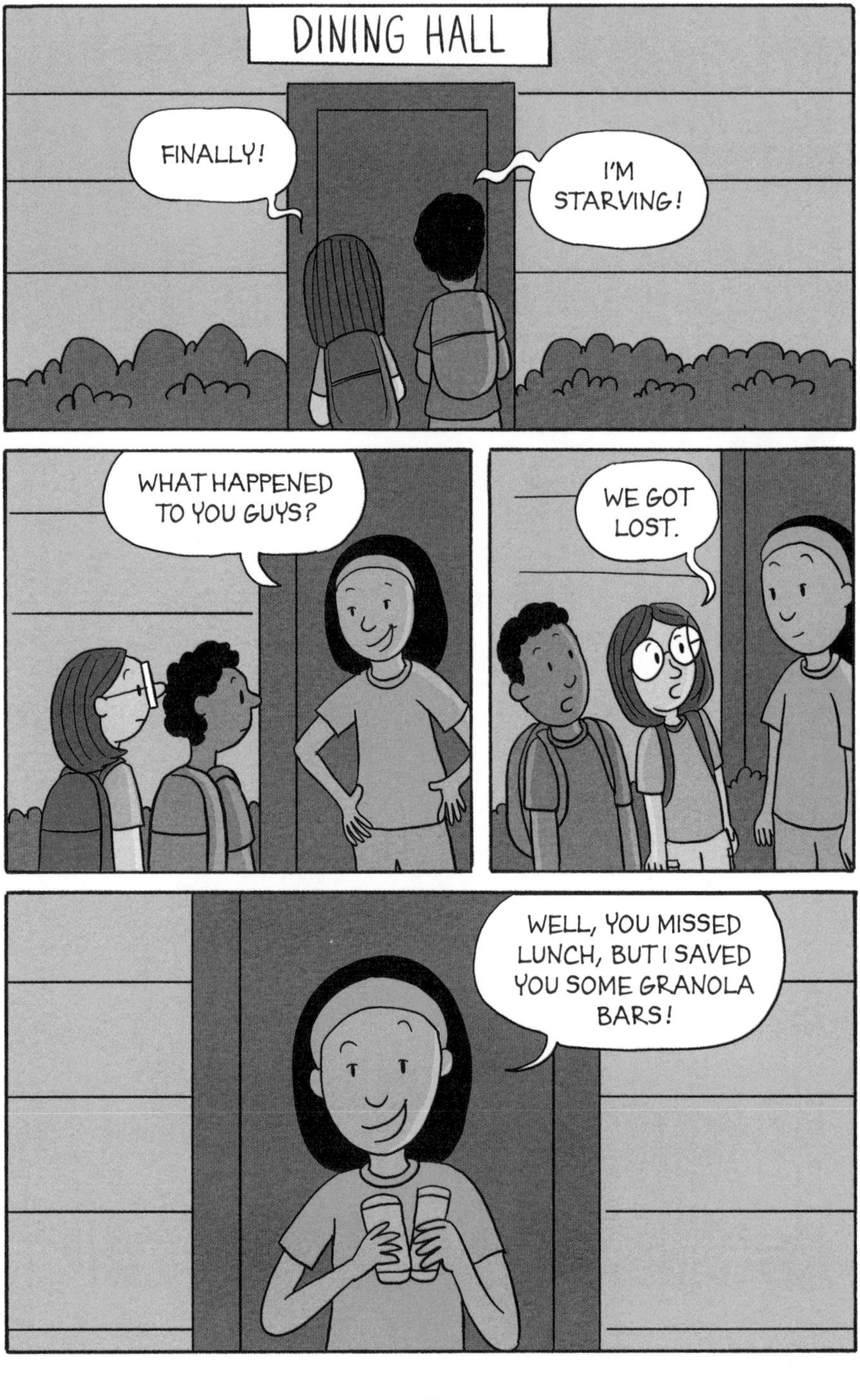
DINING HALL
FINALLY!
I'M STARVING!
WHAT HAPPENED TO YOU GUYS?
WE GOT LOST.
WELL, YOU MISSED LUNCH, BUT I SAVED YOU SOME GRANOLA BARS!

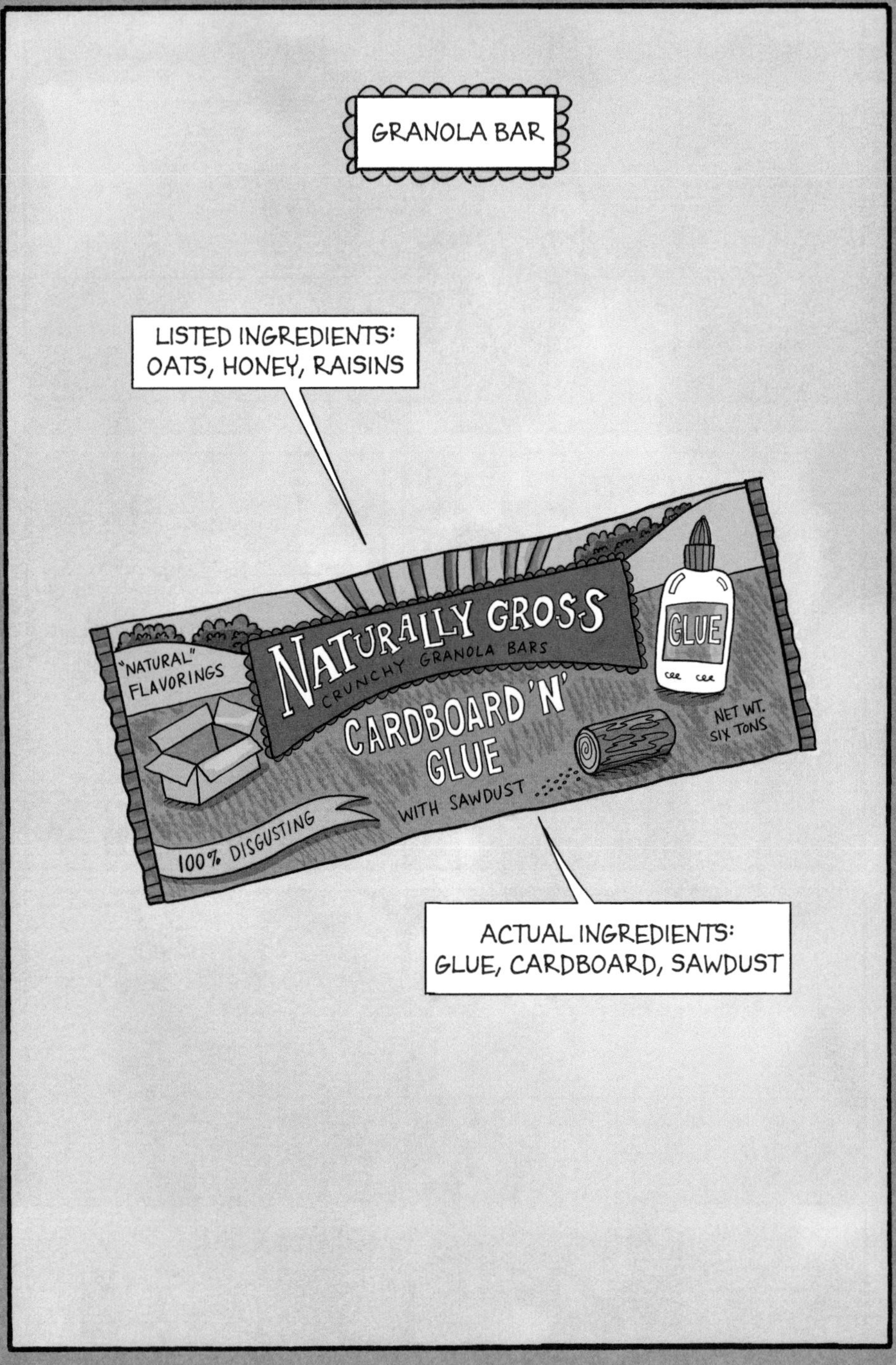
GRANOLA BAR
LISTED INGREDIENTS: OATS, HONEY, RAISINS
NATURALLY GROSS
CRUNCHY GRANOLA BARS
"NATURAL" FLAVORINGS
CARDBOARD 'N' GLUE
WITH SAWDUST
GLUE
NET WT. SIX TONS
100% DISGUSTING
ACTUAL INGREDIENTS: GLUE, CARDBOARD, SAWDUST

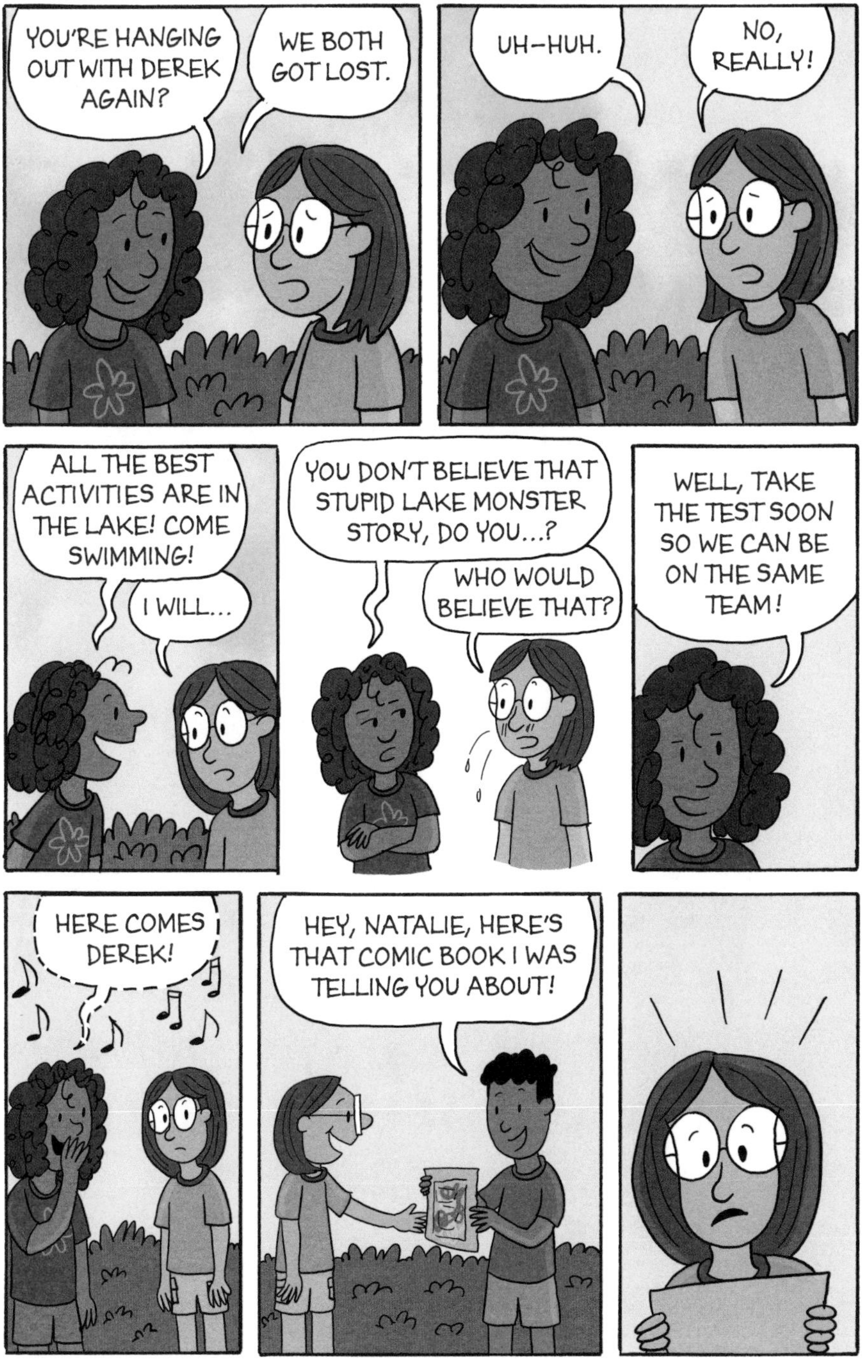
YOU'RE HANGING OUT WITH DEREK AGAIN?
WE BOTH GOT LOST.
UH-HUH.
NO, REALLY!
ALL THE BEST ACTIVITIES ARE IN THE LAKE! COME SWIMMING!
I WILL...
YOU DON'T BELIEVE THAT STUPID LAKE MONSTER STORY, DO YOU...?
WHO WOULD BELIEVE THAT?
WELL, TAKE THE TEST SOON SO WE CAN BE ON THE SAME TEAM!
HERE COMES DEREK!
HEY, NATALIE, HERE'S THAT COMIC BOOK I WAS TELLING YOU ABOUT!

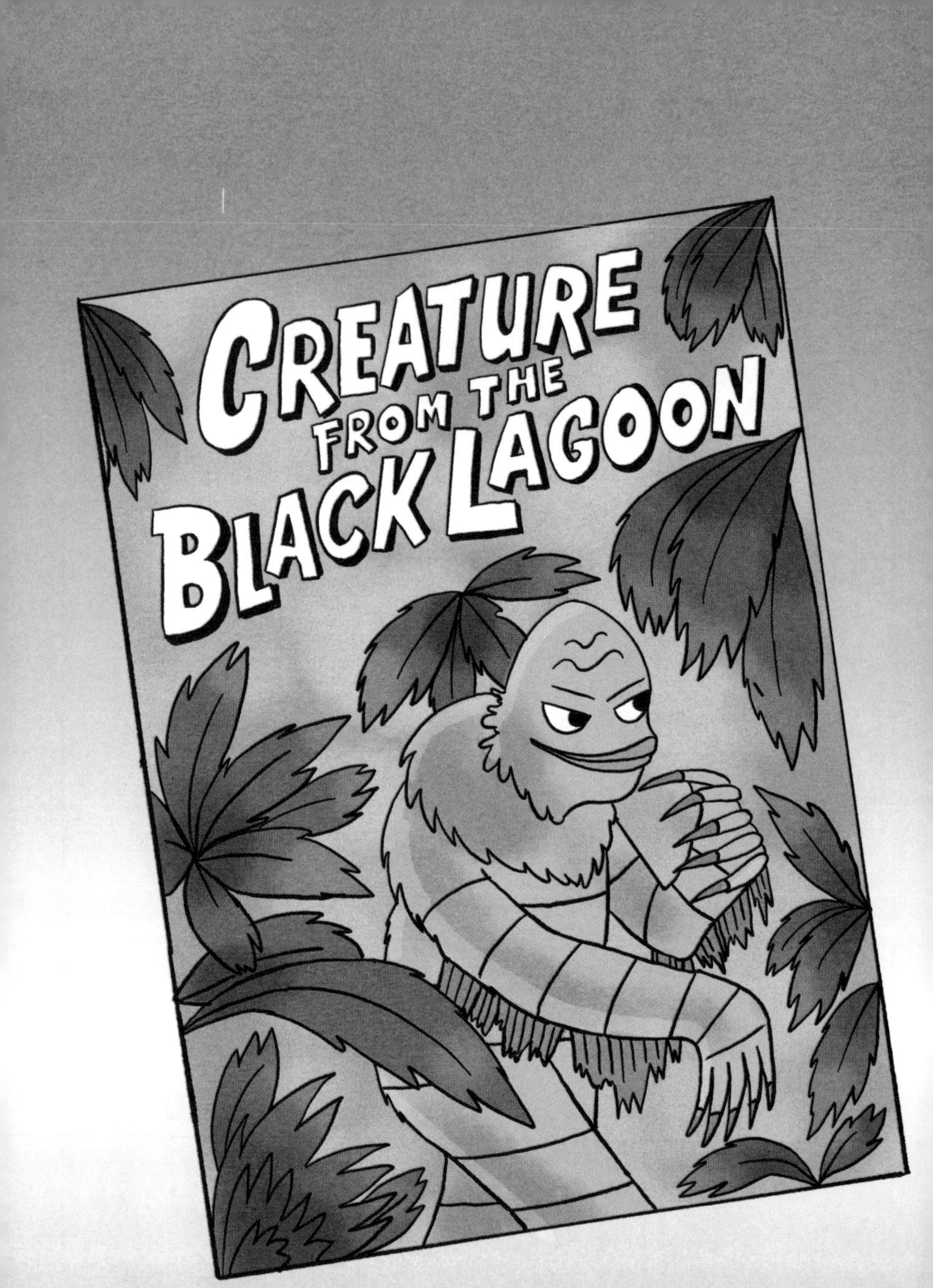
CREATURE
FROM THE
BLACK LAGOON

CHAPTER 6
AN ITCH YOU CAN'T SCRATCH

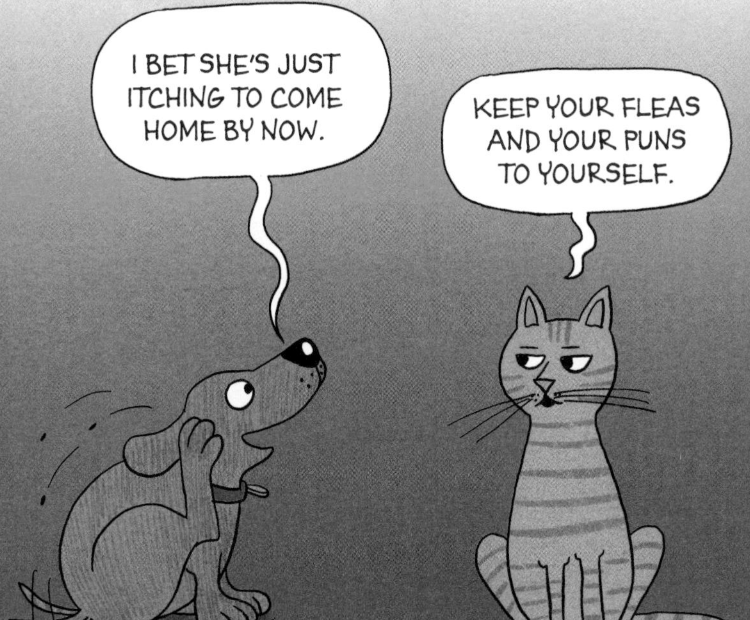
I BET SHE'S JUST ITCHING TO COME HOME BY NOW.
KEEP YOUR FLEAS AND YOUR PUNS TO YOURSELF.

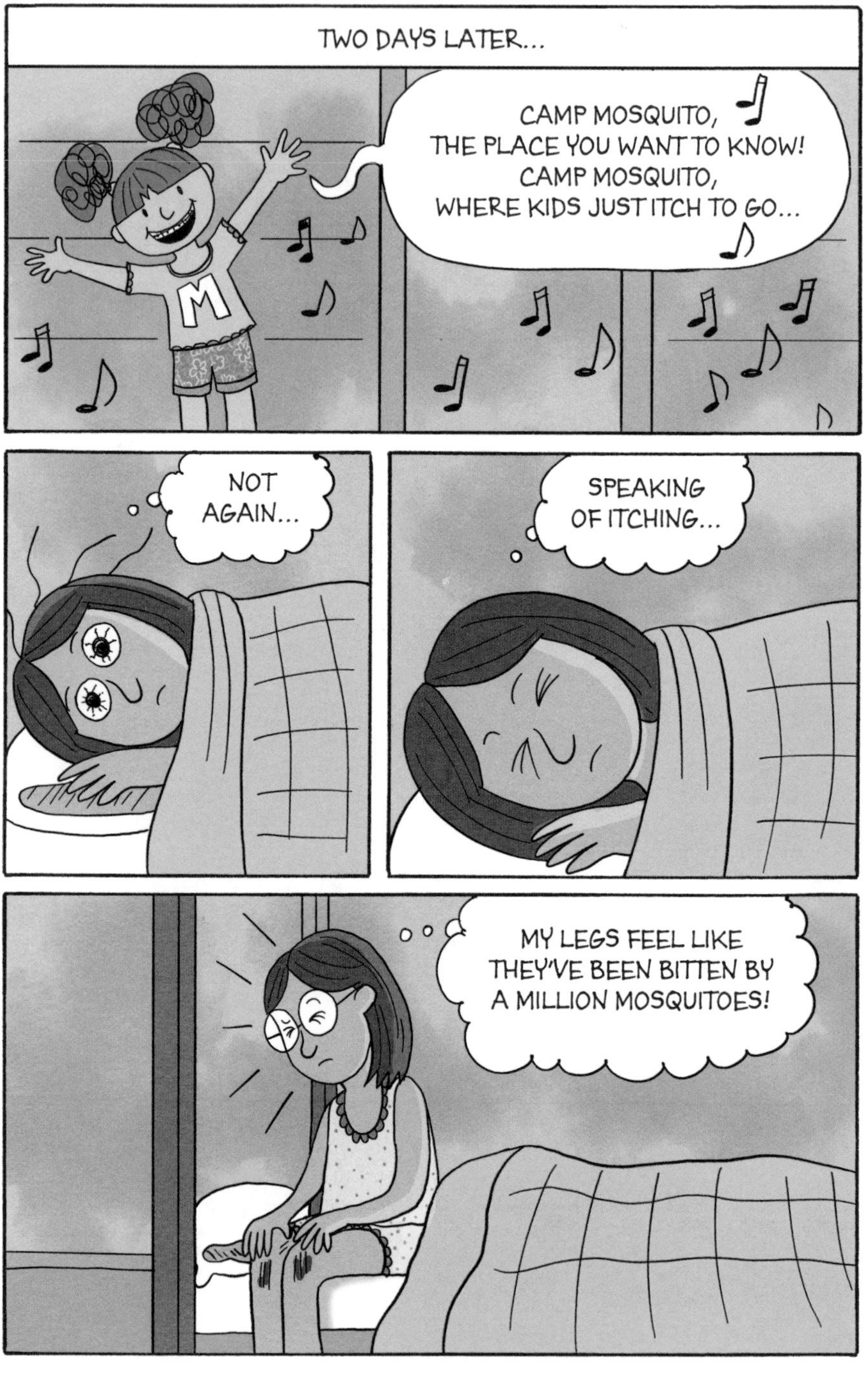
TWO DAYS LATER...
CAMP MOSQUITO, THE PLACE YOU WANT TO KNOW! CAMP MOSQUITO, WHERE KIDS JUST ITCH TO GO...
NOT AGAIN...
SPEAKING OF ITCHING...
MY LEGS FEEL LIKE THEY'VE BEEN BITTEN BY A MILLION MOSQUITOES!

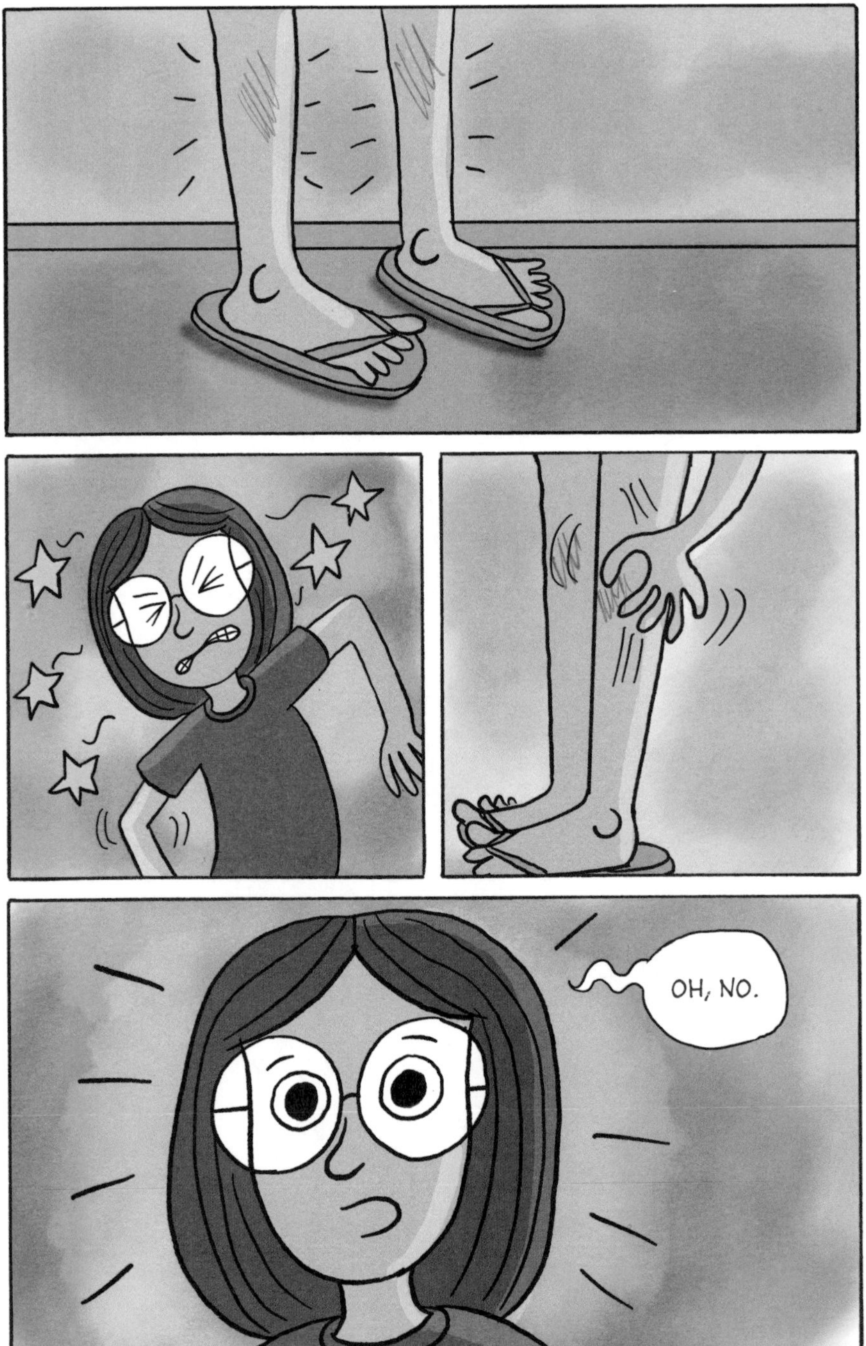
OH, NO.

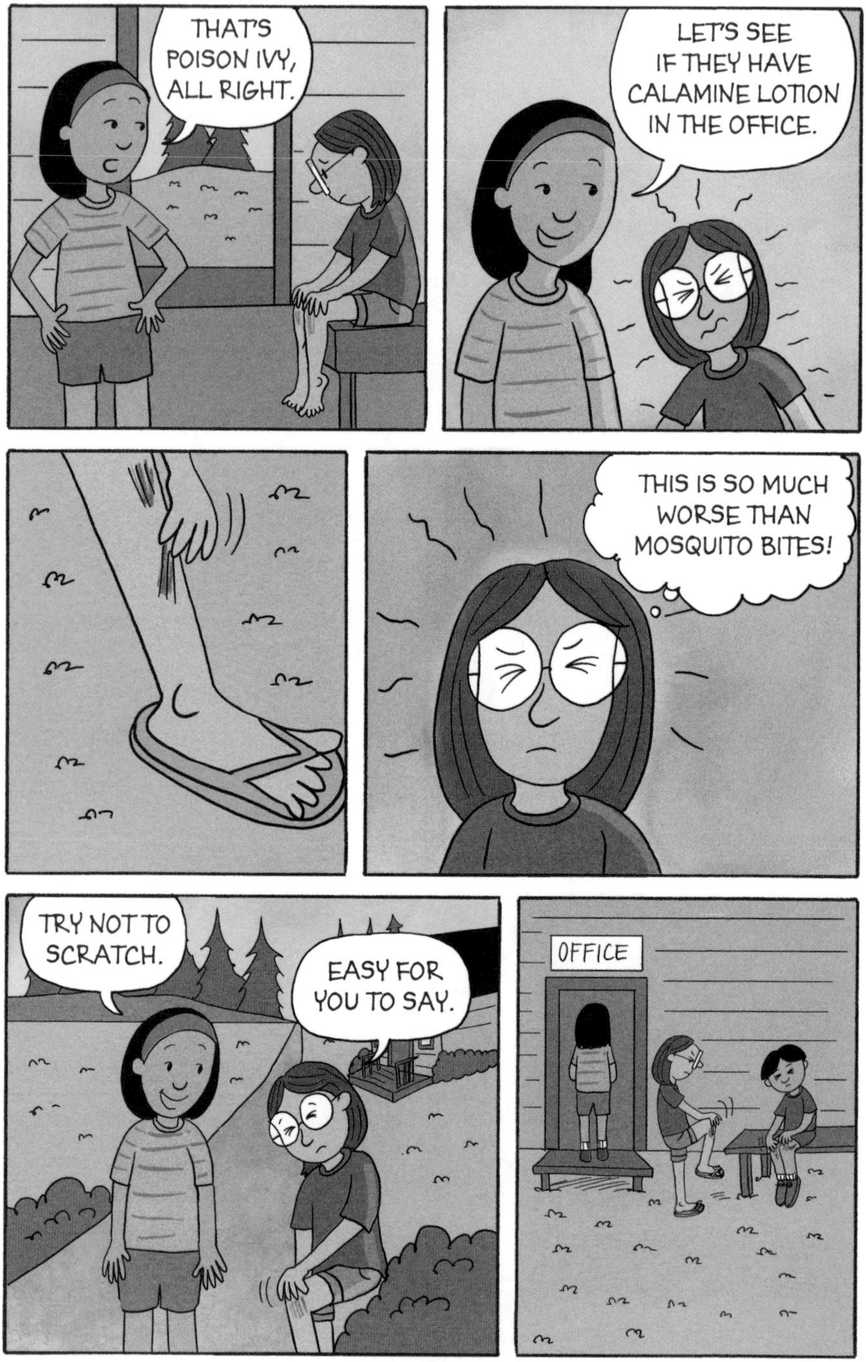
THAT'S POISON IVY, ALL RIGHT.
LET'S SEE IF THEY HAVE CALAMINE LOTION IN THE OFFICE.
THIS IS SO MUCH WORSE THAN MOSQUITO BITES!
TRY NOT TO SCRATCH.
EASY FOR YOU TO SAY.
OFFICE

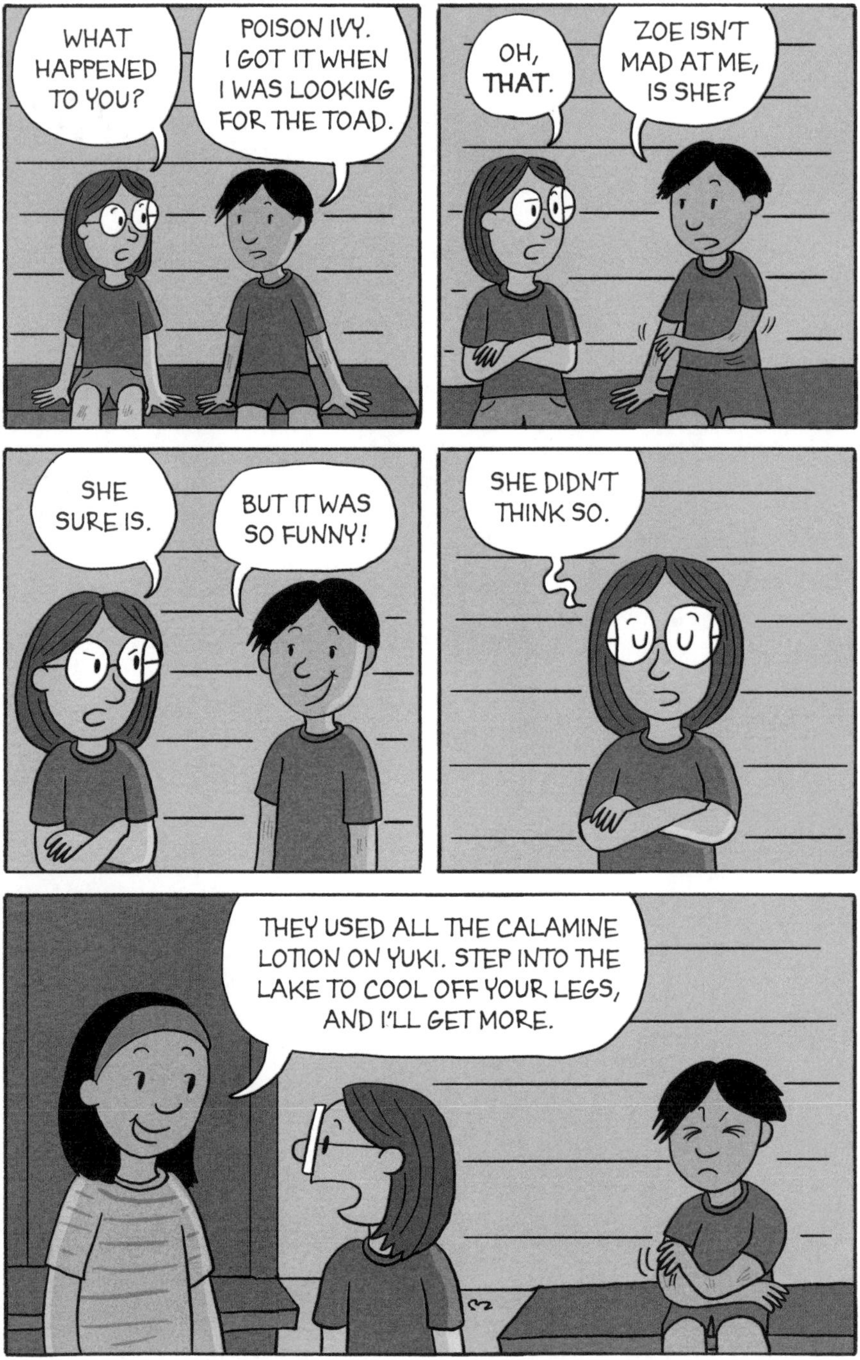
WHAT HAPPENED TO YOU?
POISON IVY. I GOT IT WHEN I WAS LOOKING FOR THE TOAD.
OH, THAT.
ZOE ISN'T MAD AT ME, IS SHE?
SHE SURE IS.
BUT IT WAS SO FUNNY!
SHE DIDN'T THINK SO.
THEY USED ALL THE CALAMINE LOTION ON YUKI. STEP INTO THE LAKE TO COOL OFF YOUR LEGS, AND I'LL GET MORE.

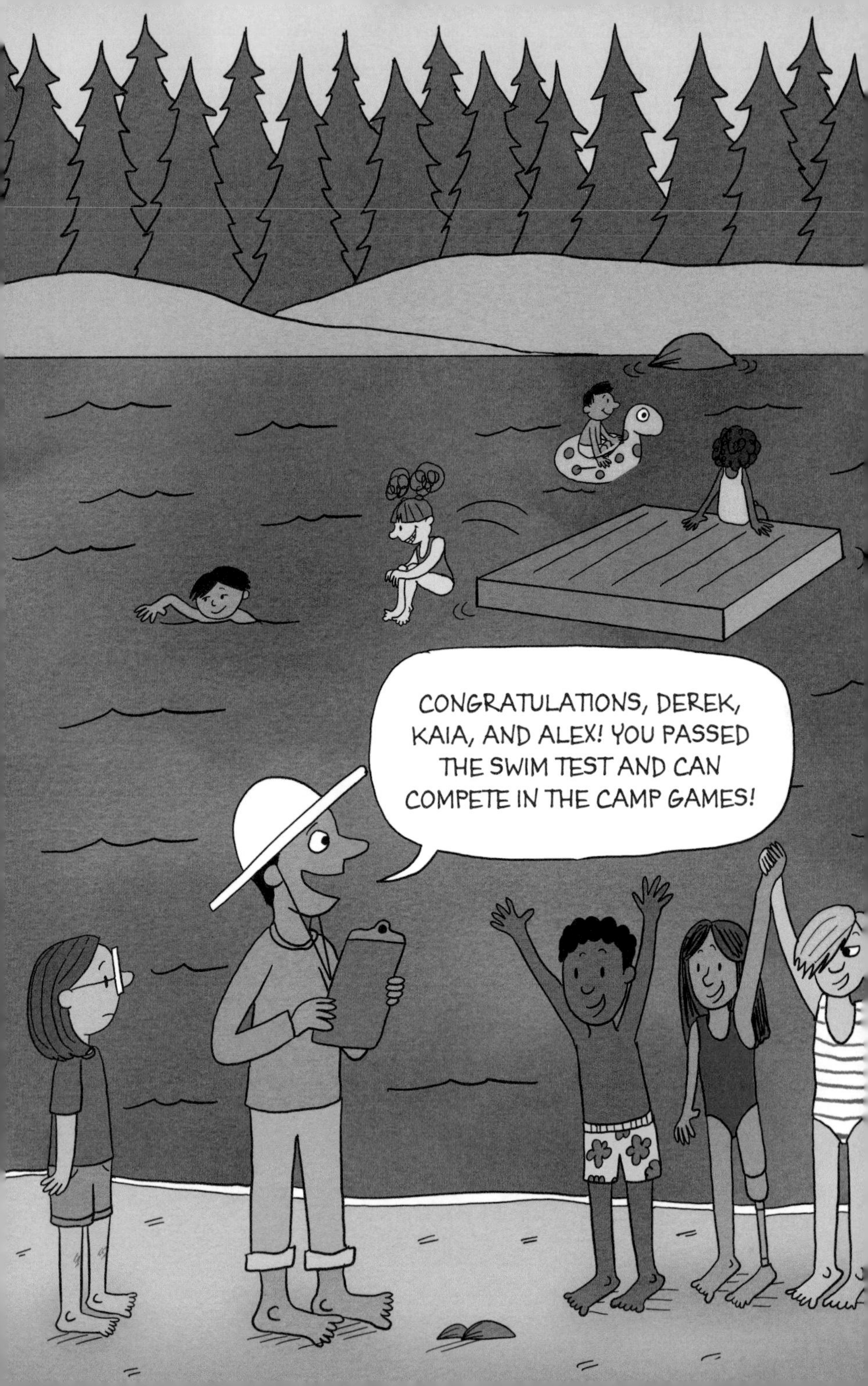
CONGRATULATIONS, DEREK, KAIA, AND ALEX! YOU PASSED THE SWIM TEST AND CAN COMPETE IN THE CAMP GAMES!

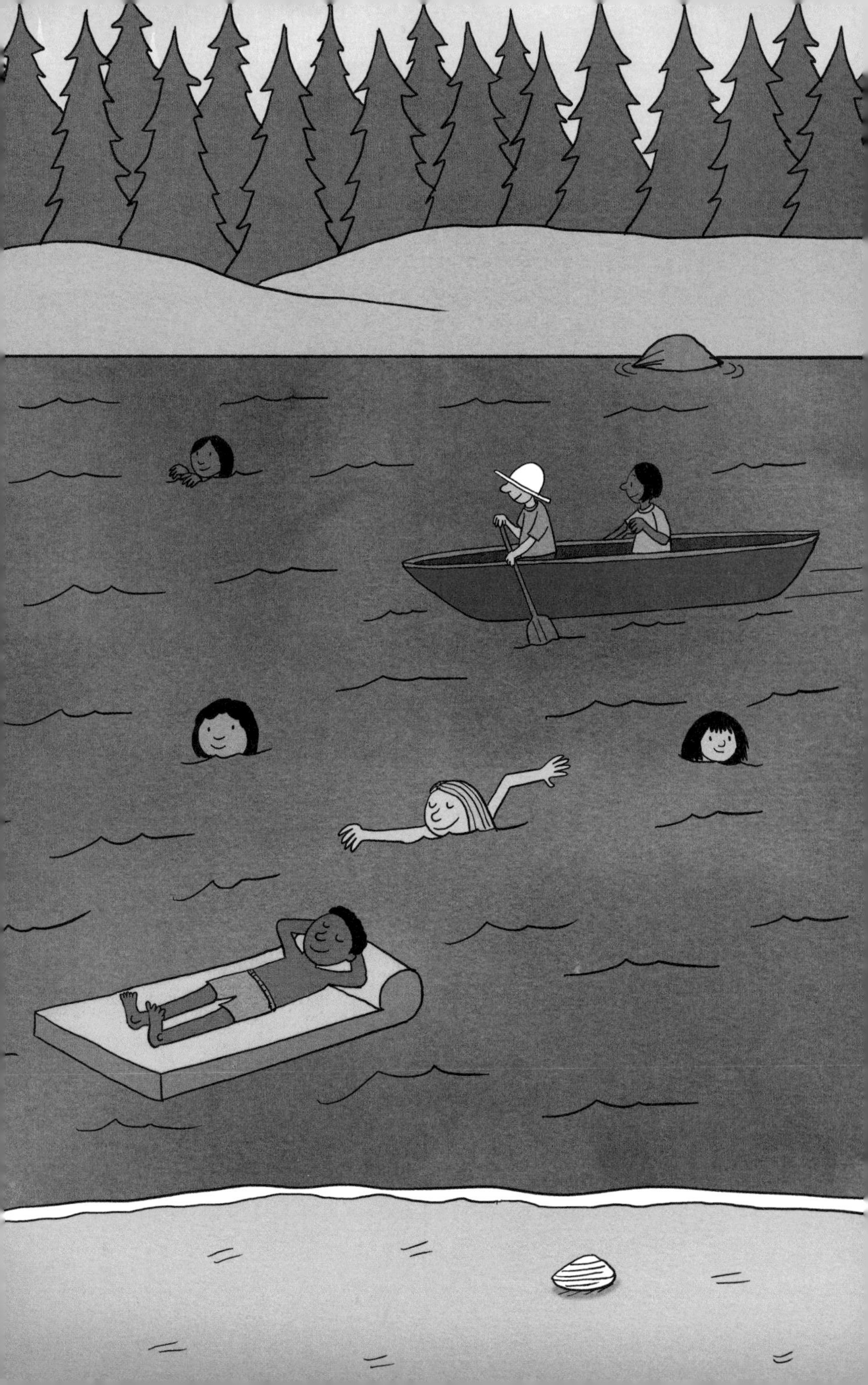

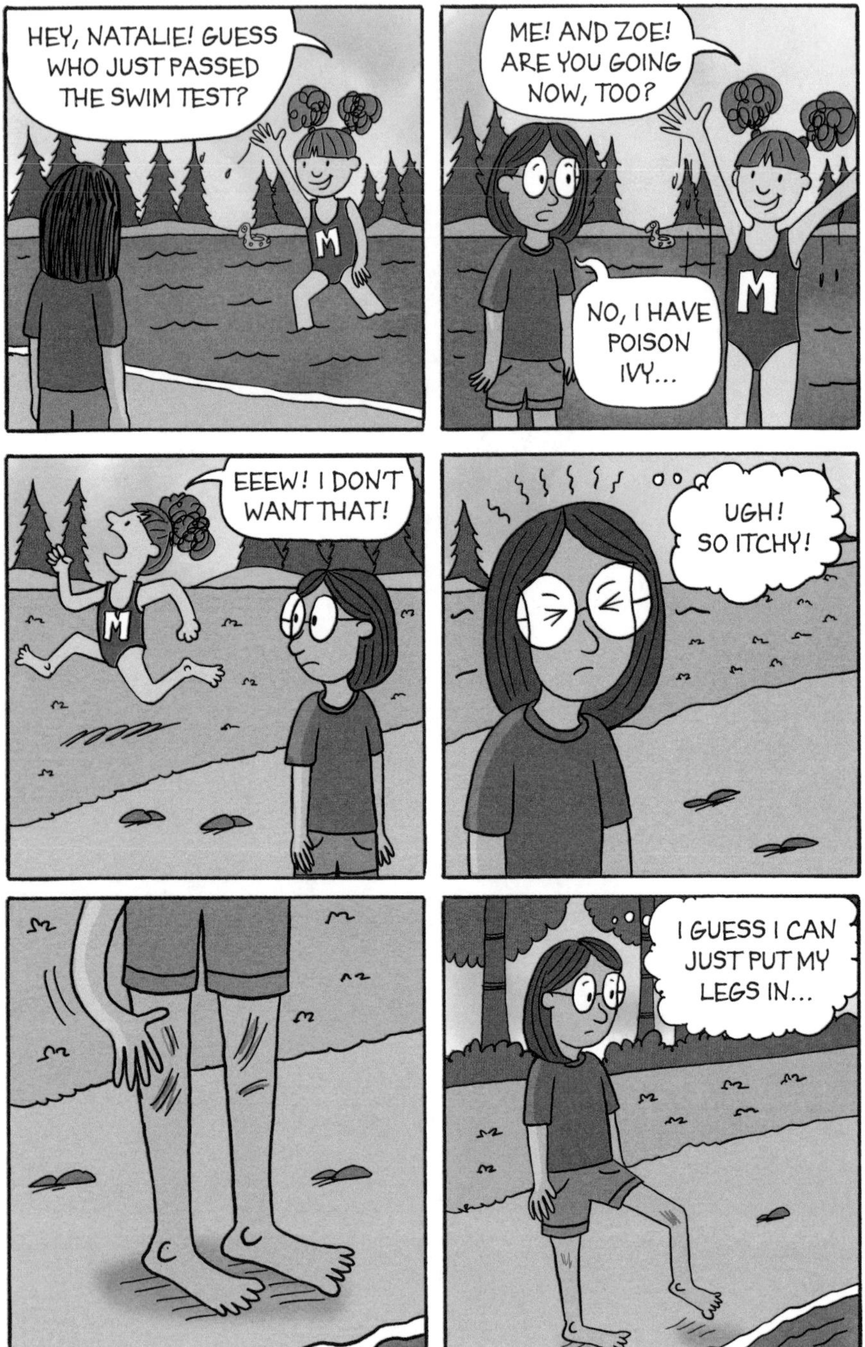
HEY, NATALIE! GUESS WHO JUST PASSED THE SWIM TEST?
ME! AND ZOE! ARE YOU GOING NOW, TOO?
NO, I HAVE POISON IVY...
EEEW! I DON'T WANT THAT!
UGH! SO ITCHY!
I GUESS I CAN JUST PUT MY LEGS IN...

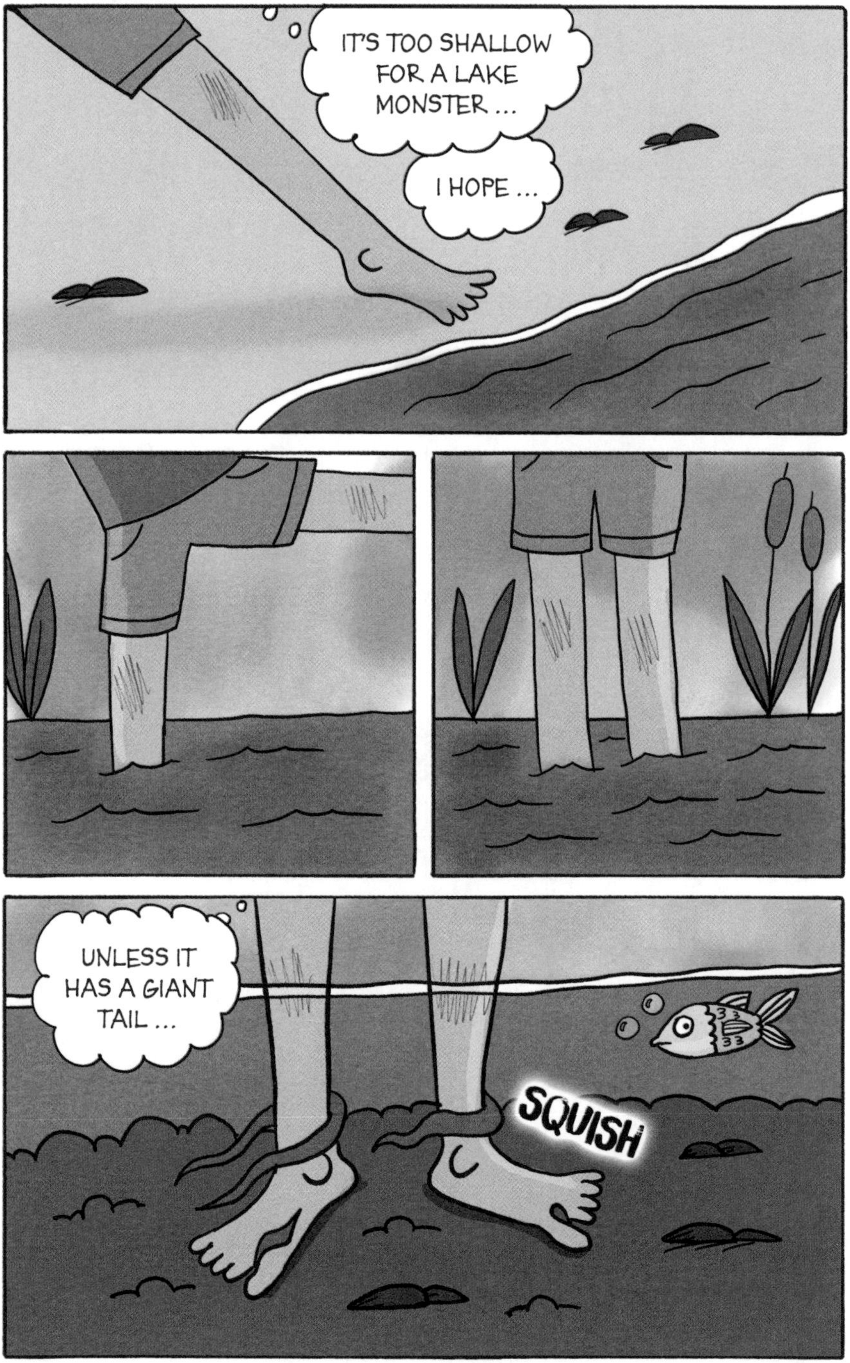
IT'S TOO SHALLOW FOR A LAKE MONSTER ...
I HOPE ...
UNLESS IT HAS A GIANT TAIL ...
SQUISH

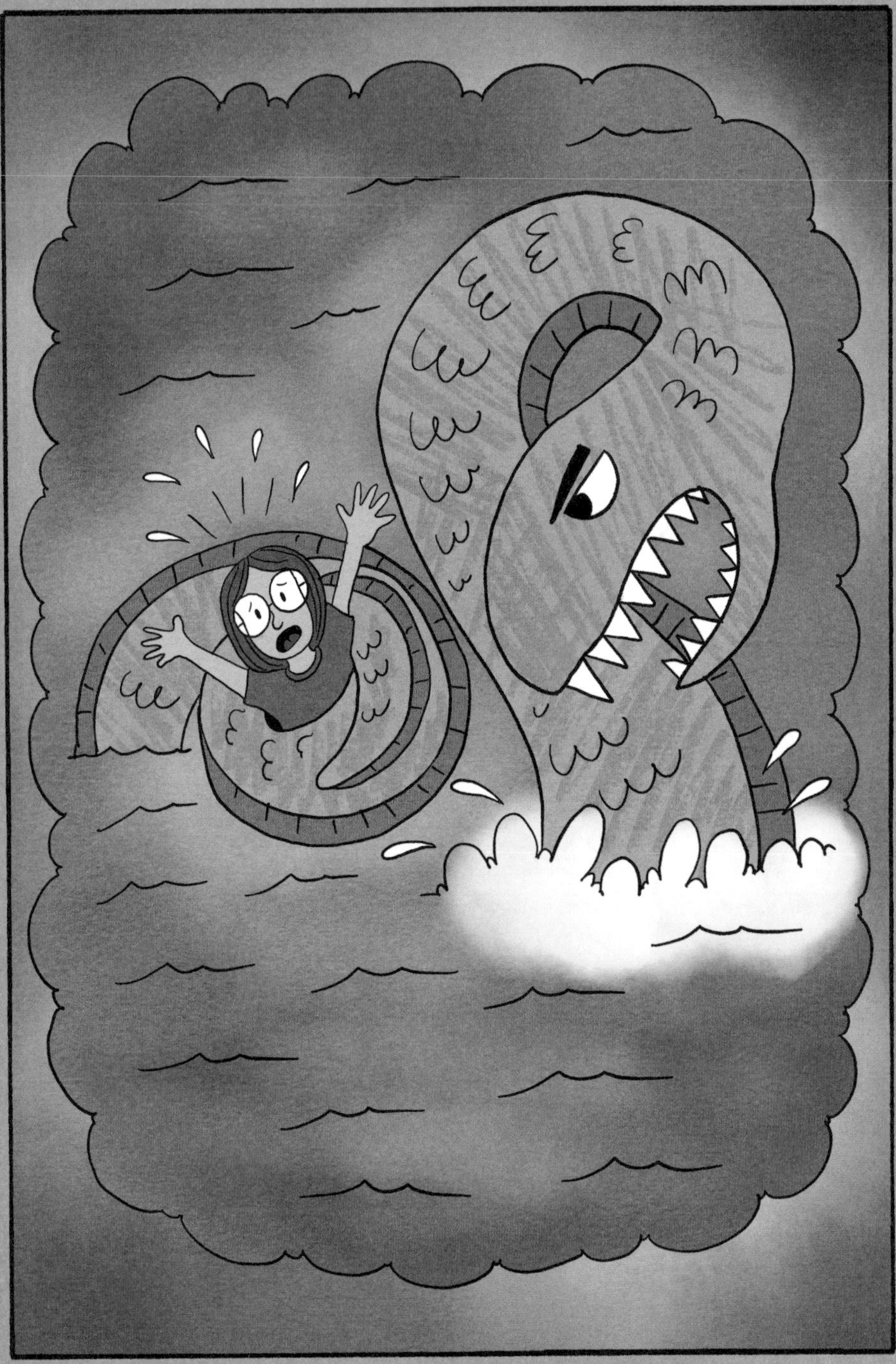

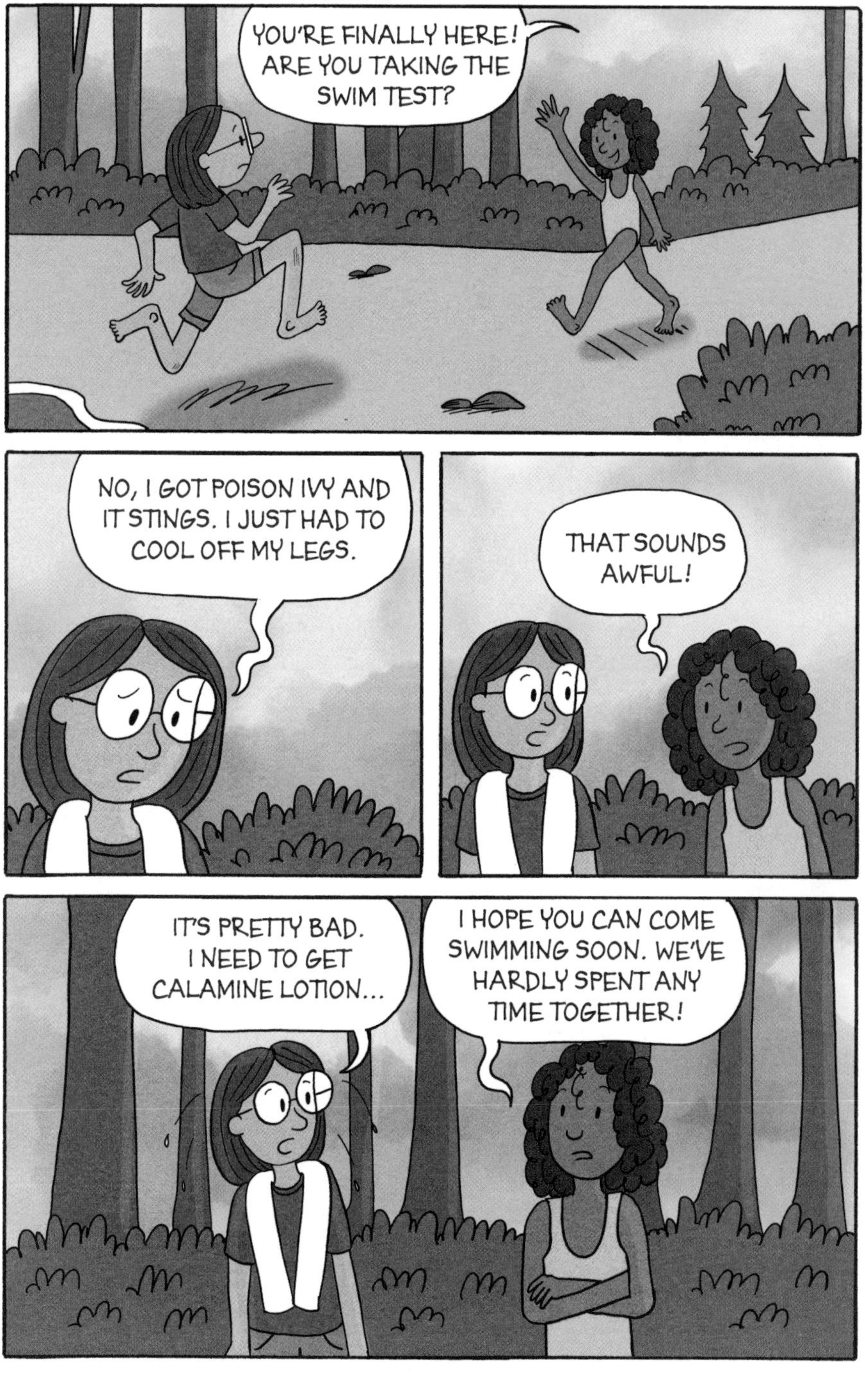
YOU'RE FINALLY HERE! ARE YOU TAKING THE SWIM TEST?
NO, I GOT POISON IVY AND IT STINGS. I JUST HAD TO COOL OFF MY LEGS.
THAT SOUNDS AWFUL!
IT'S PRETTY BAD. I NEED TO GET CALAMINE LOTION...
I HOPE YOU CAN COME SWIMMING SOON. WE'VE HARDLY SPENT ANY TIME TOGETHER!

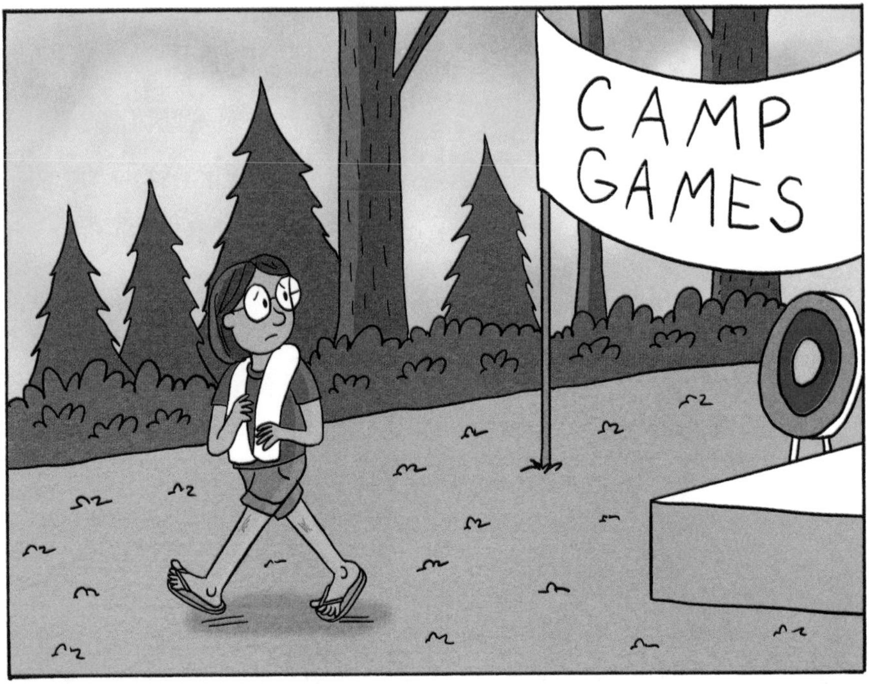
CAMP GAMES

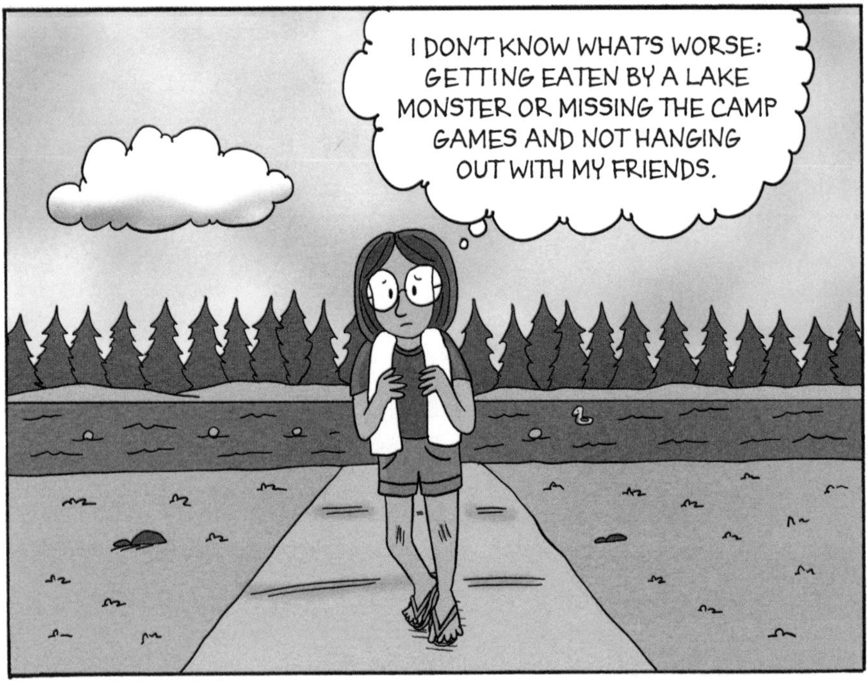
I DON'T KNOW WHAT'S WORSE: GETTING EATEN BY A LAKE MONSTER OR MISSING THE CAMP GAMES AND NOT HANGING OUT WITH MY FRIENDS.

CHAPTER 7
LETTERS HOME

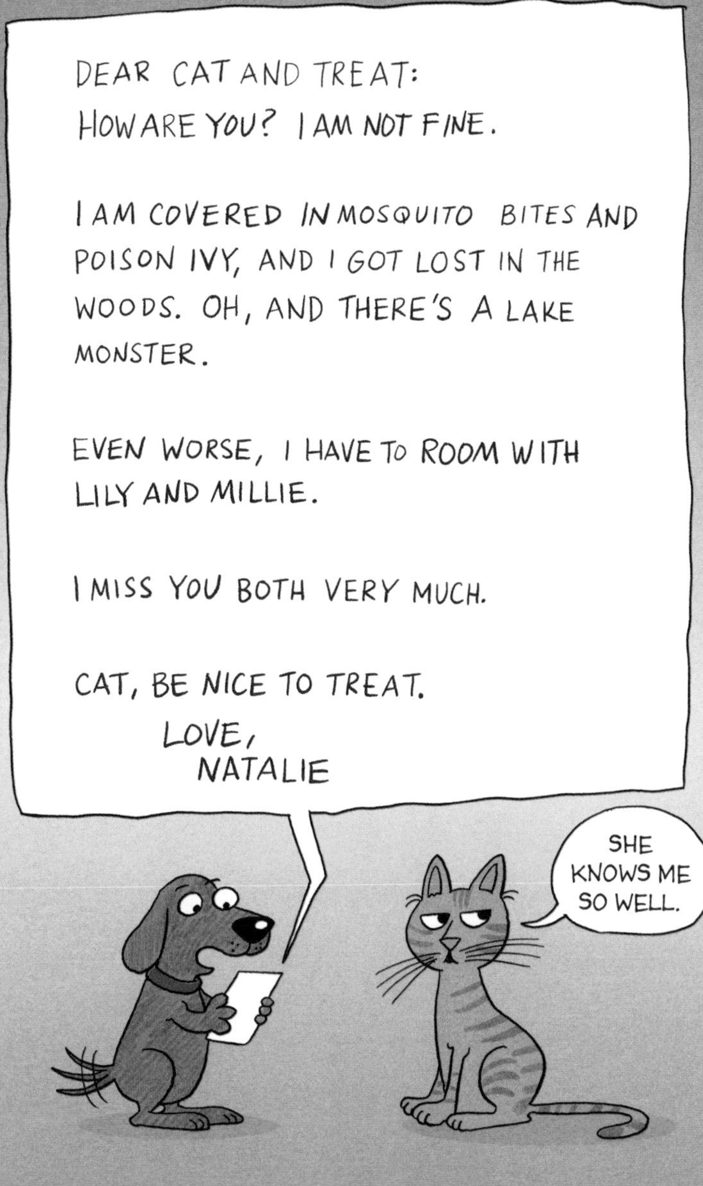
DEAR CAT AND TREAT:
HOW ARE YOU? I AM NOT FINE.
I AM COVERED IN MOSQUITO BITES AND POISON IVY, AND I GOT LOST IN THE WOODS. OH, AND THERE'S A LAKE MONSTER.
EVEN WORSE, I HAVE TO ROOM WITH LILY AND MILLIE.
I MISS YOU BOTH VERY MUCH.
CAT, BE NICE TO TREAT.
LOVE,
NATALIE
SHE KNOWS ME SO WELL.

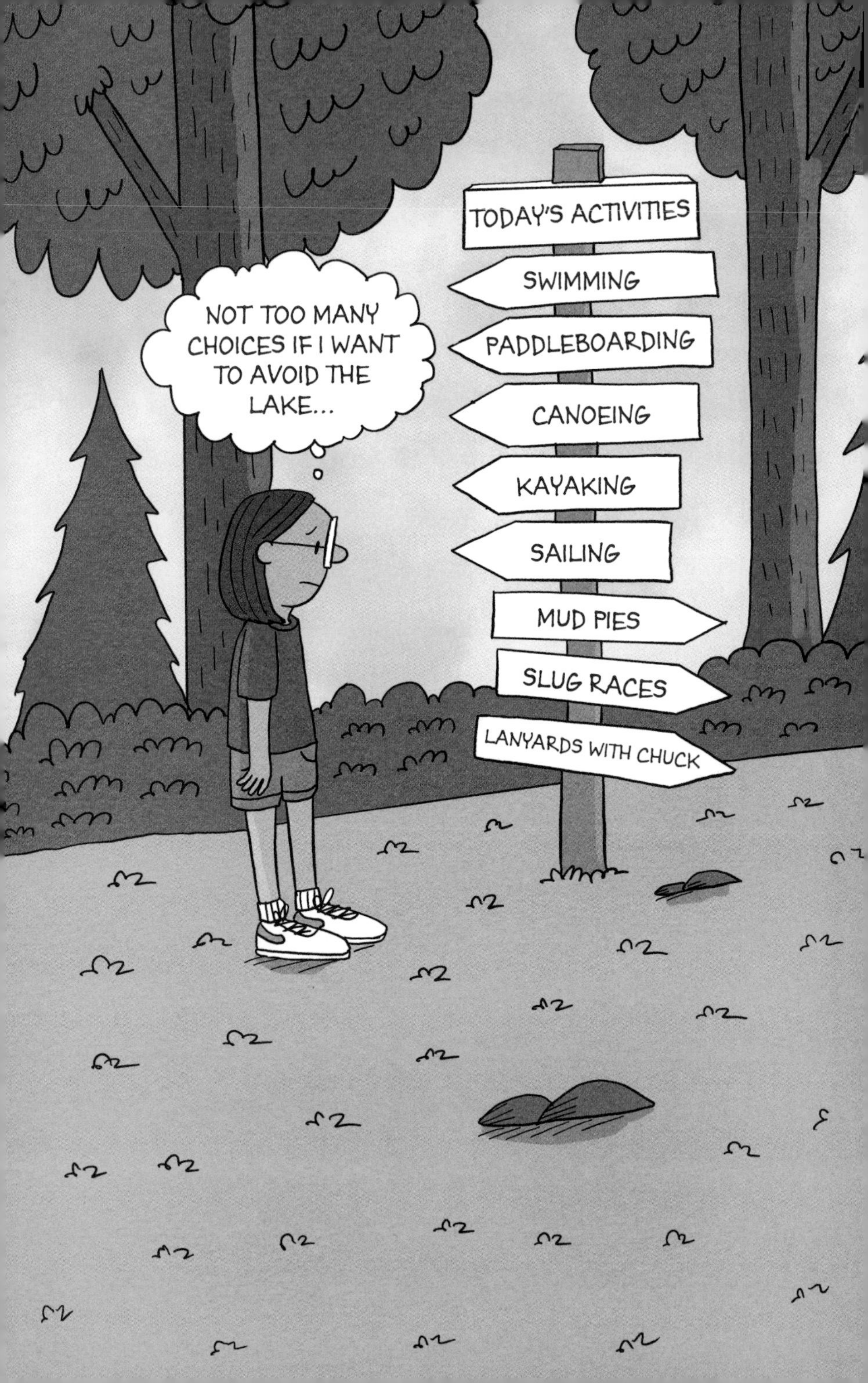

NOT TOO MANY CHOICES IF I WANT TO AVOID THE LAKE...
TODAY'S ACTIVITIES
SWIMMING
PADDLEBOARDING
CANOEING
KAYAKING
SAILING
MUD PIES
SLUG RACES
LANYARDS WITH CHUCK

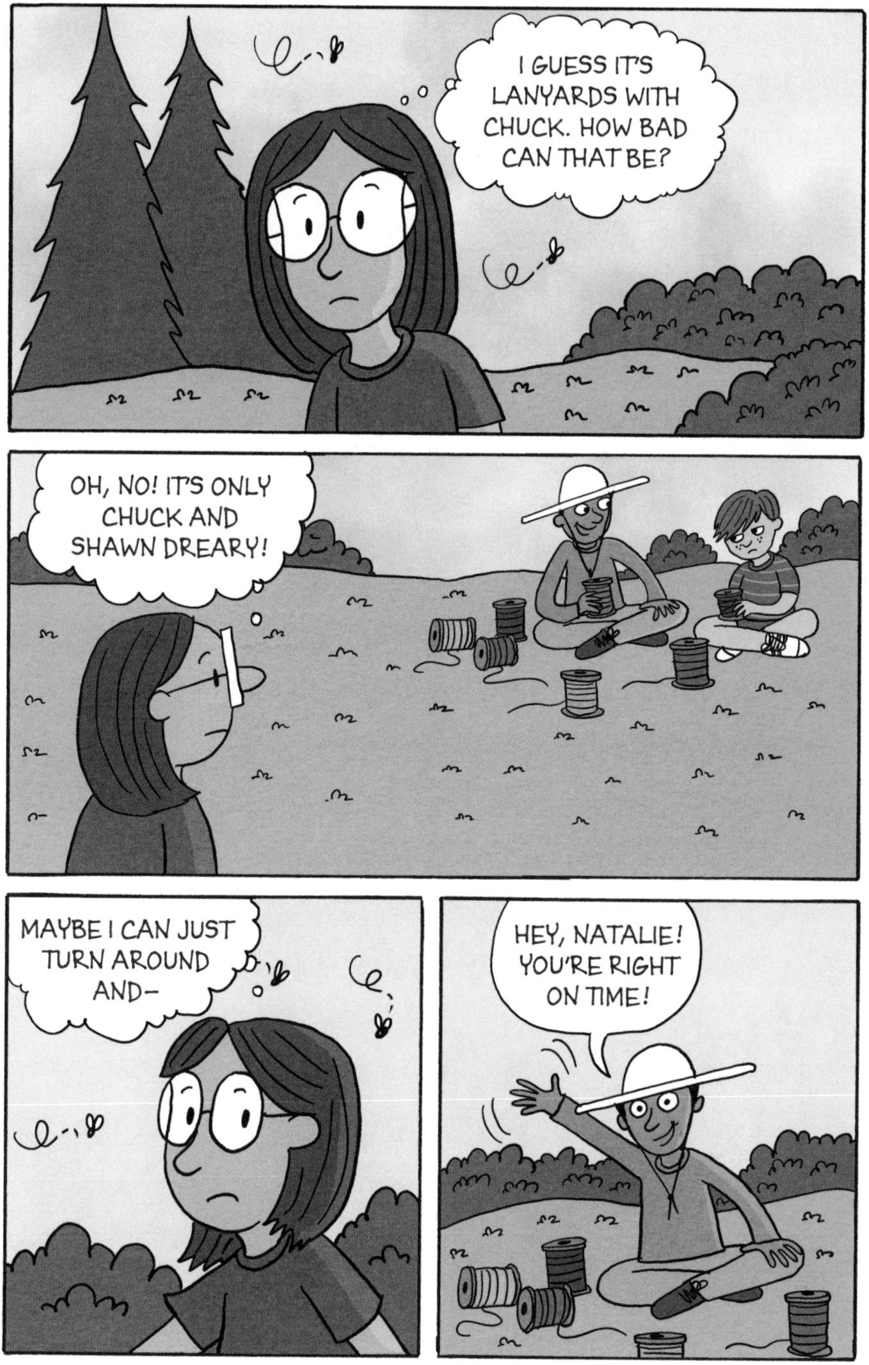
I GUESS IT'S LANYARDS WITH CHUCK. HOW BAD CAN THAT BE?
OH, NO! IT'S ONLY CHUCK AND SHAWN DREARY!
MAYBE I CAN JUST TURN AROUND AND–
HEY, NATALIE! YOU'RE RIGHT ON TIME!

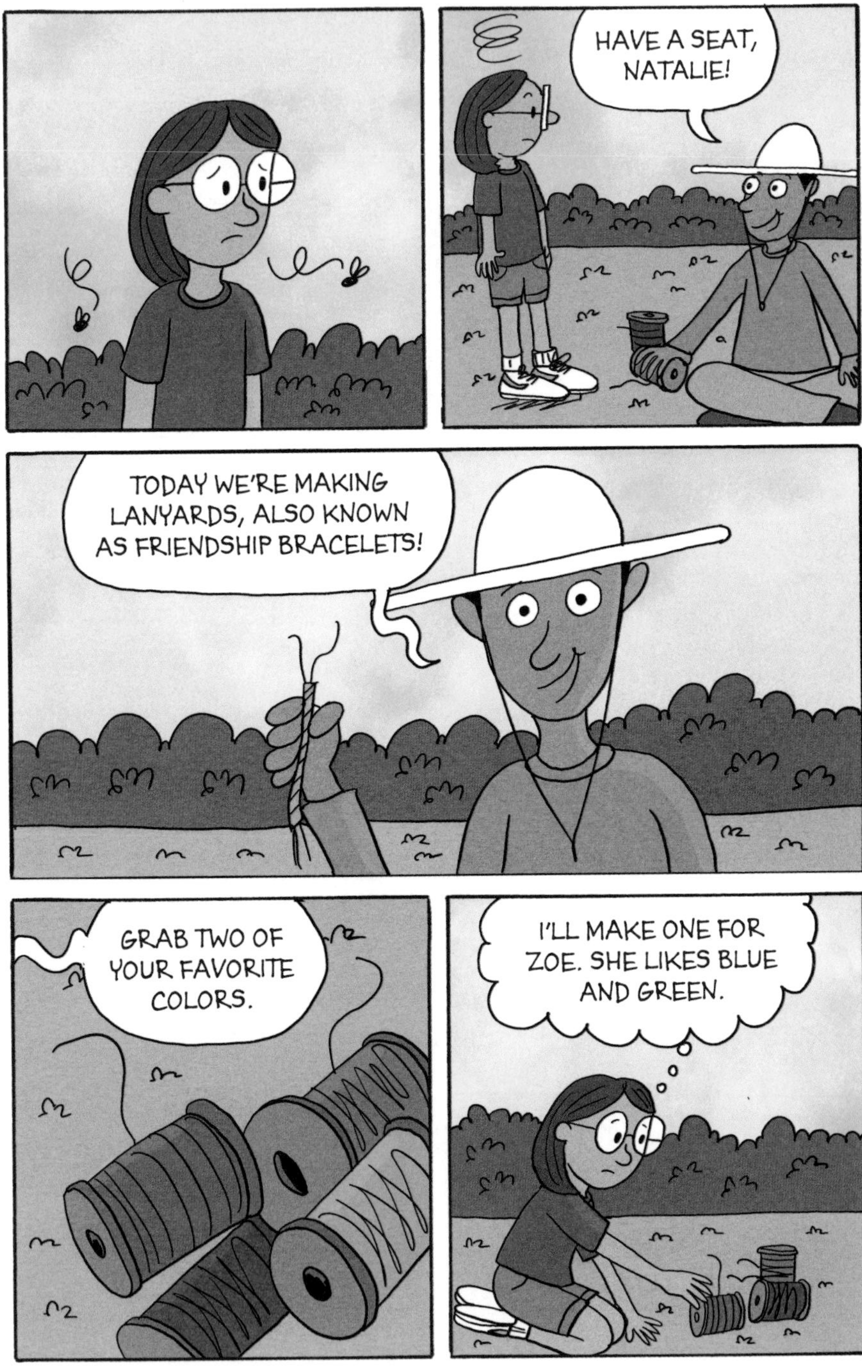
HAVE A SEAT, NATALIE!
TODAY WE'RE MAKING LANYARDS, ALSO KNOWN AS FRIENDSHIP BRACELETS!
GRAB TWO OF YOUR FAVORITE COLORS.
I'LL MAKE ONE FOR ZOE. SHE LIKES BLUE AND GREEN.

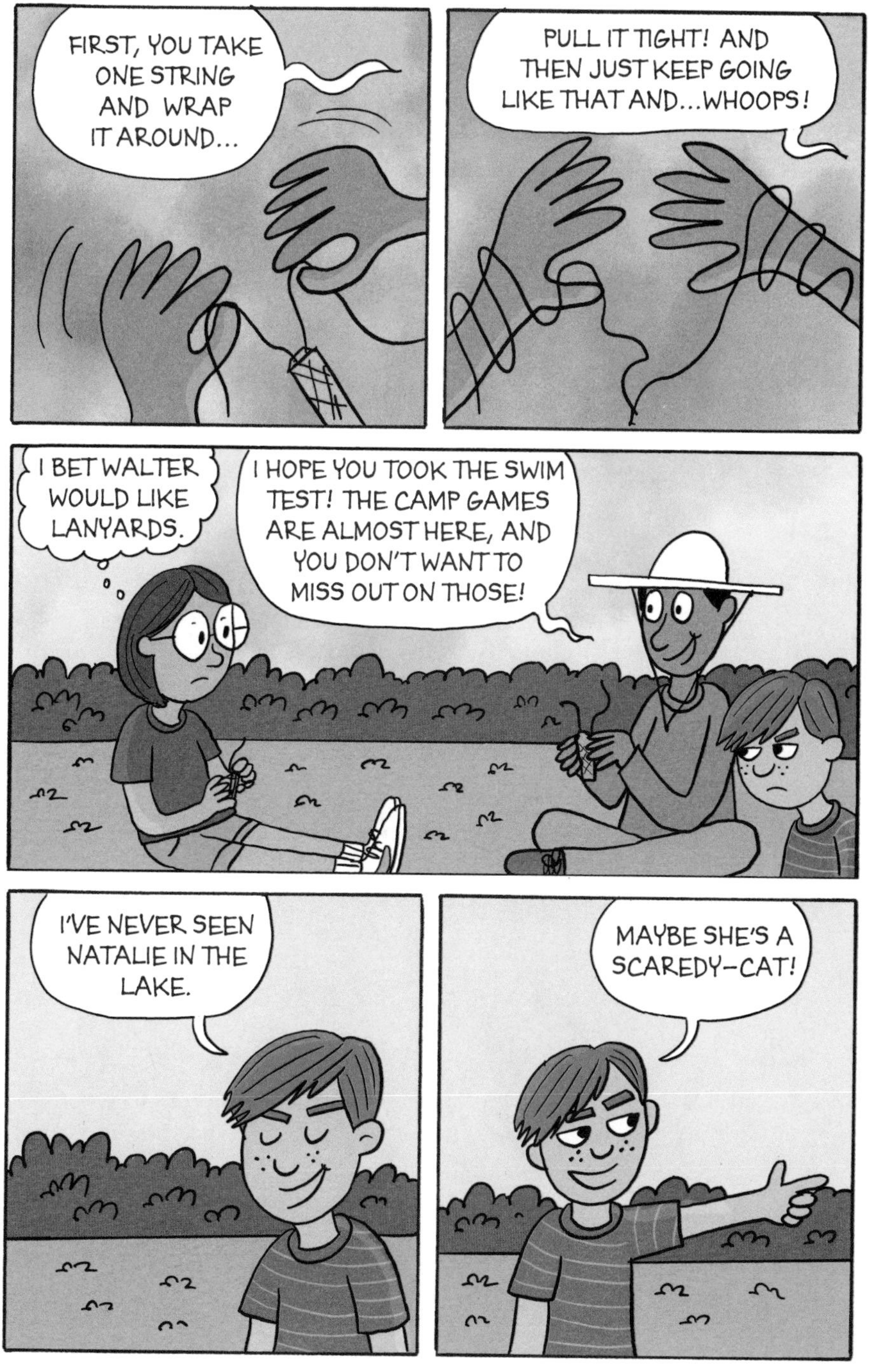
FIRST, YOU TAKE ONE STRING AND WRAP IT AROUND...
PULL IT TIGHT! AND THEN JUST KEEP GOING LIKE THAT AND...WHOOPS!
I BET WALTER WOULD LIKE LANYARDS.
I HOPE YOU TOOK THE SWIM TEST! THE CAMP GAMES ARE ALMOST HERE, AND YOU DON'T WANT TO MISS OUT ON THOSE!
I'VE NEVER SEEN NATALIE IN THE LAKE.
MAYBE SHE'S A SCAREDY-CAT!

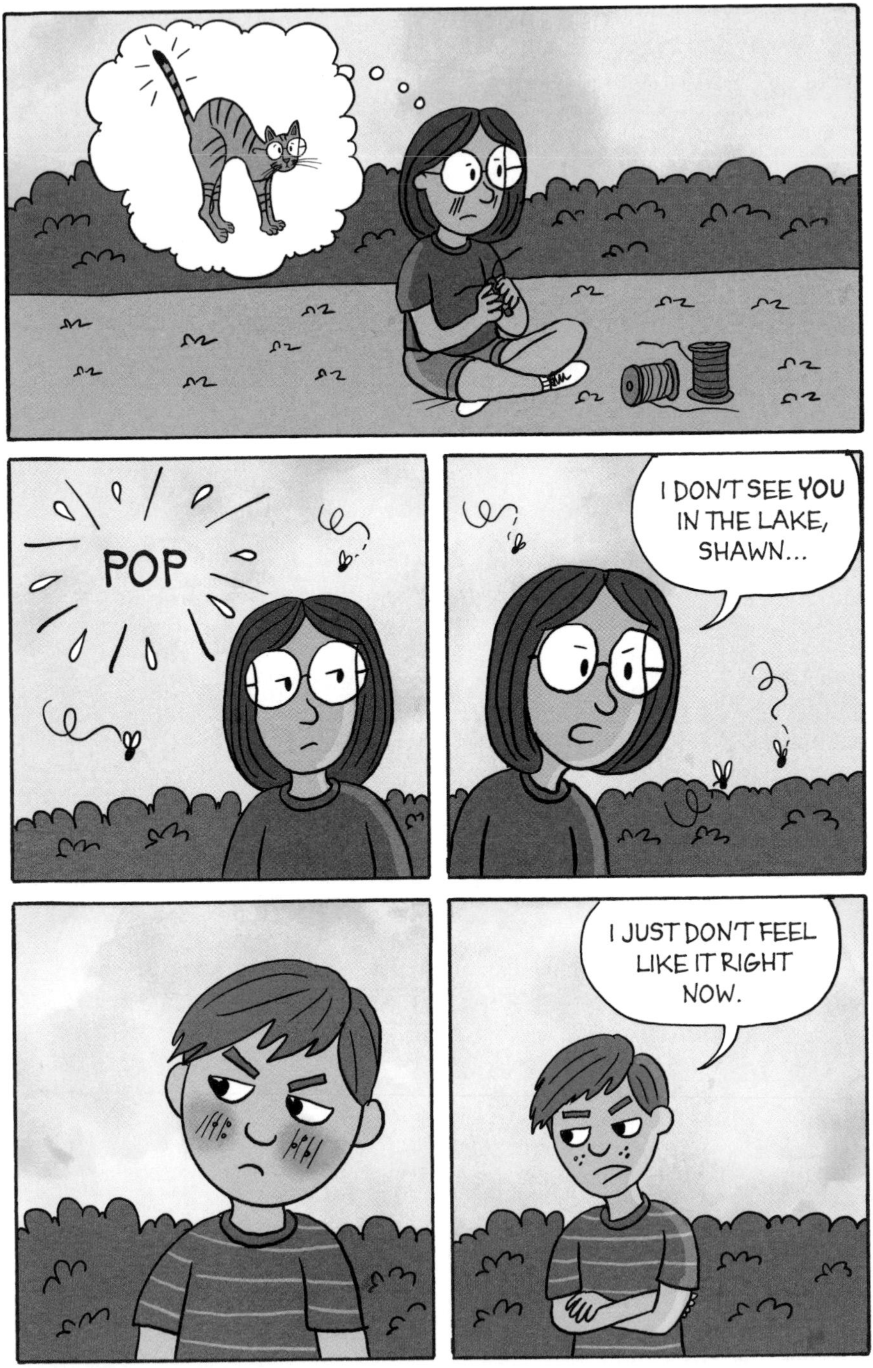
POP
I DON'T SEE YOU IN THE LAKE, SHAWN...
I JUST DON'T FEEL LIKE IT RIGHT NOW.

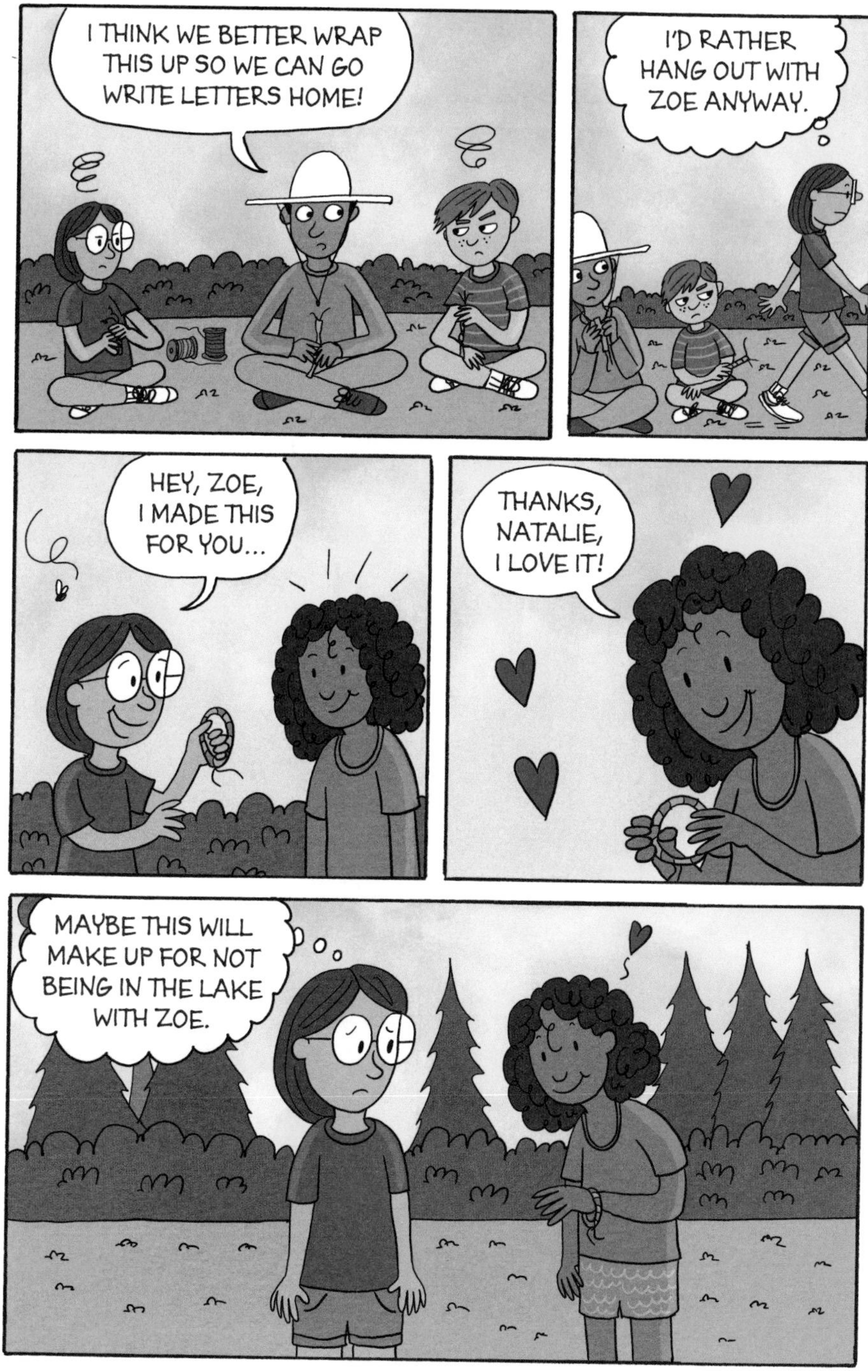

I THINK WE BETTER WRAP THIS UP SO WE CAN GO WRITE LETTERS HOME!
I'D RATHER HANG OUT WITH ZOE ANYWAY.
HEY, ZOE, I MADE THIS FOR YOU...
THANKS, NATALIE, I LOVE IT!
MAYBE THIS WILL MAKE UP FOR NOT BEING IN THE LAKE WITH ZOE.

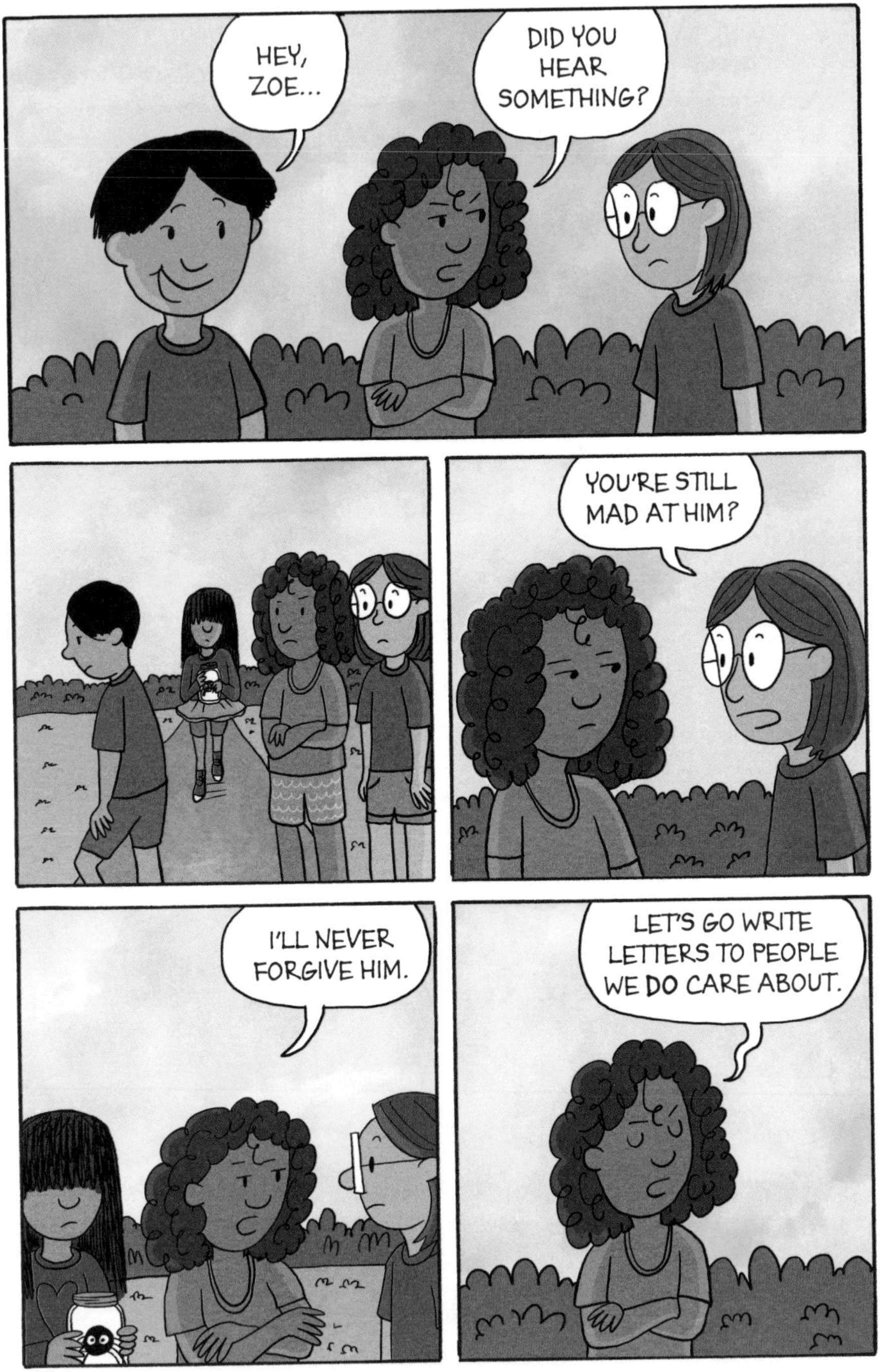
HEY, ZOE...
DID YOU HEAR SOMETHING?
YOU'RE STILL MAD AT HIM?
I'LL NEVER FORGIVE HIM.
LET'S GO WRITE LETTERS TO PEOPLE WE DO CARE ABOUT.

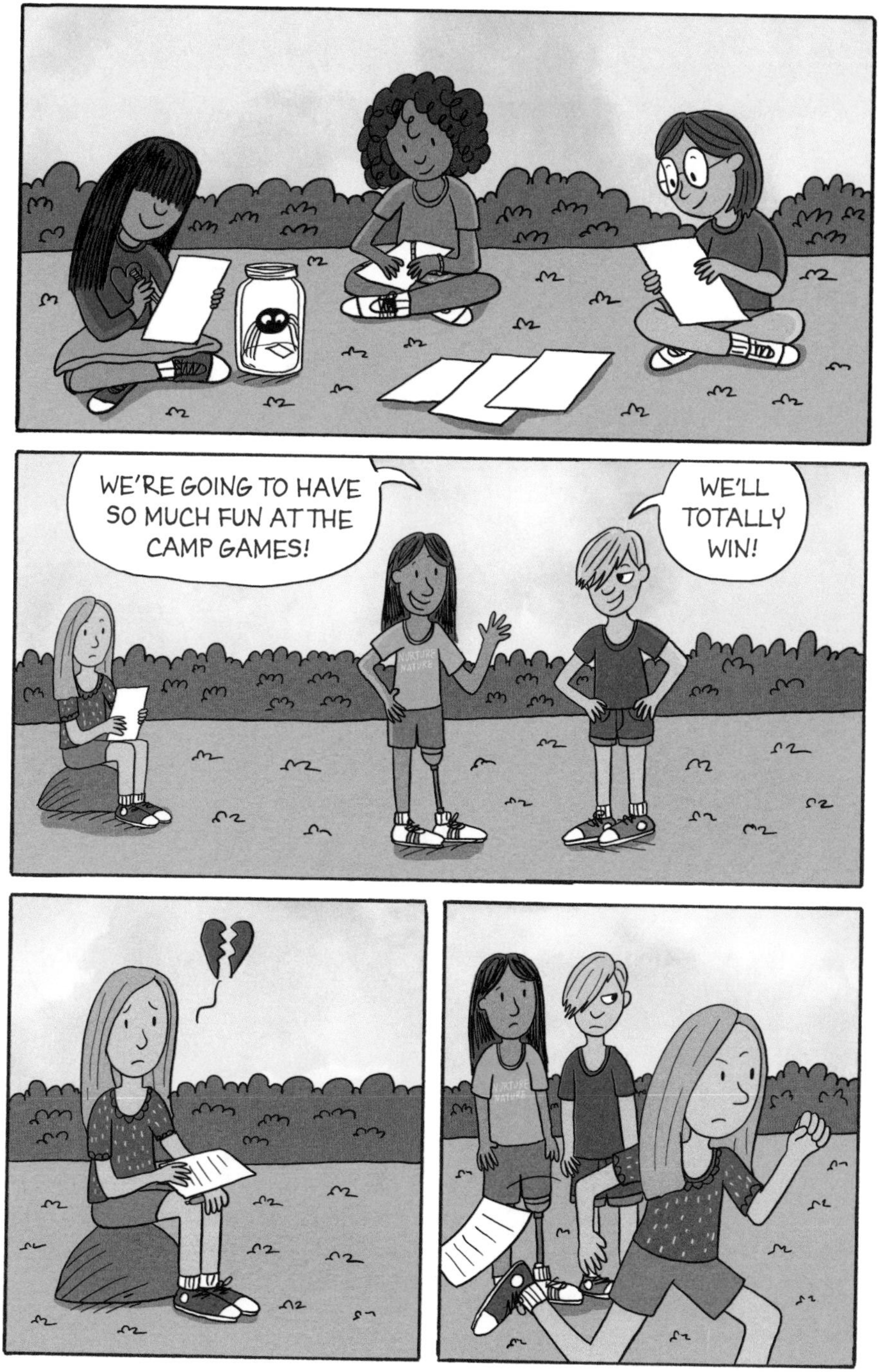
WE'RE GOING TO HAVE SO MUCH FUN AT THE CAMP GAMES!
WE'LL TOTALLY WIN!
NURTURE NATURE

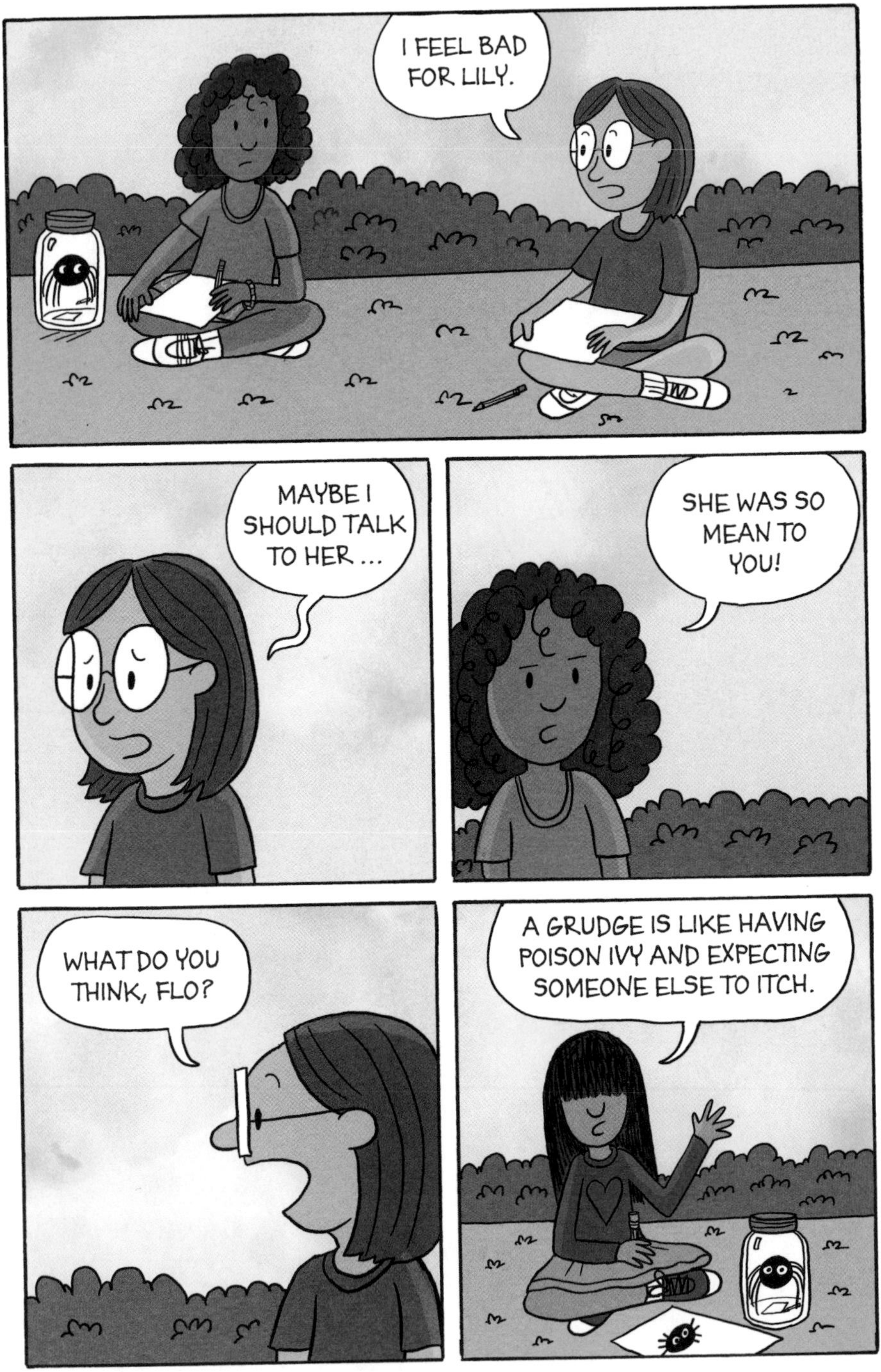
I FEEL BAD FOR LILY.
MAYBE I SHOULD TALK TO HER ...
SHE WAS SO MEAN TO YOU!
WHAT DO YOU THINK, FLO?
A GRUDGE IS LIKE HAVING POISON IVY AND EXPECTING SOMEONE ELSE TO ITCH.

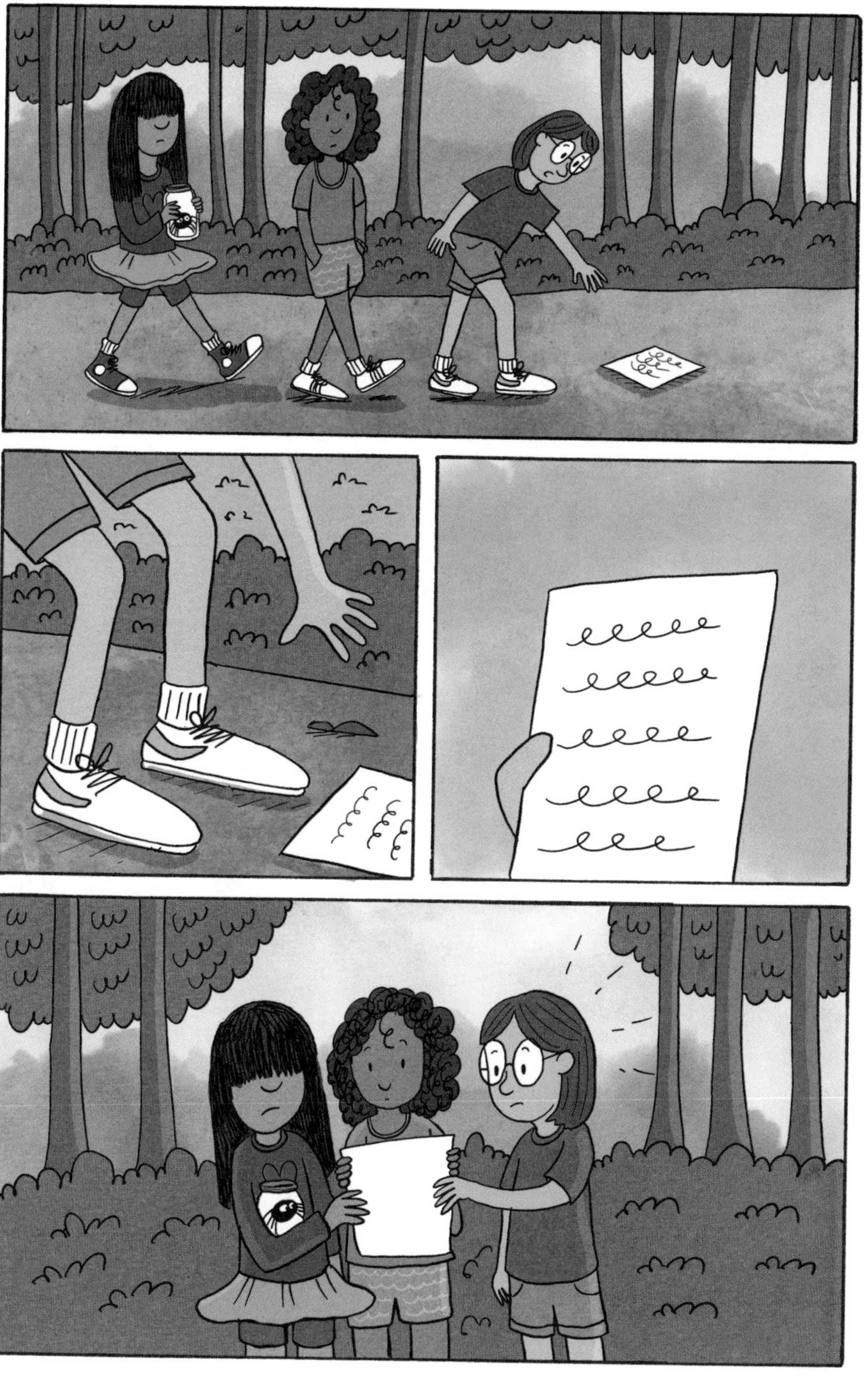

Dear Mom,
How are you? I am not fine.
I can't stand it here anymore.
Alex is being so mean and is totally ignoring me. I thought we were best friends.
I promise I'll do all my chores and more, if you will please let me come home early!
Love,
LILY
P.S. That's a tear, BTW!

CHAPTER 8
YOGA

UPWARD DOG

DOWNWARD DOG

SQUIRREL

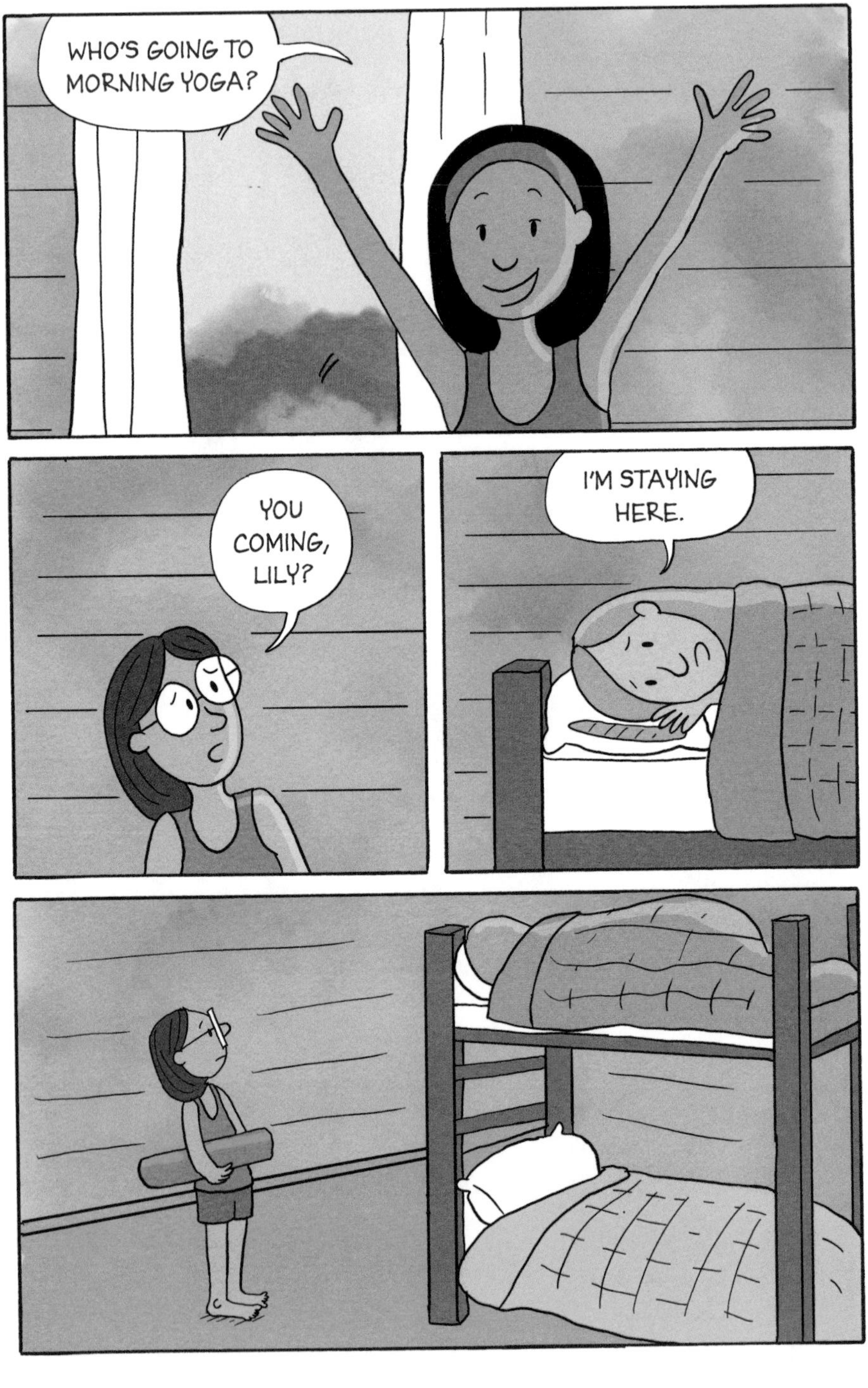
WHO'S GOING TO MORNING YOGA?
YOU COMING, LILY?
I'M STAYING HERE.

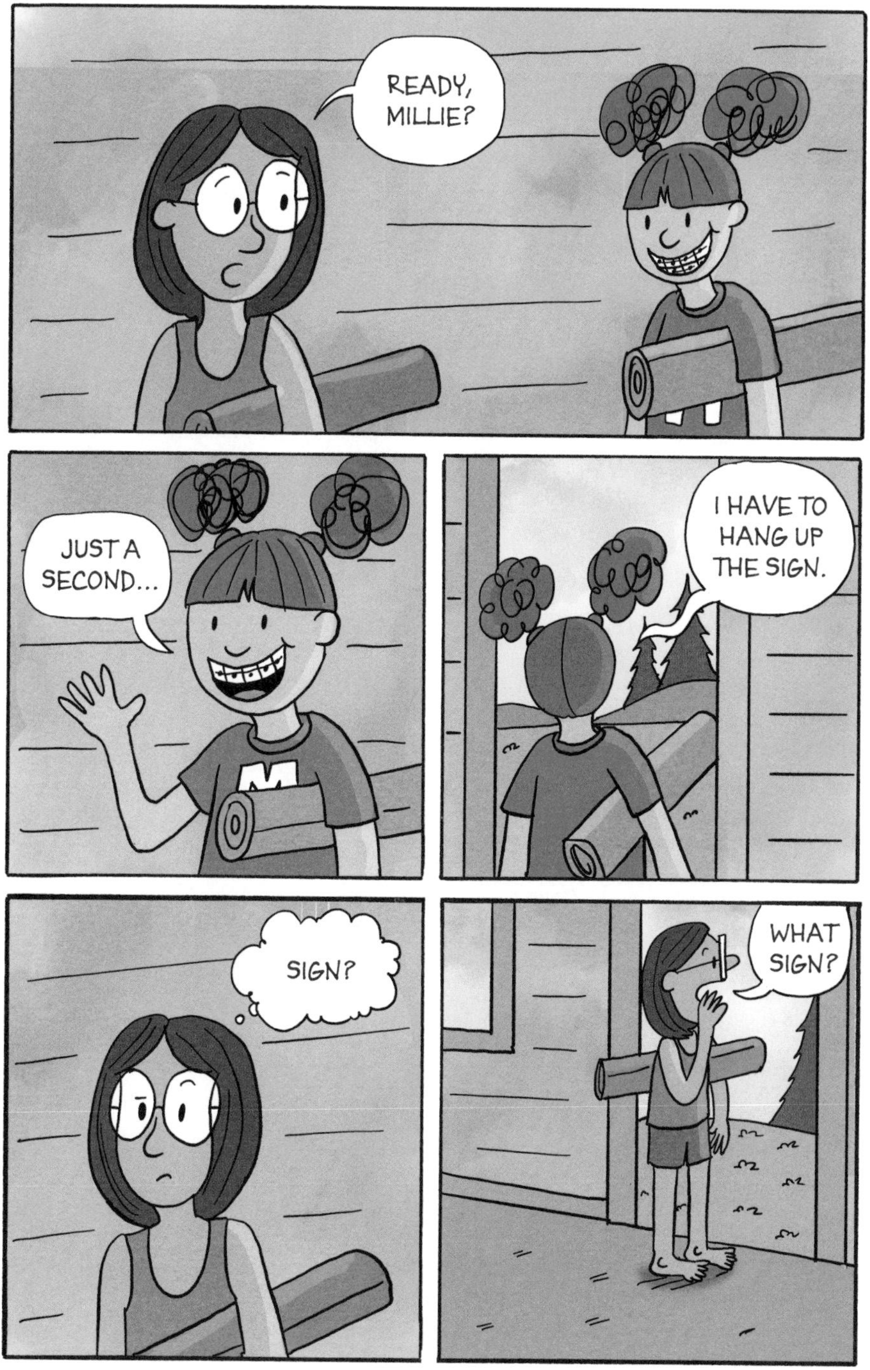
READY, MILLIE?
JUST A SECOND...
I HAVE TO HANG UP THE SIGN.
SIGN?
WHAT SIGN?

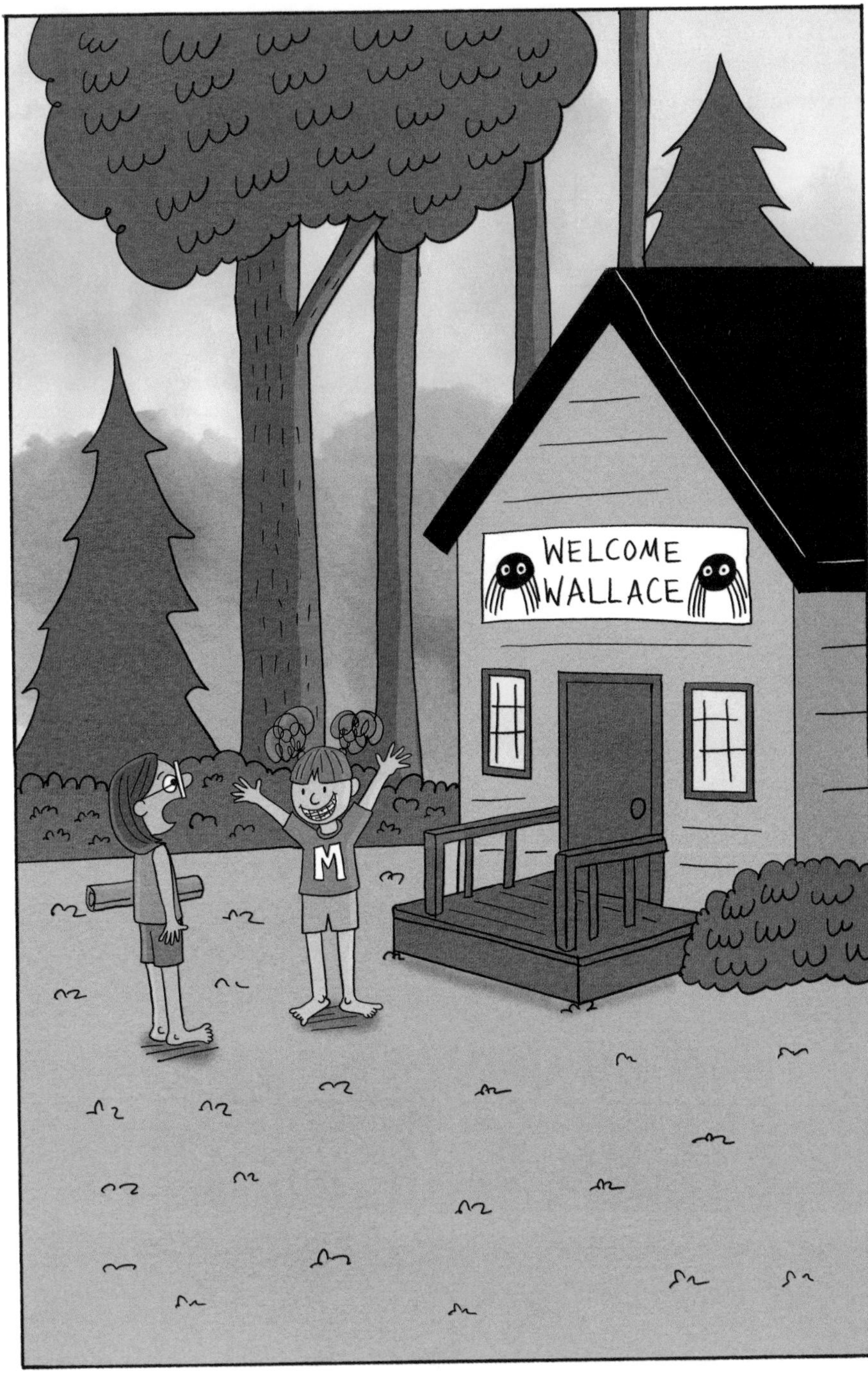
WELCOME
WALLACE

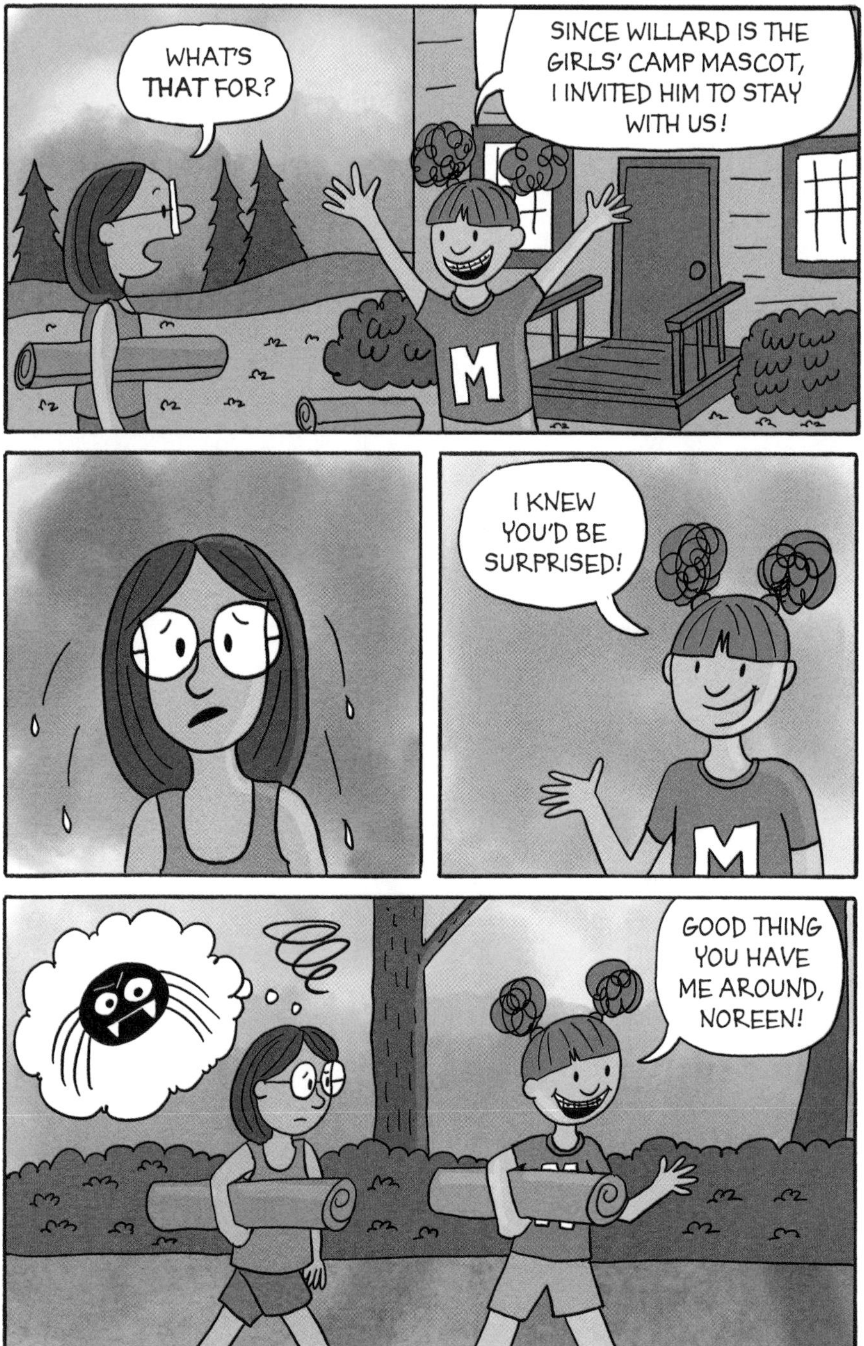
WHAT'S THAT FOR?
SINCE WILLARD IS THE GIRLS' CAMP MASCOT, I INVITED HIM TO STAY WITH US!
I KNEW YOU'D BE SURPRISED!
GOOD THING YOU HAVE ME AROUND, NOREEN!

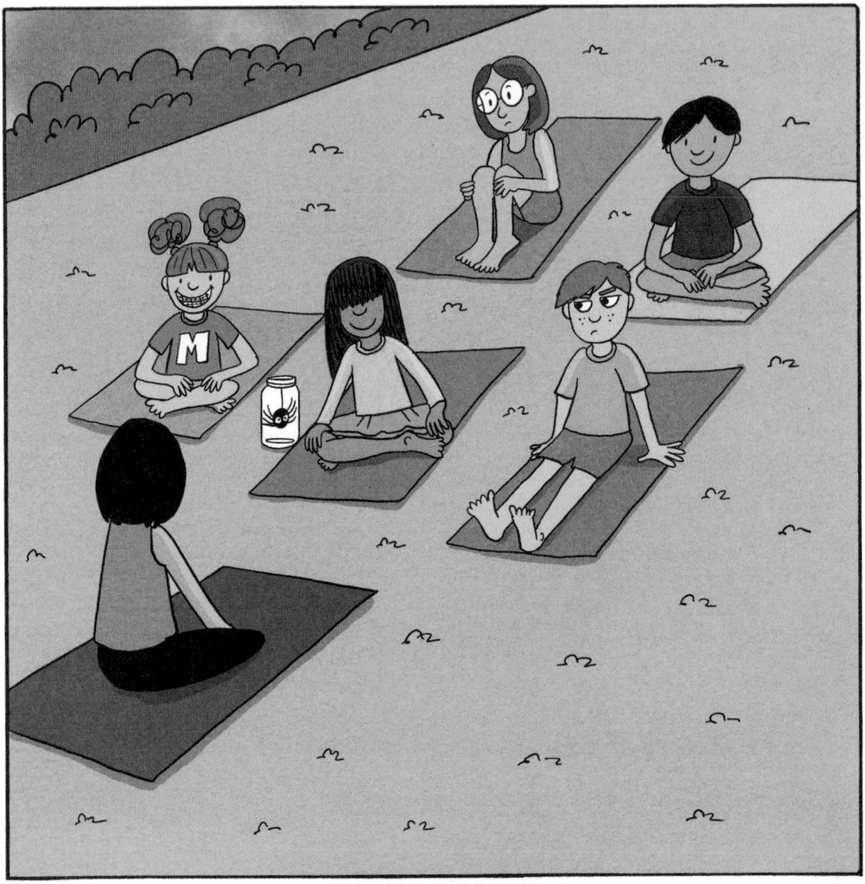

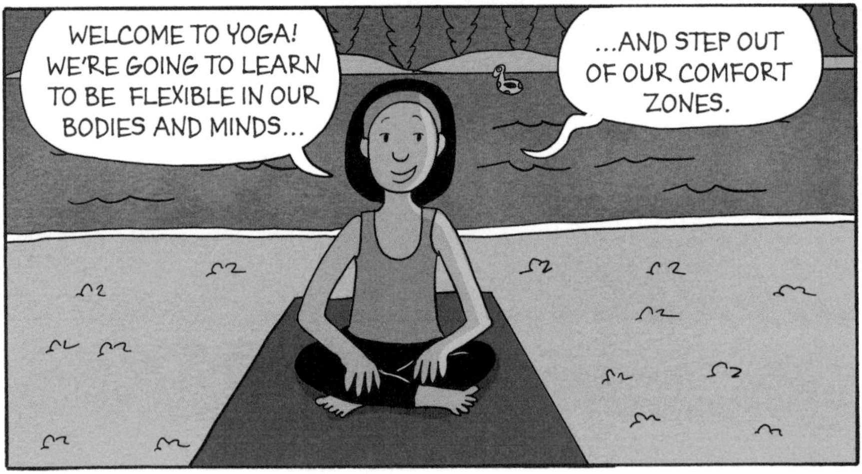
WELCOME TO YOGA! WE'RE GOING TO LEARN TO BE FLEXIBLE IN OUR BODIES AND MINDS...
...AND STEP OUT OF OUR COMFORT ZONES.

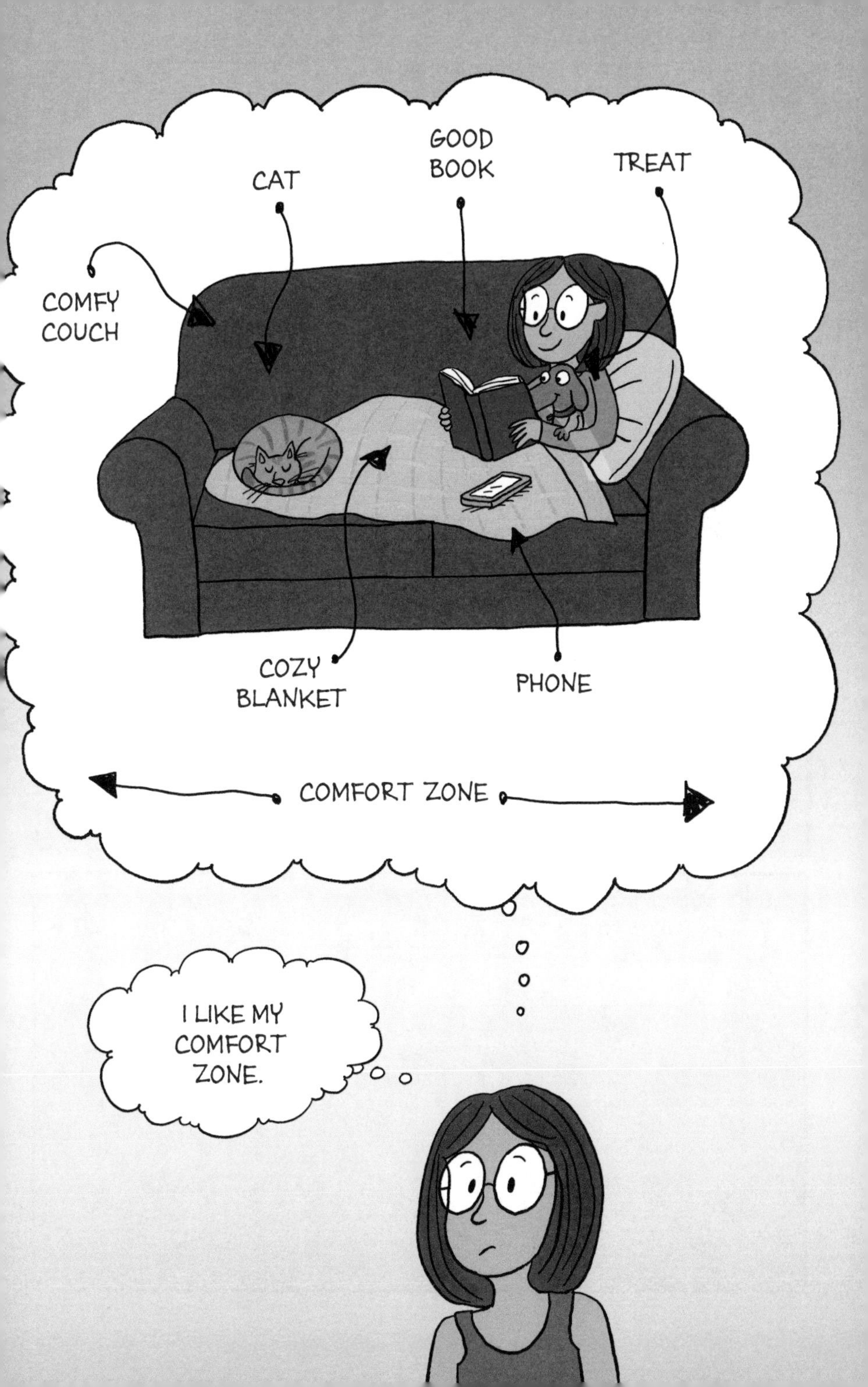
CAT
GOOD BOOK
TREAT
COMFY COUCH
COZY BLANKET
PHONE
COMFORT ZONE
I LIKE MY COMFORT ZONE.

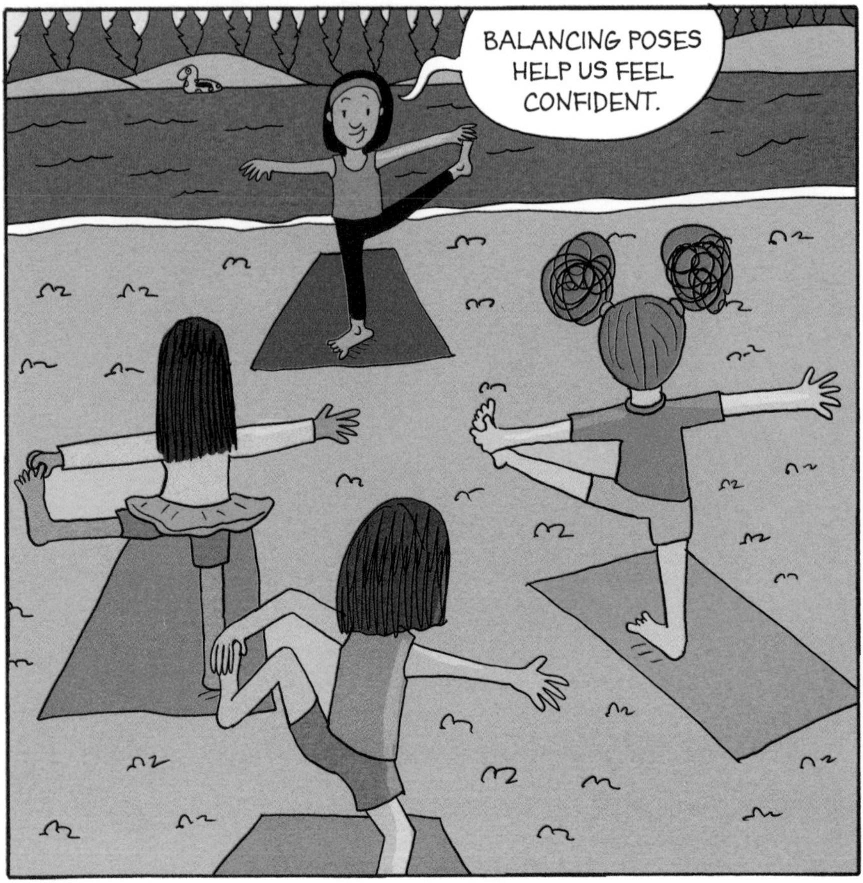
BALANCING POSES HELP US FEEL CONFIDENT.

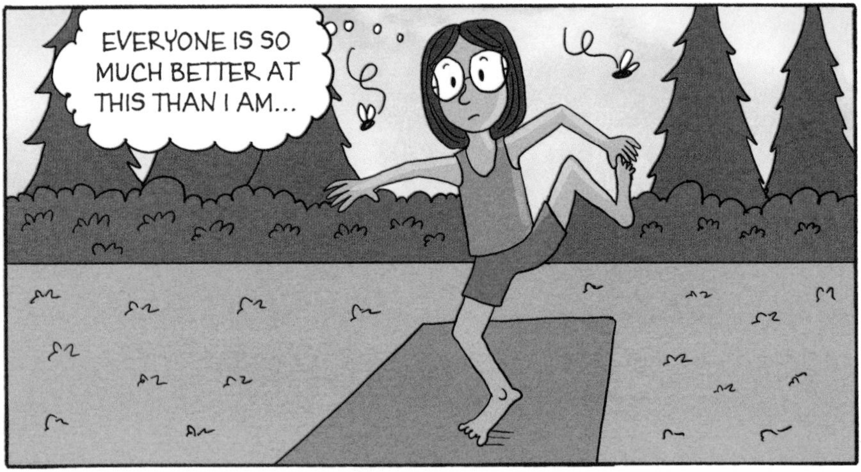
EVERYONE IS SO MUCH BETTER AT THIS THAN I AM...

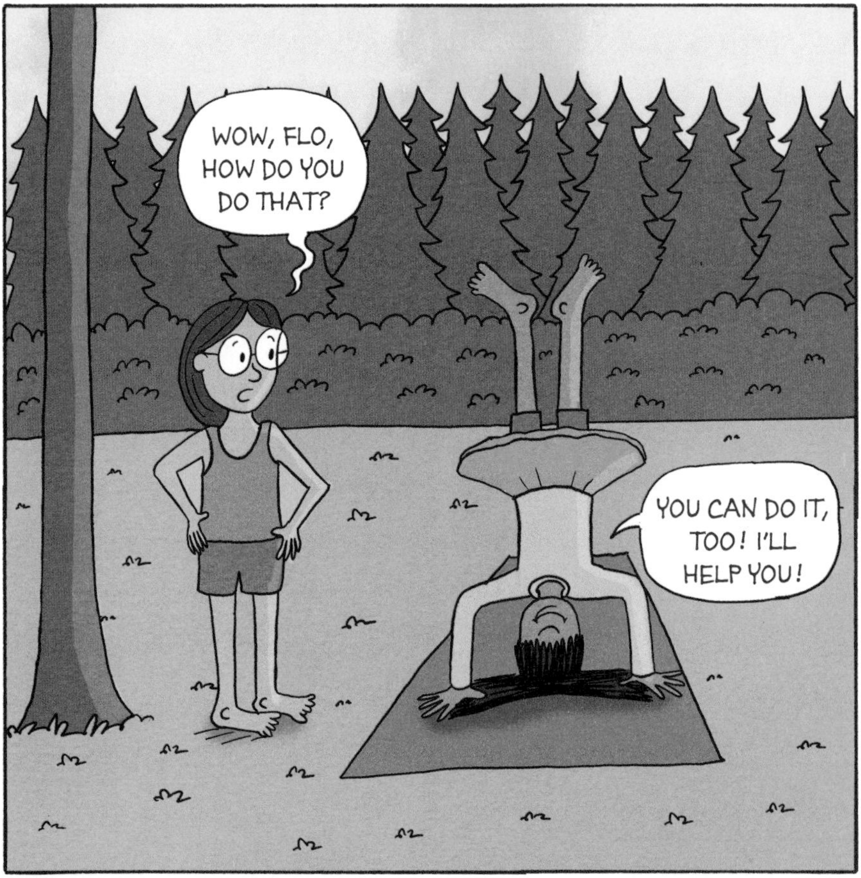
WOW, FLO, HOW DO YOU DO THAT?
YOU CAN DO IT, TOO! I'LL HELP YOU!

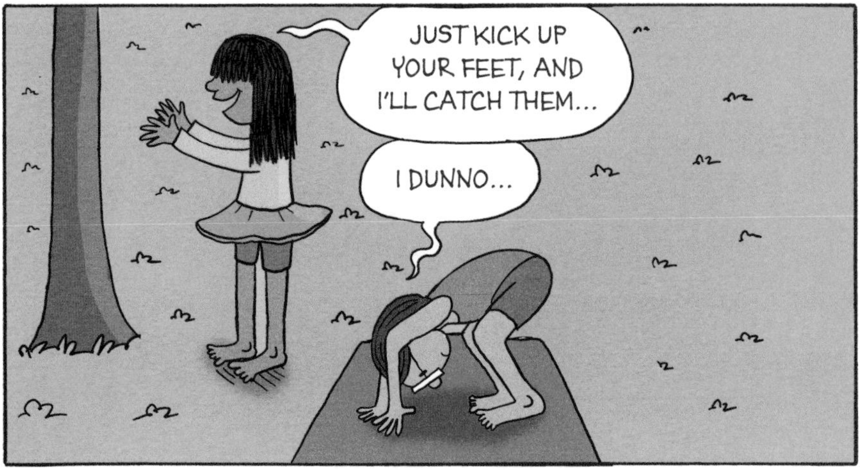
JUST KICK UP YOUR FEET, AND I'LL CATCH THEM...
I DUNNO...

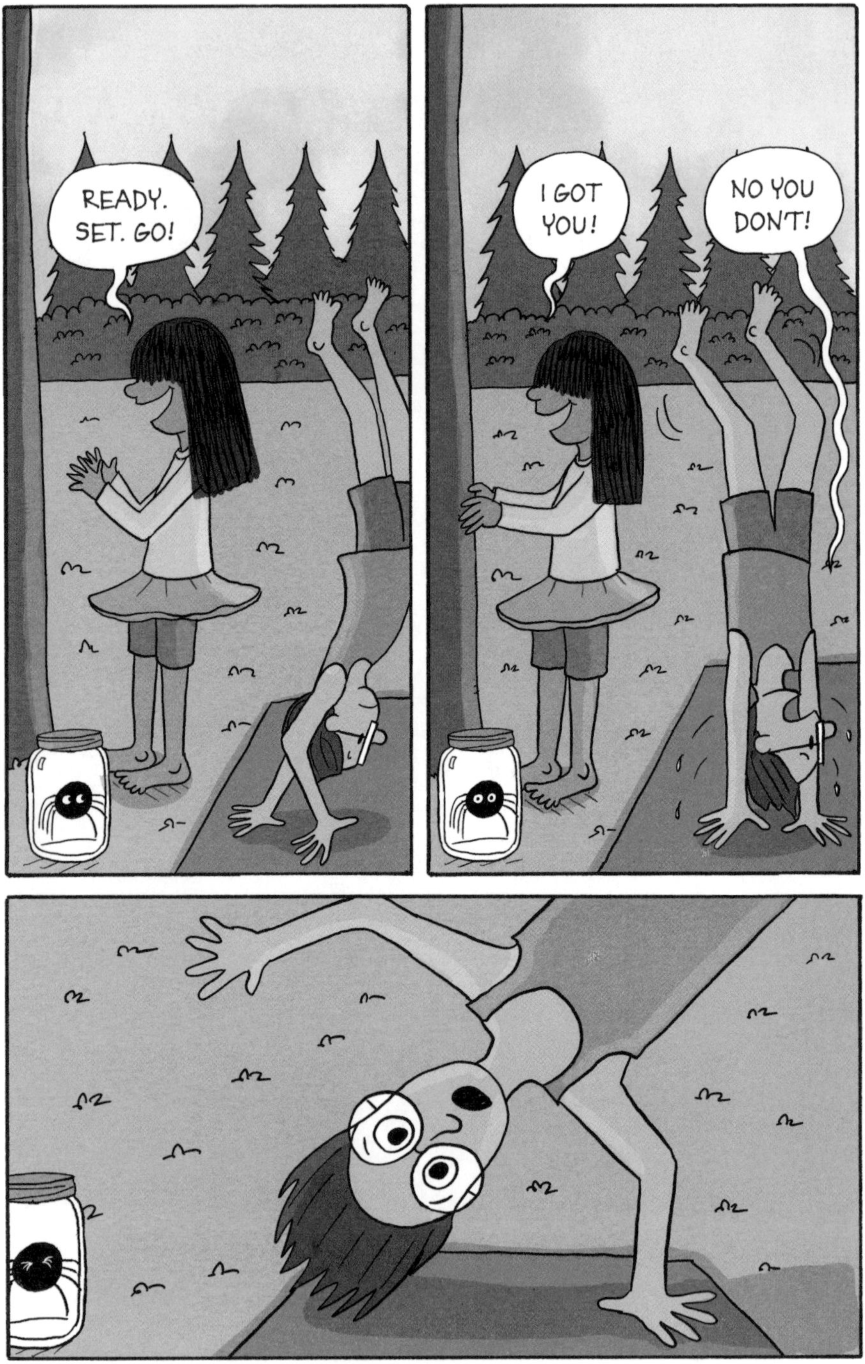
READY. SET. GO!
I GOT YOU!
NO YOU DON'T!

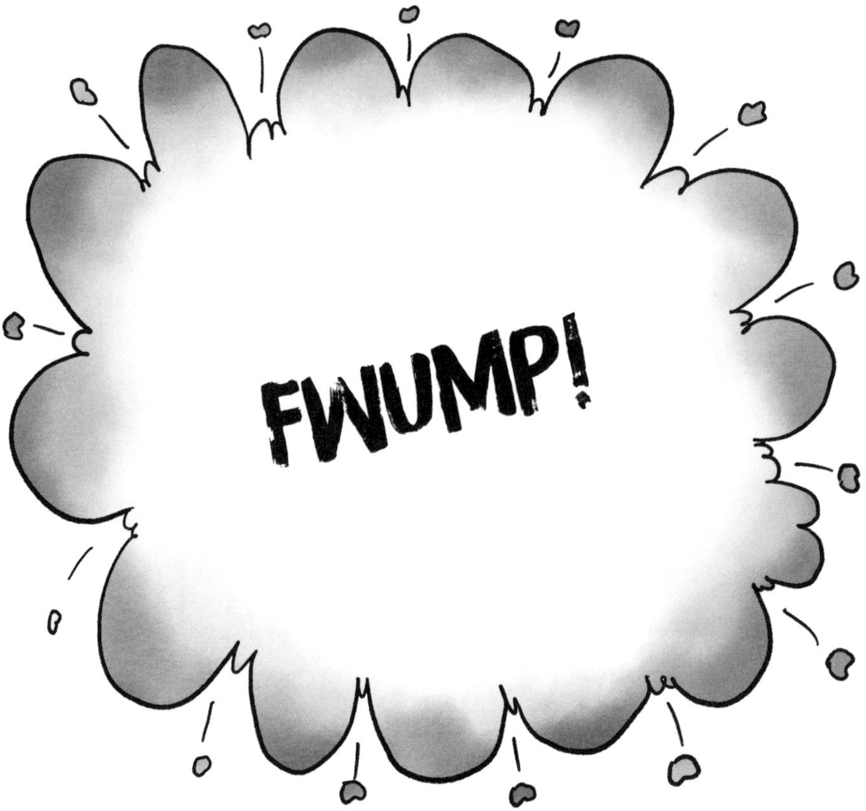
FWUMP!

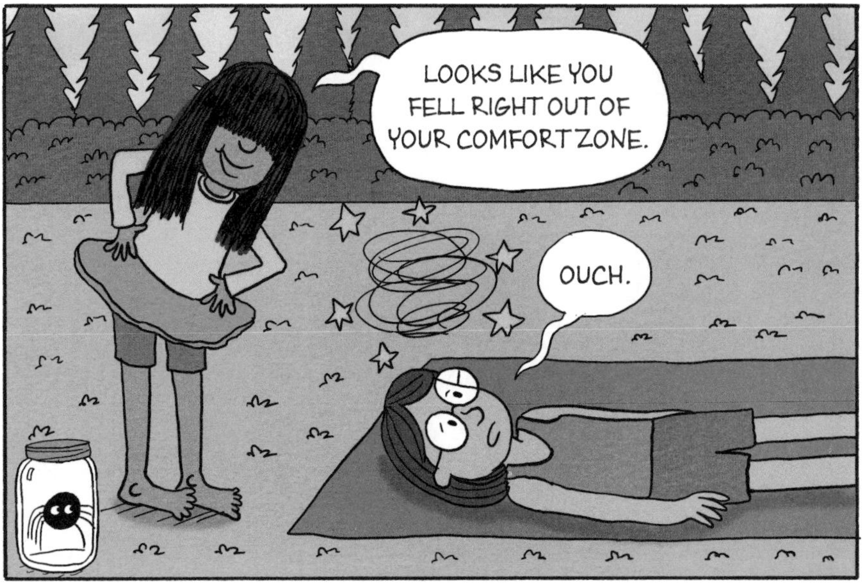
LOOKS LIKE YOU FELL RIGHT OUT OF YOUR COMFORT ZONE.
OUCH.

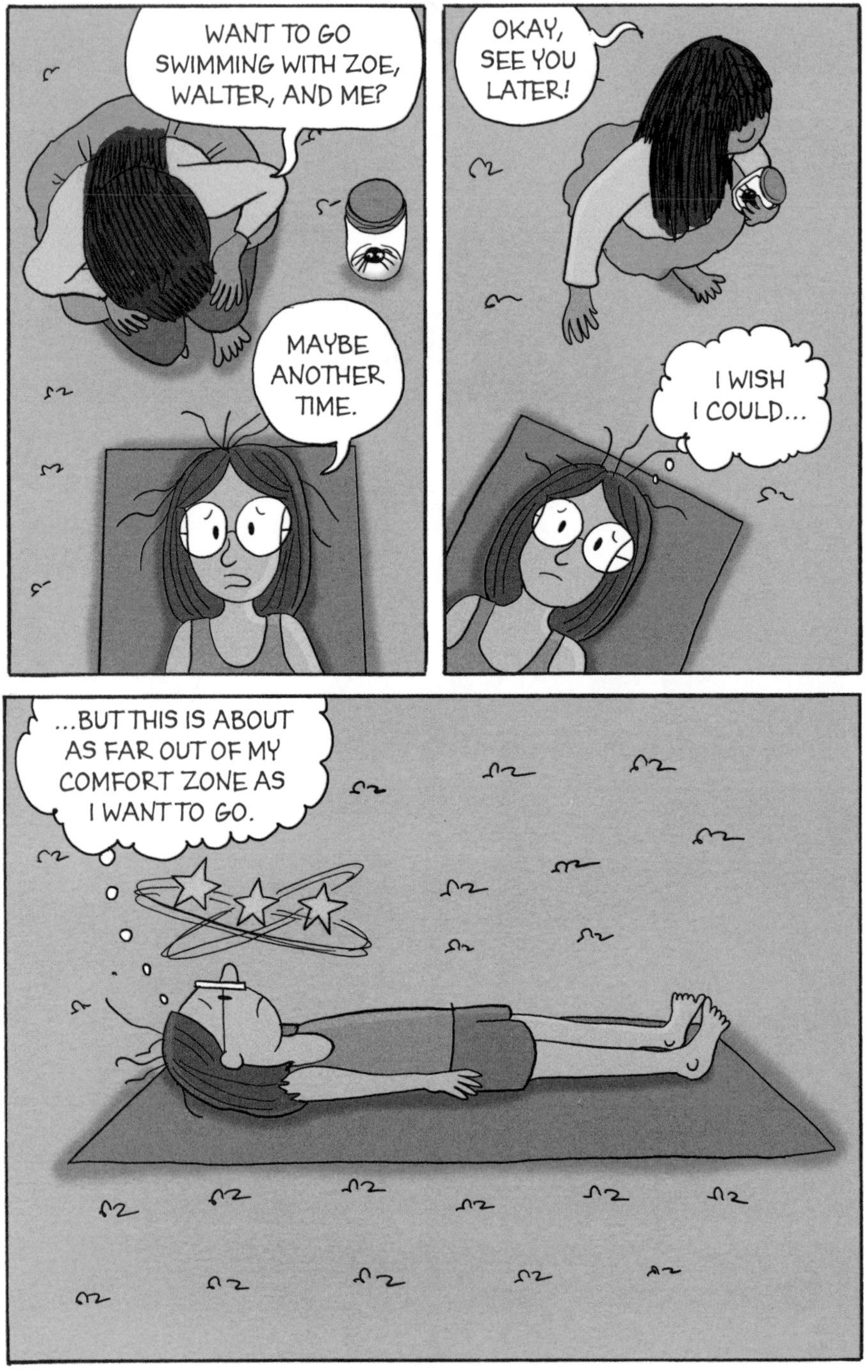
WANT TO GO SWIMMING WITH ZOE, WALTER, AND ME?
MAYBE ANOTHER TIME.
OKAY, SEE YOU LATER!
I WISH I COULD...
...BUT THIS IS ABOUT AS FAR OUT OF MY COMFORT ZONE AS I WANT TO GO.

CHAPTER 9
STUCK

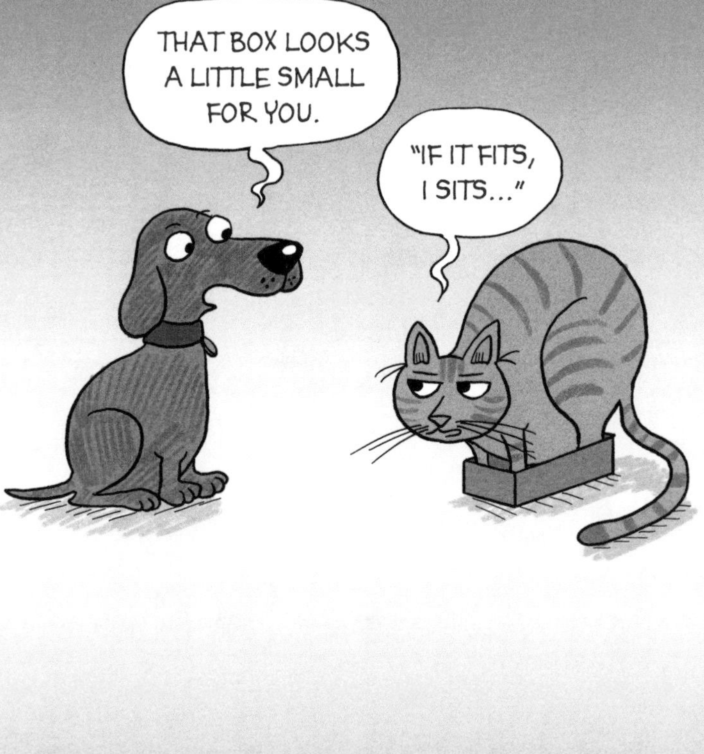
THAT BOX LOOKS A LITTLE SMALL FOR YOU.
"IF IT FITS, I SITS..."

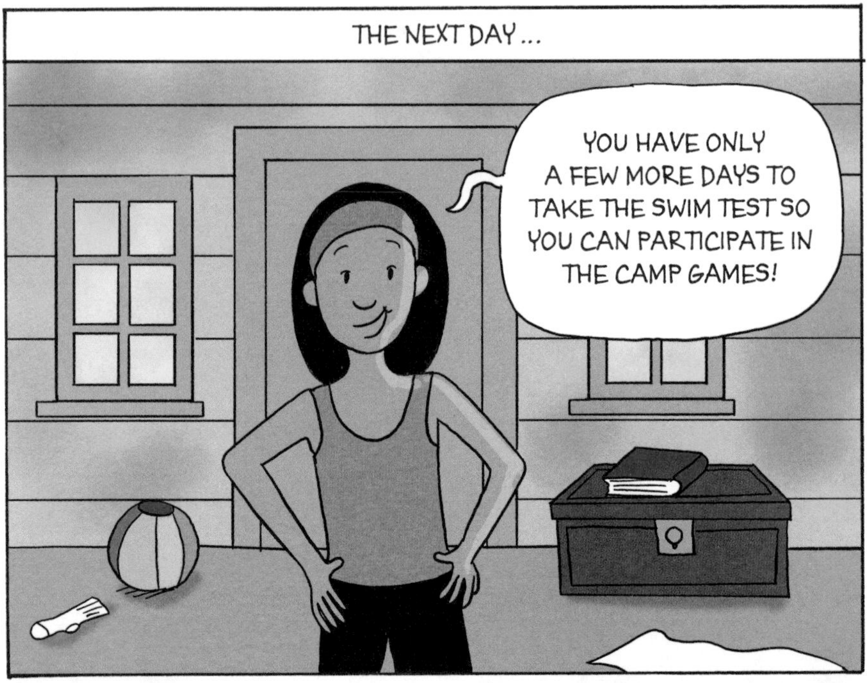
THE NEXT DAY...
YOU HAVE ONLY A FEW MORE DAYS TO TAKE THE SWIM TEST SO YOU CAN PARTICIPATE IN THE CAMP GAMES!

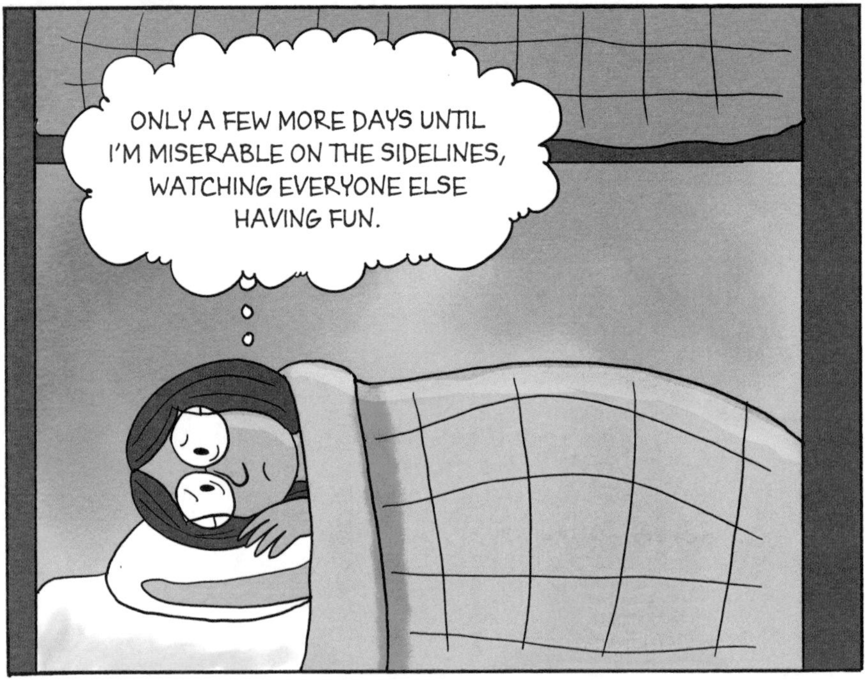
ONLY A FEW MORE DAYS UNTIL I'M MISERABLE ON THE SIDELINES, WATCHING EVERYONE ELSE HAVING FUN.

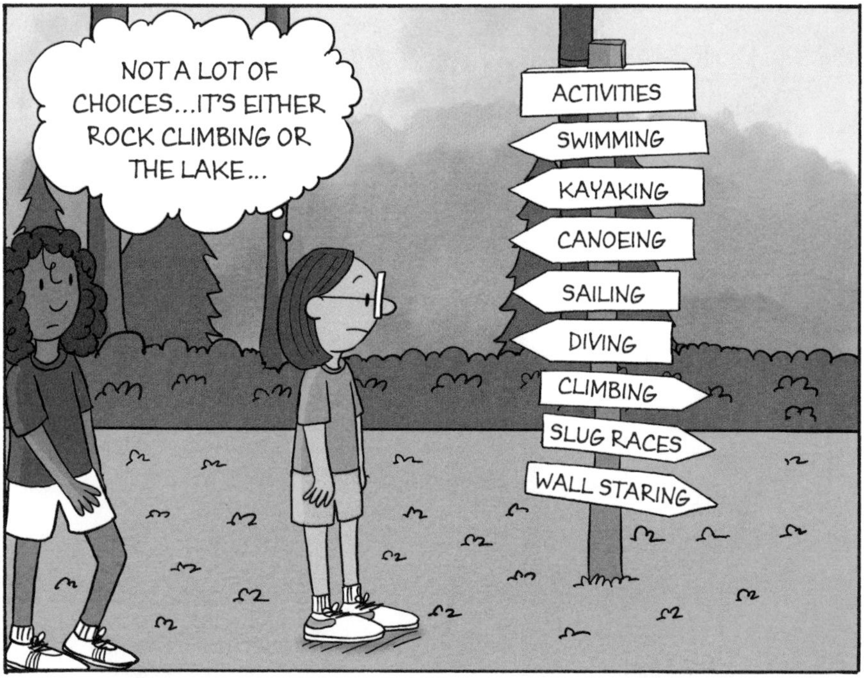
NOT A LOT OF CHOICES...IT'S EITHER ROCK CLIMBING OR THE LAKE...
ACTIVITIES
SWIMMING
KAYAKING
CANOEING
SAILING
DIVING
CLIMBING
SLUG RACES
WALL STARING

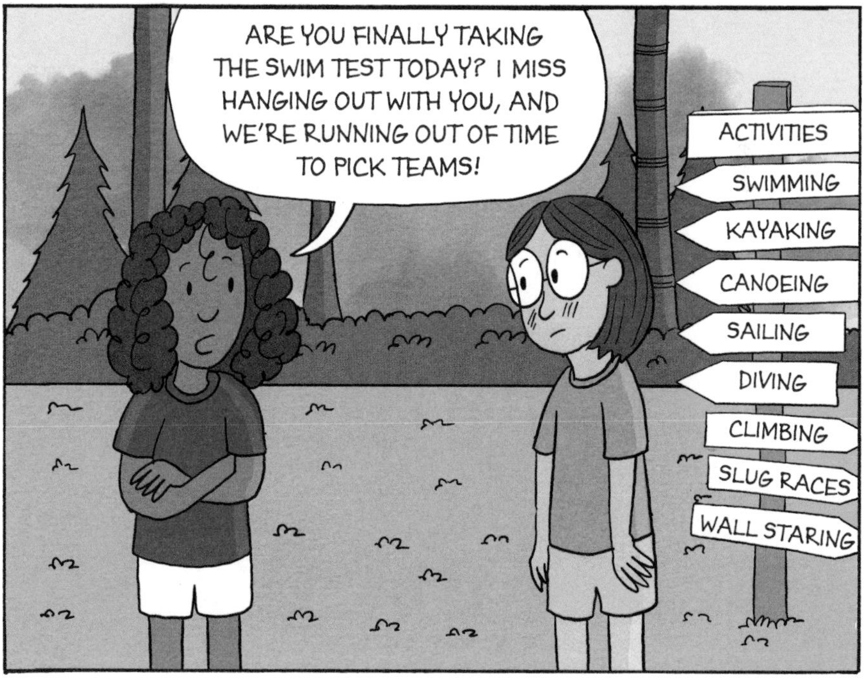
ARE YOU FINALLY TAKING THE SWIM TEST TODAY? I MISS HANGING OUT WITH YOU, AND WE'RE RUNNING OUT OF TIME TO PICK TEAMS!
ACTIVITIES
SWIMMING
KAYAKING
CANOEING
SAILING
DIVING
CLIMBING
SLUG RACES
WALL STARING

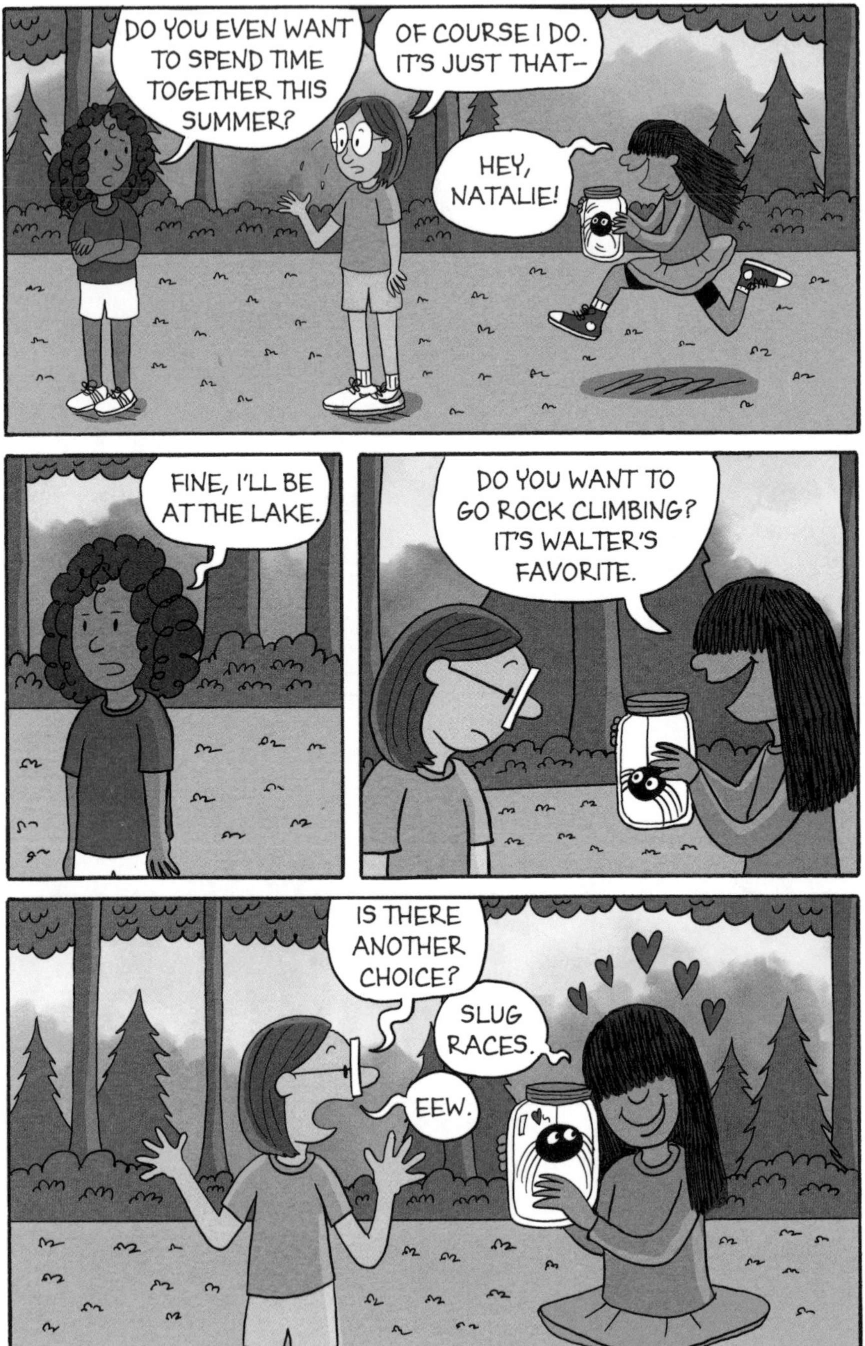
DO YOU EVEN WANT TO SPEND TIME TOGETHER THIS SUMMER?
OF COURSE I DO. IT'S JUST THAT–
HEY, NATALIE!
FINE, I'LL BE AT THE LAKE.
DO YOU WANT TO GO ROCK CLIMBING? IT'S WALTER'S FAVORITE.
IS THERE ANOTHER CHOICE?
SLUG RACES.
EEW.

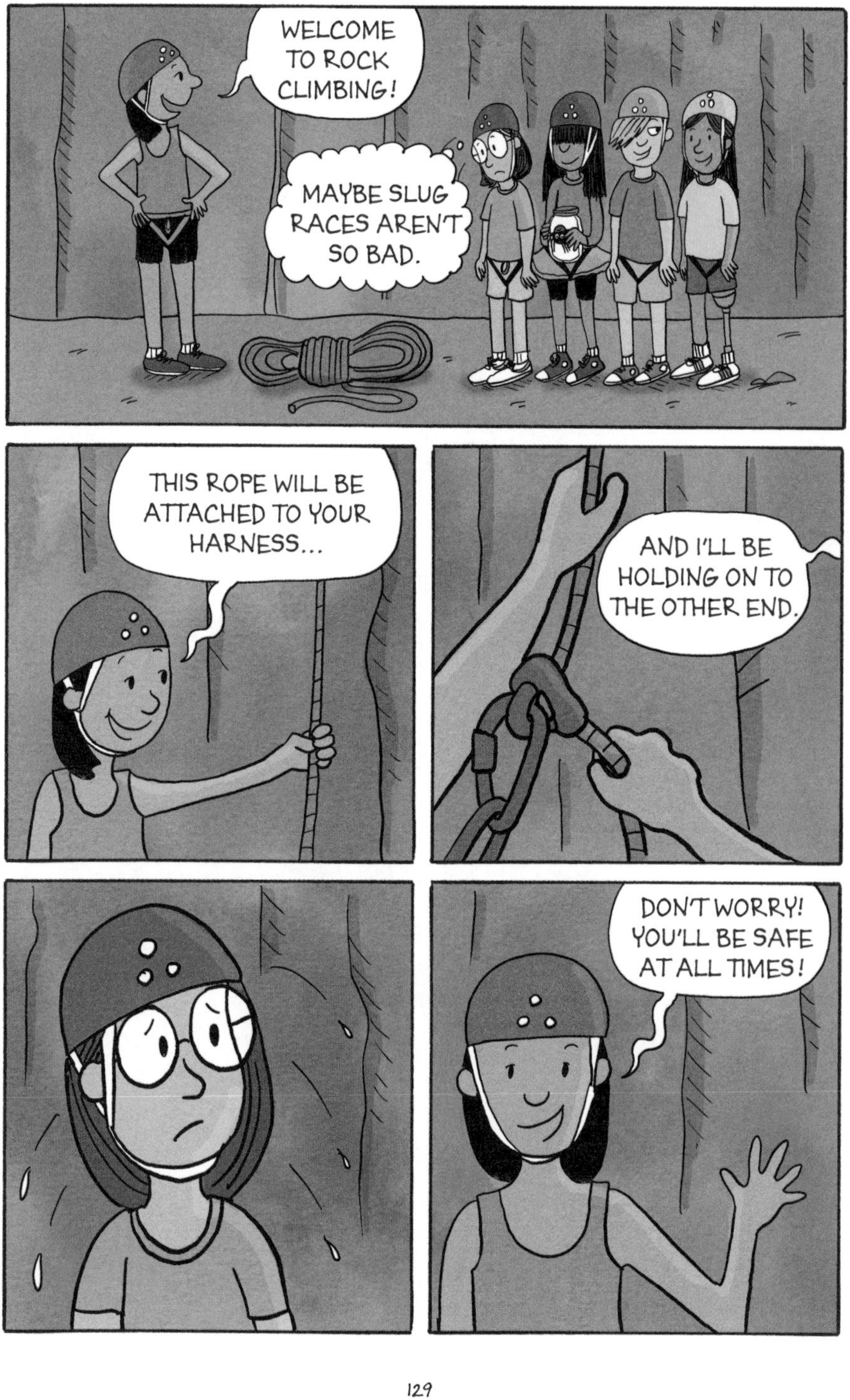
WELCOME TO ROCK CLIMBING!
MAYBE SLUG RACES AREN'T SO BAD.
THIS ROPE WILL BE ATTACHED TO YOUR HARNESS...
AND I'LL BE HOLDING ON TO THE OTHER END.
DON'T WORRY! YOU'LL BE SAFE AT ALL TIMES!

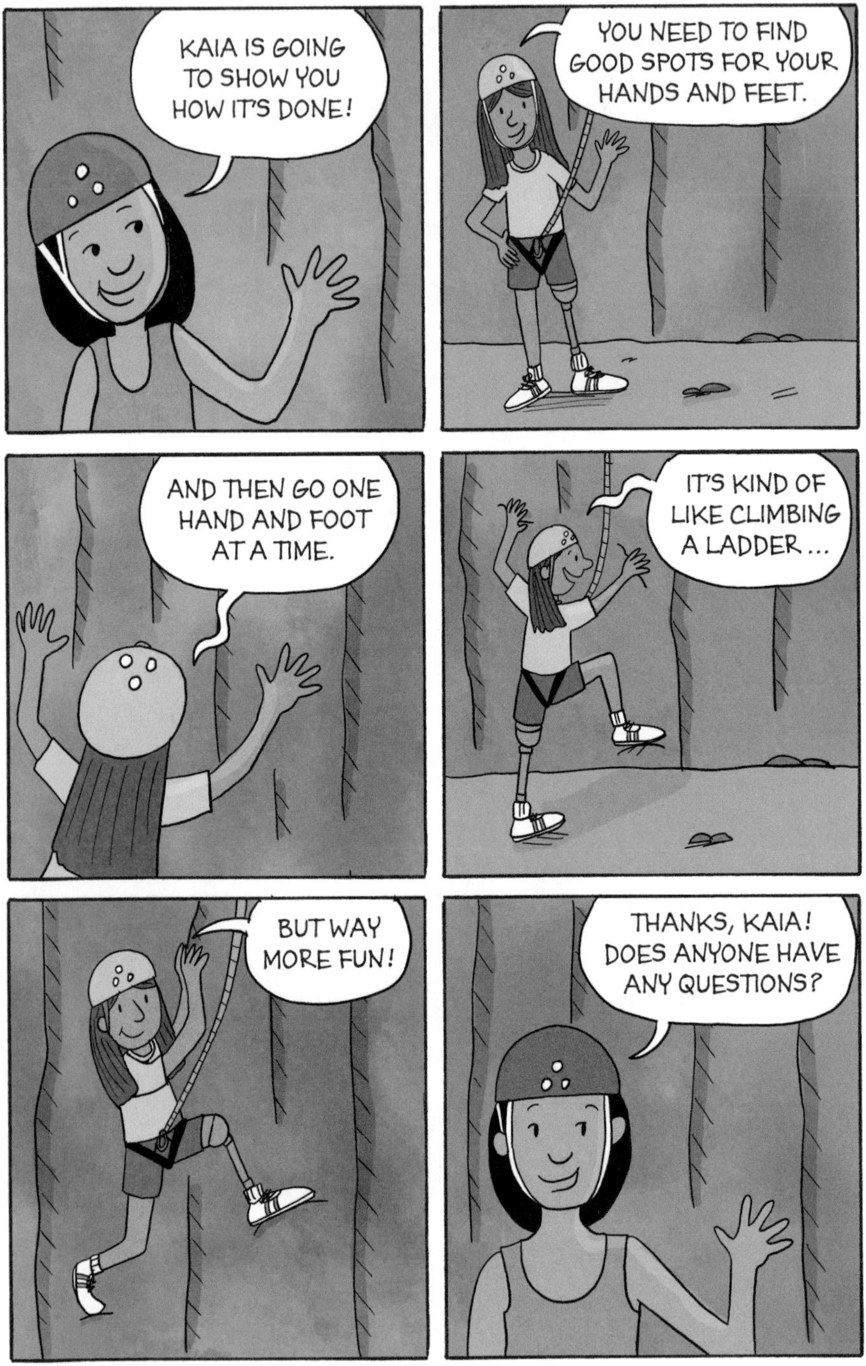
KAIA IS GOING TO SHOW YOU HOW IT'S DONE!
YOU NEED TO FIND GOOD SPOTS FOR YOUR HANDS AND FEET.
AND THEN GO ONE HAND AND FOOT AT A TIME.
IT'S KIND OF LIKE CLIMBING A LADDER...
BUT WAY MORE FUN!
THANKS, KAIA! DOES ANYONE HAVE ANY QUESTIONS?

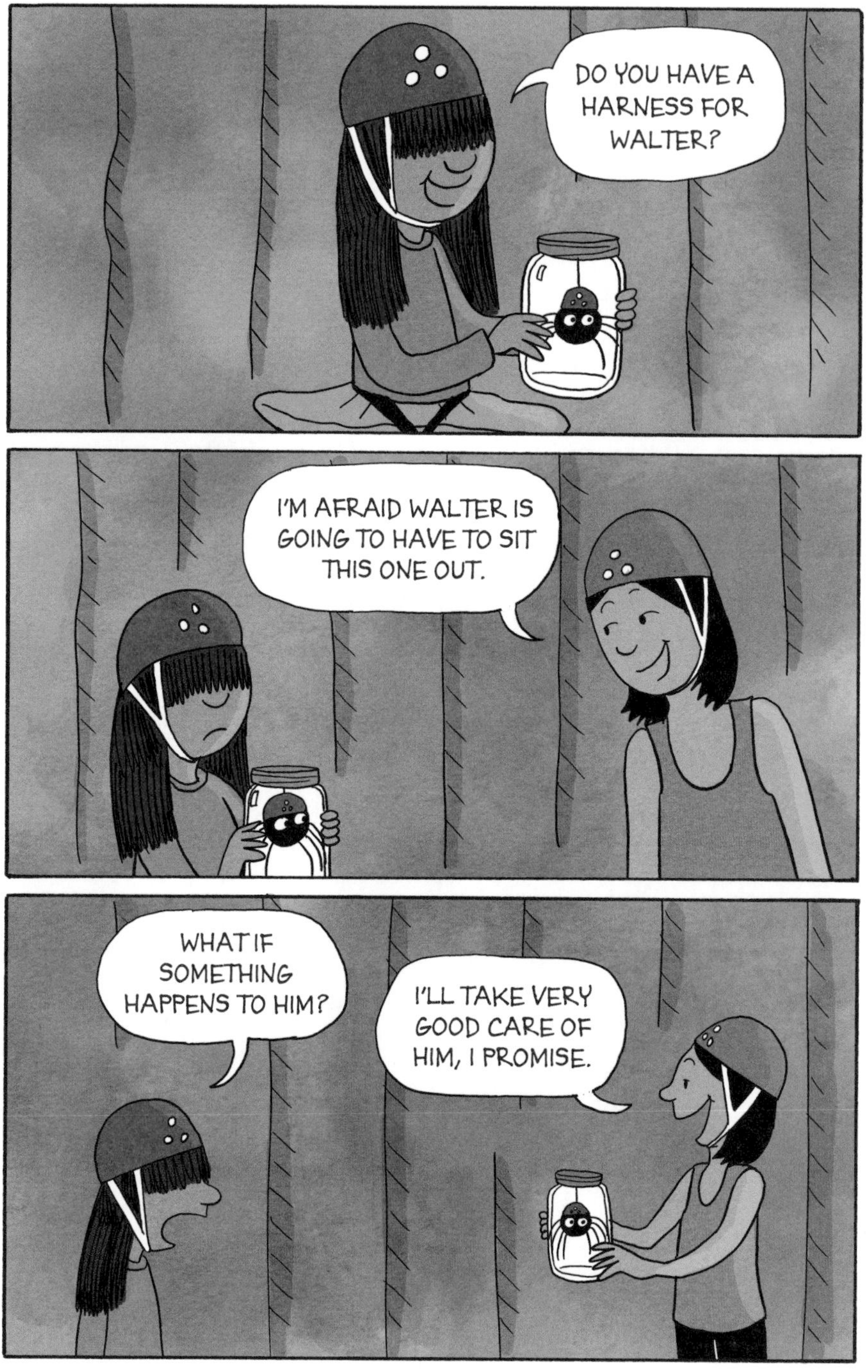
DO YOU HAVE A HARNESS FOR WALTER?
I'M AFRAID WALTER IS GOING TO HAVE TO SIT THIS ONE OUT.
WHAT IF SOMETHING HAPPENS TO HIM?
I'LL TAKE VERY GOOD CARE OF HIM, I PROMISE.

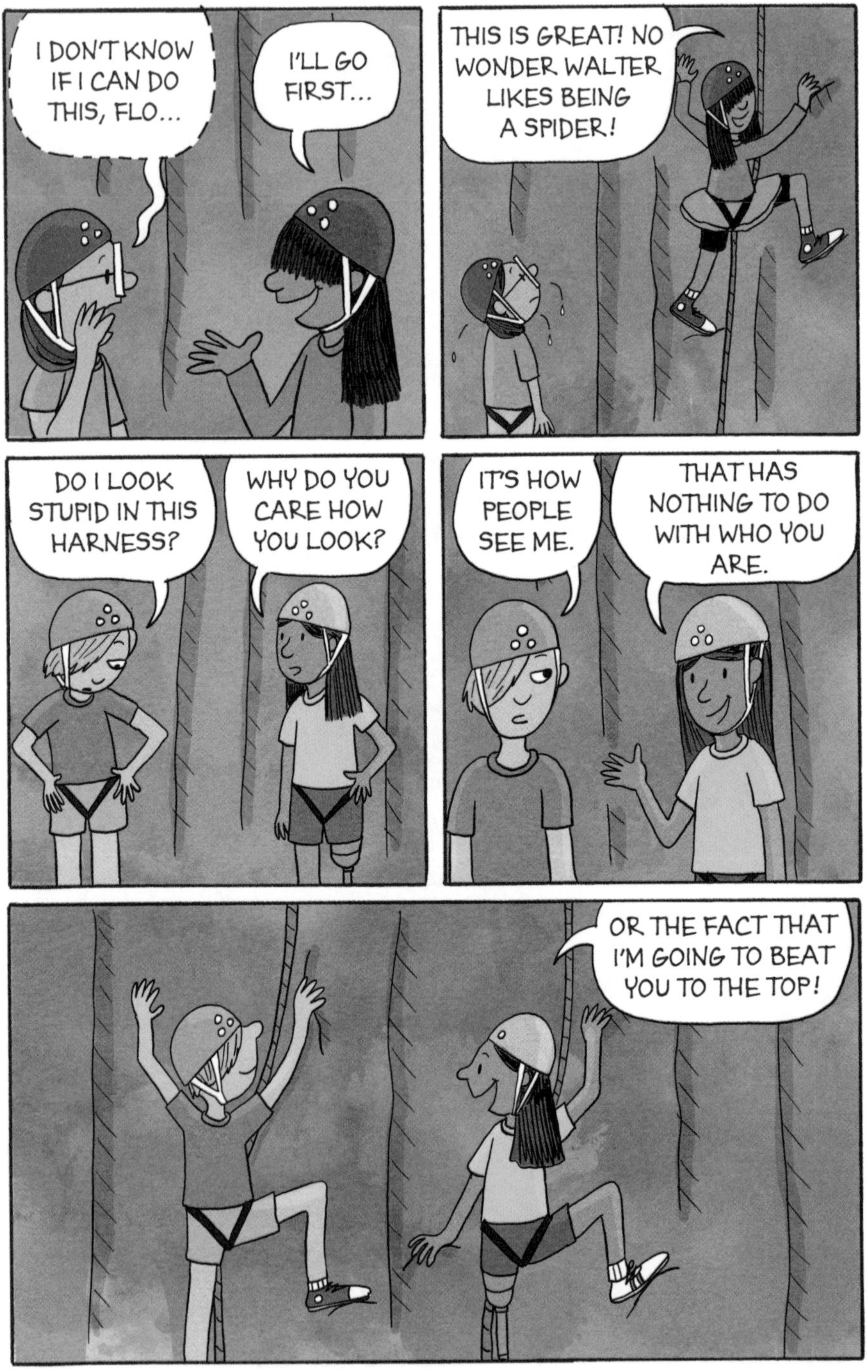
I DON'T KNOW IF I CAN DO THIS, FLO...
I'LL GO FIRST...
THIS IS GREAT! NO WONDER WALTER LIKES BEING A SPIDER!
DO I LOOK STUPID IN THIS HARNESS?
WHY DO YOU CARE HOW YOU LOOK?
IT'S HOW PEOPLE SEE ME.
THAT HAS NOTHING TO DO WITH WHO YOU ARE.
OR THE FACT THAT I'M GOING TO BEAT YOU TO THE TOP!

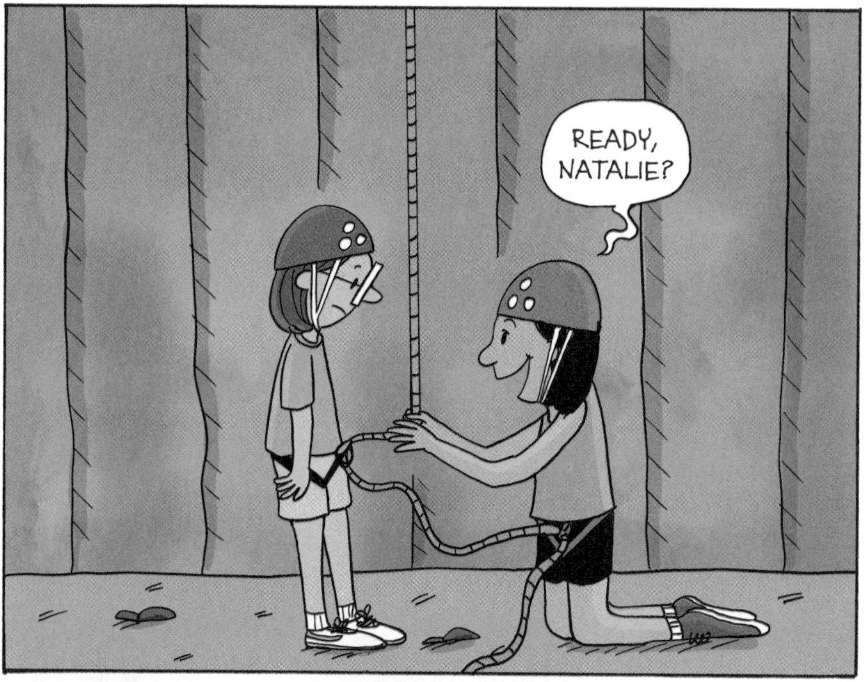
READY, NATALIE?

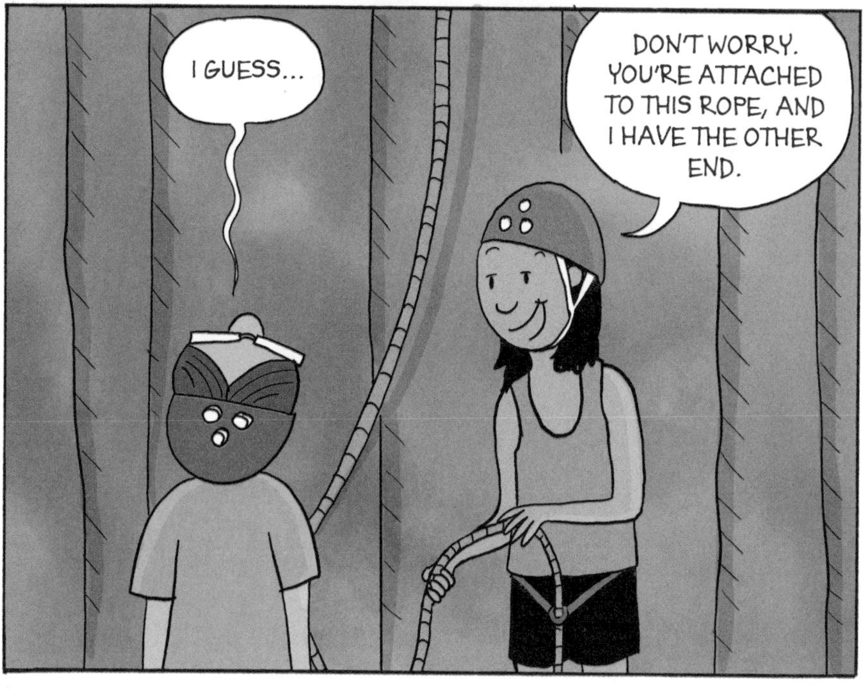
I GUESS...
DON'T WORRY. YOU'RE ATTACHED TO THIS ROPE, AND I HAVE THE OTHER END.

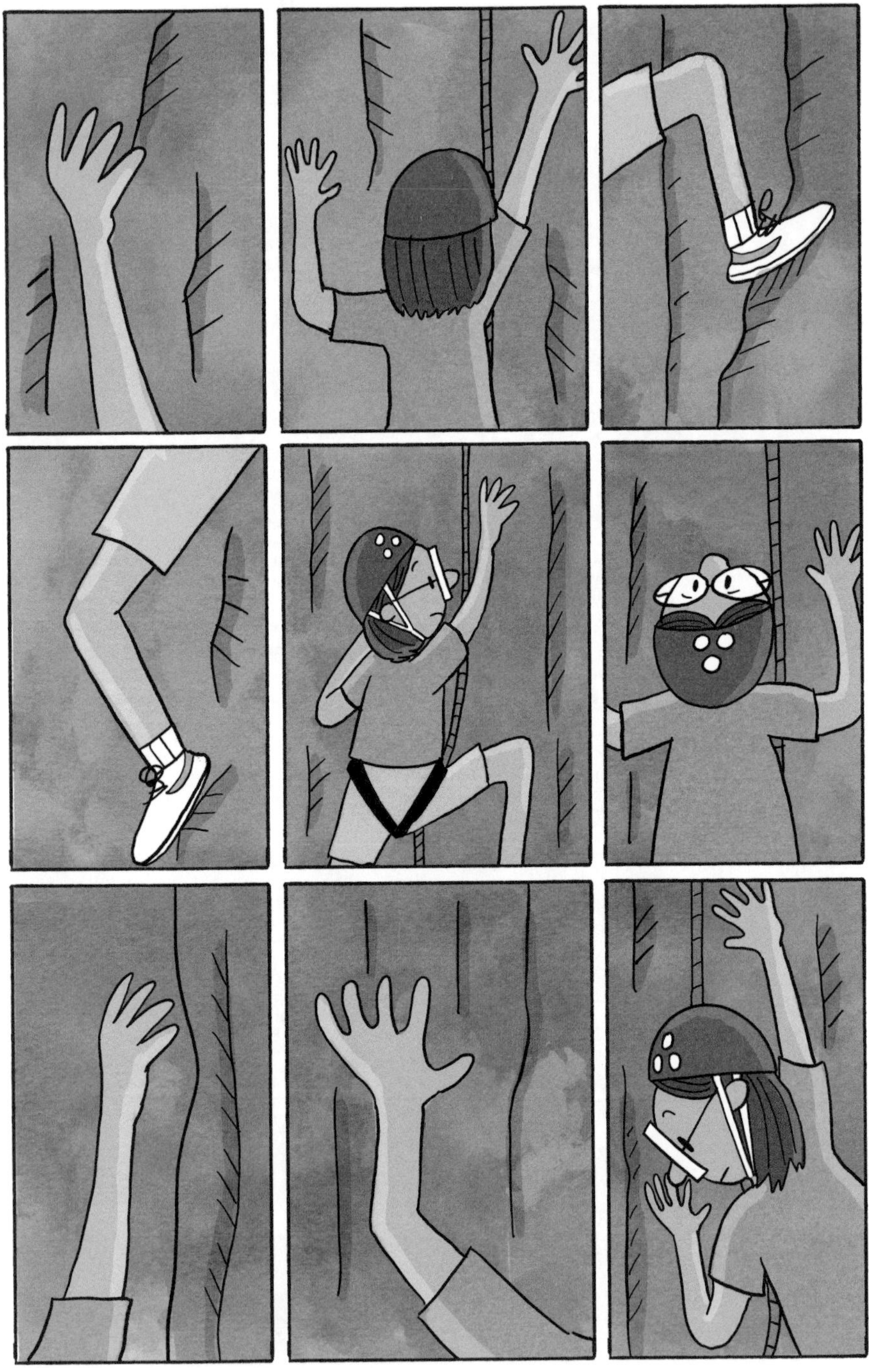

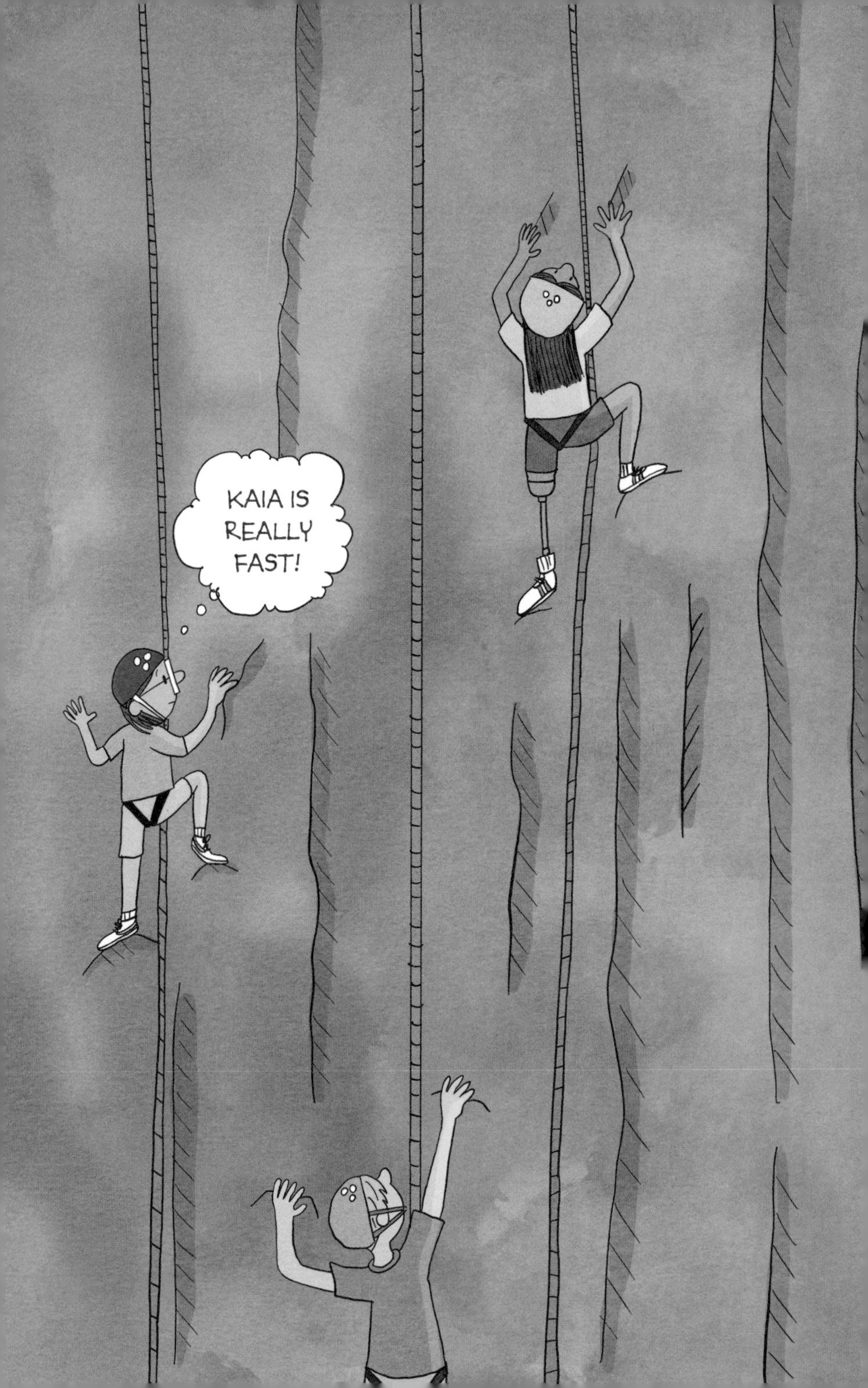
KAIA IS REALLY FAST!

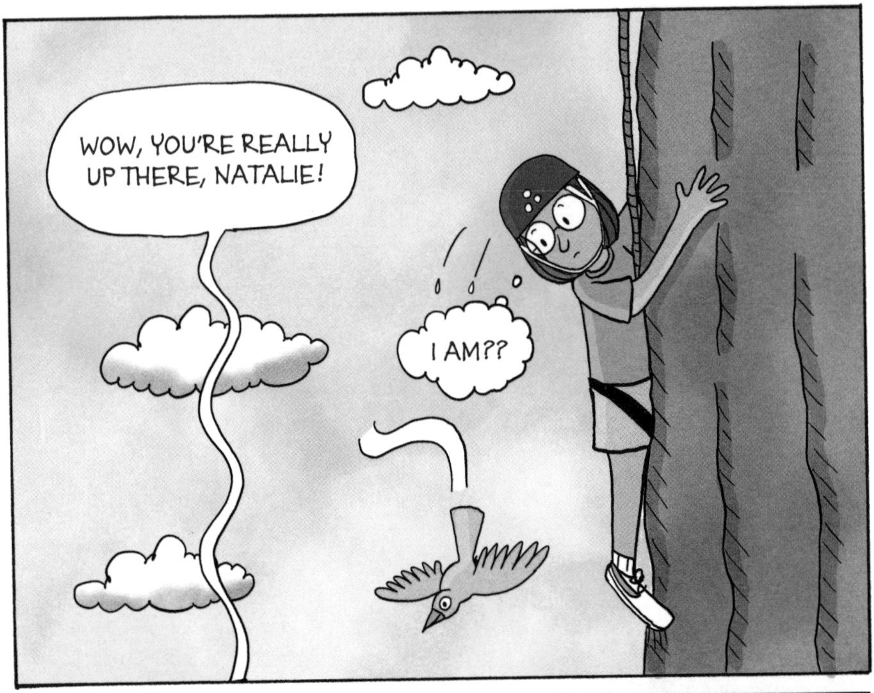
WOW, YOU'RE REALLY UP THERE, NATALIE!
I AM??

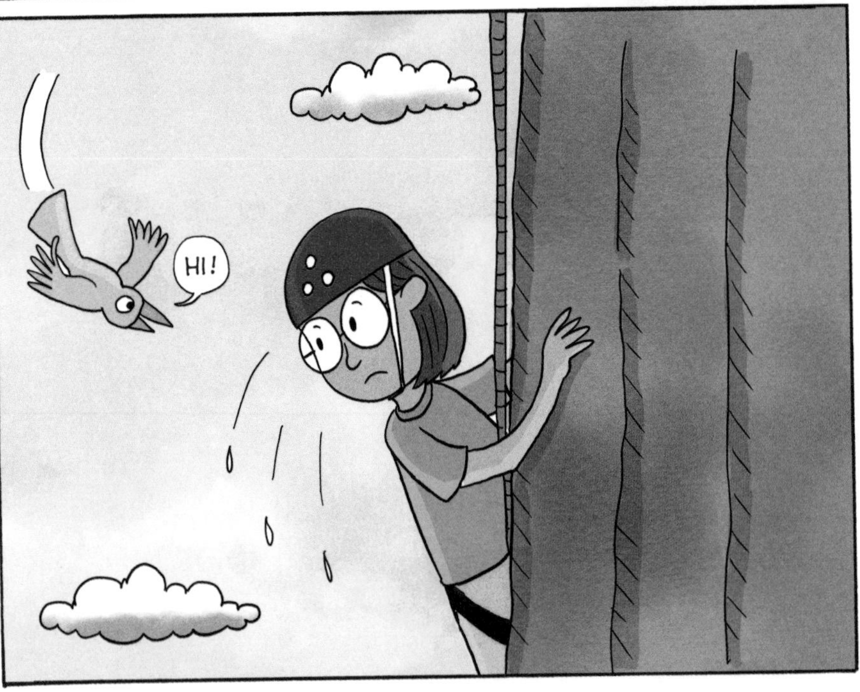
HI!

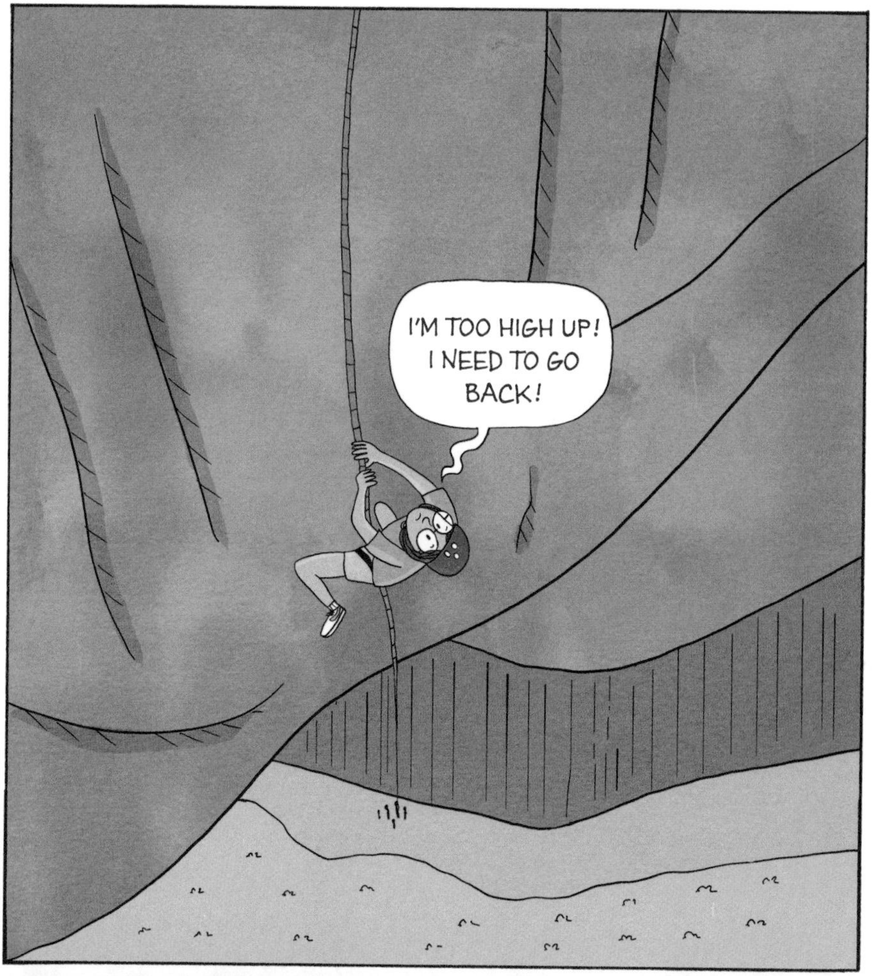
I'M TOO HIGH UP! I NEED TO GO BACK!

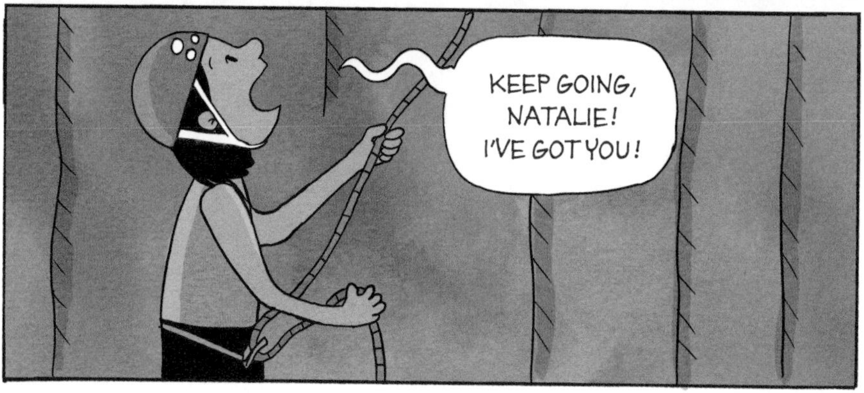
KEEP GOING, NATALIE! I'VE GOT YOU!

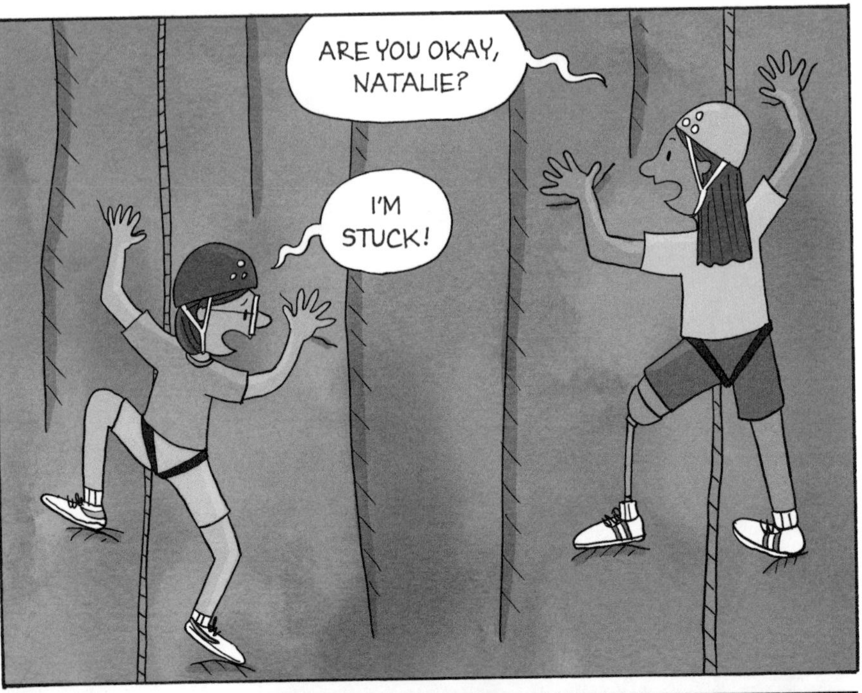
ARE YOU OKAY, NATALIE?
I'M STUCK!

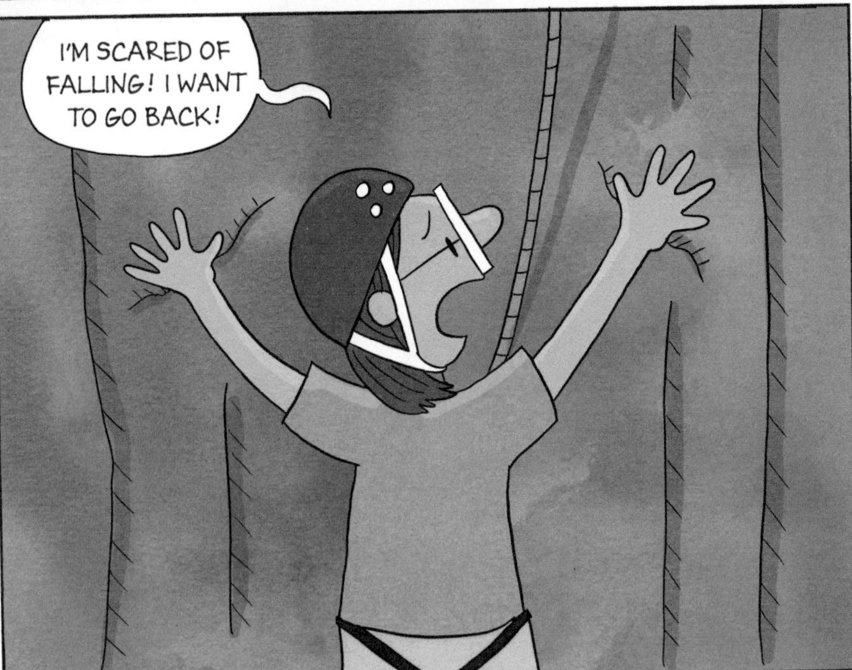
I'M SCARED OF FALLING! I WANT TO GO BACK!

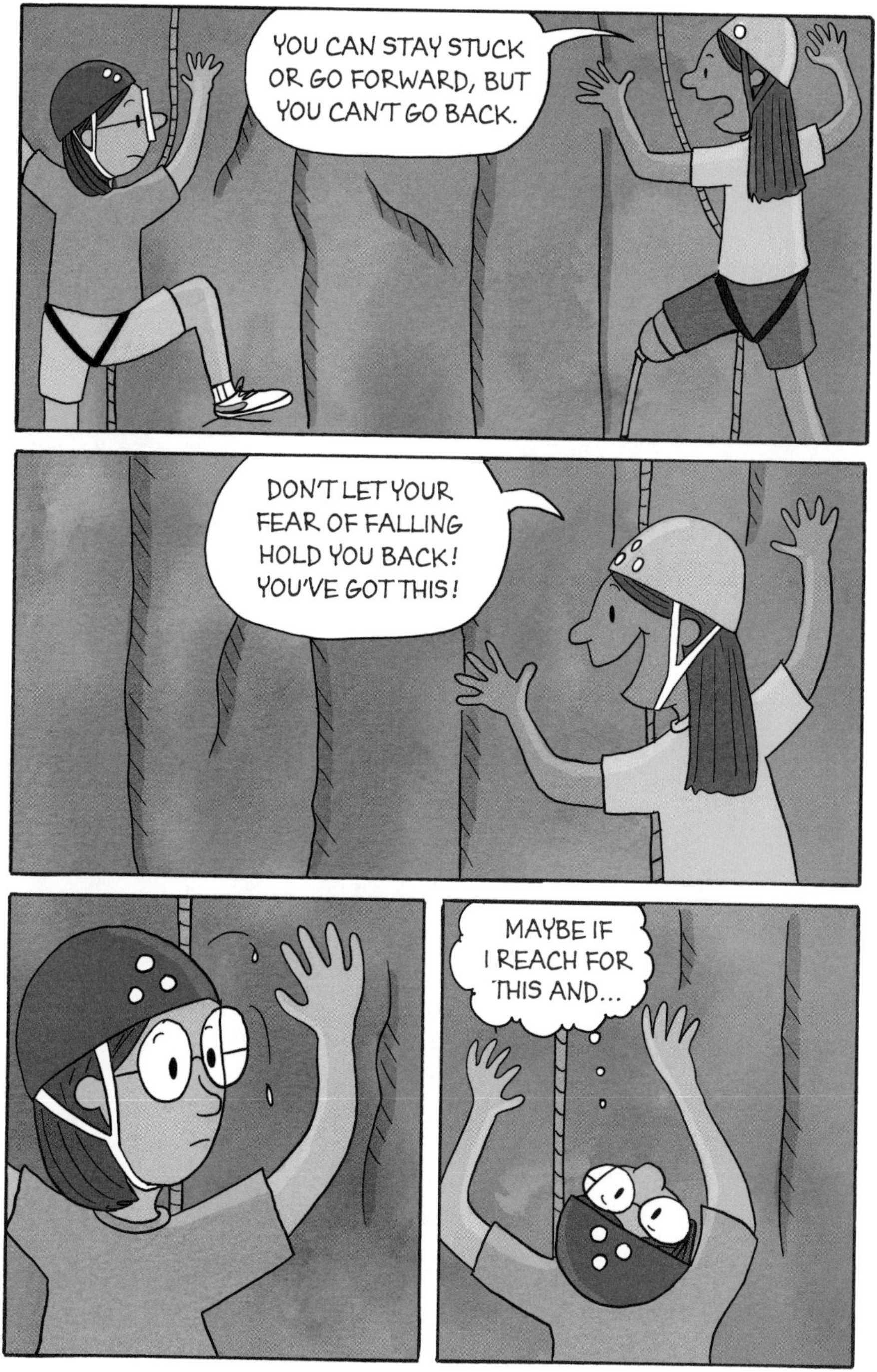
YOU CAN STAY STUCK OR GO FORWARD, BUT YOU CAN'T GO BACK.
DON'T LET YOUR FEAR OF FALLING HOLD YOU BACK! YOU'VE GOT THIS!
MAYBE IF I REACH FOR THIS AND...

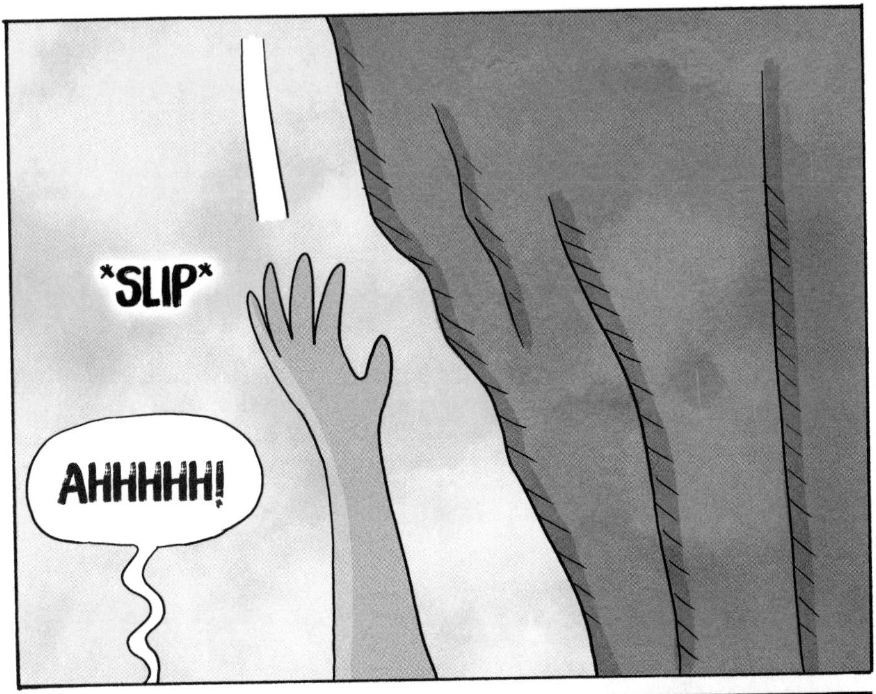
SLIP
AHHHHH!

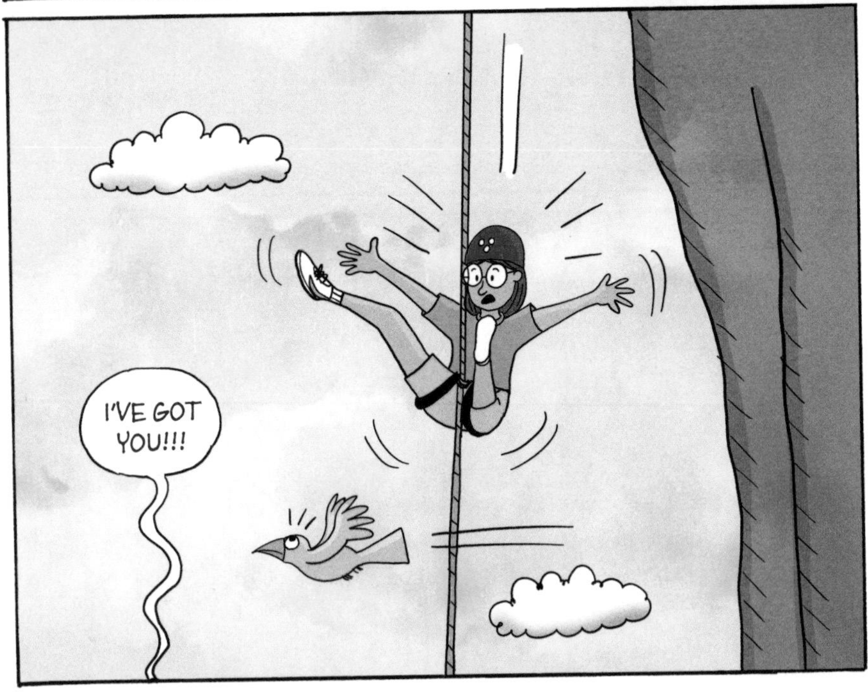
I'VE GOT YOU!!!

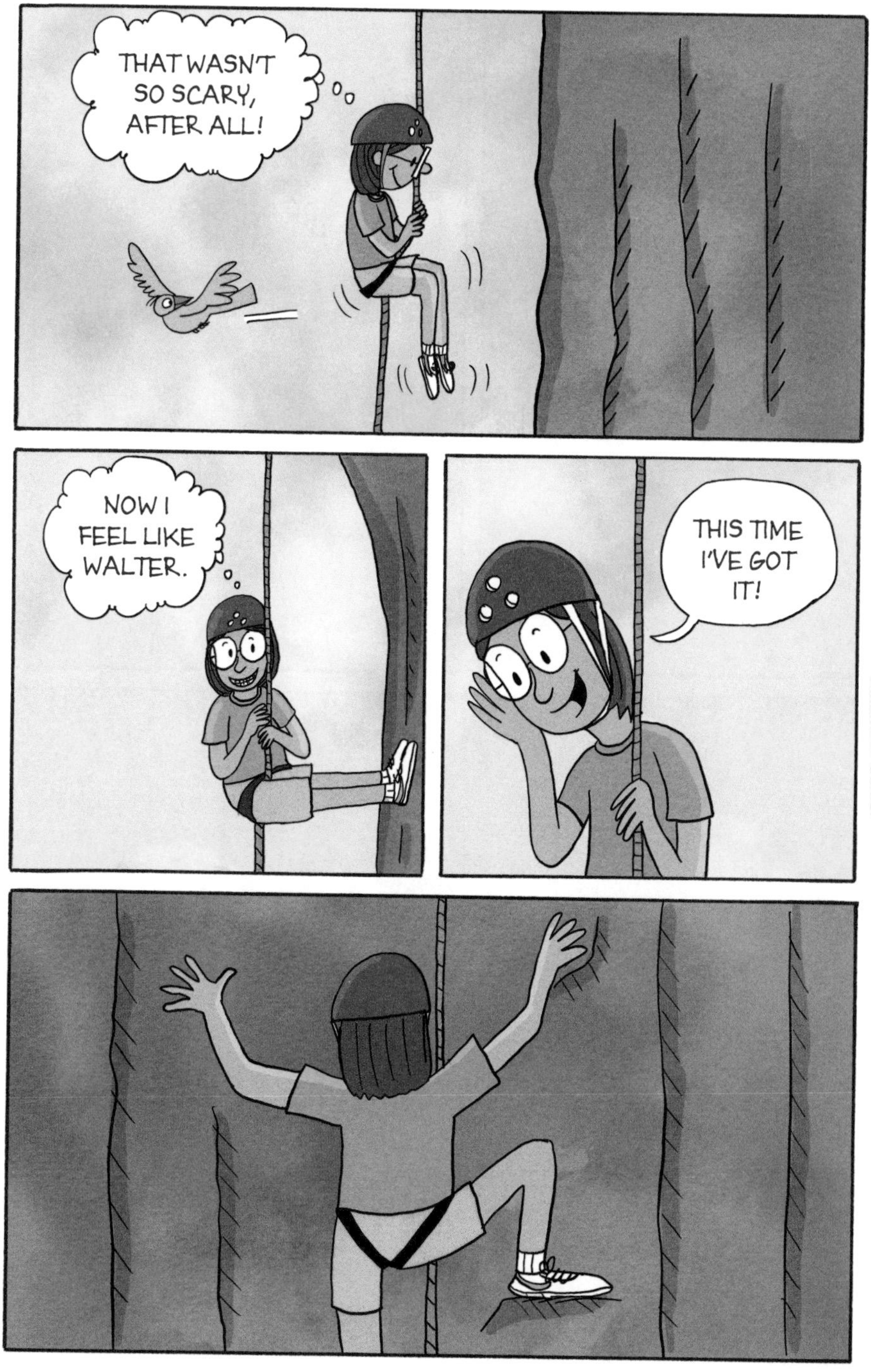
THAT WASN'T SO SCARY, AFTER ALL!
NOW I FEEL LIKE WALTER.
THIS TIME I'VE GOT IT!

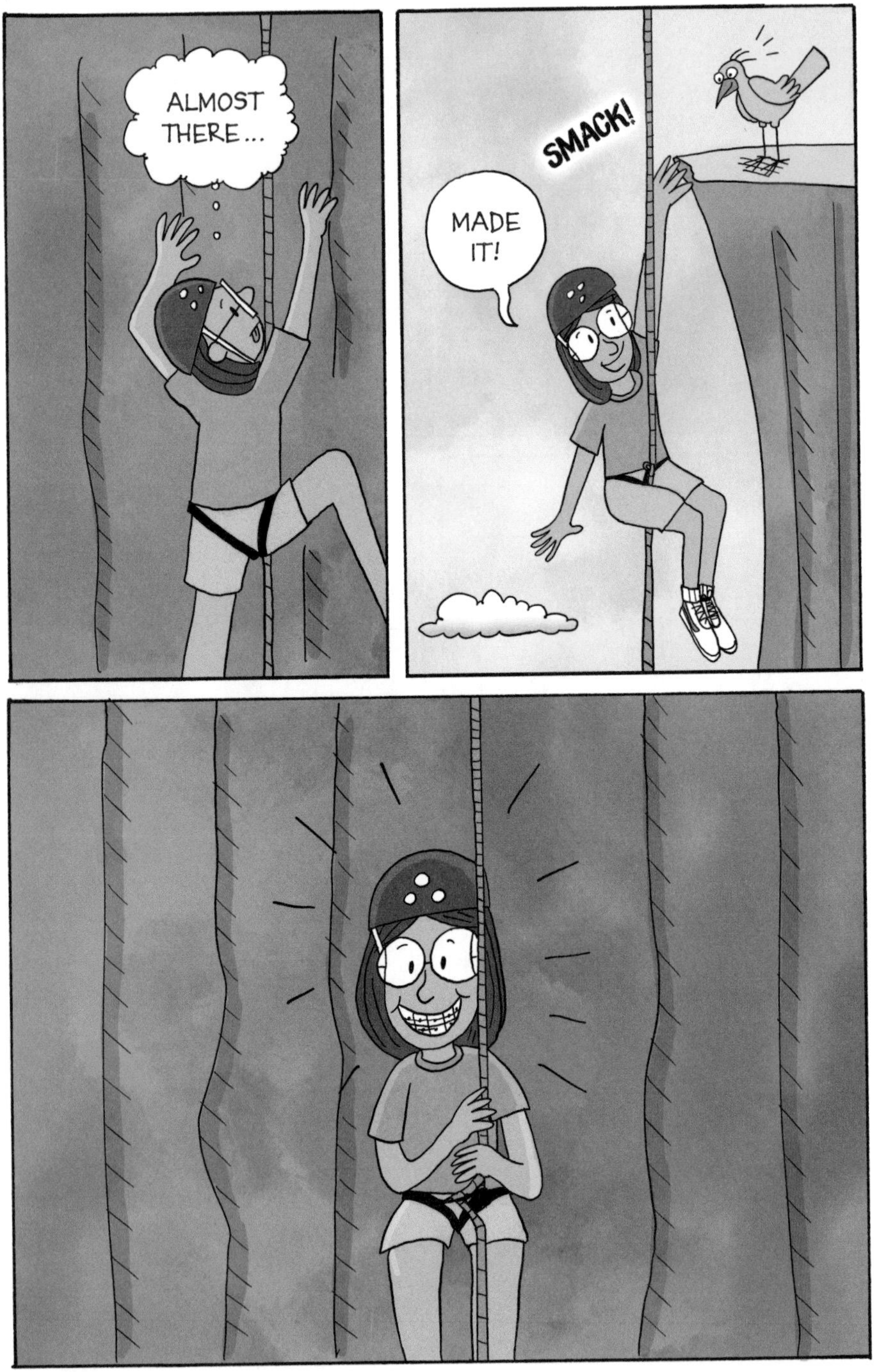
ALMOST THERE...
SMACK!
MADE IT!

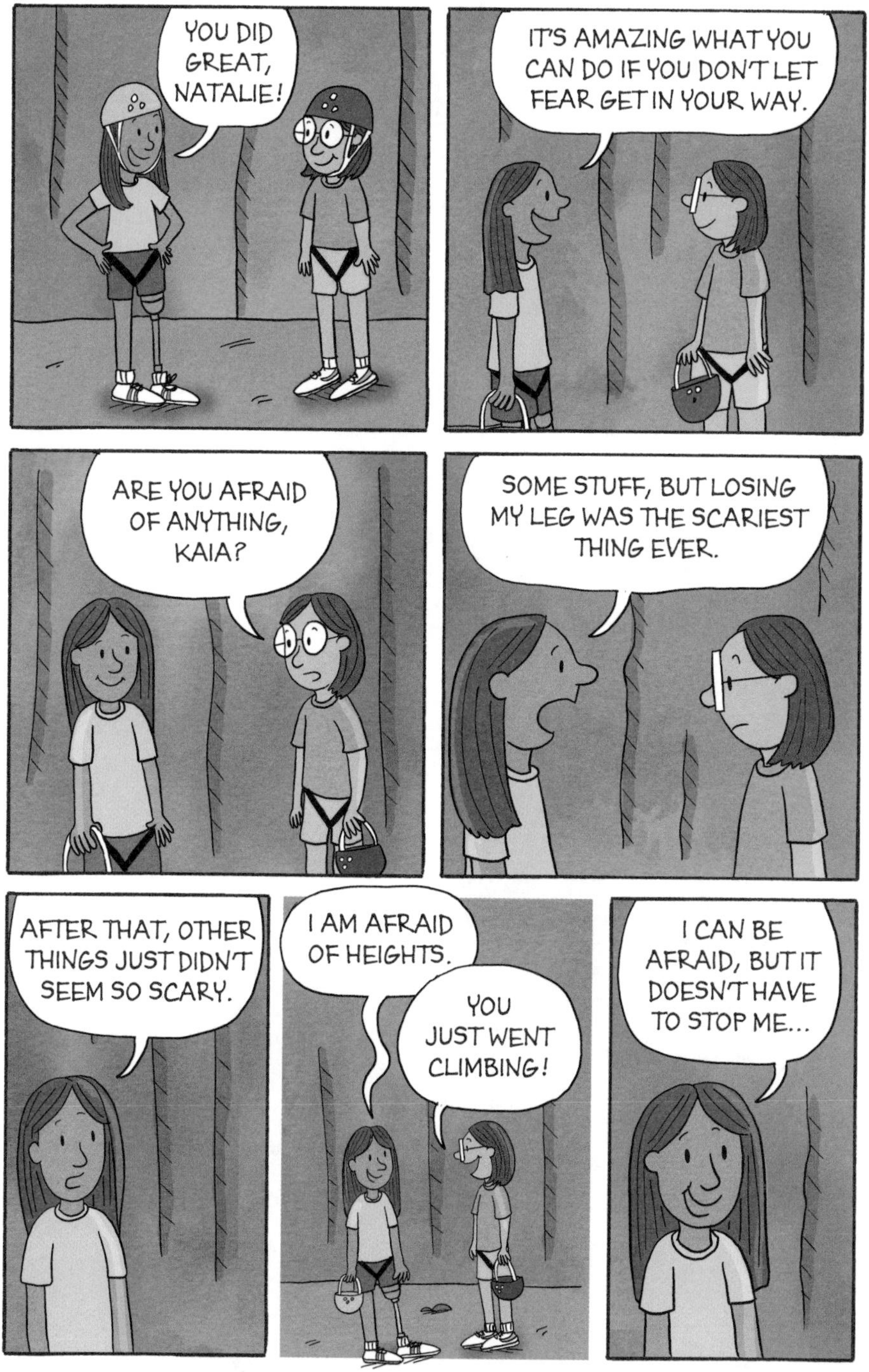
YOU DID GREAT, NATALIE!
IT'S AMAZING WHAT YOU CAN DO IF YOU DON'T LET FEAR GET IN YOUR WAY.
ARE YOU AFRAID OF ANYTHING, KAIA?
SOME STUFF, BUT LOSING MY LEG WAS THE SCARIEST THING EVER.
AFTER THAT, OTHER THINGS JUST DIDN'T SEEM SO SCARY.
I AM AFRAID OF HEIGHTS.
YOU JUST WENT CLIMBING!
I CAN BE AFRAID, BUT IT DOESN'T HAVE TO STOP ME...

FEAR

HIDES IN ALL KINDS OF PLACES...

UNDER THE BED

IN THE CLOSET

IN BASEMENTS

RIGHT BEHIND YOU...

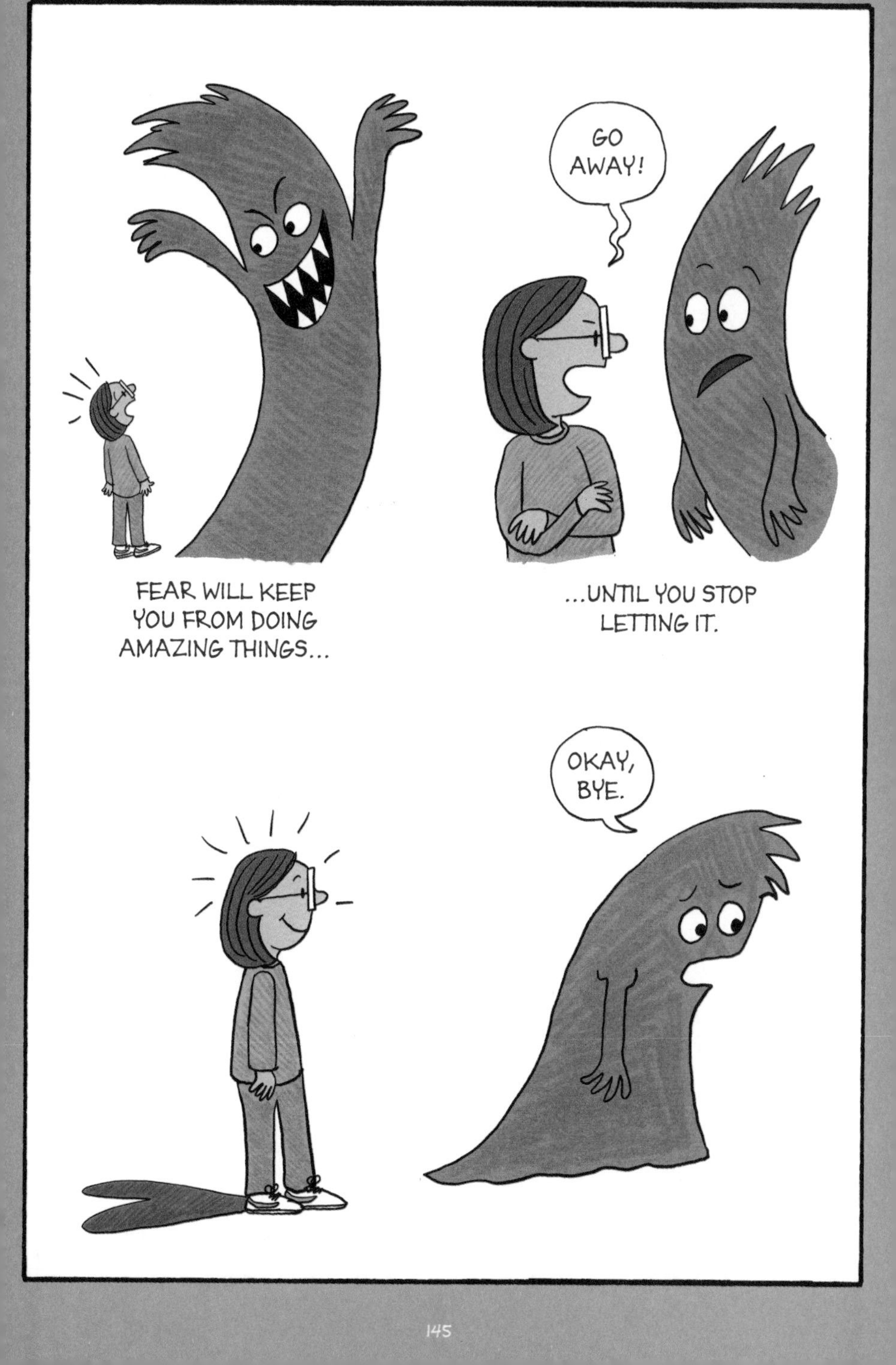
FEAR WILL KEEP YOU FROM DOING AMAZING THINGS...
GO AWAY!
...UNTIL YOU STOP LETTING IT.
OKAY, BYE.

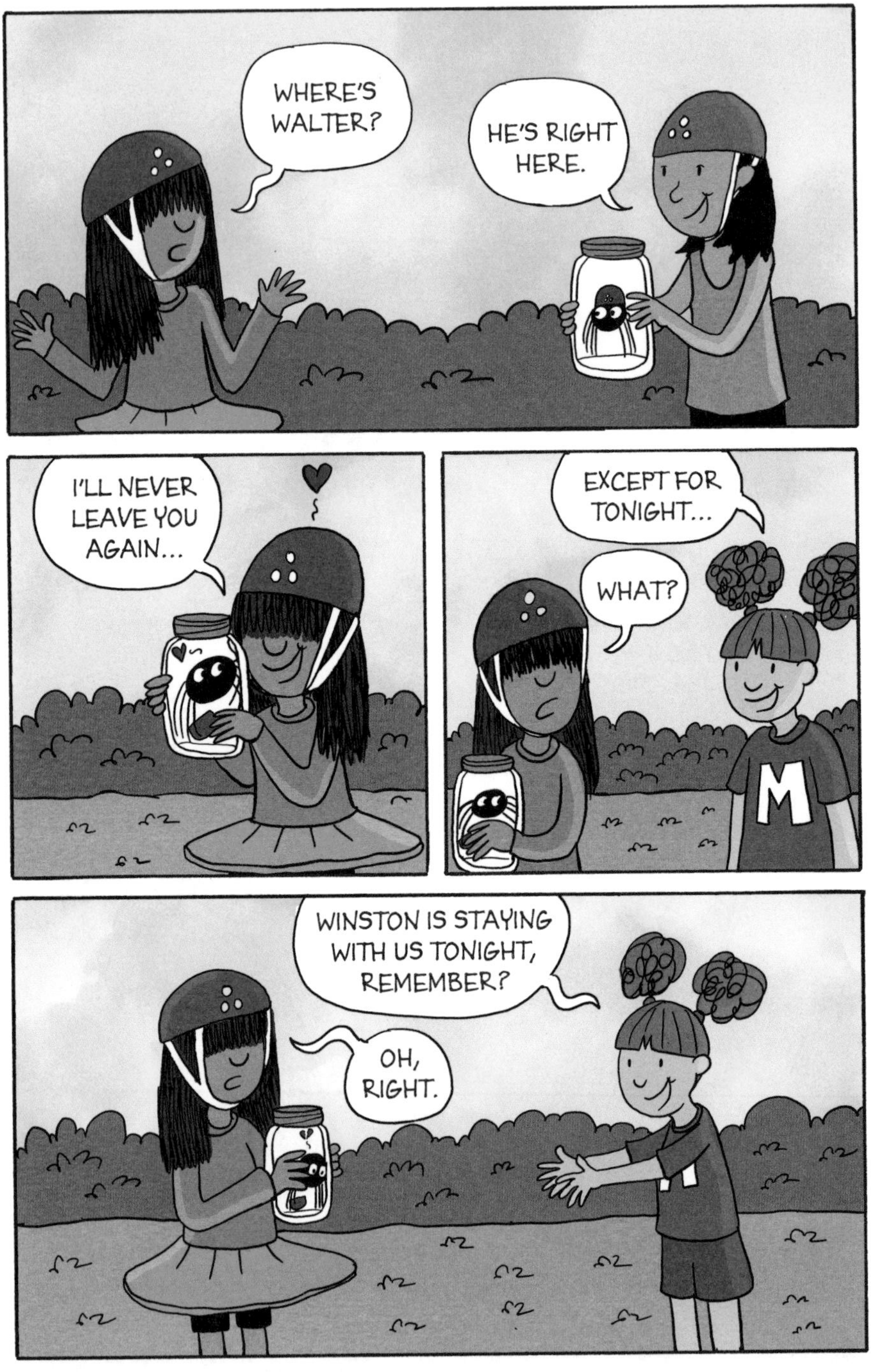
WHERE'S WALTER?
HE'S RIGHT HERE.
I'LL NEVER LEAVE YOU AGAIN...
EXCEPT FOR TONIGHT...
WHAT?
M
WINSTON IS STAYING WITH US TONIGHT, REMEMBER?
OH, RIGHT.

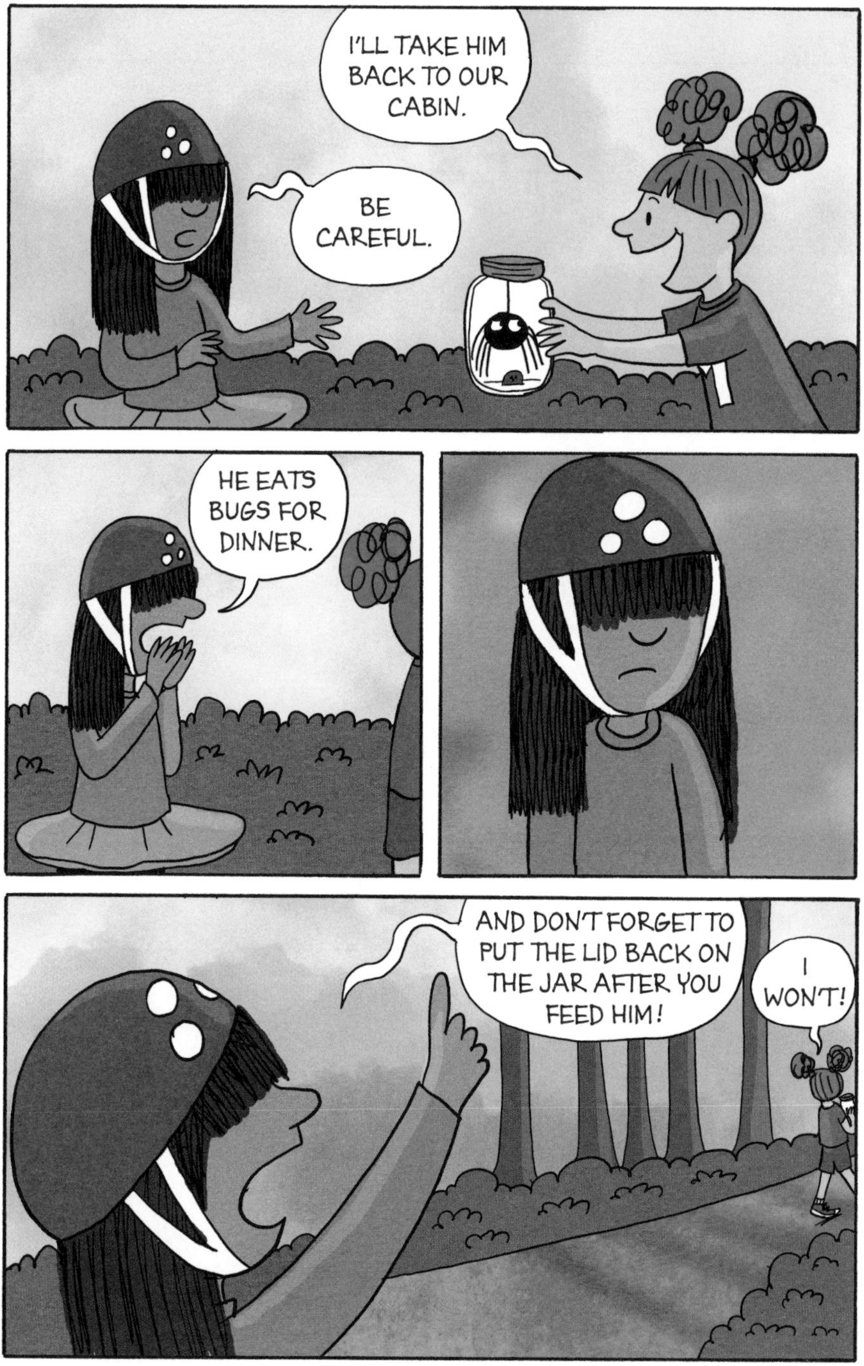
I'LL TAKE HIM BACK TO OUR CABIN.
BE CAREFUL.
HE EATS BUGS FOR DINNER.
AND DON'T FORGET TO PUT THE LID BACK ON THE JAR AFTER YOU FEED HIM!
I WON'T!

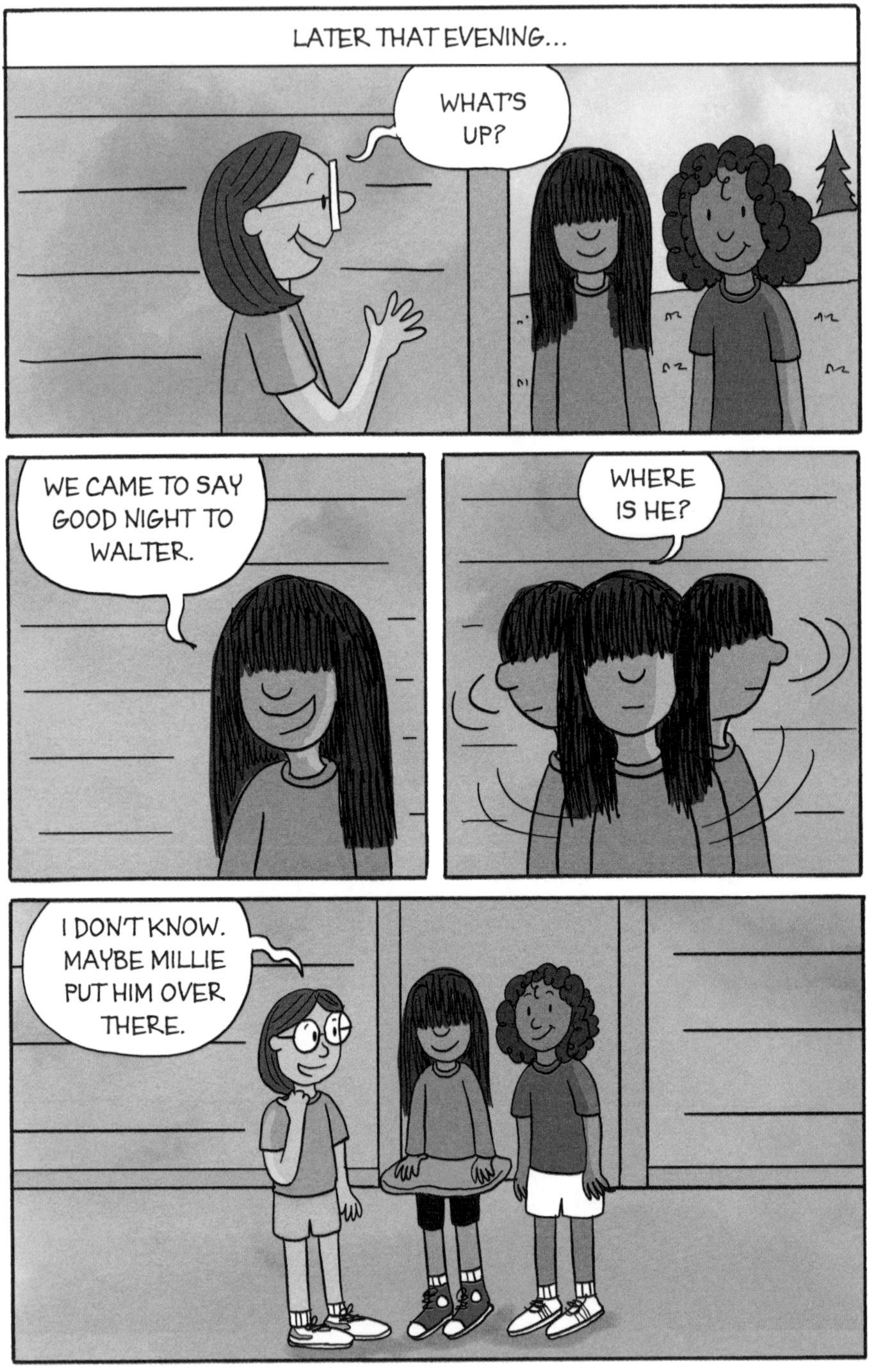
LATER THAT EVENING...
WHAT'S UP?
WE CAME TO SAY GOOD NIGHT TO WALTER.
WHERE IS HE?
I DON'T KNOW. MAYBE MILLIE PUT HIM OVER THERE.

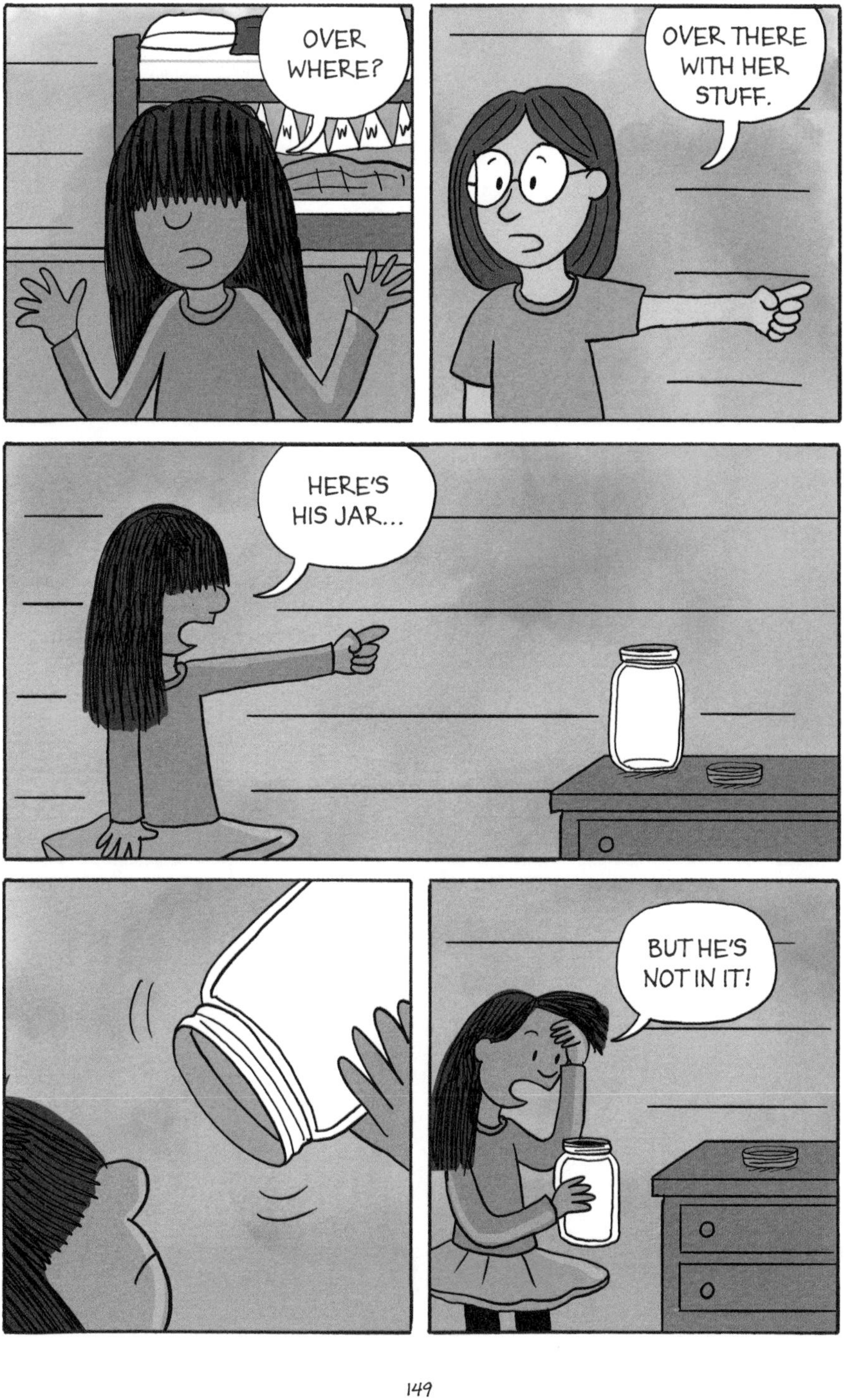
OVER WHERE?
OVER THERE WITH HER STUFF.
HERE'S HIS JAR...
BUT HE'S NOT IN IT!

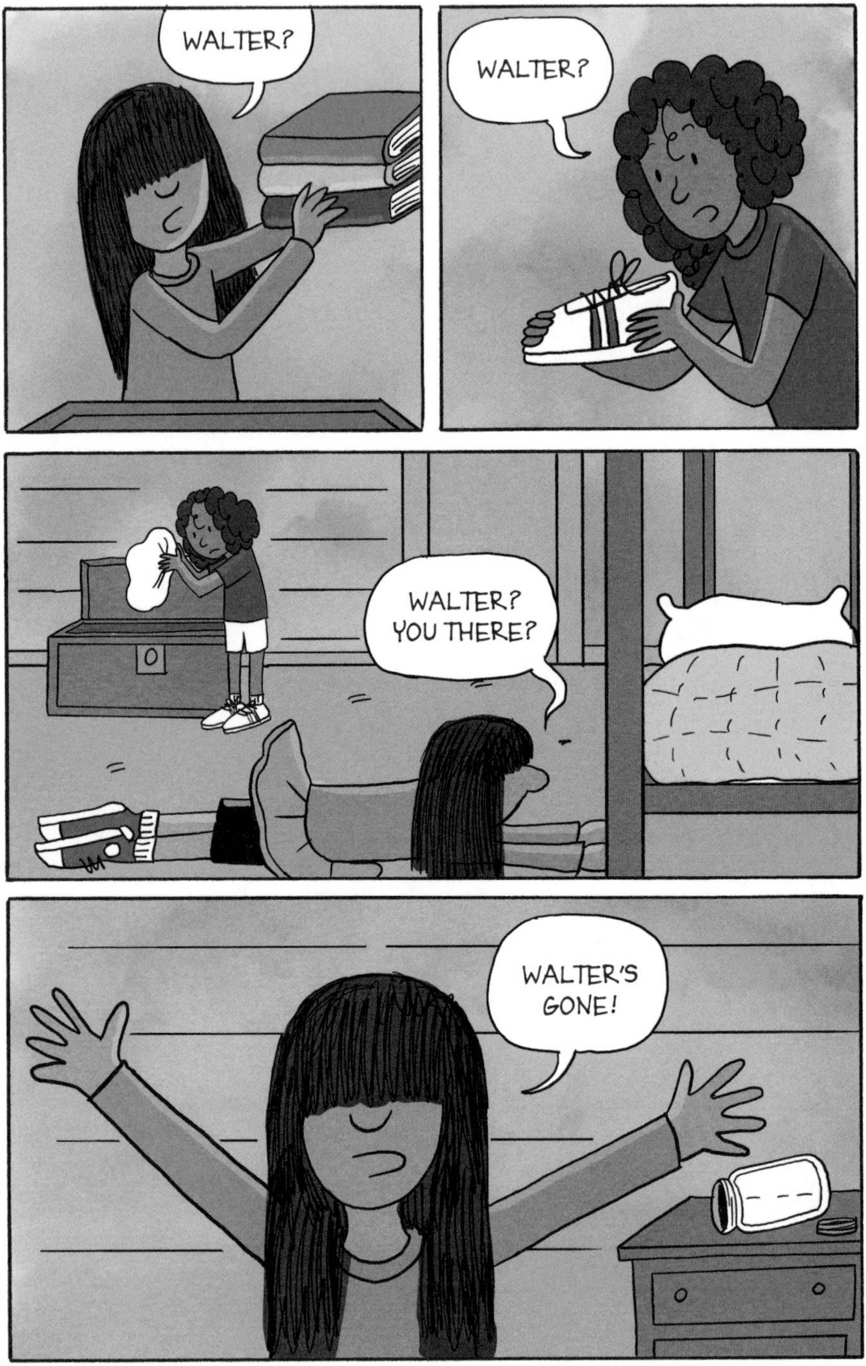
WALTER?
WALTER?
WALTER?
YOU THERE?
WALTER'S
GONE!

CHAPTER 10
OPERATION RESCUE

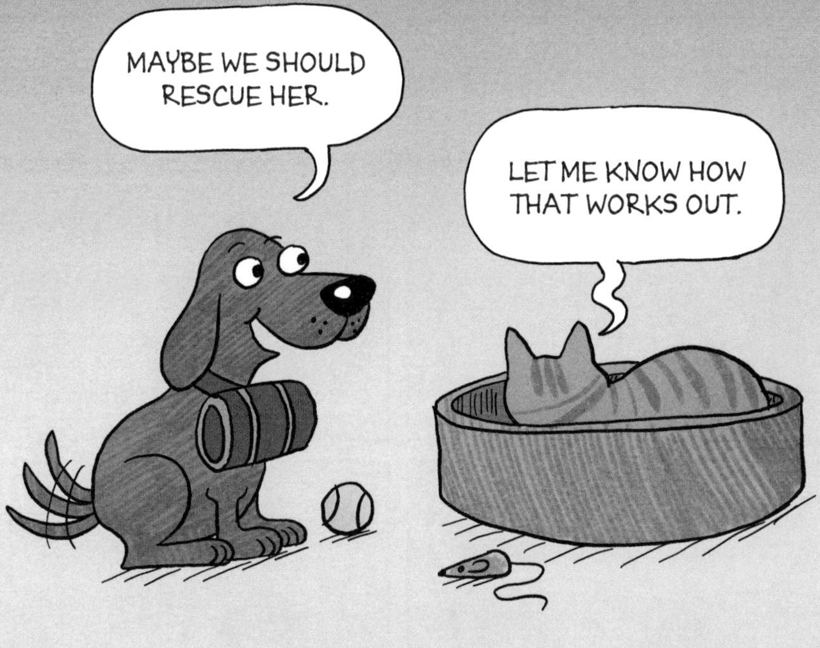
MAYBE WE SHOULD RESCUE HER.
LET ME KNOW HOW THAT WORKS OUT.

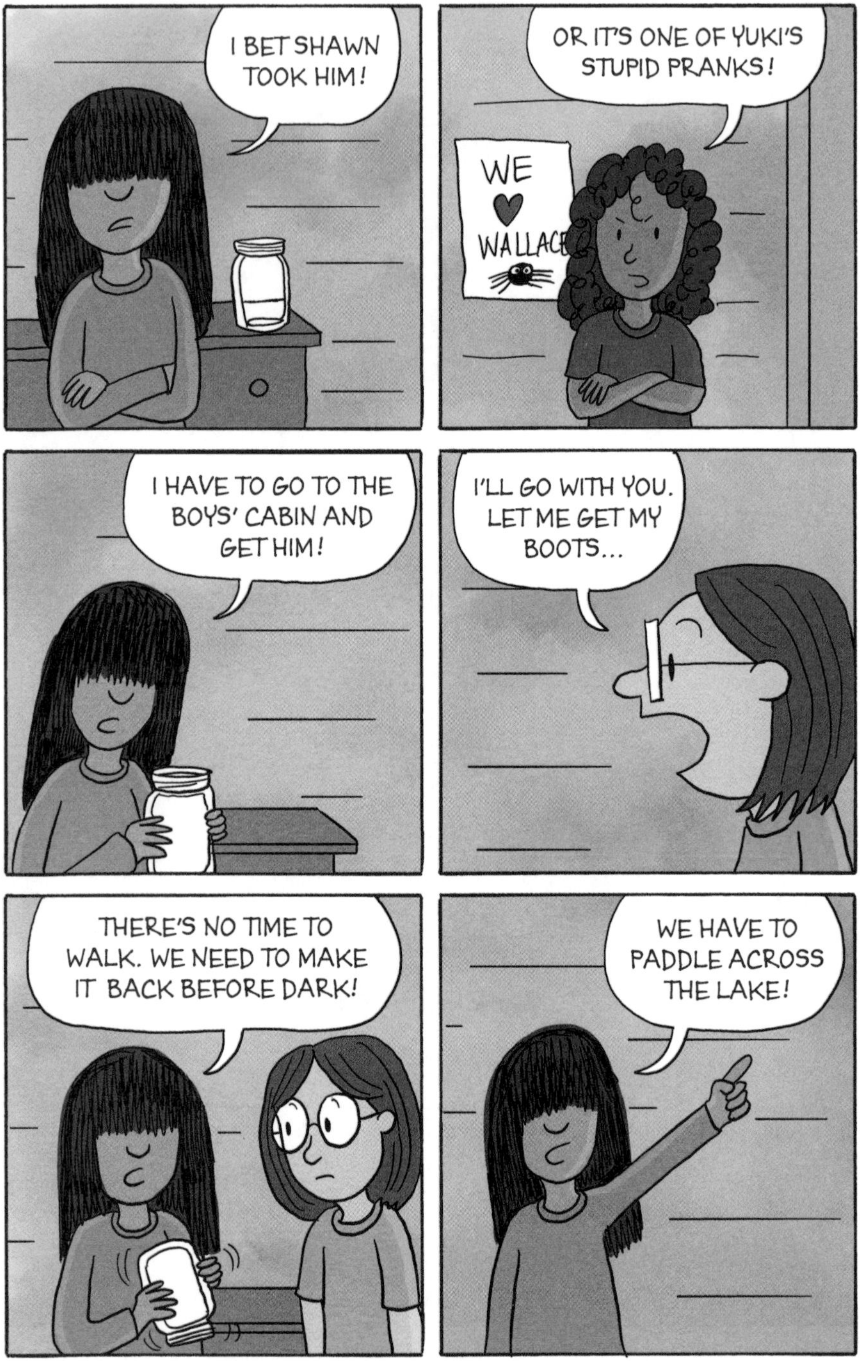
I BET SHAWN TOOK HIM!
OR IT'S ONE OF YUKI'S STUPID PRANKS!
WE ♥ WALLACE
I HAVE TO GO TO THE BOYS' CABIN AND GET HIM!
I'LL GO WITH YOU. LET ME GET MY BOOTS...
THERE'S NO TIME TO WALK. WE NEED TO MAKE IT BACK BEFORE DARK!
WE HAVE TO PADDLE ACROSS THE LAKE!

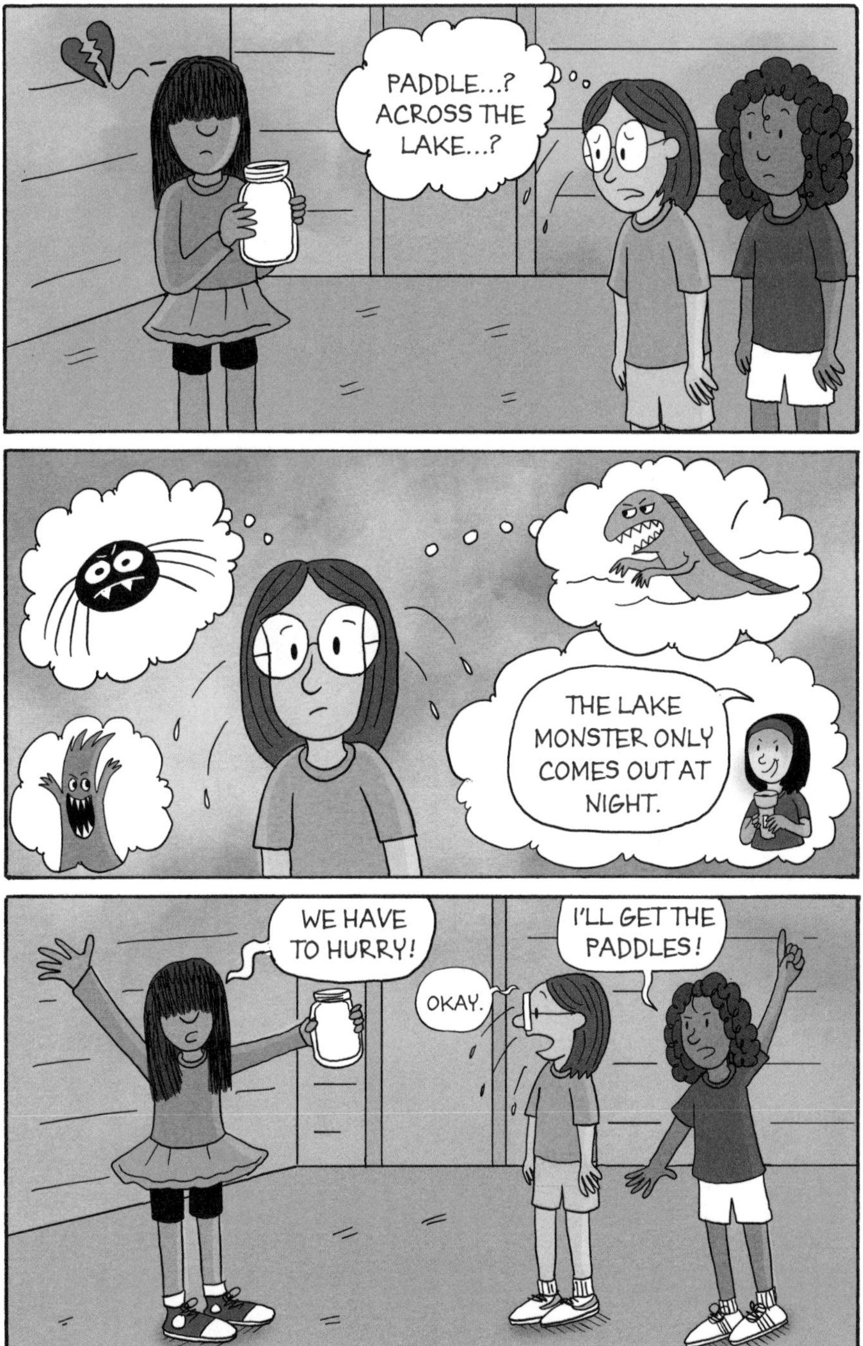
PADDLE...? ACROSS THE LAKE...?
THE LAKE MONSTER ONLY COMES OUT AT NIGHT.
WE HAVE TO HURRY!
OKAY.
I'LL GET THE PADDLES!

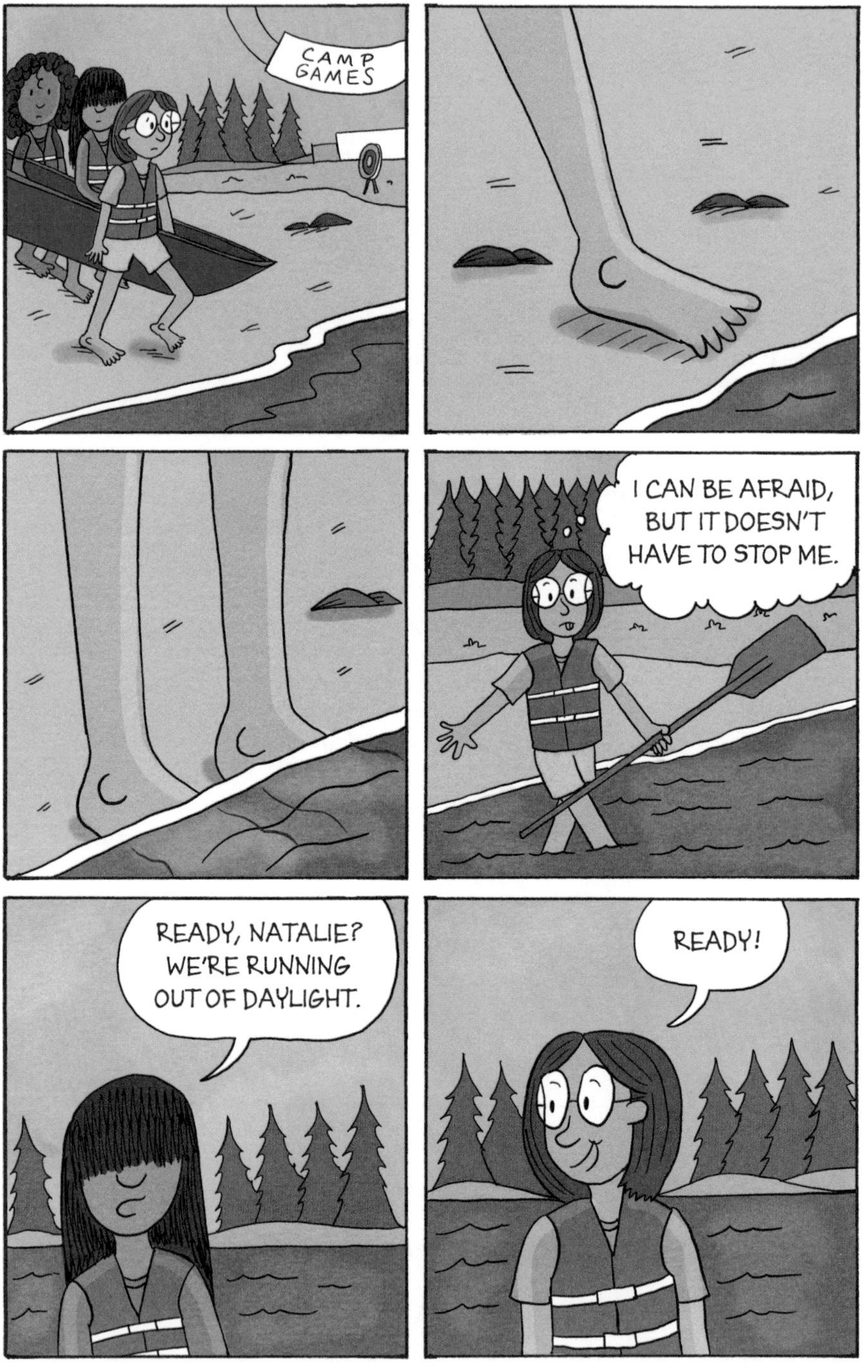
CAMP GAMES
I CAN BE AFRAID, BUT IT DOESN'T HAVE TO STOP ME.
READY, NATALIE? WE'RE RUNNING OUT OF DAYLIGHT.
READY!

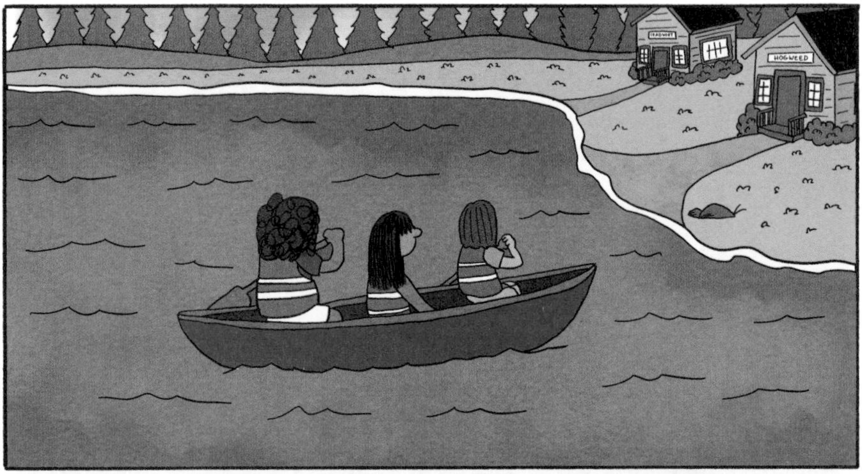
LEADWORT
HOGWEED

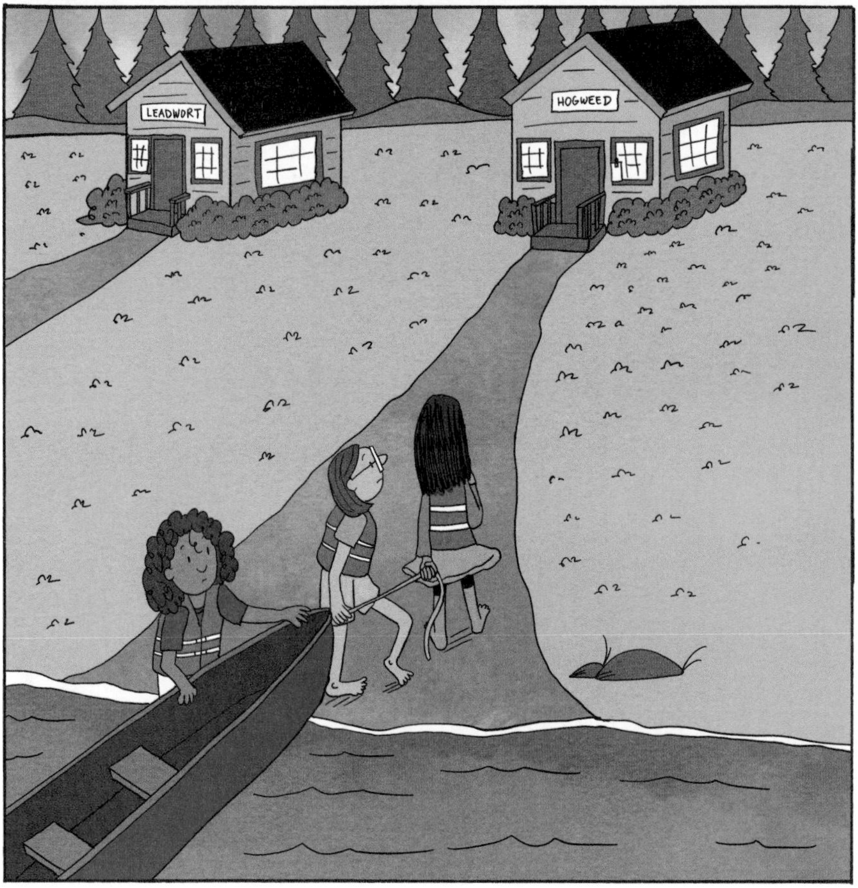
LEADWORT
HOGWEED

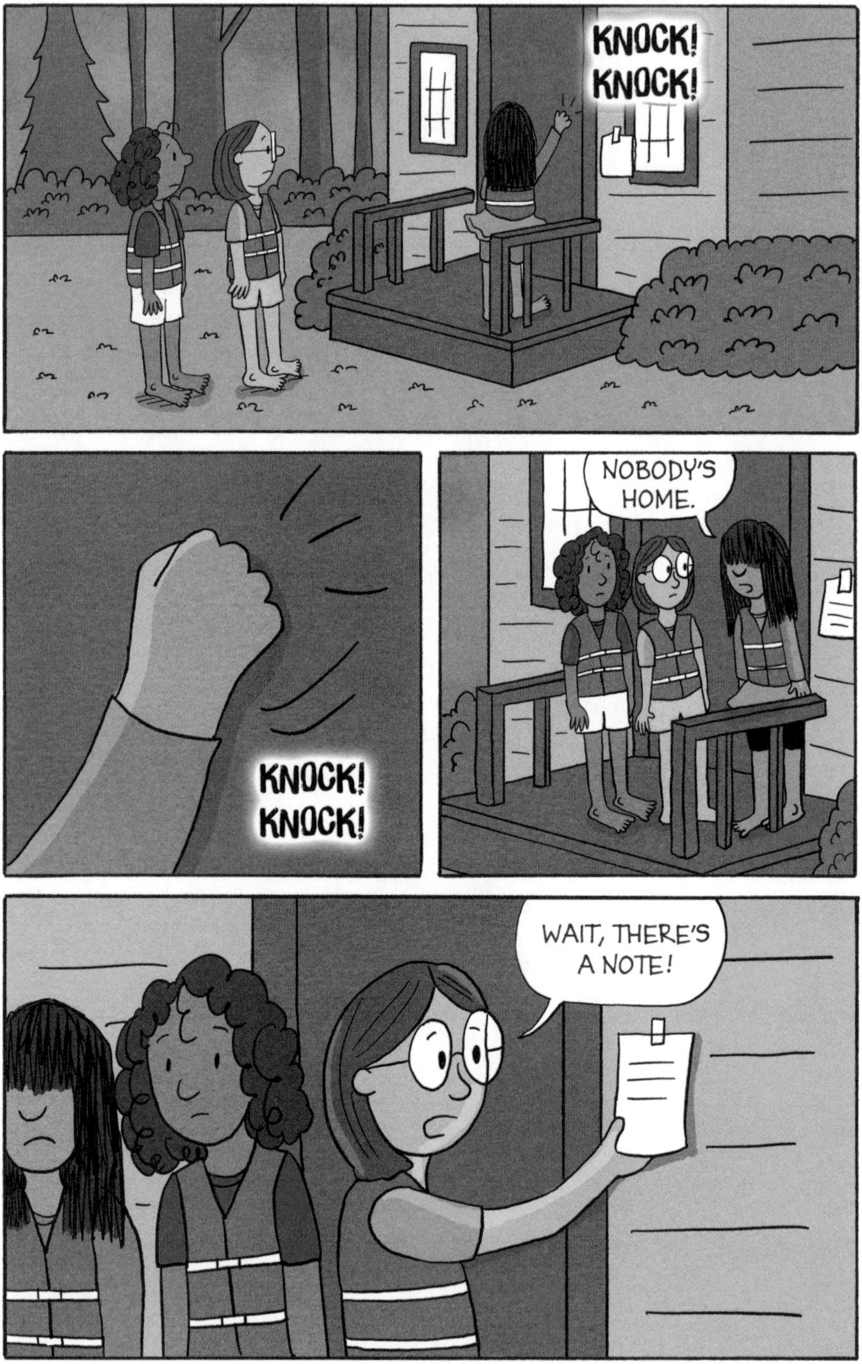
KNOCK! KNOCK!
KNOCK! KNOCK!
NOBODY'S HOME.
WAIT, THERE'S A NOTE!

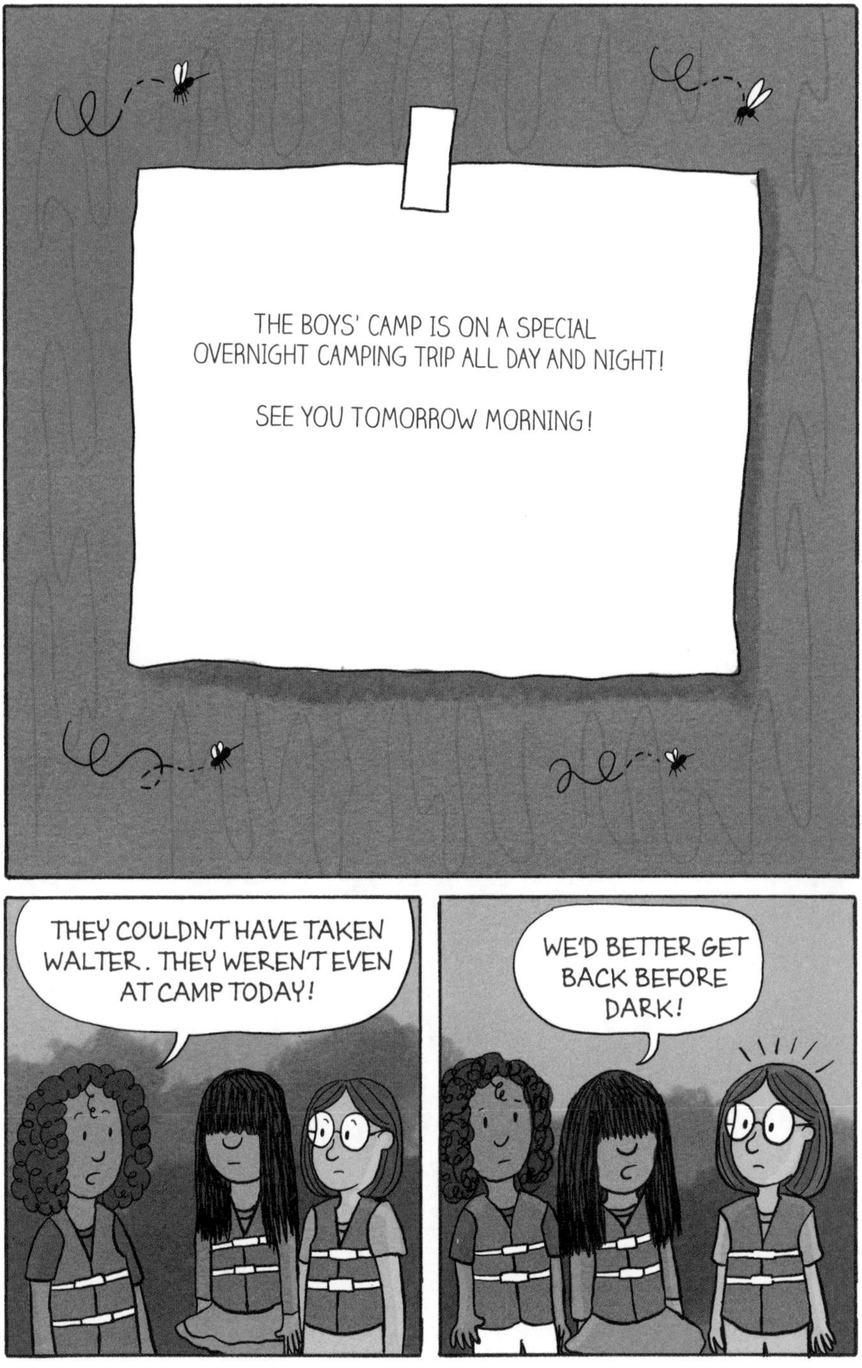
THE BOYS' CAMP IS ON A SPECIAL OVERNIGHT CAMPING TRIP ALL DAY AND NIGHT!
SEE YOU TOMORROW MORNING!
THEY COULDN'T HAVE TAKEN WALTER. THEY WEREN'T EVEN AT CAMP TODAY!
WE'D BETTER GET BACK BEFORE DARK!

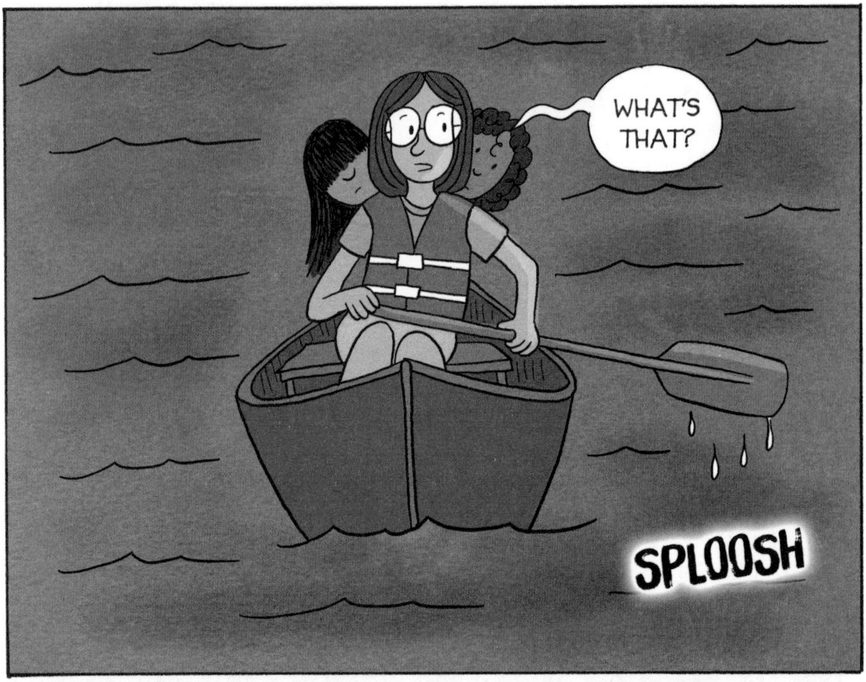
WHAT'S THAT?
SPLOOSH

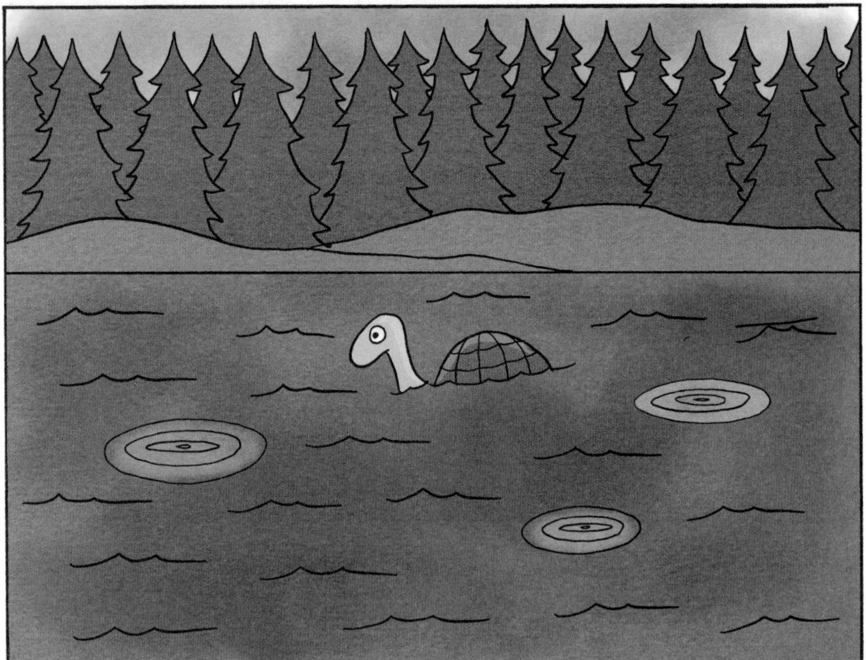

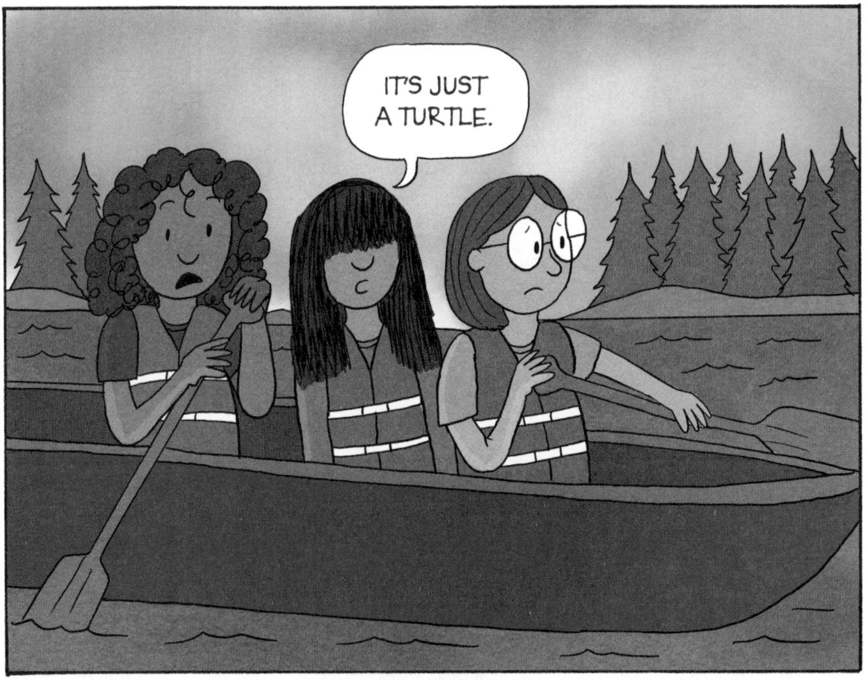
IT'S JUST A TURTLE.

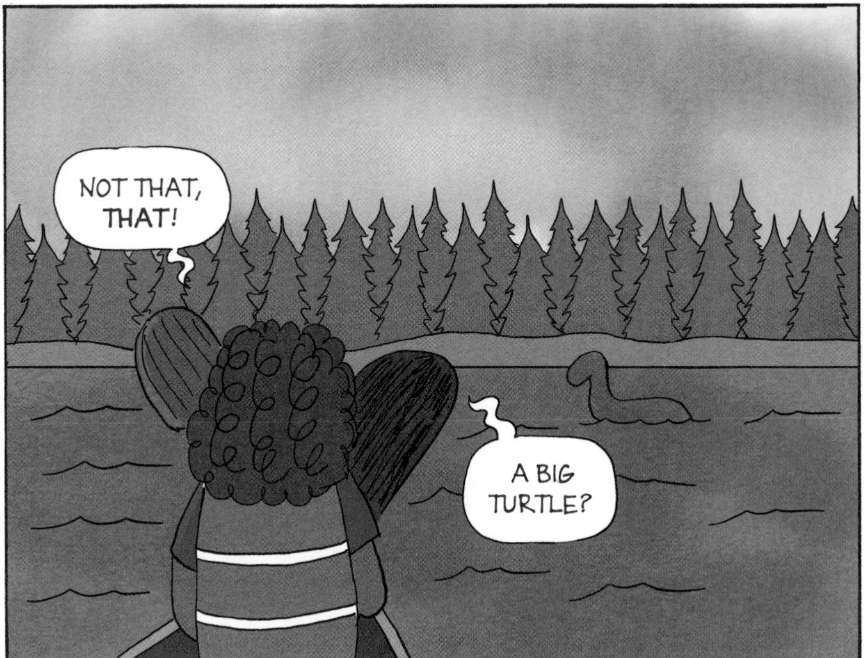
NOT THAT, THAT!
A BIG TURTLE?

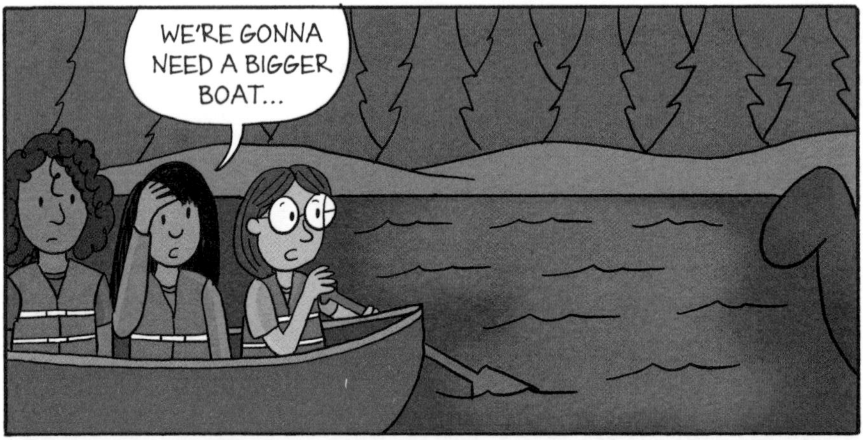
WE'RE GONNA NEED A BIGGER BOAT...

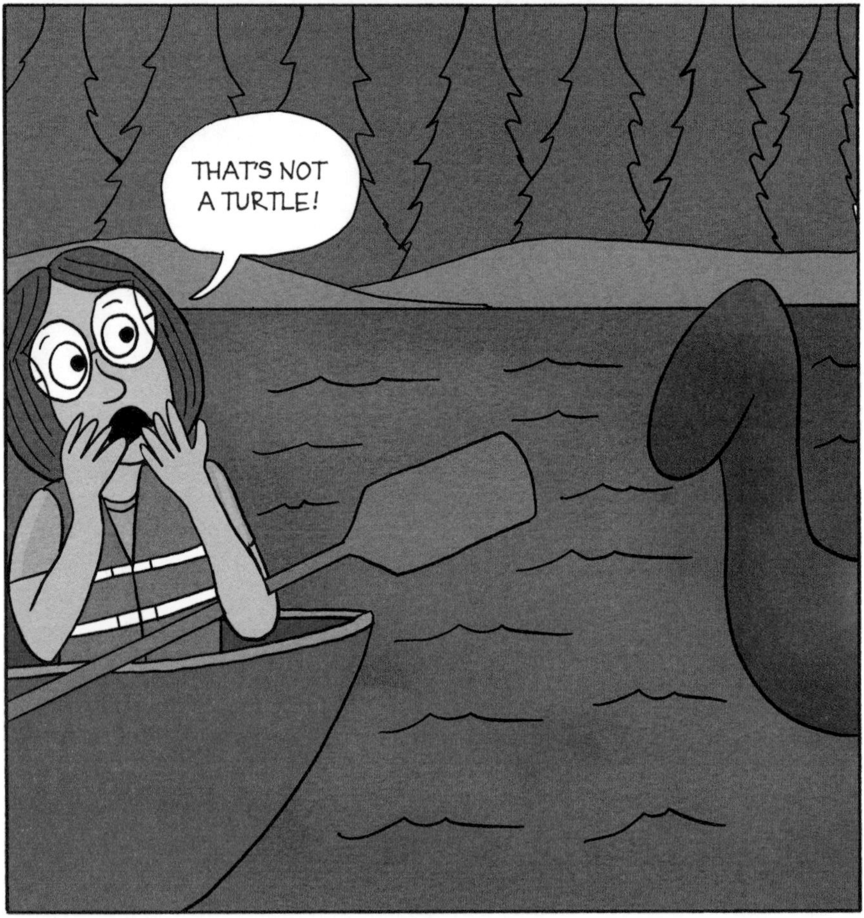
THAT'S NOT A TURTLE!

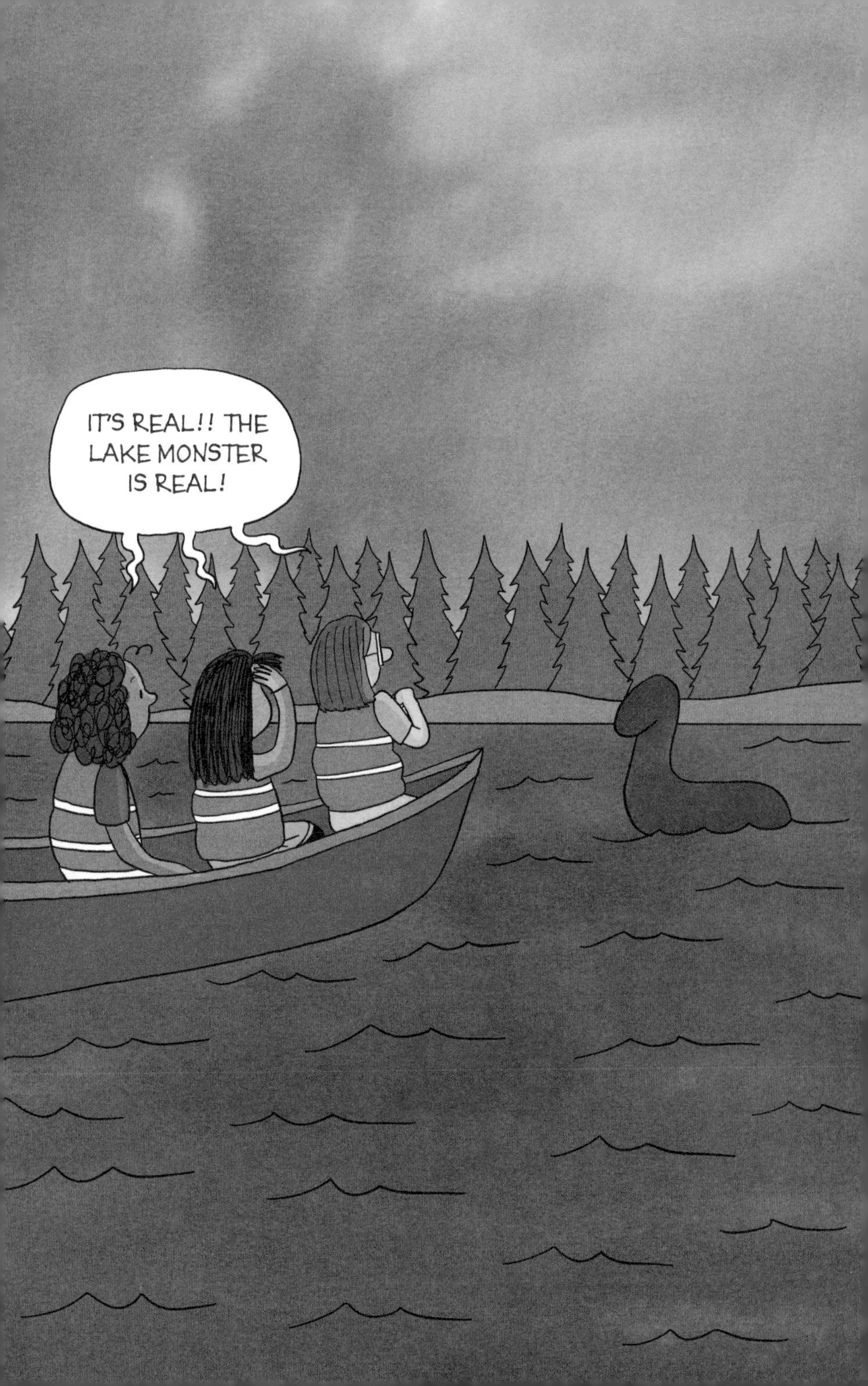
IT'S REAL!! THE LAKE MONSTER IS REAL!

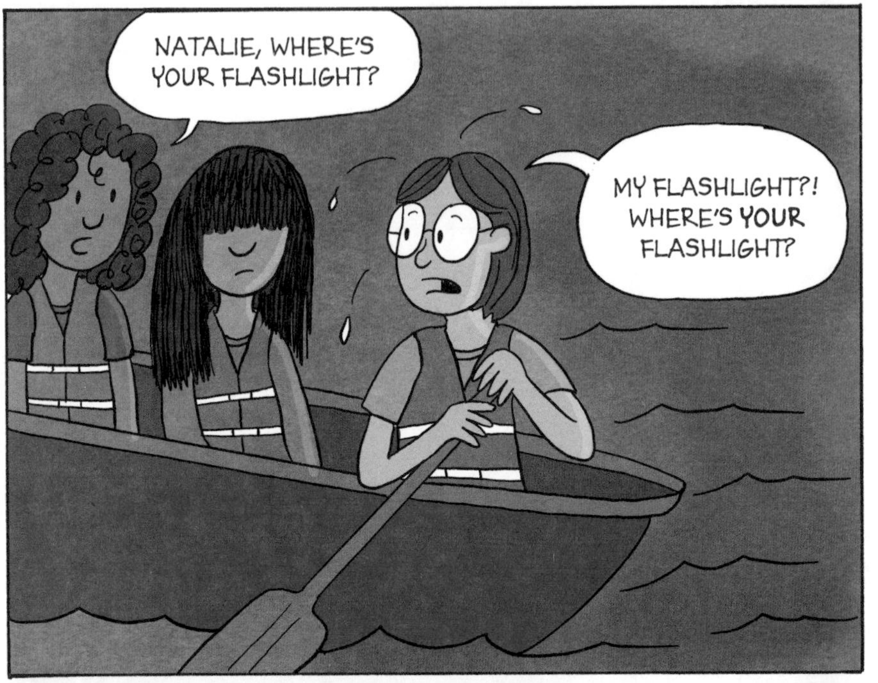
NATALIE, WHERE'S YOUR FLASHLIGHT?
MY FLASHLIGHT?! WHERE'S **YOUR** FLASHLIGHT?

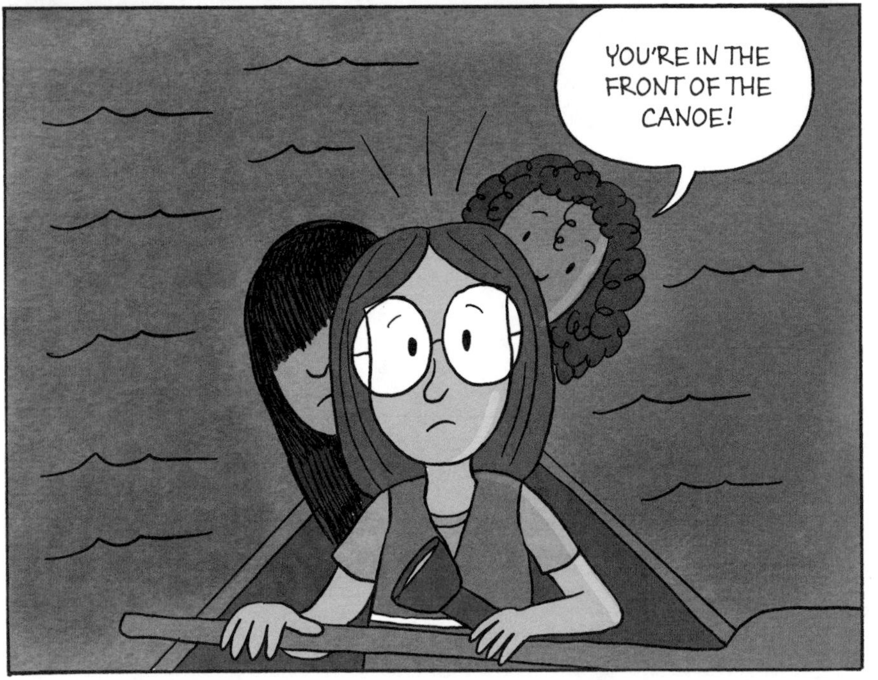
YOU'RE IN THE FRONT OF THE CANOE!

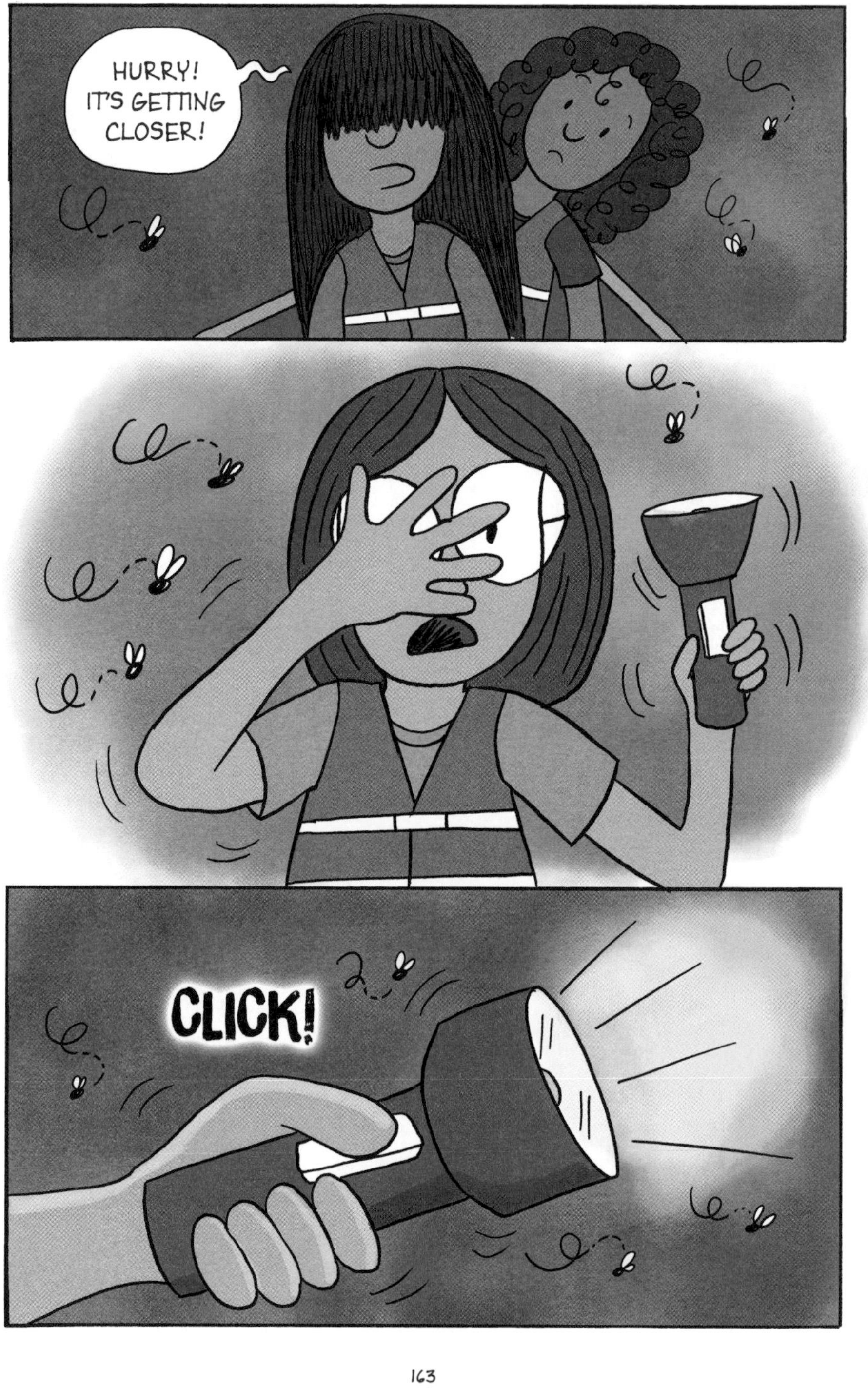
HURRY! IT'S GETTING CLOSER!
CLICK!

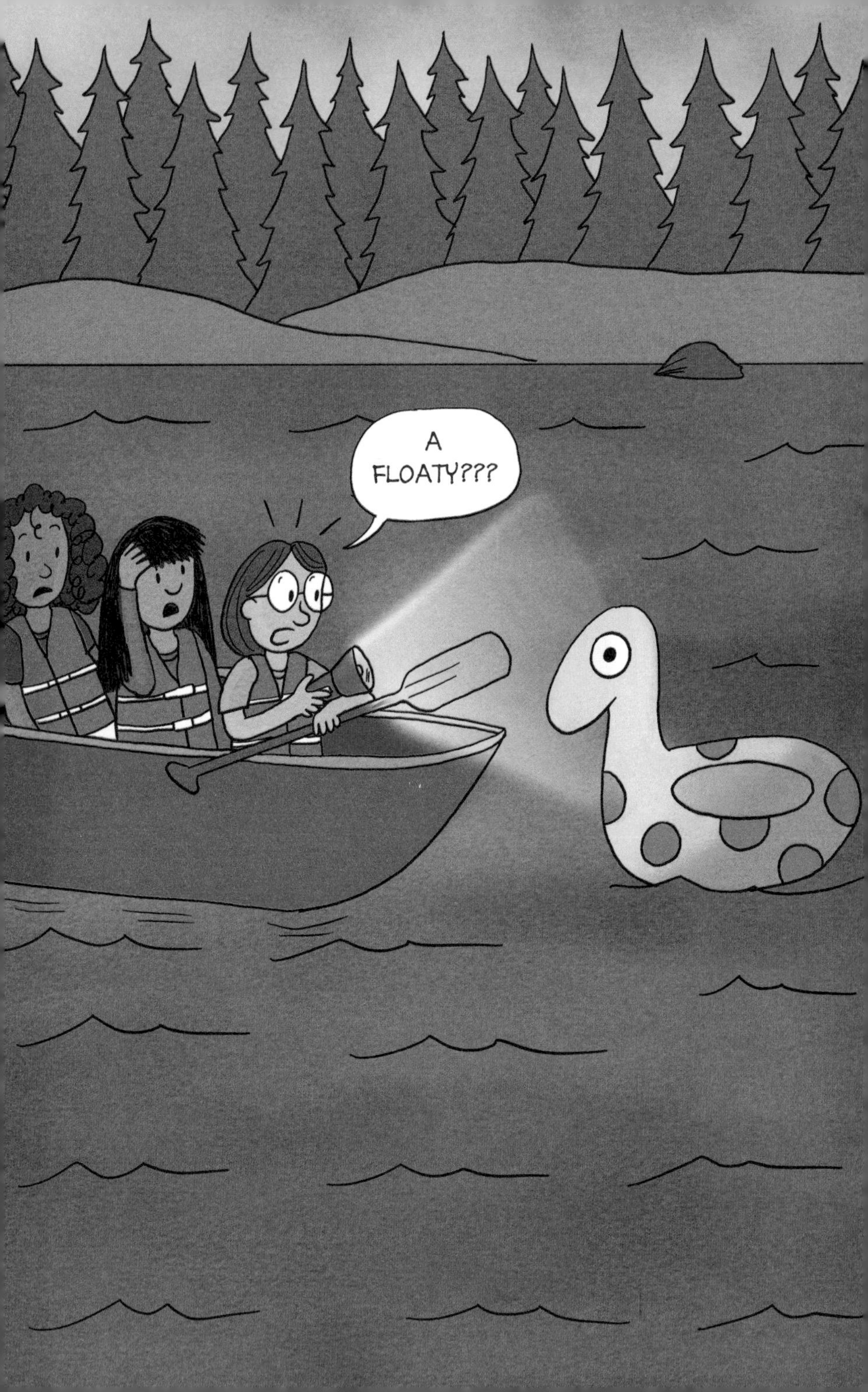
A FLOATY???

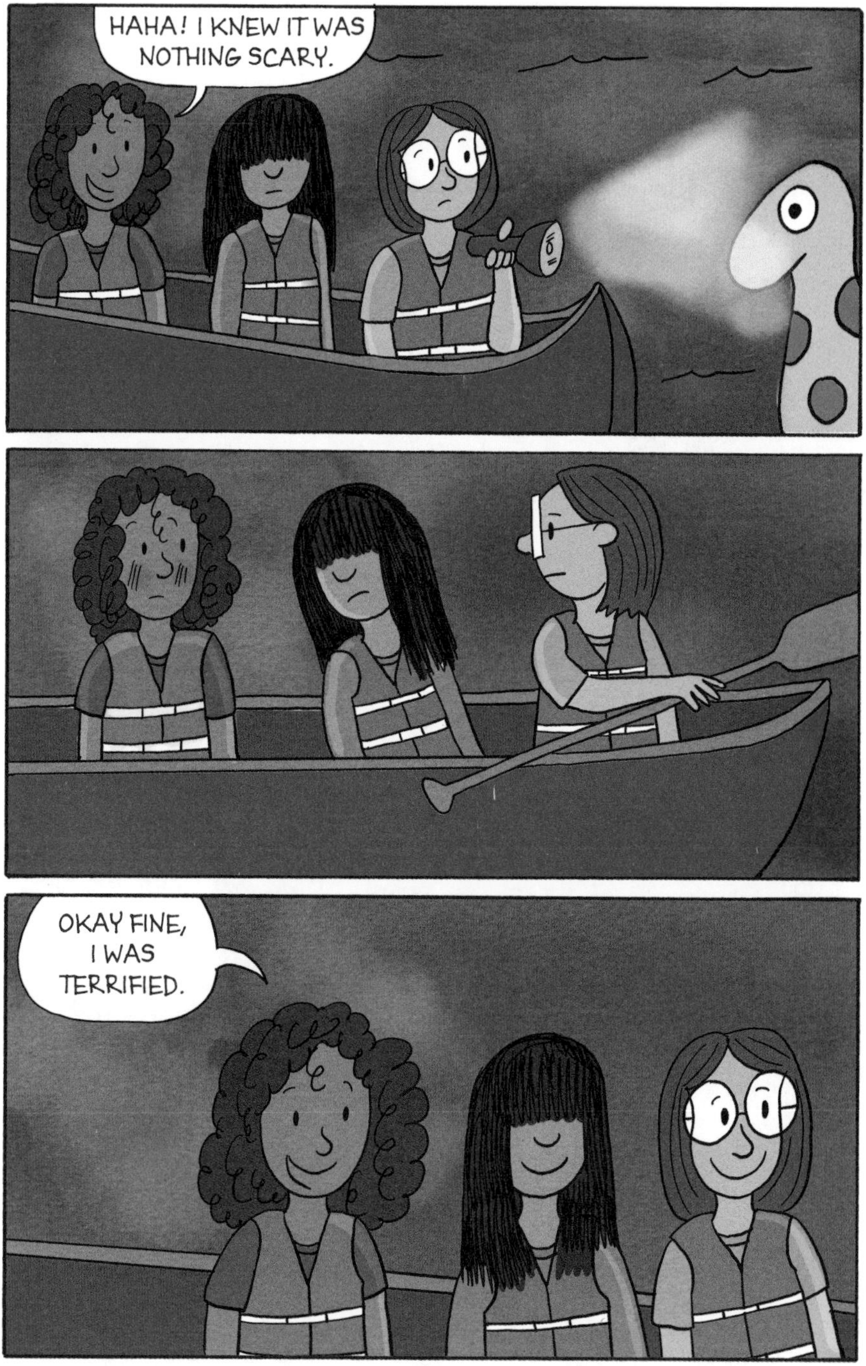
HAHA! I KNEW IT WAS NOTHING SCARY.
OKAY FINE, I WAS TERRIFIED.

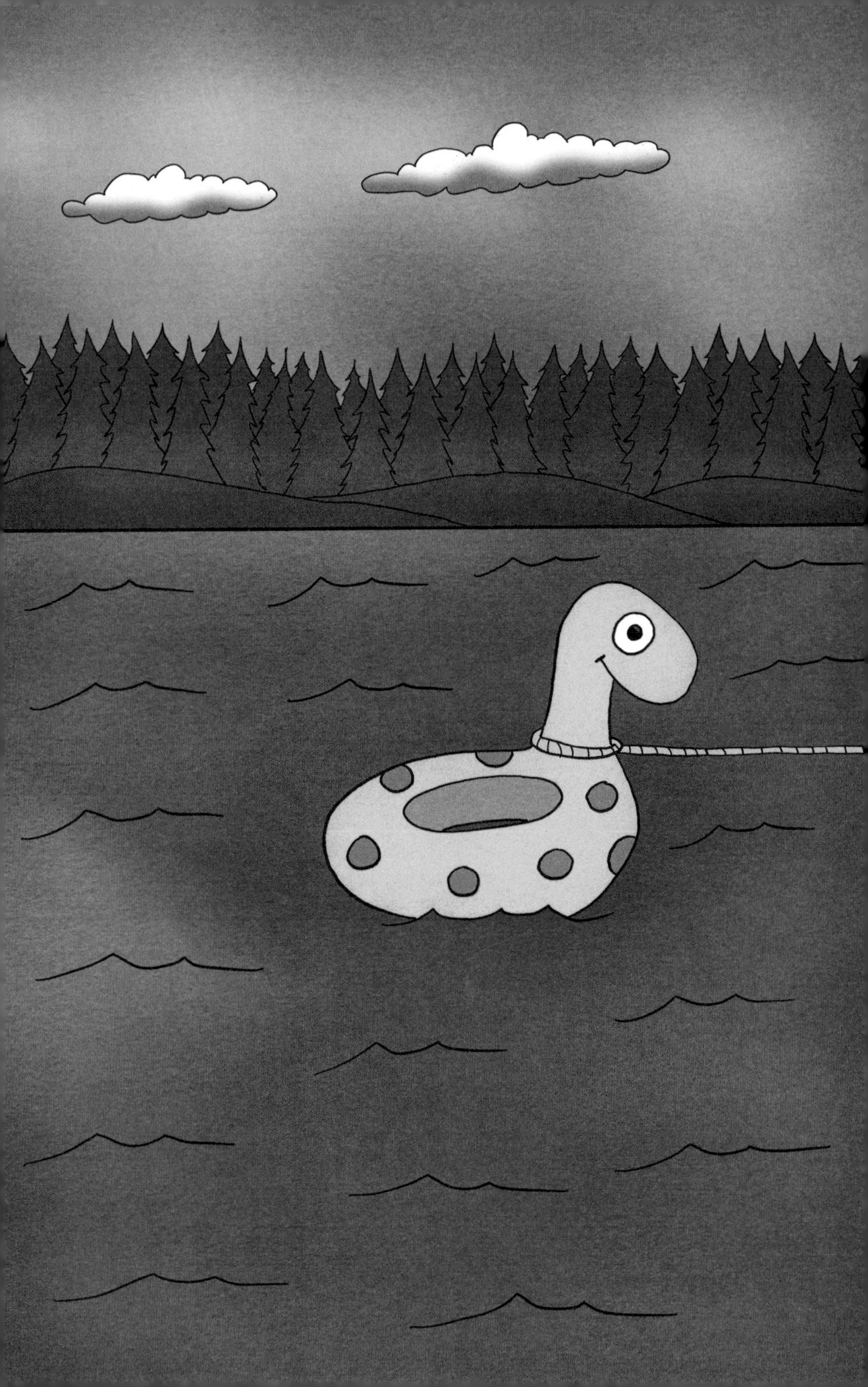

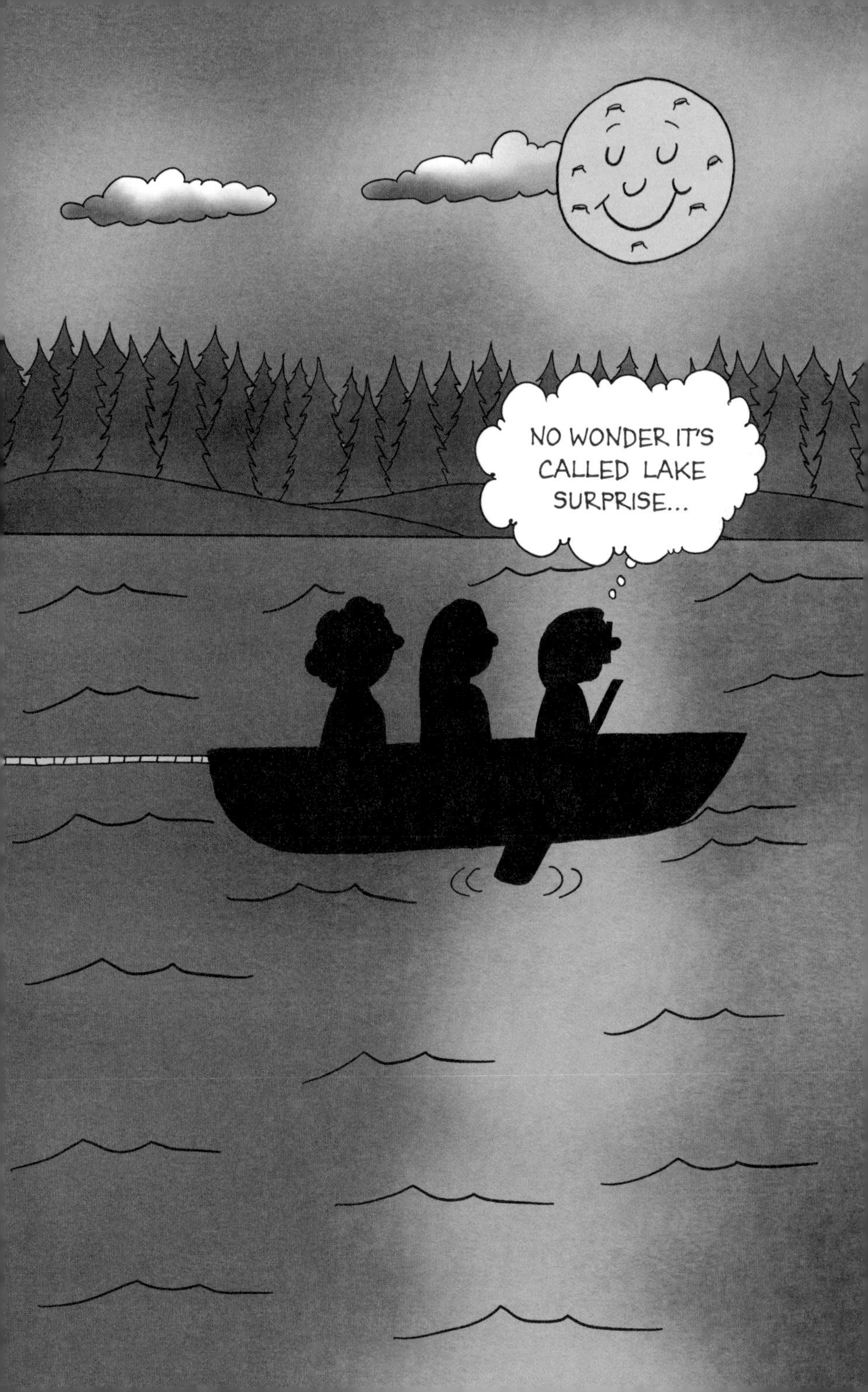
NO WONDER IT'S CALLED LAKE SURPRISE...

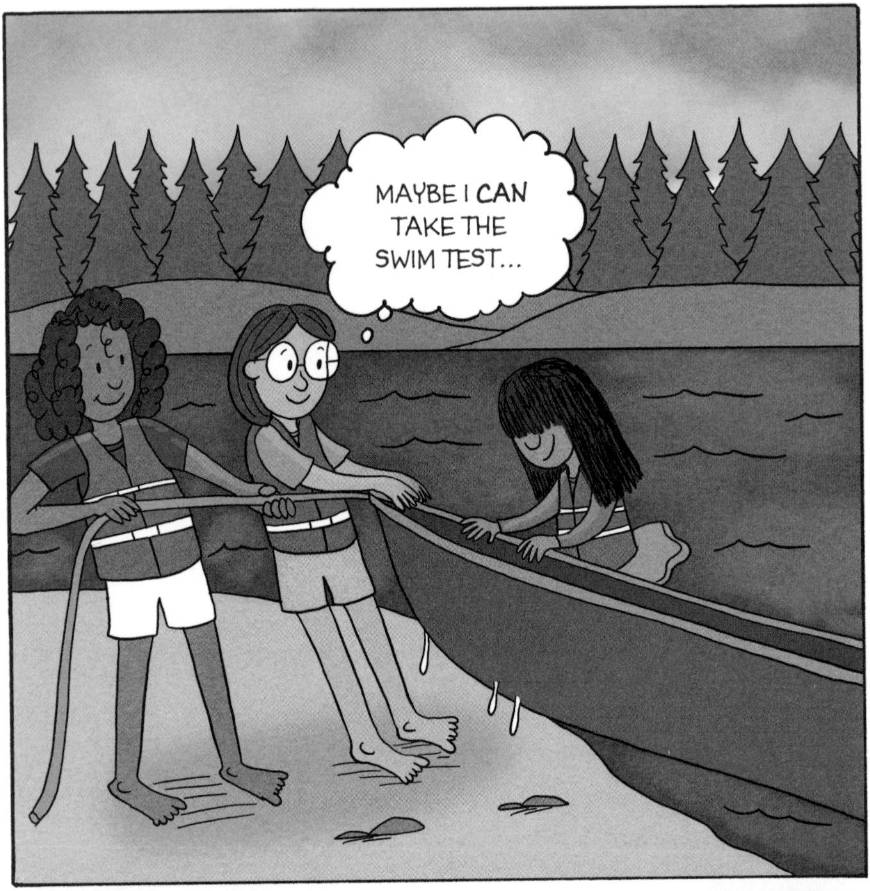
MAYBE I CAN TAKE THE SWIM TEST...

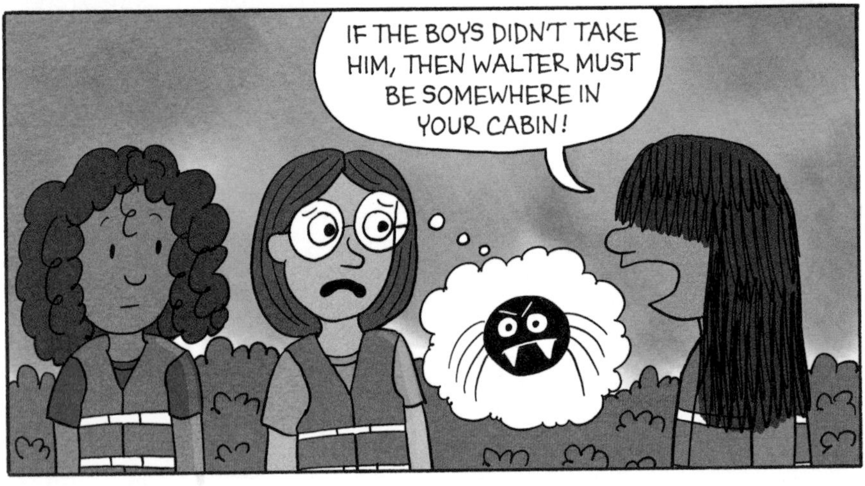
IF THE BOYS DIDN'T TAKE HIM, THEN WALTER MUST BE SOMEWHERE IN YOUR CABIN!

CHAPTER 11
HIDE-AND-SEEK

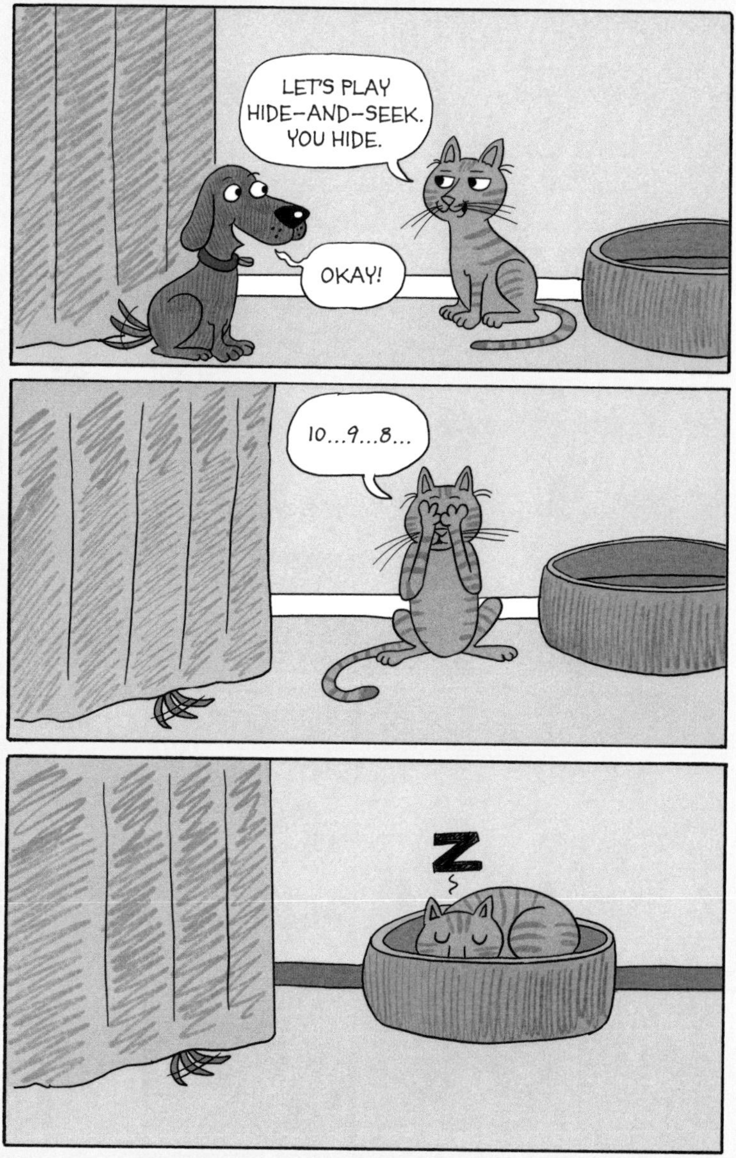
LET'S PLAY HIDE-AND-SEEK. YOU HIDE.
OKAY!
10...9...8...
Z

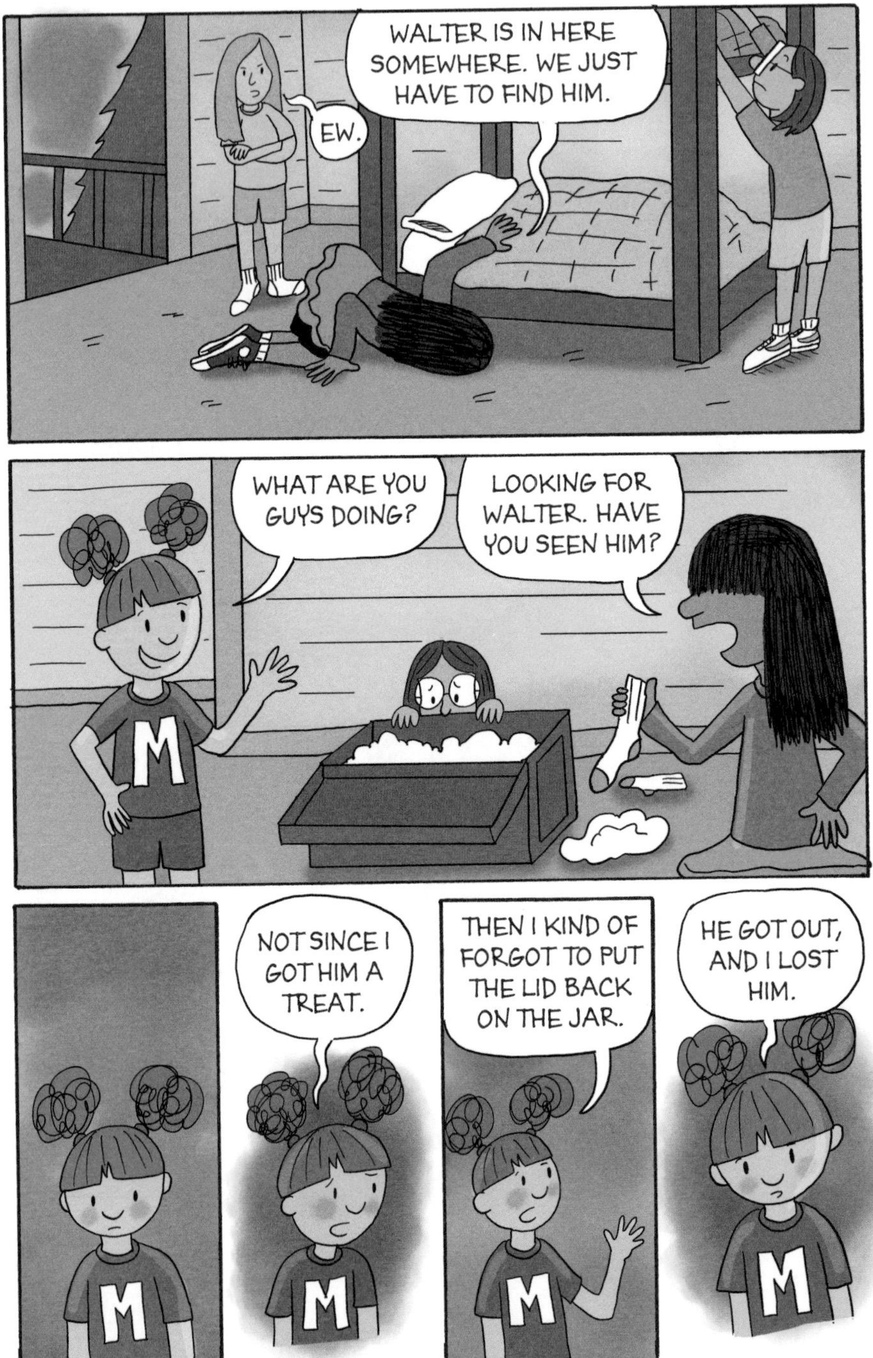
WALTER IS IN HERE SOMEWHERE. WE JUST HAVE TO FIND HIM.
EW.
WHAT ARE YOU GUYS DOING?
LOOKING FOR WALTER. HAVE YOU SEEN HIM?
NOT SINCE I GOT HIM A TREAT.
THEN I KIND OF FORGOT TO PUT THE LID BACK ON THE JAR.
HE GOT OUT, AND I LOST HIM.

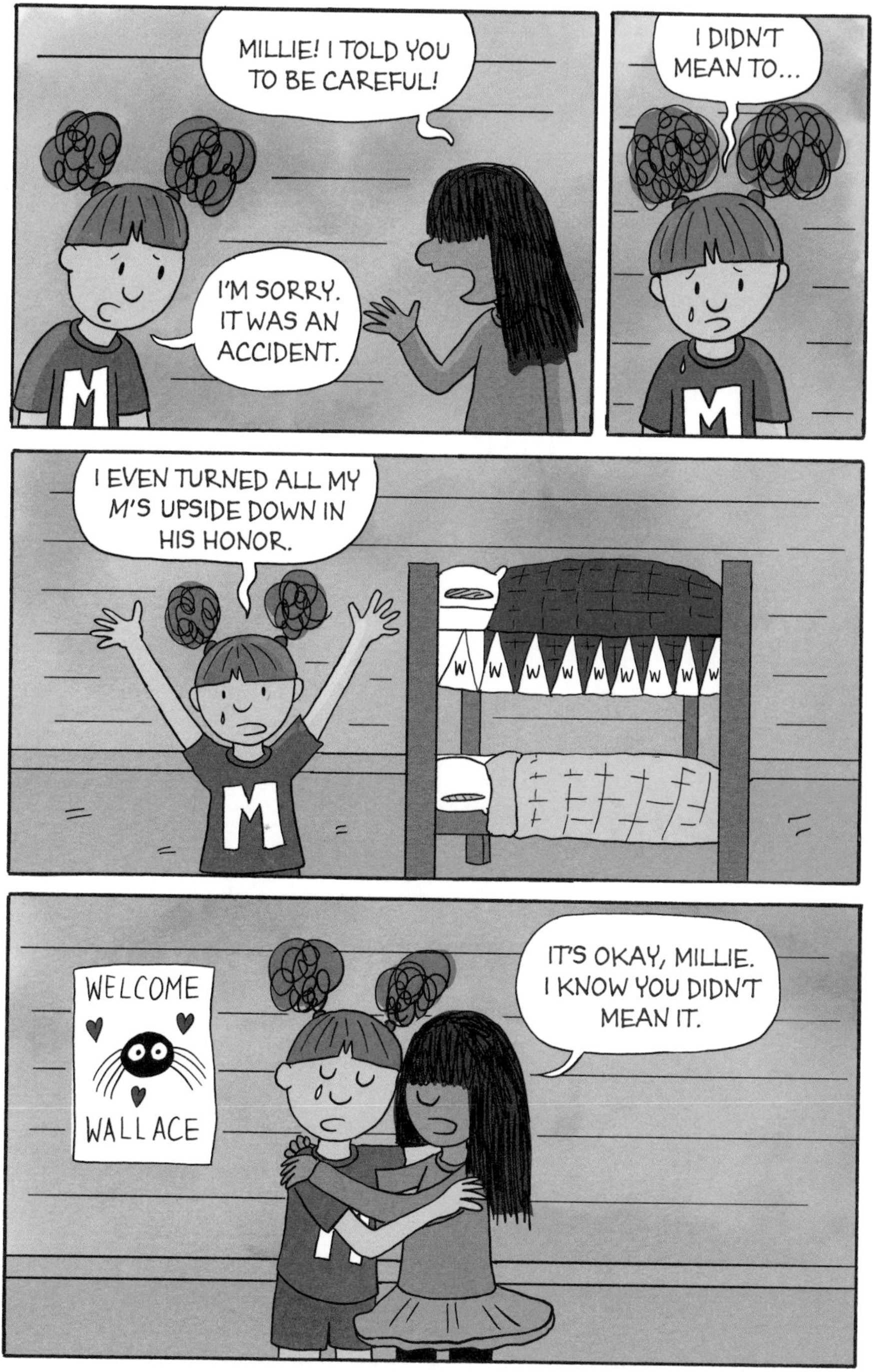
MILLIE! I TOLD YOU TO BE CAREFUL!
I'M SORRY. IT WAS AN ACCIDENT.
I DIDN'T MEAN TO...
I EVEN TURNED ALL MY M'S UPSIDE DOWN IN HIS HONOR.
WELCOME
WALLACE
IT'S OKAY, MILLIE. I KNOW YOU DIDN'T MEAN IT.

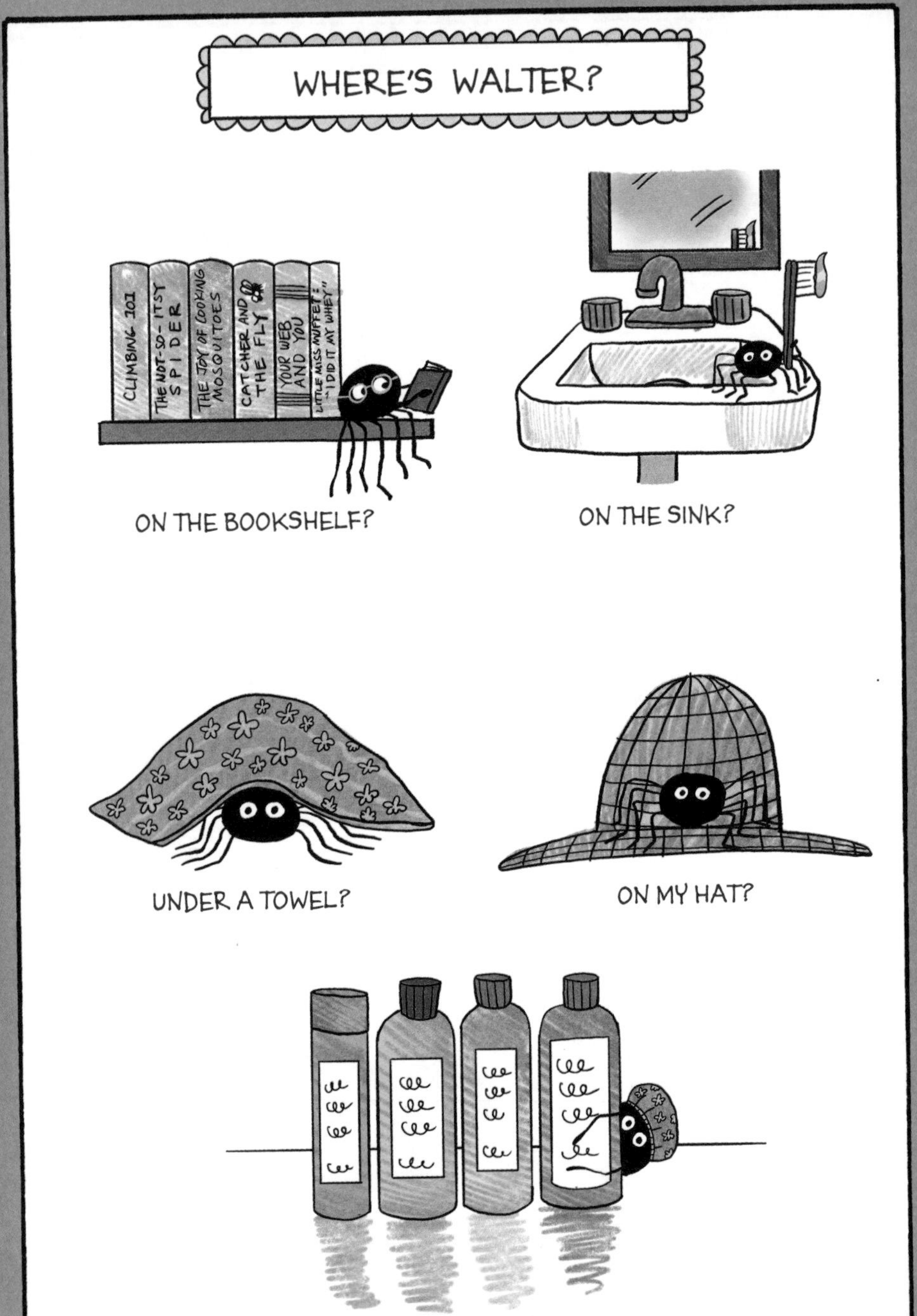
WHERE'S WALTER?
CLIMBING 101
THE NOT-SO-ITSY SPIDER
THE JOY OF COOKING MOSQUITOES
CATCHER AND THE FLY
YOUR WEB AND YOU
LITTLE MISS MUFFET: "I DID IT MY WHEY"
ON THE BOOKSHELF?
ON THE SINK?
UNDER A TOWEL?
ON MY HAT?
BEHIND THE SHAMPOO?

IN MY SHOE?

IN MY TRUNK?

ON MY SKETCHBOOK?

ON MY PILLOW?

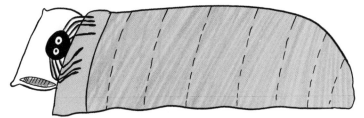

IN MY SLEEPING BAG?

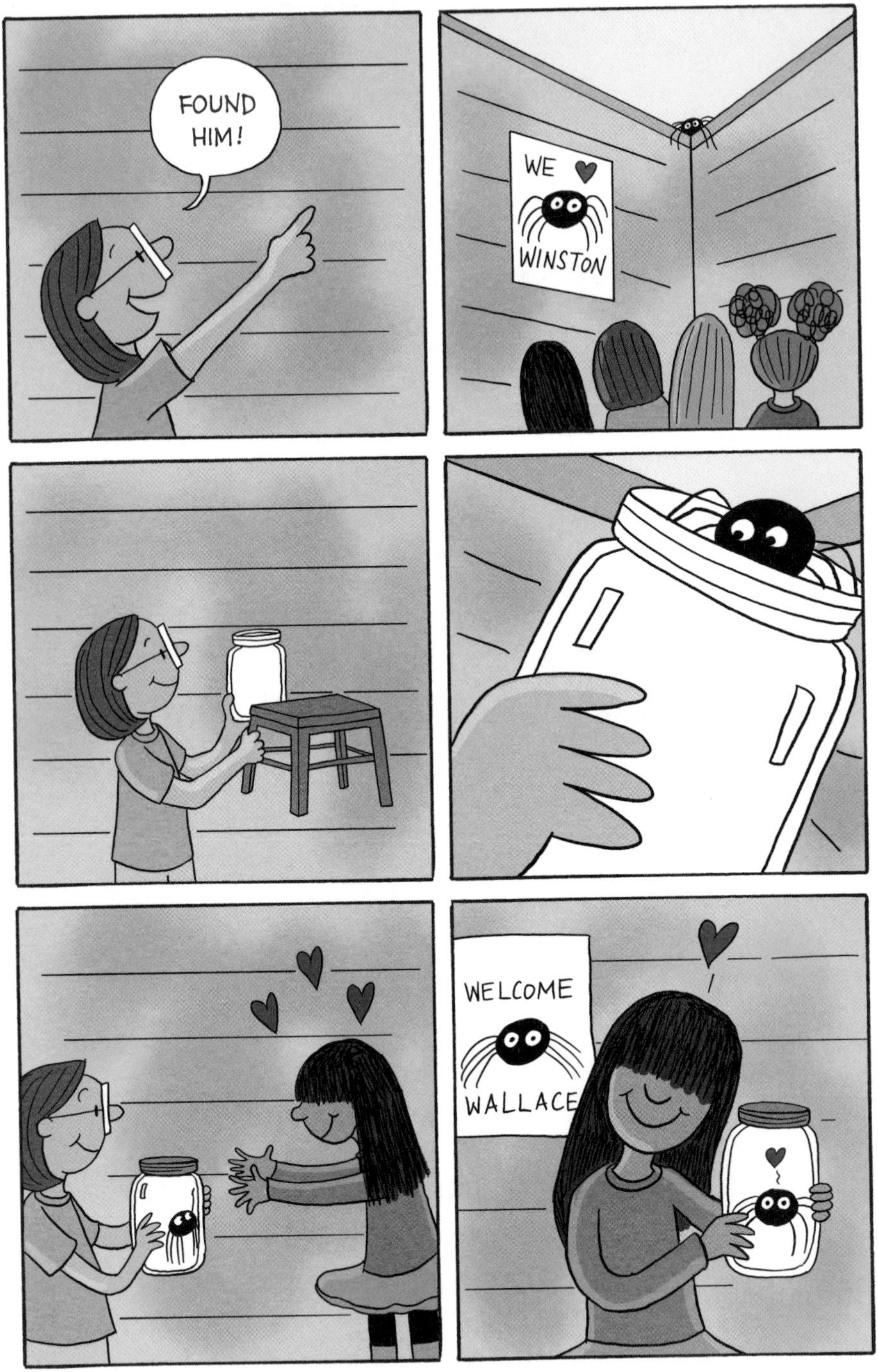
FOUND HIM!
WE ♥ WINSTON
WELCOME WALLACE

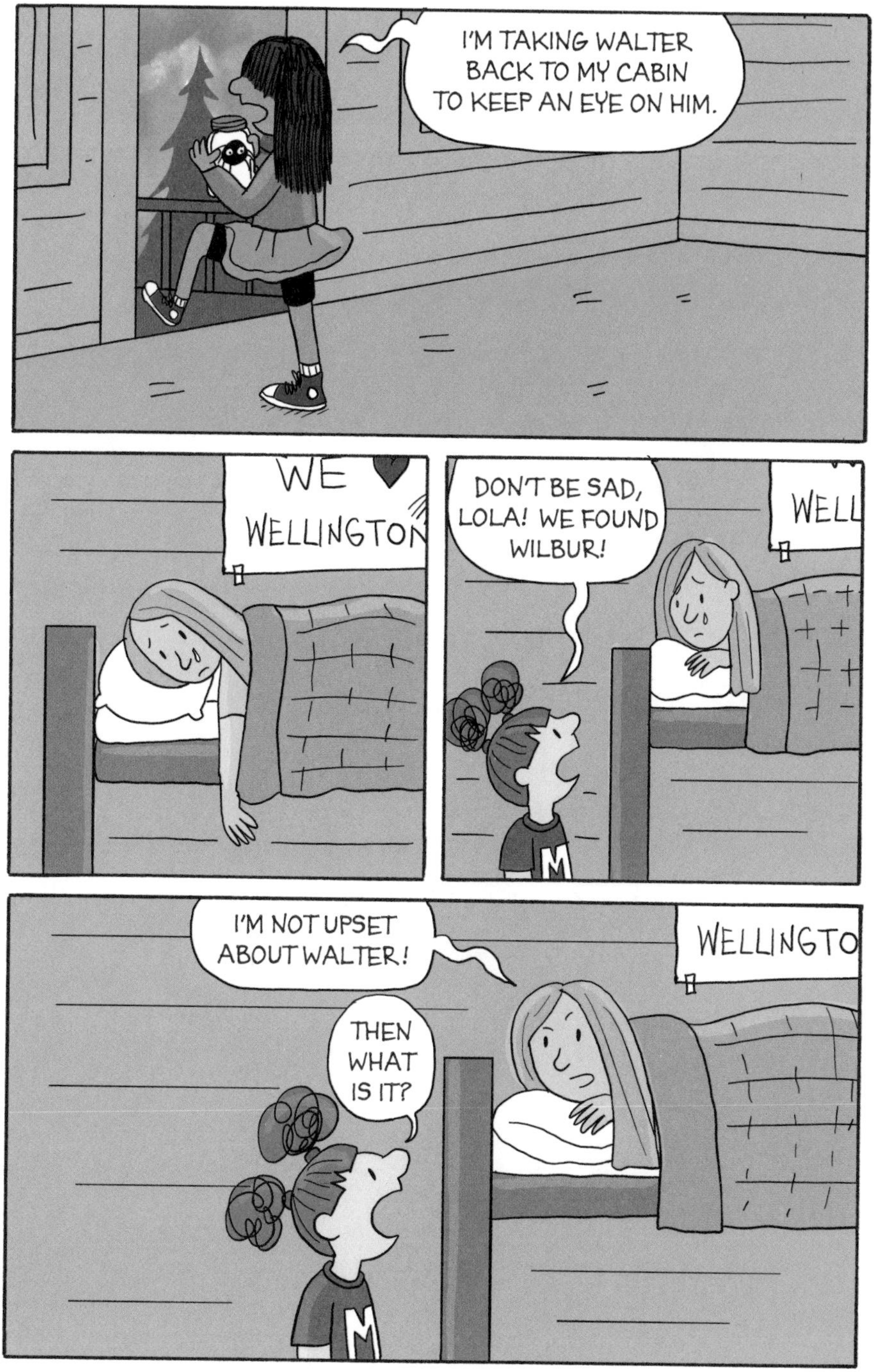
I'M TAKING WALTER BACK TO MY CABIN TO KEEP AN EYE ON HIM.
WE ♥ WELLINGTON
DON'T BE SAD, LOLA! WE FOUND WILBUR!
WELL
M
I'M NOT UPSET ABOUT WALTER!
WELLINGTO
THEN WHAT IS IT?
M

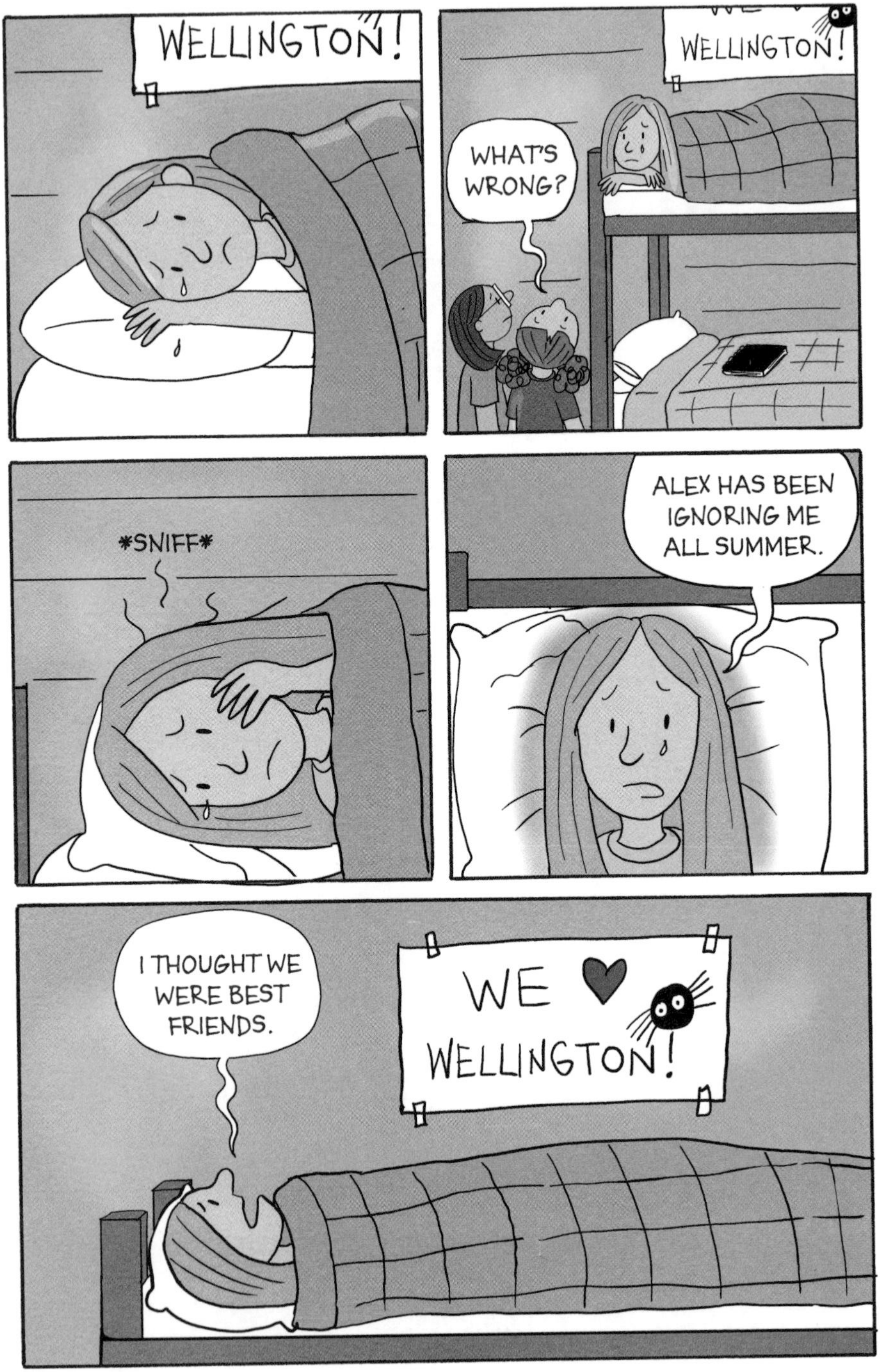
WELLINGTON!
WELLINGTON!
WHAT'S WRONG?
SNIFF
ALEX HAS BEEN IGNORING ME ALL SUMMER.
I THOUGHT WE WERE BEST FRIENDS.
WE ♥ WELLINGTON!

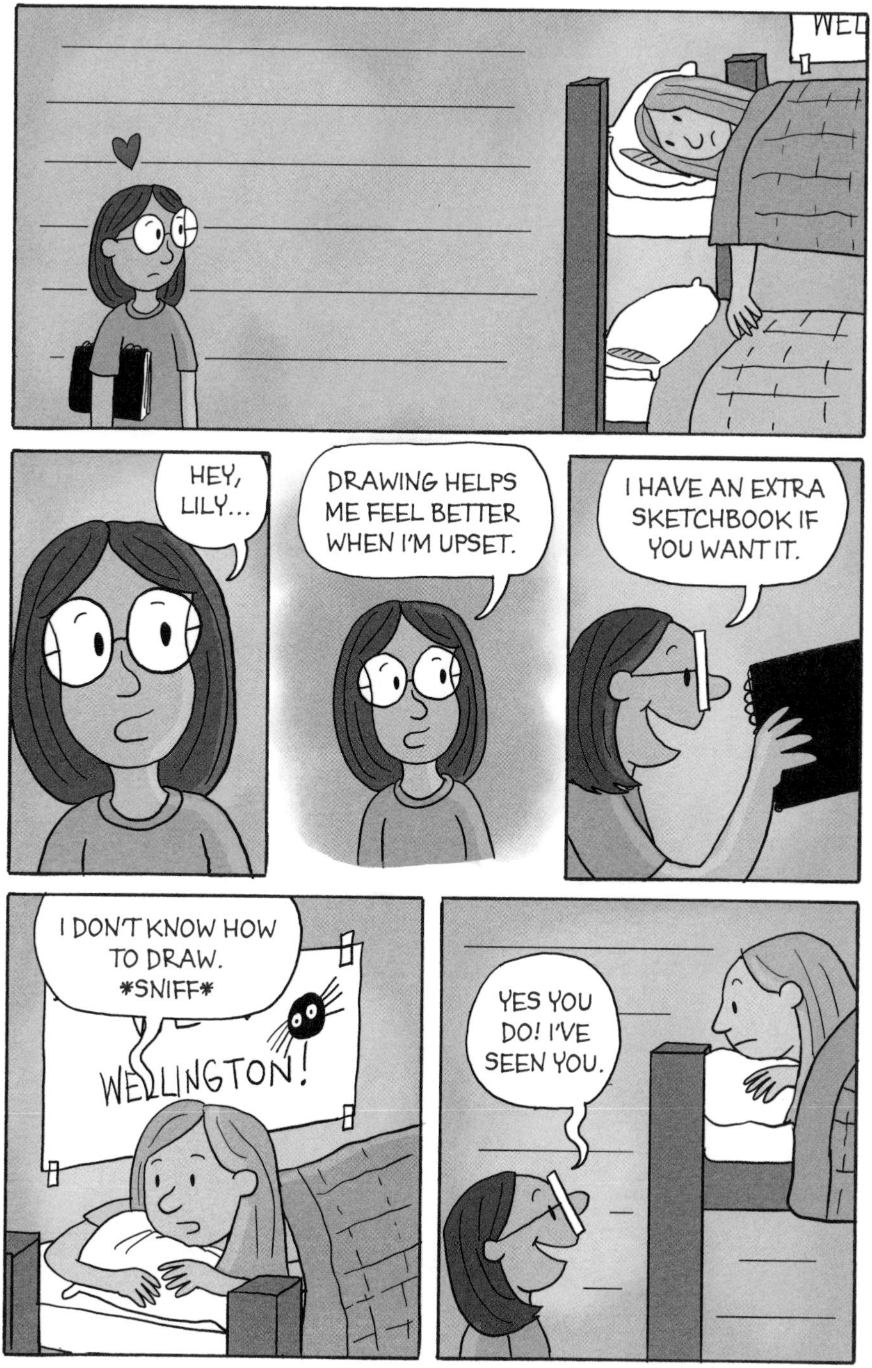
WEL
HEY, LILY...
DRAWING HELPS ME FEEL BETTER WHEN I'M UPSET.
I HAVE AN EXTRA SKETCHBOOK IF YOU WANT IT.
I DON'T KNOW HOW TO DRAW. *SNIFF*
WELLINGTON!
YES YOU DO! I'VE SEEN YOU.

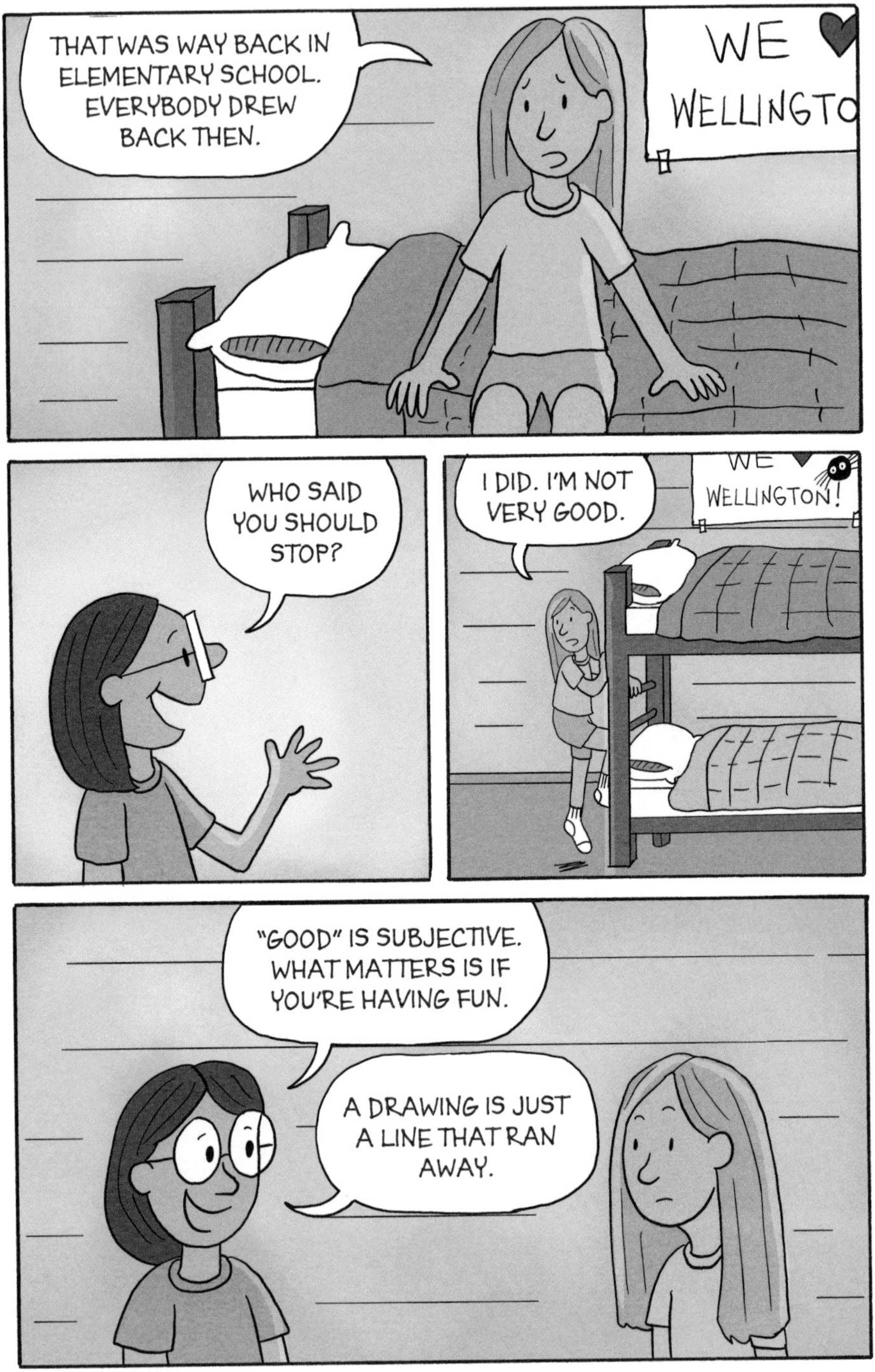
THAT WAS WAY BACK IN ELEMENTARY SCHOOL. EVERYBODY DREW BACK THEN.
WE ♥ WELLINGTO
WHO SAID YOU SHOULD STOP?
I DID. I'M NOT VERY GOOD.
WE ♥ WELLINGTON!
"GOOD" IS SUBJECTIVE. WHAT MATTERS IS IF YOU'RE HAVING FUN.
A DRAWING IS JUST A LINE THAT RAN AWAY.

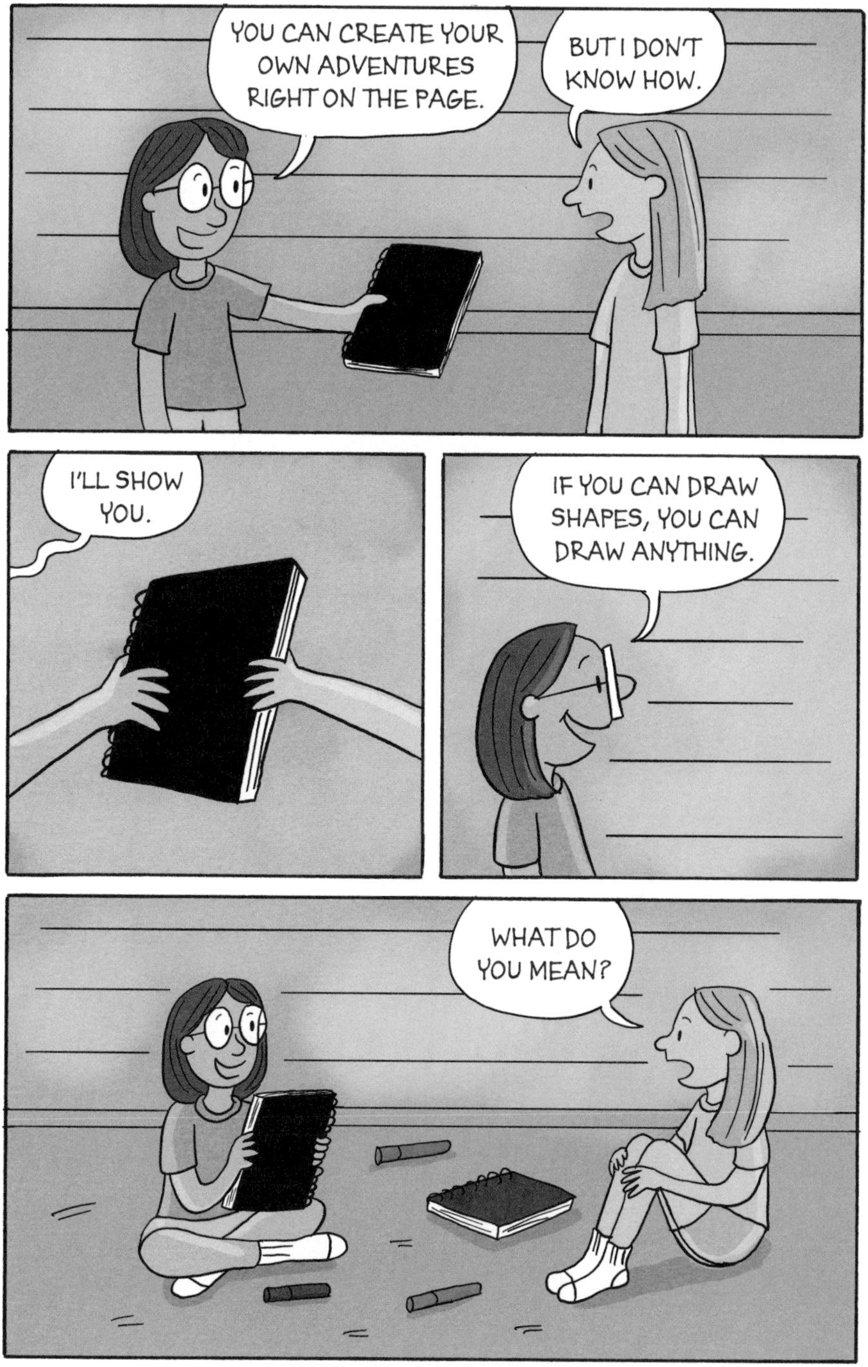
YOU CAN CREATE YOUR OWN ADVENTURES RIGHT ON THE PAGE.
BUT I DON'T KNOW HOW.
I'LL SHOW YOU.
IF YOU CAN DRAW SHAPES, YOU CAN DRAW ANYTHING.
WHAT DO YOU MEAN?

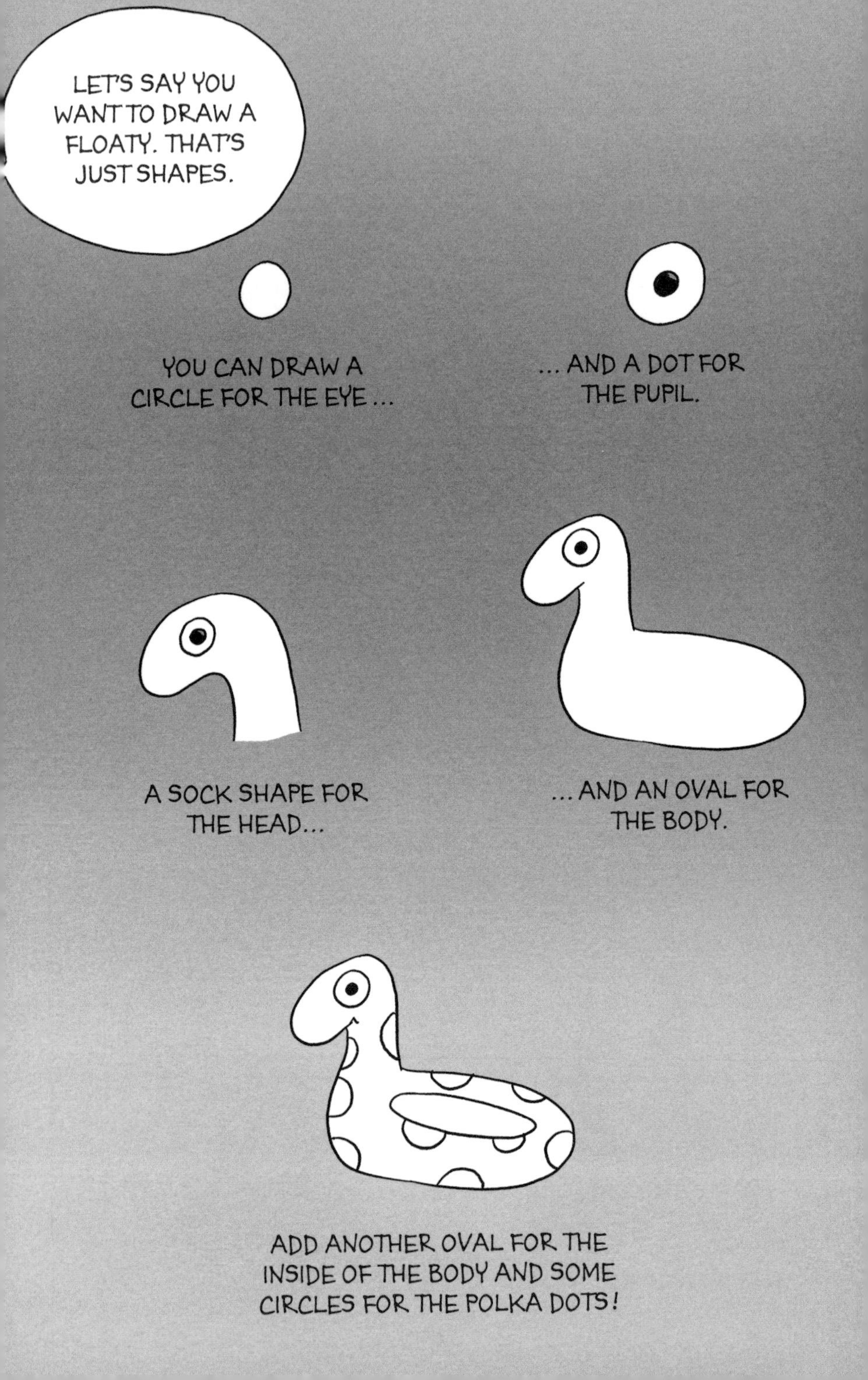

LET'S SAY YOU WANT TO DRAW A FLOATY. THAT'S JUST SHAPES.

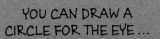

YOU CAN DRAW A CIRCLE FOR THE EYE...

... AND A DOT FOR THE PUPIL.

A SOCK SHAPE FOR THE HEAD...

... AND AN OVAL FOR THE BODY.

ADD ANOTHER OVAL FOR THE INSIDE OF THE BODY AND SOME CIRCLES FOR THE POLKA DOTS!

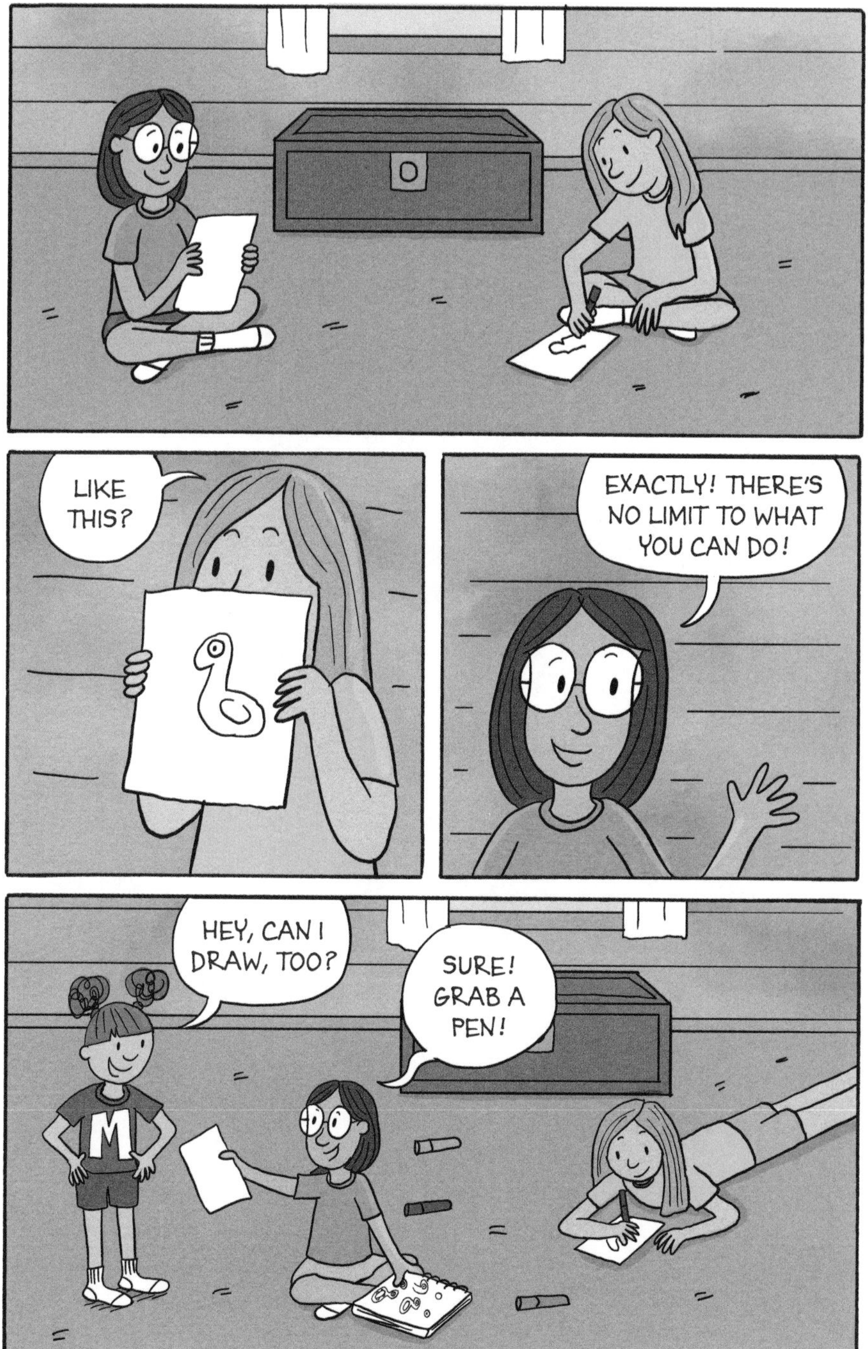
LIKE THIS?
EXACTLY! THERE'S NO LIMIT TO WHAT YOU CAN DO!
HEY, CAN I DRAW, TOO?
SURE! GRAB A PEN!

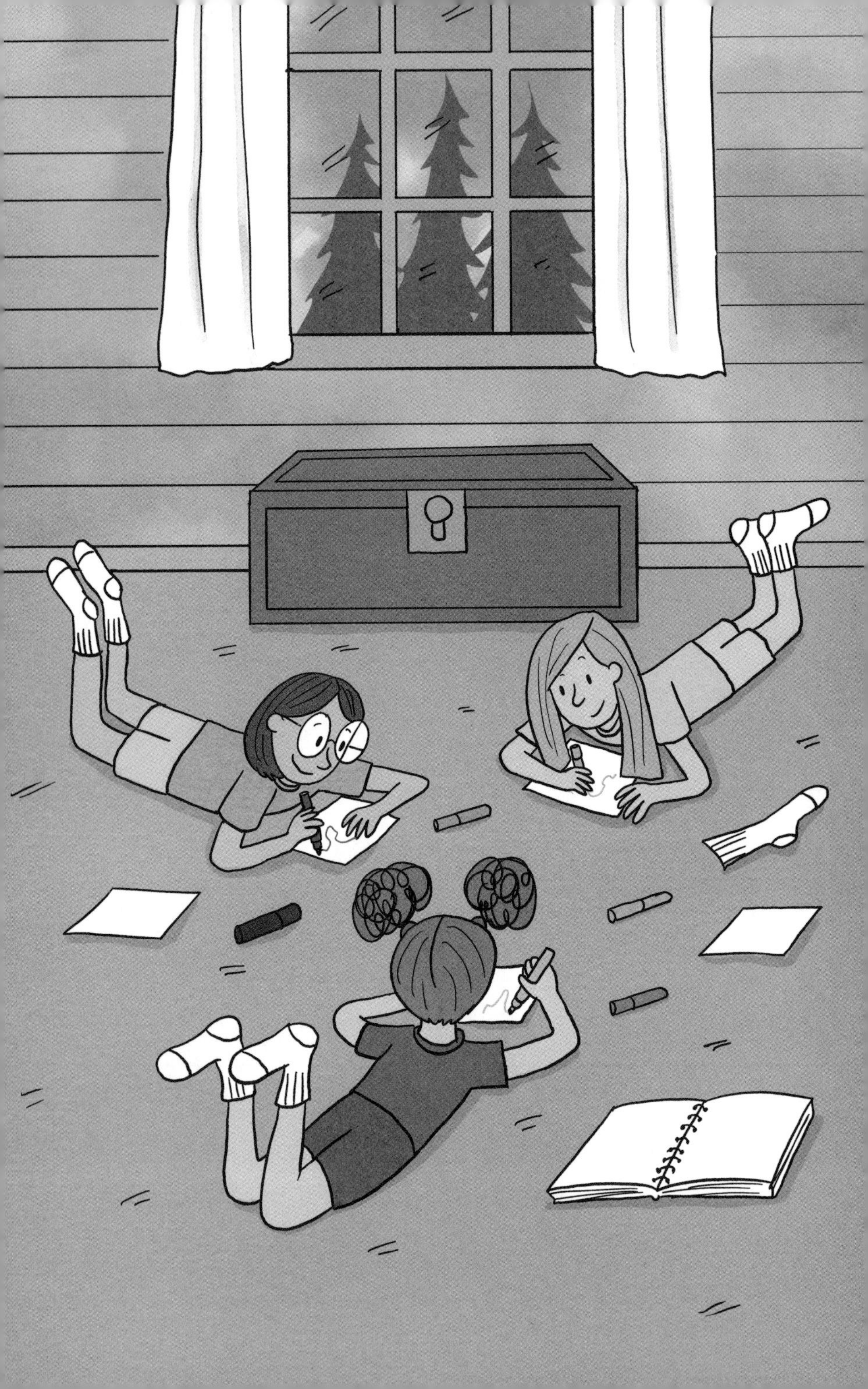

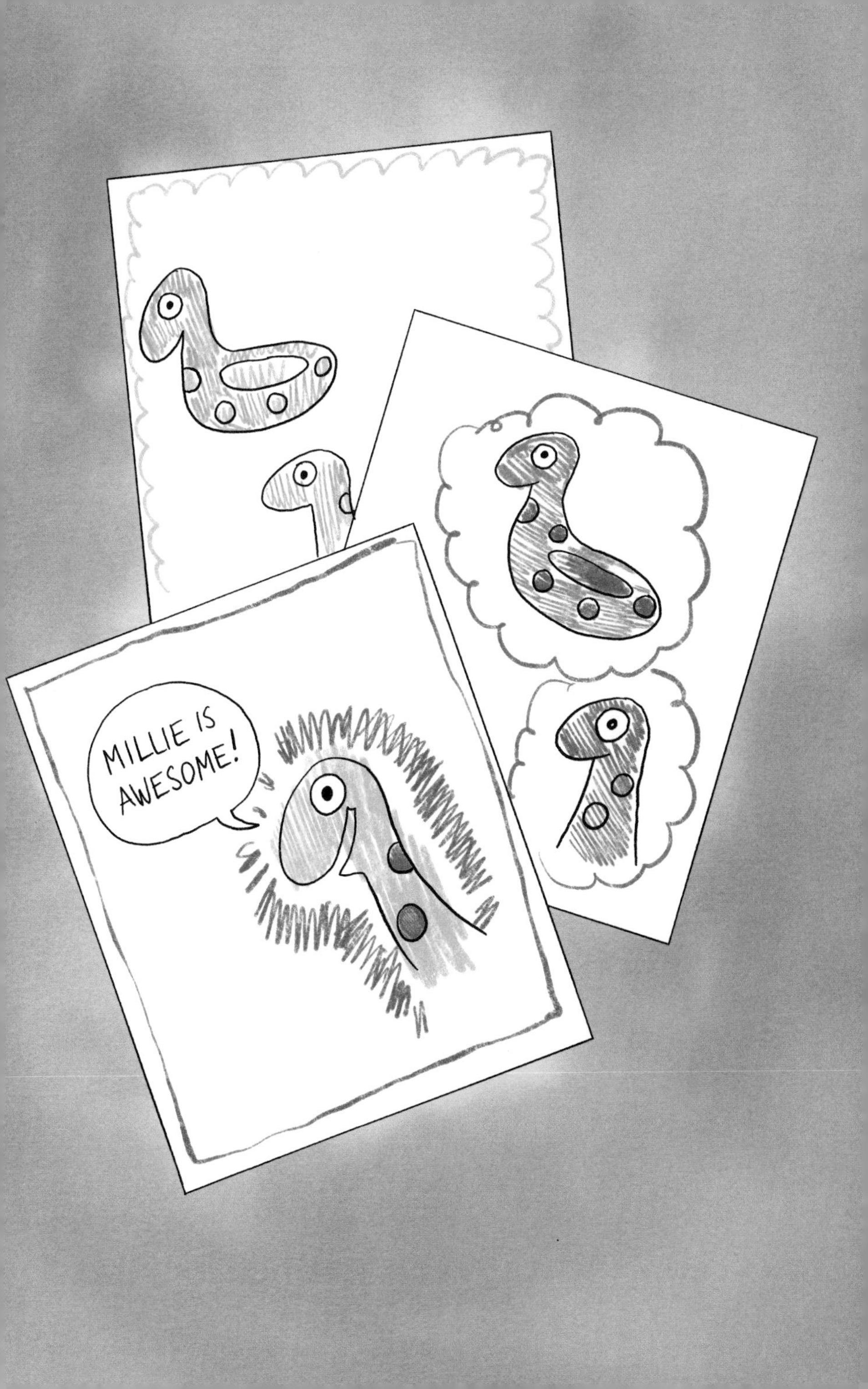
MILLIE IS AWESOME!

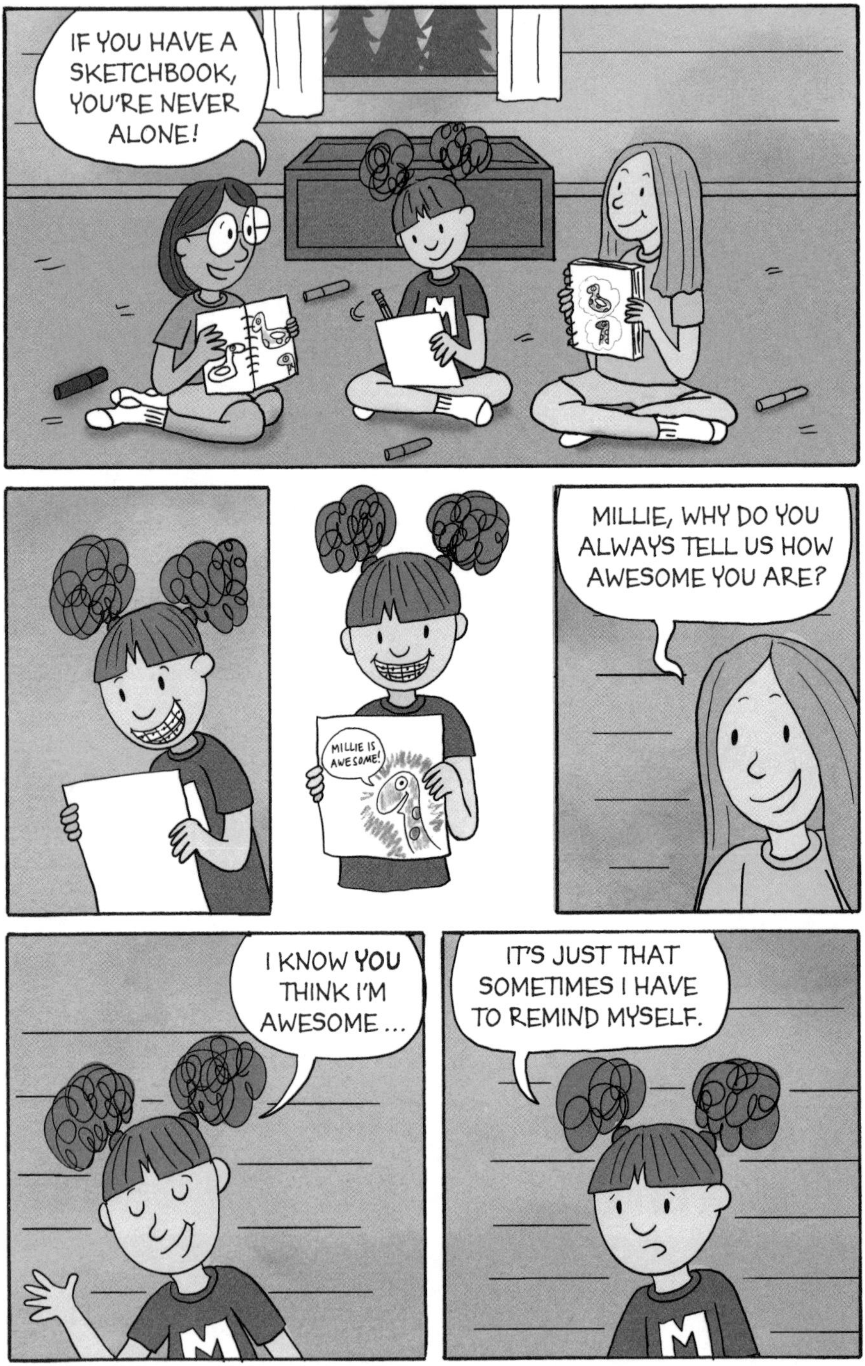
IF YOU HAVE A SKETCHBOOK, YOU'RE NEVER ALONE!
MILLIE IS AWESOME!
MILLIE, WHY DO YOU ALWAYS TELL US HOW AWESOME YOU ARE?
I KNOW **YOU** THINK I'M AWESOME . . .
IT'S JUST THAT SOMETIMES I HAVE TO REMIND MYSELF.

CHAPTER 12
SWIM TEST

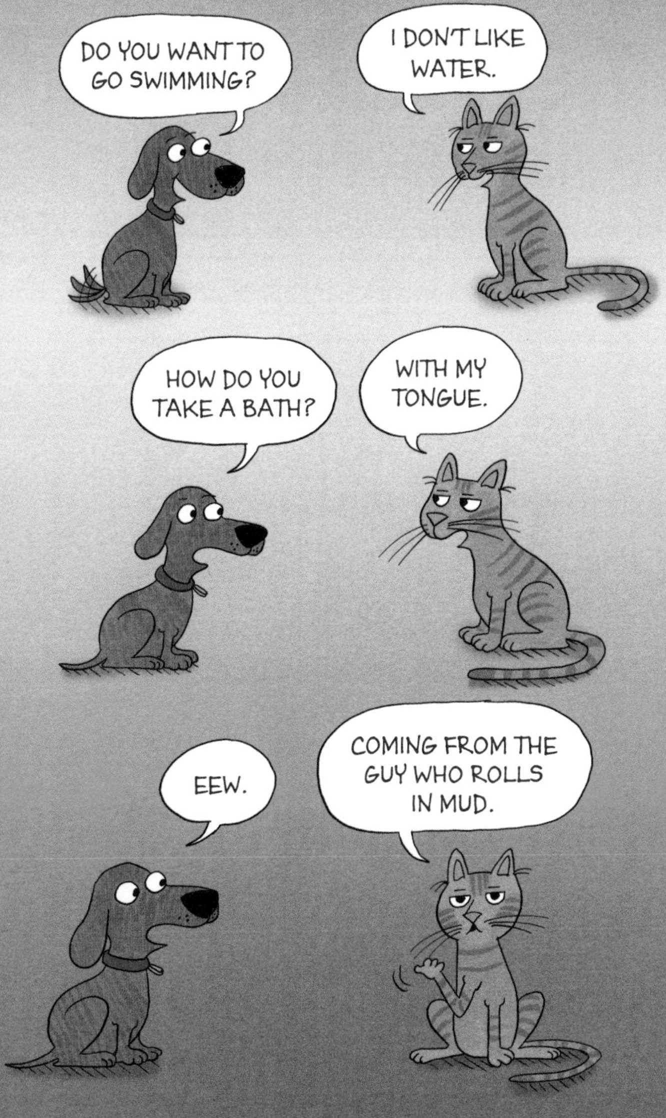
DO YOU WANT TO GO SWIMMING?
I DON'T LIKE WATER.
HOW DO YOU TAKE A BATH?
WITH MY TONGUE.
EEW.
COMING FROM THE GUY WHO ROLLS IN MUD.

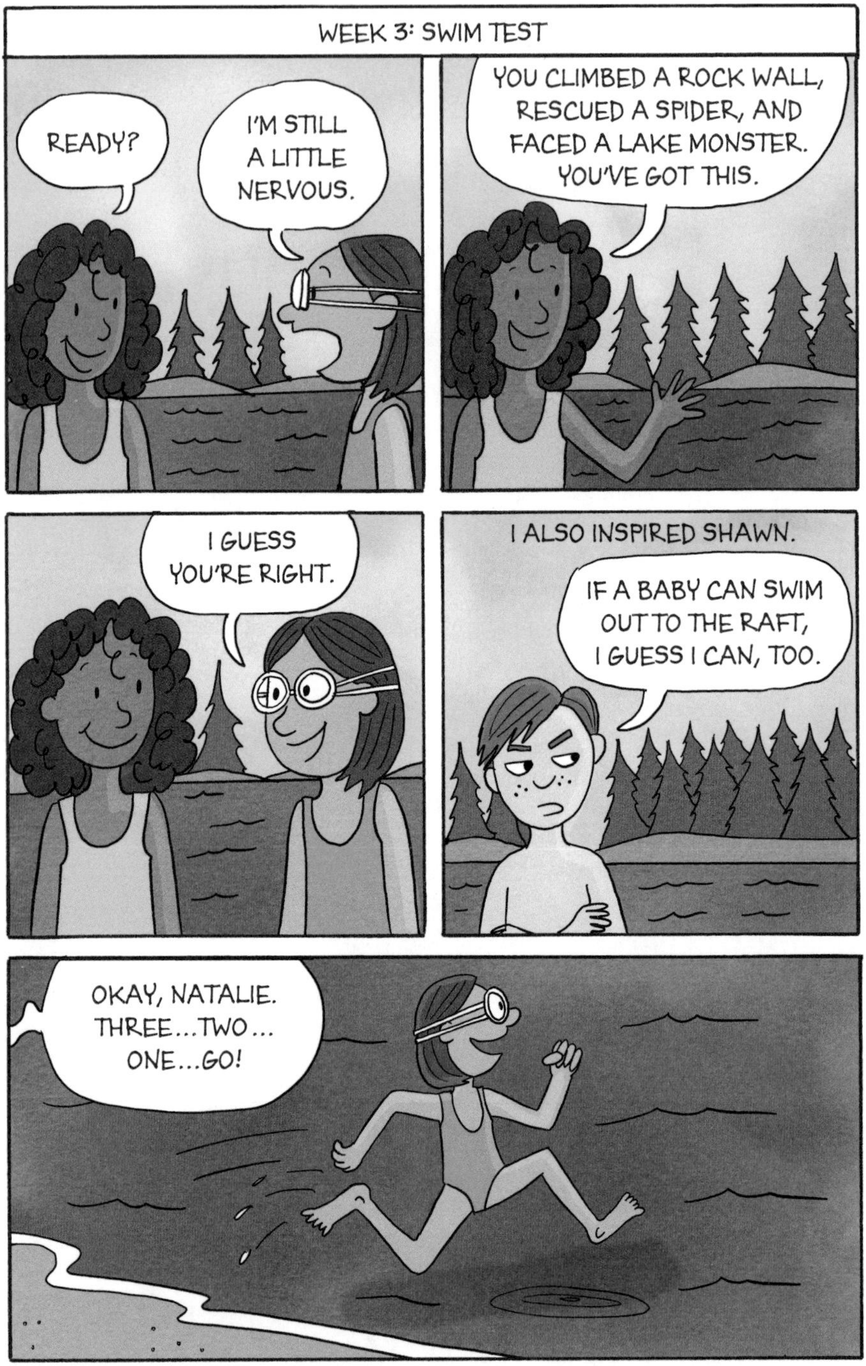
WEEK 3: SWIM TEST
READY?
I'M STILL A LITTLE NERVOUS.
YOU CLIMBED A ROCK WALL, RESCUED A SPIDER, AND FACED A LAKE MONSTER. YOU'VE GOT THIS.
I GUESS YOU'RE RIGHT.
I ALSO INSPIRED SHAWN.
IF A BABY CAN SWIM OUT TO THE RAFT, I GUESS I CAN, TOO.
OKAY, NATALIE. THREE...TWO... ONE...GO!

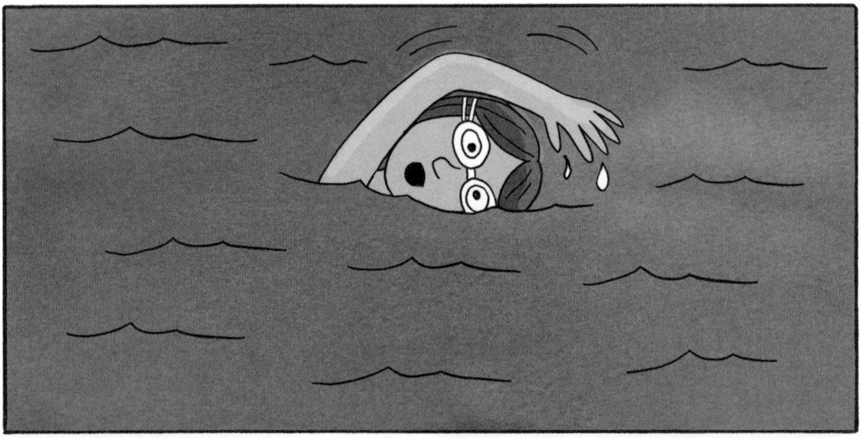

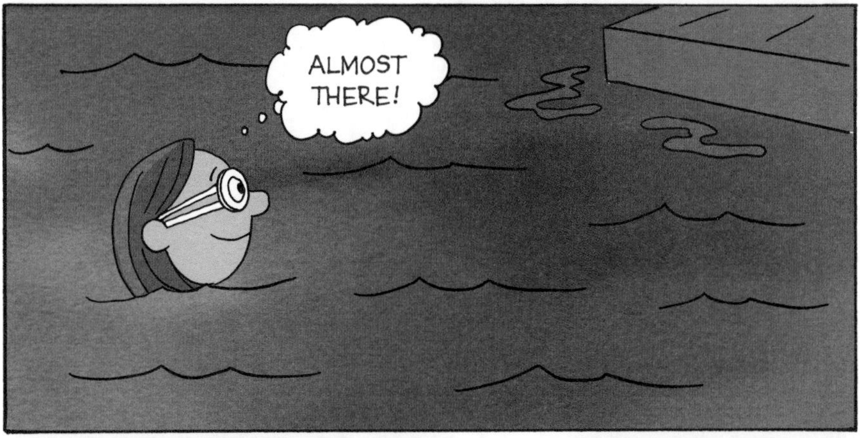
ALMOST THERE!

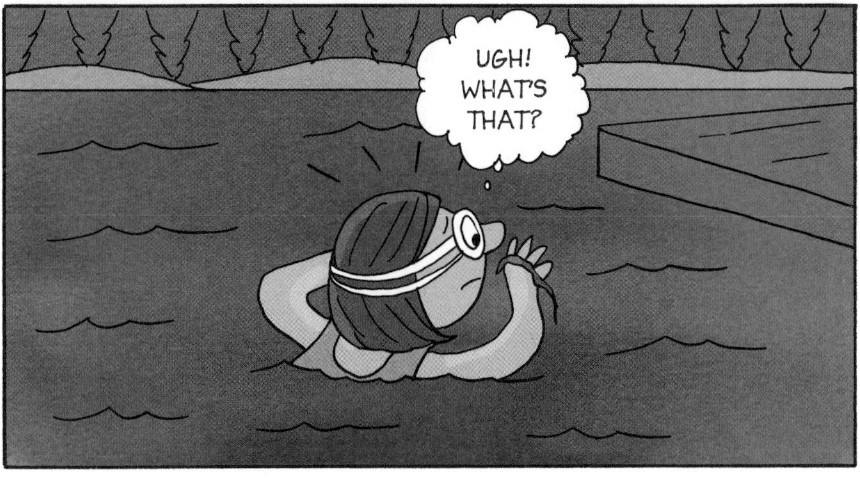
UGH! WHAT'S THAT?

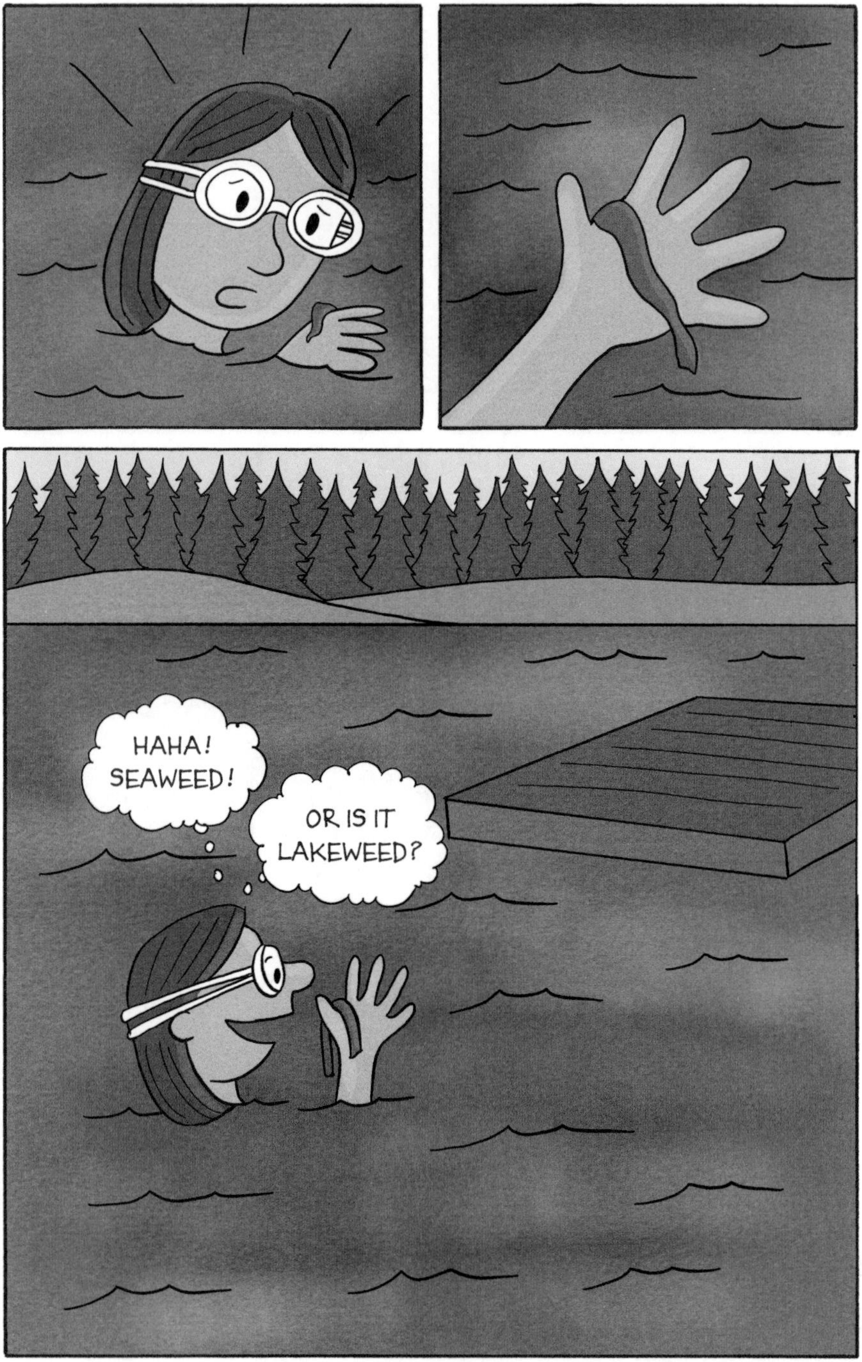
HAHA! SEAWEED!
OR IS IT LAKEWEED?

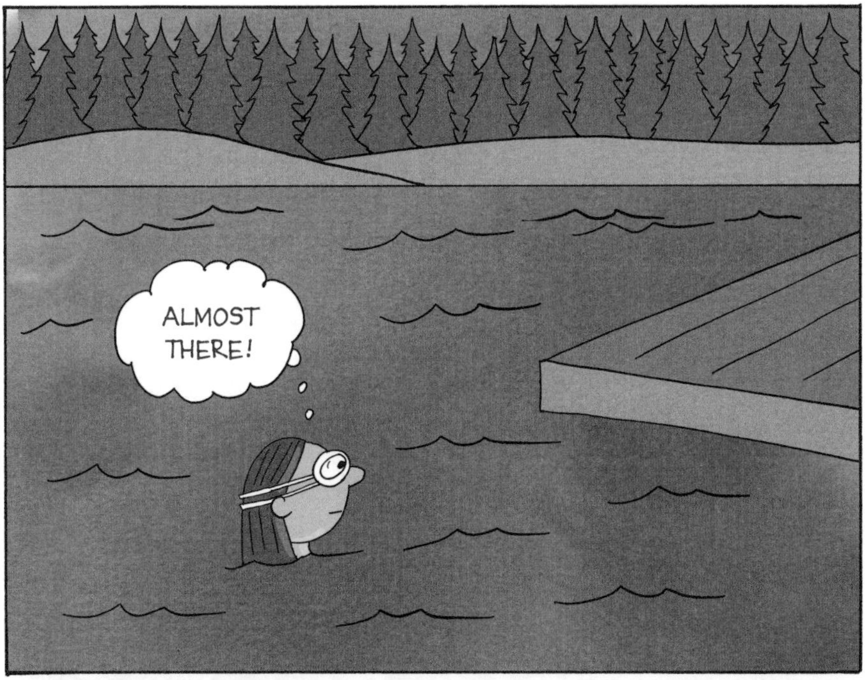
ALMOST THERE!

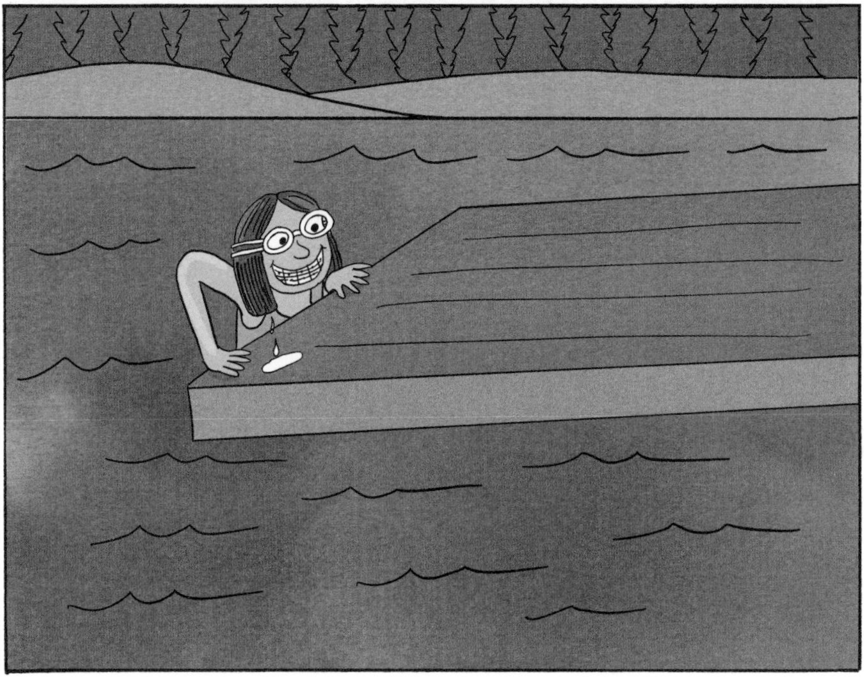

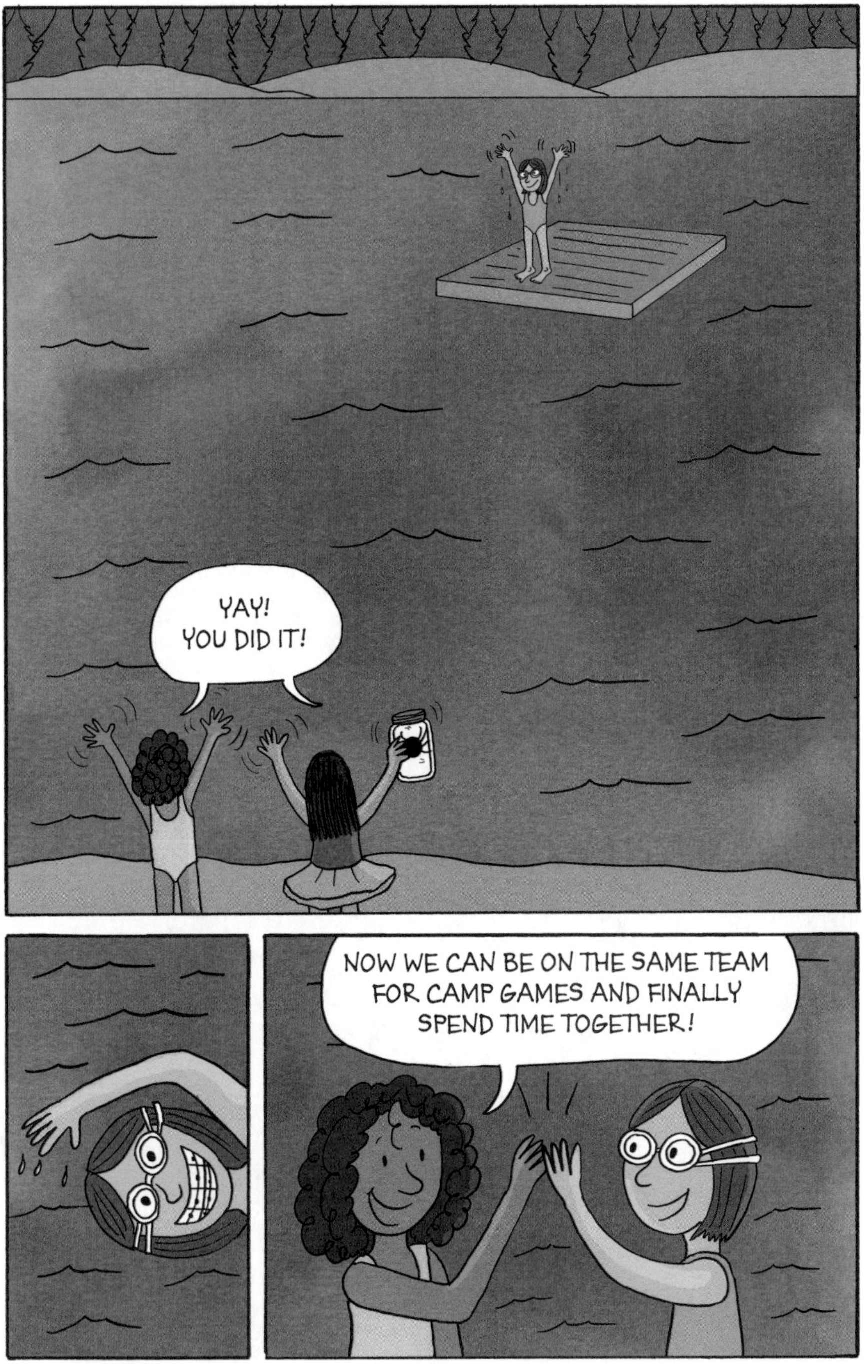
YAY!
YOU DID IT!
NOW WE CAN BE ON THE SAME TEAM FOR CAMP GAMES AND FINALLY SPEND TIME TOGETHER!

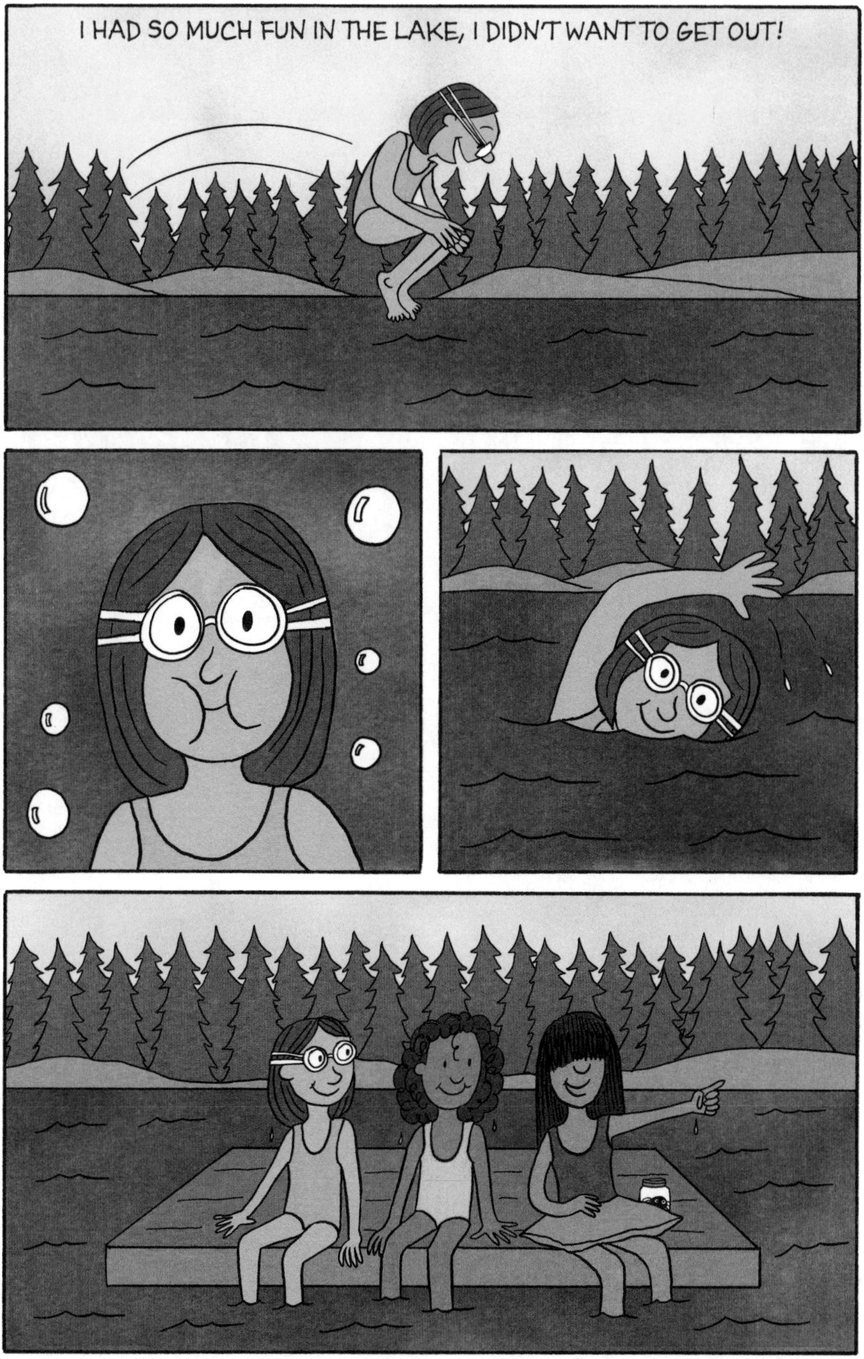
I HAD SO MUCH FUN IN THE LAKE, I DIDN'T WANT TO GET OUT!

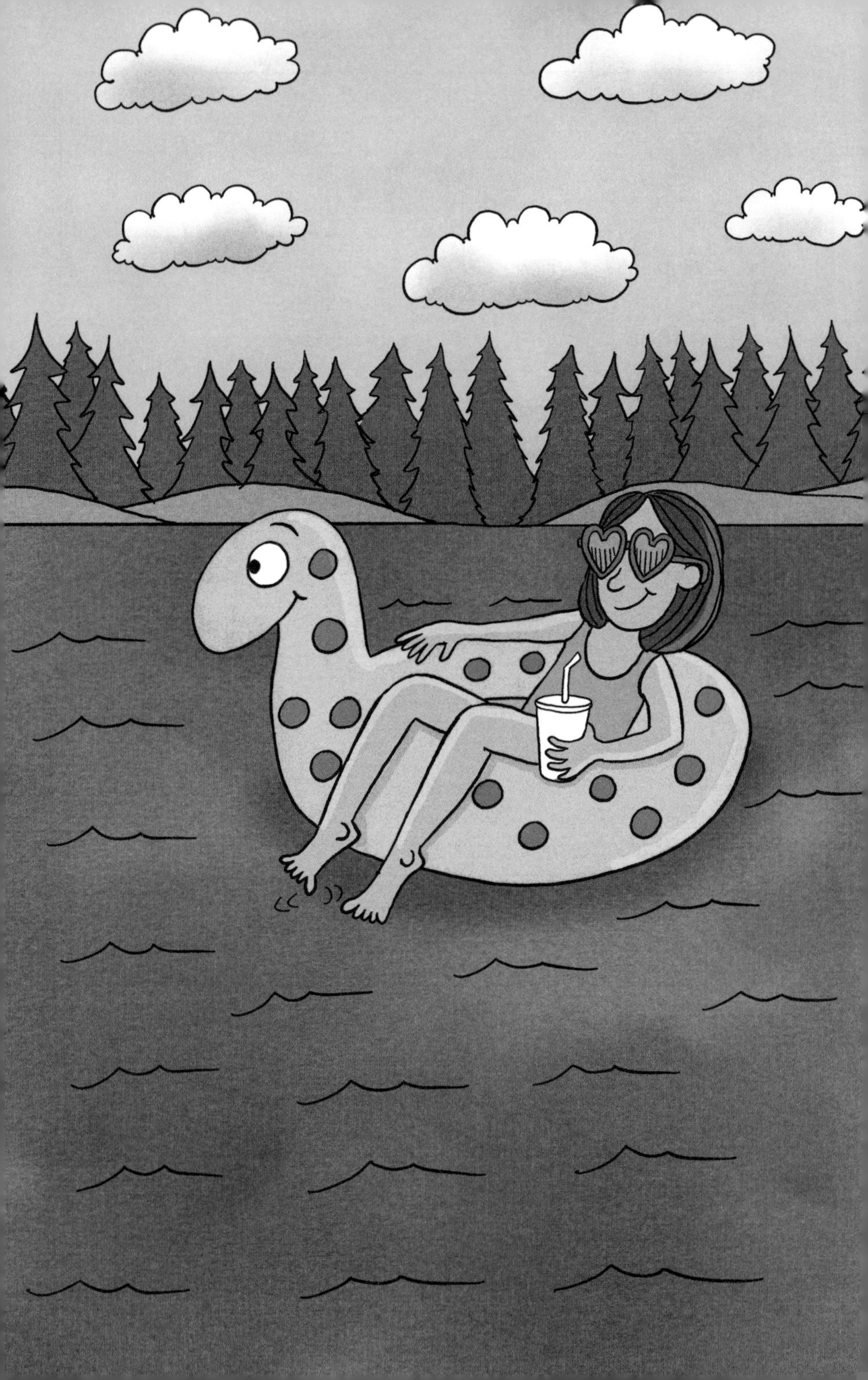

CHAPTER 13
CAMP GAMES

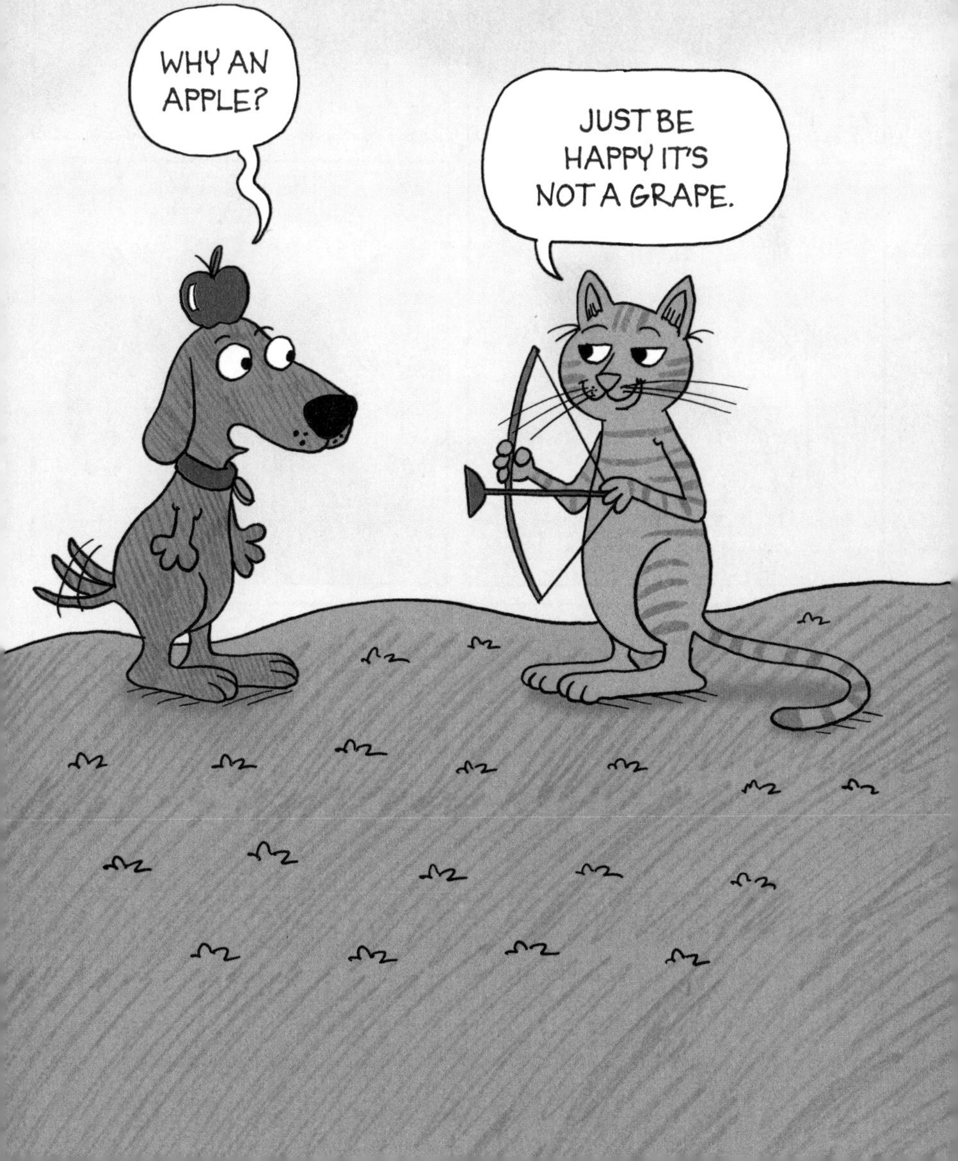
WHY AN APPLE?
JUST BE HAPPY IT'S NOT A GRAPE.

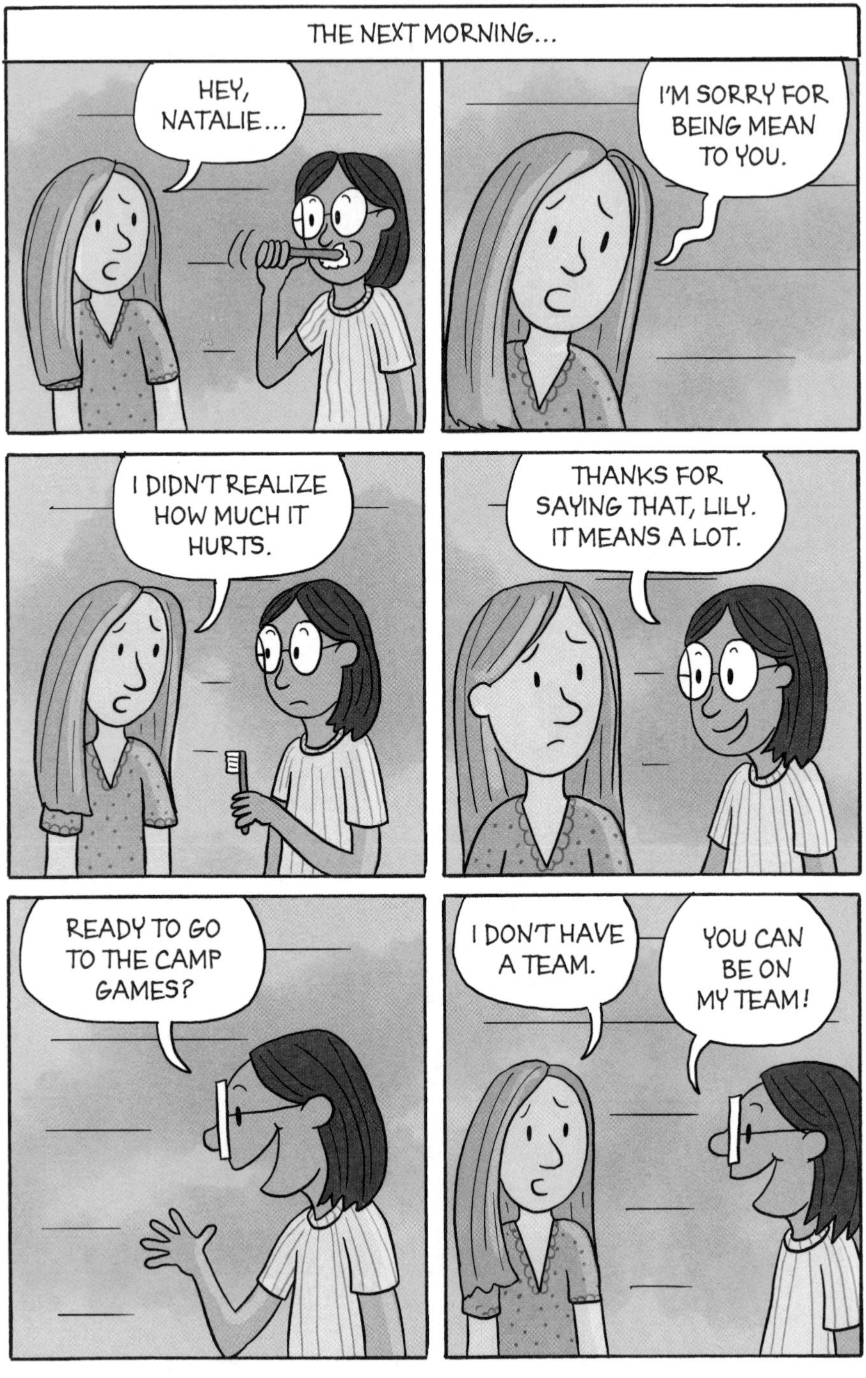
THE NEXT MORNING...
HEY, NATALIE...
I'M SORRY FOR BEING MEAN TO YOU.
I DIDN'T REALIZE HOW MUCH IT HURTS.
THANKS FOR SAYING THAT, LILY. IT MEANS A LOT.
READY TO GO TO THE CAMP GAMES?
I DON'T HAVE A TEAM.
YOU CAN BE ON MY TEAM!

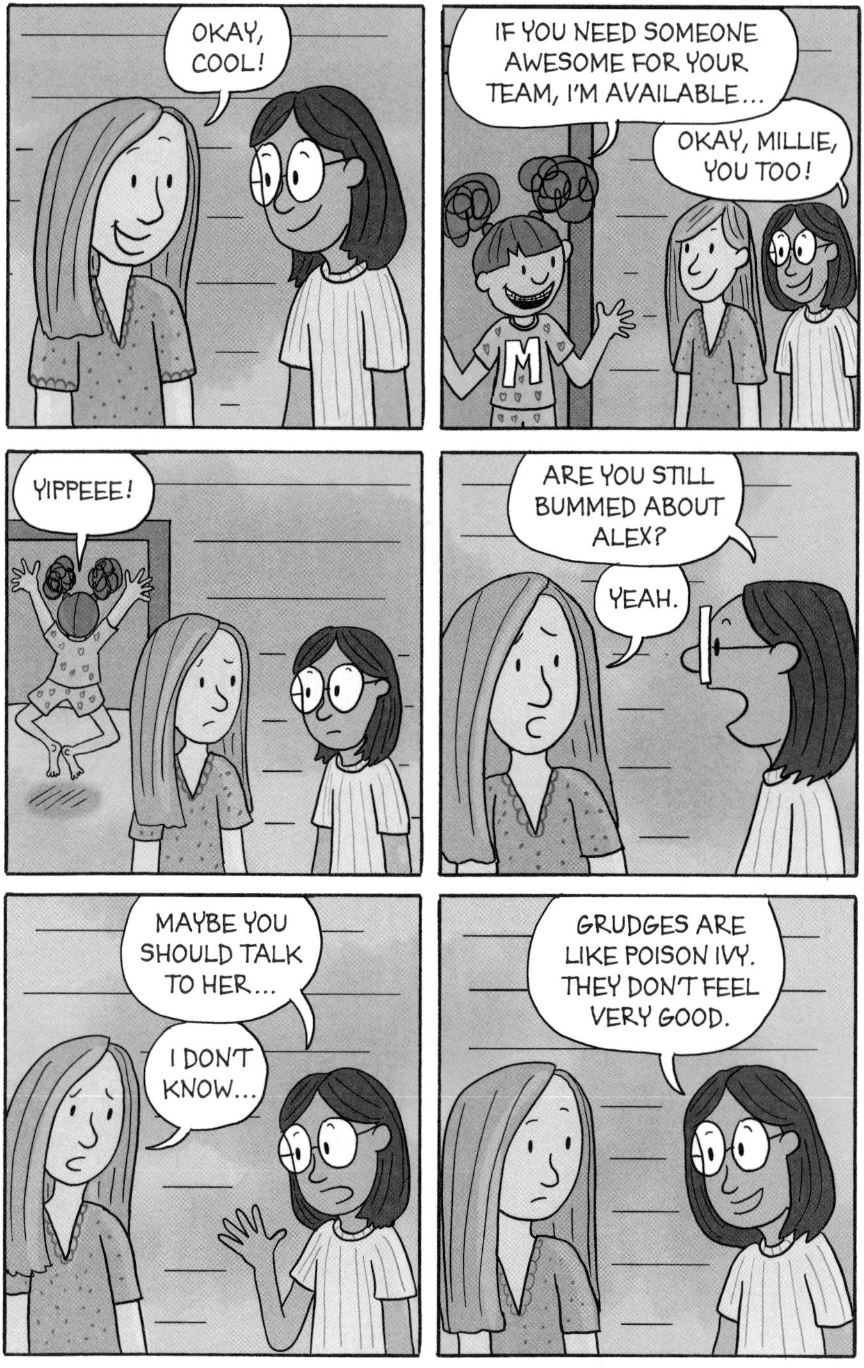
OKAY, COOL!
IF YOU NEED SOMEONE AWESOME FOR YOUR TEAM, I'M AVAILABLE...
OKAY, MILLIE, YOU TOO!
M
YIPPEEE!
ARE YOU STILL BUMMED ABOUT ALEX?
YEAH.
MAYBE YOU SHOULD TALK TO HER...
I DON'T KNOW...
GRUDGES ARE LIKE POISON IVY. THEY DON'T FEEL VERY GOOD.

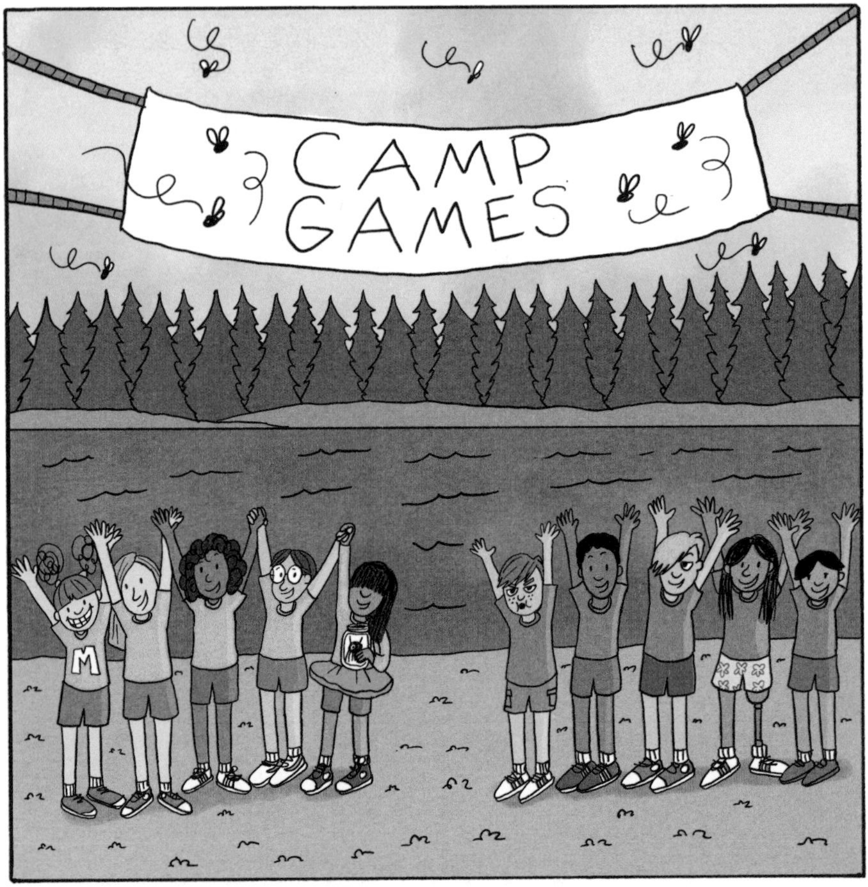
CAMP GAMES

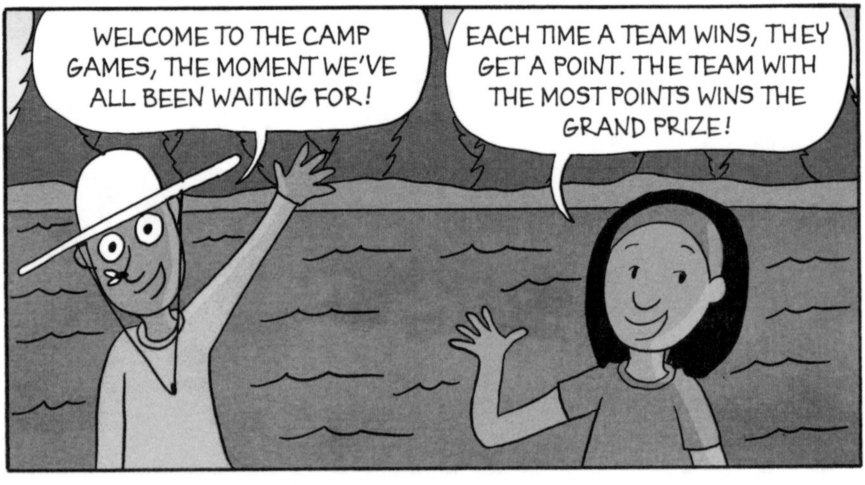
WELCOME TO THE CAMP GAMES, THE MOMENT WE'VE ALL BEEN WAITING FOR!
EACH TIME A TEAM WINS, THEY GET A POINT. THE TEAM WITH THE MOST POINTS WINS THE GRAND PRIZE!

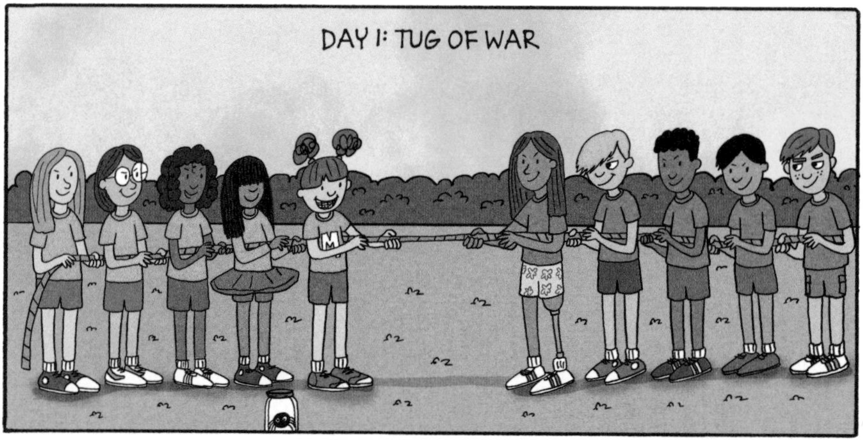
DAY 1: TUG OF WAR

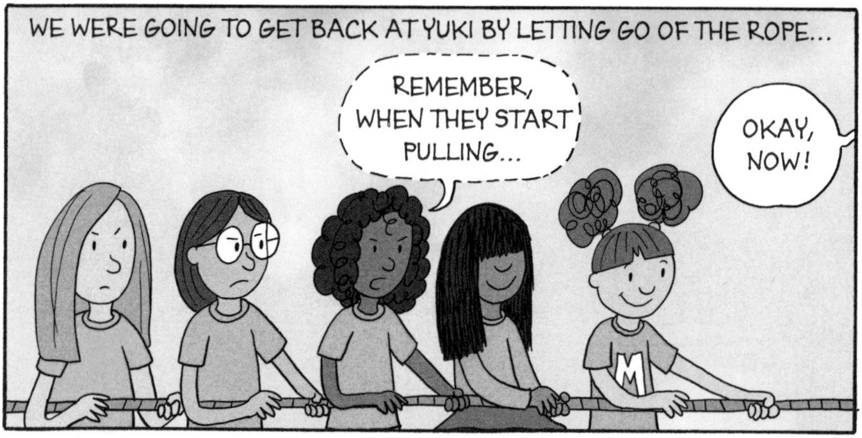
WE WERE GOING TO GET BACK AT YUKI BY LETTING GO OF THE ROPE...
REMEMBER, WHEN THEY START PULLING...
OKAY, NOW!

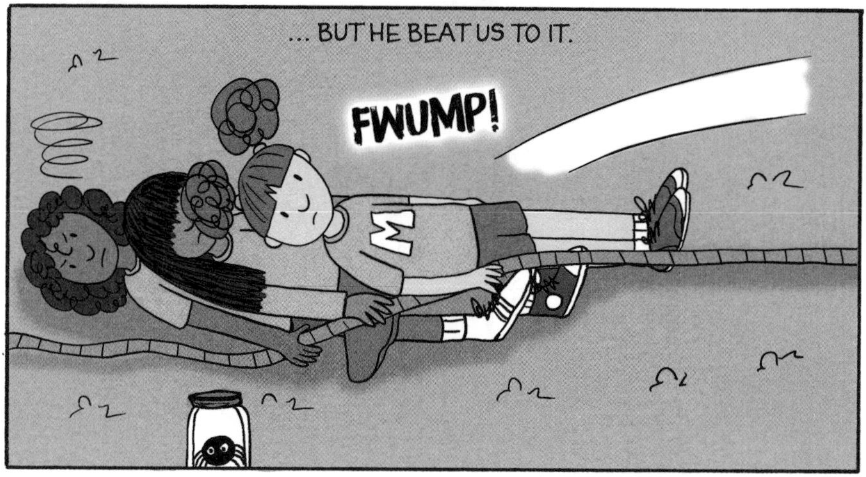
... BUT HE BEAT US TO IT.
FWUMP!

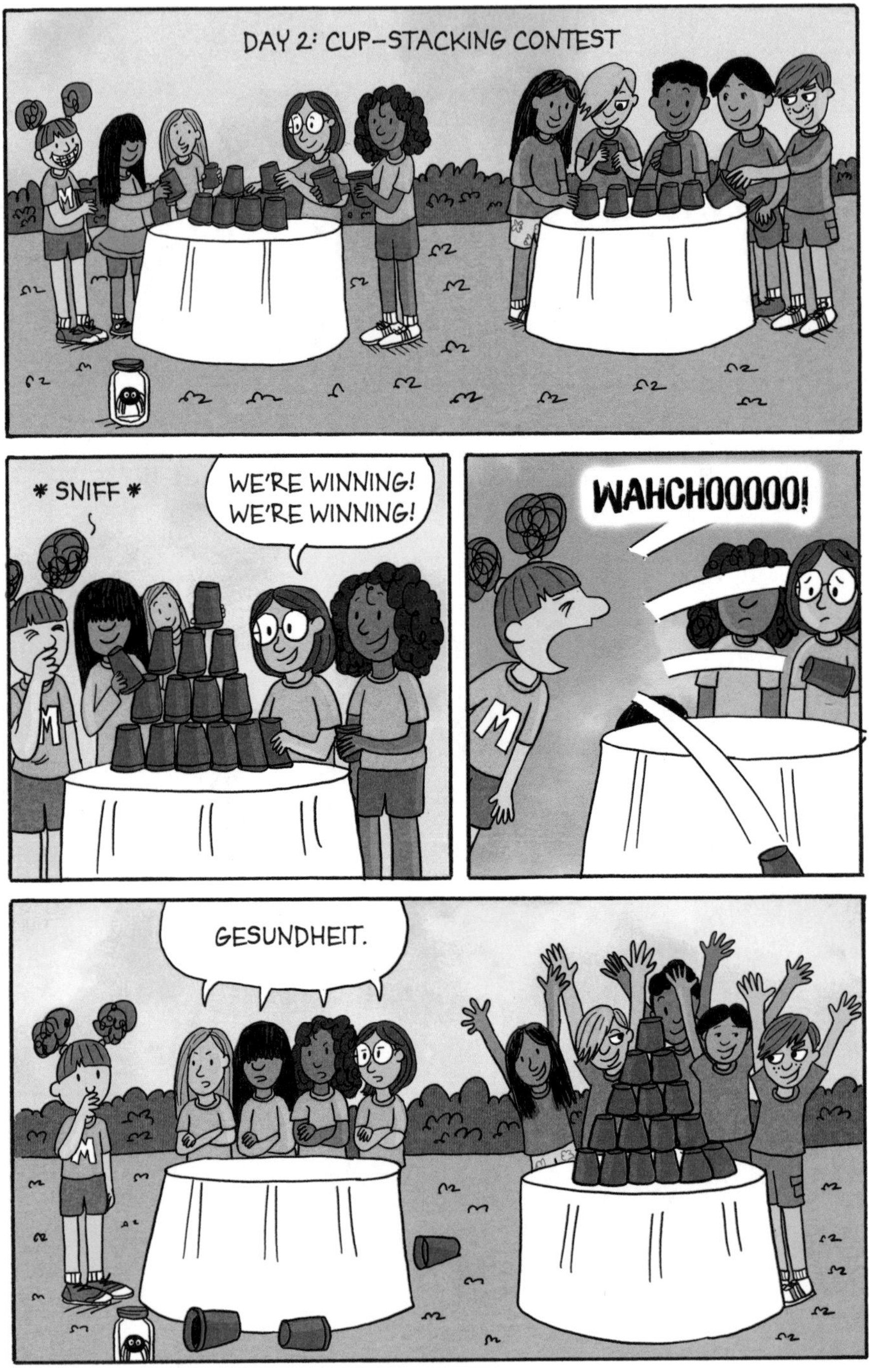

DAY 2: CUP-STACKING CONTEST
* SNIFF *
WE'RE WINNING! WE'RE WINNING!
WAHCHOOOOO!
GESUNDHEIT.

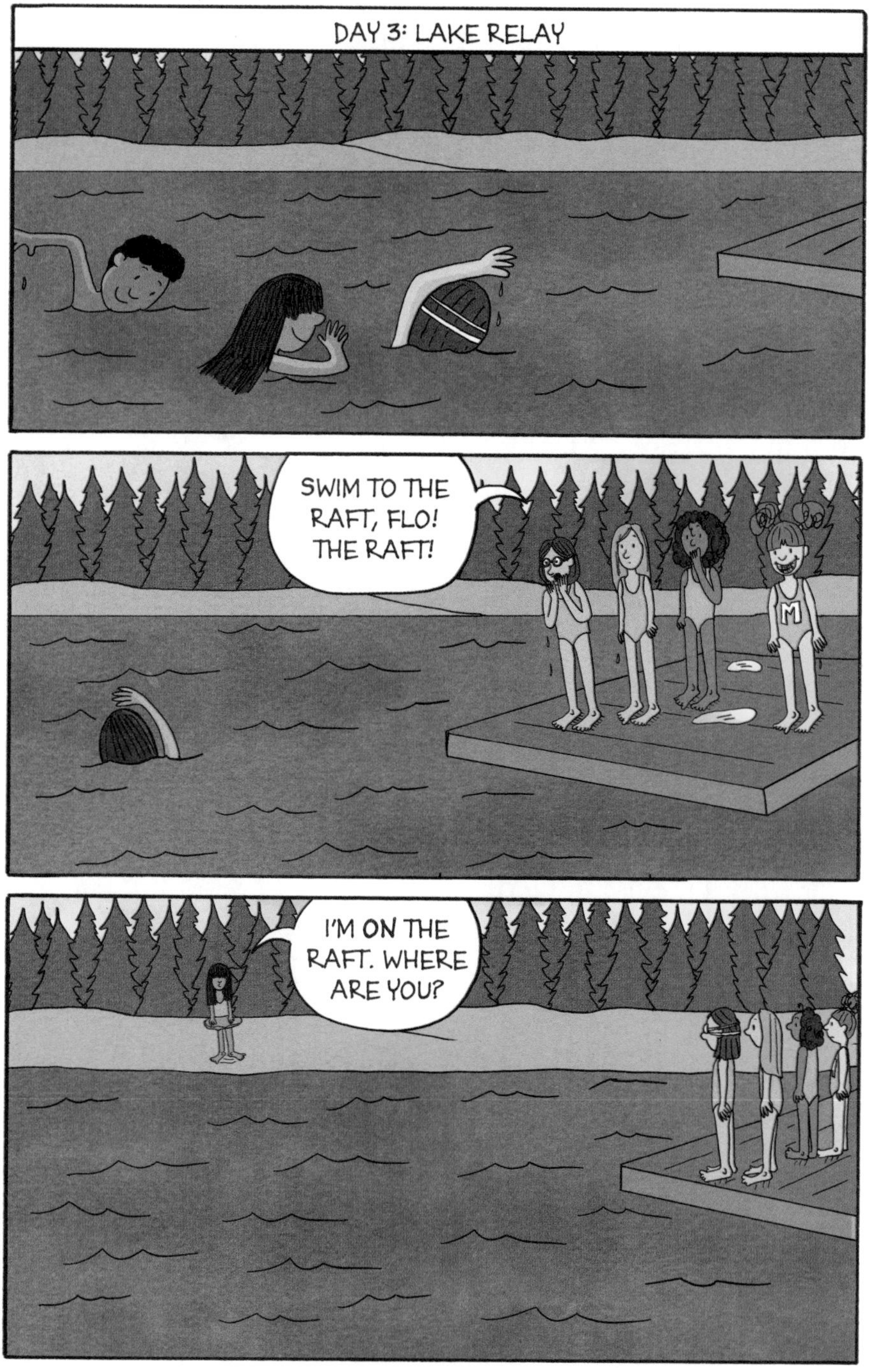
DAY 3: LAKE RELAY
SWIM TO THE RAFT, FLO! THE RAFT!
I'M ON THE RAFT. WHERE ARE YOU?

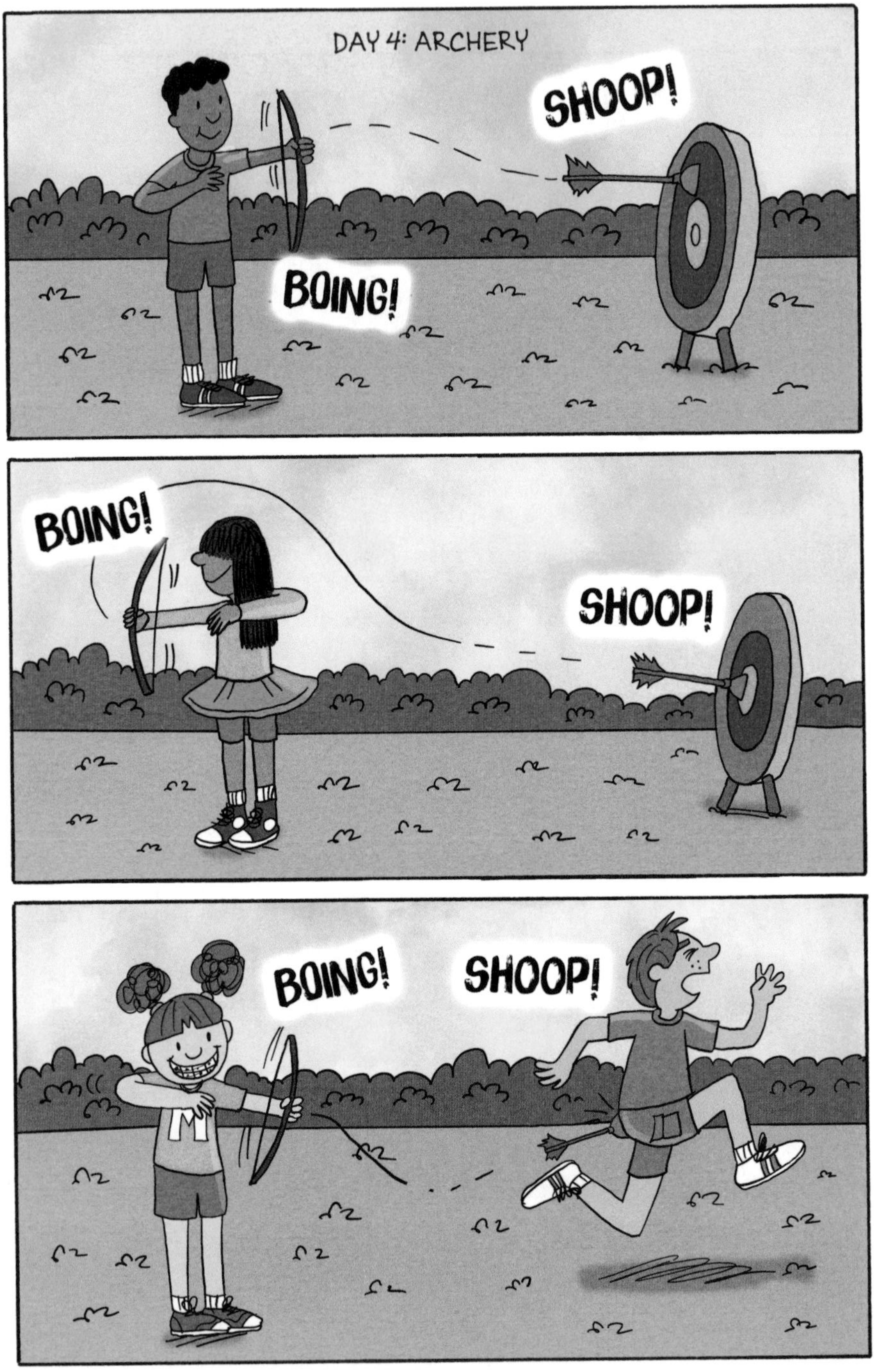
DAY 4: ARCHERY
SHOOP!
BOING!
BOING!
SHOOP!
BOING!
SHOOP!

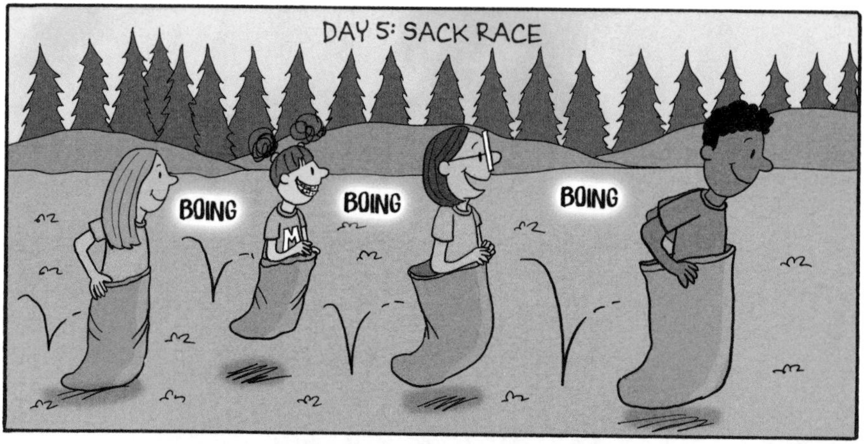
DAY 5: SACK RACE
BOING
BOING
BOING

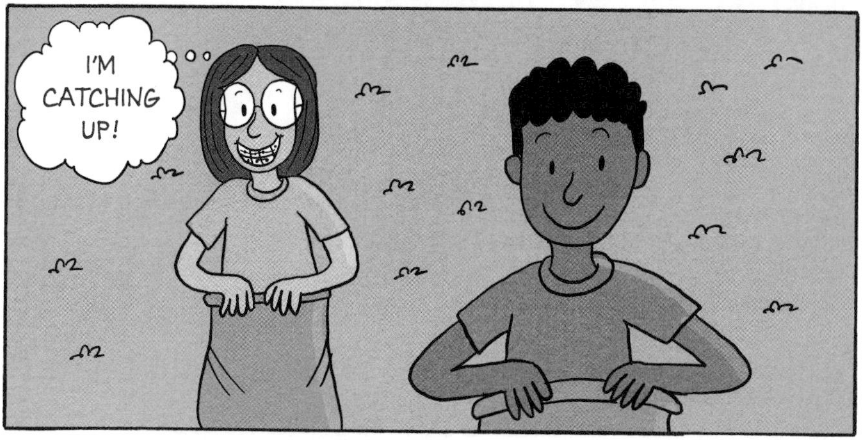
I'M CATCHING UP!

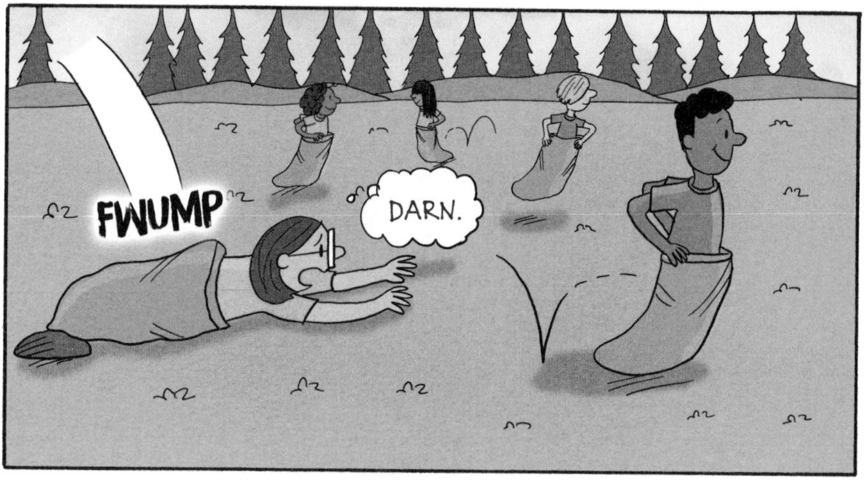
FWUMP
DARN.

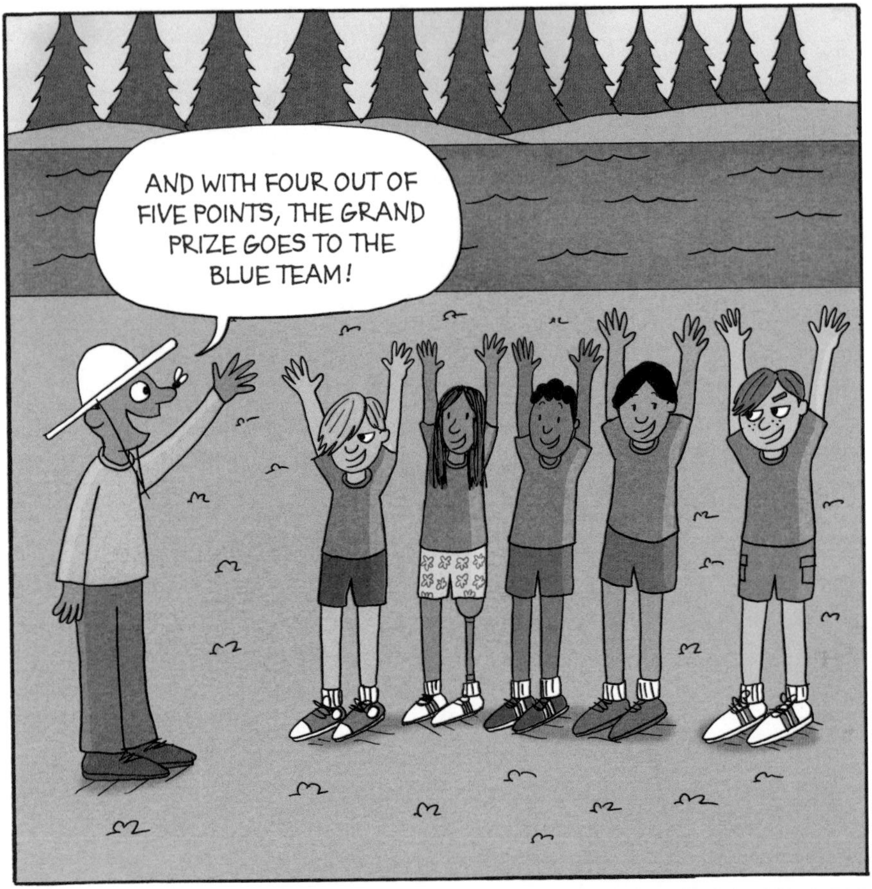
AND WITH FOUR OUT OF FIVE POINTS, THE GRAND PRIZE GOES TO THE BLUE TEAM!

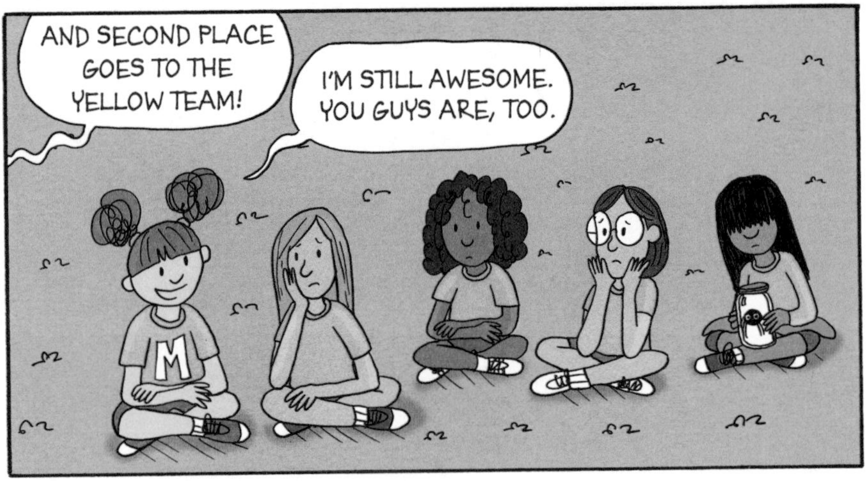
AND SECOND PLACE GOES TO THE YELLOW TEAM!
I'M STILL AWESOME. YOU GUYS ARE, TOO.

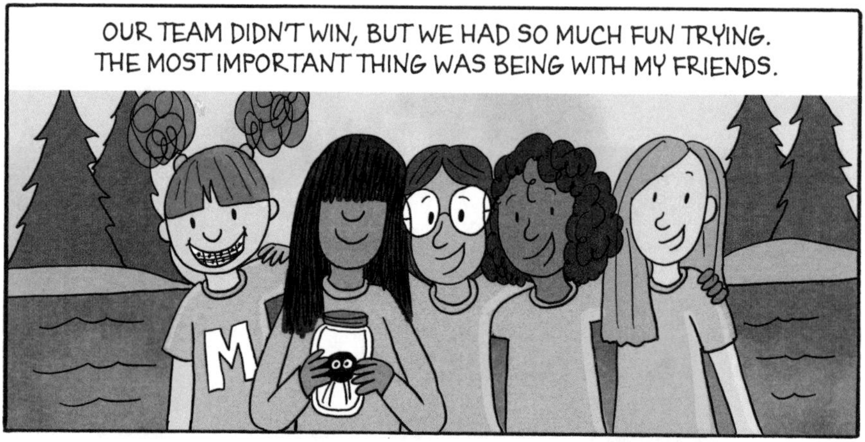
OUR TEAM DIDN'T WIN, BUT WE HAD SO MUCH FUN TRYING. THE MOST IMPORTANT THING WAS BEING WITH MY FRIENDS.
M

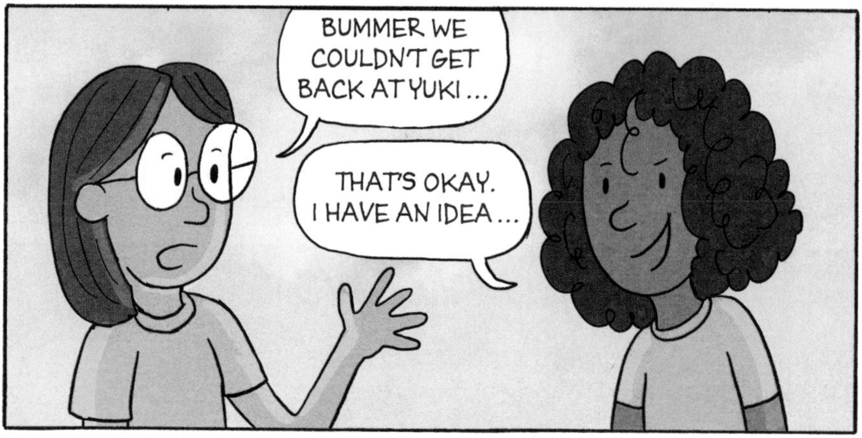
BUMMER WE COULDN'T GET BACK AT YUKI...
THAT'S OKAY. I HAVE AN IDEA...

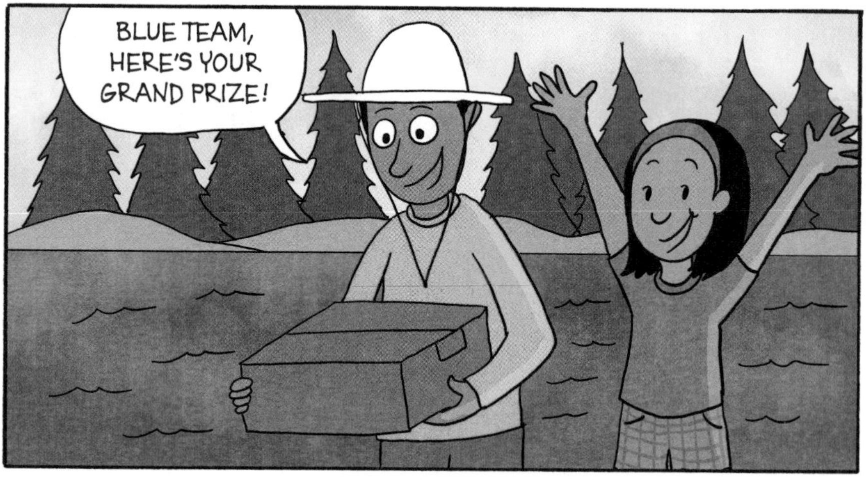
BLUE TEAM, HERE'S YOUR GRAND PRIZE!

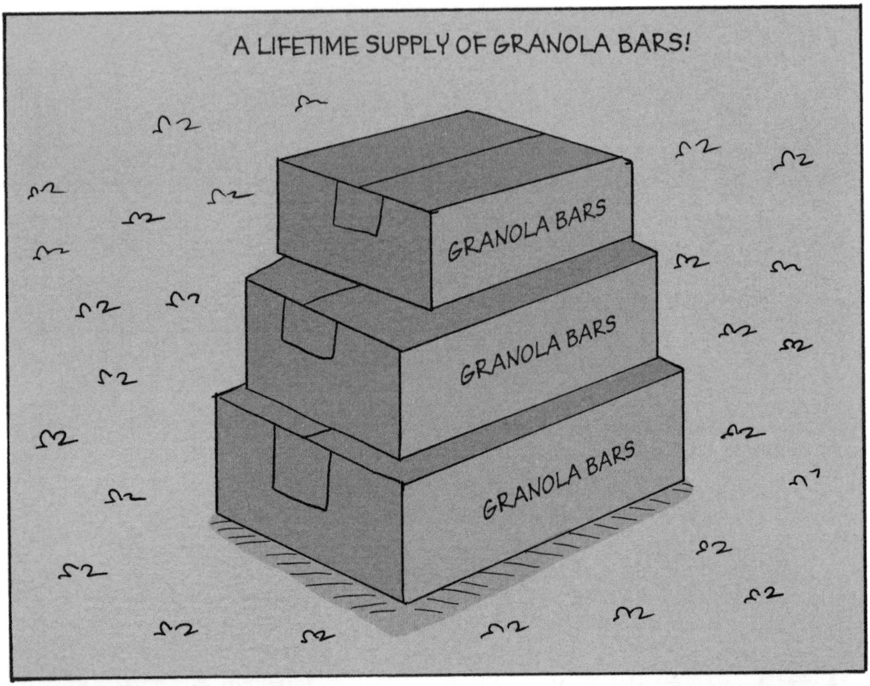
A LIFETIME SUPPLY OF GRANOLA BARS!
GRANOLA BARS
GRANOLA BARS
GRANOLA BARS

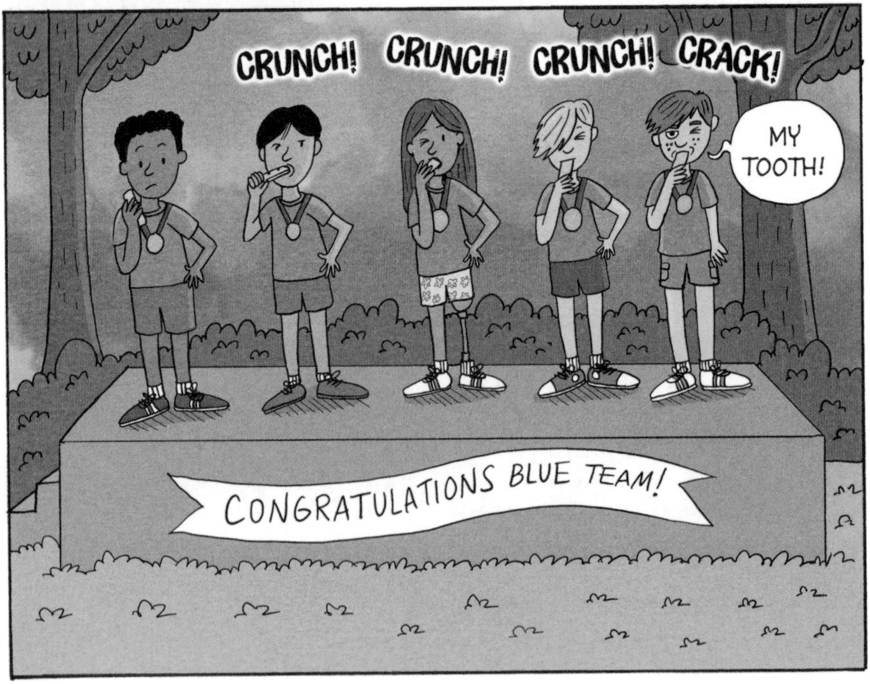
CRUNCH!
CRUNCH!
CRUNCH!
CRACK!
MY TOOTH!
CONGRATULATIONS BLUE TEAM!

CHAPTER 14
CATCH YOU LATER

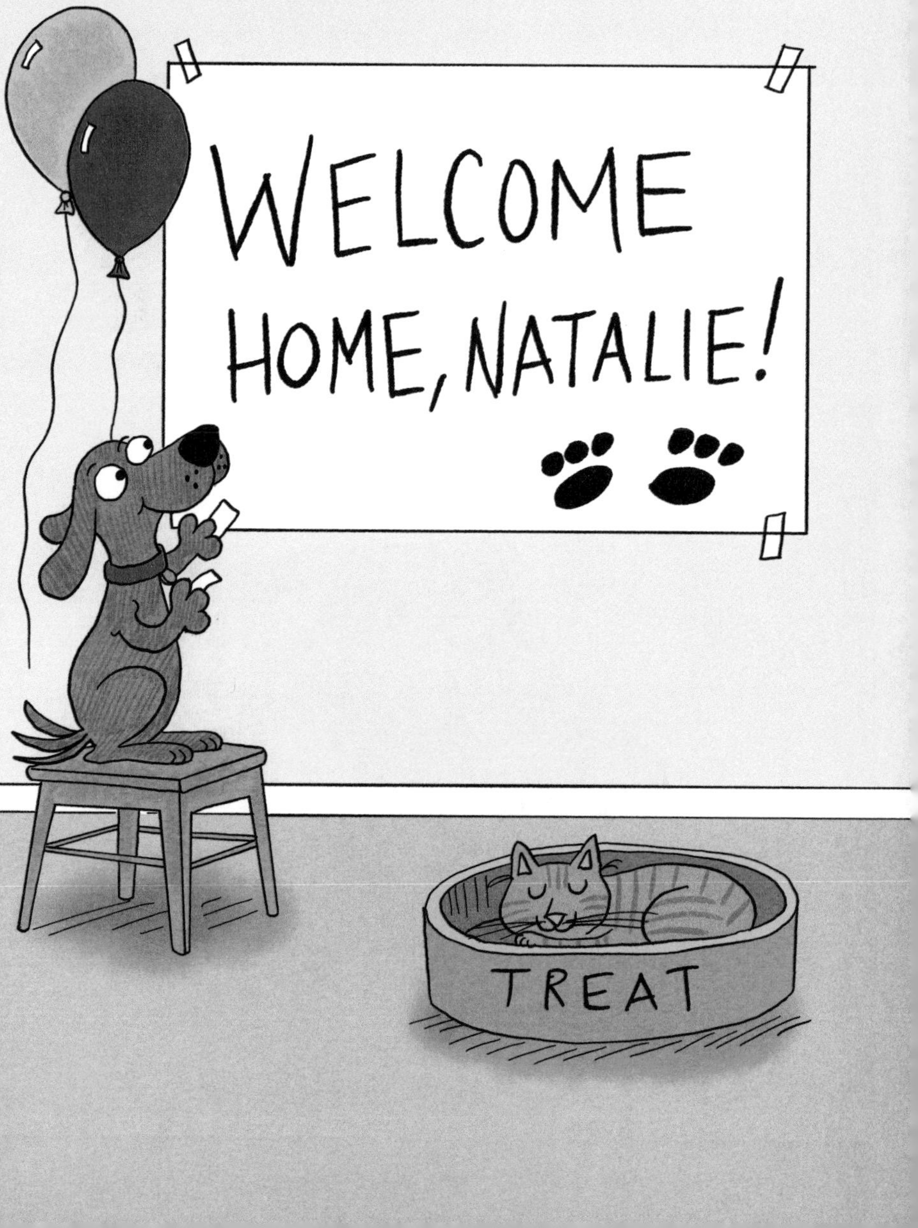
WELCOME HOME, NATALIE!
TREAT

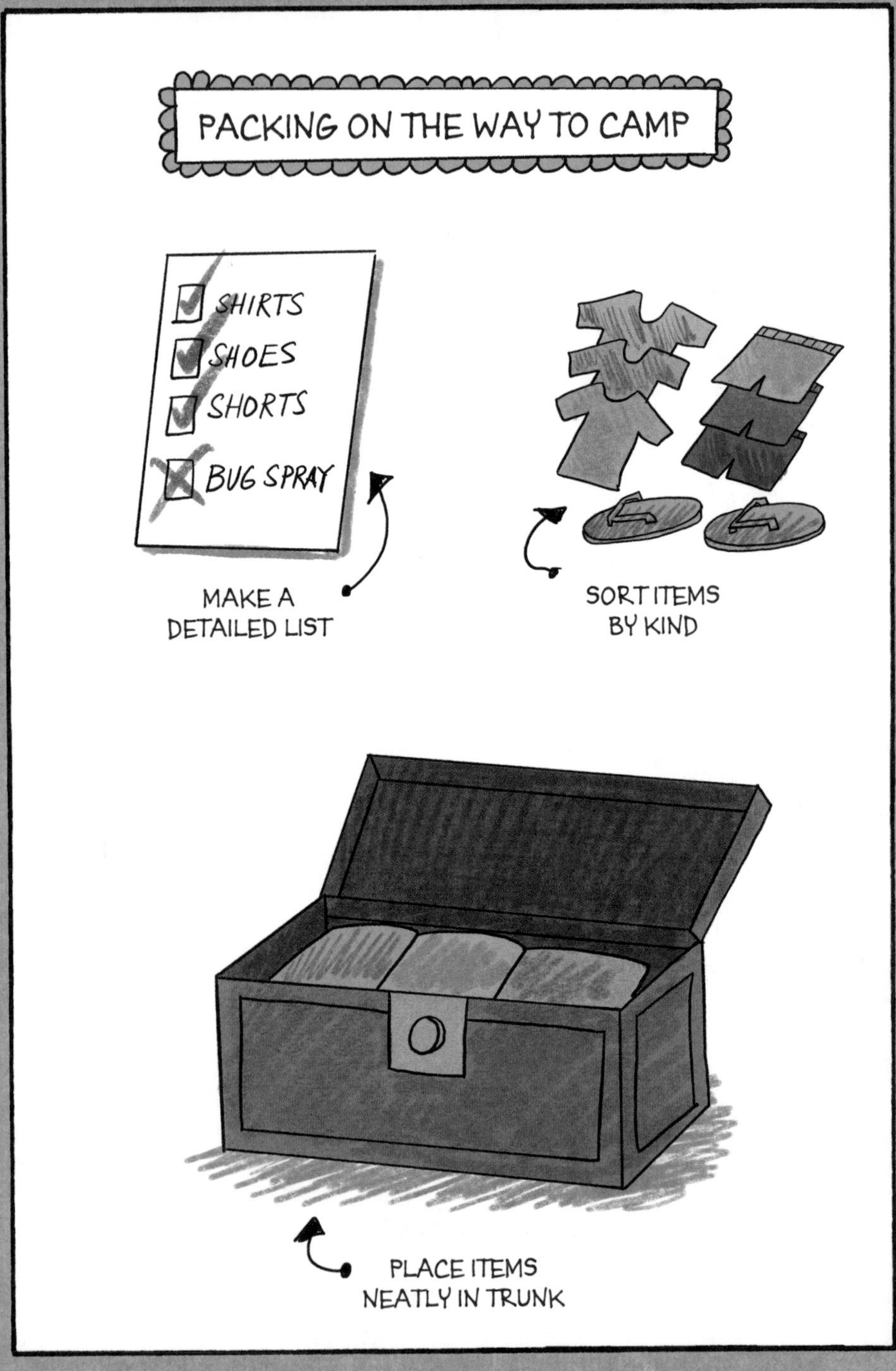
PACKING ON THE WAY TO CAMP
SHIRTS
SHOES
SHORTS
BUG SPRAY
MAKE A DETAILED LIST
SORT ITEMS BY KIND
PLACE ITEMS NEATLY IN TRUNK

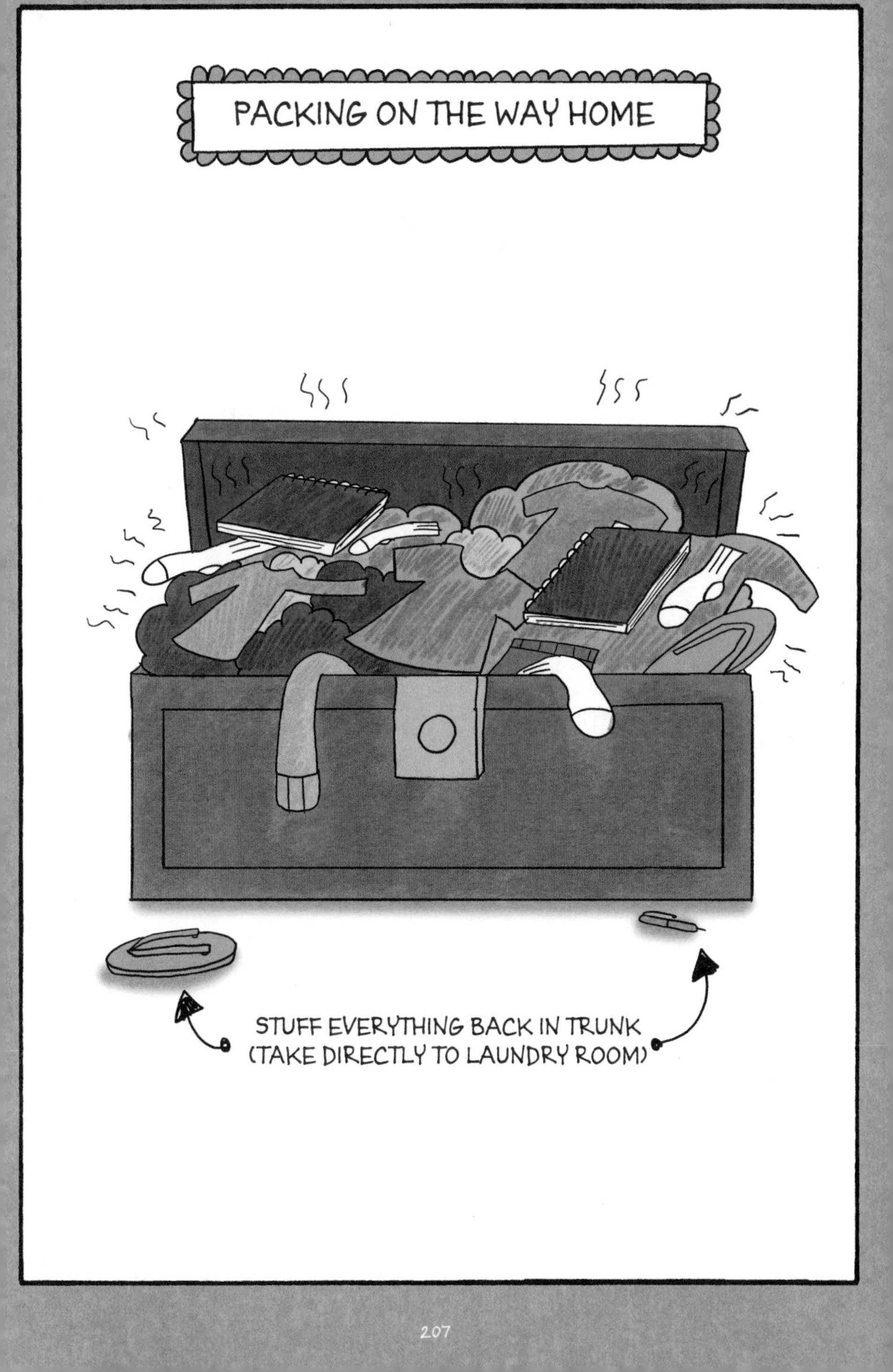
PACKING ON THE WAY HOME
STUFF EVERYTHING BACK IN TRUNK
(TAKE DIRECTLY TO LAUNDRY ROOM)

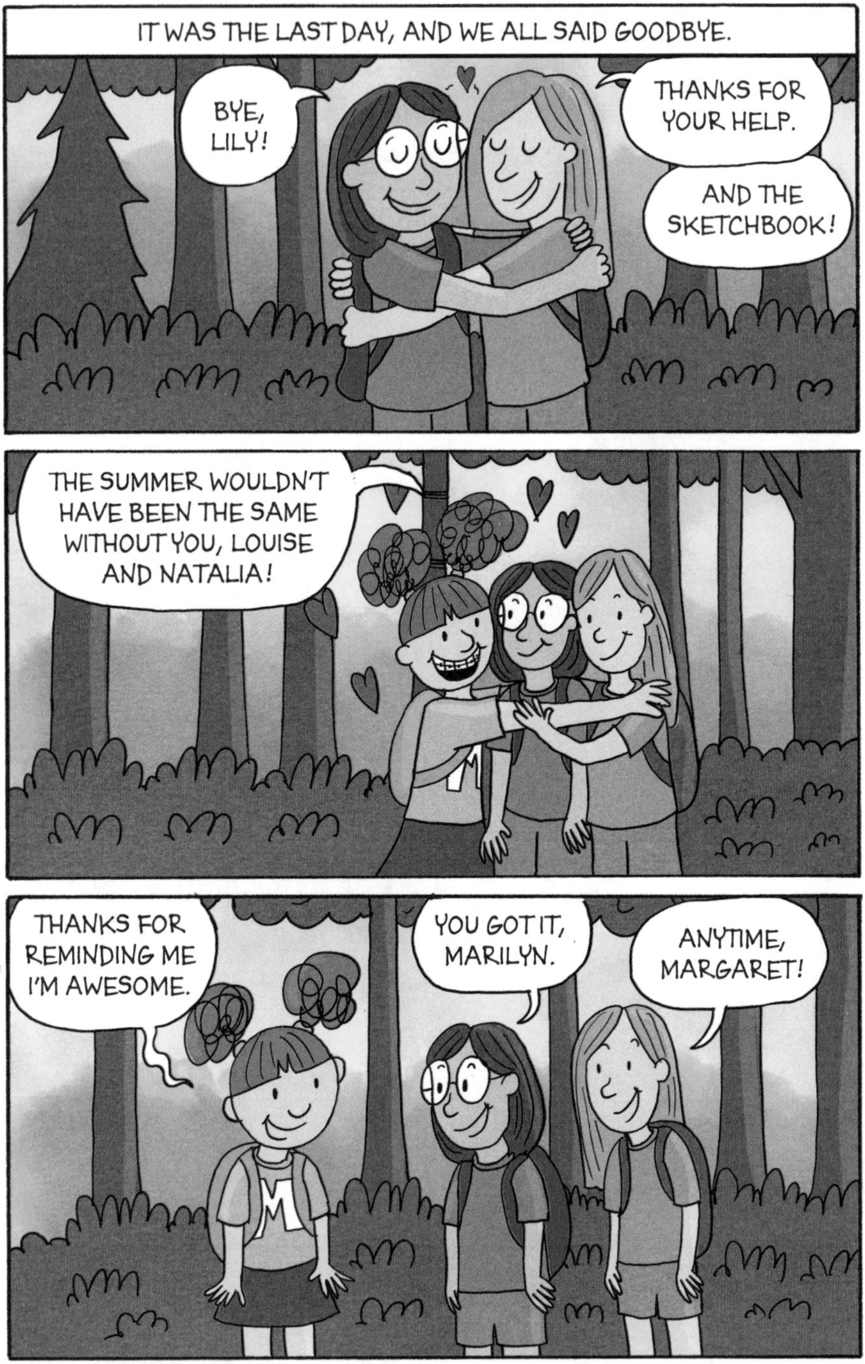
IT WAS THE LAST DAY, AND WE ALL SAID GOODBYE.
BYE, LILY!
THANKS FOR YOUR HELP.
AND THE SKETCHBOOK!
THE SUMMER WOULDN'T HAVE BEEN THE SAME WITHOUT YOU, LOUISE AND NATALIA!
THANKS FOR REMINDING ME I'M AWESOME.
YOU GOT IT, MARILYN.
ANYTIME, MARGARET!

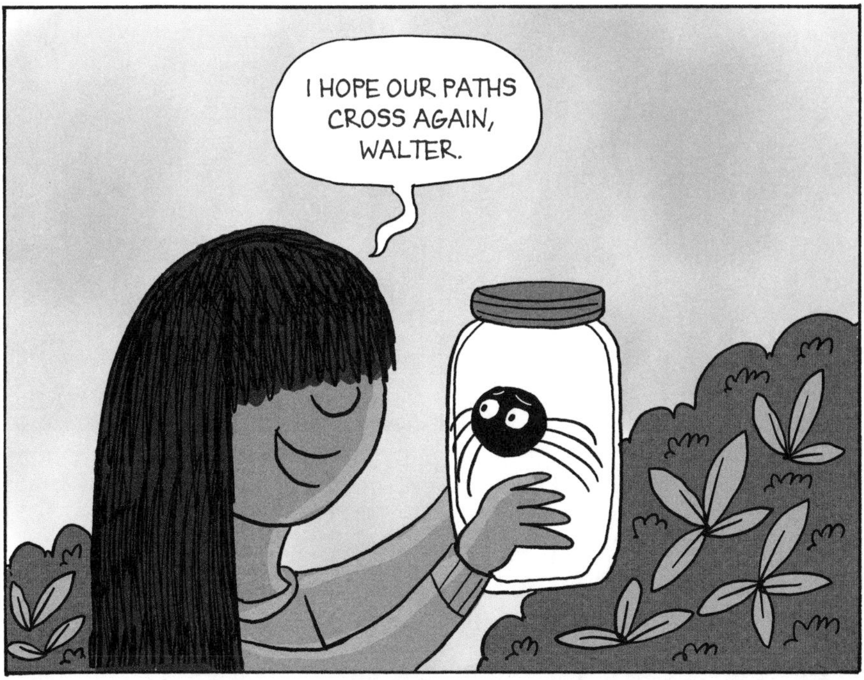
I HOPE OUR PATHS CROSS AGAIN, WALTER.

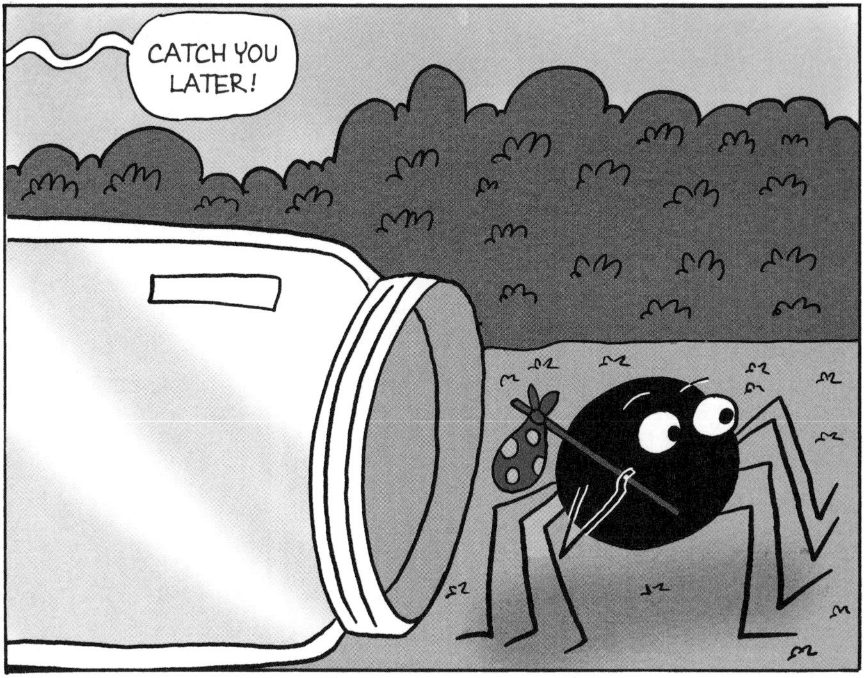
CATCH YOU LATER!

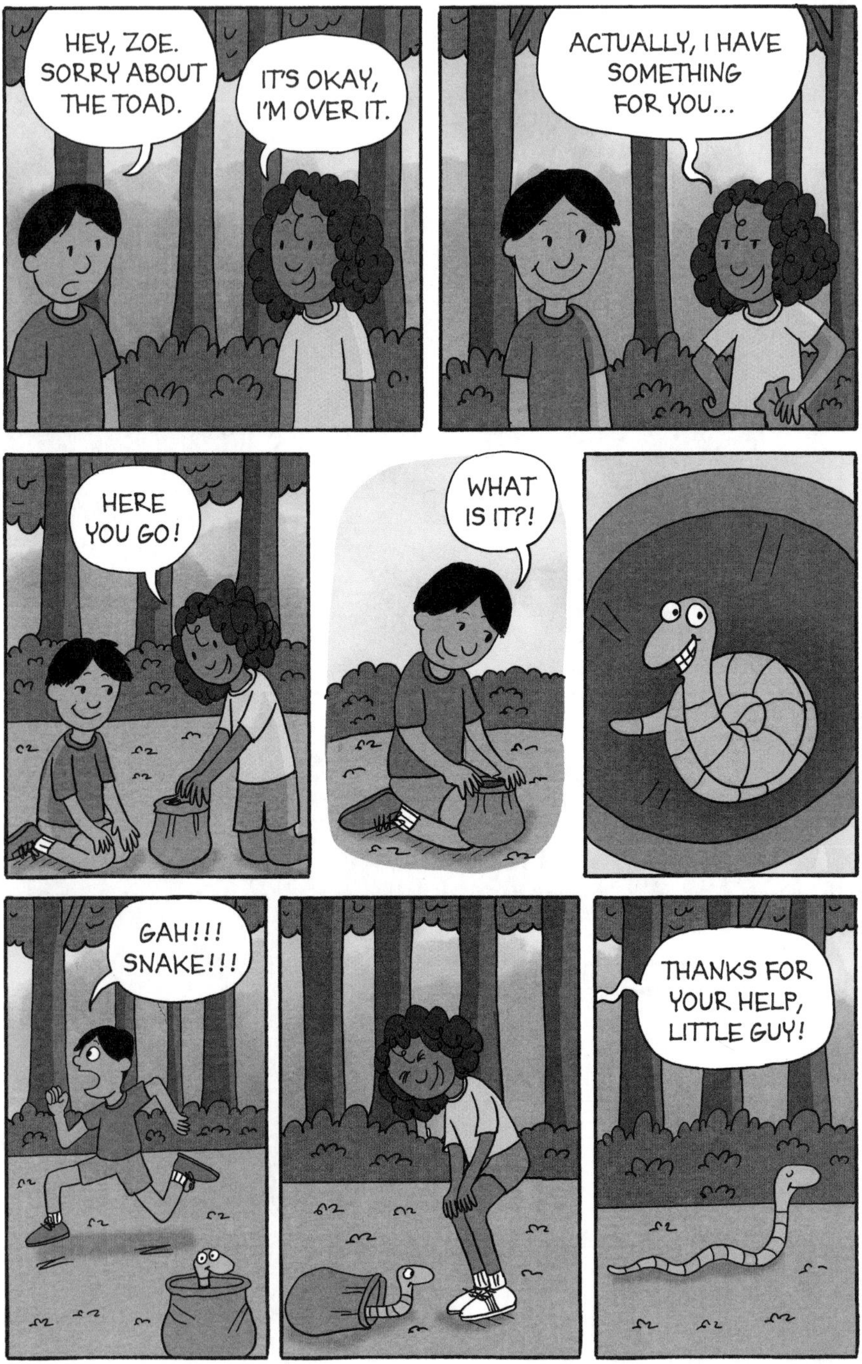
HEY, ZOE. SORRY ABOUT THE TOAD.
IT'S OKAY, I'M OVER IT.
ACTUALLY, I HAVE SOMETHING FOR YOU...
HERE YOU GO!
WHAT IS IT?!
GAH!!! SNAKE!!!
THANKS FOR YOUR HELP, LITTLE GUY!

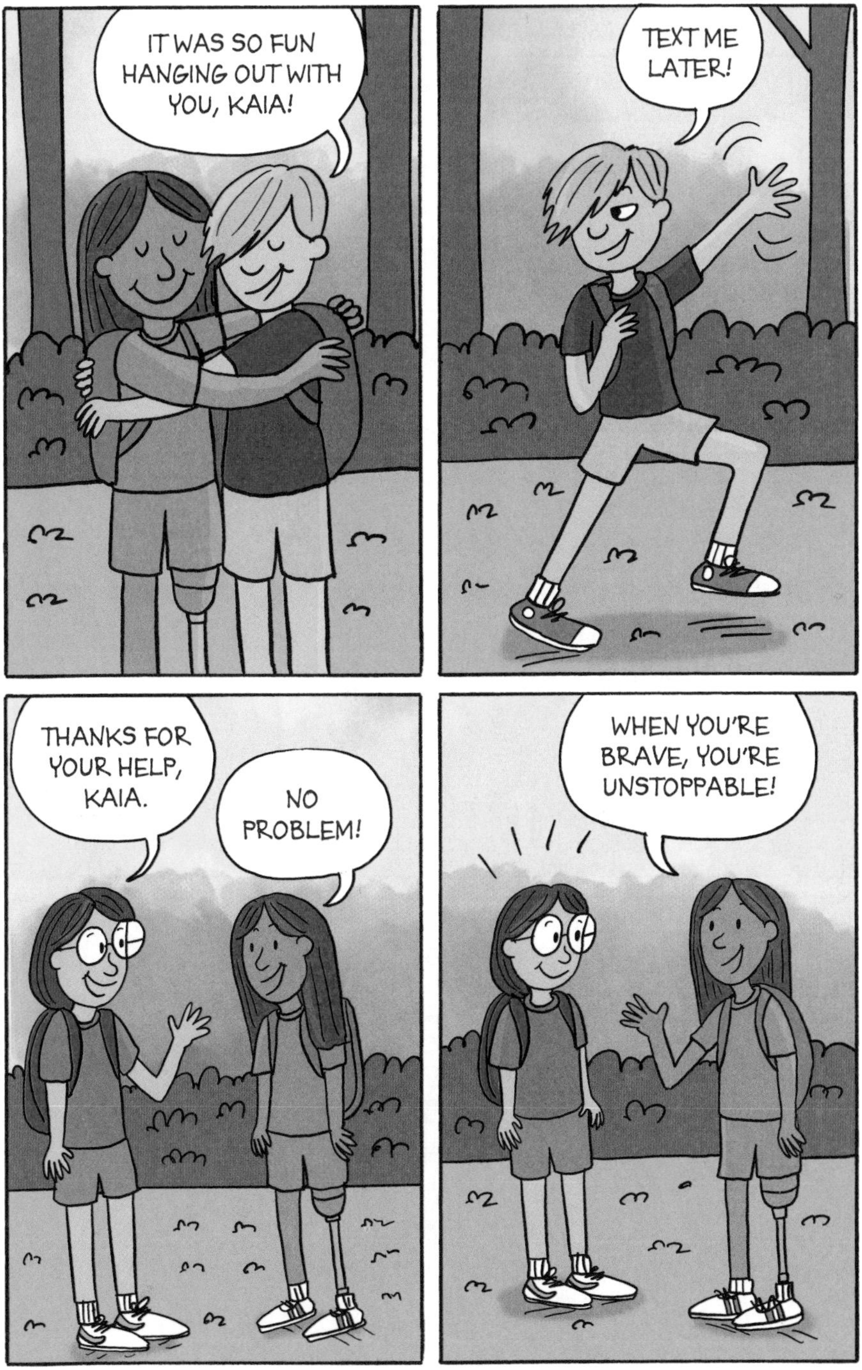
IT WAS SO FUN HANGING OUT WITH YOU, KAIA!
TEXT ME LATER!
THANKS FOR YOUR HELP, KAIA.
NO PROBLEM!
WHEN YOU'RE BRAVE, YOU'RE UNSTOPPABLE!

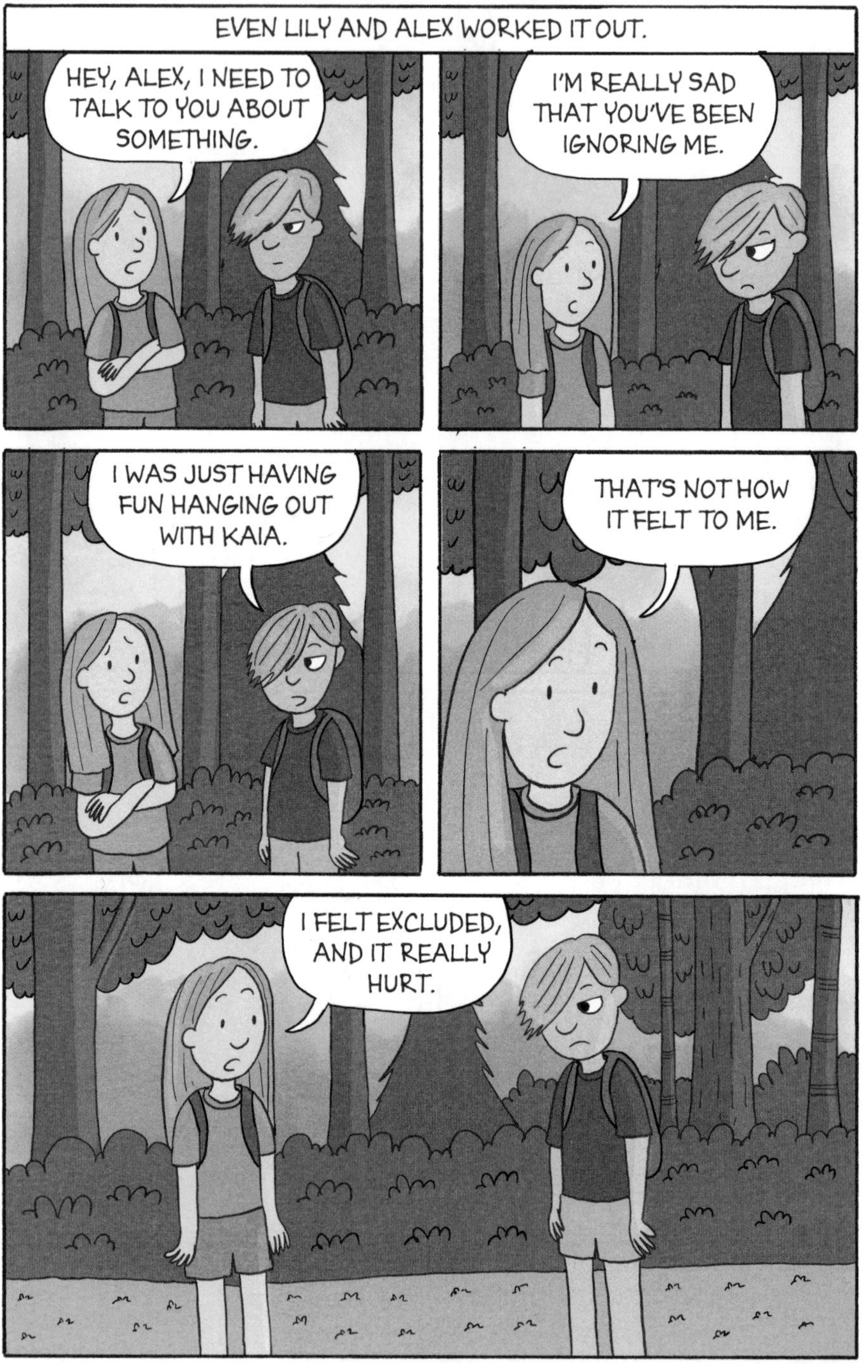
EVEN LILY AND ALEX WORKED IT OUT.
HEY, ALEX, I NEED TO TALK TO YOU ABOUT SOMETHING.
I'M REALLY SAD THAT YOU'VE BEEN IGNORING ME.
I WAS JUST HAVING FUN HANGING OUT WITH KAIA.
THAT'S NOT HOW IT FELT TO ME.
I FELT EXCLUDED, AND IT REALLY HURT.

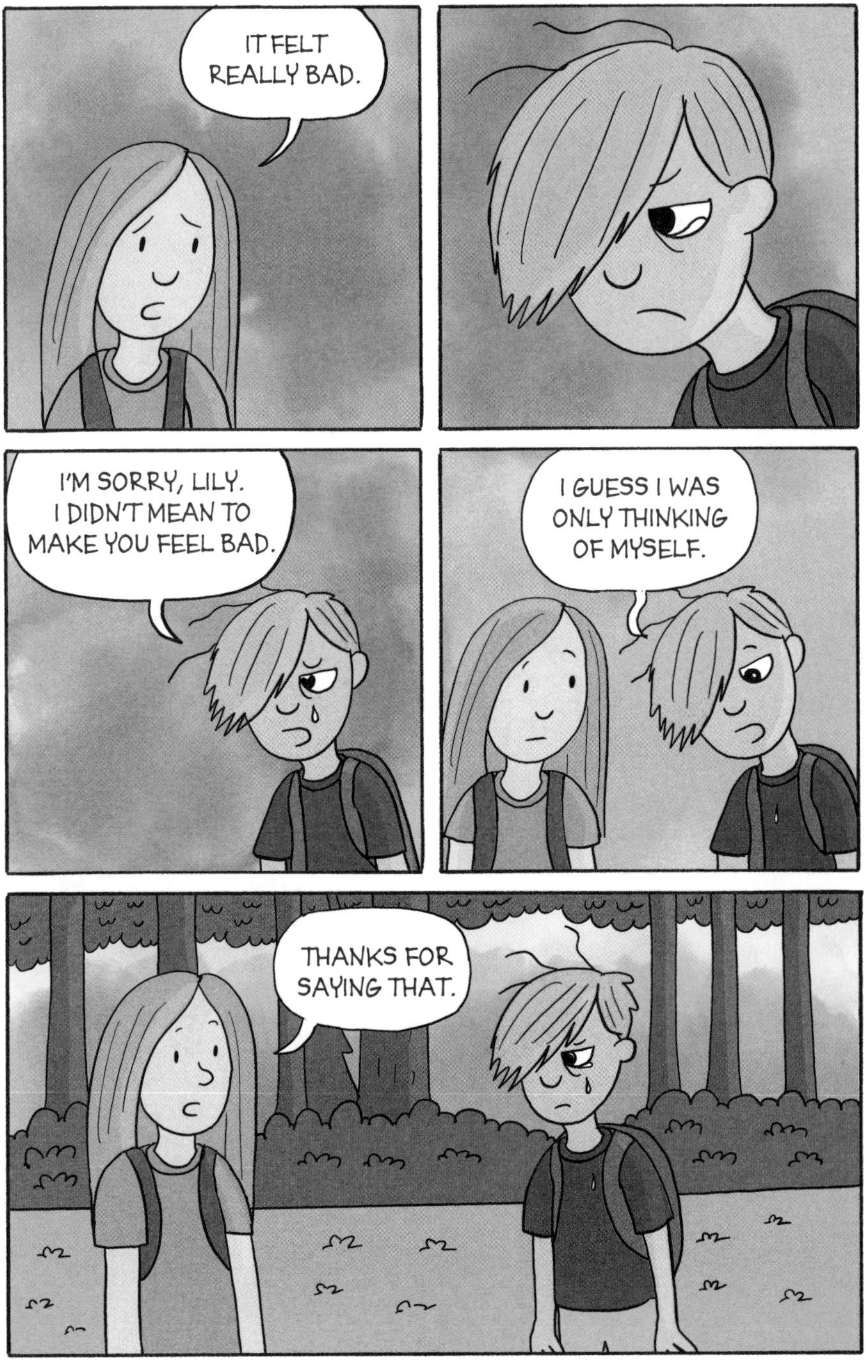
IT FELT REALLY BAD.
I'M SORRY, LILY. I DIDN'T MEAN TO MAKE YOU FEEL BAD.
I GUESS I WAS ONLY THINKING OF MYSELF.
THANKS FOR SAYING THAT.

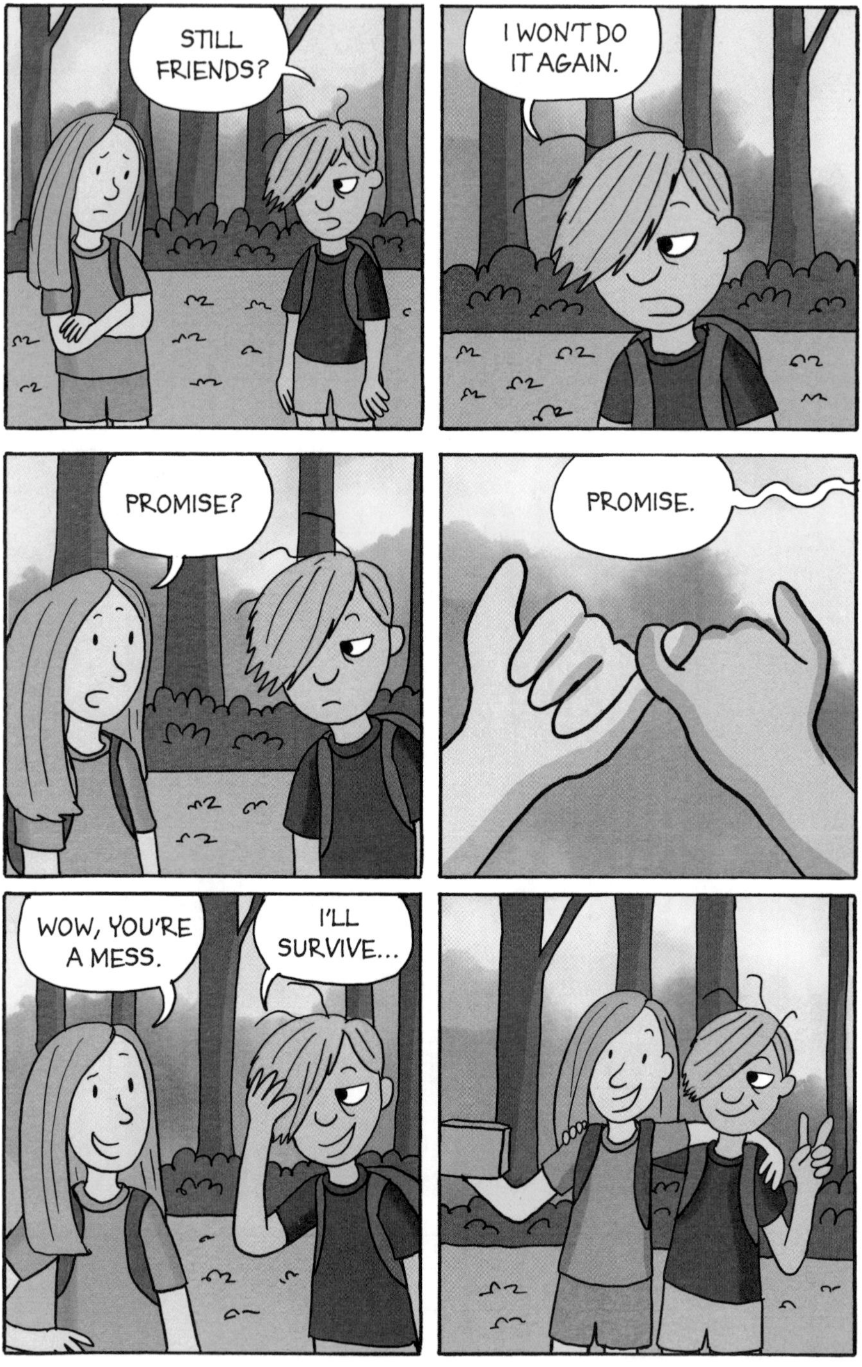
STILL FRIENDS?
I WON'T DO IT AGAIN.
PROMISE?
PROMISE.
WOW, YOU'RE A MESS.
I'LL SURVIVE...

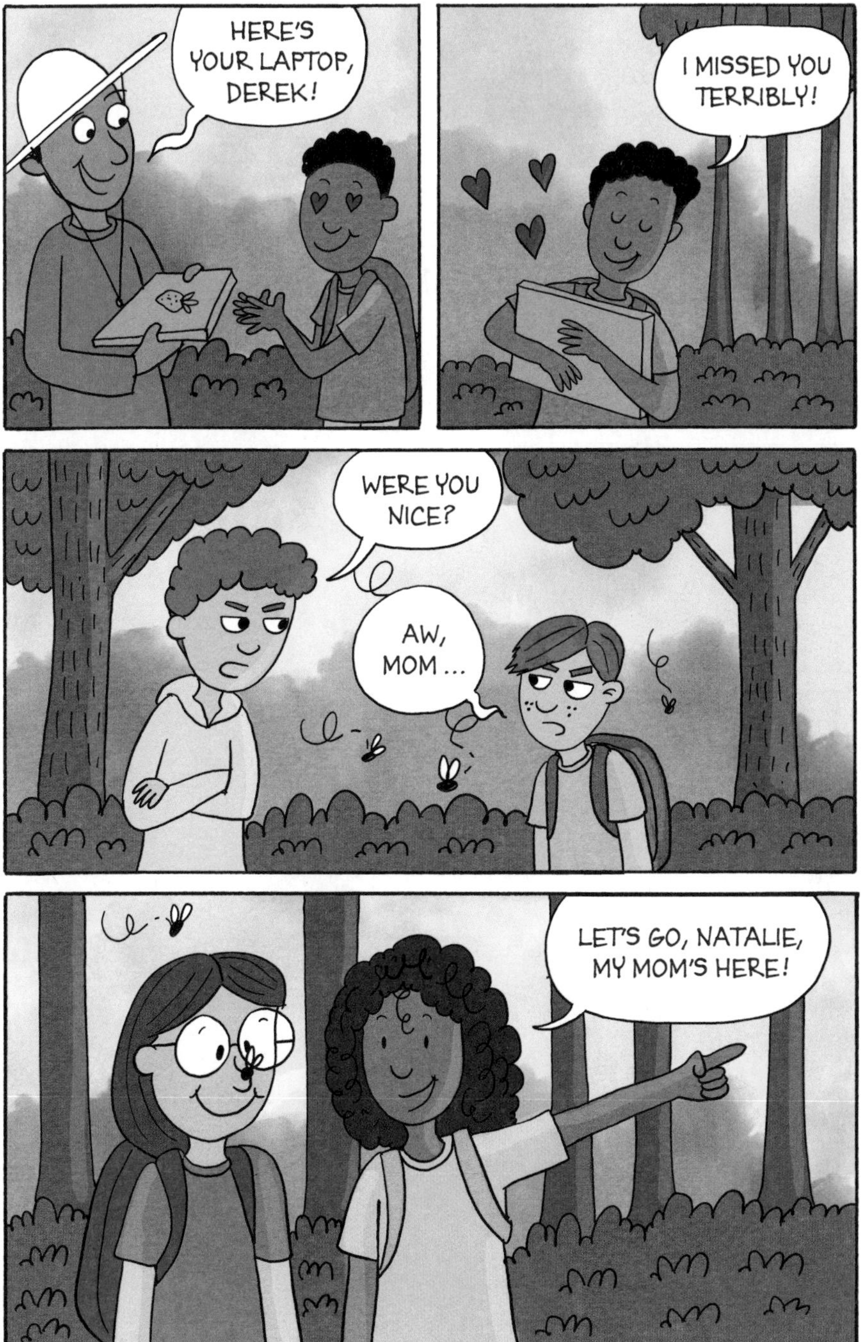
HERE'S YOUR LAPTOP, DEREK!
I MISSED YOU TERRIBLY!
WERE YOU NICE?
AW, MOM ...
LET'S GO, NATALIE, MY MOM'S HERE!

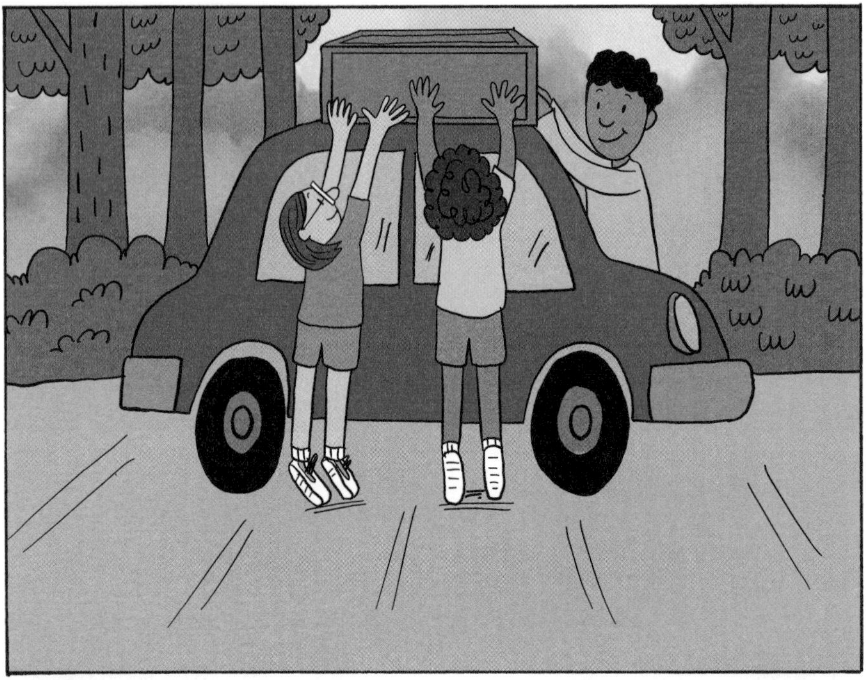

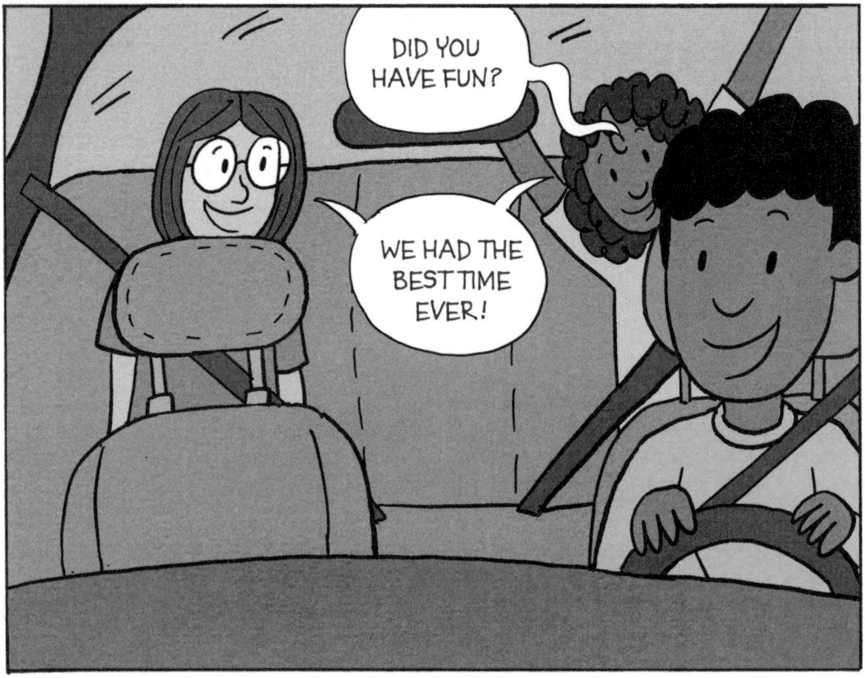
DID YOU HAVE FUN?
WE HAD THE BEST TIME EVER!

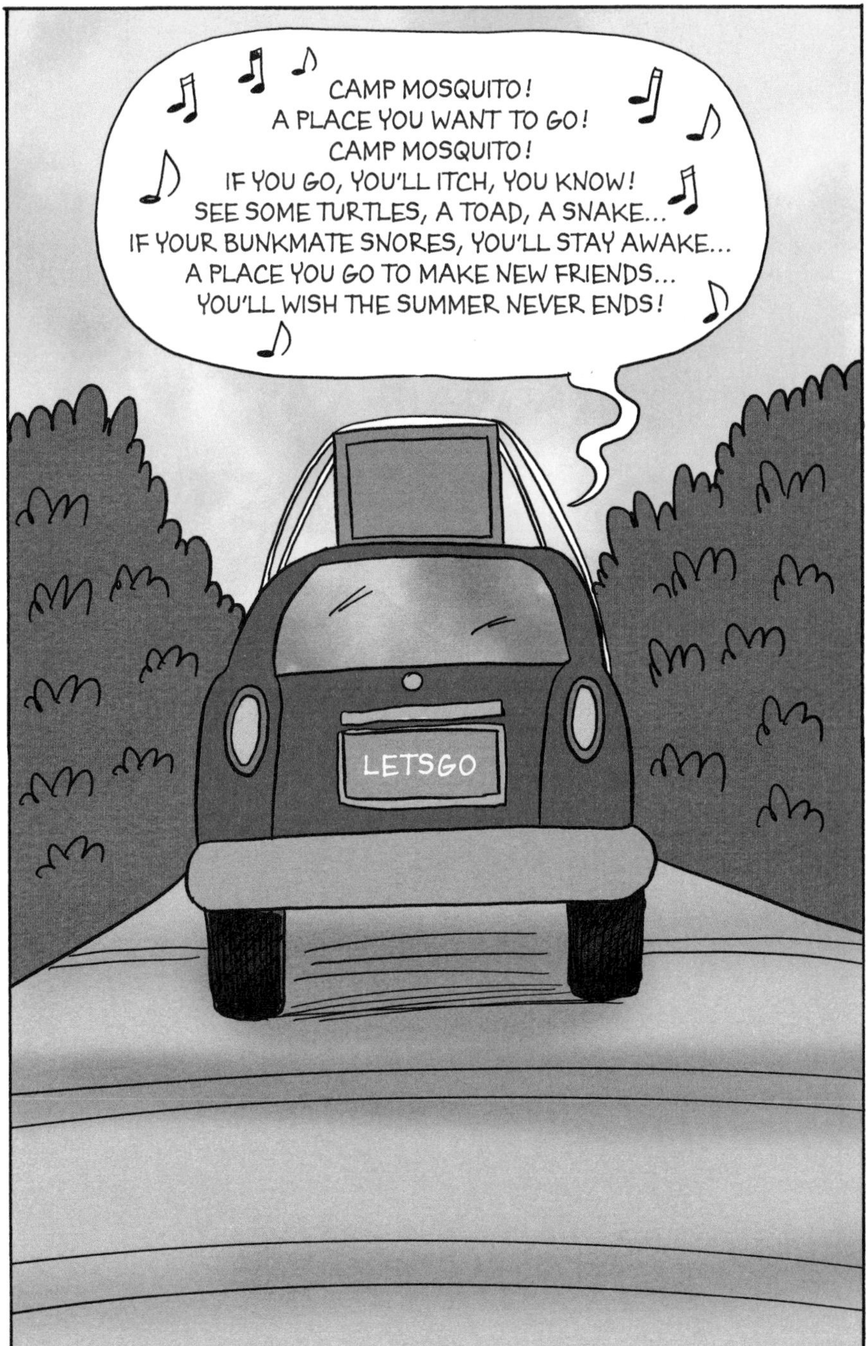
CAMP MOSQUITO!
A PLACE YOU WANT TO GO!
CAMP MOSQUITO!
IF YOU GO, YOU'LL ITCH, YOU KNOW!
SEE SOME TURTLES, A TOAD, A SNAKE...
IF YOUR BUNKMATE SNORES, YOU'LL STAY AWAKE...
A PLACE YOU GO TO MAKE NEW FRIENDS...
YOU'LL WISH THE SUMMER NEVER ENDS!
LETSGO

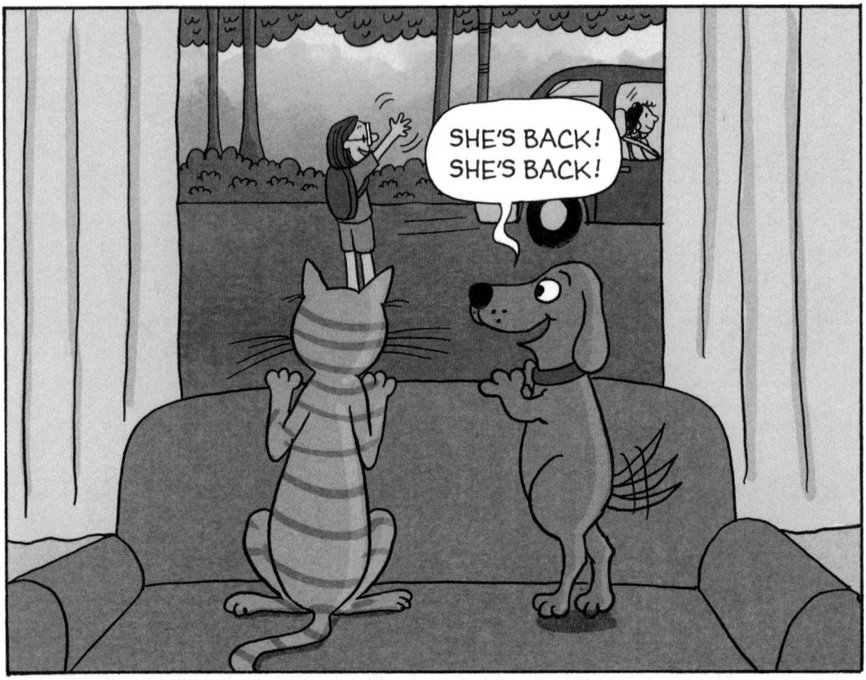
SHE'S BACK!
SHE'S BACK!

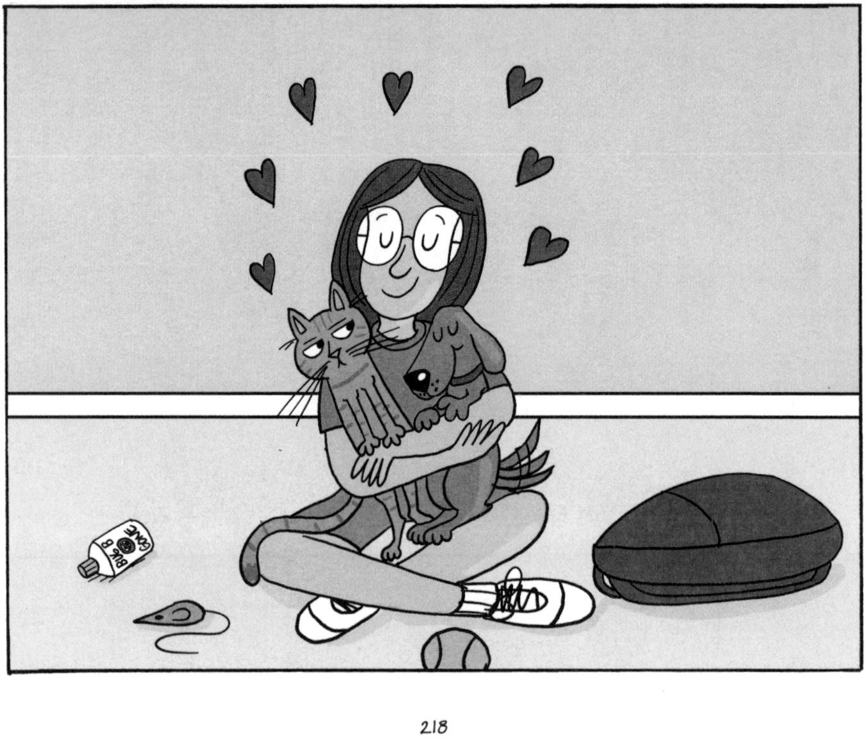

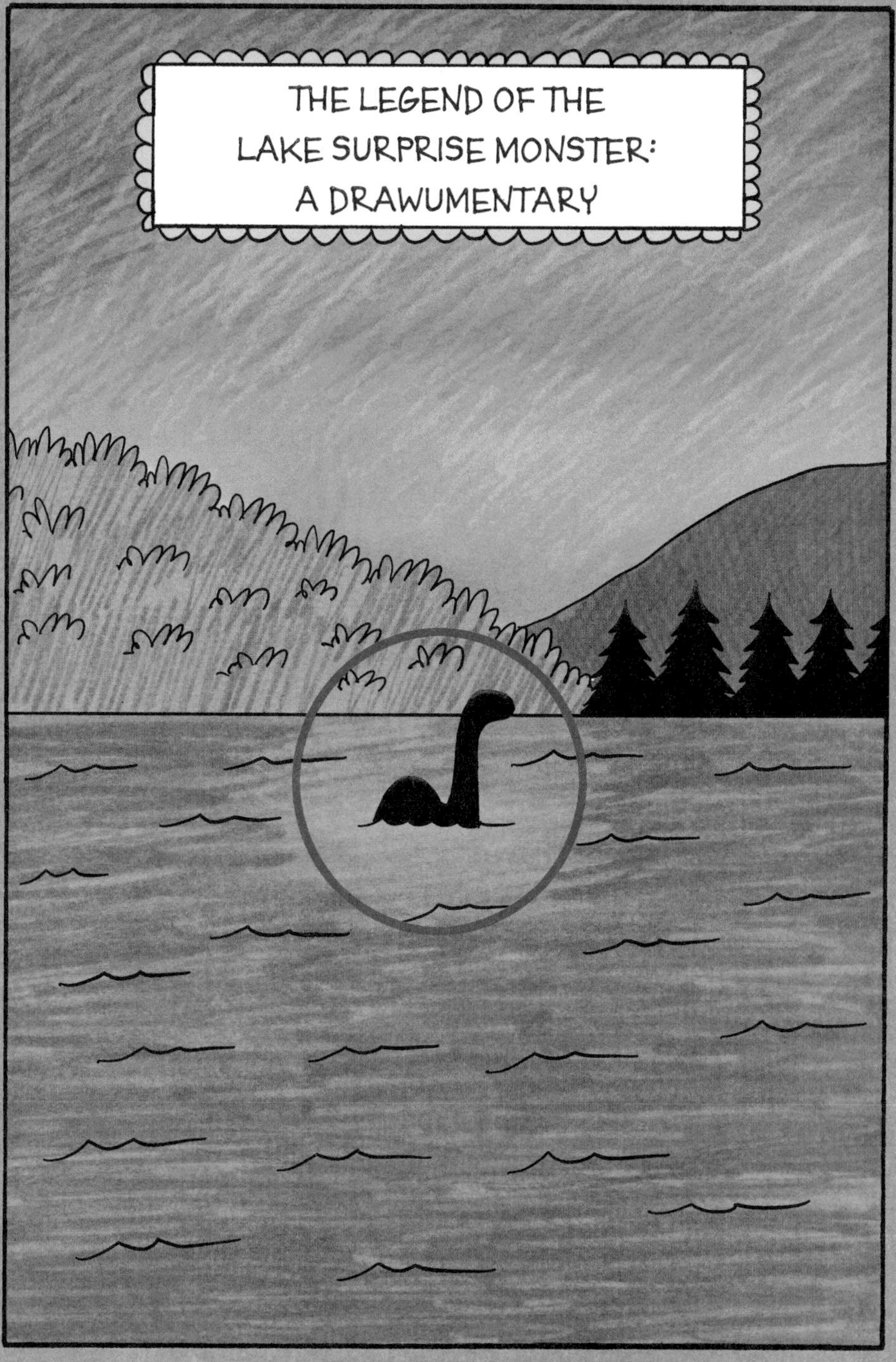
THE LEGEND OF THE
LAKE SURPRISE MONSTER:
A DRAWUMENTARY

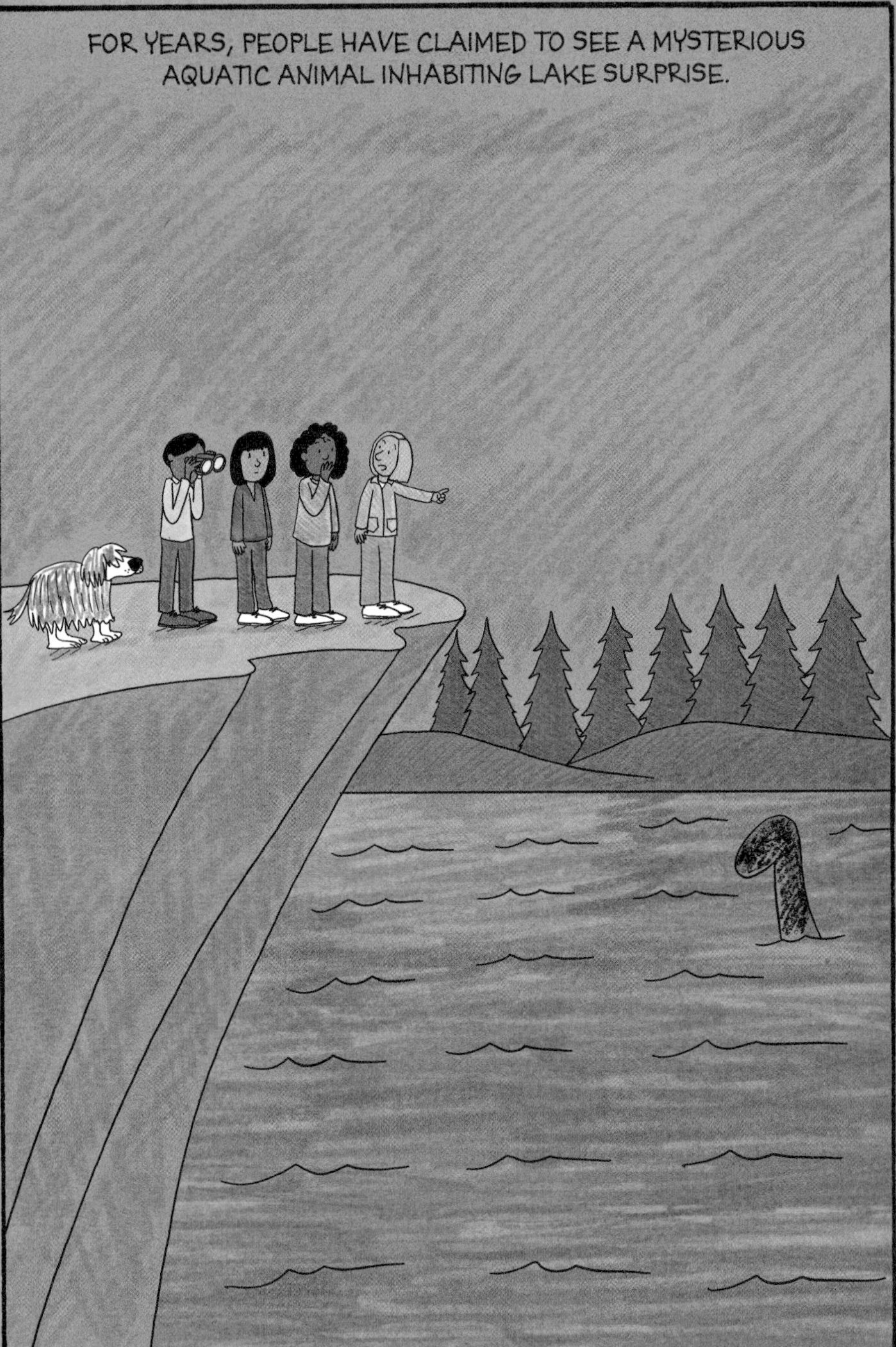
FOR YEARS, PEOPLE HAVE CLAIMED TO SEE A MYSTERIOUS AQUATIC ANIMAL INHABITING LAKE SURPRISE.

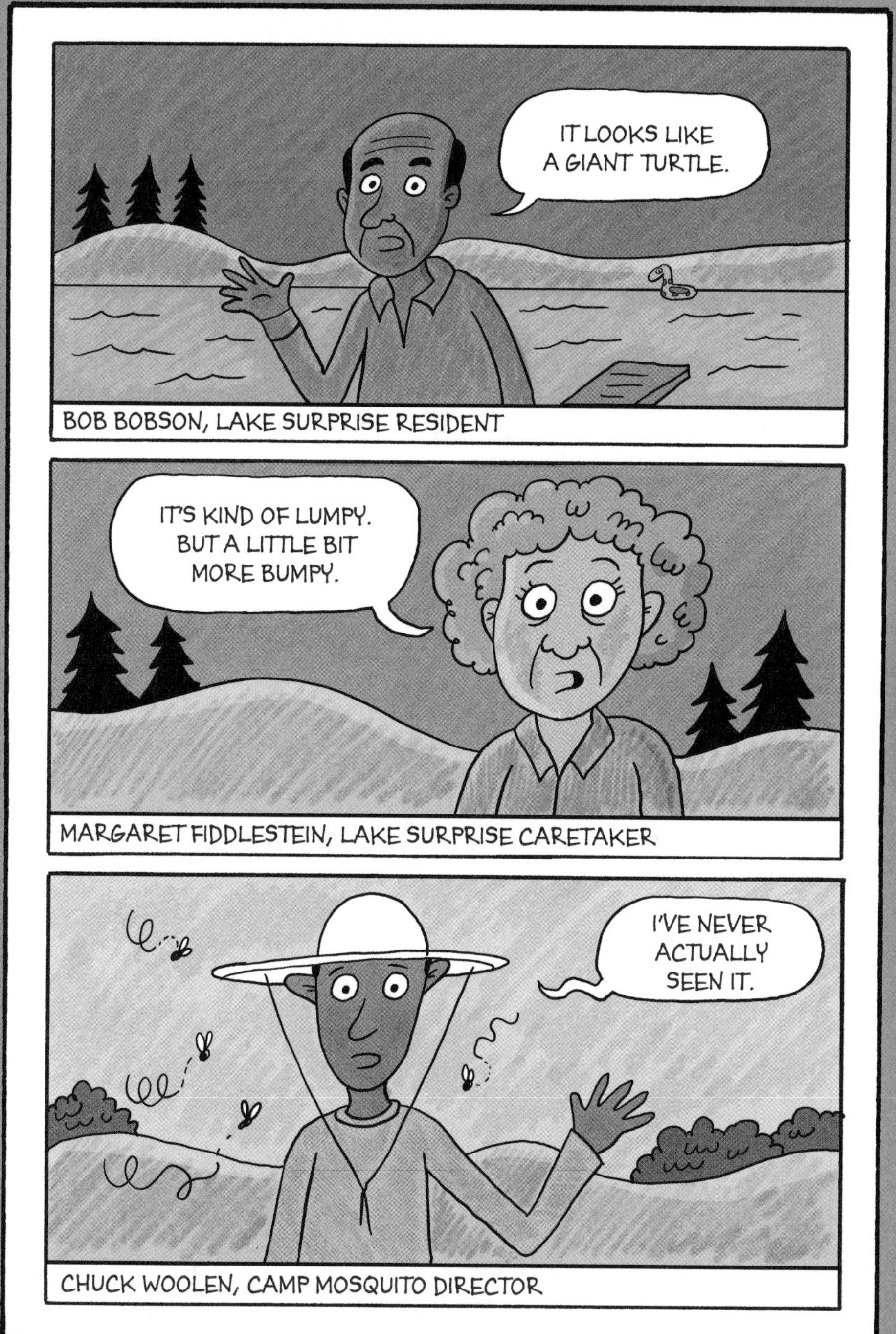
IT LOOKS LIKE A GIANT TURTLE.
BOB BOBSON, LAKE SURPRISE RESIDENT
IT'S KIND OF LUMPY. BUT A LITTLE BIT MORE BUMPY.
MARGARET FIDDLESTEIN, LAKE SURPRISE CARETAKER
I'VE NEVER ACTUALLY SEEN IT.
CHUCK WOOLEN, CAMP MOSQUITO DIRECTOR

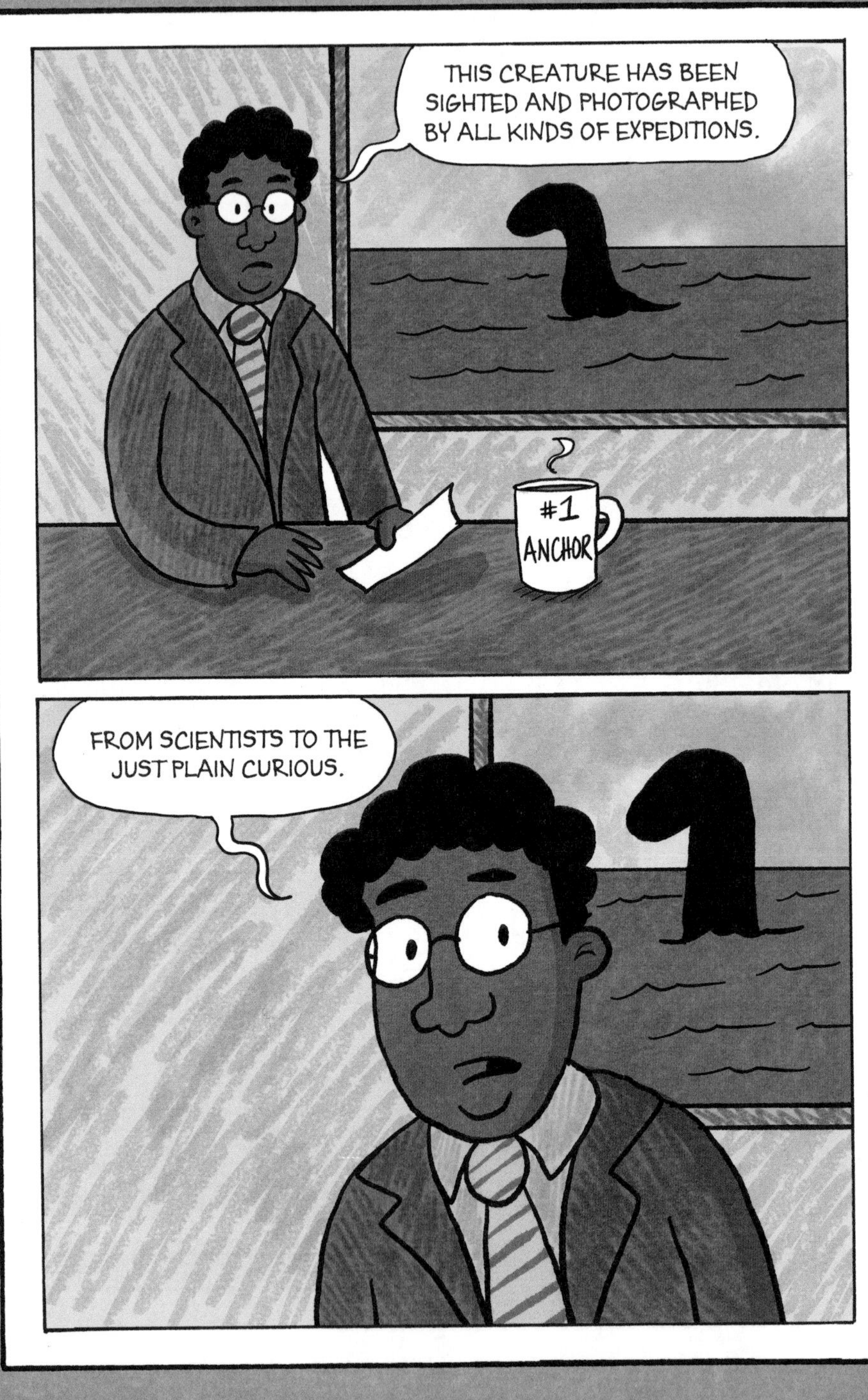
THIS CREATURE HAS BEEN SIGHTED AND PHOTOGRAPHED BY ALL KINDS OF EXPEDITIONS.
#1 ANCHOR
FROM SCIENTISTS TO THE JUST PLAIN CURIOUS.

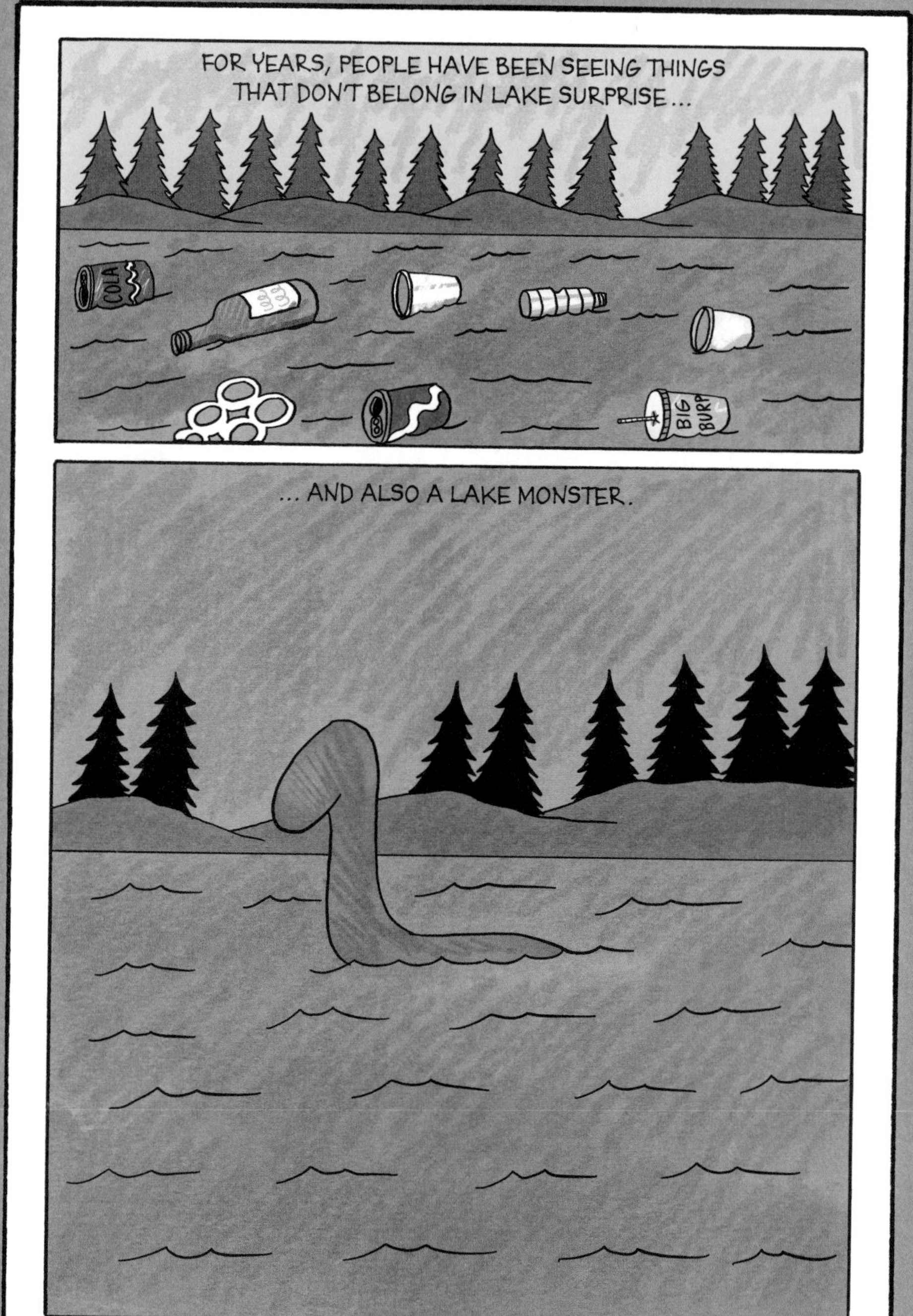
FOR YEARS, PEOPLE HAVE BEEN SEEING THINGS THAT DON'T BELONG IN LAKE SURPRISE...
COLA
BIG BURP
... AND ALSO A LAKE MONSTER.

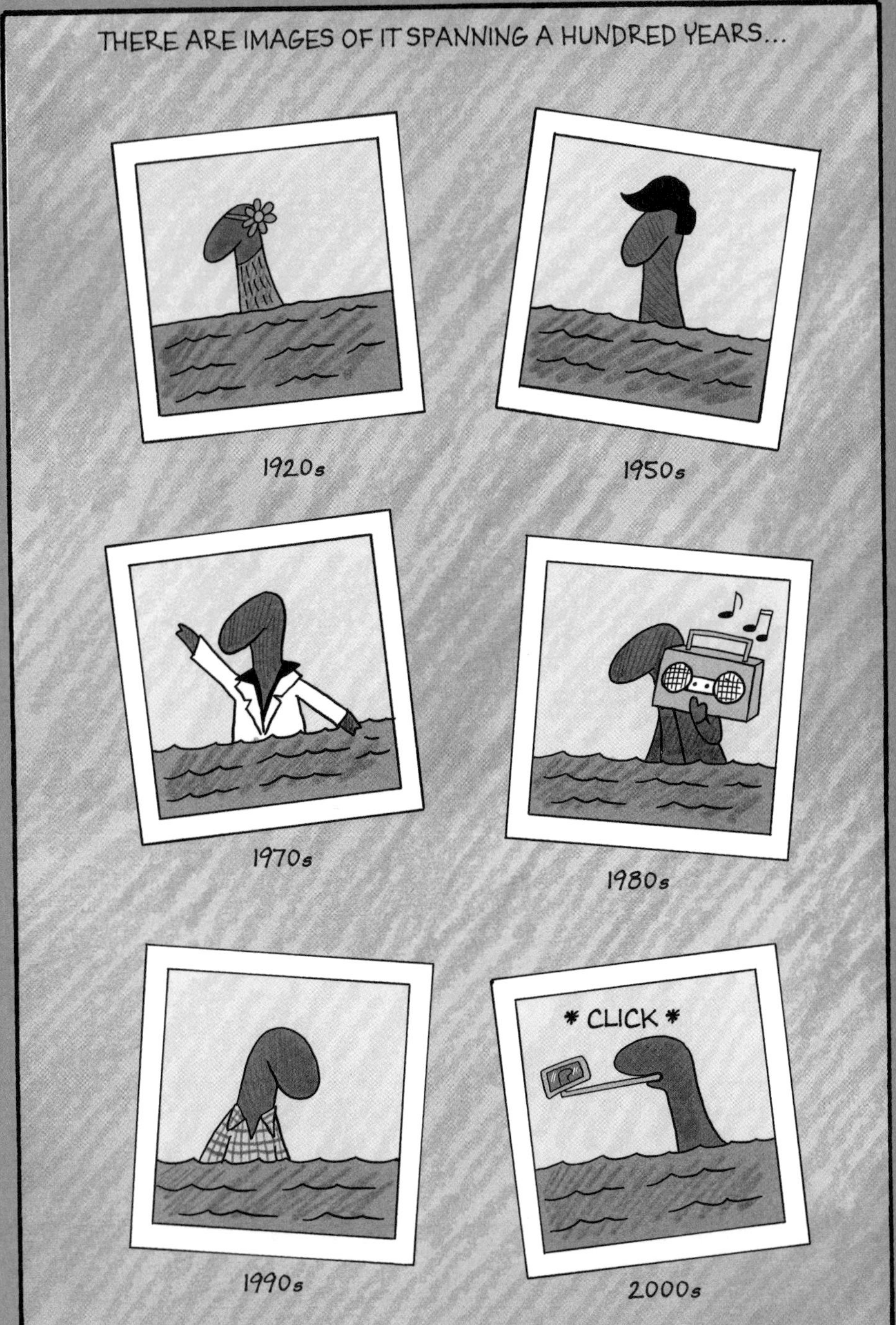
THERE ARE IMAGES OF IT SPANNING A HUNDRED YEARS...
1920s
1950s
1970s
1980s
1990s
* CLICK *
2000s

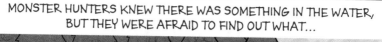

MONSTER HUNTERS KNEW THERE WAS SOMETHING IN THE WATER, BUT THEY WERE AFRAID TO FIND OUT WHAT...

SHOULDN'T WE PUT THE BOAT IN THE WATER?

NO WAY!

IT WAS THOUGHT TO BE SEEN ON SONAR...

BUT THAT WAS JUST A FLY.

SHOO!

SHEESH.

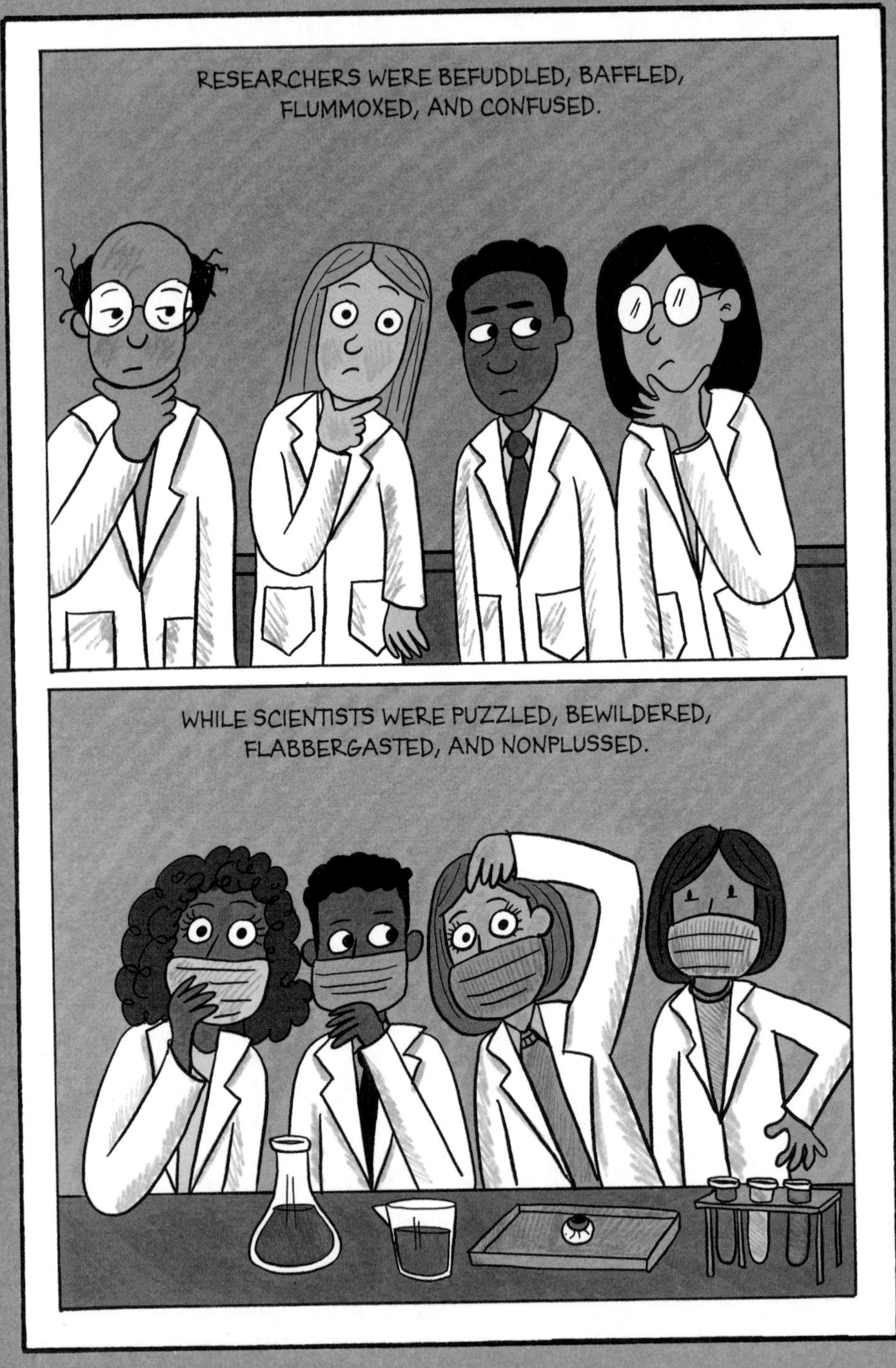
RESEARCHERS WERE BEFUDDLED, BAFFLED, FLUMMOXED, AND CONFUSED.
WHILE SCIENTISTS WERE PUZZLED, BEWILDERED, FLABBERGASTED, AND NONPLUSSED.

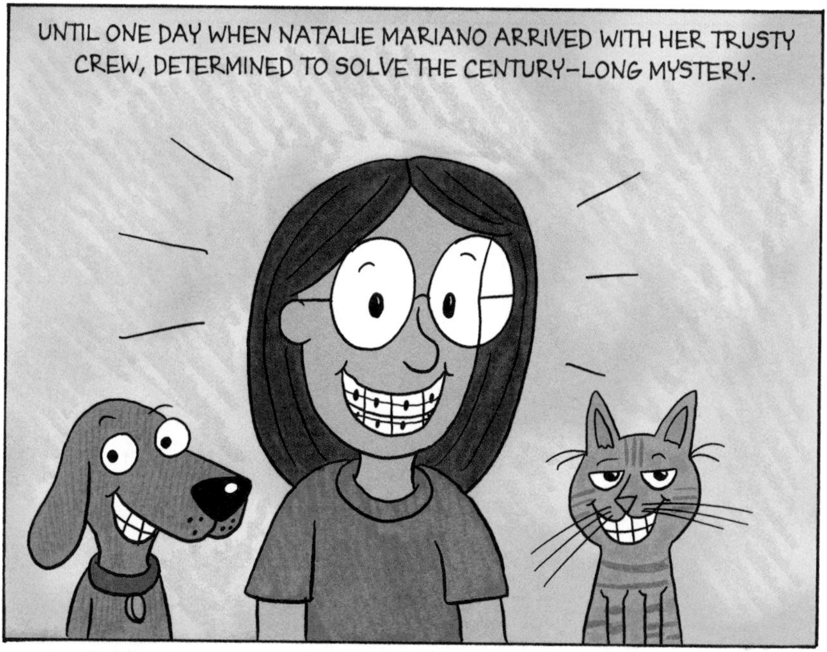
UNTIL ONE DAY WHEN NATALIE MARIANO ARRIVED WITH HER TRUSTY CREW, DETERMINED TO SOLVE THE CENTURY-LONG MYSTERY.

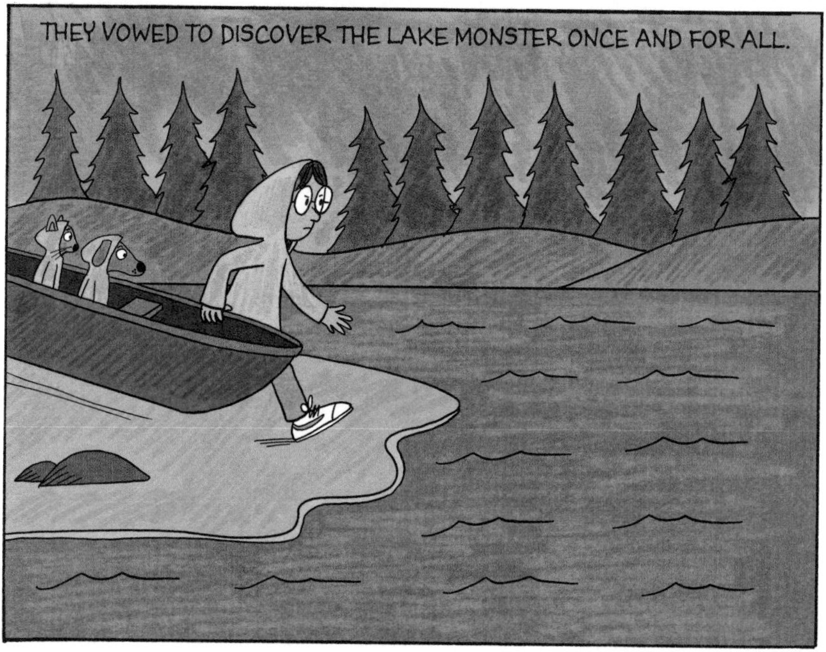
THEY VOWED TO DISCOVER THE LAKE MONSTER ONCE AND FOR ALL.

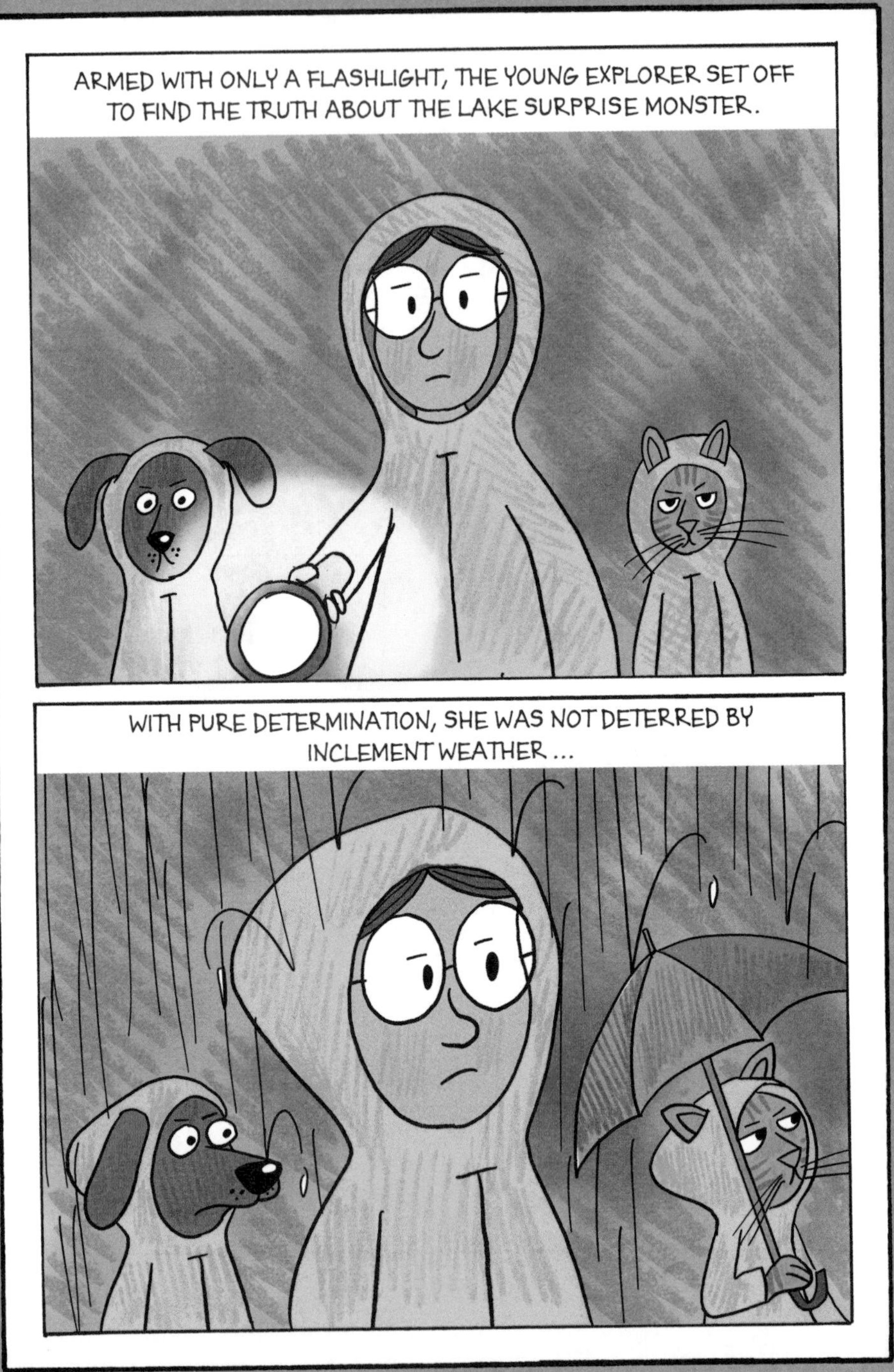
ARMED WITH ONLY A FLASHLIGHT, THE YOUNG EXPLORER SET OFF TO FIND THE TRUTH ABOUT THE LAKE SURPRISE MONSTER.
WITH PURE DETERMINATION, SHE WAS NOT DETERRED BY INCLEMENT WEATHER ...

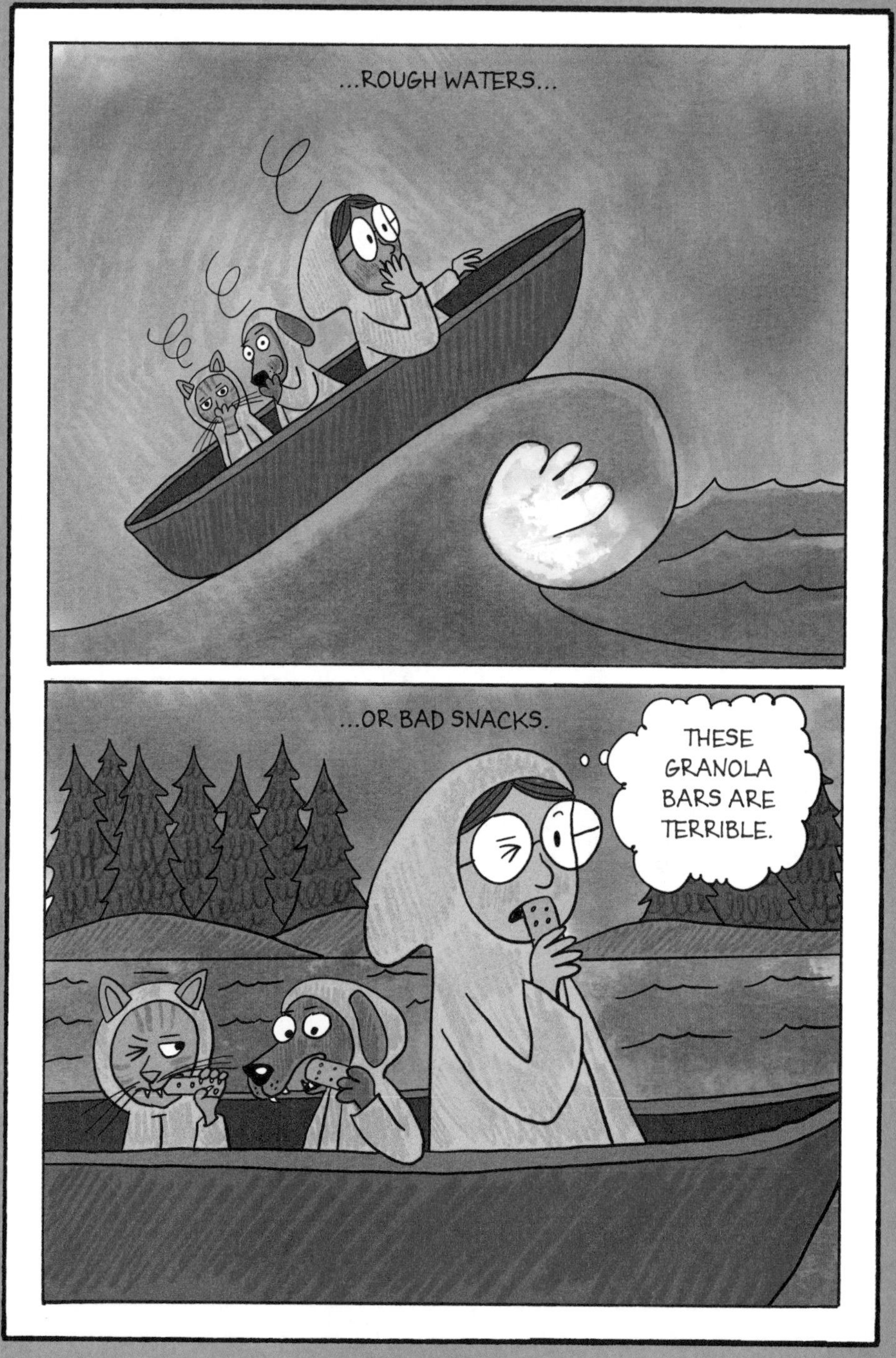
...ROUGH WATERS...
...OR BAD SNACKS.
THESE GRANOLA BARS ARE TERRIBLE.

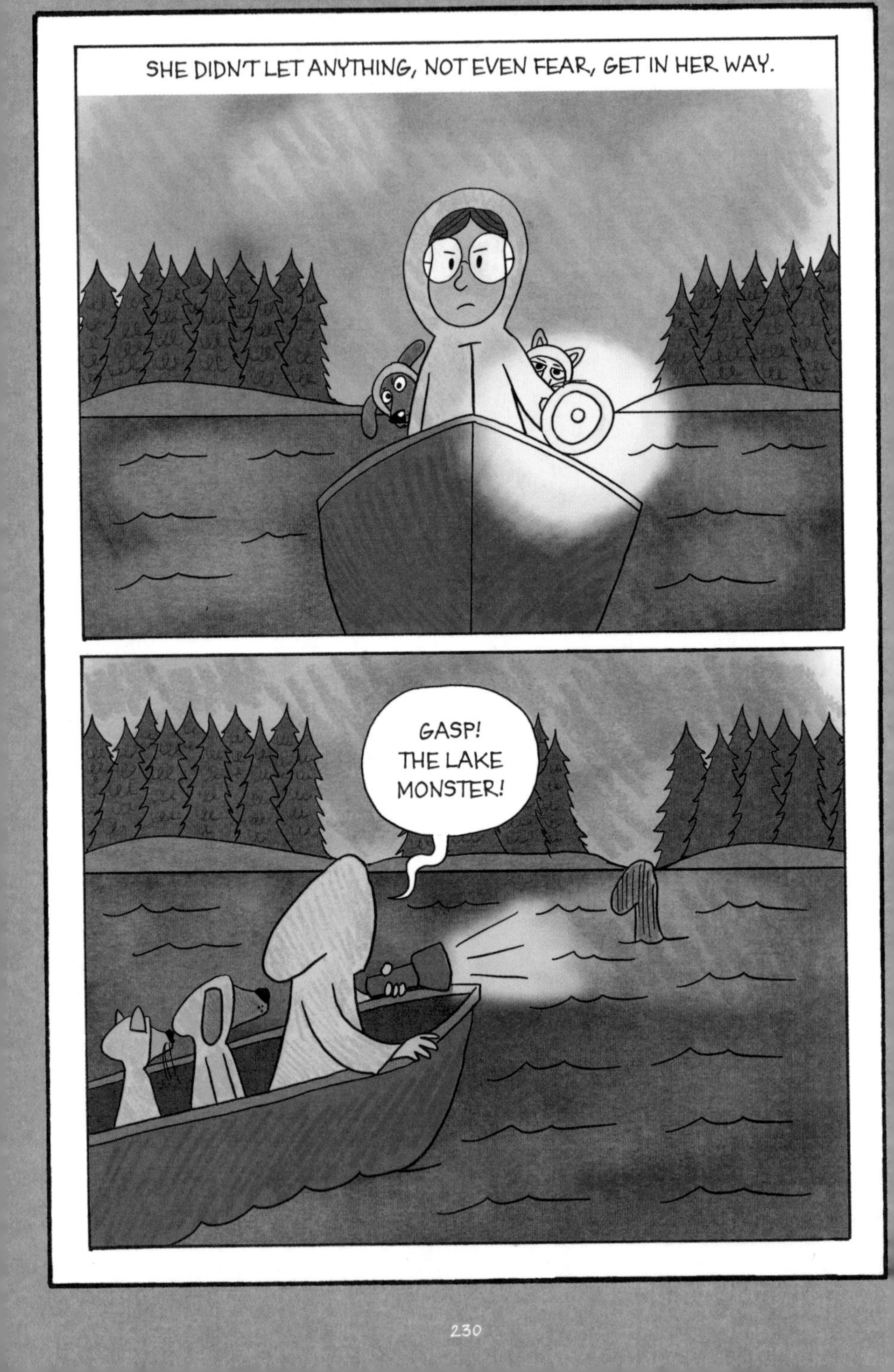
SHE DIDN'T LET ANYTHING, NOT EVEN FEAR, GET IN HER WAY.
GASP! THE LAKE MONSTER!

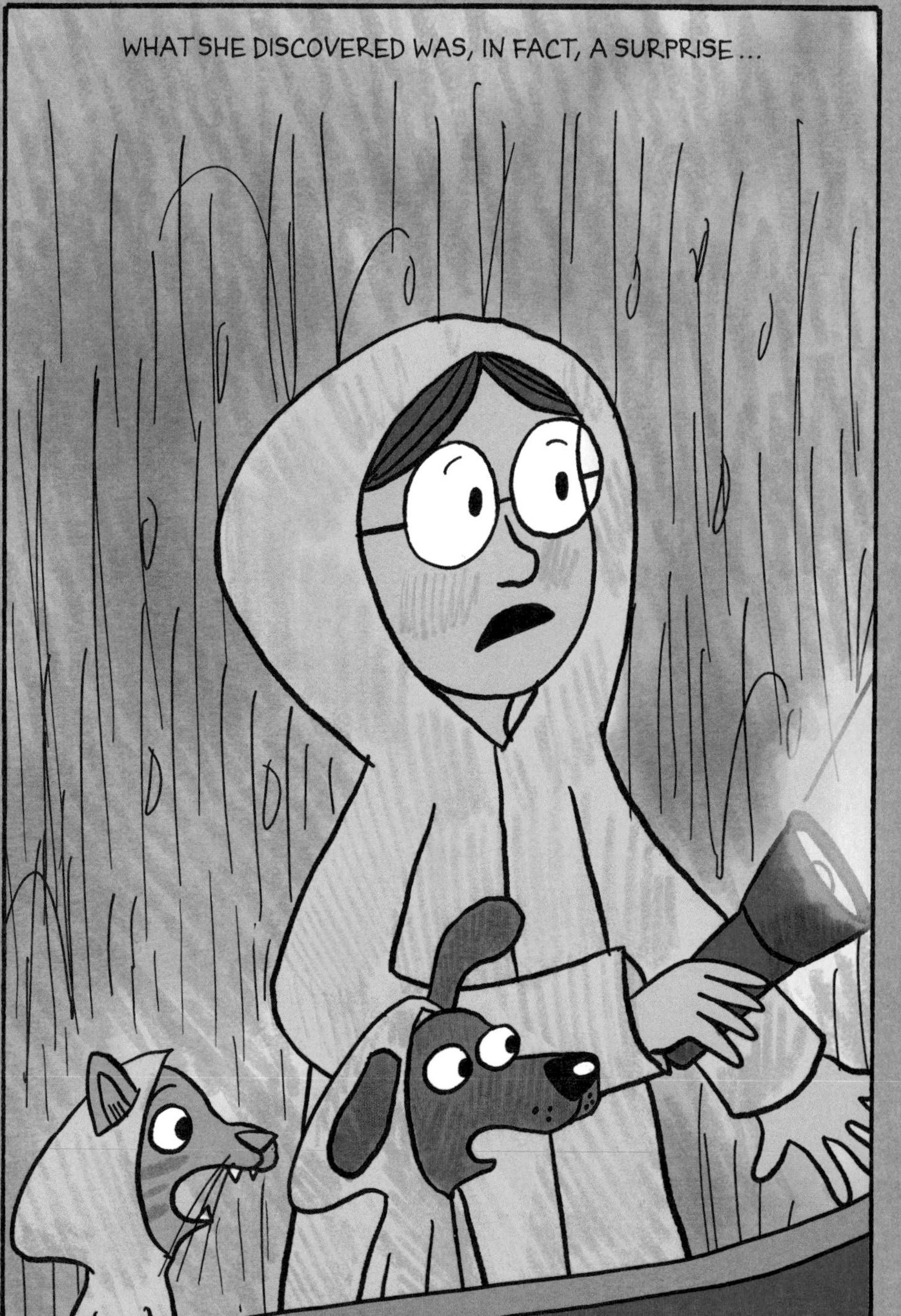
WHAT SHE DISCOVERED WAS, IN FACT, A SURPRISE...

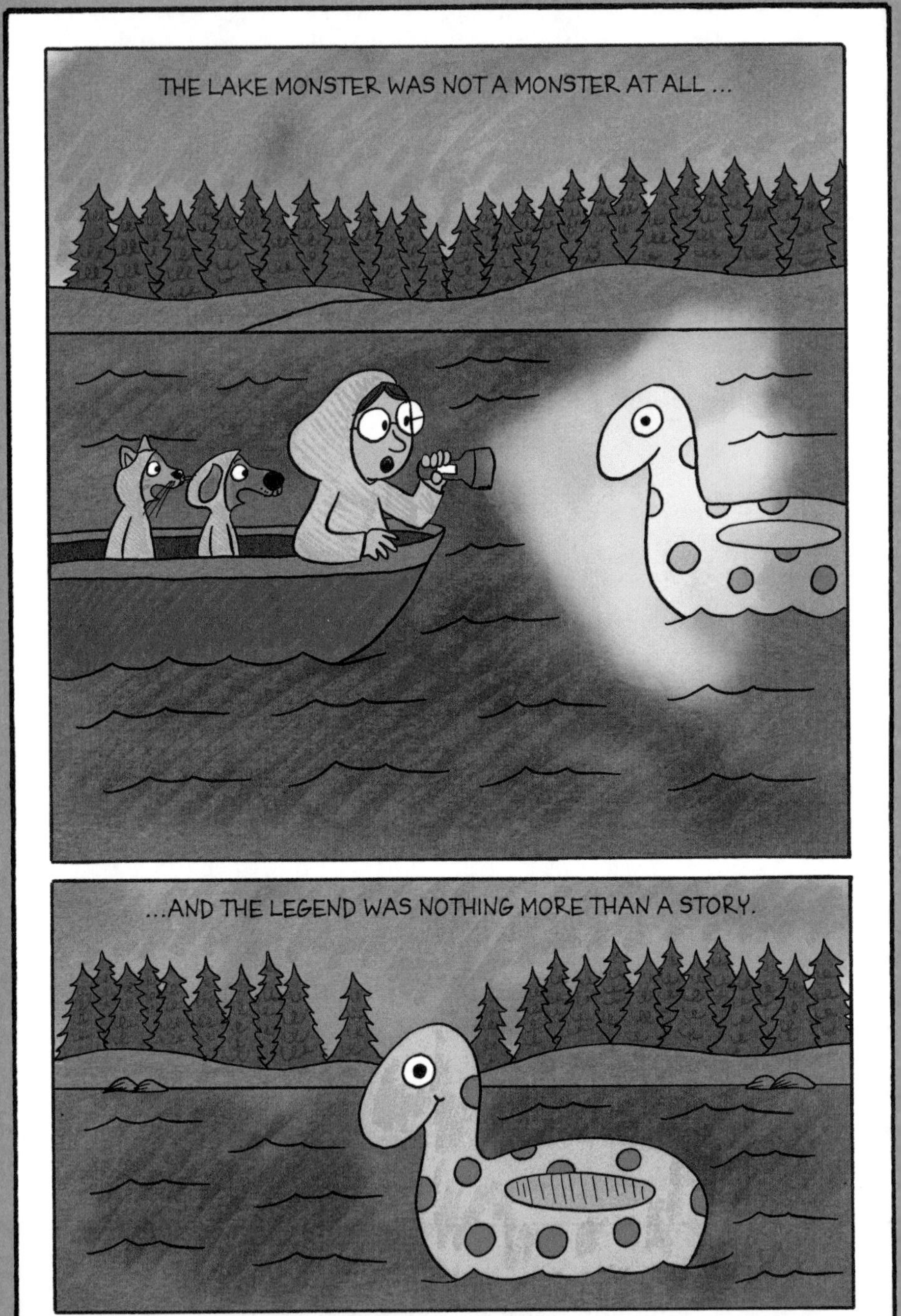
THE LAKE MONSTER WAS NOT A MONSTER AT ALL ...
...AND THE LEGEND WAS NOTHING MORE THAN A STORY.

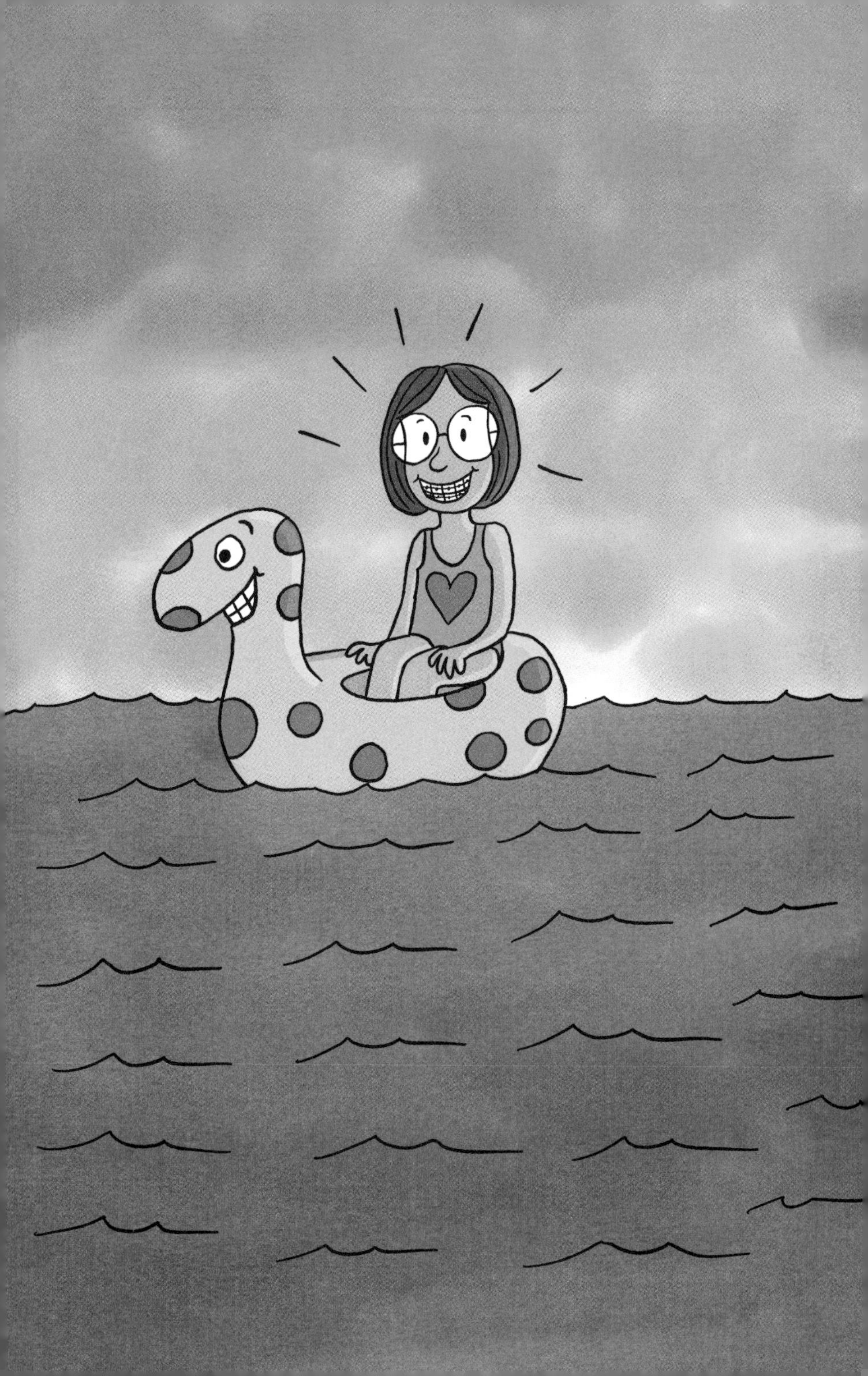

AUTHOR'S NOTE

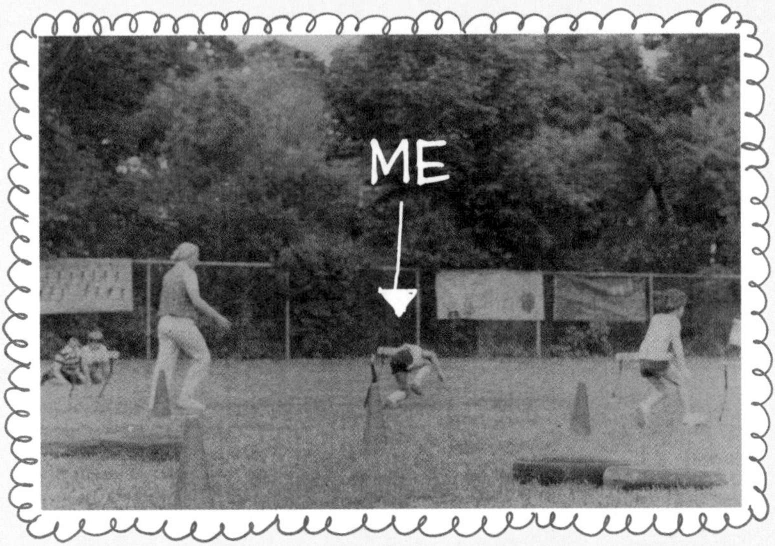
ME

Just like Natalie, I was either falling on my face or standing in my own way.

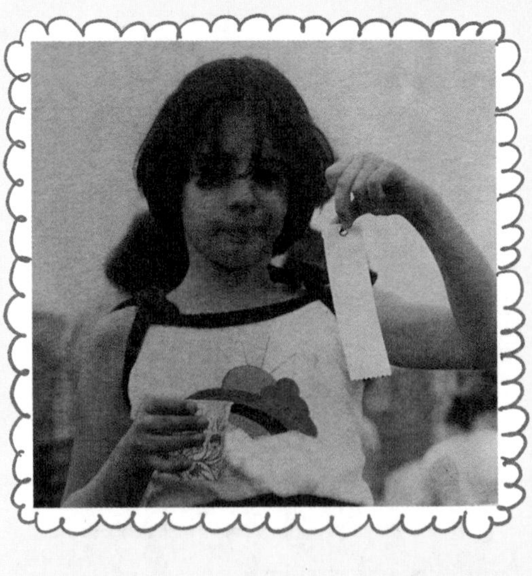

One of my biggest bullies was myself. I never felt like I was enough.

But as I grew up, I took on challenges that pushed me out of my comfort zone. I realized that courage is just feeling the fear and doing it anyway.

With so much gratitude to:

The best team on the planet: My editor, Megan Peace; Publisher, David Saylor; Creative Director, Phil Falco; and everyone at Scholastic/Graphix who helped make these books a reality.

My amazing agent, Gillian Mackenzie.

My friends and family for their unrelenting support, understanding, and encouragement.

Julie Lapin, who was my BFF before I knew what a BFF was. (I still feel bad about breaking your trophy.)

Andrew, who always reminds me it will be all right.

And my readers, for the opportunity to share these stories.

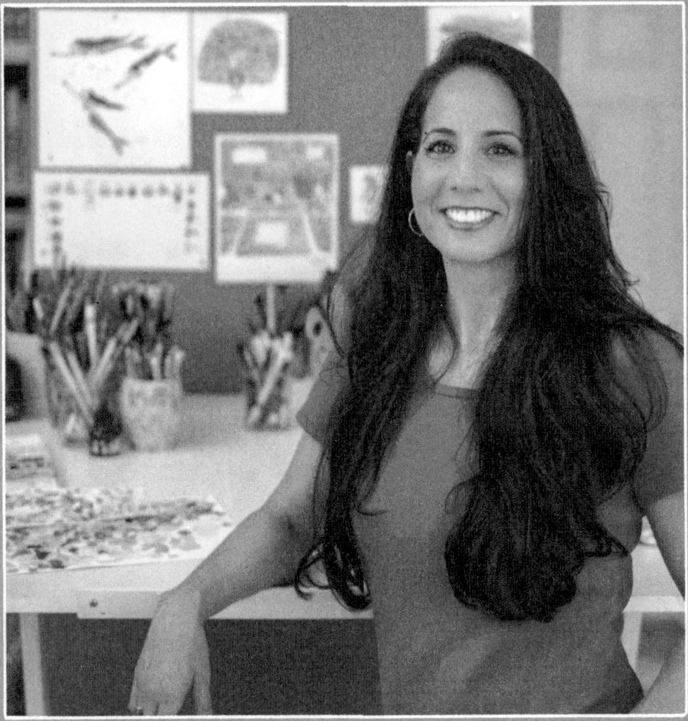

Photo credit: Don Hamerman

MARIA SCRIVAN is an award-winning syndicated cartoonist, illustrator, and *New York Times* bestselling author based in Stamford, Connecticut. Her laugh-out-loud comic, Half Full, appears daily in newspapers nationwide and on gocomics.com. Maria licenses her work for greeting cards, and her cartoons have also appeared in *MAD Magazine*, *Parade*, and many other publications. Her debut graphic novel, *Nat Enough*, was published in April 2020, and the follow-up, *Forget Me Nat*, in September 2020. Both released to great acclaim. Visit Maria online at mariascrivan.com.